A

SOUL

OF

ASH

AND

BLOOD

ALSO FROM JENNIFER L. ARMENTROUT

Fall With Me
Dream of You (a 1001 Dark Nights Novel)
Forever With You
Fire in You

By J. Lynn
Wait for You
Be with Me
Stay with Me

The Blood and Ash Series
From Blood and Ash
A Kingdom of Flesh and Fire
The Crown of Gilded Bones
The War of Two Queens
A Soul of Ash and Blood
Visions of Flesh and Blood: A Blood and Ash/Flesh and Fire
Compendium

The Flesh and Fire Series
A Shadow in the Ember
A Light in the Flame
A Fire in the Flesh

Fall of Ruin and Wrath Series
Fall of Ruin and Wrath

The Covenant Series
Half-Blood
Pure
Deity
Elixir
Apollyon
Sentinel

The Lux Series
Shadows

Obsidian
Onyx
Opal
Origin
Opposition
Oblivion

The Origin Series
The Darkest Star
The Burning Shadow
The Brightest Night

The Dark Elements
Bitter Sweet Love
White Hot Kiss
Stone Cold Touch
Every Last Breath

The Harbinger Series
Storm and Fury
Rage and Ruin
Grace and Glory

The Titan Series
The Return
The Power
The Struggle
The Prophecy

The Wicked Series
Wicked
Torn
Brave
The Prince (a 1001 Dark Nights Novella)
The King (a 1001 Dark Nights Novella)
The Queen (a 1001 Dark Nights Novella)

Gamble Brothers Series
Tempting the Best Man

Tempting the Player
Tempting the Bodyguard

A de Vincent Novel Series
Moonlight Sins
Moonlight Seduction
Moonlight Scandals

Standalone Novels
Obsession
Frigid
Scorched
Cursed
Don't Look Back
The Dead List
Till Death
The Problem with Forever
If There's No Tomorrow

Anthologies
Meet Cute
Life Inside My Mind
Fifty First Times

A

SOUL

OF

ASH

AND

BLOOD

#1 NEW YORK TIMES BESTSELLING AUTHOR

JENNIFER L.
ARMENTROUT

BLUE
BOX
PRESS

To see a full-size version of the map, visit
https://theblueboxpress.com/books/asoabmap/

A Soul of Ash and Blood
A Blood and Ash Novel
By Jennifer L. Armentrout

Copyright 2023 Jennifer L. Armentrout
ISBN: 978-1957568423

Published by Blue Box Press, an imprint of Evil Eye Concepts, Incorporated

Cover design by Hang Le

ACKNOWLEDGMENTS

Behind every book is a team of people who helped make it possible. Thank you to Blue Box Press—Liz Berry, Jillian Stein, MJ Rose, Chelle Olson, Kim Guidroz, Jessica Saunders, Tanaka Kangara, the amazing editing and proofreading team, and Michael Perlman, along with the entire team at S&S for their hardcover distribution support and expertise. Also, a huge thanks to Hang Le for her incredible talent at design; my agents Kevan Lyon and Taryn Fagerness; my assistant, Malissa Coy; shop manager Jen Fisher; and the brain behind ApollyCon and more: Steph Brown, along with Vicky and Matt. Also, the JLAnders mods, Vonetta Young and Mona Awad. Thank you all for being the most amazing, supportive team an author could want, for making sure these books are read all across the world, creating merch, helping with plot issues, and more.

I also need to thank those who've helped me keep my head above water, either by helping me work my way out of a plot corner or just by being there to make me laugh, be an inspiration, or to get me in or out of trouble—KA Tucker, Kristen Ashley, JR Ward, Sarah J. Maas, Steve Berry for story times, Andrea Joan, Stacey Morgan, Margo Lipschultz, and so many more.

A big thank you to JLAnders for always creating a fun and often hilarious place to chill. And to the ARC team for your honest reviews and support.

Most importantly, none of this would be possible without you, the reader. I hope you realize how much you mean to me.

DEDICATION

For you, the reader.

PRONUNCIATION GUIDE

Characters
Aios – AYY-ohs
Alastir Davenwell – AL-as-tir DAV-en-well
Andreia – ahn-DRAY-ah
Arden – AHR-den
Attes – AT-tayz
Aurelia – au-REL-ee-ah
Baines – baynz
Beckett – BECK-et
Bele – bell
Blaz – blayz
Brandole Mazeen – bran-dohl mah-ZEEN
Braylon Holland – BRAY-lon HAA-luhnd
Britta – brit-tah
Callum – KAL-um
Clariza – klar-itza
Coralena – kore-a-LEE-nuh
Coulton – KOHL-ton
Casteel Da'Neer – ka-STEEL DA-neer
Crolee – KROH-lee
Dafina – dah-FEE-nuh
Davina – dah-VEE-nuh
Delano Amicu – dee-LAY-no AM-ik-kyoo
Dorcan – dohr-kan
Dorian Teerman – DOHR-ee-uhn TEER-man
Duchess and Duke Ravarel – duch-ess and dook RAV-ah-rell
Dyses – DEYE-seez
Ector – EHK-tohr
Effie – EH-fee
Ehthawn – EE-thawn
Elian Da'Neer – EL-ee-awn DA-near
Elijah Payne – ee-LIE-jah payn
Eloana Da'Neer – EEL-oh-nah DA-neer
Embris – EM-bris
Emil Da'Lahr – EE-mil DA-lar
Erlina – Er-LEE-nah
Ernald – ER-nald
Eythos – EE-thos
Ezmeria – ez-MARE-ee-ah

Gemma – jeh-muh
General Aylard – gen-ER-al AYY-lard
Gianna Davenwell – jee-AA-nuh DA-ven-well
Griffith Jansen – grif-ITH JAN-sen
Halayna – hah-LAY-nah
Hanan – HAY-nan
Hawke Flynn – hawk flin
Hisa Fa'Mar – hee-SAA FAH-mar
Ian Balfour – EE-uhn BAL-fohr
Ione – EYE-on
Ivan – EYE-van
Isbeth – is-BITH
Jadis – JAY-dis
Jasper Contou – JAS-per KON-too
Jericho – JERR-i-koh
Joshalynn – josha-lynn
Kayleigh Balfour – KAY-lee BAL-fohr
Keella – KEE-lah
Kieran Contou – KEE-ren KON-too
King Jalara – king jah-LAH-ruh
King Saegar – king SAY-gar
Kirha Contou – k-AH-ruh KON-too
Kolis – KO-lis
Kyn – kin
Lady Cambria – lay-dee KAM-bree-uh
Lailah – lay-lah
Lathan – LEY-THahN
Leopold – LEE-ah-pohld
Lev Barron – lehv BAIR-uhn
Lizeth Damron – lih-ZEHTH DAM-ron
Loimus – loy-moos
Lord Ambrose – lohrd AM-brohz
Lord Chaney – lohrd chay-NEE
Lord Gregori – lohrd GREHG-ohr-ree
Lord Haverton – lohrd HAY-ver-ton
Loren – LOH-ren
Lucinda Teerman – loo-SIN-dah TEER-man
Luddie – LUHD-dee
Lyra – lee-RAH
Mac - mack
Madis – mad-is
Magda – mahg-dah
Maia – MY-ah

Malec O'Meer – ma-LEEK O-meer
Malessa Axton – MAHL-les-sah ax-TON
Malik Da'Neer – MA-lick DA-neer
Marisol Faber – MARE-i-sohl FAY-berr
Millicent – mil-uh-SUHNT
Mycella – MY-sell-AH
Naill – NYill
Nektas – NEK-tas
Nithe – NIGHth
Noah – noh-AH
Nova – NOH-vah
Nyktos – NIK-toes
Odell Cyr – OH-dell seer
Odetta – oh-DET-ah
Orphine – OR-feen
Peinea – pain-ee-yah
Penellaphe – pen-NELL-uh-fee
Penellaphe Balfour – pen-NELL-uh-fee BAL-fohr
Perry – PER-ree
Perus – paehr-UHS
Phanos – FAN-ohs
Polemus – pol-he-mus
Preela – PREE-lah
Priestess Analia – priest-ess an-NAH-lee-ah
Queen Calliphe – queen KAL-lih-fee
Queen Ileana – queen uh-lee-AH-nuh
Reaver – REE-ver
Rhahar – RUH-har
Rhain – rain
Rolf – rollf
Rune – roon
Rylan Keal – RYE-lan keel
Sage - sayj
Saion – SIGH-on
Sera – SEE-ra
Seraphena Mierel – SEE-rah-fee-nah MEER-ehl
Sera – SEE-rah
Shae Davenwell – shay DAV-en-well
Sotoria – soh-TOR-ee-ah
Sven – svehn
Talia – TAH-lee-uh
Taric – tay-rik
Tavius – TAY-vee-us

Tawny Lyon – TAW-nee LYE-uhn
Thad – thad
Theon – thEE-awn
Tulis [Family] – TOO-lees
Valyn Da'Neer – VAH-lynn DA-neer
Veses – VES-eez
Vikter Wardwell – VIK-ter WARD-well
Vonetta Contou – vah-NET-tah KON-too
Wilhelmina Colyns – wil-hel-MEE-nuh KOHL-lynz

Places
Aegea – ayy-JEE-uh
Atheneum – ath-uh-NEE-uhm
Atlantia – at-LAN-tee-ah
Barren Plains – bar-uhn pleynz
Berkton – BERK-ton
Carsodonia – kar-so-DON-uh
Cauldra Manor – kall-drah [manor]
Chambers of Nyktos – cheym-berz of nik-TOES
Dalos – day-lohs
Elysium Peaks – ihl-LEES-ee-uhm peeks
Evaemon – EHV-eh-mahn
High Hills of Thronos – hie hilz of THROH-nohs
· Iliseeum – AH-lee-see-um
Isles of Bele – IGHelz of BELL
Kithreia – kith-REE-ah
Lasania – lah-SAHN-ee-uh
Lotho – LOH-thoh
Masadonia – mah-sah-DOHN-uh
Massene – mah-SEE-nuh
Mountains of Nyktos – MOWNT-ehnz of nik-TOES
New Haven – noo HAY-ven
Niel Valley – nile valley
Oak Ambler – ohk AM-bler
Padonia – pa-DOH-nee-ah
Pensdurth – PENS-durth
Pillars of Asphodel – [pillars of] AS-foe-del
Pinelands – PINE-lands
Pompay – pom-PAY
Seas of Saion – SEEZ of SIGH-on
Skotos Mountains – SKOH-tohs MOWNT-ehnz
Solis – sou-LIS

Spessa's End – SPESSAHZ ehnd
Sirta – SIR-ta
Saion's Cove – SI-onz kohv
Stygian Bay – stih-JEE-uhn bey
Tadous – TAHD-oos
Temple of Perses – TEM-puhl of PUR-seez
The Three Jackals – thuh three JAK-uhlz
Three Rivers – three RIH-verz
Triton Isles – TRY-ton IGH-elz
Undying Hills – UN-dy-ing hillz
Vathi – VAY-thee
Vodina Isles – voh-DEE-nuh IGH-elz
Western Pass – WEST-tern pass
Whitebridge – WIGHT-brij
Willow Plains – WIHL-oh pleynz

Terms
Arae – air-ree
benada – ben-NAH-dah
ceeren – SEER-rehn
Cimmerian – sim-MARE-ee-in
dakkai – DAY-kigh
demis – dem-EEZ
eather – ee-thohr
graeca – gray-kah
Gyrm - germ
imprimen – IM-prim-ehn
kardia – KAR-dee-ah
kiyou wolf/wolves – kee-yoo [wolf/wolves]
lamaea – lahm-ee-ah
laruea – lah-ROO-ee-ah
meeyah Liessa – MEE-yah LEE-sah
notam – NOH-tam
sekya – sek-yah
sparanea – SPARE-ah-nay-ah
tulpa – tool-PAH
wivern – WY-vehrn

NOTE TO READER:

While the lives of those written on these pages are fictional, what they experience occurs in life outside of these pages—myself included. For that reason, please be aware that there are discussions surrounding self-harm and abuse.

Please know that you do not need to hurt.

There is help.
Visit crisistextline.org

PRESENT I

A sweet but stale scent drifted out from the dark corridor. My head jerked toward the sound of light, fast footsteps as I reached for my hip, drawing the bloodstone dagger.

A vampry darted between the sandstone pillars, rushing into the lamplit hall of the seemingly unending vault beneath Wayfair Castle, nothing more than a flash of streaming dark hair, alabaster skin, and crimson silk.

There was no hesitation. Neither Kieran nor I had given any of them leeway since entering the underground.

I released the dagger, sending it flying across the hall. The bloodstone blade struck true, embedding deeply in the vampry's chest, cutting off the annoying, godsawful shriek as it knocked the Ascended back. A web of fissures rapidly appeared in the Ascended's flesh, spreading across its cheeks and down its throat. Skin cracked and then peeled back, lifting from bone and turning to dust. Within a heartbeat, my dagger clanged off the stone floor beside nothing more than a pile of silk.

"Cas." It came out as a sigh, and my lips curved into a smile despite the frustration filling the breathy word.

I couldn't help it when Poppy called me that. Hearing it sometimes made my chest tight yet made me feel light as air. Other times, it made me hard as fuck. But it always brought out a smile.

"The Ascended didn't attack us," Poppy said.

"It was running at us." I went to where the dagger lay and picked it up.

"Or running *from* us," she suggested.

"That's one way to look at it." Cleaning the blade on the leg of my pants, I sheathed the dagger and faced her—and damn if I didn't feel a catch in my godsdamn breath.

Every inch of Poppy showed that she'd just fought a terrifying battle. Blood and grime smeared her cheeks, hands, and her clothing, not to mention what covered her bare feet. The braid she'd forced her unruly hair into had mostly come undone, and the strands gleamed like bold, red wine in the dim light of the gas lamps, spilling over her shoulders and down her back.

And still, she was so damn beautiful to me.

My heartmate.

My Queen.

Not a goddess but a Primal—*the* Primal of Blood and Bone. Of Life and Death.

Shock rippled through me, nearly causing me to stumble. It had been doing that every couple of minutes since she went all Primal on the Blood Queen. I imagined it would be a long damn time before it stopped happening.

"But the last thing anyone who doesn't want to end up a pile of dust should do is run in your direction." I bowed at the waist. "My Queen."

Poppy blinked slowly, clearly unimpressed by my chivalry. That brightened my smile, and her full lips twitched as she fought back a grin, revealing a hint of sharp canine.

Lust punched straight through me as my chin dipped, and my eyes locked with hers. Every time I caught a glimpse of her fangs, I wanted to feel them in my flesh. *Correction.* I wanted to feel them in my flesh while I was buried deep inside her.

A throat cleared. "May we continue?" a raspy, flat voice asked. "Or would you two like a private moment?"

Poppy's cheeks warmed, flooding her face with color that had been absent since we'd arrived at Wayfair. My gaze shifted to the speaker.

The massive mountain of a male with his black-and-silver-streaked hair raised a brow.

Fucking Nektas, the eldest and inarguably most dangerous of the draken, was starting to piss me off.

Holding his stare, I checked my desire for my wife. Not because of his presence. And not even because we were down here searching for her father. But because of Poppy.

Something wasn't right.

I rejoined her and the ever-alert Delano, who had been sticking close in wolven form. "You ready?"

Nodding, she started walking again, the stone floor likely icy against her bare feet. I'd offered to carry her.

The look she'd given me ensured I didn't ask again. That hadn't stopped Kieran from making the same offer, though. He'd received a similar look of warning—the kind that made you want to cup your balls. Lucky for us, Poppy likely preferred us with those parts undamaged.

I didn't take my eyes off her as we continued.

Out in the Bone Temple, before she unleashed unholy hell on the Blood Queen, I'd watched in unfettered horror as pure light exploded her armor. And I'd been unable to do a damn thing. I'd only ever felt such fear one other time; when the bolt had struck her in the Wastelands, and I'd watched her life slipping from her. I'd felt that same terror earlier when I saw the blood running from her mouth. She'd *changed*, even if only for a few seconds, her flesh becoming a kaleidoscope of light and shadow with an outline of wings taking shape and arcing behind her. It reminded me of the winged statues guarding the City of the Gods in Iliseeum.

I'd then watched her destroy Isbeth.

No one among us would miss the woman, but the Blood Queen had been Poppy's mother.

At some point, the realization that she had taken her mother's life would hit her, bringing out a lot of messy, complicated emotions.

And I would be there for her.

So would Kieran.

He walked on her other side, doing the same as I was. Every couple of moments, he glanced down at her, a mixture of concern and awe flashing across his blood-streaked features.

He was a fucking mess.

So was I.

Our clothing and what remained of our armor was shredded from the battle. I knew blood splattered my flesh—some of it mine, some from the dakkais. The rest was dried specks from those who'd been struck down—those who had died but hadn't *stayed* dead.

I glanced to where Delano prowled silently behind us. While most of the wolven and the others were currently moving through Carsodonia in search of the Ascended and looking for my brother, he had chosen to follow Poppy.

There was a strange, unnerving sensation I couldn't shake as Delano lifted his head and pale, luminous blue eyes met mine. I wondered if the life restored to those who'd fallen in battle had been a gift that could be stripped away at any moment. I had no real reason to feel that way. According to Nektas, the act of restoring life to so many was not only known to the Primals of Life and of Death but also aided by them.

Besides, that feeling of unease could be sourced back to a shit ton of things. We were currently moving about the enemy's nest, and while none of the mortal servants or Royal Guards who remained at Wayfair had put up a fight when we entered, and there had only been three Ascended underground so far, none of us were comfortable here. Wayfair wasn't ours. It never would be.

Another thing preying on my mind at the moment was my brother, who was somewhere out there, chasing after Millicent, who happened to be Poppy's sister. And none of us knew where Millicent stood in regard to their mother.

Then again, from my personal experience with Millie, I didn't think she knew where she stood on anything half the time.

There was also the fact that Poppy's Primal grandparents were no longer sleeping, and from what I could figure out, one of them could enter the mortal realm whenever they felt like it.

And then there was Callum, that golden fuck of a Revenant who still needed to be dealt with, which brought me to what probably should be the most disconcerting item of all. Yes, we'd defeated the Blood Crown, but the real battle awaited. We had only prevented Kolis, the original and *true* Primal of Death, from taking full corporeal form. Still, he was free, he was awake, and he wasn't the only one. All those things were hardcore pressing issues, but...

My gaze returned to Poppy's profile, and my chest tightened again. The thin, jagged scar on her cheek and the one cutting across her forehead and eyebrow stood out more starkly than they ever had. She was pale—paler than she'd been when she came to at the Temple. And shouldn't it be the opposite? Shouldn't her skin have become flushed? Other than the passing blush earlier, it hadn't, and that worried me most of all.

Poppy turned her head in my direction. Our gazes met. Her irises were the color of dewy spring grass laced with vibrant streaks of silver— eather. Was it just me, or had those luminous lines gotten brighter in the time it took us to arrive at Wayfair? Her full lips curved up in a reassuring smile, and I knew immediately that she'd picked up on my concern, either because I was projecting it, or she was simply reading me—reading all of us around her.

I reached out and took her hand. More pressure clamped down on my chest. Her hand, so much smaller than mine, was *cold*. Not icy, but also not warm.

"Are you feeling all right?" I asked, my voice low yet echoing through the cavernous hall.

Poppy nodded. "Yes." Her brows knitted as her eyes searched mine. "Are you?"

"Always," I murmured, glancing at Kieran.

There was more concern than awe in his stare. Without me having to say anything, he inched closer to Poppy.

Something wasn't right.

Starting with Nektas, who now walked silently on Kieran's other side. Poppy had asked earlier if what she had become, a Primal that had never existed before, was a good thing or bad. I already knew the answer to that. But Nektas's response?

That is yet to be known.

Yeah, I didn't like that at all.

I also didn't like his expression when he looked at Poppy. It reminded me of how we all looked at Malik—like we weren't sure we could trust him. No one wanted a draken looking at them like that.

Poppy suddenly stopped at the entrance to a long, shadowy hall. There was a musty scent to this area, one that threatened to send my mind back to darker, colder places. I stopped that before it could happen. Now wasn't the time for that shit.

Slipping her hand from mine, Poppy faced us. "Okay. Why does everyone keep looking at me?" she demanded, propping her hands on her hips as she lifted her chin. "Has something changed about me that I'm unaware of?"

"Other than your adorable fangs?" I offered.

Her eyes narrowed on me, but I grinned as I saw the skin around her mouth move as she ran her tongue over her top teeth. Then she winced, likely nicking her tongue yet again. "Other than that."

Kieran said nothing as Delano plopped his ass down, thumping his tail on the stone floor. I wasn't sure what that was supposed to translate to.

"I imagine they are looking at you with concern," Nektas answered in that gravelly voice of his.

"Why?" Poppy glanced between Kieran and me. "Aren't I the last thing any of you should be worried about?"

"Well..." Nektas drew out the word.

Kieran's head cut sharply in the draken's direction, his nostrils flaring, and it reminded me of what else Nektas had told us at the Temple. The heavy meaning to his words as he said we'd better make sure that what Poppy had become *was* something good.

"I wouldn't go so far as to say you're the last thing anyone should be worried about," Nektas continued. "You're likely the...second thing they should be worried about."

"What is that supposed to mean?" Kieran demanded.

Nektas gave the wolven a passing glance. "Kolis is our primary concern." He tilted his head. Long, silver-streaked strands slid over a bare shoulder, revealing the faint ridges of scales. "And she should be your second."

Poppy frowned. "I disagree. I think my father and your daughter are tied for first place, then Kolis. I shouldn't even be on the list of things to worry about."

Nektas opened his mouth.

"I'd be careful how you answer that," I warned.

Slowly, the ancient draken turned his head to me. Our stares locked. His vertical pupils constricted until they were thin strips of black against vibrant blue. "Interesting."

I arched a brow. "What is?"

"You," he answered. Delano's ears flattened in the tense silence that followed the word. "You stepped in front of her as if you believe she needs your protection."

I was completely unaware that I had. So had Kieran and Delano. "And?"

Poppy sighed from behind us.

"That is wise of you. Even the most powerful of beings need protection at times," Nektas advised. "But this is not one of them."

"I'm not so sure about that." My hand rested on the hilt of the dagger at my hip. It wouldn't do shit to a draken, but I would make it hurt.

"This is all really unnecessary," Poppy began.

"I'm not so sure of that, either." Sensing that she was edging to my right, I sidestepped her and held Nektas's stare. "I don't give two shits who you are. You don't need to be worried about her at all."

One side of the draken's mouth curled up, and another too-long moment of silence passed. "You are far too much like him."

"Like who?" Poppy asked.

His pupils dilated. "The one his bloodline is descended from."

"What the fuck?" Kieran muttered under his breath and then said louder, "Who was that?"

A shadow of a smile appeared on the draken's face. "You mean to ask who *is* that."

My brows shot together. "I'm going to need—"

A low rumble cut me off. Delano stood, looking around as the sound increased, becoming deeper. My gaze flew to Kieran. He turned as the very floor beneath us began to tremble. I spun toward Poppy.

Her green and silver eyes were wide. "What?"

Clouds of dust drifted like snow from the high ceiling, coating our shoulders and the floor. The rumble grew as the entire castle shook.

"It's not me," Poppy shouted over the noise, throwing up her hands. "I swear."

My gaze flew to the ceiling, where thin fractures suddenly erupted in the stone. "Shit."

I launched forward. Delano followed as I grabbed hold of Poppy, cracks forming in the pillars and quickly racing down their lengths. Afraid the entire damn castle was about to come down on our heads, my first thought was of her. I shoved Poppy between Kieran and me as Delano pressed against her legs. She squeaked as we caged her in, using our bodies to protect hers in case the ceiling ended up on top of us.

Delano whimpered as something heavy toppled somewhere in the underground lair, crashing down. More dust fell in thick clouds. The rumbling grew louder until nothing else could be heard, and the very realm itself shuddered—

Then it stopped. All of it.

The rumbling. The cracking of stone and plaster. The crashing of what were probably very important things like support beams. It all just ceased as quickly as it had started.

"Um," came Poppy's muffled voice. "I can barely breathe."

I could only see the top of her head beneath Kieran's and my arms. I wasn't quite ready to lower them.

"That wasn't her," Nektas stated, a bemused expression on his face. "That was them."

"Them?" Kieran repeated, slowly lowering his arms from Poppy.

"The gods," the draken elaborated. "One of them must've awakened nearby."

One of them must have...

Poppy shot out from under me as fast as an arrow, her eyes still wide but now lit with eagerness. "Penellaphe," she gasped, her head darting between Kieran and me. "Remember? You said the goddess Penellaphe sleeps beneath the city's Atheneum!" She shoved Kieran in the arm, causing him to stumble back a step. "Oops. Sorry."

"It's okay." Kieran caught himself, grinning. "And, yes, I did say that."

She spun toward Nektas. "Can we see her? I mean after we've freed my father and located Jadis. You see, I was named—"

"After the goddess who spoke of you so very long before you were born," Nektas finished. "Who was the first to call you the Harbinger and the Bringer of Death. A prophecy you have fulfilled."

Her arms slowly lowered to her sides. "Well, when you put it like that…" She pressed her lips together. "I think I've changed my mind."

I never wanted to punch someone more than I did the draken for stealing that brief excitement from Poppy.

Nektas chuckled. "I'm sure she will be interested in meeting you. All of them will be when the time is right," he said, his face softening in a way I had yet to see from him. "We should get moving in case there are more who slumber in the capital. I do not want to be down here if that happens again."

He was right. None of us wanted that.

"By the way," he said, glancing at Kieran and me as we started down the hall once more. "You two are…adorable."

Kieran's forehead scrunched as he brushed dust from his shoulder. "I don't think I've ever been referred to as adorable before, but thanks." He paused. "I think."

The draken chuckled once more. "All three of you raced to shield her." He nodded at Delano, who trotted beside Poppy as she led us down another hall, this one narrower. A column had toppled here, leaning against another. "The one person who would survive the collapse of a building."

I hadn't even thought of that.

Poppy grinned. "It *was* kind of adorable."

Kieran huffed, and I swore I saw a deepening in the color of his light brown cheeks.

"And unnecessary in more ways than one," Nektas went on. "The three of you are Joined, are you not?"

Delano's ears perked as Poppy's head swung toward him. Some color returned to her cheeks. His tail wagged. Clearly, he'd communicated something intriguing through the Primal *notam*. I'd have to ask him about it later.

"Yeah," she answered. "But I think it's going to take all of us a while to remember that if I'm okay, then all three of us are."

"Understatement of the century," Kieran remarked, drawing a grin from me.

The expression disappeared, though. Because as soon as her blush faded, the paleness of her skin was even more noticeable.

Something isn't right.

The feeling only intensified as we walked, traveling deeper into the underground maze of chambers and halls that Poppy had moved about as a small child. I couldn't place why I felt the way I did. The pressure remained in my chest and the back of my throat—

Click. Click. Click.

Poppy halted once more. This time, her hands opened and closed at her sides. I dragged my gaze from her to the hall in front of us. Up ahead, a soft glow spilled out into the hall, beating back the shadows.

That sound. We all recognized it. We'd heard it before in Oak Ambler. The rapping of claws against stone.

Nektas started forward, his steps fast and sure as Poppy remained frozen. I touched her shoulder, drawing her attention to me.

"Are you okay?" I asked. This time, I wasn't talking about how she felt physically.

Nodding, she swallowed as she looked at Nektas. He stopped at the cusp of the light, turning his head back to us.

"You sure?" Kieran asked, his gaze searching Poppy's.

"Yeah. Yes." She cleared her throat. "It's just that…that's my father, and I don't know what to think or even say."

I got it.

Poppy had a father she remembered: Leopold. The man she was about to set free was a stranger to her, even if she had spent time searching him out in her youth—someone who had been held captive for too long. And I was sure she was caught between excitement and guilt, feeling as if she somehow dishonored Leo's memory, and regret that she hadn't realized who had been caged beneath Wayfair and at Oak Ambler earlier. It was a lot for anyone to think about. More to act upon.

Cupping her cheek, I turned her face to mine. I smiled, even though the heaviness in my chest and throat expanded. Her skin was so damn cold. "You don't have to feel or think anything right now. All you must do is make sure he's freed." I lowered my voice. "You don't have to see him at all if you're not ready. No one will judge you for that."

Kieran nodded in agreement. "Either way, we'll be right there with you."

She glanced between us, then turned her attention to Nektas. I smoothed my thumb along her jaw. A faint tremor went through her, and then she drew in a deep breath. She squared her shoulders, and I knew what she had decided before she spoke. "I'm ready."

"Of course," I murmured, dipping to press a kiss to her cool temple. "So brave."

"I don't know about that," she said but nodded. "But I will be."

Kieran smiled, lifting a hand. "As always." He touched her other cheek, his eyes widening slightly. Over her head, his gaze shot to mine.

He'd felt how cold her skin was. I gave him a curt nod of acknowledgment.

"I'm ready," Poppy repeated, pulling away from us. She started walking with Delano at her side.

We hung back just for a second. Kieran spoke, his voice too low for her to hear. "Why is her skin so damn cold?"

"I don't know," I said. "But something—"

"Isn't right."

My gaze cut to him sharply. "You feel it, too?"

"Yeah. In my chest and here," he said, motioning to his throat.

Hell.

That didn't make me feel better about any of this, but now wasn't the time to figure it out. We'd told Poppy we'd be beside her, so we both got our asses moving, joining her as she and Delano reached Nektas's side.

The clicking had picked up.

"I know this isn't easy for you," Nektas said, looking down at Poppy. His voice was barely above a whisper. "This won't be easy for him, either. Ires has always been..." He shook his head. "We should hurry."

I could tell that Poppy wanted to ask what he had been about to say, but she stepped into the light and turned instead. The scraping of claws against stone stopped. We followed, my heartbeat picking up speed and matching the rate of hers. I lifted my gaze from her to what waited beyond.

A cage sat in the center of a candlelit chamber. Behind black bars, likely constructed of shadowstone, was a large, gray feline with bright green eyes fixed on Poppy—just as they had been in Oak Ambler. There was no doubt in my mind that he'd known who she was to him then.

Probably had all those years ago, too.

"My gods," gasped Nektas, his eyes widening as the skin around his mouth went taut at the sight of Ires.

The god hadn't looked this haggard when we'd seen him last. Ribs pressed against his dull gray fur coat. His stomach was sunken. Tendons strained in his throat as his head whipped toward Nektas.

Ires reacted upon seeing the draken, jumping weakly at the bars as his still-bright eyes shot between Nektas and Poppy when they entered the chamber.

"Are these wards?" Kieran asked, noticing the markings etched into the shadowstone ceiling and floor, symbols and letters in ancient Atlantian—the language of the gods.

"Yes." Nektas went to the bars. "No one in the mortal realm should be in possession of this knowledge."

"Callum," I surmised, watching Poppy kneel before the cage.

Nektas nodded. "But that's not the issue right now." He clasped the bars, drawing Ires's attention, but only for a moment. "He might be a bit…unstable, especially if he's been in this state for as long as I fear. He'll be more animal than anything. We need to be careful."

No one needed to tell us that as Ires kept jumping at the bars, pressing his sides and head against them as a low noise radiated from him, a sound that was a cross between a growl and a whine.

I crouched behind Poppy, forcing my hands to my knees to stop myself from grabbing her and hauling her back.

"Can you get past these bars?" Poppy asked, her hands twisting together, a sure sign she was anxious. "Or can I?"

"You will probably be able to. Eventually," Nektas tacked on. "But I can." He focused on Ires. "You're safe now. I promise you," he said to the god, voice thickening with emotion. "I just need you to stay calm. Okay?"

Ires leapt at the bars again.

"I don't think that's a yes," Kieran noted, kneeling beside me.

"It's okay," Nektas told Ires once again, but the more the draken spoke, the more the god behaved erratically, pacing and lunging at the bars. "Dammit, he's going to hurt himself."

"I can barely…barely pick up anything from him." Poppy's worry flooded her tone, and I swore I could feel it gathering in my throat like too-thick cream. "He wasn't like this before."

"He's been in this form too long," Nektas answered. "It's not like us," he added, nodding at Kieran and Delano. "We are of two worlds. He is only of one, and it's far too easy, even for a god and a Primal, to lose themselves if they stay in their animal form for too long."

Shit. How long was *too long* for a god when we were likely talking about hundreds of years? But another thought occurred to me. He'd said if a god and a Primal stayed in their animal form for too long. Did that mean Poppy would...?

I shook my head. Now wasn't the time to consider that. Rubbing Poppy's back, I watched Ires pace, hating this for her—for both of them.

"I didn't know that," Poppy responded to what Nektas had shared.

"Neither did I," Kieran added.

"And on top of that, he's probably felt the other gods awakening," Nektas explained. "It would feel like an extreme jolt of energy that he would not have been prepared for."

Kieran rose as Ires pressed against the bars in front of us. "I can try to distract him while you—dammit, *Poppy*."

A wicked sense of déjà vu swept through me as Poppy lurched forward. I reached for her, but dammit, she was fast when she wanted to be—and even faster now.

"Poppy," I shouted as she crouched and thrust her hand through the bars. "Don't—"

Too late.

Her hand was already pressed against the side of Ires's throat by the time I curled an arm around her waist. Ires swung his head back, lips peeling back over sharp fucking canines. A low growl of warning radiated from him. I started to haul Poppy's ass back. She would be pissed, but I'd rather her be angry at me than experience exactly what happened when a Primal lost a hand.

"It's okay," she said, inhaling deeply. "Just give me a second. Please."

I didn't want to, but she'd said *please*. Still, it took everything in me to keep from grabbing her again. The only reason I didn't fail was because Poppy succeeded.

Ires shuddered, the low snarl fading as he stood there, panting. I knew what she was doing, feeding good thoughts and emotions into the god. Calming him.

The first time she'd done that to me, I hadn't known what she could do. The relief—the *peace*—she had given me had been quick and stunning. A gift. Still, I wanted her pretty hand as far away from Ires as it could get. I liked her hands and the things she was learning to do with them.

Poppy's eyes were half-closed as Delano pressed against her side, his stare wary, watchful, and pinned on Ires. "It's okay. Just give him a few seconds."

"Whatever you're going to do with these bars…" Kieran said to Nektas, a dagger in hand—one I knew he wouldn't hesitate to use. "I suggest you do it quick."

"Working on it." Nektas stepped back from the bars.

A tremor went through Ires. His fur stood on end, and Poppy kept her hand on him as he lowered to his belly. His ears twitched. A bright blue flare came from our right, lighting the chamber—draken fire. Nektas hadn't shifted. I figured we would've been aware of a huge-ass draken in the chamber if he had. I was curious, but I didn't dare take my eyes off Ires and Poppy.

Ires began trembling as the scent of heated metal filled the air. Silvery light appeared in his eyes, spreading. His fur retracted and faded as patches of golden skin appeared. Muscles shrank, and bones cracked into different positions. Long, russet-colored hair appeared—hair damn near as long as Nektas's. I folded my other arm around Poppy, holding her tightly as her father struggled through the transition. It appeared as if he were fighting it. Or maybe the animal in him was. The process likely took less than a minute, but it looked painful, unlike when Kieran and the others shifted. It was as if he felt every claw sink back into his nailbeds.

Another ripple of shimmering light swept over him, and then, a male appeared in the cage where the large feline had been. He was on his knees, his upper body tucked into his lower half. Through clumps of unwashed hair, he stared at Poppy's hand resting on what turned out to be his shoulder.

Poppy lifted her hand, her fingers curling inward as she drew her arm back. She tightly gripped the arm I'd put around her waist. "Hi," she whispered.

The god's bright green eyes locked with Poppy's. Eyes that were almost identical to hers. The silvery glow in his, just behind the pupils, was faint. Much of his face was hidden, but what I could see was all sharp angles and sunken planes. He shook.

"I don't know if you…if you remember me at all," Poppy began. She was trembling, too. I held onto her. "But my name is Poppy—well, it's Penellaphe, but my friends call me Poppy. I'm your…" She trailed off, her breath catching. I ran my hand over her side, squeezing her.

Ires was silent as he stared at her, seemingly unaware of Kieran and me, even Delano, who was practically standing on us both. Ires's breathing was heavy and quick, bony shoulders rising with each inhale.

"Ires," Nektas said quietly.

His head jerked as he looked down the length of the cage. Nektas had not only melted a huge portion of the bars, he now stood inside the cell with Ires.

"I'm here now," the draken continued, softer than I would've thought him capable of as he kept his hands at his sides. "I've come to take you home."

Another shudder went through Ires, and his eyes drifted shut. Nektas carefully inched closer.

"I'm going to see if I can find something for him. A blanket or something," Kieran said, voice gruff.

"Thank you." Poppy turned her head, pressing her cheek against my chest. There was a shimmer of dampness beneath her eyes. Gods, if she was picking up on his emotions now, I couldn't even begin to imagine what she felt from him.

Actually, I could.

He was feeling everything and nothing right now. Relief but also confusion, likely due to starvation, and the gods only knew what else they'd done to him. He had to be terrified. I had been both times, fearing my rescue was a dream. He likely worried that he'd wake up and none of us would be here. That it would just be *her*. *Them*. Taunting him. Terrorizing him. He'd be terrified it wasn't an illusion and be afraid he'd hurt those trying to help him.

"This isn't a dream," I said.

Ires's chin jerked, and his eyes met mine through the tangled curtain of hair.

I nodded as I brushed my fingers under Poppy's eyes, wiping away her tears. "This is real. It's over. She's dead. Isbeth. You are free of her—from this."

A ragged breath left Ires. He swallowed. I saw his lips move, but there was just a raspy sound as he seemed to struggle to get his body and mind to communicate so he could speak. Gods only knew when he'd spoken last.

Kieran returned, handing what appeared to be one of the black and crimson cloth banners to Nektas.

The draken nodded his thanks, then knelt beside Ires. Gently, he draped the cloth over Ires's shoulders. The material seemed like it would cause the god to collapse, but after a moment, a too-thin hand appeared, and frail fingers curled around the edges of the banner. He held the material to him, and while that was only a small act, it was *something*.

"I know," came a hoarse whisper. Ires lifted his other hand, reaching it through the bars. "I know...who you are."

Poppy rocked back, her body stiffening against me before she pitched forward. "Okay," she whispered, her voice cracking. She worked an arm free and brought her hand to his. Their fingers threaded through each other's. Her shoulders relaxed. "Okay."

Dipping my head, I kissed the back of hers as Ires weakly squeezed her hand. Father. Daughter. It didn't matter that they were strangers.

"Where is...where is she?" Ires rasped, still holding onto Poppy's hand. "My...other girl."

"Millicent?" Poppy swallowed thickly. "She's not here, but..."

"She's fine. She's with my brother." I had no idea if Malik had found her yet or even if it was a good thing for either of them if he had. That was a whole different mess that Ires didn't need to know about.

A heavy exhale left the god as he slowly turned his attention to Nektas. "I'm sorry—"

"There's no need for that right now," Nektas cut him off. "I need to get you back home. You are not well."

Kieran glanced at me questioningly, and I shook my head.

"But there...is. I didn't know this...would happen. I...I would never have brought her with...me if I thought—" He coughed, shaking. "I'm sorry."

Jadis. They were speaking of Nektas's daughter. Damn.

"She's..." Air wheezed in and out of Ires as his hand slipped from Poppy's, falling limply to his side. She stretched forward, grasping the bars. "I know where...she is. The Willow..." He took a shallow breath.

"The willow?" Nektas asked, the lines of his face tensing.

"Willow Plains," Poppy exclaimed. "Are you speaking of the town there?"

"Yes. She is...she is there. I'm sorry. I'm so...damn tired. I don't know..." Ires caved in on himself. He went down, barely caught by Nektas.

"No!" Poppy shot to her feet, grasping the bars. "Is he okay?"

"I believe so." Nektas placed a palm against the unconscious god's forehead.

"I can help him," Poppy said, already reaching through the bars once more. "I just need to touch him. I can heal—"

"This is not something another can heal. He's fine," Nektas quickly added. "He just passed out."

"How is passing out fine?" Poppy demanded. "That doesn't sound fine to me."

"He's obviously been unable to feed in any way for too long." Anger thinned Nektas's lips even as he reassured Poppy. "He is far too weak."

"Are you sure that's all it is?" Her worry twisted my insides, choking me.

Nektas cradled the limp god to his chest. "He just needs to be home, where he can go to ground. That can't happen here," he explained. "Not with the shadowstone."

"Okay. All right." Poppy took a deep breath, letting go of the bars. "I think he might be speaking of Willow Plains. It's east of the capital, a bit to the north. It's where most of the soldiers are trained. There are a few Temples there, and if they're anything like—" She took a step back, lifting a hand to her head. "Whoa."

"What is it?" I was already at her side, hands on her arms.

"I don't know." Her brow furrowed. "I was just dizzy for a moment."

"You're pale." I glanced at Kieran. "She's even paler, isn't she?"

Kieran nodded. "She is."

"Probably because my head's been aching," she told us. "It started a little bit ago."

"Why didn't you say anything?" I asked, forcing my voice to remain calm, even though that was the last thing I felt.

"Because it's just a headache." She drew out the words.

"Just a headache?" I repeated dumbly. "Do Primals get headaches?" I looked at Nektas. "If so, that seems messed up."

"They can," the draken answered. "But there's usually a reason for it."

Wasn't there always a reason for a headache?

Kieran lifted a hand to Poppy's cheek. "Skin's colder." His jaw flexed. "Real cold now."

Poppy glanced between us. "What? I don't feel cold."

I touched her other cheek as she poked the skin of her chin. My stomach dipped. Cold didn't even begin to describe the iciness of her flesh. Then it hit me. "Do you need to feed?"

"I don't think so," she said, brushing our hands away. "And if my skin feels cold, it's because we're underground."

"I don't think it's because we're underground," Kieran said.

I agreed with that. "You were cold before we even came down here."

Poppy gave us both an exasperated look. "Guys, I appreciate the concern, but it's not necessary. We have more important things to worry about."

"Disagree," I stated. "No one is more important than you."

"Cas," she warned, eyes narrowing—eyes that were now shadowed. Faint purple bruised the skin beneath them.

"Did she sleep?" Nektas asked.

Her frown deepened. "Uh, last night."

"I'm not talking about that kind of sleep." Nektas shifted the unconscious god in his arms. "Have you entered a deep sleep? A stasis at the end of your Ascension?"

"No." Her nose scrunched.

"She slept for a bit at the start, but that was because..." Kieran looked at Ires, then clearly changed his mind about how much detail he'd go into, even though the god was out cold. "No, she hasn't slept like that."

"Well, damn." There was a grim twist to Nektas's mouth. "So, you're telling me that you went through the Ascension and completed the Culling *without* going into stasis?"

"Yeah. I mean, I did pass out there for a few moments," Poppy said. "But you already know that."

"I really don't like where this conversation is heading," Kieran muttered.

Neither did I.

"This is inconvenient timing," Nektas grumbled.

I tensed. "What is?"

"What's likely to happen any moment now," he said.

"You need to give us some more detail," I said, frustration burning its way through me.

"I'm fine," Poppy insisted, turning to Nektas. "Can we please get him out of this cage?"

Nektas nodded. "I'm planning to do just that, but I think you should probably sit down."

"You should listen to him," Kieran urged, his stare intense. The shadows were even darker beneath her eyes.

"Please don't worry about me," Poppy said. "I feel totally—" She sucked in a sharp breath as she pressed her hand to her temple.

"Is it your head?" I grasped her shoulders, turning her toward me as a sharp slice of fear cut through my chest and stomach.

Her eyes were squeezed shut. "Yeah, it's just a headache. I'm—" Her legs went out from under her.

"Poppy!" I caught her around the waist as Kieran lurched forward, bracing the back of her head. "Open your eyes." I cupped her cheek—gods, her skin was far too cold. Shifting my arm under her legs, I lifted her to my chest. "Come on. Please—"

"She's not going to wake, no matter how much you beg."

"What the fuck does that mean?" Kieran whipped his head toward Nektas.

"It basically means I was wrong in my assumption that she's fully completed the Culling. She's gone into stasis to finish it," Nektas explained. "I'm surprised it took this long for it to happen—or that she even woke up earlier. I suppose the eather is strong in her. That's why—"

"I don't give a fuck about the eather in her," I snarled. "What's happening to her?"

"You should care about the eather in her, especially since you've Joined with a Primal. But that's neither here nor there at the moment," Nektas responded too damn calmly. "She's in stasis, just like her father. It happens when Primals, even gods, finish their Culling. Or when they're weakened and unable to recoup their strength. You would know if she were injured or in danger in any way."

"What do you mean by that?" Kieran turned, his gaze falling to Poppy as Delano whined, pacing nervously at my side. "How would we know?"

"The very land itself would seek to protect her," Nektas said. "She would—"

"Go to ground," I murmured, remembering the roots that had come out of the ground, attempting to cover her when she was mortally wounded in the Wastelands. We hadn't understood what was happening then.

"She *sleeps*," Nektas repeated. "That is all."

That was all? I looked down at Poppy. Her cheek rested against my chest. Except for the bruises under her eyes and her cold skin, she did look like she simply slept. "How—?" I cleared my throat. "How long will she sleep?"

"That I cannot answer. And, yeah, I know that doesn't make either of you happy," he said as Kieran growled. "It could be a day or a couple of days. A week. It's different for everyone, but it's likely her body is now catching up with the whole process. She'll awaken once she fully finishes the Culling."

Kieran cursed under his breath, rubbing a hand over his hair. I stared at Poppy, the pressure in my chest tightening. Had this been what both Kieran and I sensed through the bond we'd forged during the Joining? That she was on the verge of going into stasis? And she could be out for days? A week?

"Gods," I bit out, feeling fucking helpless and hating every moment of it.

"Get her someplace comfortable and wait it out. That is all you can do," Nektas said. "I'll take care of Ires."

Somewhere comfortable? Here? I shared a look with Kieran. Poppy wouldn't be comfortable anywhere in Wayfair, but what choice did we have?

"We'll find a place," Kieran assured, slipping into the role he always did. The logical one. The calm and supportive one when shit went south. But I knew that was far too often a façade. I started to turn.

"There is just one thing you should be aware of," Nektas added, stopping all of us in our tracks. "The stasis that comes at the end of a Culling can have…unexpected and lasting side effects."

A fist seized my heart. Trepidation rose. "Like what?"

"Loss of memory. Lack of knowledge of who they and those around them are," he explained.

That invisible fist…

It fucking crushed my heart.

Kieran's entire body jerked back a full step. "It's possible she…" The calm began to crack. "She won't know who she is? Who we are?"

"It is, but it is very rare. I can only think of twice that it has happened," Nektas said, tension bracketing his mouth. "You just need to be aware of the possibility."

And what if it became a reality? Kieran's stare met mine. I swallowed. "And if it does happen?"

Nektas didn't answer for a long moment. "Then she will be a stranger to herself and you."

Kieran's eyes closed.

Mine couldn't. I looked down at Poppy. She was my heart—my everything. I couldn't even consider her not knowing who she was—not knowing *us*.

"Talk to her." Nektas's voice had softened. "That's what Nyktos did when *she* was in stasis. I don't know if she heard him, but I think it helped." His head tilted as he looked down at Ires. "I know it helped him."

I nodded, turning from the draken. I knew I should've asked when or if he'd be back. I imagined he would be. His daughter was in this realm, but given the single-minded bastard I was, my only priority was to get Poppy somewhere comfortable. I wasn't thinking about Nektas and his daughter. Nor Poppy's father, or the Crown we'd just overthrown—the kingdom we'd conquered, yet only in the most technical sense. All those things were important, but none of them mattered.

I carried Poppy back through the underground maze and to the first floor, my heart calm and steady because it followed the rhythm of hers. I kept reminding myself of that as Kieran walked ahead and Delano stuck close to my side. Other than that, the surroundings were a blur. All I knew was that Kieran and a member of the castle staff had a hushed conversation, and I thought I heard Emil's voice as we climbed a narrow set of stairs. I didn't know how many floors we went up. There were only whitewashed stone walls and a few windows until we entered an empty hall lined with heavy, black drapes. A door opened ahead, and I followed Kieran into a darkened chamber. He went straight to two large windows framing a bed and grabbed the brocade curtains, tearing them from their rods.

"This is a guest room," Kieran explained, tossing the drapes aside. "It hasn't been used in a while, but it has been recently cleaned."

A faint breeze drifted in through the windows as I looked around. The chamber was outfitted with several couches and chairs, and there appeared to be access to a bathing chamber. It would do.

Kieran followed me as I carried Poppy to the bed. He grabbed hold of a cream-hued blanket and pulled it back. I didn't want to let her go. It was like I was physically incapable of doing so. My arms trembled as I laid her down.

"She hasn't stirred once," I heard myself saying as I forced my arms out from under her. I sat beside her, shaking my head. "Her eyelashes haven't even fluttered."

"She'll be okay," Kieran said as Delano jumped onto the bed and lay down on her other side by her hip, placing his head between his front legs. His gaze was trained on the door. "I don't think Nektas would lie to us."

"Does that make you feel better about this?"

"Hell, no."

Drawing my lower lip between my teeth, I kept shaking my head. So much shit was running through it. "I don't like being here, in this godsforsaken place, when she's in this vulnerable state."

"I will make sure no staff even enters this floor," Emil said from the doorway.

I looked over at the Atlantian. I'd been right about hearing his voice, but I hadn't realized he'd followed us. Shit. I needed to get it together. "Thank you."

Emil's golden eyes flicked to Delano. "Neither will he."

I nodded. Poppy looked so damn…lifeless. I briefly closed my eyes, ordering myself to chill the fuck out. She couldn't be comfortable like this, with weapons strapped to her and her feet filthy with blood and dirt. I glanced over my shoulder at the bathing chamber. "Is Hisa near?" I asked, speaking of the Commander of the Crown Guard.

Kieran nodded. "Want me to see if she can find something for her to wear?"

"Yeah." Clearing my throat, I ran my hand over the harness at her thigh, undoing the snaps. There was something strangely calming about the task. It made all the roaring thoughts slow enough for me to remember who I was—who we were. "Emil?"

"Yes," he answered immediately.

"We're going to be out of commission for a bit, but no one other than our people needs to know why," I began, slipping the harness and the dagger from her leg. "First thing we need to do is make sure Wayfair is secure."

"Already on it," Emil answered. "The wolven were already guarding the premises when you were all below, along with Hisa and the Crown Guard."

"Perfect." I watched Kieran take the harness from me, placing it on the nightstand. "We need to find my brother and…and Millicent."

"Naill went after them," Emil shared.

"I…" I met Kieran's stare. "I don't want either of them near this floor."

"Understood," Emil said. There were no jokes or teasing from him. Not now. "And what do you want us to do about the Ascended? We haven't found any more in the castle, but I have been made aware of several clusters in the manors near the Golden Bridge and within the Garden District."

Kill them. That was my first response. *Make it quick and neat.* But as I brushed a smudge of dirt from Poppy's hand, I knew she wouldn't want that. Especially since I couldn't say that any of them were running in our direction. "Keep them in their homes." The words tasted like ash on my tongue. "Make sure all know the Ascended are not to be harmed until we discuss what to do with them."

"Will do," Emil answered. There was a pause. "And what of your father?"

Fuck. I hadn't even thought about him and the others in Padonia.

"We need to send word to him." Kieran had knelt at our side. "Let him know the status of everything. We don't have to tell him about Poppy, though."

"Agreed." I exhaled heavily, knowing he would be on his way the moment he received word of our success. I didn't know if Poppy would be awake by then. I thought about her friend. "Make sure Tawny comes with him."

"And what of the people of Carsodonia?" Emil asked after a moment. "They are still locked down in their homes, by choice currently, but I don't think that will last for long."

No, I didn't either.

What to do with them was a damn good question. "Many of them have spent their entire lives believing we're monsters. They're going to be scared. We will...we will need to address them."

Kieran nodded his agreement. "I think we'll have some time before that becomes necessary."

"We'll cross that bridge when we're ready to set it on fire," I said with a dry laugh, dragging the back of my hand across my chin. "It's important that we locate Malik. He knows a lot of the Descenters here."

"They could be of help." Kieran turned to Emil. "Anything else?"

"Nothing I can think of, but I'm sure I will in about five minutes." Emil stepped back, then stopped. "Actually, it only took a second for me to think of something else."

A faint smile tugged at my lips.

"Did you find him?" Emil asked. "Her father?"

"Yes." I smiled then, wider and a little stronger. "Nektas will take him...home."

"Nektas," Emil repeated, letting out a low whistle. "He is one big motherfucking draken."

A rough laugh left me. Yeah, he was.

"And I just thought of something else," Emil said, and Kieran cracked a grin. "There was some kind of...event that occurred at the city Atheneum, almost like an explosion. It's being checked out now."

"It's fine," I said, counting Poppy's breaths. "It's the goddess Penellaphe."

"Come again?" Emil's voice pitched high.

"You heard him right," Kieran said. "The gods are awakening. She was asleep beneath the Atheneum." He paused. "There may be more coming awake, here or throughout Solis, if they haven't already."

"Oh. Okay. That's a whole bunch of completely normal and expected things to speak out loud," Emil replied slowly. "I'll...I'll let everyone know. And I'm sure none of them will have a single question or potentially overreact to such news." He started to leave.

"Emil?" I twisted at the waist, looking him over and actually paying attention. I saw him standing there, but I couldn't get the image of seeing him speared through the chest out of my mind. "How are you feeling?"

"I'm..." Emil looked down at the jagged tears in his armor. He swallowed, then looked past me to Poppy. "I'm glad to be alive. Tell her she has my everlasting devotion and utter, complete adoration when she wakes."

My eyes narrowed.

Emil winked and then turned to leave.

"Fucker," I muttered, turning to Poppy. I wasn't telling her shit.

Kieran chuckled, but the sound was quick to fade. Gods, she'd hate this—us staring at her while she slept. She'd probably stab one or both of us upon waking. I wanted to laugh, but I couldn't get the sound out.

"She'll be fine. She'll wake, and she'll know herself. She'll know us." Kieran placed his hand on my shoulder. "We just need to wait."

"Yeah." Thick emotion clogged my throat and tightened my chest.

Kieran squeezed my shoulder and then dropped his hand. He cleared his throat. "What do you think Nektas meant when he was talking about the eather and us having Joined with a Primal?"

I rubbed my chin, needing a moment to recall what he was talking about. "Man, I totally forgot about that. I have no idea. And, of course, he didn't go into any detail."

"I'm beginning to think vagueness is a unique ability when it comes to the draken," Kieran muttered.

A rough laugh left me. "Yeah, but all of us had way more important things on our minds."

We still did.

"Talk to her." I glanced at Kieran. "That's what Nektas said."

"He did."

But what did I talk to her about? I shook my head as I stared at her face. She looked too damn peaceful, when my entire being felt like it was being ripped apart. I ran the tips of my fingers over her cold cheek. *Talk to her.* I grazed the scar that started at her temple and thought of the first time I'd seen her unveiled for some reason.

Then I thought about the first time I'd seen *her*.

I didn't know if that was what Nektas had meant, but it was something. I forced a deep, steady breath as Kieran straightened the sleeve of her shirt. "Did I ever tell you what it was like when I was in Masadonia?" I said to her, feeling Kieran's and Delano's attention moving to me. "I can't remember, but I don't think I've told you what it was like before I became your guard. Everything I did." A heavier breath left me this time because I'd done *a lot*. "And how it all changed—how *I* changed—because of you."

I tucked a strand of hair behind her ear. "But where do I start?" I searched my memories. They were hazy at first. But then… "I think I'll start on the Rise."

ON THE RISE

A chill reached the Rise, chasing away what remained of the late-season warmth that had lingered far into autumn. The hint of coming snow was in the night air.

That wasn't the only thing.

I turned at the waist and propped a booted foot on the ledge, looking down at the ramshackle buildings in the shadow of the massive wall enclosing the cesspool of a city known as Masadonia. The homes were all drab shades of gray and brown, stained with dirt and smoke and stacked atop one another, leaving little room for the wagons to travel the streets, let alone enough space for the people to breathe anything but the stench of sewage and decay.

And death.

There was always death in the air near the Rise.

My lip curled in disgust as I scanned the rows and rows of homes in the Lower Ward. Lit by torches and a few sporadically placed streetlamps powered by oil instead of electricity, the packed buildings appeared one wind gust away from crumbling in on themselves. Clearly, Duke and Duchess Teerman, the Ascended who ruled Masadonia, believed only the wealthy deserved such luxuries as clean air and space, electricity, and running water.

Masadonia was one of the oldest cities in the kingdom, and I was sure it had once been beautiful when Atlantia ruled the entirety of the mortal realm—before the War of Two Kings, the Blood Crown, and the Rises were erected around cities and villages as prisons to keep out the consequences of the evil that lived within. Before my people retreated east of the Skotos Mountains for the greater good of the realm.

But no real good had come of it.

The Ascended, those who now ruled everything west of the Skotos, were expert revisionists, rewriting history by calling themselves the heroes and damning Atlantians as the villains. They'd managed to convince the mortals they were *Blessed* by the gods and installed themselves as rulers of what they now called the Kingdom of Solis.

A too-abrupt scream echoed from the shadows of the Lower Ward.

That evil didn't find its way in. It now lived among the mortals.

My grip tightened on the hilt of the broadsword at my hip as I lifted my gaze to the twinkling lights of Radiant Row, seated at the base of Castle Teerman. Now, the only beauty to be found was beyond the heavily wooded Wisher's Grove, where the elite of Masadonia lived in large manors on sprawling acres. Most were Ascended. Only a few were mortals who'd benefited from generational wealth. And they were likely aware of precisely *what* the Ascended were.

One would think the vamprys would take better care of their people, considering they would simply shrivel up and waste away without them. However, as a whole, the Ascended appeared to lack foresight as much as they did empathy. They treated their people like cattle, keeping them alive in shit conditions until it was time to be butchered.

"You never quite get used to the smells or the sounds." The voice intruded on my thoughts. "Not unless you grew up in the Lower Ward."

I turned my head to Pence. The blond-haired guard couldn't be more than a year or two into his second decade of life. I doubted he'd make it much further if he continued on the Rise. Most of the guards didn't. "Did you grow up down there?"

In the light of a nearby torch, Pence nodded as he stared at the homes lined up like uneven, jagged teeth. His answer came as no surprise. There wasn't much opportunity in Solis unless one was born into wealth. You either worked as your parents did, barely scraping by, or you joined the Royal Army hoping to be one of the lucky fools to live long enough to move off the Rise and into something like a position in the Royal Guard.

Pence frowned as several shouts broke out, coming from an area near the Citadel, where coin was spent in gambling dens and houses of pleasure. Only the gods knew what was going on. A deal gone wrong? Senseless, unprovoked murder? The Ascended themselves? The possibilities were endless.

"How about you?" he asked.

"Grew up on a farm in the east." The lie slipped easily from my lips, and it wasn't just because I did, in fact, hail from the east—the Far East—but because I was as good at lying as I was at killing.

The crease between Pence's brow deepened. "Heard you were from the capital."

"I worked on the Rise in Carsodonia." Another lie. "But I'm not from there."

"Ah." The skin between his eyes smoothed as he returned to stare at the Lower Ward and the plumes of smoke coming from chimneys.

I wasn't at all surprised that he didn't press harder about what I'd said. Most mortals rarely questioned anything. Generation after generation was groomed to simply accept what they were told. That was one thing I could thank the Ascended for. It made what I'd come to do much easier.

"Bet Carsodonia looks nothing like this," Pence said, sounding wistful.

I almost laughed. The capital was just like Masadonia, though even more stratified and worse. But I squelched the sound that wanted to rise in humor. "The beaches along the Stroud Sea are…nice."

A brief smile appeared on Pence's face, making him seem even younger. "Never seen the sea before."

He probably never would.

A gnawing pang radiated through my chest and stomach, reminding me that I needed to feed.

"My brother will, though," he added with a smile. "Owen is a second son, you know."

Anger replaced the ache, flooding my system, but I kept it in check as I turned my attention back to the Lower Ward. "He's a Lord in Wait, then?"

"Yeah. He's at the castle. Been there since he turned thirteen, learning to be a Lord."

I smirked. "How does one *learn* to be a Lord?"

"I imagine it's all about which fork and spoon is the correct one to eat with. Fancy shit like that." Pence let out a raspy laugh, reminding me that he'd only just recovered from one of the many sicknesses that ran rampant through the Citadel and the Lower Ward. "Probably bored out of his mind learning the histories and how to act right, not realizing how lucky he is."

"Lucky?" I glanced at him.

"Fuck, yeah. All the second sons and daughters are." Pence adjusted the hilt of his sword. "He'll never have to worry about being up on the

Rise or going out beyond it. He's got it made, Hawke. He really does."

I stared at the fool—no, not a fool. Pence may not be educated—none of the first sons or daughters were unless they were wealthy—but the man wasn't a fool. He'd just been fed the same bullshit the Blood Crown doled out in spoonfuls. So, of course, he thought his brother was lucky to be given to the Royal Court upon his thirteenth birthday during the godsforsaken Rite—as all second sons and daughters were. They were raised at Court and then, at some point, received the Blessing of the gods. They were Ascended. But I supposed Owen was luckier than the third sons and daughters, those given over at infancy during the Rite to serve the gods in the various Temples throughout the kingdom.

I ground my molars. The faith the people had in the Ascended was strong, wasn't it? In truth, the Lords and Ladies in Wait didn't receive jack shit from the gods when they Ascended, and those babes weren't being raised to serve the gods because the gods had been resting for centuries.

But most of the people of Solis didn't know that, and if I were being fair, it wasn't all that hard to understand how the Ascended had so many believing in them. If one only looked at the surface, you wouldn't doubt the gods had Blessed the Ascended. Not when they *appeared* to have been gifted strength, longevity, wealth, and power that mortals could only dream of. However, nothing about the Ascended—the Blood Crown and all their Dukes and Duchesses and Ascended Lords and Ladies—was a blessing.

It was all a fucking waking nightmare.

An odd noise came from behind us, a low wail easily mistaken for the wind, but everyone on the Rise was trained to listen for that sound. The warning. We turned at once, facing the moonlight-drenched lands beyond the Rise.

I crossed to the other side of the wall and looked out over the barren lands. Clouds had gathered, blocking most of the moonlight, but my eyesight was far better than the others on the Rise and below, just outside the wall, where the horses whinnied nervously, I saw what that sound warned of. Beyond the row of torches placed about halfway out from the Rise, a thick mist gathered at the edges of the Blood Forest, a lone shadow in the mist.

Pence joined me, scanning the darkened land. He was paler now, but his shoulders were straight as he withdrew the bow strapped to his back. The guard was afraid, but that didn't make him any less brave.

The Blood Crown didn't deserve him or the men below, those who began riding forward. Some of them wouldn't return.

Another low, keening cry echoed from the Blood Forest, and a second shadow appeared in the mist. Then another. The mist didn't thicken or rise, though. There didn't seem to be a horde, but three Craven could be dangerous enough.

"Fucking Atlantians," Pence spat.

My head cut to him, and I had to stop myself from knocking his ass off the Rise—or laughing, considering he cursed those whose blood would be used to Ascend his brother when the time came since the gods weren't Ascending anyone. The Blood Crown simply used Atlantian blood.

And the Craven had nothing to do with my people. They weren't the product of our poisonous kiss as the mortals were led to believe. That was just more shit the Blood Crown used to cover up their misdeeds and make sure the people hated Atlantians. *They* were solely responsible for the creatures that slaughtered indiscriminately in their hunger for blood.

"I really hope my brother Ascends soon," Pence said, swallowing. "He'll be safer then, you know?"

Yeah, he would be safer.

He'd also be creating more Craven that could one day kill Pence.

"How old is your brother now?" I knew the Blood Crown didn't typically Ascend the Lords and Ladies in Wait until they reached adulthood.

"Just turned sixteen." Pence squinted. "Not sure if he'll Ascend during the Maiden's Ascension or if they'll wait. But it's coming up. That is if it actually happens."

I stiffened, forcing my grip on my sword to relax.

The Maiden.

Breathing in deeply, I ignored the stench I could practically taste. She was the reason I was in this shithole of a city. Her Ascension was to happen within the year, and it should've been the largest one to take place since the end of the war some several hundred years ago.

Should've been the key phrase there. Because Pence was smart to question if the Ascension would happen.

It wouldn't.

My voice was level as I asked, "What makes you think the Ascension won't happen?"

"Seriously? You don't think the Descenters will try something?" He sent me a sharp look as he lowered the bow. "They want to usurp the Crown. At the very least, cause trouble. Preventing the Maiden's

Ascension would be one way to do just that."

"And why would the Maiden's Ascension have that much impact on the Crown?" I angled my body toward his, doubting he could answer what I or any of my spies had yet to figure out.

His eyes narrowed. "Because the Maiden is Chosen by the gods," he said with the reverence that often filled the voice of anyone who spoke about the Maiden and the confidence of every single motherfucker who spewed that bullshit. Except Pence's words included a tone that said he thought me half-idiotic to even ask the question.

It was a good thing I stopped myself from shouting, "*Why?*" in his face. *Why* was this Maiden Chosen? The Blood Crown never elaborated beyond her Ascension ushering in a new era. No matter who we questioned or how many Ascended we interrogated, we never learned the reason beyond the belief or how she would be this…this harbinger of a new era.

"I've been hearing the Duke's worried about the upcoming Rite," Pence said after a moment, his slender face drawn. "I'm guessing there've been credible threats. Fear the Dark One will get the Descenters here riled up into doing something."

The Duke had every right to be concerned about the upcoming Rite. One side of my lips twisted up as I turned from Pence, thinking the guard would likely piss himself if he knew who he stood beside and spoke to.

The so-called Dark One.

The Prince of a fallen kingdom the Blood Crown claimed was hellbent on murder and mayhem. Many believed that, but the false King and Queen hadn't been able to convince everyone in Solis. The Descenters knew that the Kingdom of Atlantia hadn't fallen. Instead, we'd thrived and rebuilt in the four centuries following the war, strengthening our armies.

If Atlantia invaded Solis, something many within Atlantia wanted, Solis would be taken. Thousands, if not millions, would die in the process. And that was exactly what would happen if I didn't get off this fucking Rise and get my hands on the Maiden.

Because unbeknownst to the people of Solis, the Blood Crown had stolen someone very important to Atlantia. Not just their Prince but the heir to the throne. If he wasn't freed, there would be war. And this time?

This time, there would be no retreat for the greater good of the people.

THE SCENT OF ROT

Six guards had ridden out on horseback to take care of the Craven before they reached the Rise.

Three returned.

It was rare for those who fell outside the Rise to be brought back for burial rites. Sometimes, there was simply nothing left of the body for their loved ones to mourn. Usually, it was all due to the Ascended not wanting the people to know exactly how many were lost while fighting the Craven.

In other words, they didn't want the people to know how little control they had of the situation.

I tensed as I watched one of the guards dismount just inside the Rise. The man was unsteady on his feet. I inhaled deeply, catching the stale-sweet scent of...*rot*. Shit. Not liking the look of what I'd seen or smelled, I walked to the edge and waited for the guard to turn.

"Hawke Flynn." The high-pitched, nasally voice of Lieutenant Dolen Smyth cut through the low chatter of those on the Rise. "You weren't at roll call this afternoon."

Pence bowed as was required for one of Smyth's position. I didn't. Instead, I tracked the dark-haired guard's movements as he spoke with several other guards on the ground. "I was there."

"I just said I didn't see you," Lieutenant Smyth snapped, which was utter bullshit. He'd seen me. I knew he had because he'd been eyeballing me like he wanted to see my head on a spike. "So, exactly how were you there, Flynn?"

"I'm not sure how to answer that question." The guard I was tracking had started walking, leading his nervous horse to the stables. He turned briefly, his profile blanched in the firelight. I recognized him. Jole Crain. He was young. Fuck, he was younger than Pence. "I think it would be a question better asked of a Healer."

"And why the hell would you think that?" Lieutenant Smyth demanded.

"Because if you didn't see me…" I began, catching sight of Pence out of the corner of my eye. He looked as if he were attempting to disappear into one of the curved parapets. "Then there appears to be something wrong with your vision." I turned to the Lieutenant then, smiling tightly. The white mantle of the Royal Guard flapped from his slender shoulders in the wind like a flag of surrender. While Smyth lorded his authority over others like far too many in his position, he'd earned that coveted spot among the Royal Guard. Only the strong and the skilled stayed alive long enough to make it off the Rise. "And I would suggest you have that checked out immediately."

"There is nothing wrong with my vision." The blond Lieutenant sputtered, and his normally ruddy cheeks flushed even more in anger.

I reminded myself that throwing his ass off the Rise would not do me any favors. "Then you did see me. Perhaps there is an issue with your memory, then."

His nostrils flared as he took a step toward me, but then he stopped himself. The knuckles of his right hand turned white from how tightly he clenched the hilt of his broadsword. He didn't draw it. It was clear he wanted to, though. Whatever instinct the man possessed had prevented him from making an entirely foolish choice. Or perhaps it was smarts. Smyth was as intelligent as he was a bastard.

And I was beginning to think he was perhaps too wise. Too observant.

Because he'd been on my ass from day one, watching my every move and asking too many questions.

"Your disrespect will be reported," he said finally, his tone pitching even higher than usual. "And we'll see what Commander Jansen has to say."

My smile kicked up a notch. "I suppose we will."

"Just so you know," he bit out, lifting his pointed chin, "I've got my eye on you, Flynn."

"Most do," I replied, then winked.

Lieutenant Smyth's shoulders stiffened. It appeared as if he wanted to say more, but disappointingly, he stalked forward, bumping my shoulder as he continued on the patrol path.

Chuckling, I looked to where Pence had nearly blended into the shadows of the parapet.

"Exactly how big are your balls?" the guard asked.

I snorted. "Normal size, the last I checked."

"I don't know about that." Pence crossed the battlement, dragging a hand through his windblown hair. "Smyth is a prick."

"I know that."

"Then you have to know he's going to do exactly what he said. He'll go to the Commander."

"I'm sure he will," I said, straightening the strap of my baldric as I glanced at where I'd last seen the guard. "Jole Crain has a chamber in the dorms, right?"

"Yeah. He's on the third floor." Pence's brow knitted. "Why do you ask?"

I shrugged.

Pence eyed me for a moment. "You aren't worried at all about the Lieutenant, are you?"

"Not at all." And I wasn't.

Lieutenant Smyth didn't even register on the list of things I was concerned about.

I lifted my gaze to the Citadel's stone towers, then looked farther out past the edges of the Lower Ward and Wisher's Grove, beyond the wider, nicer streets and lush manors. My stare fixed on the sprawling, arched walls of Castle Teerman, where the Maiden likely slept peacefully, safe in her stone and glass cage, out of reach.

But not for long.

HE DIED WITH HIS DREAMS

I cut across the Citadel's courtyard, where patches of grass struggled to grow, having been stomped out from years of training.

Lucky for me, only the new guards trained at the Citadel. The rest took part in daily sessions at Castle Teerman. I didn't mind the training. I actually looked forward to it. The time spent in the yard gave me the opportunity to familiarize myself with the castle.

It also gave me chances to see *her*.

Kind of.

The Maiden wasn't seen in public outside the City Council sessions. But I had caught sight of her watching from one of the castle's many alcoves that faced the training yard. Usually, it was just a glimpse of the white of her gown or veil. I'd yet to see anything of her features beyond a slightly sharp chin and surprisingly lush mouth the color of berries. I hadn't even heard her voice.

To be honest, I was beginning to think she had no vocal cords or that she spoke only in whispers like a mouse terrified of any loud sounds. Wouldn't surprise me if that were the case. After all, the so-called Chosen had to be either a submissive, frightened creature to allow herself to be veiled and have every aspect of her life controlled, or she believed the bullshit the false Queen—the Blood Queen—fed her. The latter was the likeliest explanation for her willing submissiveness, especially since she had a brother who had Ascended.

I'd seen the Maiden in the alcove with the Duchess a few times, the Ascended watching the men training as if she wished to feast on their flesh more than their blood. Ladies and Lords in Wait did the same, usually tittering from behind silk fans between sending not-so-coy glances at those on the field. Attraction drove them to watch, but the Maiden's presence was an intriguing mystery, and so very little intrigued me these days.

Everyone in Solis knew the Maiden was *untouched* in both the literal and figurative senses and was to remain so. I couldn't even begin to fathom what kind of archaic reasoning the Ascended had to justify that or why. To be honest, I couldn't give two fucks, but there had been absolutely no gossip indicating that the Maiden rebelled against the cage she had been placed in. So, I doubted she watched for the same reasons the Duchess and the others did.

Then again, there was no actual gossip about the Maiden at all, likely due to the fact that most were forbidden to speak to her. There were even stories of guards having been relieved of their positions or demoted to work beyond the Rise for merely acknowledging her presence with a smile or a harmless hello.

What I knew of her was minimal. The Maiden was supposedly born in the shroud of the gods, which was yet more Ascended bullshit. Those of the working and lower classes harbored a fondness for her, which was clear in how they spoke of her in the same reverent tones as Pence had the other night. And she was said to be kind. How they would know that since they weren't allowed to acknowledge her was anyone's guess. Their foolish superstitions likely drove their loyalty, not anything based in reality.

The Maiden was likely as unworthy of the people's support as the Blood Crown she represented. Because at the end of the day, there was no way she was unaware of what the Ascended truly were—how the Ascension actually came to be and that they were responsible for the monsters that had stolen so many lives.

Shoving thoughts of the Maiden aside, I entered the back hall of the dormitory and hung a left, entering a staircase. I was tired, but even if I was headed to my chamber, I wouldn't be going to sleep. It took several hours for my head to get in the right space to shut down, which usually occurred a handful of hours before dawn—if I was lucky. Hell, I couldn't remember the last time I'd slept an entire night.

Tonight, I had a real reason for avoiding the silence of my single bedchamber and its bare, lifeless walls.

I took the steps three at a time, wondering what Kieran was up to. We'd made a point not to cross paths, especially since the Lieutenant was on my ass like white on rice. With Kieran planted in the City Guard, there weren't a lot of chances for us to happen upon each other.

He had a bit more freedom to move about, but it also meant he saw far more shit than I did. Abuses I knew he wanted to do something about but couldn't without drawing attention to himself. And the exploitation and mistreatment of the most vulnerable in Masadonia was only getting worse.

Because that was also how the Ascended kept the people of Solis in line and not asking questions. They used fear.

Reaching the third floor, I walked out into the wide hall. It didn't take long for me to find the room I was looking for. The stench of rot wouldn't be noticeable yet to the others, but it *was* stronger. I continued forward, wondering exactly what in the wide realm of fucks I was doing.

The problem brewing in this hall wasn't mine.

In fact, it was a boon. I could keep walking and let what would happen come to pass. After all, fewer guards made everything easier. And if I were smart, I would see every single mortal even loosely tied to the Blood Crown as an enemy.

But I could hear snores coming from behind closed doors and understood that most guards who served the Blood Crown knew no better. This floor was full of innocent men, and if I did nothing, half of them would be dead by the time the sun rose.

Or worse.

I stopped at the door, rapping my knuckles on it. There was silence and then a muffled, "Yeah?"

I reached for the handle and turned, finding it unlocked. Pushing it open, I stepped inside. My vision immediately adjusted to the narrow, dimly lit chamber, and I found who I'd come for.

Jole Crain sat on the edge of his bed that was barely more than a raised cot, his dark hair hanging forward, shielding his face as he clasped the back of his neck. Something about the way he sat reminded me of my brother after he returned from an evening of enjoying far too many spirits. A pain that was akin to a knife wound sliced through my chest. It had to be the hair. My brother's was a bit lighter, a shade stuck somewhere between blond and brown, but it was the same length as Jole's.

Thinking about my brother was the very last thing I needed at this moment.

I closed the door behind me as I glanced around the chamber. His armor had been left by the entrance, his weapons placed on the chest at the foot of his bed—all but one. A dagger lay beside him on the blanket, its blade the color of crimson in the low light. Bloodstone.

Jole lifted his head. Sweat dampened the wisps of hair at his forehead, a sign that the fever had taken hold. He squinted. Shadows had already blossomed under his eyes where the skin was thin and quick to decay.

And that was exactly what was happening to Jole. He was decaying. Rotting. He was already dead.

"Flynn?" he asked.

I nodded, propping myself against the wall. "Saw you return from outside the Rise."

"Yeah?" He dropped his hand to his knee. His arm trembled.

"Thought I'd check on you and see how you were doing."

Jole blinked and then looked away. "Feeling just…peachy."

"You sure about that?"

He opened his mouth, but all that came out was a ragged laugh.

"You were bitten, weren't you?" I asked.

Another laugh came from him, but this time it was shaky and harsh. I waited, and it didn't take long for him to do the right thing. Silently, he lifted his left arm and shoved up the sleeve of his tunic.

There it was. Further confirmation of what I already knew.

Two jagged indents on his wrist. The torn flesh oozed an oily, dark substance. Reddish-blue lines already radiated from what should be a rather minor wound, running up his forearm and disappearing under his sleeve.

Jole was going to turn, becoming what he'd been dispatched to kill. A violent, rage-fueled beast with a hunger that couldn't be satiated, and he would do it sooner rather than later.

Bodies handled the infection differently. Many made it a day or two without showing any obvious signs. Others turned in hours. He was one of the latter, and I bet that where the Craven had gotten him had a lot to do with that. It had likely hit a vein or nicked it at the very least.

Jole shuddered. "I'm cursed."

"You're not." I tilted my head. "You're just unfortunate."

He turned his head to me. The hollows of his cheeks had deepened. "If you knew I was bitten while you were on the Rise, you should've reported me. It's treasonous not to."

It was.

I pushed off the wall, glancing at the bloodstone dagger. The stone was fashioned from the ruby-red rocks that had littered the coast of the Seas of Saion centuries before I was born. As a child, my father had told my brother and me that they were the angry or sad tears of the gods left to petrify in the sun. It was one of the few things in the realm that killed a Craven or those infected by them.

It also killed their makers.

The Ascended.

"You were going to try to handle it yourself?" I nodded at the dagger.

He wearily followed my gaze. "I was going to, but I couldn't. I can't even touch it."

The infection wouldn't allow it. It was kind of awe-inspiring to think about—that the bite could seize that much control of a person, preventing them from ending their life.

"I...I was going to go to the Commander," Jole added, his shoulders shaking. "But I sat down to take a breather, and I...I thought I'd have more time. I really did. I was going to turn myself in." His watery eyes met mine. "I swear."

I didn't know if that was the truth. Probably wasn't, but I couldn't blame him. Turning himself in meant a horrific death since the Ascended liked to make a public spectacle of executing the infected. They burned them alive, which was one hell of a way to respect and honor their sacrifice. If I reported Jole, his very last memory—if he were even still himself by then—would be his screams.

I came to stand in front of him. "Do you have family?"

A breath shuddered out of him as he shook his head. "Ma and Pa both died a few years back. It was something like a...a cold. They were fine...one moment and not the next. Died the same night." He looked up at me, looking older with each moment that passed. "I have no brothers or sisters."

I nodded, thinking that was at least fortunate. It was always better when no one was left to mourn.

"If I did, I would've gone to them," he continued. "They...would've known what to do. She would've...come for me. Given me dignity."

Was he speaking of someone who answered the silent call of the white handkerchiefs hung on windows and doors? It had taken a godsawful long time to learn what they represented. Half the people asked behaved as if they had no knowledge of their existence. Once I found out what those scraps of white that sporadically appeared—only to then quickly disappear—meant...I understood why. They signified that a so-called cursed resided within, one likely infected by a Craven in the same manner as Jole Crain had been. The piece of white cloth was used to alert those throughout Masadonia who risked treason to provide quick, dignified deaths to the infected.

The fact that the act was even considered treasonous and therefore punishable by death blew my mind but did not surprise me. The Blood Crown excelled at senseless cruelty.

"She?" I asked.

He nodded, swallowing hard. "The child of the gods."

The Maiden. The people believed she was the child of the gods, but I had no idea why he thought his family, if they'd been alive, would've gone to her. "And how would she have done that? Given you dignity?"

"She...she would've given me peace," he told me.

My brows lifted as another coughing fit hit him. Given him peace? I wasn't sure how that was possible. The infection was addling his mind.

"What are...you going to do?" Jole wheezed, his breath rattling in his chest.

Crouching in front of him, I smiled. "Nothing."

"W-what? You have to do something." Confusion and a hint of panic filled his now-sunken features. "You—" He twisted his neck to the side, the veins standing out starkly as he closed his eyes. "You have to—"

"Jole," I said, clasping his clammy, feverish cheeks. The young man's entire body jerked. "Open your eyes."

Lashes fluttered and then lifted. His irises were blue. No hint of red appearing in them. Yet. He started to lower his lids again.

"Look at me, Jole," I whispered, my voice dropping even lower as the elemental power of my ancestors—the gods themselves—spread through me, filling my veins, washing over the room and Jole. "Don't close your eyes. Keep looking at me and just breathe."

Jole's gaze met mine.

"Be calm." I held his stare. "Just keep breathing. Focus only on that. Inhale. Exhale."

A long, steady breath left him. Tension eased from his rigid body. He relaxed. He inhaled.

"Tell me, Jole, what is your favorite place?"

"My dreams," he mumbled.

His dreams were his favorite place? Fucking gods, what kind of life was that? A ball of anger lodged in my chest, but I didn't let it grow. "What is your favorite dream?"

There was no hesitation. "Riding on horseback, going so fast it feels like I have wings. That I can take to the air."

"Close your eyes and go there. Go to your favorite dream, where you are on horseback."

He obeyed without hesitation. His jaw slackened beneath my hands. The rapid flickering behind his closed lids stilled. His breaths evened out more, becoming deeper.

"You're riding so fast you have wings. You're in the air."

Jole Crain smiled.

I gave his head a sharp twist. Bone cracked, severing the brain stem. He died in an instant, as himself and with his dreams instead of screams.

AN OMEN

Wind swept through the field, gusting against the walls of Castle Teerman and through the many alcoves and balconies overlooking the training yard. Crisp white rippled from within the darkness of one of those recesses like the specters rumored to haunt Wisher's Grove, but what had caught my attention this morning was no spirit haunting the castle.

It was her, like clockwork.

The Chosen.

The Maiden.

She appeared in the various shadowy alcoves, usually two hours past dawn. Since I was a betting man, I was willing to wager she thought no one saw her.

But I always did.

Other than the times I managed to follow her from the inner wall surrounding the castle while she walked in the garden, this was as close as I got to her.

That, however, would change.

One side of my mouth curled as air stirred to my right. I brought the broadsword up, blocking the blow. Dipping under the next attack, my gaze flicked back to the recess. What sunlight managed to penetrate the alcove glinted off the golden chains securing the Maiden's veil.

My partner's footsteps gave away his movements before he struck. Pivoting, I cut his sword down, nearly knocking it from his grasp even though I checked my strength. I glanced at the second floor as I leaned back, dodging the swipe of a thick blade.

Another row of golden chains glinted from the shadows. She

must've turned her head. For what? Who knew? She was alone. Well, relatively speaking. No one was right beside her, but Rylan Keal, one of the two Royal Guards who served as her personal guardians, stood farther back in the alcove. She was never truly alone. When she was with the Lady in Wait that I usually saw her with, a guard followed. When she was in her chambers, her doors were manned.

I couldn't understand how she dealt with that—how anyone could. Being constantly surrounded as she was would drive me mad.

Then again, the quiet wasn't all that favorable either, now was it? Not when too much silence made me think of damp, cold stone, and pain. Made me think of my brother. So, I guessed I was sort of fucked—

"*Hawke*," the man snapped as I stopped his blade with mine when it was about an inch from my throat.

Slowly, I turned my head toward my sparring partner, giving him what he apparently desired: my full attention.

Unease flashed in the sea-blue eyes of the seasoned Royal Guard who'd likely seen some shit in his time. He took a slight step back, an instinctive reaction he couldn't help nor even begin to understand. That gut instinct usually sent most mortals scurrying off before they could question the cause, but not him. He caught himself before he conceded further, the skin at the corners of his eyes pulling taut. Irritation quickly settled in the weathered face of the Maiden's other personal guard.

"You should be paying attention," Vikter Wardwell bit out, knocking back a strand of blond hair that had blown across his face. "Unless you're in the mood to lose a limb or your head."

Dust from the packed dirt whipped around us as another gust of wind funneled through the yard. "I'm paying attention." I paused, glancing down to where our swords remained locked. I then gave him a tight-lipped smile. "Obviously."

Tension bracketed his mouth. "Let me rephrase. You should be paying more attention to the field."

"Versus what?"

"Versus wherever your eyes and attention may be wandering to," he said, holding my stare. He didn't look away, not for a damn second. "Masadonia is far more susceptible to attacks than the capital. The enemies you will face here will take full advantage of any distractions."

My smile didn't fade. I knew that ticked off the prickly bastard. I also knew he had a damn good idea of where my eyes had wandered to. Which meant I also had to give him credit for knowing exactly where the Maiden was, even though Keal protected her right now.

A whistle sounded, signaling the end of training. Neither Vikter nor I moved.

"Not sure I know what you speak of," I replied, sparing one more look at our swords before forcing his tip to the ground. "But I appreciate the sage advice, nonetheless."

"Glad to hear." A muscle ticked in his jaw. "Because I have more *sage advice* for you."

"Is that so?"

Vikter stepped in, his head tilting back to meet my stare. The man was brave, but he didn't realize he was one of two obstacles that stood between the Maiden and me.

And one of them had to go.

"I don't give two shits about the glowing recommendations you arrived with from the capital," he said.

I arched a brow, aware that the Commander of the Royal Guards was eyeing us as the others began filing out of the training yard. "That's your advice?"

His free hand clenched, and I had a feeling he wanted nothing more than to introduce that fist to my face. "That was just the start of my advice, boy."

Boy? I almost laughed. Vikter appeared to be in his fourth decade of life, and while I looked as if I were in my second, I hadn't been a boy in over two centuries. In other words, I was already skilled at wielding a sword when this man was a swaddled babe.

"All it takes is a second for your enemy to gain the upper hand," he said, stare unflinching. "Nothing more than the length of a heartbeat, given to either arrogance or vengeance, to lose all which truly matters. And if that isn't something you've yet learned,"—Vikter sheathed his sword—"you will."

I said nothing as I watched him turn his back and stalk across the yard, the cold press of unease settling in the center of my chest.

What he'd said was something I'd already learned the hard way, but his words...

They felt like a warning.

An omen of things to come.

PRESENT II

"Vikter," I said, laughing roughly as I wrung the water from the towel. "He was not a fan of mine even before I became your guard."

Silence was my only answer.

I looked up from where I sat at the foot of the bed to where Poppy's head rested on the pillow. Her lips were slightly parted, and the thick fringe of her lashes framed the heavily shadowed skin beneath her eyes.

There had been no change in Poppy, but it had only been a few hours.

A few hours that felt like a lifetime.

It reminded me of how deeply she'd slept after Vikter was killed. I felt as helpless then as I did now.

My gaze moved to the thin blanket covering her chest and stayed there until I saw it rise with her deep, steady breaths. It was idiotic. I knew she was okay. I knew her heart beat calmly because mine did, but I couldn't stop myself from checking every so often. The quiet of the chamber didn't help my paranoia.

Delano was out in the hall, giving us some privacy while I removed Poppy's dirty and bloodied clothing. Kieran had gone to talk to Hisa while I did my best to bathe the dirt and remnants of battle from her.

Talk to her.

I cleared my throat. "You know, it was almost like Vikter sensed my motivations or something because, from day one, he was not at all impressed." I ran the cloth over her foot, paying close attention to the bottom. "But what he said to me? It felt like an omen. Almost like he was warning me of what was to come. And he had."

Rinsing the towel, I moved on to her other foot, placing it carefully in my lap. "When we were in the Wastelands, after you were taken, I was distracted in those ruins—diverted by rage and the need for vengeance. I should've been focused solely on you, but I wasn't. And you were hurt because of it."

I looked up at her, seeing her as she'd been that night, bloody and in pain, so afraid yet desperately trying not to show it. The memory came far too easily.

I swallowed. "Looking back, I wonder if Vikter knew what would happen. He was, well, he *is* part of the Arae—the Fates—in a way. Did he know on some unconscious level?"

There wasn't a speck of dirt left on her feet by the time I tucked them beneath the blanket and rose. I replaced the water in the basin with fresh before returning to sit at her side. Her hands were the last to be cleaned.

I picked up her left hand, her skin still so cold. Dirt and blood smudged the top and between her fingers. I turned her hand over, drawing the towel over the shimmering, golden swirl of the marriage imprint. What if...what if she forgot this? The ceremony. Everything that it took for us to get to that moment.

I cut off those thoughts, forcing myself to move past the fear.

"So maybe that was why Vikter didn't like me from the get-go," I continued, washing away the blood and dirt from her palm. "What he was—a *viktor*—could sense what I was about." I smiled a little. "I wonder what he thinks now? Bet he had a few choice words about me."

I lifted her clean palm to my lips and pressed a kiss to the imprint. "But I couldn't blame him for not having the greatest opinion of me back in Masadonia. Even if he never suspected who I was, I *was* there to take you away."

Lowering her hand to my lap, I rinsed the towel and then moved on to her fingers. "And I killed those he trusted. Hannes. Rylan." I pressed my lips together as I shifted my gaze to her features. "It could've been Vikter that night. If he had taken Rylan's place for whatever reason, it would've been him."

Shaking my head, I returned my attention to her hand. I cleaned the ring. "I wouldn't have cared then. I mean, I didn't like ending the lives of good men, but it would've been a passing regret. Little to no guilt. I had a goal. That was all that mattered, and I..."

I sighed, placing her hand on her stomach as I moved on to her right. "I didn't know you yet. I hadn't even heard you speak, and I seriously thought you were this submissive creature who only spoke in whispers." I laughed for real. "Or that you were a cohort in the Ascended's plans. Gods, I couldn't have been more wrong if I tried."

The grime was far more stubborn on her right hand. "That's the thing. I had all these preconceived notions about you—ones based on absolutely nothing. Because no one really talked about you. I think I just...well, I needed you to either be the enemy or weak. It made everything I planned to do easier." I frowned. "Which actually makes *me* the weak one."

If Poppy were awake, she would likely agree with that moment of self-realization.

I dragged the cloth between her fingers, oddly moved by how fragile her hand felt in mine, despite knowing how deadly it could be.

Looks could be deceiving, couldn't they?

"But I was about to begin learning just how wrong I was about you," I told her. "Because I was about to finally meet you, and you..." I looked at her still, serene features. "You were about to meet who I used to be."

WHO I WAS

"The Maiden's guards are good men."

I lifted my gaze from the glass of whiskey I held to the man standing by the empty fireplace. "Good men die all the time."

"True," Griffith Jansen, the Commander of the Royal Guard, replied. He'd been in Solis longer than most Atlantians could tolerate, managing to keep his true identity hidden. He was the only reason my men were now firmly rooted in the Royal Army, serving both at the Rise and in the city. But he would be killed or worse if anyone ever learned where Jansen's loyalties lay or what he was. "But far too few good men are left in Solis."

"That, we can agree on." I watched Jansen for several moments. "Is one less good man going to be a problem?"

His gaze met mine. "If it was a problem, I wouldn't be here. I'm just saying it will be a shame to lose one of them."

"Shame or not, I need to get close to her." I took a drink of whiskey. The smoky liquor went down far smoother than any other spirit this miserable land had to offer. "Being on the Rise won't help me. You know that. You also understand what is at stake here." My head tilted. "And since there's no current opening in those who guard her, we need to make one."

"I do understand." Jansen dragged a hand over his head, his shoulders tight under the plain brown tunic he wore. "That doesn't mean I have to like what must be done."

I smiled faintly at his response. "If you did, then you would be of better use to the Ascended since they enjoy pain and senseless death."

His chin rose slightly at the reminder that we may be casually discussing the death of an innocent man. However, we were not the enemy. No amount of evil from me would surpass what the Ascended had done to our people or theirs.

At least that's what I kept telling myself.

"What do you know of the Maiden?" Jansen asked after a moment.

I almost laughed because what a silly fucking question. There wasn't much to know about her.

I knew her name was Penellaphe.

I knew her parents had been killed in a Craven attack.

I knew she had a brother who'd Ascended—one I had eyes on in the capital.

But what I knew next was all that mattered. She was the Queen's favorite, and that made her the only thing in this entire kingdom that could be used as leverage against the false Crown. She was the only possible route to preventing war.

"I know enough," I stated.

Jansen stretched his neck from side to side. "She's favored by many people, not just the Queen."

"How is that possible?" the other who stood by the window asked. "She is rarely seen in public, and even more rarely does she speak."

"He makes a good point." Which was likely a shock to everyone in the chamber.

"To be honest, I don't know. But many speak of her kindness," Jansen answered. "And her guards care for her. They protect her because they want to, whereas most of the Royal Guards protect their charges because it puts food on their family's tables and keeps their heads on their shoulders. That's about it."

"And the same people believe she was Chosen by the gods—which we both know is impossible since they've been at rest for several centuries. I'm sorry if I don't necessarily trust their judgment regarding what they think of the Maiden."

Jansen gave me a wry grin. "My point is, when she goes missing, it's going to cause a stir. Not just with the Ascended. People *will* be looking for her."

"What will cause a great stir is my father's armies descending on Solis and laying waste to every city and village he comes across. All in retribution for what the Ascended did to me and are currently doing to Prince Malik," I told him. "Now, tell me, which stir would you rather see? Questions about a missing Maiden? Or war?"

"What I want to see is the godsdamn Ascended eradicated," Jansen snapped. The only reason I allowed that was what came out of his mouth next. "They killed my children. My first son and then my second—" He cut himself off with a thick swallow, briefly looking away as he did whatever he needed to help contain the kind of pain that never healed. "I will do anything to stop them and protect our kingdom."

"Then give me the opening I need." I dragged my thumb over the rim of my glass. "Once I free the true Prince, I will kill the false King and Queen. That, I promise."

Jansen exhaled roughly, and it was obvious he didn't like this. My respect for the man grew. None of this business was pleasant. If someone enjoyed any part of this, they were living on borrowed time. "She walks the garden every night at dusk," he said.

"I already know that." I'd stalked her and her guard through the gardens many times at nightfall, getting as close as I could without being seen. Which, unfortunately, wasn't nearly close enough.

"But do you know she goes to see the night-blooming roses?"

I stilled. I didn't know that. Oddly unsettled by the revelation that she sought flowers native to Atlantia, I shifted on the settee. Throughout the day, I'd often found myself wondering what she found so interesting in those gardens.

I now knew.

"Or is it that they're located near the jacaranda trees?" Jansen added.

A smile slowly tipped the corners of my lips. "Where a section of the interior wall has collapsed."

Jansen nodded. "The same part I've told the Teermans to repair a time or five hundred."

"Lucky for me, they haven't."

"Yes." Jansen moved from the fireplace. "Do what you must, and I will take care of the rest."

"You're sure you can secure his spot as a Royal Guard?" the wolven spoke up again, stepping out from the shadows.

"I can." Jansen glanced at the wolven with the shaggy dark hair and then refocused on me. "You have such glowing accolades from the capital," he replied dryly, referencing the recommendations he'd fabricated. "And the Duchess finds you…pleasant to look upon. It won't be hard."

My lip curled in disgust as I looked at the wolven. "You know what to do, Jericho."

He smiled and nodded. "She'll be less one guard after her next visit to the garden."

"Good." *The sooner, the better* went unsaid.

"Anything else?" Jansen asked, and I shook my head. He stepped forward, clasping my forearm. "From blood and ash."

"We will rise," I promised.

Jansen bowed his head slightly, then turned. My gaze lifted to the men as they reached the door. Jericho was a bit of a wild card, more so than most of his kind, but of all those who'd traveled with me, he was unknown to the guards. The wolven wouldn't be recognized. "No harm comes to the Maiden. Do you understand me?"

The Commander remained quiet as Jericho nodded.

I held the wolven's pale blue gaze. "I mean it, Jericho. She is to be unharmed in this."

His jaw, covered with a hint of a beard, lifted. "Message clear."

Watching them leave, I admitted to myself that my demands made little sense as I leaned back on the settee.

I planned to take the Maiden from everything and everyone she knew. Kidnapping her wouldn't exactly be pleasant business, but the idea of harming a woman made my skin crawl. Even when I had to. Even when it was an Ascended. But what I planned for her was far better than what my father would do if he got his hands on her. He'd send her back to the Blood Crown in pieces—and my father was someone Commander Jansen would also consider a good man.

"I don't like him."

Looking up from my glass of whiskey, I raised my brows.

Kieran Contou leaned against the wall; the warm beige brown of his features set in an ever-present mask of indifference. He had been so silent during the meeting that I doubted Jansen even realized he was there. The wolven couldn't look more bored if he tried, but I knew better. I'd seen him look as if he were an instant away from falling asleep, then rip out the throat of whoever was speaking a second later.

"Which one?" I asked.

He cocked his head. "Why would I have a problem with the Commander?"

I lifted a shoulder. "Jansen asked a lot of questions."

"If he hadn't, you'd rethink working with him," Kieran replied. "I don't like Jericho."

"Who does? He's reckless, but he has no qualms when it comes to killing."

"None of us do. Not even you." Kieran paused. "At least when we're awake."

But when we slept, a far different story could be told.

"I can kill Jericho," he offered, his tone the same as if he were asking if I wanted to grab a bite to eat. "And take care of the guard."

"I don't think that'll be necessary. I suspect he'll end up dead at some point anyway."

"I have a feeling that's true."

I smirked. Kieran's *feelings* often had a way of becoming a reality. Just like his father. "Besides, with you in the City Guard, you risk being recognized if things go south."

Kieran nodded, and a moment passed. "It is a shame, though. From what I've heard of the Maiden's guards, Jansen is right. They're both good men."

"It's the only way," I repeated, thinking of Hannes. He'd been taken out before I arrived in Masadonia. His replacement had opened the door for me to enter the Rise Guard. The death of another personal guard was simply one more door opening.

I glanced back at Kieran. We were dressed the same, wearing the black of the Royal Army and carrying weapons bearing the heraldry of our enemies—a circle with an arrow piercing the center. The Royal Crest of the Kingdom of Solis. Supposedly, it stood for infinity and power, but in ancient Atlantian, in the language of the gods, the symbol represented something else.

Death.

Which was also fitting for the Blood Crown.

"By becoming one of her personal guards, I would have the closest thing to unfettered access to her, and you know we can't simply grab her and run," I reminded him. "We'd be lucky to make it out of the city. And even if we did, we wouldn't make it far." I leaned, draping my arm along the back of the settee. "Getting close to her allows me to gain her trust so that she won't put up a fight and slow us down when we do make our move."

Turning his gaze to the darkened city streets beyond the window, Kieran was quiet. He knew if we moved now, we wouldn't make it past the Rise encircling Masadonia before our deeds came to light. And that meant the only way out was with a whole lot of blood and death.

Because I would not be captured.

Ever again.

And if that meant slaughtering innocents, then so be it. I was trying to avoid that, though. Kieran understood. He wasn't *that* bloodthirsty. Jericho, on the other hand…

"We don't have much longer to wait," I assured him.

"I know. The upcoming Rite."

I nodded. The Rite provided us with the perfect opportunity to strike. Most of the Ascended would be at the castle, which meant the most skilled and seasoned guards would be there, leaving the Rise and the city poorly guarded. My lips curved up. Those guards would find themselves occupied, dealing with the distraction the Descenters created, and we'd make our move then. The key was gaining the Maiden's trust so that when I told her I'd been given orders to remove her from the city, she wouldn't question me. Eventually, she would, but by then, we would be on our way to a more secure location where we could negotiate with the Blood Crown.

The plan would work, but it would also take time.

And it would cost more lives.

Kieran's shoulders rose with a deep breath. "It's just that…it's too bad so few of the guards can be called good, and we'll be causing those numbers to be even less."

That we would.

"Have you learned anything that explains why the Maiden is so important to the Blood Crown?" he asked. "Other than her supposedly being a child of the gods."

"All I can figure is that she is somehow key to the Ascensions of all those Lords and Ladies in Wait. Why? Not even Jansen, who has been here for years, can answer that, so your guess is as good as mine." I snorted, knocking back a strand of hair that had fallen forward. "I assume you haven't learned anything new, either?"

"You assume correctly. Anytime I casually bring up the Maiden, it incites suspicion. You'd think she was some sort of benevolent goddess based on how people speak of her. Even the City Guard." He glanced to where I'd placed my weapons by the door. "It has to be the shroud."

I raised a brow. "Come again?"

"You've heard that she was born in a shroud."

"I have." I frowned.

"Then you also know what that means."

It was believed that Atlantians born in a shroud at birth—a caul—were Chosen by the gods. Blessed. There hadn't been an Atlantian born in one since the time of the gods. But besides that… "She doesn't have Atlantian blood in her, Kieran." I stated the obvious. There was no way she was even half-Atlantian, unless her brother wasn't related to her by blood. But none of the digging we'd done had indicated that he was a half-brother. "She's mortal."

"No shit," Kieran replied dryly. "But who's to say mortals cannot be born in such?"

Who *was* to say? "I suppose it's not *im*possible," I decided. "But since the vamprys are pathological liars, I'm sure this is yet another lie."

"True," Kieran murmured. "But there has to be a reason they keep her cloistered and well-guarded at all times."

"Perhaps that is something I will discover once I become one of her guards."

"I would fucking hope so."

I cracked a grin. "And if not, maybe we will find our answer in one of the Ascended we…befriend."

"Befriend?" Kieran scoffed. "What a lovely way to frame capturing and torturing vamprys for information."

"Isn't it?"

Shaking his head, he scratched at his jaw. "By the way, exactly how are you going to earn the trust of someone you haven't even spoken to?" he asked.

"Besides using my irresistible charm?"

"Besides that," he replied dryly.

"I'll use any means necessary."

Kieran's stare sharpened. "I think you mean that."

I lifted my chin. "I do."

"She could be innocent in all of this," he stated.

I tamped down my rising irritation. Kieran's words came from a good place. They almost always did. "You're right. She could be, but her possible innocence or even her complicity doesn't matter. The only thing that does is being able to use her to free Malik without setting the entirety of Solis on fire. That's all that matters."

Silent, he eyed me for several moments, his head cocked. "Sometimes I forget."

My brows knotted. "Forget what?"

"That the Dark One was a fabrication the Ascended created to frighten the mortals. That you really aren't that."

I laughed, but it didn't sound right to my ears. Nothing about the rough, low noise did.

I looked away, my jaw working. The Blood Crown may had spun tales about how murderous and violent the Dark One was before I even got to Solis. They created a shadow figure to hold up as an example of how evil Atlantians were, using the mere threat of such a specter to further frighten and control the kingdom's people.

But how far off were they?

My hands were soaked in blood. I'd racked up more kills than all my men combined. Those I'd struck down upon my arrival in Solis. The high-ranking guards in Carsodonia. The lives I took in the town of Three Rivers. Throats I slit in all the many villages. Hannes. The yet unnamed guard who would also find their life cut short. Some of them deserved it. Too many were simply in the way.

I wanted to regret taking those lives.

In the bright light of day, I thought I did. At least those who were only an obstacle between me and freeing my brother. But at night? In the silence when there was no liquor to quiet the thoughts or a warm body to forget what I'd experienced and what I'd lost at the Blood Crown's hands? I didn't think I felt a damn bit of guilt then.

And didn't that make me a type of *tulpa*—created in the minds of others and then willed into existence? Because the truth was, the Dark One hadn't been real. Not in the beginning.

But he existed now.

THE ONLY WAY I KNEW HOW

"You okay?" Kieran asked, eyeing me closely.

Nodding, I picked up the glass.

"You sure about that?"

I sent him a look of warning. "Don't you have something to do? Or someone?"

Kieran huffed out a low laugh. "I'm going to see if the others have arrived." He stepped forward. "You staying here?"

"For a little while." I wasn't in the mood to return to the dorm, where I would lay in bed, damn near praying to sleeping gods that *I* could find rest.

"Expecting company tonight?" he asked as he moved to the door.

"No." My gaze returned to the whiskey. Tension crept into the muscles of my neck. "Not tonight."

"The Red Pearl is a strange place to spend one's evening alone."

"Is it? I imagine you wouldn't know what it's like to be here alone."

"As if you do?" he countered.

A tight smile twisted my lips, but I stopped as he reached the door. "Real quick—how is Setti?" I asked.

Kieran smiled. "Your horse is fine. Though I don't think he's all that pleased with the offerings of hay."

I smiled at that. That horse was a picky bastard at times. I was surprised he hadn't nipped at Kieran while he kept him stabled.

"Anything else?" he asked.

"Goodbye, Kieran."

The wolven let out a soft, knowing laugh as he slipped quietly from the room. Anyone else would've thought twice about that laugh, but I didn't with Kieran.

And he was right.

The Red Pearl *was* a strange place to spend your time alone. These rooms were used for the kinds of meetings you didn't want others to know about. Sometimes, words were exchanged. Other times, a different type of communication happened, one with far less clothing that didn't usually end with discussions of the likelihood of someone's death. Then again, those types of meetings had become few and far between, hadn't they?

I finished off the whiskey, welcoming the burn as I tipped my head back against the settee. A heavy restlessness settled into my bones. I stared at the dark ceiling, wondering exactly when a few hours of mindless pleasure stopped having the desired effect of shutting down my mind.

Had it ever really worked, though? For longer than a handful of seconds? I could occupy my hands and tongue and every other part of my body with soft curves and warm, hidden places, but my mind would always end up exactly where I sought to escape.

That damn cage with the unending hunger.

The feeling of being dead yet still breathing. As if everything that made life about more than just existing was still in that cage.

Even now, I could feel the cold, bruising hands and hear the taunting laughter as the Ascended slowly sliced away a part of who I was. And Malik? He was likely experiencing everything I had and more, and it was all my fault.

I was the only reason the Blood Crown held him captive. The only reason Atlantia had gone long past the time to name a new King. If I hadn't thought I could end the threat to the west on my own, he would be free. Instead, he'd rescued me at the cost of his freedom.

When the Blood Queen held me, it had been for five decades. They'd had him twice that long, and I knew exactly what they were doing to him.

To my *brother.*

How could he even still be alive?

I stopped myself. Malik had to survive. He *would.* Because he was strong. I knew no one stronger, and I was so close to freeing him. I just needed—

The sound of footsteps stopping outside the door snapped my head up and my eyes open. The handle on the *unlocked* door started to turn.

I moved fast, placing the glass on the small table beside the settee and retreating to the shadows clinging to the wall. I curled my fingers around the hilt of one of the short swords I'd left near the door. None of my men would dare to enter the room without knocking. Not even Kieran.

Apparently, someone had a desire to die tonight.

The door cracked open just enough for a body to slip through. Immediately, curiosity washed away the tension creeping into my muscles as I watched the slight, hooded figure close the door. The cloak was familiar. I inhaled deeply as the intruder backed up, walking right past me. The cloak belonged to a maid I knew, but she—and it was definitely a *she*—didn't smell like Britta. Everyone had a unique scent, something Atlantians and the wolven were sensitive to. Britta's reminded me of rose and lavender, but the smell that teased me now was something else.

But who would be in her cloak and in this room? Annoyance flared as I watched her look around, but quick on the emotion's heels was a looming restlessness. Britta or someone else, the unexpected intrusion at least offered entertainment. No matter how fleeting, it was still a reprieve from all the damn thoughts in my head.

From the memories.

From the...*now*.

Watching her, I let go of the sword. She started to turn, and I made my move. Even quieter than a wolven, I was on her before she even had a chance to realize that someone was in the room with her.

Clamping an arm around her waist, I drew her back against me. I dipped my head as she stiffened and caught her scent again. It was fresh. Sweet. "This," I said, "is unexpected."

And this didn't feel like Britta, either.

The maid was of average height for a mortal, barely reaching my chin. But the hip under my hand was fuller, and that scent...

It reminded me of honeydew.

Then again, it wasn't like I'd committed much about the maid to memory. The amount of whiskey I'd consumed when I met with her last probably hadn't aided in that. "But it's a welcome surprise."

She spun toward me, her right hand lowering to the area of her thigh as she lifted her head and froze. The sharp breath she took was audible.

A long moment stretched as I tried to see within the darkness of the hood. Even with the thick shadows of the candlelit room, my vision surpassed that of a mortal's; however, I couldn't make out her features. But I *could* feel the intensity of her stare, and as foggy as my memories were of the hours spent with Britta, I did not recall her keeping her hood up.

"I wasn't expecting you tonight," I admitted, thinking of what Kieran would say if he returned. A half grin appeared on my lips when I heard another soft inhale. "It's only been a few days, sweetling."

Her cloaked body gave a little jerk, but she said nothing as she continued watching me from the depths of her hood.

"Did Pence tell you I was here?" I asked, referring to the guard Britta knew that I often worked with on the Rise.

A moment passed, and she shook her head. Britta wouldn't have known what room I could be found in. Each time I was here, I requested a different one.

"Have you been watching for me, then? Following me?" I asked, tsking softly under my breath as annoyance flared once more. "We'll have to talk about that, won't we?" And we would because that could not happen again. But now...? She was here. The memories and the restlessness were at bay for the moment, and she...she smelled so different. Good. "But not tonight, it seems. You're strangely quiet."

Which was odd.

I *did* remember that Britta was the opposite of quiet. A chatterbox. Cute, if a bit overwhelming, especially as the bottle of whiskey had grown lighter. This was an entirely different side to the maid. Perhaps she sought to be more mysterious tonight. If so, I knew better than to look a gift horse in the mouth.

"We don't have to talk." I reached for the hem of my tunic, pulling it over my head and tossing it aside.

She was incredibly still, but that fresh and sweet scent of hers heightened and became heavier, strengthening with her arousal. The promise of a quiet, primal pleasure was a lure that drew me toward her.

"I don't know what kind of game you're about tonight." Gripping the back of her hood, I folded my other arm around her waist, drawing her against me. She gasped, and I liked the breathy little sound. "But I'm willing to find out."

I lifted her, and her hands—her *gloved* hands—landed on my shoulders. The tremor I felt course through her heightened my senses. Everything about her felt different, and I was beginning to wonder exactly how much I'd drunk the last time I was with her as I took her to the bed, guiding us down and laying her on her back. Sinking into her, I was suddenly caught off guard by the enticing mixture of hardness and softness beneath me.

That was another thing I didn't remember.

I recalled Britta being slim, but there were curves here—lush ones I couldn't wait to unwrap and explore.

And hell, as wrong as it was, a part of me was glad I'd been three sheets to the wind the last time I was with her. Because this…this felt new and not like a chore that was all about the end result. Those moments that washed away the memories. But already, I wasn't thinking about those cold, bruising hands as I dipped my head, pouring my gratitude into the kiss, showing my thanks the only way I could.

The only way I knew how.

Her mouth was soft and sweet under mine, and when she gasped, I deepened the kiss as much as I could without revealing what I was, slipping between those parted lips the way I hoped I would later between her thighs. I flicked my tongue over hers, drawing the taste of her into my mouth. Her fingers dug into my shoulders as she shuddered against me. And like lightning, it hit me then as the scent of her arousal rose, and I felt what could only be described as a tentative touch of her tongue against mine.

The body truly didn't feel like what I remembered.

The taste on my tongue, and the sweet, fresh scent of honeydew wasn't at all what I recalled.

The hesitancy of how she returned the kiss. There was nothing even remotely tentative about the way Britta kissed. That much, I did remember. She kissed like she was starving, from the moment our lips touched to the very second our mouths parted. The female under me kissed like…

Like someone who had far less experience than those I usually spent my time with.

Heart thumping heavily, I broke the kiss and lifted my head. "Who are you?"

There was no response. Irritation flared. Whatever game this girl was about, I was done playing it without knowing what cards I'd been dealt. I tugged the hood back, exposing her face—

Holy shit.

For a moment, I couldn't believe what I was seeing. I was caught in a state of shock that was so rare I almost laughed, but no sound parted my lips as I stared down at her face—at what I could see of it, anyway. She wore a white mask, as many did while in the Red Pearl, but I still knew whose body cradled mine, whose taste still tingled on my lips. I just couldn't believe it as my gaze tracked over the wide mask that covered her from cheek to brow.

It was impossible, but it was *her*.

I'd recognize the curve of that jaw and that mouth—those full, bow-shaped lips the color of berries—anywhere. It was all that was ever visible of her. And the gods knew I'd tried to catch a glimpse of what she looked like beneath that fucking veil when I followed her and her Royal Guards through the gardens or the castle or when I watched her with her Lady in Wait. I'd seen her smile a few times. I'd seen her lips move even less, but I knew that mouth.

It was who I'd just sat in this very room discussing.

It was her.

The Maiden.

The Chosen.

The Queen's *favorite*.

THE MAIDEN AND THE RED PEARL

The Maiden was here, in the godsdamn Red Pearl, in a room with me—*under me*—someone she had to fear more than the gods themselves. Because there was no doubt in my mind that she'd heard the whispers about me. The name the Blood Crown had given me.

The name I'd become.

I'd spent years planning to take her, had orchestrated many deaths and just sealed the fate of another, all so I could get close enough to take her. And she'd practically fallen into my lap.

Or I'd fallen into hers.

Whatever.

Another disbelieving laugh built in my throat because what in the wide kingdom of fucks was the *unreachable, unseen,* and *untouched* Maiden doing in the Red Pearl? In a private room. Kissing a man.

The laugh was never given life because something else snagged my attention. Her hair. It had always been hidden beneath the veil, but in the candlelight, I could tell that it was the color of the richest red wine.

I drew my hand out from behind her head, noting how she tensed as I picked up a strand, drawing it out. The tendril was soft as it slipped through my fingers.

The Maiden was a redhead.

I had no idea why that surprised me, but it felt like a discovery just as startling as finding her here.

"You are most definitely not who I thought you were," I murmured.

"How did you know?" she demanded.

So, she does speak. Her voice was stronger and earthier than I'd expected.

The shock of the situation forced an honest answer out of me. "Because the last time I kissed the owner of this cloak, she damn near sucked my tongue down her throat."

"Oh," she whispered, and what I could see of her nose wrinkled.

My gaze flicked to hers, and I made another discovery. Her eyes, which were always hidden by the veil, were a stunning shade of green, as bright as spring grass.

I stared down at her, still trying to wrap my head around the fact that this was the Maiden, and that the Maiden was a green-eyed redhead, when something occurred to me. "Have you been kissed before?"

"I have!"

One side of my lips kicked up. "Do you always lie?"

"No!" she exclaimed.

"Liar," I teased, unable to help myself.

The skin below the mask deepened to a rosy color as she pushed against my chest. "You should get off."

"I was planning to," I muttered, thinking she probably had no idea what that meant.

But then her eyes narrowed behind the mask in a way that told me she knew exactly what I meant, and that was another shock.

She had...the Maiden had a dirty mind.

The laugh that had been building broke free, and it was a real one that came from a warm place that hadn't existed since I made the foolish decision to go after the Blood Crown myself. The laugh shocked the hell out of me, filling me with emotions I'd long believed dead.

Interest.

Awe.

Genuine curiosity.

A feeling of...contentment.

Contentment? Where in the fuck did that even come from? I had no idea, but at the moment, I didn't care. I was interested. And, gods, I couldn't even remember the last time I'd been focused on anything but my brother. The warmth in my chest iced over.

"You really should move," she said.

Her demand pulled me from the disaster my thoughts were veering toward. "I'm quite comfortable where I am."

"Well, I'm not."

I could feel my lips twitch, and I didn't know if it was the desperation to reclaim those fleeting emotions or something else that propelled me to behave as if I had no idea who she was. "Will you tell me who you are, Princess?"

"Princess?" She blinked.

"You are quite demanding." I shrugged, thinking it was a far more fitting name than Maiden or Chosen. "I imagine a Princess to be demanding."

"I am not demanding," she argued. "Get off me."

I arched a brow, feeling that warmth again—that…enjoyment. "Really?"

"Telling you to move is not being demanding."

"We'll have to disagree on that." I paused. "Princess."

Her lips curved and then flattened. "You shouldn't call me that."

"Then what should I call you? A name, perhaps?"

"I'm…I'm no one," she replied.

"No One? What a strange name. Do girls with a name like that often make a habit of wearing other people's clothing?"

"I'm not a girl," she snapped.

"I would sure hope not." Wait. I had no idea *what* the Maiden's age was. I'd been teasing when I called her a girl, but… "How old are you?"

"Old enough to be in here, if that's what you're worried about."

The amount of relief I felt was a warning. "In other words, old enough to be masquerading as someone else, allowing others to believe you're another person and then allowing them to kiss—"

"I get what you're saying," she interrupted, surprising me yet again. "Yes, I'm old enough for all those things."

Did she know what *all those things* were? Truly? If so, there was a whole hell of a lot I did not know about the Maiden. But I didn't think that was the case. She didn't kiss like someone who knew from personal experience what *all those things* were. "I'll tell you who I am, although I have a feeling you already know. I'm Hawke Flynn."

She was quiet for a moment and then squeaked out, "Hi."

That… That was cute.

I grinned. "This is the part where you tell me your name." When she said nothing, my interest only grew. It wasn't like I expected her to admit who she was, but I was dying to discover what she *would* share. "Then I'll have to keep calling you Princess. The least you can do is tell me why you didn't stop me."

Remaining stubbornly quiet, she drew her plump lower lip between her teeth.

Every part of me focused on that—on her mouth. And hell, that filled my head with all kinds of things my body was shamefully on board with. I shifted slightly, hiding my reaction. "I'm sure it's more than my disarming good looks."

Her nose wrinkled. "Of course."

I laughed, surprised yet again by her—by myself. "I think you just insulted me."

She winced. "That's not what I meant—"

"You've wounded me, Princess."

"I highly doubt that. You have to be more than well aware of your appearance."

"I am." I grinned at her. "It has led to quite a few people making questionable life choices."

I hoped it would lead *her* to make some questionable life choices, which, considering where she was, she wasn't unfamiliar with.

"Then why did you say you were insulted—?" Her mouth snapped shut, and she pushed against my chest again. "You're still lying on me."

"I know."

"It's quite rude of you to continue doing so when I've made it clear that I would like for you to move."

"It's quite rude of you to barge into my room dressed as—"

"Your lover?"

I stared at her for a moment. "I wouldn't call her that."

"What would you call her?"

Hell, how was I supposed to answer that? "A...good friend."

She returned my stare. "I didn't know friends behaved this way."

"I'm willing to wager you don't know much about these sorts of things."

"And you wager all of this on just one kiss?"

"Just one kiss? Princess, you can learn a wealth of things from just one kiss."

She quieted, and I...needed to know why she was here, at the Red Pearl, in this room, wearing a maid's cloak. And where were her guards? I seriously doubted they'd allow her to come here. If so, I needed to know which one did so I could make sure that wasn't the one who found themselves dead.

But I started with the most pressing question. "Why didn't you stop me?"

As I waited for an answer, my eyes tracked over her mask and then lower, to where the cloak had parted...

It felt like a punch to the chest when I saw what she wore.

Or what she *wasn't wearing* to be more exact.

The neckline was low, exposing the surprising swells of her breasts, and the gown, whatever silky material it was made of, was now my favorite. It was nearly transparent and thin enough that I thought for a moment the gods had woken from their slumber to bless me.

Or curse me.

But if this was the idea of a curse, then being damned wasn't all that bad.

However, none of that answered why the untouched, pure Maiden would be at the Red Pearl, a notorious pleasure house in Masadonia, by herself. In a room with a man she believed thought her to be someone else, no less. Someone who had kissed her without one word of protest falling from her lips. Hell, she'd kissed me back. Started to, at least. And she was dressed...

She was dressed for utter debauchery.

It suddenly seemed hard to breathe as my gaze lifted to hers. A sense of understanding swept over me, quickly followed by disbelief. There was only one reason she would be here.

And I was more interested in all the reasons *why* than I had been interested in anything in...forever. I shouldn't be. I had just been handed the golden goose. This was the perfect chance for me to take her. I could slip out of the city right now.

There'd be no need to continue the ruse of being a dutiful and loyal Rise Guard. No need to get close to her. Hell, I couldn't get any closer than I was right now.

Well, yeah...I could.

I could get *way* closer.

But if I took her now, I'd never hear from her lips why she was here. And I *needed* to know that. If I made my move, I would lose the strange pounding in my chest. The warmth. The enjoyment. And I was a selfish son of a bitch when it came to something I wanted.

Besides, it wasn't me who'd found her. She had found me. And in an instant, I was more than willing to let this play out for as long as possible.

Because it would all be over soon enough.

"I think I'm beginning to understand," I told her.

"Does that mean you're going to get up so I can move?"

I shook my head. "I have a theory."

"I'm waiting with bated breath for this."

The Maiden...she had a mouth on her.

I liked that.

A lot.

"I think you came to this very room with a purpose in mind," I said. "It's why you didn't speak or attempt to correct my assumption of who you were. Perhaps the cloak you borrowed was also a very calculated decision. You came here because you want something from me."

She dragged that lip between her teeth again.

I shifted once more, lifting my hand to her right cheek. The simple touch sent a shudder through her. "I'm right, aren't I, Princess?"

"Maybe...maybe I came here for...for conversation."

"To talk?" I almost laughed again. "About what?"

"Lots of things."

Fighting a smile, I said, "Like?"

Her throat worked on a delicate swallow. "Why did you choose to work on the Rise?"

"You came here tonight to ask that?" I asked more dryly than anything Kieran could've said, but it was clear by her stare alone that she expected an answer. So, I gave her the same one I gave anyone who asked. "I joined the Rise for the same reason most do."

"And what is that?" she asked.

The lie came all too easily. "My father was a farmer, and that was not the life for me. There aren't many other opportunities offered than joining the Royal Army and protecting the Rise, Princess."

"You're right."

Surprise flickered through me. "What do you mean by that?"

"I mean, there aren't many chances for children to become something other than what their parents were."

"You mean there aren't many chances for children to improve their stations in life, to do better than those who came before them?"

She gave a short nod. "The...the natural order of things doesn't exactly allow that. A farmer's son is a farmer or they—"

The natural order of things? For Solis, perhaps. "They choose to become a guard, where they risk their lives for stable pay that they most likely won't live long enough to enjoy. Doesn't sound much like an option, does it?"

"No," she said, sending yet another ripple of surprise through me. I hadn't, even for one moment, considered that the Maiden spent a second thinking about those who guarded the city. None of those close to the Blood Crown did. "There may not be many choices, but I still think—no, I know—that joining the guard requires a certain level of innate strength and courage."

"You think that of all the guards? That they are courageous?"

"I do."

"Not all guards are good men, Princess," I said, meaning the words.

Her eyes narrowed. "I know that. Bravery and strength do not equal goodness."

"We can agree on that." My gaze lowered to her mouth.

"You said your father was a farmer. Is he…has he gone to the gods?"

My father was a god among men to many. "No. He is alive and well. Yours?" I asked, even though I already knew.

"My father—both of my parents are gone."

"I'm sorry to hear that," I said, knowing that her parents had died many years ago. "The loss of a parent or a family member lingers long after they're gone, the pain lessening but never fading. Years later, you'll still find yourself thinking that you'd do anything to get them back."

Her gaze flicked over my face. "You sound like you know firsthand."

"I do," I said, refusing to think about any of that.

"I'm sorry," she whispered. "I'm sorry for whoever it is that you've lost. Death is…"

I tilted my head. "Death is like an old friend who pays a visit, sometimes when it's least expected and other times when you're waiting for her. It's neither the first nor the last time she'll pay a visit, but that doesn't make any death less harsh or unforgiving."

"That it is." Sadness colored her tone, tugging at a part of me that needed to stay deadened.

I lowered my head, noting the catch in her breath as my lips neared hers. "I doubt the need for conversation led you to this room. You didn't come here to talk about sad things that cannot be changed, Princess."

Her eyes widened under her mask, and I felt her stiffen under me. I didn't need to know her thoughts to realize that she was battling what she knew she should be doing versus what she wanted.

That very same battle had briefly raged inside me, except reckless curiosity had won out—as did my selfishness. Would she be the responsible one and end this? If so, I would walk away from this room.

And I would.

I wouldn't take her tonight, even though that made more sense than leaving this room without the one person I'd come to this kingdom for. What stopped me was some kind of twisted sense of chivalry, as ridiculous as that sounded. But I knew why she was here.

The Maiden wanted to know pleasure.

And that meant many things—things I couldn't give any critical thought to. Things that would really make me change what I knew, or assumed, about the Maiden. All I could acknowledge was that there was something so…innocent behind her reasons for coming here. Something courageous. Unexpected. I didn't know what had gone into her choice to come here, what she'd had to do, how she'd prepared herself, or even why. And if I revealed who I was—who she was to me—in a society like the one the Ascended had created, where women needed to hide their faces when they sought pleasure and happiness, it could be seen as a punishment. As if this were what happened when you engaged in such behaviors, and I…I didn't want to be a part of ruining that for her.

I sensed the moment she made up her mind. Her body relaxed under mine as she drew that lower lip between her teeth once more.

And gods, I didn't expect that. I figured she would end this. She should have. But hell, I was a bastard because I was…too captivated—too intrigued—not to follow through.

Drawing in a breath that felt strangely shallow, I drew a finger across the satin ribbon of her mask. "May I remove this?"

She shook her head.

Disappointment sparked. I wanted to see her face and the expressions she made, but that mask…it was just a silly piece of cloth. Yet sometimes, silliness fed bravery, and who was I to judge? After all, I was constantly pretending. My life in this kingdom was a façade. Everything about me was a lie. Well, mostly.

I trailed my finger along the line of her jaw and down her throat, over her wildly pounding pulse. My fingers stopped where the cloak was fastened. "How about this?"

She nodded.

I'd never removed a cloak quicker in my life.

The shiver I saw, the sudden rise of her breasts as I skimmed the tip of my finger over the wonderfully indecent neckline, sent a bolt of raw, pounding desire through me. In a flash of heat, I saw that gown of hers in shreds, and me between her thighs, first with my tongue and then with my cock. And that desire was nearly as potent as the need to remain where I was—warm and interesting and alive.

I checked myself then.

Clenching my jaw, I willed the gathering throb to cool it. I was willing to go wherever this led, but not *there*. That was taking too much, and it didn't matter if it was willingly given. I was a monster, but not that kind of monster.

But there was so much we *could* do.

"What do you want from me?" I asked, toying with the small bow between the sweet swells on her chest. "Tell me, and I'll make it so."

"Why?" she asked. "Why would you...do this? You don't know me, and you thought I was someone else."

It wasn't like I could answer that question honestly, and it had nothing to do with who she was. Or maybe it did. At this moment, I couldn't be sure. "I have nowhere to be, and I'm intrigued."

"Because you have nowhere to be at the moment?"

"Would you rather I wax poetic about how I'm charmed by your beauty, even though I can only see half your face?" I asked. "Which, by the way, from what I can see is pleasing. Would you rather I tell you I'm captivated by your eyes? They are a pretty shade of green from what I can tell."

The corners of her lips turned down. "Well, no. I don't want you to lie."

"None of those things were a lie." Tugging on the little bow, I dipped my head, brushing my lips over hers. Her fresh and sweet scent heightened. "I told you the truth, Princess. I'm intrigued by you, and it's fairly rare anyone intrigues me."

"So?"

"So," I said, chuckling against the curve of her jaw, "you've changed my evening. I'd planned to return to my quarters. Maybe get a good—albeit boring—night of sleep, but I have a suspicion that tonight will be anything but boring if I spend it with you."

It would be nothing short of a miracle.

"Were you...were you with someone before me?" she asked.

I lifted my head. "That's a random question."

"There are two glasses by the settee."

"It's also a random, *personal* question asked by someone whose name I don't even know."

Her cheeks warmed.

And I...I could understand her inquiry, couldn't I? Her concern. "I was with someone," I answered. "A friend who is not like the owner of the cloak. One I hadn't seen in a while. We were catching up, in private," I explained, and it shocked me. I rarely ever did such a thing.

But my response wasn't exactly a lie. I hadn't seen Kieran in a few days, and since we'd been together since birth, that did feel like a while. That was the longest we'd been separated since I—

I cut those thoughts off before they could take hold and become something darker, harder to cast off. "So, Princess, will you tell me what you want from me?"

Her breath caught again. "Anything?"

"Anything." I slid my hand down, cupping the surprisingly full weight of her breast. The white robes I normally saw her in had hidden a lot.

But now, with the thin material of her gown pulled taut against her skin, I could make out the deep, rosy hue, and the oh-so-very-intriguing hardened peak. My thumb followed my gaze.

She gasped as her back arched, pressing her breast more firmly into my palm. My chest tightened with a surge of need.

"I'm waiting." I swept my thumb once more, thoroughly enjoying the breathy sound she made and the curl of her body. "Tell me what you enjoy, so I can make you love it."

"I..." She bit down on her lip. "I don't know."

My gaze flew to hers as I froze. Her words were a reminder. They were also a spark that lit a fire under the need I felt to show her exactly what she wanted.

"I'll tell you what I want." I moved my thumb again, slower, harder. "I want you to remove your mask."

"I..." Her lips parted. "Why?"

"Because I want to see you."

"You can see me now."

"No, Princess." I lowered my head. "I want to really see you when I do this without your gown between you and my mouth."

Keeping my gaze on her face because I refused to miss a moment, I flicked my tongue over the tip of her breast. The silk was barely a barrier, and as I closed my mouth over the turgid peak, I could easily imagine doing something that rarely ever occurred to me when I was with a mortal.

I could see myself sinking my teeth into the plump flesh, discovering if she tasted as sweet as she smelled. I bet she did. My body answered the cry of pleasure that parted her lips, thickening and hardening.

"Remove your mask. Please." I slid a hand over the lush curve of her hip and down her thigh to where the dress parted. Her skin felt like the silky material, smooth as I curled my fingers—around something hard. "What the...?"

My hand closed over the hilt of a *dagger*. What in the hell? I unsheathed the blade, rocking back as she sat up, reaching for the weapon.

The Maiden had a dagger. And not just any ordinary kind.

"Bloodstone and wolven bone."

"Give that back," she demanded, scrambling to her knees.

My gaze shifted from the dagger to her. "This is a unique weapon."

"I know." A tumble of red-wine waves and curls fell forward over her shoulders.

"The kind that's not inexpensive." And one that carried a particular purpose. "Why are you in possession of this, Princess?"

"It was a gift, and I'm not foolish enough to come to a place like this unarmed."

That was a smart decision. "Carrying a weapon and having no idea how to use it doesn't make one wise."

Her eyes narrowed with irritation. "What makes you think I don't know how to use it? Because I'm female?"

I stared at her. "You can't be surprised that I would be shocked. Learning how to use a dagger isn't exactly common for females in Solis."

"You're right, but I do know how to use it."

The confidence in her words told me that she spoke no lies. So, the Maiden knew how to wield a dagger. That was wholly and gloriously unexpected. Instead of concerning me, it made me all the more interested.

The right side of my lips curved up. "Now, I'm truly intrigued."

Her eyes widened as I thrust the dagger blade down into the mattress and then went at her. I took her down to the bed, settling between her thighs and letting her feel exactly how *intrigued* I was—

A fist pounded on the door. "Hawke?" Kieran's voice rang out. "You in there?"

I halted and closed my eyes, telling myself that I did not just hear his voice.

"It's Kieran."

"As if I didn't know that already," I muttered, and a small giggle left her. The sound opened my eyes and brought a grin to my lips.

"Hawke?" Kieran pounded some more.

"I think you should answer him," she whispered.

"Dammit." If I didn't, he would likely barge in out of concern. "I'm thoroughly, happily busy at the moment."

"Sorry to hear that," Kieran replied as I refocused on her. The wolven knocked again. "But the interruption is unavoidable."

"The only unavoidable thing I see is your soon-to-be broken hand if you pound on that door one more time," I warned, causing her eyes to widen. "What, Princess?" I lowered my voice. "I told you I was really intrigued."

"Then I must risk a broken hand," Kieran replied, and a growl of frustration rumbled from deep within me. "The...envoy has arrived."

Gods.

I cursed again, under my breath this time. This couldn't have happened at a worse time.

"An...envoy?" she asked.

"The supplies we've been waiting for," I explained, which was sort of true. "I need to go."

She nodded.

And I did need to leave, but I didn't want to. It took several moments for me to force myself to move. Standing, I grabbed my tunic from the floor as I told Kieran I'd be out in a few. He wouldn't be waiting for me in the hall. He'd go somewhere quieter. I yanked the shirt over my head, glancing over my shoulder to see that she had retrieved the dagger. I grinned.

Clever girl.

I shrugged on a baldric and picked up the two short swords from the chest near the door, and it was like I had no control over what came out of my mouth. "I'll come back as soon as I can." I sheathed the blades flat to my sides, realizing that what I said was the truth. I *would* come back. "I swear."

She nodded once more.

I stared at her. "Tell me that you'll wait for me, Princess."

"I will."

Pivoting, I walked to the door and then stopped. Slowly, I turned back and soaked in the sight of her—that surprising mass of red waves and those parted lips, the way she sat there, clutching the edges of her cloak around her, brave yet vulnerable. It was an interesting mix, one I wanted to continue exploring.

"I look forward to returning."

She was silent again, and I knew it was unlikely that she'd be here when I returned, but I would come back. I would look for her. And if she wasn't here?

I would find her again.

Sooner rather than later.

She would be mine.

TOO BRIEF
MOMENTS

I walked through the thickly forested Wisher's Grove at a fast clip, wanting to get this meeting over with. Only the thinnest sliver of moonlight made its way through the sweeping pine branches. The woods were unsettling enough during the day, eerily silent except for a bird's distant, shrill call or the quiet rustle of some small woodland creature. At night? Even I was uneasy here. But due to the fact that very few entered this part of the Grove during the day, something I only knew occurred because of the pathways I'd spotted worn into the soil, it was one of the few places in the entirety of Masadonia where words could be spoken freely without the threat of being overheard.

And from Wisher's Grove, it would take me only mere minutes, if that, to return to the Red Pearl.

To *her*.

"You know," Kieran began, "I wouldn't have interrupted you if it weren't for this."

I nodded. These *supplies* weren't exactly what one would typically think of.

"It's been far too long since you've fed," Kieran added.

His words were like a siren's call, reawakening a slumbering giant. My upper jaw throbbed as an ache blossomed in my gut.

"And since you don't like to use those who are only part Atlantian—"

"I know my preferences, Kieran," I interrupted. A cold breeze stirred the branches overhead, sending a few needles to the ground. And he knew why I didn't like using them. Half-Atlantians weren't accustomed to feeding. They were also a hell of a lot easier to injure—or worse—and because of the Blood Crown, I…I'd taken enough lives that way to last me a lifetime. I preferred not to repeat that. "You know, the older you get, the more of a mother hen you become."

Kieran snorted behind me. "Someone has to make sure you don't descend into madness." He paused. "More so than normal, that is."

If he knew who I'd been with minutes ago, he would think I'd reached all new heights of madness.

And he'd be right.

That was exactly what the time spent with the Maiden had felt like. Madness.

The all-too-fresh memory of the Maiden's soft body under mine told me it would be one hell of a way to go, though, and I planned on doing just that after I was done here. I would go a little mad when I returned to the chamber. That was if the Maiden honored her promise to wait for my return.

She had to.

I cleared my throat. "Who came?"

"Emil," Kieran answered.

My brows shot up. "Didn't expect that."

"Yeah, me neither, especially since he's not that familiar with Solis. But Naill couldn't make the trip."

I nodded, not liking any of them to be this far into Solis, but all of them were loyal to me. Too loyal.

"You going to tell me what that was all about?" Kieran asked after a moment.

"Not sure what you're speaking of." I kept my gaze trained ahead, a little surprised it had taken him so long to ask.

"Sure." He drew out the word, walking ahead of me.

I said nothing.

"In case you've forgotten," Kieran said, lifting a low-hanging branch to dip under it, "I can smell another on you."

Hell, I could still smell the Maiden. I was drenched in her sweet scent—

Cursing, I caught the branch Kieran let go of before it smacked me in the face. "Asshole."

"You weren't alone," he said, glancing over his shoulder. "And I don't recognize that scent."

"Do you know the scent of everyone in Masadonia?" I brushed past him.

"I know the scents of those who frequent the Red Pearl." Fallen needles and twigs crunched under our steps. "And I know the scents of who you typically spend your evenings with."

"Fucking wolven noses," I muttered. Even I could decipher differences between those I usually spent my nights with. Considering that, I should've known it wasn't Britta the moment the Maiden walked into that chamber.

But never in a thousand years would I have guessed it would be her. Nor would I have thought she had such a biting tongue on her. And that intrigued me.

As did her sympathy for me when I spoke of loss. She didn't know me, nor did she know anything about what I'd lost, but her compassion had been genuine. "Cas."

I halted, the nape of my neck tightening. Not once since we'd been in the Kingdom of Solis had Kieran used that name. Not even in these woods or at the Red Pearl.

"The fact that you're being all cagey about who you were with has me worried."

I slowly faced the wolven I'd known since birth. He had a right to be worried. We were bonded, but our connection ran deeper than that. Always had. I kept nothing from Kieran. He shared everything with me, but I found myself in a strange position of being unwilling to tell him what had occurred in that room in the Red Pearl and with whom. I didn't know why. I trusted no one more than him, but this was…

This was the fucking Maiden.

Another ripple of lingering shock went through me. If I weren't still able to taste her sweetness on my lips, I would've believed I'd hallucinated her unexpected arrival.

I looked away, my shoulders stiffening. If I didn't tell him, he wouldn't let it go. This meeting with those who'd just arrived would take longer than necessary, and knowing Kieran, he'd follow my ass back to the Red Pearl. "I was with the Maiden."

Silence.

Absolute, dead silence.

And Kieran always had a response, no matter what came out of my mouth.

My gaze flicked back to him. He stared at me as if I'd spoken garbled ancient Atlantian while drunk off my ass. I arched a brow. "You okay? Or did I just fry your brain?"

Kieran blinked. "What. In. The. Actual. Fuck?"

A low laugh left me. "Yeah. Pretty much my thoughts."

"You're not bullshitting me, are you?" Kieran's head tilted. "You were with the actual Maiden—" He stopped, inhaling deeply. His eyes narrowed. "You were *really* close with the actual Maiden?"

"I wouldn't go so far as to say I was *that* close," I lied, and fuck if I knew why. "But, yeah, it was her."

Kieran opened his mouth, then closed it. He started to turn away but then faced me. "You know I have questions about this, right?"

I sighed. "I do."

"I'm going out on a limb and assuming she was unguarded."

I shot him a droll look. "You'd assume correctly."

Once more, he appeared as if he didn't know what to say. "How? Why? What in the—?"

"I'm guessing she snuck out," I cut him off. "And based on how far she got, I imagine this wasn't her first time."

"What in the hell was she doing at the Red Pearl?" Kieran asked.

Surprise flickered through me as a bird shrieked from somewhere above us. "*That's* the question you're going to ask? Not why we're standing here without her?"

"Oh, I'm getting to that question next, but I'm just trying to wrap my head around why the *untouched* Maiden was in a *private* chamber at the Red Pearl, a known gambling den and *brothel.*"

She'd come to that chamber to learn what pleasure felt like.

She'd gone there tonight to *live.*

I still found that courageous and boldly innocent. And it was also private. Intimate enough that I couldn't share it with anyone. Not even Kieran.

"That, I cannot answer," I said, and Kieran's eyes narrowed. "She just walked right into the chamber. I don't know if she knew I was there."

Kieran was quiet for a moment. "Is it possible she was expecting someone else to be there or went into the wrong room?"

Based on her inexperience—the innocent and hesitant but very eager responses—I didn't think she was there to meet anyone in particular. I could be wrong, though. After all, I'd obviously been wrong about a few things regarding the Maiden.

"I don't know." I scratched my fingers through my hair. "Wasn't like my presence there was known to many."

Kieran appeared to think that over. "Well, there are only a couple of reasons why she would be there, and I doubt she would be willing to risk coming face-to-face with a guard. It had to be coincidental."

I observed him, watching the corners of his lips turn down. "Except you don't believe in coincidences."

"Do you?"

"There's always a first time."

He shook his head. Another moment passed. "Why didn't you take her, even with the risks involved?"

A muscle flexed at my jaw. "Because if I did, I would have had to quiet her. Used compulsion. And that wouldn't have lasted long enough to get her out of the city."

Kieran eyed me. "You sound entirely too reasonable."

I did.

And yet, I didn't.

Because that wasn't my only reason.

It was also the fact that if I had taken her, she likely would have seen it as some sort of punishment for breaking the rules of the society the Ascended fostered and for stepping out of the cage I was no longer sure she willingly submitted to.

And for some reason, allowing her to have those all-too-brief moments wasn't something I was willing to taint.

At least, for now.

NECESSARY SUPPLIES

Emil Da'Lahr was a motherfucker.

One either enjoyed being in his presence or spent the entirety of that time plotting various ways to murder him, something I truly believed brought Emil a perverse level of joy.

Either way, I routinely alternated between those two states of being.

But when push came to shove, the auburn-haired Atlantian had my back, and I had his. He was loyal, as quick with a sword and dagger as he was with his retorts, and although he had jokes for days, he was a beast if crossed.

He was waiting for us on the bank of a quiet lake nestled deep within the Grove, seated on a flat boulder.

And Emil wasn't alone.

Crouched at his feet was a large, silver-and-white wolven. He rose upon our approach, nearly as tall as the boulder Emil sat upon. The wolven's size alone would've stopped the heart of any mortal upon sight, so he would've traveled as a mortal, but I bet he'd shed that form the moment he could. None of the wolven liked to remain in their mortal forms for long stretches of time, even if it was by choice or forced by a situation.

"Arden," I acknowledged, smiling.

The wolven trotted from Emil's side, brushing against Kieran's legs first and then coming to nudge my hand. I ran my fingers through the fur between his ears as Emil stood and gave an overly elaborate, sweeping bow.

"You're not going to greet me with that handsome smile of yours?" the auburn-haired Atlantian asked as he straightened. "Flash those dimples?"

"Not now."

Arden let out a low huffing noise that sounded like a laugh.

Emil pressed a hand to his chest. "You wound me." He paused. "My Prince."

I shot him a narrowed-eye glare, and the man's smile deepened.

"Sometimes, I really think you have a death wish," Kieran muttered under his breath.

Everyone who met Emil thought that.

Chuckling, Emil leaned back against the boulder. There was no sword on his hip. Dressed as he was in the dull brown breeches of a Solis commoner, a sword would've drawn too much attention. Still, I knew he had an armory of weapons beneath the plain black coat.

"How was your journey here?" I asked as Arden turned his attention to the dark woods. "Run into any problems?"

"Nothing that Arden and I couldn't take care of. Just a few Craven and a nosy guard or five," he answered. "All these years I've lived, and I've never seen a wolven basically eat a person before."

My brows knitted as I glanced at Arden. The wolven chuffed, keeping his stare on the trees.

"We don't usually make a habit of that," Kieran replied. "Mortal meat is…gamey."

"*Mortal meat?*" I repeated under my breath.

"It was morbidly fascinating to watch. Couldn't look away. Also, very disgusting." Emil crossed his arms. He glanced toward the east. "Anyway, got to say, I'm not impressed with what I've seen of Masadonia so far, especially what you get an eyeful of upon entering the city." His lip curled. "Gods, I can't believe they have people living like that."

"Most wouldn't believe it unless they saw the Lower Ward." Then again, even if the Blood Crown took better care of their people, their cities would be a dull comparison to Atlantia.

I was eager to return to the Red Pearl, but there were things I needed to know. "How are things in Spessa's End?" I asked of the Atlantian city that sat upon the Stygian Bay, within a day's ride of the Skotos Mountains. The once-busy trading post was believed to have been destroyed in the war, just like the nearby city of Pompay, and since it was so far east, the Blood Crown had no knowledge of the city's current state. It had to stay that way.

"Good. I think some of the crops are about to be harvested. At least that's what Vonetta was talking about when I left," he said, referencing Kieran's sister. "Many more homes have been built. You'll barely recognize the place when you return." His amber gaze met mine. "Which we all hope is soon. Not me. But others, yes. They hope it will be soon."

Laughing, I shook my head and then shifted the subject to a far more delicate one. "Any word from Evaemon?"

"The King and Queen are...concerned about your current whereabouts and your motives for being gone so long," he shared, the humor fading from his features. "Alastir's commentary on the matter hasn't been helpful in easing those worries."

Dragging a hand through my hair, I sighed. I wasn't at all surprised to hear that. As the Advisor to the Crown, Alastir Davenwell's duty was to keep the King and Queen informed about all things. However, the elder wolven did very little to quell my father's temper or de-escalate plans for war. He wanted to see the Blood Crown burn. I couldn't exactly blame him for that. He, like many others, had his reasons.

"We'd better get on with this." Emil nodded at Arden. I glanced at the wolven. His ears were flat once more as he nervously paced near the boulders. "I don't believe he likes these woods very much. I fear he will start eating one of us."

Arden growled at the Atlantian, and Emil simply smiled. I imagined their journey here had been...interesting and long.

"Bad vibes," Kieran murmured, turning his stare to the still lake.

Emil raised his brows at me.

I shook my head. "Kieran believes these woods are haunted."

"I don't believe," Kieran countered. "I know."

"Well, then, we really need to hurry." Emil began rolling up the sleeve of his coat. "Because if I see even one ghost, you will never see an Atlantian run faster."

Kieran smirked. "You can't outrun the dead."

Fingers halting around the sleeve, Emil turned his head to the wolven. "That was an...exceptionally creepy statement."

He shrugged. "Just the truth."

Emil frowned. "That didn't help."

"Thank you for doing this," I cut in, stopping them before the conversation went any further. I took Emil's hand as I looked down at the slightly shorter male. "The risk you took coming here is appreciated."

"Anything for you." Emil met my stare. "You know that."

"I do." I squeezed his hand. "I won't take more than is needed."

Kieran's stare sharpened on me. I knew he didn't look away. Not as

I lifted Emil's wrist to my mouth. I hesitated, even as my jaw began to ache more furiously. His blood would surely erase the lingering taste of the Maiden, and damn if that wasn't an idiotic as hell thing to even think about.

Even more so was the fact that I hesitated *because* of that.

Biting fast and clean where Emil's pulse beat strongly, he only jerked a little as I quickly withdrew my fangs. I smoothed my thumb along the inside of his wrist, soothing away the brief sting of pain. Feeding could be painful or bring pleasure. It could also be as impersonal as a business transaction. This was the latter as I drew his blood, his very life force, into me. The moment the rich, earthy taste hit my tongue, every cell in my body seemed to vibrate. It was like going too long without food or water. I wanted to gulp but forced myself to take slow, steady draws as Emil stood still.

Feeding and being fed on were quite common among our kind, but if one didn't trust another, there was an instinctual reaction that couldn't be hidden—a physical one. Emil showed no signs of such. He didn't pull away. He didn't tense or even make a sound. Emil trusted me. Irrevocably. And I wasn't sure what I'd done to earn that.

As I drank, bits and pieces of images formed in my mind. Thick, dark green trees. The smell of freshly tilled soil and sawdust. Memories. This was one of Emil's. I heard his teasing laugh as I saw a girl with long, dark braids that reached her waist, and skin the color of the night-blooming roses the Maiden sought in the evenings. I recognized her at once.

It was Vonetta—Kieran's sister. Why the fuck would Emil be thinking of her right now? Well, the answer was an obvious one.

I grinned against Emil's wrist. Man, he really did have a death wish.

Several more moments passed before I forced myself to withdraw. I lifted my head, chasing away a lone drop of blood that had dampened my lip as my eyes found Emil's. I raised a brow and grinned. His jaw locked as he glanced at Kieran. My grin spread.

"That's not enough," Kieran began.

"It was." I offered my other hand to Kieran. "See for yourself."

He folded his fingers around my wrist, his thumb pressing into my pulse. Being that Emil was like me, one of the elemental bloodlines that could be traced back to the first Atlantians created by the gods, his blood was pure and powerful. Already, my skin felt warmer. The faint fogginess clouding my mind was gone. My heart rate had slowed.

Kieran dragged in an audible breath of relief.

"Are you sure?" Emil's gaze searched mine. "If you need more, I'll be fine."

"I'm sure." I squeezed his hand once more before letting go. "Thank you again."

"You know, I can stay." Emil began rolling down his sleeve. "Keep a low profile while doing some sightseeing. No one will even know I'm here."

"I thought you said you weren't impressed with the city."

"I'm willing to hang around and see if a longer look will change my mind," he said.

I smiled, knowing that Emil, like all of us, had no real desire to spend time in any place controlled by the Blood Crown. He offered so he could be available in case I needed to feed again. Hopefully, that wouldn't be necessary. Elemental Atlantians could go for long periods without feeding if we remained uninjured and kept ourselves well-fed through typical mortal means.

"I appreciate the offer, but there is something else I must ask of you. Another favor," I said, shifting my weight. The growing tension seizing my muscles had also faded. "I would like for you to return to Atlantia and Evaemon."

Emil's head tilted as Arden listened. "I assume there is a more detailed purpose behind this request."

"There is. I would like for you to keep an eye on Alastir."

Surprise flickered across Emil's face. "Are you suspicious of him?"

"No. I've known Alastir since I was a babe. He's like a second yet more demanding father," I said, earning a snort from Kieran. "But the very last thing we need is for him to discover what I'm planning."

"At the very least, we need to delay his knowledge," Kieran added. "Alastir has eyes and ears everywhere. He's bound to find out."

"So, you want me to run interference?" Emil surmised, and I nodded. "I can do that." He glanced over at Arden, who was nosing a fallen leaf as if it were a pit viper. "Out of curiosity, why do we want to keep Alastir in the dark for as long as possible?"

"Alastir wants war. Possibly more so than even my father. If he learns of my plans to take the Maiden, he will want to use her to strike back at the Blood Crown."

Just as my father would.

Emil turned his attention back to me. "And how does that differ from what you are doing?"

"I don't plan to kill her," I stated flatly. "And that is exactly what they would do."

The Atlantian said nothing for several moments. "Well, I hope your plan doesn't turn out to be what you expect of *them*. Truly."

"As do I," I said. The unease I'd felt the other morning while training with Vikter returned, plopping its ass on my chest, now too cold and heavy for having just fed.

Wishing Emil and Arden safe travels back to Atlantia, we parted ways. Kieran returned to the city, where Jansen had set him up with somewhat private lodging in a small apartment over one of the various workshops. And I, well, I made my way back to the Red Pearl, picking up enough speed that I was free of the Grove within seconds. Moving too fast for mortal eyes to track, I forced myself to slow once I reached the alley outside the Red Pearl. My heart began pounding, and it had nothing to do with physical exertion.

I climbed the back steps, taking three at a time to reach the hall outside the chamber. I'd only been gone an hour, if that, but before I reached the door, I already knew. Still, I had to check. I pushed the door open, finding only her lingering sweet scent. The room was empty.

The Maiden hadn't waited.

HUNTED

The bitter surge of disappointment upon the Maiden's broken promise quickly gave way to one of concern as I stared at the rumpled bed.

Her not being here meant she was out there somewhere, on the too-often-vicious streets, by herself, at a time of night when those often up to no good roamed. The kind of people who preyed upon the weak and helpless.

But the Maiden wasn't exactly helpless. A wry grin twisted my lips. She carried a dagger—a wolven-bone and bloodstone dagger, no less—and handled it in such a way that backed up her claim that she knew how to use it.

Still, I stalked forward. Grasping a fistful of the blanket, I lifted it and inhaled deeply, taking in the sweet and earthy scent. Honeydew. Dropping the cover, I turned and left the Red Pearl. Outside, I scanned the dimly lit streets, quiet except for the muted hum of laughter and bawdy shouts coming from inside the numerous businesses.

She could be anywhere if she left the Red Pearl immediately upon my departure. I lifted my gaze to the distant glow of lights radiating from the numerous windows of Castle Teerman. The streets didn't get safer the closer one got to the castle.

They actually got more dangerous because mortals no longer populated the areas. The closer to the castle you got, the closer you were to the Ascended, and after sunset, they would be moving about freely.

With her traveling dressed not as the Maiden but as a commoner, I doubted any Ascended would hesitate before helping themselves.

Anger took root in my gut, but I wasn't exactly sure who it was meant for. The Maiden for foolishly endangering her life? The Ascended, who were truly to blame? Or myself for not ensuring she stayed put until she could be safely returned?

The Maiden was entirely too valuable to lose to a bloodthirsty Ascended.

Crossing the street, I headed for the bridges and pathways that cut through the portion of Wisher's Grove that had been thinned out and used as a park by the most privileged of Masadonia. The entire Upper Ward surrounding Radiant Row, the homes, shops, and the park, were brimming with activity, my sensitive ears picking up on the distant sounds of carriage wheels and chatter. It struck me halfway there, bringing me to a complete stop.

The Maiden was clever.

She must be to have successfully evaded her guards and made it to the Red Pearl. I also doubted that was her first time escaping her personal guard and her pretty cage. She wouldn't travel public roads, especially those that would be busy with the Ascended, who could only live their lives once the sun had set. She wouldn't avoid them out of fear of harm, simply because she knew no better, but rather out of concern of being found out. She would…

Outside a quiet row of narrow townhomes, I looked back to the edges of where I'd just come from. The one place very few traveled.

Wisher's Grove.

A smile spread along my lips. The deepest part of the Grove led right to the inner walls of Castle Teerman.

Cutting across the street, I hit the shadows of the townhomes and started to run. I reached the low stone wall separating the homes from the woods and vaulted over it, entering the Grove once more. I slowed, having moved too fast when I left to pick up on her scent. I still might not be able to catch it. Those wolven senses I'd been damning earlier would've come in handy now.

Recalling the faint trails where the grass had been beaten down from the tread of footsteps, I cut through the trees, coming upon the winding path of packed earth within a few moments. Sticking to the darkness, I followed the trail as it curved closer and closer to the edges of the area they'd cleared for the park. Only a handful of heartbeats later, I picked up on a scent that didn't belong among the damp, rich soil of the woods.

Sweet. Slightly fruity.

My instincts hummed as I prowled forward, my pace increasing as I scanned the trees ahead, every sense on high alert. I moved silently through the woods like a predator tracking its prey. It was one of the only things Atlantians shared with the Ascended—the vampry. Our single-minded focus when we were on a hunt.

There.

A figure moved quickly in the shadows several yards ahead—a cloaked figure. My smile returned as I hit a burst of speed, coming within a dozen feet or so of...her. And it was definitely her. The breeze had her scent and was tossing it in my face.

I followed, treading lightly as I tracked her. The Grove was a maze I could navigate simply because of my vision, which was leagues above a mortal's. How in the world the Maiden found this path at night was beyond me, but her steps were sure. More than once, she skirted jutting rocks and fallen branches I knew she couldn't see, but she obviously knew they were there.

My hearing picked up the low murmur of speech and softer, sultrier sounds from the park. Noises I would've preferred to hear coming from the Maiden if I had my way.

However, it was probably a good thing I hadn't. For I liked to believe I was capable of such restraint that I wouldn't have taken things too far. That I wasn't that kind of monster. But truthfully? Would I have stopped if she wanted to experience more? Would I have been the kind of *good man* my mother had raised me to be? Or would I have been selfish and greedy? A low rumble came from my throat as I followed her. Even now, there was a baser part of me, a primal one, that rode me hard, urging me to cross the distance between us. To reveal myself. What would she do? Be angry that I followed? Pleasantly surprised? Would she talk to me about sad things that clearly weighed on her mind? Would she welcome me, my body against hers once more? Or would common sense prevail, as it must have done for her to leave? Would she run? If so, she wouldn't have a chance. I would catch her. I would—

A twig snapped to my left, jerking my head in that direction. It was too quiet for her to have heard. I scanned the crowded trees, picking up on the sound of quick, almost silent footsteps. The noise came from ahead, between the Maiden and me.

I wasn't the only one following her.

Hunting her.

My eyes narrowed as I dipped under several branches, inching closer. A shadow moved to her left, crossing briefly out of the darkness. The thin stream of moonlight glanced over light hair; round, almost boyish features, and bare shoulders. The glimpse was enough for me to know that what crept up behind her was no mortal who had recently turned Craven—something I'd discovered was an unfortunate occurrence within a week of being here. People like Jole, who thought they had time to turn themselves in but didn't in the end. The same thing happened in Carsodonia and every city within Solis. But the thick, glossy hair and smooth, pale skin meant that what followed her while she blissfully forged ahead was a different sort of death.

An Ascended.

One who likely had no idea who he stalked. And by the time he realized who he was sinking his teeth into, it would be too late. Only the oldest among the Ascended could show restraint and stop before they took the last drop of their victim's blood. That was why so many Craven surrounded the city. It was what happened when a vampry drained a mortal.

Like with most lies, that bit of history had started out as some truth. But the Ascended had the so-called poisonous kiss, not the Atlantians.

Only a few Ascended here were old enough to have that kind of restraint. The Duke and Duchess. A few of the Lords I'd seen creeping around the grounds. This wasn't one of them. This one wouldn't stop. He would kill.

Knowing that we were nearing the section of the garden wall I exploited, the one Jericho would soon make use of and the Maiden was obviously familiar with, my muscles tensed.

Then, I made my move.

I bolted through the narrow spaces between the trees like a streak of lightning, leaping over a toppled pine. As the Maiden slipped from the edge of the Grove, where the stone of the castle wall gleamed dully in the moonlight, I landed behind the Ascended.

The vampry spun, his pitch-black eyes even more bottomless in the darkness. His features twisted into a snarl, lips peeling back to reveal two canines sharpened into fine points.

I bared my fangs. "Mine are bigger."

The vampry's mouth opened wider, and I knew he was gearing up for a big-boy roar—one that would not only alert any of his nearby friends but also possibly the Maiden.

"Nope." I grasped him by the throat, cutting off his growl. It crossed my mind that I *should* question him as we did with those we'd snagged in the past, but I quickly dismissed it.

I had been in the mood for pleasure.

Now, I was in the mood for violence.

He swung, but I caught his arm as I lifted him off his feet and twisted, slamming him to the ground. The vampry immediately jerked upright at the waist as I came down on him, digging my knee into his stomach. I didn't reach for the dagger strapped to my chest—the *bloodstone* blade. Much like the one the Maiden carried, except for the wolven-bone hilt. It was the cleanest way to kill an Ascended, leaving nothing but dust behind.

But I was in the mood for messy.

I smacked my hand down on his mouth, silencing his screams as my other hand slammed into the vampry's chest, punching through bone and cartilage. My fingers sank into the bastard's heart. With a savage yank, I tore the organ from his chest. The Ascended squirmed, his eyes wide as blood gushed from his chest and coursed down my arm.

"Should have stayed out of the woods tonight," I said, squeezing the heart until there was nothing but gore and mush left behind. Until the vampry ceased its useless thrashing.

I rocked back as clumps of tissue fell from my hand. I wiped it as clean as I could on the Ascended's breeches, and then I grabbed the fucker by the hair and dragged him toward the edge of the Grove. I hauled him up and tossed his corpse over one of the heavier, low-hanging branches, where others of his kind would eventually discover him. If not, the sun would finish him off when it rose.

Stepping back, I returned to the worn path, glancing at the spot where the Maiden had disappeared. Smiling, I started back toward the Citadel, whistling softly.

HAUNTED

Sinking into the hot water of the hip bath, I thought about what I'd do for a shower, but since Atlantian infrastructure was apparently the only thing the Ascended hadn't been stealing, I'd have to make do.

Except I couldn't even extend my damn legs.

Cursing under my breath, I grabbed the soap from the nearby stool and got down to scrubbing it through my hair and across my skin. I'd already gotten most of the blood off since I wasn't in the mood to soak in what remained of the vampry on my flesh.

My thoughts wandered as suds gathered on the surface of the hip-deep water, revisiting Emil's news about Alastir and my parents. Knowing Emil, he was already well on his way out of the city with Arden. He would do as I asked, delaying the inevitability of Alastir discovering what I'd been up to.

What I would soon do.

With my knees bent, I leaned back and rested my head on the copper rim. My eyes closed, my thoughts veering to the Maiden—not to what I planned to do, but to what had happened only a handful of hours ago. Not the best of decisions since a throb hit my dick, thickening it.

I was getting hard thinking about the Maiden.

"Gods," I muttered, a rough laugh leaving me as I dragged a hand over my forehead.

A month ago, it never would've crossed my mind. It wouldn't have even been possible, and that had nothing to do with the shapeless white gowns I'd seen her in or the fact that I had no idea what she truly looked like. It was *what* she was. A virginal, untouched Maiden and nothing about seducing or being with an actual maiden was my kind of thing. Not because of her lack of experience. I could give two shits about that. Pleasure could be learned. It was the value placed upon such a thing. The idea that her entire being was tied to her virginity. *That* prevented me from even looking at her in such a way.

It was *what* she symbolized.

The Ascended.

I'd assumed she was a fully willing participant in the role she played. I should've known better than to assume shit because I'd obviously been wrong.

My eyes cracked open into thin slits. It made me wonder what else I could be wrong about when it came to her. Like maybe what she knew about the Ascended. Or what she really thought about how she lived.

I shook my head, not wanting to think about any of that because it led to nowhere good. Just as thinking about how she'd felt beneath me, soft and warm, was leading nowhere good. My dick didn't agree with that, though. It was all on board with my thoughts and memories, hardening and quickly feeling full and too damn sensitive as the tip jutted from the water.

"Fuck," I muttered, running my palm over my face as the fingers of my other hand pressed into the copper side of the tub.

My hand dropped from my face and fell beneath the water. Thinking of how instinctually and eagerly she'd responded to my touch, I gripped myself at the base of my erection. The breath I took was too shallow. She'd seemed so shocked by the prospect of asking for anything and receiving it, as if doing so had never occurred to her. Had never been possible. Clearly, it hadn't because she hadn't known what to ask for. She hadn't known how to put into words what her body ached for.

But she'd shivered in anticipation when I unfastened her cloak. In my mind, I could still see the sweet swells of her chest rising sharply and straining against the tight material, revealing the darker skin beneath, the deep, rosy hue of the tips of her breasts clearly visible through the thin fabric of her gown. Never in a thousand years would I have thought the Maiden had such glorious breasts, soft, strong thighs, and a blade-sharp tongue.

The bolt of raw desire returned, pounding through me. Gods, what I would've given to get my mouth between those thighs. More than what I'd do for a shower because I bet she tasted as sweet as she smelled.

If we hadn't been interrupted, I would've shown her that if allowed. I groaned, thinking of how I would've tasted her, sipped from her—not her blood, but the dampness I knew had been gathering between those lush thighs.

I should be finding another way to slake my need, either through violence or with another—those willing were easy to find in Masadonia. But neither appealed to me as I stroked myself.

Staying with my memories appealed. Those minutes in the chamber where I wasn't Hawke Flynn. When everything about me wasn't a lie, and I hadn't become a phantom of darkness and madness made real. Where I was only living in the moment, not in the past or the future. And good gods, I hadn't existed in the now—I hadn't been interested in that in…in fucking *decades*.

I'd be out of my mind to want to leave that.

I'd be mad not to recognize the dangers of remaining.

But still my hand tightened, my thoughts needing little effort to return to that chamber and to see myself there. To conjure up the image of her, those berry-hued lips parted, and green eyes bright with desire as my mouth closed over the tip of her breast, the silk a decadent barrier.

My head fell back again as my hand pumped. I swore I could hear her voice—that surprising, cutting mouth of hers that was just as arousing as her soft curves. The way she'd grabbed that bloodstone dagger, yanking the blade free of the mattress. She'd handled it like she knew how, which was another surprise that should be concerning yet had the absolute opposite effect.

That tight, curling sensation came out of nowhere and hit me hard, whirling down my spine. My hips reared, splashing water onto the stone floor. I gritted my teeth as I came, the rush of arousal an intense wave, taking a bit of my breath with it as pleasure rippled through me.

Breathing deeply, I lay there, heart slow to calm. Damn, I hadn't come that quickly or hard in…

Fuck if I could remember.

Opening my eyes, I stared at the dull white ceiling, body too lax to even attempt getting out of the tub. The release had eased the tension in my muscles, quieting my mind.

It was only temporary, though.

No different than when the warmth of another brought me pleasure. Because my thoughts were already firing up, drifting back to the same shit. This was precisely what happened when I tried to sleep. Why I lay in bed for hours, doing exactly what I was now: staring at the godsdamn ceiling as if it could answer what I couldn't.

But that didn't stop me from trying to remember the last time a release hadn't felt mechanical. Just a thing my body wanted to be done with when the need hit. When was the last time it didn't feel like anything more than simply getting off? An all-too-brief escape? Was it before I'd so foolishly thought I could end the threat of the Blood Crown all by myself and got taken? Had it been when I was with her—*Shea*? My hand fisted in the water against my thigh.

I didn't want that to be true as I searched my memories. Sex was both nothing and everything to Atlantians and the wolven. Intimately sharing oneself with another was something to be celebrated. The pleasure came from the closeness and not so much the actual release.

But that had become all kinds of fucked up while the Ascended held me, hadn't it? Taking something that was an expression of mutual lust and sometimes fondness—or even love—and turning it into an act to be dreaded. I wasn't sure what had been worse about my time in that cold, dank cage. The numerous cuts made along my body as they stole my blood from me, pouring it into vials and chalices and then into mouths. Knowing they were using a part of me to create more Ascended. The *bites* while that bitch Queen and the bastard King watched, getting off on my pain. Or was it how the King forced me to watch while he killed, but not before committing every atrocious act one could do to another? He'd let them turn and have at me until one of them finally ended the poor soul's life. There were the half-Atlantians they found, and the full-blooded ones who'd remained in Solis after the war, those they'd kept in other cages since before I was even born. The things they did to them. The blood I had to drink to stay alive. Or was it the touching? The caresses that started off cruel and then became tender with no warning.

The copper began to dent under my fingertips as the image of the auburn-haired bitch formed in my mind, no matter how much I wanted to forget what she looked like because *that* was her specialty.

Queen Ileana.

The Blood Queen.

She was living proof that beauty was nothing more than an outer façade because she was the worst of them all. Her touch was scraping, sharp nails that carved into my flesh and then turned to almost loving strokes, always seductive, always so very... *effective*.

That was what she enjoyed more than taking my blood: watching my body give in to her demands while I cursed her and struggled against the chains that bound me, throwing every insult I could think of at her. Even after she grew tired of being the one to inflict such damage, and others just like Ileana took her place, I still heard her laughter, soft and tinkling like the windchimes that once hung in the gardens of Evaemon—the ones I'd torn down in a blind rage upon returning home, frightening my mother and leaving my father silent for days.

Five decades of having pieces of who I was broken off, bit by bit. Five decades of surviving on the promise of revenge, of retribution, kept on the verge of bloodlust, always hungry, until the day my brother came for me. I barely recognized him. I barely recognized Shea.

And I no longer knew myself.

Lowering my gaze to my hands, I saw them. I saw what I'd done with them. The first act I'd committed after my wrists were no longer bound. A shudder went through me. I didn't want to think about what Shea had done—the bargain she'd made with the Ascended.

I didn't want to think about what I'd done to her.

Lifting my hands, I pressed my fingers against my temples instead of what I had done in the past too many times to count when I was alone and the memories wouldn't go away. When the thoughts wouldn't stop coming.

Pleasure wasn't the only temporary escape.

There was also pain.

And if my skin scarred as easily as a mortal's, my arms would be a coarse map that led the way to all the times I'd sought to feel something—*anything*—but what those memories dredged up.

Neither the pleasure nor the pain had worked. I knew that, even though the years after my rescue were a blur of doing everything I could to forget by any means necessary.

My fingers slipped from the sides of my head. I stared at them once more, thinking of the unending stretch of waking nightmares. The long nights of drinking. The even longer days of smoking the unripe poppy seeds until I was either drunk or high enough to forget who I was. And the countless nameless and faceless bodies I'd been with in those dark years afterward. Atlantian. Mortal. Women. Men. Those I fucked just to prove to myself that I decided who touched me. Who I touched. That I had control. That I could still find pleasure in the act. But hell, I'd been a mess. It didn't matter how many times I proved it, how many times I looked at my hands as I did now, a near century later, and didn't see chains cutting into my flesh.

I'd *still* be in that headspace if not for Kieran and others. If they hadn't done everything they could to remind me who I was and who—*what*—I wasn't. Kieran had done a whole lot of the heavy lifting. Damn if he still didn't. But they'd woken me up. They'd pulled me out of the darkness and into a new life that held one purpose only.

To free my brother.

And that was who I'd become.

All I'd become.

Not exactly who I was before. I would never be him again, but this was the closest I would ever get.

Now, the nightmares only really found me in sleep, and there *had* been times since then when sex was about the pleasure of sharing myself with another and not about control or proving a godsdamn thing to anyone—not even myself. A few moments where it had been about something deeper. But the other times? There were still many where I couldn't clearly recall anything about their features. Too many.

There was no feeling of pride accompanying that realization. No smug satisfaction or arrogance. Because, truth be told, I still hadn't forgotten that darkness. It lingered. Haunted. Just as cold as all those releases.

Just as empty.

PRESENT III

I sat with my eyes closed, back against the headboard, holding Poppy to my chest. The top of her head was tucked against my shoulder, and her hips and legs were nestled between mine. Kieran had returned some time ago with a pale blue slip that Hisa had found for Poppy. It had taken so long because she had to search for something that wasn't white. Hisa likely hadn't understood why that mattered, but Kieran hadn't wanted Poppy to wake in the color of the Maiden.

I focused on the weight of her against me. Could she feel my heart beating, even in this deep sleep? This stasis?

"I had…I had a lot of trouble processing everything. The foolish mistakes that led to my capture. What I went through. Shea. What I did afterward. Sometimes, it was like I felt too much—the rage and also relief because I was free. And that felt wrong. There was also guilt. And all of it was so all-consuming that I couldn't feel anything else."

I smoothed my hand over her hair. "Sometimes, the sex, drugs, and drinking didn't silence those feelings. The memories. So, that's when I…" It was like my throat sealed up. Words failed me.

No, the words hadn't failed me. They were still there, pushing against my lips. What stopped them was the…the godsawful shame, even after all these years. Even though I knew that what they'd done to me and what I'd been forced to do to others wasn't my fault. I knew that.

But the mind, man…it liked to ignore that.

Still, I wouldn't forget that the shame wasn't mine.

"It was by accident—the first time I realized that pain could stop it all, just like sex," I forced myself to say. I needed her to know, even if she couldn't hear me. I needed to hear myself say it aloud. "I was training, getting my muscles to relearn how to be quick with a sword and even quicker with my feet, but it was too soon. I was still stuck too deep in my head. I wasn't that present, even though Naill, who was working with me, didn't notice."

A dry, hateful laugh left me. "I learned how to hide it well from those I could. So, I slipped up, and he cut my chest. It wasn't deep, but that bright, sharp pain didn't thrust me back into the cage like I thought it would. Instead, it just...it *silenced* everything. It stunned me enough that it got through all that shit in my head. It stopped the thoughts, and gods, just having a minute of not being back there, not thinking about Malik or what I did or didn't do... Just a fucking minute of silence was like getting release. Not just a physical one, but a mental one. Because there was this sense of calm afterward. Clarity."

A tremor went through me. "Sometimes, I used a blade. Other times, my fangs." My jaw worked. "Relief came the moment I saw red. Clearness. And it took way less effort than the sex did." Another hard laugh left me as I shook my head. "The thing, though, Poppy? It didn't last. It was only another escape. Except I was now hurting myself instead of another hurting me. You'd think I would've realized that right off the bat, but it took getting it out. Talking. I know that sounds cliché as fuck, but it's the truth. Because while that was painful in a different kind of way, the release of putting all that nasty shit into words actually lasted."

And it really had.

Of course, talking hadn't been an immediate miracle fix. Talking that shit out took time. A whole lot of redirection. It took being honest, which wasn't always easy when the natural reaction was to say that I was okay, even when I was a storm waiting to ignite on the inside.

I brushed my lips over the top of her head. "No one knows about any of that—what I used to do to escape everything." My throat felt thick. "Except for Kieran. He knows. He had no choice with the bond." And here came the real fucked-up thing to acknowledge. "What I was doing to myself was weakening him. You'd think that would've been enough to snap me out of it, seeing what it was doing to him, but it wasn't. I was too lost in my head, though not lost enough that I didn't know how fucking selfish it made me."

"You weren't selfish, Cas. You were in pain."

A ragged breath went through me as my arms reflexively tightened around Poppy.

"Please, tell me you know that now."

Opening my eyes, I looked down at the hand that held one of Poppy's, one belonging to the only person I would trust irrevocably to touch her that way—to stay with her earlier while she was most vulnerable as I hastily cleaned the blood and sweat from myself. "I do."

"Really?"

Taking another breath, I turned my head to where Kieran sat beside me, his shoulder against mine. He looked too damn solemn. "I forget that sometimes, but I do."

"It's okay to forget," he said, his gaze searching mine. "As long as you remember later."

A wry grin tugged at my lips. "Yeah, I know." I swallowed. "I just wished I hadn't put you through that."

"I wish you hadn't had to go through any of that shit," he countered. "We can't change anything, though."

"No, we can't."

Kieran held my stare, then looked down at Poppy. "Does she know the truth about Shea?"

I shook my head.

"You ever going to tell her?" he asked.

"I will."

"She's not going to judge you." He moved his thumb over her knuckles as his gaze rose to meet mine. "If anyone understands, I think it will be her."

"I know." I tipped my head back against the wall. "It's just…that's something she needs to be awake to learn."

Kieran was quiet for a moment. "I still can't believe you were with her in the Red Pearl." He laughed quietly. "Shocked the hell out of me."

"You and me both."

He grinned, and a little bit of silence seeped into the chamber. It wasn't bad like before. I was a little more relaxed with Kieran here, knowing that everyone was doing everything they could to give Poppy time.

Time.

It made me think of how my plans had begun to snap into motion after the Red Pearl.

My mind went to what had followed the meeting at the Red Pearl. I thought of the good man who'd had to die. The innocents who'd been slaughtered. The bad ones who needed to be punished.

And the bravery of a Maiden.

EMPTY GARDEN

The Maiden had not gone into the garden the previous night, nor had she been in the shadowy alcoves this morning while I trained. No doubt her late-night…adventures explained her absence. She didn't realize I knew who she was, but I imagined she'd do her best to avoid me.

However, that would soon change—hell, it should've changed already.

But our plans got delayed when I received word from Jericho that she hadn't shown in the garden just before dusk.

What had prevented her from going into the garden?

Had she been caught upon her return to the castle? I didn't think so. Jansen hadn't mentioned it when I saw him earlier. He would've heard if the Maiden had gotten herself into trouble and relayed the information to me.

I tore my attention from the ancient willow. The damn thing fascinated me. Atlantia had none of those trees that I could recall. Stars blanketed the sky as I walked the castle's inner wall, scanning the grounds below. Impatience made my skin as tight as hunger did. The garden was empty, and it shouldn't be. The only signs of life were in the courtyard near the stables, where Lieutenant Smyth currently berated a group of guards for something as irrelevant as unpolished boots. As if the Craven or any other enemy would notice someone's footwear.

My attention flicked to the white mantle draped around Commander Jansen's shoulders. He stood with a few Royal Guards outside one of the halls. The doors were open, the bright light shining out. From the wall, I could see groups of servants huddled together. That wasn't something I saw often. The Teermans were notoriously demanding when it came to their servants. If one wasn't actively busy, they knew to appear as if they were. None simply stood around.

Something had occurred.

A tall, dark-haired figure strode out from the hall, dressed in all black. My eyes narrowed as I gave the male's pale, handsome features a once-over. I didn't know much about this Lord, but I knew his name.

Lord Mazeen.

And he wasn't alone.

The equally dark-haired Duchess Jacinda Teerman walked beside him, dressed in some frock of cyan blue. The Ascended was beautiful, no one could deny that, and when she smiled, she almost looked mortal. Alive. Compassionate. She was better at faking than most. Nearly as good as their Blood Queen, but her eyes were as cold and soulless as the rest. Three Royal Guards followed them.

I came down the inner steps, keeping to the shadows of the wall as the Duchess and Lord Mazeen reached the group near the door. Jansen and the others bowed, the former's movements stiff. I smirked, slipping behind a wide pillar on the main-level breezeway. I didn't have to get too close to hear them.

"We've searched the entire grounds, Your Grace. As His Grace requested," Commander Jansen said as I leaned against the cool stone. "We have found no signs of a Descenter or an intruder of any type."

They were looking for a Descenter? I knew Jericho hadn't been spotted. He would've alerted me if that were the case.

"Someone must have been here," the Duchess said as the Lord hung back, her voice deceptively soft. "That neck didn't break itself."

Behind her, the Lord let out a low laugh.

"I would think not," Jansen replied, his tone all politeness and professionalism. "But no one saw anything. We'll question those assigned to the main floor once more, but I doubt their answers will change."

"Descenters are as clever as they are violent, Commander Jansen. You know this." She looked up at the Commander, her hands clasped primly at her stomach. "We could have them working among us right now, as our guards or in our home."

They most certainly could. They did. Though I had no idea who they spoke of, nor why a Descenter would attack who I assumed was a mortal. Contrary to what the Ascended claimed or liked to believe, though I wasn't aware of all their plots and ploys, they didn't often attack others, even those close to the Ascended.

"And if any are, we will discover them," the Commander assured her, so genuinely I almost believed him. "But I'm not sure if a Descenter is responsible for this attack."

"What do you mean?" the Duchess said, her brows knitting as Lieutenant Smyth crossed the yard to join them.

"Did you...?" Commander Jansen cleared his throat, appearing unwilling to ask what he needed to. What a consummate actor, he was. "Did you see the body, Your Grace? Or hear of her condition?"

"I saw her body briefly." She tilted her head, sending curly raven hair spilling over one shoulder. "Long enough to know she is no longer of this realm."

"There were puncture wounds on her throat," Jansen shared. "Deep ones."

Every muscle in my body went rigid as the Duchess feigned shock— and she was definitely faking that gasp if there were fucking bite marks on the woman's throat. The broken neck now made sense. The woman's blood had probably been drained, and her neck then broken to ensure she died before she turned Craven within the castle walls.

"I'm sorry to be the one to share this news with you," Jansen said, knowing damn well there was no way she'd missed that, no matter how briefly she'd seen the body. "A Descenter would have no reason to drain a mortal of blood."

"No, they string bodies from trees," Lord Mazeen spoke. "Like one of them did to Lord Preston at some point last night."

My lips curved up in a smile. So, he *was* found before the sun got him. That gave me savage satisfaction.

"But that doesn't mean they can't make it seem like someone else is culpable," Lieutenant Smyth suggested, proving exactly what a fucking imbecile the man was.

"Unless someone was running around with an ice pick or another small, sharp object, I find that unlikely," Jansen replied dryly.

Lieutenant Smyth huffed. "I'm just saying it's not impossible."

The Duchess stared at Jansen for long enough that wariness brewed in my chest, but her expression smoothed out. "No, it's not, but it is unlikely. That leaves us with only one other suspect."

Them?

"An Atlantian," Smyth surmised—incorrect yet again.

Because outside of *my* ass, no other full-blooded Atlantians were roaming anywhere even close to the castle. Besides that, we could drink from mortals, and sometimes it happened during heated, passionate moments, but mortal blood provided no sustenance. It wasn't something we sought out.

"The Dark One," the Duchess whispered.

Oh, come the fuck on.

Jansen's expression was devoid of emotion as he said, "We will check the grounds once more, Your Grace." He turned to Smyth. "Alert the Rise and City Guards to be on the lookout for any signs or evidence of the Dark One having arrived in Masadonia."

Lieutenant Smyth nodded, then bowed to the Duchess and Lord before hurrying off to do just that. The man walked as fast as his knobby legs would carry him, all too eager to do the Ascended's bidding.

All too happy to ignore the obvious and spread falsities that would inevitably lead to innocent people being accused of crimes they had taken no part in nor had any knowledge of. Because he knew exactly what the Ascended were. They didn't hide their true natures from the upper crust of the Royal Guard. I'd learned that from my time in captivity in the capital.

After all, those within the Royal Guard usually disposed of the bodies when the Ascended drained them, leaving them to turn Craven outside the city walls.

But this was how they operated, blaming their crimes on Descenters, the Dark One, and Atlantians. They gave the people something to fear so they didn't look too closely at *them*. I eyed Smyth as he climbed the Rise. Mortals who aided in the Ascended's deception were a unique breed of evil fuckery.

"We must make sure something like this doesn't happen again," the Duchess said to Jansen, putting on an act for the other guards who flanked the Commander. Ones who were unaware of the truth. Hopefully, she would have this same conversation with the other Ascended since one of them had ended the woman's life. "It must be safe for the upcoming Rite. But most importantly, it must be safe for the Maiden."

The Maiden.

I stiffened.

"Of course. She is far too important," Jansen answered, this time speaking honestly. "Her safety is always paramount."

Except that none of them, not even Jansen, realized how close she'd come to harm last night.

They parted ways then, Jansen turning his head slightly in my direction. He either sensed my presence or saw me. There was just a slight upward turn of his lips before he disappeared inside Castle Teerman.

Duchess Teerman and Lord Mazeen went in the opposite direction, heading toward the gates leading to Radiant Row. Neither they nor their guards were aware of me as they neared the spot where I remained hidden in the shadows.

I stiffened again.

My gaze fixed on the Lord and narrowed as he passed. Most Ascended had the same scent, but Lord Mazeen smelled different tonight. Beneath that stale-sweet scent they usually had was a hint of jasmine, iron, and…something else. It wasn't the flowery smell or the faint trace of blood that I picked up from him that caused my hand to tighten around the hilt of my broadsword, and it should've, considering what they'd just been discussing. It was the sweeter, slightly earthy scent that caused my nostrils to flare and a low growl to rumble from my chest. He carried *her* scent on him.

The Maiden's.

Soft, quick footsteps came from my left as I watched the Lord disappear into the night.

"Hawke?" came a soft voice. "Is that you?"

Dragging my focus from where I last saw the Lord, I turned to see Britta inching her way along the wall.

"I thought I was well hidden," I answered.

"It is you," she said, her arms folded tightly over her chest. "I saw you from up there." She tipped her rounded chin to one of the windows on the second floor. "I thought I'd say hi."

Tamping down my irritation, I smiled as her scent reached me. It was tart. Lemony. My gaze drifted over her willowy frame as she drew near. How I hadn't immediately recognized it wasn't her last night was beyond me. It was likely due to my needing to feed. Our senses weakened when we went too long, but damn. Britta was a beauty, but she wasn't anything like the Maiden.

"Something happen tonight?" I asked, using the interruption to my benefit.

Several flaxen curls bounced from below the edges of her cap as she nodded. "There was a death." One hand went to her slender throat. "A…a murder."

"That's what I heard." I glanced at the gates. The Lord and Duchess were long gone. "Was it a servant?"

"No. It was Malessa Axton." Britta lowered her voice *and* stepped in close enough that we nearly shared the same breaths. Considering how quietly she spoke, the latter had little to do with what she said. "She is the widow of one of the merchants and fairly close to Lady Isherwood."

"Was she here with the Lady?"

Britta shook her head as she leaned in, her chest brushing my arm. "As far as I know, Lady Isherwood isn't here tonight." Her head tilted back as she looked up at me with cornflower-blue eyes. "Mrs. Axton was alone…"

The way she trailed off told me she knew more than what she was saying. But, then again, Britta always knew a lot about everything.

Except for the Maiden.

When I asked Britta about her, she had very little information to share. That was no different than any other person, but how did the Maiden get her hands on Britta's cloak?

I angled my body toward her, noting how her breath caught as my arm dragged across her chest. I dipped my chin, watching her lashes sweep down. "I heard a Descenter was at fault."

"I don't know about that." The hand at her throat lowered. Her fingers curled around the collar of the maroon uniform the servants wore.

"Because she wasn't alone?" I pressed.

"No." Reaching out with her other hand, she fixed the strap of my baldric that didn't need fixing as she drew her lower lip between her teeth. Her lashes lifted. Little flirt. "I heard she was in one of the sitting rooms with a Lord." Her finger lingered on the strap that crossed my chest. "The chamber she was found in. Her neck was broken."

"And she was drained of blood?"

Her pert nose scrunched. "I hadn't heard that. Only about her neck." Swallowing, she drew her hand back. "Her blood was drained?"

"That's what I heard, but I could be mistaken," I added, not wanting to disturb her. "Do you know what Lord she was with?"

"Lord Mazeen," she answered.

I took a breath. "I don't know much about him." That was all I said. I fell quiet, giving her the opportunity to elaborate.

Britta took it. "He can be…very friendly," she said tentatively, cautiously. The servants, even her, knew better than to speak ill of the Ascended. Her throat worked on another swallow. "Some would say a little too friendly."

I liked that he smelled of the Maiden even less. "Is this something you've had personal experience with?"

"I tend to make sure I'm very busy when he's near."

"Clever girl," I remarked, and she gave me a grin. "Is he at the castle often?"

She lifted a shoulder. "Not any more than the others, but he is usually with the Duke. They are good friends."

Duke Dorian Teerman.

That Ascended was part ghost. I rarely saw him.

I couldn't outright ask Britta if Lord Mazeen was often too friendly with the Maiden. "And does he show the same...attention to others in the castle? The Duchess? Ladies or Lords in Wait...?"

"I don't know, but he seems to have little awareness of personal space with whomever he comes into contact with," she said, her smile strained as she gave a visible shake of her head. Pretty blue eyes met mine once more. "Will you be visiting the Red Pearl soon?"

My smile was a little more genuine. "Perhaps."

"Good." She stepped back, glancing over her shoulder. "I'll keep an eye out for you. Good evening."

"Good evening," I murmured, watching her make her way back into the castle before returning my gaze to the gate, having no intention of returning to the Red Pearl anytime soon.

Or keeping an eye out for Britta.

Which made little sense. Britta was a good time, and sometimes, like tonight, her chattiness came in handy. But the idea of that kind of a good time left me...disinterested.

My gaze flicked to the garden wall, where the Maiden should've been tonight. Now, I knew why she was absent.

But I didn't know why the Lord, who was likely responsible for what had happened with this Axton woman, smelled of the Maiden.

IT IS DONE

"It is done."

I stopped at the top of the Rise, facing the moonlight-drenched-crimson leaves of the Blood Forest. I didn't necessarily feel satisfaction or relief upon learning of another death, one that had happened upon my orders. I only felt determination.

"Which one?" I asked.

"Keal."

Jansen's tone and the way he chewed up the guard's name and then spit it out caused the back of my neck to tighten. "What happened?"

The changeling exhaled harshly. "Did the plans change?"

My brows snapped together as I looked over my shoulder. "What do you mean?"

The Commander stood a few feet behind me, but he stared out over the city. "As far as I recall, the plans were to open a position among the Maiden's personal guards. Not to attempt to take the Maiden. There was to be no contact with her."

Son of a bitch.

I stretched my neck to the left and then the right. "That would be correct."

There was a pause as he angled his body closer, aware of the others on the Rise. "He tried to take her."

Anger heated my blood so fast that it took a moment for me to fully realize what he'd said. Jericho had *tried* to take her. "He failed?"

"She fought back."

My head snapped to his as icy shock doused some of the anger. "Explain."

"She cut him. Got him good in the side based on the amount of blood he left behind. The only reason she remains safely in the castle is because she fought back. If she hadn't, the guards wouldn't have arrived in time to stop him from taking her." His gaze briefly met mine. "Or causing her more harm."

I went completely still. Everything in me. "He harmed her?"

"He struck her." Jansen looked away, and I stopped seeing him at that point. "Would've likely done it again if Kieran hadn't signaled to him."

Darkness descended as a flood of icy rage rose within me. Jericho, that motherfucker, literally had one job: Take out one of her guards and do so without being seen. He was not to interact with the Maiden. He had been warned not to touch her. Not to harm her.

"Cover for me." I pivoted and started walking. "There is something I must attend to."

Jansen was on my heels, keeping his voice low. "Hawke—"

I stopped long enough to meet his stare.

Whatever he saw caused him to draw up short. He gave me a curt nod. "I'll cover for you."

Saying nothing more, I left the Rise, coming down by one of the gatehouses. A few guards lingered near, but none looked at me as I grabbed one of the cloaks left hanging. Donning it, I didn't care who or how many had worn it last. I lifted the hood and quickly blended into the darkness of those who lived in the shadows of the Rise.

Knowing exactly where Jericho would be, I wasted no time crossing the smoke-and-sewage-riddled streets of the Lower Ward, my rage increasing with each step as I neared the Three Jackals, a gambling den known for its blood sports and violent clientele.

I was about to become the most violent patron they'd ever seen.

A shadow peeled away from the walls, drifting quietly past an unconscious man on the sidewalk. Kieran approached me in the dim light of the lanterns that framed the windowless entry, dressed in the dull brown trousers and worn jacket of a commoner, a cap pulled low to hide his features. "I know you want to do something irresponsible and reckless, but you can't kill him," he said. There was no greeting. No need to ask questions. He knew why I was here.

"I'm not going to kill him," I replied. "I'm only going to murder him."

Kieran sidestepped, blocking me. "That's the same thing."

"No, it's not. Killing someone implies it could've been an accident.

What I'm about to do will be completely intentional."

"I get your anger. I do—"

"I don't think you do." I started to brush past him, but Kieran planted a hand on my shoulder, stopping me. I looked down at his hand and then lifted my gaze to his. "I *really* don't think you do."

"He didn't listen, and he stepped way out of line. I'm pissed, too." His pale blue eyes brightened beneath the brim of his cap. "But you cannot murder, kill, or unalive him."

A rumble of warning rose from my chest. "I can do whatever I please," I growled, stepping into Kieran and forcing his arm to bend. "I am his fucking Prince, and he disobeyed me."

"Oh, so *now* you claim ownership of that title?" Kieran countered, his voice as low as mine. "Bear all the responsibilities of such? Good. About damn time. Your parents and Atlantia will rejoice. Alastir will likely come in his pants from happiness, and blah, blah, what-the-fuck-ever, but you aren't just going to go in there as his Prince. You will be going in there as the Prince of Atlantia—the Prince who governs us all."

I knocked his arm aside. "I can't believe you're out here defending him."

"You know damn well I can't stand the jackass, but it's not about me. It's not about you," he shot back.

"Then educate me on what this is about because, right now, the world is my fucking playground."

"He was acting upon your orders—and, yes, he wasn't supposed to attempt to take her." Having no concern for his well-being, he clasped my shoulder again. "But do you think anyone will see the harm in him attempting to speed this shit up? Even if it *was* a foolish attempt?"

"That's not the only reason," I spat. "You were there."

"I was." His grip on my shoulder firmed. "I saw what he did. I saw what she did. She cut him, deeply enough that if he were mortal, he would be dead."

My head tilted. "Do you think I give a fuck about him being cut? I told him she was to remain unharmed."

"I know, and I knocked him on his ass for it already. But how do you think any of those with him, those who traveled into Solis with you and are risking their lives for you, will handle seeing him die at their Prince's hands?"

"They are risking their lives for my brother," I seethed.

"Is there a difference?"

There was in my mind.

108/Jennifer L. Armentrout

Kieran leaned in until the brim of his cap brushed the hood of my cloak. "No one in there will care that he struck the Maiden. Right or wrong, they don't see her as a person. When they look at her, all they see is a symbol of the Ascended, of those who have killed many of their kin and drove their people to near extinction. That doesn't mean they all agree with what he did, but you need to think about what it will do if you walk in there and kill him—a wolven who descends from one of the eldest families."

I inhaled sharply, some of what he was saying breaking through the fog of anger.

"I know what's got you so fired up. It's not because he tried to grab her," Kieran repeated, squeezing my shoulder. "I *know*."

The next breath I took was too shallow. The idea of harming a woman disgusted me; however, it was sometimes an unfortunate necessity, even when it came to the Ascended. Still, Kieran knew most of what the Blood Crown had made me do when they held me. He'd gotten a lot of it out of me when I was on one of my benders. He knew the lives I'd been forced to take, those I'd had to end slowly and painfully. My stomach churned.

I took a step back, exhaling roughly. Kieran was right. None of the others would expect me to be angry enough to slaughter the idiot wolven for attempting to take the Maiden. And he was also right about how they saw her.

Just as I did.

A symbol for the Ascended, a reminder of the bloodshed and loss we'd all dealt with and were still experiencing. My time with her at the Red Pearl didn't change that. Neither did the Maiden wanting to experience pleasure. Not a damn thing had changed.

"You level?" Kieran asked.

I nodded. "Thank you."

"I didn't do anything you should thank me for," he said.

"Not true." I met his stare. "You did everything. Like always."

HE EARNED IT

Anger somewhat in check, I cut through those crowding the ring where two men duked it out to a bloody and broken finish, and headed for one of the back rooms. None of the working girls made any grabs for us, nor did anyone attempt to stop us. It could've been the way I walked or the look on Kieran's face. Whatever it was, everyone gave us a wide berth.

Entering a narrow hall, we passed men drunkenly receiving pleasure they likely wouldn't remember, rooms with gambling, and chambers where various weapons were sold to those forbidden to carry. Men and women were given life and death in these back spaces.

I reached a closed door at the end of the corridor, slamming my hand on the center. It swung open, banging off the wall.

Several men immediately jumped from their chairs. I quickly scanned them. The two wolven who'd traveled with Jericho, one of them the brown-haired Rolf. Two Descenters: a half-Atlantian, and a blond-haired mortal. My gaze settled on Jericho as Kieran closed the door behind us.

Jericho stood, bare from the waist up. He held a crimson-stained cloth to his side. A half-empty bottle of whiskey and several glasses sat on the table.

Jericho paled as I stalked forward. "Cas—"

I grabbed his arm, pulling it from his side as I mentally repeated what Kieran had told me outside the Three Jackals. Don't *kill* him. Don't *murder* him. Don't *unalive* him. I gave the ragged wound a brief once-over. My lips twisted into a satisfied smile. She *had* gotten him good, right up under the rib, too. Likely hit an organ. The wound was already healing, though, barely seeping blood at this point.

"You'll live," I bit out, lowering the hood of my cloak. The blond mortal swallowed nervously as he got a look at my face. Lev was his name, I believed.

There seemed to be a collective release of breath from those around the candlelit chamber.

"I will." Jericho tossed the bloodied rag onto the table. His scruffy chin lifted. "Wasn't expecting her to have a blade on her. A bloodstone dagger with wolven bone, at that."

"I wasn't expecting you to attempt to take her," I said, choosing my words carefully.

"I know," he admitted, at least not attempting to lie. "There were no other guards close by. I saw an opportunity and acted on it."

My hand curled into a fist, and I forced it open. "I didn't ask you to look for opportunities."

Jericho nodded, dragging the back of his hand over his mouth. "I fucked up."

"You did." Aware of Kieran moving closer to my right, I reached for the bottle of whiskey. "And...you didn't. You did what I asked." I jerked my chin at the chair. "Sit."

Jericho was listening to me now, sitting his ass right down.

"You opened the spot for me." I poured a shot's worth of whiskey into a glass. "And for that, I am grateful."

The wolven eyed me from behind the lengths of his shaggy hair.

Kieran inched even closer.

"You sure about that?" Jericho asked, resting both of his forearms on the table.

"I am. Now, I will be able to proceed correctly and safely with our plan." I set the glass in front of him. "Drink. You've earned it."

Relief seeped into his features, easing the tension in the set of his jaw. "Thank you," he said, reaching for the glass.

"One thing." I smiled, and he halted. "You're right-handed, correct?"

"Yeah." Wariness skittered across Jericho's features. "Why?"

"Just curious," I told him, nudging the glass closer to him. "Drink."

I watched him reach for the glass. Kieran realized what I was about a second before I moved. He cursed under his breath, but I was faster. Reaching inside the cloak, I unsheathed one of the short swords. Jericho hadn't even picked up the glass—he didn't see it coming. All he felt was the clean, quick slice of *my* blade as I brought it down on his left wrist, severing his hand. Blood spurted, spraying across the table.

"Holy fuck," someone gasped.

Jericho jerked back so quickly he knocked over his chair as he stared at where his hand had once been.

"The next time, do as I order, not as you see fit. We need the Maiden unscathed when *I* take her. Disobey me again, and it will be your head." I looked around the room, meeting stares. "That goes for everyone."

There were quick nods of agreement.

Jericho began to scream.

Stepping back, I cleaned the blade of my sword on my cloak as Jericho doubled over, pressing his arm to his chest as his howls became pitiful whimpers. I sheathed the sword, then reached for the cloth Jericho had been using. "You're going to need this." I tossed it at him, then turned and left the room.

Kieran followed, stepping out into the hall. I looked over at him. He'd stopped, his arms crossed over his chest. "What?" I questioned. "I didn't kill him, *and* I poured him a drink."

Kieran's lips twitched.

"I wanted to do much worse," I reminded him.

He sighed. "I know."

"I want him gone from the city," I said. "Send him to New Haven."

"Will do." Falling quiet until we reached the outside, Kieran then asked, "How in the hell did she get her hands on a bloodstone dagger crafted with wolven bone?"

"Damn if I know." I stopped near where the man had been passed out upon our entry, but he was now gone. A heartbeat passed. "She had it with her the other night at the Red Pearl."

"Really?" He drew out the word.

I nodded. "Shocked the piss out of me. She said she knew how to use it." I tilted my head. "Guess she does to some extent."

Kieran shook his head as he turned his stare to the moon. "A Maiden with a wolven-bone dagger and, at the very least, no fear when it comes to using it?" One side of his lips tipped up. "Why do I have a feeling we may have underestimated her?"

I let out a short, low laugh. "Because I think we did."

A GOOD MAN

The rites of death in Solis weren't all that different from those held in my home. Performed either at dusk or dawn, the bodies were carefully wrapped and then set on fire as it was recognized in both kingdoms that what remained upon death was nothing more than a shell. The soul had already moved on to the Vale or the Abyss, depending on what kind of life one lived.

The Ascended hadn't completely butchered that, at least.

The main differences were that those who stood in attendance as the sun began its climb above the Undying Hills, its bright glare reflecting off the black stone of the Temple walls celebrating Rhahar, the Eternal God; and Ione, the Goddess of Rebirth, believed Rhahar was waiting for Rylan Keal's soul. Rhahar, like Ione and all the other gods, even the King of Gods and his Consort, slept. I had no idea how souls were ushered, but one would think they had some process in place before they went to sleep.

The second difference was that no one representing the Crown was in attendance. At home, the King and Queen, along with the Council of Elders who aided in ruling Atlantia, attended the last rites of all the guards who served them. In other cities, the Lords and Ladies tended to the funerals, paying the respect due to a life either served or ended in service of the kingdom. Here, no one from the Crown attended. Not the Duchess, the Duke, nor the numerous members of Court. Granted, none of them could step foot in sunlight without going up in flames. Of course, they had an excuse for that, claiming they couldn't walk in the sun because the gods couldn't.

Which had to be the most uncreative excuse ever.

They could've held the funerals at dusk. Or, at the very least, sent Lords and Ladies in Wait, those who hadn't yet Ascended.

However, they hadn't.

They didn't care enough.

I rubbed a hand on the back of my neck as I stood among the other guards, fully aware of the hypocrisy of my irritation regarding the Blood Crown's lack of respect when I was attending the last rites of a man whose death I'd ordered.

One who was said to be good.

Who didn't deserve to die.

Whose blood would forever stain my hands.

A hushed murmur swept through the line of guards before me, drawing me from my thoughts. A few turned, looking over their shoulders. Brows furrowing, I followed their stares.

My lips parted as shock rippled through me. I blinked, thinking I was hallucinating, likely due to the single hour of sleep I'd gotten, courtesy of old memories deciding to pay a visit. It was the only logical explanation for what I saw. Or who.

The *Maiden.*

She walked beside Vikter in her white robes and veil, the golden chains holding the latter in place gleaming in the rising sun.

I stared, as dumbfounded as the others clearly were. No one expected her to attend. I sure as hell hadn't. It didn't matter that Rylan Keal had been her guard. The Maiden was never seen in public like this, not without the Duke or Duchess. I watched her and Vikter come to a stop near the back of the crowd. He stared straight ahead. She stood with her chin bowed slightly, hands clasped.

I quickly looked away as the murmurings quieted. An odd feeling hit me as I stood there while Keal's linen-wrapped body was carried forth and lifted onto the pyre. It was…a churning in my gut and chest. Her presence *unsettled* me.

The respect she showed the fallen guard.

I glanced over at her, my heart thumping. She stood so still I would've thought her one of the statues lining the gardens she liked to visit at dusk. I doubted she could see much of the pyre from her position, as nearly all those who stood before her were taller. As the Maiden, she could've walked right to the front and stood among the Royal Guards. That was where Vikter should be, but he remained affixed to her side. She could sit at the feet of that damn pyre if she wanted to, but I thought her quiet arrival right before the beginning of the service said she didn't want to draw too much attention.

That she knew this wasn't about her presence and didn't want it to turn into that.

Unlike me, where I had made last night about my anger.

Well, if I were being fair to myself, my anger had been more about her being struck than it had been about Jericho disobeying my orders. My gaze narrowed on what I could see of her face, just the lower half. Anger flared back to life as my eyes narrowed more. The skin at the corner of her lip was red and a faint blue.

I should've cut off his fucking head, but that would've been *irresponsible and reckless,* at least according to Kieran.

I watched her as one of the white-robed Priests began speaking monotonously, going through the rites as if he were half-asleep. He flung salt and oil onto the pyre, the air filling with a sweet scent.

Then she moved.

Not a lot. A slight jerk as she glanced at Vikter and then back to Keal's body. Her hands unclasped and then came back together.

At the pyre, my gaze skipped from Lieutenant Smyth to where Jansen waited, the breeze stirring his white mantle as he held a torch. He was looking at...

Vikter.

Shit.

The tradition among the guards dictated that the one who worked closest with the deceased should be given the honor of lighting the pyre, but as Vikter started to take a step forward, he stopped and returned his attention to the Maiden. I understood what she had also realized.

Vikter wouldn't leave her unprotected.

The Maiden's hands twisted as she shifted from one foot to the other, her stance practically vibrating with anxiety after standing so still.

I was moving before I realized what I was doing, silently cutting in and out of the guards. The fact that it was forbidden for guards other than her personal ones to approach her didn't stop me.

Coming up behind them, I kept my voice low as I said, "I have her."

The Maiden went incredibly still again, so much so that I wondered if she had stopped breathing. Vikter's gaze lifted to mine. For a brief moment, I thought of what he'd said to me the other morning during training. The cold press of unease returned.

"Do you?" Vikter asked.

I moved to stand at the Maiden's side, speaking the words that belonged to Atlantia and had since been stolen by the Ascended. "With my sword and with my life."

Her chest rose suddenly and deeply, confirming that she did, in fact, still breathe. Thank the gods.

"The Commander tells me you're one of the best on the Rise. Said he hasn't seen your level of skill with a bow or sword in too many years," Vikter said.

I already knew what he thought of all of that. He'd made it clear the morning we trained together. But I answered, nonetheless. Now wasn't the time for me to be an asshole. "I'm good at what I do."

"And what is that?" he countered.

"Killing," I answered with the truth. I'd always been good at that, even before my captivity. I'd just gotten better since.

"She is the future of this kingdom," Vikter said after a moment, and out of the corner of my eye, I saw the Maiden twisting her hands so fiercely it wouldn't have surprised me if she bruised herself. "That is who you stand beside."

Something about how Vikter said that struck a nerve. Did he say it because of who she was or what she symbolized? I wasn't sure why it even mattered, but in that moment, it did to me. "I know who I stand beside."

Vikter said nothing.

Then I spoke my first lie of what I was sure would be many. "She is safe with me."

Vikter got done eyeballing me and then turned to the Maiden. I quickly realized that he was waiting for her to tell him it was okay.

Damn.

I honestly had no idea how she would handle this. I wouldn't have known even before her little adventure at the Red Pearl, but it could go either way now. It didn't matter that she was unaware that I knew it had been her. She knew it was me, and I imagined that was somewhat...awkward for her.

The Maiden nodded.

A little surprised, I barely caught the look of warning Vikter sent me before he turned and went to Jansen. It was another reminder that she wasn't here for herself. She'd come to show Rylan Keal the respect he deserved. If she protested, it would've drawn attention and would've prevented Vikter from honoring the man he'd served beside.

I kept my head facing forward, but I still caught the slight turn of hers. She was looking at me. I had no idea what she saw. I'd wondered more than once how much she could see through the veil, but I *felt* her stare, as strange as that sounded.

She wasn't the only one who eyed me. The Lieutenant did, too, and he looked pissed, as if he were on the verge of stalking through the guards and squirming his body between the Maiden's and mine. But he could go fuck himself.

As Vikter took the torch, the Maiden continued looking at me. Was she wondering why I had stepped forward? Or did she worry that I recognized her? Had she believed me when I'd told Vikter that she was safe with me?

She shouldn't have, not when the only reason she was standing here was because of me. A stone sank to the pit of my stomach. It felt like guilt. That muscle in my jaw ticked more.

The Maiden's attention shifted away from me then, just as I turned to look down at her. The veil rippled in the breeze, giving me just a glimpse of one nostril. My gaze lowered, fixating on the corner of her mouth. My hand closed into a fist at my side. The reddish-blue bruise marring her skin wasn't so faint to me now, not when I stood so close.

I didn't feel an ounce of guilt for chopping off Jericho's hand. Not a damn bit.

At the pyre, Vikter lowered the torch. I'd expected the Maiden to look away, but she didn't. She breathed in deeply, watched, and…

Right then and there, I stopped *expecting*. Stopped *assuming*. Kieran had said we might've underestimated the Maiden, and I'd agreed, but it didn't hit me until right now that we truly had. It was clear I had no clue about who was beneath that veil. I only had the scant knowledge of her I'd gained, and now what I had learned.

The Maiden was adept at sneaking out. She clearly didn't want to remain all that untouched. She carried a wolven-bone and bloodstone dagger and had either gotten lucky with it when Jericho attacked or knew the basics. She clearly wasn't like the Ascended here, at least not when it came to showing the guards the most basic respect.

The Maiden drew in a shaky breath as fire ignited on the pyre, quickly sweeping over the linen-wrapped body.

Did she know what it probably meant to the other guards that she was here? Even the Royal Guards? If not, she should know.

"You do him a great honor by being here," I told her as Vikter knelt at the pyre. Her attention cut to me, and she tilted her head back. The edge of the veil danced above her mouth. "You do us all a great honor by being here."

Her lips parted, and…fuck me, I held my breath, waiting to hear if her voice was as smoky and warm as I remembered it being at the Red Pearl.

But she didn't speak.

She wasn't allowed.

Her mouth closed, once more drawing my attention to the mark my orders had inadvertently left behind. "You were hurt," I said, tamping down the fury that was far too easy to ignite. "You can be assured that will never happen again."

WHAT WAS NECESSARY

Muffled conversations echoed from the rows of closed doors as I followed Kieran through the narrow, cramped hall of the low-rise building near the warehouse district. The cloying scent of sandalwood was heavy in the air, smothering the stench of too many people crammed into one spot. It was the best the people of the tenement housing could do.

Word had gotten to Jansen that something had gone down in the housing building—something they hadn't seen before. And based on the telltale scent of death that no incense could cover, I knew it was something bad.

At the back of the dark hall, Lev Barron waited, a brown cap pulled low. The mortal Descenter pushed off the wall upon our approach. Although Kieran and I both wore cloaks hiding our garb of guard and patrol, he recognized us at once.

"What's going on?" Kieran asked.

"It's something you have to see," Lev answered, his gaze darting between us. The mortal, who'd lost one brother to a fever and another to the Rite, reeked of anxiety. "I can't…" He cleared his throat. "I can't put it into words."

Kieran exchanged a look with me. I stepped forward, keeping my voice low. "Show us."

Nodding, Lev dragged the back of his hand over his chin and then crossed the hall, reaching for the handle. The door beside him inched open. "There's nothing to see here, Maddie," Lev said to the small figure who appeared in the crack of the door. "Go back to your momma."

Lev waited until the child closed the door and then opened the one we stood in front of. The smell of death about knocked me over.

"Gods," Kieran muttered, lowering a hand to the hilt of his short sword.

Lev stepped inside, stopping to turn on a nearby gas lamp. Dull yellow light flickered to life, casting a faint glow across the front room. A body lay on the floor, wrapped in white linen.

"Who is that?" I asked, eyeing the pool of red that had coagulated on the wood floor beneath the head.

"Werner Argus," Lev said, his hand pressed to his nostrils. "He turned Craven."

"Was he a guard?" Kieran asked as a faint sound came from the back of the apartment. "A Huntsmen?"

Lev shook his head. "From what the neighbors say, he was a sweeper—cleaning the streets. Born and raised here. Never been out of the city. Not once."

"So he was fed on and left to turn here?" Kieran surmised, his tone thick with disgust. "The vamprys are getting even sloppier."

Lev said nothing as I stepped over the poor soul who'd spent his days cleaning the streets of all manner of shit for the ones who inevitably slaughtered him.

I glanced into the small cooking area. The countertops were clear, the fire long extinguished in the hearth. I checked the kettle, finding broth that had cooled. There was no mess. The people who'd lived here did their best to keep the place tidy. The sound came again, drawing my attention to the closed door of the back area, likely the bedchamber. I couldn't quite place the odd…gurgling sound.

"Where is the wife?" I asked, knowing damn well that Lev wouldn't have summoned anyone for a mortal being turned within the city. Sure, it was always somewhat shocking that the Ascended were so damn reckless, but it wasn't that uncommon.

"Through there." Lev nodded at the closed door. "She's dead in there." He wiped a palm across the linen shirt and vest he wore. His hand shook. "With…with *it*."

"It?" Kieran repeated.

I approached the door, noting that Lev didn't move any farther. A dead Craven or a victim of one wouldn't have caused the man to linger back as he was. His reluctance had to do with whatever *it* was.

I pushed open the door, lowering a hand to the dagger at my hip. The foul odor of rot nearly gagged me as I scanned the one-windowed chamber lit by muted sunlight.

"Shit," Kieran cursed from behind me, picking up something from the floor. It rattled. "There's a babe here?"

I stepped inside the chamber and looked to the side of the bed. I'd found the wife. She lay curled in a fetal position on the floor, her brown hair matted to the side of her face. One arm was outstretched, baring deep scratches. Her fingers curled as if she'd died reaching for the…

A small bassinet lay upon the floor. Inside, a *lumpy* white blanket stained by a rusty brown substance *stirred*.

And that sound came again—a soft gurgling noise that gave way to a low, keening wail from inside the bassinet. The hair on the nape of my neck rose.

I went still, staring at the fallen crib, unable to move for what felt like an eternity. It wasn't until I felt Kieran draw near that I could even speak. "Please, tell me that isn't what I think it is."

"I…I wish I could," Kieran said, sounding hoarse. "But I'm likely thinking the same as you."

Neither of us budged as what appeared to be two arms beneath the blanket moved. Two small arms. Tiny ones.

"They had a babe," Lev said from beyond the open door. He'd come close enough to be seen. Not too far, though. I couldn't blame him. "A little… A little girl. Less than a year old, according to Maddie's momma."

"There's no way," Kieran denied. "They wouldn't have…"

"I want to believe that." I swallowed. "That not even the vamprys could be that depraved and cruel, but I would be lying."

I forced myself forward, walking around the mother. A guttural noise came from beneath the blanket, a distorted cooing sound. *My gods*, I thought as I reached down, taking hold of the edge of the once plush blanket with gloved fingers. I tore it aside.

"Fucking gods." Kieran staggered back, his hand falling from the hilt of his short sword.

A half-swaddled babe stared up at me with eyes the color of blood, the sockets like the darkest night set in ghastly pale chubby cheeks streaked in dried blood. It strained, lifting those small arms toward me, almost as if it wanted me to pick it up. But those tiny fingers had sharp fingernails—claws that had dug at its skin.

The babe hissed and whined, opening its mouth wide. There were only two bottom teeth—incisors that had sharpened. They appeared fragile, nothing more than grotesquely disfigured baby teeth, but they were strong enough to tear into flesh. To infect.

I tilted my head, seeing the marks on one inner arm, at the inside of the elbow. Puncture wounds. Just two of them. The arm was too small for the Craven to lodge all four canines into it. That hadn't been necessary, though.

"The babe was drained and left to turn," I stated flatly, keeping myself in check, locked down. "And it did."

"That's what I think," Lev said. "The babe infected the father and…"

And the rest was history.

The child squirmed, thrashing at the air. I turned my head, closing my eyes. I'd seen a lot of messed-up shit. Things I thought could never be topped. But this? This was something else entirely.

Feeding on babes wasn't anything new, as sick as it was. It was what they did in the Temples to all the third sons and daughters—to Lev's brother. But letting them turn? There were no words. None.

I opened my eyes at the low, softer sound of a Craven's wail.

"They have to be stopped." Lev took off his hat, thrusting a hand through his blond hair. "They have to be."

"They will be," Kieran swore. "And they will pay for this."

I looked back at the babe, anger tightening my gut. Did the Maiden have any knowledge of this? That this kind of horror occurred while she was sneaking off to the Red Pearl or taking her lessons with the Priestess?

I didn't know.

And it didn't matter as I withdrew the bloodstone dagger and did what I had to. What was necessary.

Just like I would continue to do.

MEETING WITH THE DUKE

"So, this is the Hawke Flynn I've been hearing about," Dorian Teerman, the Duke of Masadonia, observed from where he sat upon a settee of crimson velvet.

"I hope you've heard only good things," I replied as I eyed the vampry before me.

With the heavy curtains drawn over the windows to block out the fading afternoon sun and the chamber lit by only a few scattered oil lamps, Teerman looked about as bloodless as one could get. Even his hair, so blond that it was nearly white, was devoid of color—of life.

I didn't like the man.

It wasn't just because he was an Ascended—an old one that must have been created shortly after the war.

The predator in me recognized the predator in him.

And it wanted at Teerman.

I didn't show it as I stood in a chamber connected to the Teermans' private quarters, which seemed to have been constructed entirely of mahogany. The walls. The desk. The credenza stocked with decanters of liquor. There were several canes propped against one wall, all but one made of mahogany. The other was a deep, dark red and appeared to have been fashioned from the wood of a Blood Forest tree.

"Glowing recommendations from both the capital and the Commander," he said, his obsidian gaze briefly flicking to where Jansen stood beside me. "And my dear wife."

I tilted my head to the side, thinking of the family in the tenements. The babe. Did the Duke even know that one of his vamprys was leaving infants to turn Craven? If so, I doubted the bastard cared.

"She likes to look at you," he added, sipping from his glass of whiskey. How alcohol affected the Ascended always amused me. Despite no longer needing food or water for their bodies to survive, the Ascended had to enjoy libations carefully as they were far more susceptible to the effects of liquor. "Though I imagine that's something you're not entirely surprised to hear."

I wondered how careful he was being with that whiskey today, especially ahead of the City Council session that would be held shortly. "It is not."

Teerman chuckled, the smooth skin at his eyes not even crinkling. The sound was as cold as the close-lipped smile I was sure he believed was warm and friendly. Instead, the curve of his lips reminded me of a pit viper. I half-expected a forked tongue to appear.

"No false modesty? Refreshing. I approve." He inclined his chin. "I'm of the opinion that those who deny what is obvious to all around are most disingenuous."

I could give two fucks about his opinions.

"And that takes assertiveness and confidence," he continued. "Two things needed if you are to join the Royal Guard as one of the Maiden's personal guards. But one needs more than just that."

I doubted he knew what it took to protect a newborn hare, let alone an actual person, but that didn't stop him from detailing what he believed. One thing most Ascended had in common—they so enjoyed hearing themselves speak.

"One needs not only mastery of a weapon and strength but also the skill to foresee any possible threats. The latter was something Ryan Keal, unfortunately, did not possess."

Wait. My brows knitted. Keal's first name was Rylan. Not Ryan. However, I was not even remotely surprised to hear that Teerman didn't know the man's first name.

"But more is needed if one is to take on the duty of protecting one of the most valuable assets to the kingdom. Nothing you have accomplished or will is as important as what the Maiden will do for our kingdom. She will usher in a new era," he went on, and of course, he didn't elaborate on exactly what this *new era* was or how it would be accomplished. "Any who guard the Maiden must be willing to forsake their lives for hers without hesitation. They must have no fear of death."

"I disagree with that," I said. The pathetic excuse of a smile froze as Jansen tensed beside me. "With all due respect, Your Grace," I added, holding his dark, bottomless stare, "if one does not fear death, then they do not fear failure. They rely too heavily on being rewarded with a hero's welcome upon that death. I fear death, as it means I have failed."

Teerman's head cocked to the right.

"I also believe that the duty of guarding the Maiden does not require one to sacrifice their life," I said. "As those who guard her should be skilled enough to defend their life as well as hers."

"Interesting," Teerman murmured, falling quiet as he took a short drink of his whiskey. "And how would you have handled what occurred in the gardens?"

The irony that it wouldn't have even happened if I'd been there didn't pass me by. "The attempt to take the Maiden occurred where the night roses bloom, correct?" I already knew the answer but waited for his nod. "That is also where the jacaranda trees have damaged the inner curtain wall of Castle Teerman, a location in the garden that is particularly dangerous."

"So, you would not allow her to view the roses, then," Teerman surmised.

"Restricting her access to where she would like to go in the garden is unnecessary," I said. "I would simply position her so that she remained out of sight of anyone seeking to exploit that weakness."

"You would then take the arrow in place of her, as Keal did?" Teerman smirked. "Did you not just say sacrifice was unnecessary?"

"Positioning her so she cannot be struck from afar does not equate to me being felled by an arrow," I countered. "There are ways to view those roses that require neither of us to be in danger."

Teerman's stare shifted to Jansen.

"He is correct, Your Grace," Jansen spoke. "There are several natural barriers that would've made any attack difficult. Unfortunately, Keal may have grown...too at ease guarding the Maiden since no attempts have been made against her."

"And that is why he is dead," Teerman stated. "He forgot that the threat of the Dark One has not lessened and paid that price in blood." His attention returned to me. "And you believe that's not a price you will inevitably pay?"

"Yes," I answered without so much as a hint of amusement.

Teerman shifted, resting an ankle on the opposite knee. "With the upcoming Rite, there are already heightened concerns regarding the Descenters and the Dark One. And as she nears her Ascension, there will likely be more attempts."

"There most definitely will be," I agreed. "After all, if what people believe is true, and the Dark One wishes to stop her Ascension, then what occurred in the garden is only the beginning."

"It is true," the Duke confirmed. "The arrow used was engraved with their…" His lip curled. "With their rally cry. Or, more accurately, their dying whimper."

I smiled. "From blood and ash?"

"We will rise," the Duke finished for me, much to my amusement. He was silent as his fingers tapped the calf of his boot. "With the recent attempt to take the Maiden and the growing…unrest here, it is likely that King Jalara and Queen Ileana will request the Maiden be brought back to the capital. Which means, you could be required to leave and make the journey to Carsodonia at any time."

It would be a damn blessing if such a thing occurred. Being granted permission to leave with the Maiden was a hell of a lot easier than absconding with her through the city. But I wouldn't be traveling alone. There'd be a team of guards, which would present an issue.

"Would that be a problem?" the Duke asked.

"I have no ties here," I answered.

"You say all the right things, Hawke," he said after a moment. "And Commander Jansen believes you're not only qualified but also ready for such an enormous duty. However, I admittedly have concerns. You would be considered young for such a position, and I find it hard to believe that none older are better suited. Though I do recognize that is not necessarily a detriment. Younger, fresher eyes carry different experiences. But you are also handsome."

"Thank you," I replied.

A faint smile appeared. "The Maiden is no child. She is a young woman with very little experience and knowledge of the world."

I *almost* laughed at how incorrect he was.

His fingers continued tapping. "Nor has she interacted closely with a man of her age."

"I have no interest in seducing the Maiden if that is what concerns you, Your Grace."

Teerman laughed with a dismissive wave of his hand. "I'm not concerned about that," he said, leaving me to wonder exactly why he was so confident. "I am more concerned with her getting infatuated and therefore becoming a distraction. She does have a…habit of not setting boundaries between her and others."

What he said and what he hadn't stoked my curiosity. "I also have no intention of becoming a companion or friend to her."

He raised a brow. "She can be surprisingly charming—her innocence, that is."

While he was correct about her being charming, it had nothing to do with her innocence. "She and I would have absolutely nothing in common to bond over or even speak of." That was the truth. "She is a job. A duty. One I would be honored to have, but nothing more."

"All right, then," Teerman drawled. "I have some things I need to discuss with the Commander. He will let you know my decision."

"Thank you, Your Grace." I bowed, then straightened and turned for the door.

"One more thing," Teerman called out.

I faced him. "Yes, Your Grace?"

"If you do become the Maiden's guard, you need to know that if she were to become harmed while under your care..." The lamplight reflected off his black eyes. "You would be flayed alive and hung so the entire city could bear witness to your failure."

I nodded. "I would expect nothing less."

NATURAL ORDER
OF THINGS

Every time I looked at the eleven gods painted across the ceiling of the Great Hall, I had questions.

Starting with who in the fuck was the pale, white-haired God of Rites and Prosperity? The Ascended called him Perus, but he'd never existed. I supposed they had to make up a god for their Rites.

My gaze swept over the ceiling as city folk entered the long, white chamber of marble and gold, carefully navigating the silver urns full of white and purple jasmine flowers. Whoever had painted this had talent, capturing the somber expressions of Ione, Rhahar, and then Rhain, the God of Common Men and Endings often depicted in Atlantia. The red hair of Aios, the Goddess of Love, Fertility, and Beauty, was as vibrant as fire, not having faded in the years since the ceiling was painted. Penellaphe, the Goddess of Wisdom, Loyalty, and Duty, appeared peaceful and serene, while Bele, the Goddess of the Hunt, looked as I imagined she would if awake: like she was about to whack someone across the head with her bow. Even the different shades of skin, from the rich-brown-hued Theon, the God of Accord and War, and his twin, Lailah, the Goddess of Peace and Vengeance, to the deeper, cooler black skin of Saion, the God of Sky and Soil, were rendered with exquisite detail. It made me think the artist had been an Atlantian, or at least one who'd descended from Atlantia.

But Nyktos, the King of Gods, was painted as he was throughout the entirety of Solis, his face and form showing only as silvery moonlight. Why they hid him was beyond me, as was the fact the Ascended appeared to have erased every mention of his Consort. Her name and visage weren't even known to us, but we knew of her existence. Legend said it had to do with Nyktos being overly protective of his Queen, but for the Ascended to completely cut her out always struck me as a purposeful act. An odd one, just as the decision to hide Nyktos's appearance was. There had to be a reason. Alastir had once said it was because, deep down, the Ascended feared the wrath of the King of Gods and couldn't bring themselves to look upon him. And maybe that was true, but it didn't explain removing all record of his Consort, to the point where most within Solis had no knowledge of her.

My gaze lowered, skipping over the white banners bearing the golden Royal Crest that hung from the ceiling to the floor, between the numerous windows that lined the entirety of the Hall. Old anger festered. White and gold were the colors of Atlantia's sigil. Modeling theirs after ours was also purposeful.

Eyes narrowing, I looked at the raised dais as the hum of conversation filled the chamber. From where I stood in the alcove, I had an unobstructed view. Several Royal Guards already flanked the two chairs the Duke and Duchess would soon sit upon. I leaned against a marble pillar, wondering what this session would bring. Usually, it was nothing more than a show of the wealthy kissing the Ascended's asses. As a Rise Guard, I didn't have to attend these events, but I did because the Maiden attended. It was the same reason so many of those crowding the main floor came each week yet never spoke.

They were here for her, too.

Likely because they believed she was even closer to the gods than the Ascended. I wondered what she thought of that. Did she believe it? That the gods had Chosen her? A handful of days ago, I would've assumed she did. I had assumed many things—

The crowd quieted.

The Duke and Duchess entered to a wave of applause that was notably halfhearted. Interesting. My attention remained on the side door as the Ascended took their seats.

Vikter came out first, his hand on the hilt of his sword, alertness etched into every line of his weathered face.

Then the crowd went completely silent and still as the Maiden appeared. There wasn't a single sound, not even a cough, as she walked to stand to the left of the chairs. The silence was one of… I quickly scanned the faces I could see. All stared up at the dais, focused on her, even the members of the Court—the Ascended and the Lords and Ladies in Wait that stood at the front. I recognized the Lady in Wait often seen with the Maiden, the one with the warm brown skin and curly hair. She looked half-asleep. The mortals, though, they smiled. Some looked close to joyous tears. Others just stared in open-mouthed awe. The smiles were ones of reverence.

Gods.

The Duke spoke, starting as he always did by reading a letter sent from the capital. I doubted King Jalara or Queen Ileana had written it. They were too busy being absolute menaces.

The Maiden was as still as she had been the morning before while Keal was laid to rest. Spine straight, looking straight ahead, and hands clasped at her waist. That changed once one of the Duke's stewards announced those in attendance and summoned them to step forward to speak. It started with her shifting her hands, moving her left atop the right and then back to the right atop the left. My brows knitted as I watched her. While people began the weekly tradition of ass-kissing, she shifted from foot to foot while standing in place. She fidgeted during these sessions at times, but usually at the very beginning, and then she always seemed to calm. Was she uncomfortable? Anxious? Or was it the lingering effects of what had happened to Keal? Clearly, she'd liked the man enough to honor him by attending his funeral.

Vikter leaned in behind her, whispering something. The Maiden nodded, then stilled. I glanced out at the crowd, seeing that many weren't paying attention to what the people said to the Duke and Duchess. Instead, they were as focused on her as I was. Was *that* her source of discomfort? But why would it be more of a bother to her today than any time before? My gaze inched its way to the ceiling and her namesake. Penellaphe. I knew no one else named after the gods. No one in Atlantia would even dare to do so. Her parents had, and I was sure her naming was one more purposeful act initiated by the Blood Crown—

"Are you fucking the Duchess?" Lieutenant Smyth's low, nasally voice came from behind me.

I smiled at his question, keeping my stare on the dais. On the Maiden. "Not that I'm aware of."

There was a beat of silence, and I knew my refusal to turn to him had the Lieutenant bursting with quiet rage.

Smyth moved to stand at my side. "Then how in the hell were you nominated to replace Keal?"

"You'll have to ask the Commander that," I replied.

"I did," he snapped. "All he would say was that you were the best qualified."

"Well, there you go. You have your answer."

130/Jennifer L. Armentrout

"That's a bunch of bullshit. You've only been here a few months. There are plenty who are more qualified."

I looked at him then. "Like you?"

His ruddy cheeks deepened in color. He didn't answer. Didn't need to. I smiled, returning my attention to the dais. To her. The Maiden was beginning to fidget again.

Smyth leaned in close enough that his shoulder touched mine. I wanted nothing more than to turn and snap his neck. It wasn't morality that stopped me, even though that should've been why. Killing people because they were annoying likely wasn't considered a good enough reason. He lived only because murdering him in front of hundreds of people would cause a bit of unnecessary drama.

"Something about this isn't right," Smyth hissed. "And I will get to the bottom of it."

"Good luck with that," I murmured.

He cursed under his breath and turned from me, sulking as he moved along the edge of the alcove. I watched him, thinking there was a good chance he would have to die.

Oh, well.

I returned my attention to the Maiden. Some man spoke of how great the Duke's and Duchess's leadership was.

She turned her head slightly toward where I stood, and though I couldn't see her eyes, I knew our gazes locked. The nape of my neck tingled as the strangest damn feeling hit me. I could *feel* her stare peeling away the layers of who I was. Muscles tensed throughout my body. Several moments passed, and then her head tilted away. As a couple approached the dais, the inexplicable and undeniably silly sensation was slow to pass. I looked at the mortals. I believed the steward had introduced them as the Tulises.

I continued studying the Maiden as the couple spoke. She'd found me in the crowd, and that was intriguing.

Because I had lied to Duke Teerman about many things during our meeting, including what my relations with her would entail.

I fully planned on getting as close to her as possible. Gaining her trust was as necessary as receiving theirs. I would use any tactic. Friendship? A confidante? More? A faint smile tugged at my lips. Despite what I had said to Kieran the night at the Red Pearl, I'd had no real plans of seducing the Maiden—or any interest—but that was before meeting her. Tasting her lips. Feeling her beneath me. Seduction was definitely not off the table.

"Is he your first son?" the Duke asked, drawing me from my thoughts. He spoke to the couple at the foot of the dais. The woman held a small bundle to her chest—a babe.

Mr. Tulis swallowed. "No, Your Grace, he isn't. He's our third son."

Fuck.

An image of the babe in the tenement formed.

The Duchess had the absolute opposite reaction, clapping joyfully. "Then Tobias is a true blessing, one who will receive the honor of serving the gods."

"That's why we're here, Your Grace." Mr. Tulis slipped his arm from around his wife. "Our first son—our dear Jamie—he...he passed no more than three months ago." He cleared his throat of emotion. "It was a sickness of the blood, the Healers told us. It came on real quick, you see. One day, he was fine, chasing around and getting into all kinds of trouble. And then, the following morning, he didn't wake up. He lingered for a few days, but he left us."

Sickness of the blood? The ever-present anger boiled deep. The only sickness was the Ascended who preyed upon mortals at night while they slept. It was likely what had taken Jole Crain's parents. It was what had turned that babe. Neither the young nor the old understood that what visited them in the night was no phantom or dream.

"I'm incredibly sorry to hear that," the Duchess said as she settled back in her seat, her delicate features fixed in sympathy. "And what of the second son?"

"We lost him to the same sickness that took Jamie," the mother answered. "No more than a year into his life."

Fuck.

"That is truly a tragedy," the Duchess said. "I hope you find solace in the knowledge that your dear Jamie is with the gods, along with your second born."

"We do," Mrs. Tulis shared. "It's what's gotten us through his loss. We come today to hope, to ask..."

Oh, *fuck*.

I knew it before they even spoke. I knew what they were about to ask for.

"We came here today to ask that our son not be considered for the Rite when he comes of age," Mr. Tulis said, and a rolling gasp hit the Great Hall. His shoulders tensed, but he pressed on. "I know that it's a lot to ask of you and the gods. He is our third son, but we lost our first two, and my wife, as much as she desires more babes, the Healers said she shouldn't have more. He is our only remaining child. He will be our last."

"But he is still your third son," Duke Teerman responded. "Whether your first thrived or not doesn't change that your second son and now your third are fated to serve the gods."

"But we have no other child, Your Grace." Mrs. Tulis's voice trembled as her chest rose. "If I were to get pregnant, I could die. We—"

"I understand that," Duke Teerman interrupted. "And you do understand that while we've been given great power and authority by the gods, the issue of the Rite is not something we can change."

"But you can speak with the gods." Mr. Tulis stepped closer but stopped when several Royal Guards shifted forward.

This was...

It was fucking heartbreaking.

"You can speak with the gods on our behalf. Couldn't you?" Mr. Tulis's voice roughened. "We are good people."

Of course, they were.

It just didn't matter to the Ascended. They needed that small bundle held in the mother's arms to feed upon.

"Please." Mrs. Tulis cried openly, her cheeks streaked with tears. "We beg of you to at least try. We know the gods are merciful. We have prayed to Aios and Nyktos every morning and every night for this gift. All we ask is that—"

"What you ask cannot be granted. Tobias is your third son, and this is the natural order of things," the Duchess cut in, drawing a broken sob from the mother that cut up my chest. "I know it's hard, and it hurts now, but your son is a gift to the gods, not a gift from them. That is why we would never ask that of them."

There was nothing natural about this, and as I glanced over the crowd, I saw that I wasn't the only one thinking that. Many in the audience stood in shock, unable to believe the Tulises would dare to make such a request. But others watched the horror unfold, their faces full of sympathy and barely leashed anger as they stared up at the dais—at the Ascended and the Maiden. My hand clenched into a fist as I pushed off the pillar. Vikter stepped in closer to her, likely sensing the brimming anger.

And she—the Maiden—looked *uncomfortable*. Her fingers were twisting incessantly, and her chest moved rapidly. She appeared as if she were on the verge of running away...

Or stepping forward.

"Please. I beg of you. I beg," Mr. Tulis pleaded, dropping to his knees.

This was...gods, this was one of the worst things I'd ever witnessed, and I'd seen some shit. Done some of it. But seeing a father and mother beg for the chance to keep their child was something else entirely.

Turning from the nightmare, I slipped through the crowd in the alcove and made my way toward the exit. I had to because I was on the verge of doing something extremely irresponsible and reckless.

Like slaughtering the Ascended right then and there.

But there was something I *could* do. Purpose filled me as I left the Great Hall. Something that had nothing to do with my brother. I could make sure the Tulis family remained whole and together and that Tobias didn't become yet another victim of the Ascended.

THE MAIDEN
UNVEILED

After showing me my new living quarters in the servants' wing of the castle, a floor below the Maiden's, Commander Jansen and I crossed the grand foyer. According to him, I still had a room at the dormitory, but the Maiden's personal guards tended to stay in the castle. That was fine by me.

"Just so you know," Jansen said, his voice low, "the Duke agreed to make you one of the Maiden's guards, but he was still hesitant. He will have others watching you."

I nodded as we passed the limestone statues of the goddess Penellaphe and the god Rhain. I wasn't surprised to hear that, nor did it do anything to hinder the surge of satisfaction at finally getting what I wanted. Or at least being on the path to doing so. "I imagine Smyth will be one of those obsessively tracking my movements."

"You would be correct."

I was quiet as we walked through the archway, where servants dressed in maroon gowns and tunics with white caps hung an ivy garland. A dark-haired woman stopped, her hands tangled in greenery as she caught my gaze and smiled, leaving me to wonder as we walked on if I knew her—if she was one of those nameless, faceless people I'd spent time with.

I pushed that aside. "He's becoming a problem."

"I know."

I glanced at Jansen as more castle staff hurried by on all sides, carrying baskets of fresh linen and dirty glassware. "He will likely need to be dealt with at some point."

"Figured," the Commander answered, not bothering to argue as he had the night at the Red Pearl. He knew Smyth wasn't a good man.

The banquet hall was less busy. Only an older woman with gray hair curling around the edges of her cap arranged night-blooming roses in a golden vase upon the long table. "Did you check on what I asked?"

He nodded. "We'll get them out before the Rite," Jansen assured me. "Move them to New Haven. They can decide what they want to do from there."

"Thank you." I allowed myself to feel a bit of relief at knowing that what was left of the Tulis family would remain together.

"No need to thank me," he replied gruffly, dragging his hand over his chin.

He was wrong. Setting up the Tulises' escape from the city came with great risk, but I got why he didn't want anyone's gratitude for doing what felt like the barest expression of common decency.

"Ready?" Jansen asked as we came upon one of the many meeting spaces on the main floor.

"Been ready, my friend."

A quick grin appeared, something rare from the changeling, then he opened the door. Having never been in this space before, I quickly glanced over the marble walls, bare except for the black chair rails and the Royal Crest painted in white and gold behind where the Duke sat at a slick, shiny black desk. The Duchess sat in a cream chair near him, and before them were three rows of limestone benches.

Both Jansen and I stopped upon entering and bowed.

The Duchess smiled. "Please, rise."

Aware of her stare, I straightened. "You look lovely today, Your Grace," I said, the lie slipping smoothly from my lips. Of course, the Duchess was lovely, but it was barely skin-deep.

"You are far too kind," she replied, rising as we came forward. She clasped her hands at her waist in a manner that caused her breasts to strain against the tight satin of her bodice. I half-expected one of the pearl buttons to snap off and take out one of our eyes.

Her husband gave a bare smile. "The others will be joining us very shortly. Would either of you care for something to drink?"

"Thank you, but that won't be necessary," Jansen answered, moving to stand at the Duchess's side. I followed. She must've nearly drowned herself in gardenia because I *almost* couldn't detect the sweet and stale scent of the Ascended. "Has the Maiden been informed?"

The Duke leaned back in his chair. "She will be in a few moments."

My attention sharpened on him. There was an odd, eager glint to his eyes, which were like shards of obsidian as he eyed the door. He gave me the distinct impression that he was up to something while the Duchess spoke to Jansen about the next set of guards who would be leaving training soon. The Duke wasn't paying attention to the conversation, instead returning his gaze to the papers on his desk. Then again, it was suspected that he had little interest in running the castle or the city.

Approaching footsteps from outside the chamber caught my attention, but I gave no sign of it as a spirited burst of anticipation buzzed through me. I had no idea how the Maiden would take this.

The door opened, and she entered. Immediately, her steps faltered. Though most of her face was hidden, the shock was evident in the parting of her lips.

Tawny Lyon, the tall and lithe Lady in Wait often seen with her, entered next. She came to a complete stop the moment her dark-eyed gaze landed on me. Surprise flickered across her rich brown features as her head jerked back, causing gold and brown curls to bounce. Tawny quickly looked to the Maiden, the corners of her lips tilting up slightly.

The Maiden still hadn't proceeded any farther. Her chest under the white robes rose sharply, and her right hand twitched, repeatedly opening and closing at her side, where her dagger had been sheathed the night she'd come to the Red Pearl.

Was she carrying it now?

Heat hit my blood as my gaze shifted to the shapeless bottom half of her robes. The quick pounding pulse of arousal was extremely problematic.

"Please," the Duke spoke. "Close the door, Vikter." He waited as the guard fulfilled his request. "Thank you." Teerman lowered the paper as his attention shifted to the Maiden. That odd, eager glint returned to his eyes as he motioned her forward. "Please sit, Penellaphe."

Penellaphe.

My head gave a slight jerk. Obviously, I knew her name, but I'd never heard anyone speak it. I silently repeated it, preferring it to *the Maiden*. Immediately, I recognized that was an irrelevant preference.

The Maiden came forward with a cautiousness that hadn't been present while she was at the Red Pearl. No longer looking in my direction, she sat on the edge of the middle bench, her posture impossibly rigid as she placed her folded hands in her lap. The Lady in Wait situated herself behind the Maiden. Vikter, however, moved to the Maiden's immediate right, almost as if attempting to put himself between her and me.

"I hope you're feeling well, Penellaphe?" the Duchess spoke as she returned to the chair beside the desk.

The Maiden nodded.

"I'm relieved to hear that. I was worried that attending the City Council so soon after your attack would be too much," the Duchess continued, sounding surprisingly genuine.

The Maiden's response was minimal, a slight incline of her head.

"What happened in the garden is why we're all here," Duke Teerman stepped in, and even though it seemed impossible, the Maiden's posture became even stiffer. "With the death of…" His brow furrowed. "What was his name?" he asked of his wife, whose brows pinched in confusion. "The guard?"

Was he fucking serious?

"Rylan Keal, Your Grace," Vikter answered flatly.

The Duke snapped his fingers. "Ah, yes. Ryan," he said.

The Maiden reacted then. I doubted anyone else noticed because no one watched her as intently as I did at the moment. Her hands balled into fists—tight ones that bleached the knuckles of her hands white.

"With Ryan's death, you are down one guard. Again," the Duke added, smirking. "Two guards lost in one year. I hope this isn't becoming a habit."

Well, he would be disappointed because it likely would be.

"Anyway, with the upcoming Rite, and as you draw closer to your Ascension, Vikter cannot be expected to be the only one keeping a close watch on you," the Duke said. "We need to replace Ryan."

A muscle at the curve of her jaw flexed.

"Which, as I am sure you realize now, explains why Commander Jansen and Guard Flynn are here."

The Maiden gave no sign of even hearing him.

"Guard Flynn will take Ryan's place, effective immediately," the Duke announced. "I'm sure this is surprising, as he's new to our city and quite young for a member of the Royal Guard."

The corners of my lips twitched.

"There are several Rise Guards in line to be promoted, and bringing on Hawke is no slight to them." The Duke leaned back, crossing one leg over the other. "But the Commander has assured us that Hawke is better suited to this task."

"Guard Flynn may be new to the city, but that isn't a weakness. He's able to look at possible threats with fresh eyes," Jansen spoke then, mostly for Vikter's benefit, I guessed. "Any number of guards would've overlooked the potential of a breach occurring in the Queen's Gardens. Not due to lack of skill—"

I could've sworn I heard Duke Teerman murmur, "*Debatable.*"

"But because there is a false sense of security and complacency that often comes with being within one city for too long," Jansen continued. "Hawke does not have such familiarity."

My eyebrow rose at how Jansen addressed me, using my first name. Setting a tone. Smart.

"He also has recent experience with the dangers outside the Rise," the Duchess added. "Your Ascension is a little less than a year from now, but even if you're summoned sooner than expected or at the time of your Ascension, having someone with that kind of experience is invaluable. We won't have to pull from our Huntsmen to ensure that your travel to the capital is as safe as possible," she said, referencing those whose task it was to escort travelers from city to city. "The Descenters and the Dark One are not the only things to fear out there, as you know."

She was right.

Yet I didn't think the Maiden realized who was the true danger in this chamber or in the city and beyond.

"The possibility of you being summoned to the capital unexpectedly played a role in my decision," Jansen explained. "We plan trips outside the Rise at least six months in advance, and there could be a chance that when and if the Queen requests your presence in the capital, we'd have to wait for the Huntsmen to return. With Hawke being assigned to you, we would be able, for the most part, to avoid that situation."

The Maiden's head moved then to where I stood. The nape of my neck prickled. Her clenched hands relaxed, the fingers straightening. I inclined my head, watching the pace of her breath quicken.

"As a member of the Maiden's personal Royal Guard, it is likely that a situation may occur where you will see her unveiled." The Duchess spoke, but her tone gave me pause. Her voice was always soft, but there was sympathy there now. "It can be distracting, seeing someone's face for the first time, especially a Chosen, and that could interfere with your ability to protect her. That is why the gods allow this breach."

My attention flew back to the Maiden, and my damn heart gave an unsteady skip. Holy shit, I was going to see her with no veil and without a mask.

"Commander Jansen, if you will please step outside," the Duke asked.

Jansen nodded, quickly obeying the request. The eager look in the

Duke's eyes was now in his smile, and it struck me what he'd said the day before. How confident he'd been when he said that he wasn't concerned about me having any sort of interest in the Maiden.

"You are about to bear witness to what only a select few have seen," the Duke said, his gaze on her. "An unveiled Maiden."

The Maiden's hands trembled in her lap.

"Penellaphe, please reveal yourself," the Duke requested, and his fucking smile had warning bells ringing.

Something was off.

She didn't move for several seconds. No one did. My gaze flew to her companion. Tawny had closed her eyes, and when they reopened, I saw a faint sheen to them. I glanced at Vikter. He looked stoic as he stared down at her.

The Maiden still hadn't moved.

"Penellaphe," the Duke warned, and my hands fisted. "We do not have all day."

"Give her a moment, Dorian." The Duchess twisted to him. "You know why she hesitates. We have time."

What in the actual fuck was going on here?

The lower half of her face turned pink, but that slightly pointed chin of hers lifted, jutting out stoically. She rose at the same time Tawny did. Her companion reached for the chains and clasps, but the Maiden got to them first.

My skin started to chill as I watched her *yank* the chains apart, her movements quick and jerky. The material loosened, then slipped. Tawny caught it, easing the veil off.

Then the entire right side of her face was revealed to me.

It was oval-shaped, cheekbones high and defined, the one eyebrow bold and naturally arched. There was that red hair I'd glimpsed at the Red Pearl, wrapped in some sort of complicated braided knot that looked like it took way too fucking long to create. With the veil gone and in the well-lit chamber, the strands gleamed with a deep, red-wine hue. Her profile was strong.

Beautiful.

One side of her lips tipped up as she stared at the Duke. Just a small bit, a faint smile, but my stomach clenched.

Tawny returned to her seat, holding the veil as the Maiden faced me. Fully.

And I saw.

The entirety of her full mouth. The stubborn chin and sharp curve of her jaw. Her nose dipped at the bridge, and the tip was slightly upturned. Both brows carried that natural arch, framing clear green eyes.

That was where the similarities between the two sides of her face ended.

There was a lingering bruise from Jericho, one I doubted was noticeable to anyone else, but there was also a jagged streak of flesh, a pink a bit paler than her skin. It started below her hairline and sliced across her temple, coming damn close to her left eye, then ending at the side of her nose. A shorter, long-since-healed gouge cut across the left side of her forehead and her eyebrow, right through that arch. Again, so damn close to that emerald eye.

My gods, she was so damn lucky to have both of her eyes. But the pain the wounds that left those scars likely caused… It must have been unbearable. Especially those kind. Because I knew what had caused those scars. The Craven. I'd felt those claws dig into my body more times than I could count, but the only difference was that my flesh *almost* always healed. A mortal's would not. But godsdamn. The inner strength she must have to survive such an attack was inconceivable.

The Maiden had *strength*. An inner kind of resiliency that many didn't have. She was also…fuck me. She was *beautiful.*

And those two things felt like a problem. A big one.

Pink crept over her cheeks as I continued staring at her. Her lower lip trembled before she pressed both together. Our eyes locked. Her gaze was unflinching, and there was no ignoring her obvious discomfort. I didn't get it. She was lovely, and those scars didn't detract from that. Fuck, they actually added to her features, but…

But she lived in the world of the Ascended.

One where flawless beauty was coveted and worshiped. A world where some would only see those flaws, but not all. Not even every Ascended would see nothing but those scars. But those who did…

Suddenly, I understood why the Duke had said what he did about my interest in the Maiden. I figured out that fucking nasty eagerness in his stare and smile because he, too, saw how uncomfortable she was. Everyone in the damn chamber did. But he *reveled* in it.

"She's truly unique," Duke Teerman said pleasantly. "Isn't she? Half of her face is a masterpiece," he went on, drawing a tremor from her. "The other half a nightmare."

For a moment, I no longer saw her, even though I hadn't taken my eyes off her. All I saw in my mind was the Duke and my fist punching repeatedly into his fucking face. I saw myself ripping out that tongue and then shoving it down his throat so he choked. His commentary was unnecessary. The *Duke* was fucking unnecessary.

"The scars aren't a nightmare," the Duchess said. "They are...they are just a bad memory."

They weren't a nightmare or a bad memory. They were proof of what she'd survived. Badges of strength. There was nothing wrong with them or her.

I stepped forward, absolutely done with these comments. "Both halves are as beautiful as the whole."

The Maiden's lips parted on a sharp inhale as she watched me place my hand on the hilt of my broadsword. I bowed, my gaze still holding hers as I recited the pledge given by the Royal Guards that Jansen had instructed me to speak earlier—the vow I already knew because it was part of those spoken by the King and Queen of Atlantia to their subjects.

"With my sword and with my life, I vow to keep you safe, Penellaphe." Speaking her name caused that prickle at the nape of my neck to return and spread across my shoulders and down my spine. In the back of my mind, I knew I shouldn't have said it, but it was important that she knew *someone* saw her in this moment when the Duke sought to humiliate her. It had nothing to do with my plans and maybe a bit to do with the fact that I knew exactly what it was like to be stripped of everything that made you who you were, becoming not someone but some*thing*. And maybe it also had to do with wanting her to know that I found her utterly exquisite because my tone deepened, and I heard it in my voice. "From this moment until the last moment, I am yours."

POPPY

There was no easing into the transition from Rise Guard to one guarding the Maiden. My new role kicked off immediately as Vikter and I accompanied Penellaphe and Tawny to…

Actually, I really didn't know.

The four of us had walked out of the chamber and were currently making our way through the dining hall.

Stopping, I faced them. The Maiden and Lady halted. Vikter's stare narrowed. Her companion's eyes were wide, and she had both lips sucked between her teeth, appearing as if she'd been caught doing something she shouldn't. The Maiden was once more veiled, hidden again.

"Where would you like to go?" I asked her.

The Maiden said nothing as Vikter's eyes slitted even more. Her silence reminded me of when she'd first entered the Red Pearl, back when I thought her incapable of speaking above a whisper. But I now knew better. She could speak quite clearly and sharply.

When she wanted to.

Seconds ticked by in increasingly strained silence, and it hit me that everything that had gone down in that chamber had followed us out here. I wanted her to answer, to speak to me, but she was clearly still troubled.

I glanced at Tawny.

Her lips popped out from between her teeth. "Her chambers…" She paused. "Mr. Flynn."

One side of my lips kicked up. "Hawke is fine."

A smile appeared as she glanced at the Maiden. "We would like to return to her chambers, Hawke."

"That all right with you?" I asked the Maiden.

She nodded quickly and then hurried past, leaving behind a faint trace of her fresh, sweet scent. Tawny walked much more sedately, her smile easing into a grin. Vikter was the only one who didn't seem to be able to walk past me without making contact. His shoulder bumped mine. I bit back a laugh as I fell into step behind them.

We entered the foyer, and right off, I got a small taste of what it was like to be in the presence of the Maiden. Two women were dusting the statues, talking among themselves. Upon our arrival, both stopped, their eyes widening and chatter ceasing. One dropped her feather duster. Their gazes followed as we made our way to the main staircase that led to the floors above. The servants we passed on the steps did the same, all staring at the Maiden, not taking their eyes off her until she was no longer in view. It was like she had some special power that froze people upon sight of her.

My brows pulled together. While I was used to drawing some level of attention from women and men, young and old, this was different. I knew those who looked at me, those who had no idea who I was, still saw me as a person. Usually, someone they wanted to waste a few hours with. But when they looked at the Maiden, they clearly only saw *what* she was—the Maiden—and *what* she symbolized to them—the one Chosen by the gods.

Just like when the King and Queen had me caged and chained, the Ascended had only seen *what* I was—the Prince of a kingdom they wanted destroyed—and *what* I symbolized to them—the vessel that carried the blood they needed to survive and multiply.

I eyed her hands. They were clasped in front of her, but I bet she was twisting them as she had in the Great Hall. She was aware of what her presence invoked.

But was she aware that they didn't see her? They only saw what she represented.

I didn't know.

We finally reached her floor. Why she was housed in the vacant wing of the castle, one of the oldest parts of the structure, was beyond me. The halls up here were narrower, and I bet the chambers were drafty in the winter. The only sound was our footsteps. Even I couldn't hear the near-constant flutter of activity that pervaded every other floor and wing.

I didn't have a chance to say much when we reached the door to her chambers before she opened it and practically flew inside. I only caught a brief glimpse of bare stone floors and a chair before Tawny gave us a parting nod. Then, I was left staring at the closed door to the chamber I needed to get inside. The Maiden had been able to get out of that room and make her way to the Red Pearl. I doubted she'd walked out this door to do it.

My head cocked to the side at the sound of a soft thud against said door. "Should we be worried about that?" I asked as I turned to the man I knew wasn't my fan.

"They're fine." He glowered at me from behind a lock of sandy hair. "I need to speak with the Commander, which means you will be guarding the Maiden."

I nodded.

"From the hall," he added as if that were necessary. "And don't leave your station. Not for anyone or anything."

"Understood."

"Not even for the gods," he insisted.

"I know what's expected of me." I met his glare. "Both of them are safe while I'm here."

Vikter looked like he wanted to say something more, but he must've decided it wasn't worth it. He turned stiffly, stalking down the length of the hall. I figured he wanted to see Jansen to bitch about my appointment.

Wouldn't do him any good.

I started to move so I faced the door when I heard Tawny's faint, muffled voice.

"Hawke Flynn is your guard, Poppy."

My brows flew up. *Poppy?* That was what Tawny called her? Not Penellaphe. But...Poppy. The poppy fields of Spessa's End flashed in my mind.

"I know," came the softer, even fainter voice.

That was her. *Poppy.* The prickle at my nape came once more. I hadn't heard her voice since the night of the Red Pearl.

"Poppy!" Tawny's voice was loud enough that I blinked. "That is your guard!"

The corners of my lips curved up as I shifted so I stood even closer to the door.

"Keep your voice down," the Maiden said as I drew my lower lip between my teeth. They'd have to whisper for me not to hear them, and as I heard their footsteps retreating, I really hoped her companion continued to practically shout. "He's probably standing outside—"

"As your personal guard," Tawny interrupted.

"I *know*," came the exasperated response.

"And I know that this is going to sound terrible," I heard Tawny say as I angled my head closer, never having been more thankful for my heightened hearing than now. "But I have to say it. I can't contain it. It's a vast improvement."

A silent laugh left me.

"*Tawny.*"

"I know. I recognize that it was terrible, but I had to say it," she replied. "He's quite…exciting to look at."

I grinned.

"And he's clearly interested in moving up in the ranks," the Maiden countered.

The curve of my lips flattened. Did she not agree with her companion? She had to. I *knew* I was quite exciting to look at.

"Why would you say that?"

There was a beat of silence. "Have you ever heard of a Royal Guard that young?"

Well, I couldn't fault her for saying that. It was a valid question.

"No. You haven't. That's what befriending the Commander of the Royal Guard will do for you," the Maiden said. And, man, she didn't know how right she was. "I cannot believe that there was no other Royal Guard just as qualified."

Tawny didn't respond for a few moments. "You're having a very strange, unexpected reaction."

Crossing my arms, I had a feeling her response had more to do with what had happened at the Red Pearl than it did with anything else.

"I don't know what you mean," the Maiden said.

Sure, I thought, smirking.

"You don't?" Tawny, who was quickly becoming one of my favorite people in the kingdom, challenged. "You've watched him train in the yard—"

"I have not!" The Maiden's voice rose.

Such a little liar. She totally had been.

Tawny had my back, even if she didn't know it. "I've been with you on more than one occasion as you watched the guards train from the balcony, and you weren't watching just any guard. You were watching *him.*"

I really liked this Tawny.

"You seem almost angry about him being named your guard," Tawny continued. "And unless there's something you haven't told me, then I have no idea why."

There was silence.

"What haven't you told me?" Tawny demanded as it became clear the Maiden hadn't shared details about her trip to the Red Pearl with her companion. "Has he said something to you before?"

My lips pursed. What a rather uncalled-for leap of logic.

"When would I have had a chance for him to speak to me?" the Maiden said.

"As much as you creep around this castle, I'm sure there is a lot you overhear that doesn't actually require you speaking to someone," Tawny said, sharing another interesting tidbit while proving one of my suspicions correct. One that said the Maiden had a habit of sneaking around. "Did you overhear him say something bad?"

My eyes narrowed. Tawny was quickly losing that coveted spot in my favorites.

"Poppy…"

There was a long stretch of silence where I briefly considered moving farther from the door so I wasn't eavesdropping, but I quickly dismissed that idea.

Then the Maiden announced, "I kissed him."

My jaw unlocked as my head cut to the door. I couldn't believe she'd actually admitted it.

"What?" Tawny said.

"Or he kissed me," the Maiden added as a bit of concern started to blossom in my chest. Was this wise of her? Could she trust this Lady in Wait with such information? I sure as fuck hoped so. Not only did it jeopardize what I'd been working toward, I doubted the Teermans would take kindly to learning such information. However, the way Tawny spoke to the Maiden said there was a level of closeness there. "Well, we kissed each other. There was mutual kiss—"

"I get it!" Tawny shrieked, causing me to blink as I glanced down the empty hall. "When did this happen? How did this happen? And why am I just now hearing about this?"

The sound of footsteps came again, and then the Maiden shared, "It was…it was the night I went to the Red Pearl."

"I knew it." There was another thud, this time sounding like someone, who I guessed was Tawny, stomping their foot. "I knew something else had happened. You were acting too weird—too worried about being in trouble. Oh! I want to throw something at you. I can't believe you haven't said anything. I would be screaming this from the top of the castle."

Okay. I was flattered, and Tawny was now working her way back into my favorite-person spot.

"You'd be screaming it because you could," the Maiden replied wryly. "Nothing would happen to you. But me?"

What exactly would happen to her? She didn't elaborate, and their voices disappointedly dropped too low for me to hear, but I did pick up the Maiden's voice a few moments later.

"It's just that…I've done a lot of things I shouldn't do, but this…this is different," she said, and I wondered what the *other things* were. "I thought if I didn't say anything, it would, I don't know…"

"Go away? That the gods wouldn't know?" Tawny said, and my eyes rolled. "If the gods know now, they knew then, Poppy."

She had a point. Except the gods didn't know shit, and if they did, this whole Maiden and Chosen business was a load of bullshit anyway. Despite what the Ascended said. Despite even what Kieran wondered about the whole shroud crap.

If the Maiden responded, I didn't hear her, but I heard Tawny as if she were standing next to me.

"I'll forgive you for not telling me if you tell me what happened in very, very graphic detail."

I waited with bated breath to hear exactly what she said.

"I wanted to, you know, experience something—anything—and I thought that would be the best place. I saw Vikter there," the Maiden shared. While I wasn't surprised to hear that, I'd seen him there myself, I was surprised to hear her call him by his first name. "So there was this lady there, and she recognized me."

"What?" Tawny nearly yelled again.

"I don't know," the Maiden said. "But I think she was like a…a Seer or something."

Huh. I frowned. There were no Seers that I knew of in Masadonia. Or changelings other than Jansen.

"I could be wrong, though. Maybe she just recognized me someway else," the Maiden said. That had to be it because there was definitely no Seer at the Red Pearl. I would know. "I was probably just so awkward it became obvious. Anyway, I went into this chamber I thought was empty, and he…he was in there."

"And?" Tawny pressed.

"He thought I was Britta."

"You look nothing like her," Tawny explained. A pause. "Her cloak.

You were wearing it."

"I guess the rumors about them are true, because he grabbed me—not in a bad way, in a…passionate, familiar way," she said, her voice lowering to the point where I had to really strain to hear her. Which meant I was really eavesdropping now.

It was wrong. I knew that.

But I rarely behaved right, so here I was.

"It was…it was my first kiss," she said.

Every muscle in my body tensed. I knew that already but hearing her say it now… It made my chest feel off. Light and heavy at the same time.

"And did he continue doing so while thinking you were someone else?" Tawny asked. "If so, I'm going to be thoroughly disappointed."

"In me?" Her voice peaked then.

"No, at him. And I'll also be concerned for your safety if he didn't realize after getting all up in your personal space that you weren't Britta. Nice to look at or not, he shouldn't be your guard if that's the case."

I cracked a grin. She was right.

"He realized pretty quickly that I wasn't her. I didn't tell him who I was, but he… I think he must've sensed that I wasn't, you know, that experienced. He didn't like tuck tail and run. Instead, he…" The Maiden's voice lowered again. "He offered to do anything I wanted."

"Oh," Tawny uttered. "Oh, my. Anything?"

"Anything," the Maiden confirmed.

And I would have done *nearly* anything she wanted of me. Who wouldn't when they had her soft, warm body beneath theirs, her lips plump from kissing, and her eyes bright with desire?

Dammit.

A pulse of want pounded through me, hitting my cock just enough for it to stir.

I should stop listening. It would be really awkward if Vikter arrived and I was rocking a hard-on.

"We just kissed. That's all," the Maiden said. But that wasn't all. I'd kissed her elsewhere.

Not that I needed to think about that at the moment. I shifted my stance, widening my legs as I frowned. For fuck's sake, her talking about kissing, and me thinking about what had honestly been very tame activities, shouldn't be getting me hard.

"Oh, my gods, Poppy," Tawny said after a few moments. "I so wish you'd stayed."

"Tawny," she said with a sigh.

"What? You can't say you don't wish you'd stayed. Not just a little bit."

I tilted my head again, waiting...and waiting.

"I bet you wouldn't be a maiden any longer if you had," Tawny remarked.

No, she would still be one. I wouldn't have crossed that line in a godsdamn brothel. I wouldn't have crossed that line with *her* anywhere.

"Tawny!" I heard her shock and my lips twitched.

"What?" Tawny laughed. "I'm kidding, but I bet you'd *barely* be a maiden," she added, and yeah, she would've barely been that. "Tell me, did you...enjoy it? The kissing?"

"Yes," came the almost-too-quiet-to-hear reply. "I did."

I knew that, but I still smiled.

"Then why are you so upset that he's your guard?" Tawny asked.

"Why?" Disbelief dimmed the Maiden's voice. "Your hormones must be clouding your rational thought."

"My hormones are always clouding my rational thought, thank you very much."

I chuckled under my breath.

"He's going to recognize me," the Maiden said. "He has to once he hears me speak, right?"

Too late for those concerns.

"I imagine," her friend replied.

"What if he goes to the Duke and tells him that I was at the Red Pearl?" the Maiden wondered, clearly worried, but she didn't need to be. "That I...allowed him to kiss me? He has to be one of the youngest Royal Guards, if not *the* youngest. It's clear he's interested in advancement, and what better way to secure that than to gain the Duke's favor? You know how his favorite guards or staff are treated! They're practically treated better than those on the Court."

That was the utter last thing she had to worry about when it came to me.

"I don't think he has an interest in gaining *His Grace's* favor," Tawny argued. "He said you were beautiful."

"I'm sure he was just being kind."

My eyes narrowed. I was not. It was one of the rare times I'd been telling the truth since I returned to this shithole kingdom. She was stunning.

"First off," Tawny began, "you are beautiful. You know that—"

"I'm not saying that to fish for compliments."

"I know, but I felt the overwhelming need to remind you of such," Tawny countered, and I was glad she did. "He didn't have to say anything in response to the Duke being a general ass."

Tawny was definitely back in my favorite-person spot.

"He could've just ignored it," she continued. "And proceeded on to the Royal Guard oath, which, by the way, he made sound like…*sex.*"

I smiled.

"Yes," the Maiden agreed. "Yes, he did."

The curve of my lips spread wider, revealing a hint of my fangs to the empty hall.

"I almost needed to fan myself, just so you know," Tawny said. "But back to the more important part of this development. Do you think he's already recognized you?"

"I don't know. I wore a mask that night, and he didn't remove it, but I think I would recognize someone in or out of a mask."

"I would like to think that I would, and I would definitely hope that a Royal Guard would," Tawny retorted.

"Then that means he chose not to say anything," the Maiden mused. "Although, he might not have recognized me. It was dimly lit in that room."

I would recognize her anywhere.

"If he didn't, then I imagine he will when you speak, as you said. It's not like you can be completely silent every time you're around him," Tawny stated. "That would be suspicious."

"Obviously."

"And odd."

"Agreed," the Maiden said. "I don't know. Either he didn't, or he did and chose not to say anything. Maybe he's planning to lord it over my head or something."

"You're an incredibly suspicious person."

Damn straight, she was.

"He probably just didn't recognize me." The Maiden was silent and then said, "You know what?"

"What?"

"I don't know if I'm relieved or disappointed that he didn't recognize me. Or if I'm excited that he might have." There was a soft laugh. "I just don't know, but it doesn't matter. What…what happened between us was one time only. It was just this…thing. It can't happen again. Not that I'm even thinking he'd *want* to do any of that again, especially now that he knows it was me. If he does."

"Uh-huh," Tawny said.

"But what I'm trying to say is that it's not a thing to even consider," the Maiden forged on. "What he does with the knowledge is the only thing that matters."

"You know what I think?" Tawny said.

"I'm half-afraid to hear it."

I wasn't.

"Things are about to get so much more exciting around here."

Tipping my head back, I smiled as I stared at the bare rafters of the ceiling. Yes, things were *definitely* about to become more exciting.

ARROGANT AND COCKY

Vikter returned not long after Tawny had entered her room through a connecting door within the Maiden's chambers. He strode down the hall with a white cloth clenched in his grip, which he all but shoved into my hands.

Glancing down at the crisp white with its gleam of gold, I could barely contain my disgust as I realized it was the mantle of the Royal Guard. "Thanks," I muttered.

"Try not to look too thrilled," Vikter replied.

I lifted my gaze to him. "The same could be said about you."

He stood across from me, the faint light catching the nicks and grooves in the black armor covering his chest. "Would you prefer that I pretend I approve of this decision?"

"No." I tossed the mantle over one shoulder, wondering if he called the Maiden *Poppy*. "As long as you understand that no matter how many times you complain to the Commander, it won't undo his decision."

Vikter huffed out a short laugh. "You think I'm not aware of that?"

"You think I believe you went to see the Commander just to graciously retrieve the mantle for me?"

"I don't give two shits what you think," Vikter retorted.

"Well," I drawled, my head tilting, "won't that make working together a bit difficult?"

"Nah." He shook his head, his blue eyes as cold as the ice that capped the High Hills of Thronos near Evaemon. "I don't need to know what you think for either of us to carry out our duties. I already know enough."

"And what is it that you know?" I asked.

"The Commander thinks you're not only ready but also capable enough to take on this responsibility. You're obviously skilled, quick with a sword, and strong as an ox."

"Flattered," I murmured.

A blade-sharp smile appeared. "And you're also arrogant and cocky."

I arched a brow. "I do believe they are the same thing."

"And a smartass," Vikter added.

My lips twitched as unwanted respect grew for the man. Something warned him to be wary of me. An innate instinct, which was spot-on. "You forgot to add wickedly handsome."

He huffed a breath. "What I forgot was that you don't know when to shut your mouth, but that's something you're going to learn."

Biting back a laugh, I turned my head to face the end of the hall, where specks of dust caught in the fading sunlight coming through a small window. "You wouldn't be the first to wish I'd learn how to do that."

"Not surprised at all to hear that," he said. "The difference with me is that you either learn the easy way or the hard way."

A grin snuck free.

"You think I'm fucking with you?" Vikter sneered. "Accidents have a way of happening around here, even with Royal Guards—even with newly promoted Royal Guards."

My head turned back to him. Was he actually threatening me? The burst of disbelief gave way to another ripple of amusement. "I'm not fucking with you, Vikter. You just remind me of someone I know."

"Doubtful," he muttered.

"Let me guess, the hard way involves breaking my jaw or worse?" A short laugh left me as Vikter's eyes narrowed. "So, I'm right. He's said the same thing quite a few times."

Vikter was silent for a moment. "And who is this clearly astute person?"

"A father of a friend." I met his stare, my humor fading. "Look, we don't have to like each other. We don't even really need to get along. You have your duty, and I have mine, and we share that responsibility. I will not fail her. That's all you need to know."

He held my gaze, then let out a low, gruff noise as his attention shifted over my shoulder to the door. A moment passed. "Is Tawny still in there?"

"No, she left a little bit ago." I rested my hand on the hilt of the broadsword, assuming we'd reached some sort of understanding. "Will the Maiden remain in her chambers for the rest of the day?"

"If that is what she chooses," he replied. "What did the Commander prepare you for in terms of your role?"

"The basics," I answered. "As for her schedule, he didn't go into that much detail on what's prohibited and not."

Vikter nodded. "We will alternate days and nights. That's what we've always done," he explained, some of the tension easing from his shoulders. "There is something you should know—to prepare for when you guard her at night. Sometimes, she has…unpleasant dreams."

The tautness that left him seized me. "Nightmares?" I thought of what I'd seen when she was unveiled. "What causes them?"

He just stared at me.

"Are they about how she was scarred?" I surmised.

Silence.

I pushed back the frustration. "Look, I get you're protective of her. Even more so than I'd expect a guard to be," I said, and his eyes narrowed. "But I need to know everything about her to do my job."

"You don't need to know anything to protect her other than what your damn job is," he snapped, then cursed low. "She got the scars when she was a child. Six years old. In a Craven attack that killed her parents and nearly ended her life."

"Fuck," I rasped, rubbing my hand over my chin. I knew about the Craven attack, but I hadn't heard this, and if I had, I must've forgotten it. "She was six? How the fuck did she survive?"

"She's Chosen," he answered.

I looked at him, shaking my head. "She must be," I muttered, glancing over my shoulder. She'd been six years old? Good gods. "No wonder she has nightmares."

"Yeah." He cleared his throat. "You may hear her scream," he said, each word stated slowly as if he were taking the time to choose them. "She will be fine, but I ask you not to bring it up to her."

As someone who had spent way too many decades with unpleasant dreams, I quickly understood what he was saying. He didn't want her embarrassed. I could respect that, except…

"How am I to know when a scream is due to a nightmare or her being under duress?"

Vikter snorted. "She won't scream if she's under duress," he said, leaving me wondering exactly what the fuck he meant by that as he went on. "In terms of her schedule, she is not to be disturbed in the early hours of the morning. That time is for prayers and meditation. She normally takes her meals in her chambers." He gave the rough times for when the staff served them, usually handing the meal over to whoever guarded her door. "Servants generally enter her chambers to clean when she is taking her lessons with Priestess Analia, which you will attend on the days you're guarding her. Sometimes, she will be present when the servants need access. We try to avoid that, but…" He trailed off, clearing his throat. "She is to be veiled during those times, and you will be required to enter her chambers if she is present when servants or any of the other staff are there. The only ones allowed to be in her chambers without you are the Teermans and Tawny. As far—"

"Wait," I interrupted. "Does the Duke visit her chambers?"

"He hasn't, but it is not an impossibility." A muscle ticked in Vikter's jaw, and I didn't like the looks of it. He quickly moved on. "She will sometimes sit in the atrium, usually in the early afternoons when it's empty. She also likes to take walks on the castle grounds in the mornings, and especially after supper. When she is moving about the grounds, she will not interact with others…"

My brows inched closer and closer together as he spoke and had to be nearly connected by the time he reached the very short list of things the Maiden did. That couldn't be it, but something he said made me think of Lord Mazeen.

"What about the Lords and Ladies?" I asked. "Do they interact with her?"

"Some do," he confirmed. "They do not see her unveiled."

"But is she to be alone with them?" I pressed.

"Not usually. They could, of course, request to speak with her in private, but that is rare." He studied me. "Why do you ask?"

"Just want to make sure I know exactly what is and isn't allowed." I folded my arms. "And I've heard that some of the Lords and Ladies are known to disrespect personal boundaries."

Vikter's left eye squinted. "A few are known for that."

"Any that I should be aware of when it comes to the Maiden?"

A moment passed. "I do not let the Maiden stray too far in Lord Mazeen's presence."

My jaw tightened. For the Lord to have carried the Maiden's scent, someone had allowed it, but I didn't believe it was Vikter. "Is he a…problem?"

"He can be." He drew a hand over his armored chest. "But only to the point where he makes a nuisance of himself."

From what Britta had shared, I wouldn't consider Lord Mazeen's behavior a nuisance. But there was only so much Vikter could say about the Ascended—or *would*, considering he didn't exactly trust me.

But I knew enough to know to keep an eye on Lord Mazeen. I changed the subject. "So, that's all she does?"

"Other than attending the City Councils, that's about it," Vikter confirmed. "She doesn't go out in public."

Oh, yes she did, but that was beside the point. I glanced at the closed doors behind me as Vikter continued on with a much longer list of things she couldn't do. She was not to speak to others, eat among company, leave the castle grounds—the list went on and on until I wondered if she was allowed to visit the bathing chambers without permission for fuck's sake. "What does she do with the rest of her time?"

He frowned. "Why do you ask?"

"Why?" I faced him. Was he serious? "She spends the majority of her time in her chambers? Alone?"

That muscle was ticking double-time now. "Yes, and other than the situations I listed above, it will be rare for you to find yourself in her chambers." His chin dipped. "*Very* rare. And when you do, the doors should be left open. She is aware of this."

I didn't respond to his clear warning, and silence descended between us. I was stuck on the fact that the Maiden truly spent the entirety of her time alone or being watched. I'd known the latter, but I'd assumed her days were spent doing…well, whatever it was the so-called Maiden did.

Apparently, this…this was it.

Damn. I dragged a hand over my head. Her existence had to be a lonely one. *Damn.*

"You used her name."

My attention cut to the Royal Guard. "What?"

"When you spoke your vow," Vikter said, "you used her given name. Why?"

A slew of lies rose to the tip of my tongue. I could just claim that I didn't know why, but after what I'd learned? "I just wanted her to know that someone saw her."

Vikter inclined his head, but there was no other acknowledgment. No reprimand, either. I didn't think he had an issue with it, and my reluctant respect for him grew.

And that was a damn shame.

Because if we were summoned to the capital, he would be one of the guards escorting her. Which meant it was likely that Vikter Wardwell would have to die for me to succeed in what I'd come to do.

MADE A NEW FRIEND

The acrid scent of cold-cut steel filled the air as I lifted a gloved hand and removed the loosened brick on the blacksmith's shop. A slip of parchment passed through an intricate chain of supporters and spies had been tucked behind the loose block. It was unsigned and included only five words.

I've made a new friend.

My lips curled as I tucked the note into the interior pocket of my cloak. I'd destroy it later, leaving no trace of its existence. I made my way to the mouth of the alley, where puddles from the quick, drenching downpour formed narrow streams in the pitted cobblestones.

I quickly slipped in with the throng of people hurrying through the clogged streets at dusk, some heading home while others were just starting their days. There was a chill in the air, so many were cloaked like me. I blended in, unseen or forgotten the moment I passed another as I crossed the twisted, convoluted network of streets in the Lower Ward. There was always gloom in the shadows of the Rise, but even more so with thick clouds choking out the sun earlier and now the moon.

I took note of the white handkerchiefs tacked onto the doors of the squat, narrow houses—three of them. My jaw clenched, but I forced myself to keep going, telling myself that someone would answer the silent calls. I thought of what Jole had said about the Maiden and shook my head.

Cutting between two tarp-covered wagons, I crossed the street and was suddenly swallowed by the stench of slaughter and animals. One smelled the meatpacking district before they actually entered it. The rain did nothing to quell the scents. Many of the shops here didn't close for the night, so the streets were just as filled with commoners and the unhoused.

Since I'd been here, the number of those without shelter had doubled, if not tripled. The Blood Crown did nothing for them, not even as the coldest months approached. In Atlantia, everyone who wanted a home had one. Providing for those who were unable to do so themselves for whatever reason wasn't easy, but it wasn't impossible. Atlantia had always done it, even when we ruled the entire continent.

I skirted a vendor hawking smoked pork, reaching a tight lane between two smoke-stained warehouses. In the flickering yellow glow of the streetlamps as I headed for the side entrance to one of the buildings, I almost didn't see the two small, young children—a boy and a girl. They couldn't have seen more than their tenth year of life. Their faces were smudged with dirt, their bodies slender beneath their too-thin shirts and pants. They had managed to press themselves into an unused stoop, their eyes sunken, but they still watched those on the sidewalk with the wariness of an adult who'd seen war.

Gods, they were too young for this kind of life.

Slowing my steps, I pivoted and returned to the vendor, buying a package of pork.

One of the children leaned forward, using their body to shield the other as I approached. Were they siblings by blood or circumstance?

I knelt, keeping myself at arm's length so I wouldn't frighten them. Though all they saw was a cloaked and hooded figure in black, crouching before them, so I doubted much I did *wouldn't* scare them.

"Here." I extended the package. The one who'd leaned forward watched me with brown eyes. Behind him, the other child peered over his shoulder. "It's yours."

The boy looked at the package, hunger sparkling in his hollow features. He didn't take the pork, though. I didn't blame him. Nothing on the streets was given for free.

Except for tonight.

I placed the package by the child's dirty boots, then saying no more, I rose and backed off. A second passed, and then the boy snatched up the package before disappearing into the shadows of the stoop. The pork was salty, likely tasted like shit, and not the healthiest, but it was better than an empty belly, and smarter than handing over coin, which would only make them a target. It was the best I could do.

For now.

Walking through the building's side entrance, I entered the busy warehouse. Wooden crates thumped off tables, and sharpened cleavers sliced through bone and tissue. Heads rose as I strode between the tables, discarded parchment wrapping crinkling beneath my boots. There were a few smiles. No one said a word. They'd seen me before.

They could guess who I was.

At the back of the space, a large man I only knew as Mac sat on a stool by a closed door, head bald and apron stained with dried blood. He, too, said nothing, but he did nod. He knew who I was, and I knew exactly who *he* was. He was the unofficial leader of the Descenters here.

I pushed open the door. The hall was cramped with unused crates, and the sound of pigs rooting around in the outdoor pens silenced the sounds of the meatpacking floor. Two doors were at the end, and one led outside. I took the other to the right, going down a steep, unlit set of stairs that one without light or my vision would break their necks attempting to descend. There was one more door, and dull yellow light and cold air seeped out from the frame. Pushing it open, I entered the underground ice cellar packed with large blocks of the frozen water used to keep the slaughtered meat hanging from the rafters fresh for long enough it could be packaged on the floor above. The spot was cold and smelled like fresh kill, but what happened down here wasn't heard above.

"About time," I heard Kieran say as I walked between two slabs of hanging meat. "I think all my bits are about to freeze off."

I snorted, knowing Kieran was fine. Wolven's bodies ran hotter than any I knew. It would take a lot longer for these kinds of temps to do any real damage to him. I reached the pool of yellow light and found Kieran leaning against a bare wooden table, his arms crossed. He was dressed as I was, minus the hood. I left mine up. It had proven scarier that way. My attention shifted to the male slumped in the chair he was tied to.

"I'm pleased to introduce you to Lord Hale Devries," Kieran announced, following my gaze. "He was arriving from Pensdurth," he said, referencing the nearby port city. "But he is from Carsodonia, and according to all who had to listen to his insufferable boasting during the trip here, he is well connected to the Blood Crown."

I smiled as I eyed the unconscious vampry. He was dark-haired and appeared somewhere in his second or third decade of life, but I'd bet he was a few decades older. "Gods, how I love a boaster." We had Descenters in the Guard and among those escorting travelers among the cities. Not many, but enough that a few Ascended found their way down here. I prowled around the Lord, spotting a nasty bluish-purple bruise on his temple. "How long has he been out?"

"Since he was dumped here. Want me to wake him?"

"Sure." I came to stand behind him.

Kieran pushed off the table and dipped below to where a bucket sat beneath it. He lifted a large ladle. Sending me a grin, he went to where the Ascended sat limply. "Wakey. Wakey," he murmured, dumping a cup's worth of icy water atop the Ascended's head.

The vampry came awake with a gasp, shaking his head and sending drops of water spraying in every direction. "What the—?" Whatever the Lord had been about to say, it died a hundred deaths when he spotted Kieran standing in front of him.

"Hello." Kieran tossed the ladle onto the table. "Did you have a nice nap?"

"Who...who are you?" the Lord demanded as he turned his head left and right, his body going rigid as he saw the slabs of hanging meat. "Where am I?"

"I think it should be obvious where you are." Kieran's face was devoid of emotion, but his eyes were a bright, luminous blue. "And you shouldn't be concerned with me. You should be asking about the one behind you."

The Lord's head jerked to the side. "Who's there—?"

Planting my hand on the top of his head, I stopped him. "I'm so glad to make your acquaintance, Lord Devries. I have a few questions for you that I do hope you can answer."

"How dare you?" he sputtered.

I grinned as I pressed my gloved fingers into his head. "How dare I?"

"Do you know who I am?" the Lord demanded.

"I believe that's been established," Kieran stated.

"I doubt you understand—"

"Look at him when you speak," I turned his head so he faced Kieran.

The Lord fought but lost. He ended up looking right at Kieran as he warned, "I'm a Lord, a member of the Royal Court, and you have made a grave mistake." Devries spat on the floor. "*Descenter.*"

Kieran raised a brow.

"What is it you want that has driven you to make such poor choices?" Devries demanded in that annoying air of haughtiness all Ascended seemed to come equipped with. "Land? Coin?"

"We have no need of your coin," Kieran said. "The land, though? Yes, but that will have to wait."

I chuckled.

"You laugh now, but you risk the wrath of the gods," Devries hissed, pushing his head against my grip as he tried to turn toward me. "You risk bringing the Crown down upon your head."

I bent so I was close to his ear as I whispered, "Fuck the Crown."

"Bold words from the coward who stands behind me," the Lord snapped.

Grinning, I shoved his head and stepped back. He cursed as he and the chair toppled forward. Kieran caught him with a boot to the chest, and I prowled around him, setting the chair to rights.

"You stupid heathen. You will burn…" He trailed off as I came into view. Pitch-black eyes widened as he watched me stand in front of him.

"Do you know who I am?" I asked.

He took in the black cloak, the heavy hood that hid my features, and my gloved hands. That alone would not be of concern, but combined with the predicament he found himself in, it took no time for him to figure it out.

The Lord's head snapped forward, and his lips peeled back over his teeth, all pretense vanishing in an instant as he bared sharpened canines. "Dark One."

I bowed. "At your service."

"Dramatic," Kieran muttered.

Smiling, I straightened. "As I was saying before you had your little meet and greet, I have questions for you."

"Fuck your questions," he snapped. "You're going to die."

"Let me cut in here since it's fucking cold and it stinks," Kieran interjected. "You're going to threaten us. We're going to laugh. You're going to swear you won't answer our questions, but we'll make you."

The Lord's head swiveled in the wolven's direction.

"And right now, you think there's no point in cooperating since you know you're not walking out of here," Kieran went on. "But what hasn't sunk in yet is that there is a difference between dying and a very long, drawn-out, and painful death."

Devries' nostrils flared as his gaze darted between us.

"And if I have to stay down here longer than necessary? I can promise you will beg for death," Kieran continued. "You have a choice."

"He speaks the truth," I said, my eyes narrowing on Devries. "I want to know where they're keeping Prince Malik."

"I know nothing about Prince Malik," he growled, his arms flexing.

"But you told everyone on the journey here you were well connected with the Crown," Kieran said.

Vamprys were strong—strong enough to break the ropes holding him in place.

I sighed. "He's going to choose unwisely."

The bindings snapped, and the vampry came out of the chair faster than a mortal could move.

But not faster than a wolven.

Kieran caught him by the shoulders, holding the vampry back. "Why do they always do this?" he asked as his chin dipped.

"Maybe they think it's fun," I mused.

"It's not." A growl rumbled up from Kieran's chest as his nostrils flattened and the skin of his features thinned. The hand on the Ascended shoulders lengthened, the nails growing and sharpening, plunging deep into the vampry's shoulder.

The Lord howled as Kieran clawed through flesh and muscle. He threw Devries to the cold, stone floor, sending him skidding back into a hunk of meat. "You're a..." He gasped, clutching his mangled shoulder. "Wolven."

"You can call me that." Kieran inhaled deeply, reining himself back in. His skin filled out, his hand returning to its normal size. Blood and tissue dripped from his fingertips. "Or you can call me death. Whichever you'd prefer."

I glanced at him. "Bet you've been waiting all day to say that."

Kieran lifted a bloody middle finger.

"How about I call you a filthy dog?" Devries retorted.

I snapped forward, bringing my boot down on his ruined shoulder. The Lord screamed. "That was rude." I kept pressing. "Apologize."

"Fuck you."

"Apologize." I dug my foot in, cracking bone. "You have a hell of a lot more bones to go."

He swung with his other hand, reaching for my legs I supposed, but I wasn't sure what he thought that would accomplish. Kieran easily caught his arm, snapping it back and cracking the bone in the process. Devries howled, kicking his foot at Kieran as he jerked upright, fangs bared as he went for my thigh.

I sighed.

This continued for a while, proving that the Lord was not all that wise. Both legs were broken when he finally stopped trying to bite us. So was his left arm. The right hung on for dear life. He was a messy heap of flesh and bone, leaking all over the floor.

Cleanup would be a bitch.

"Tell me where Prince Malik is being kept," I said for what had to be the hundredth time.

"There is no kept Prince," the vampry moaned, and that was, at least an improvement over telling me to go fuck myself.

I kicked him in the chest, knocking him flat on his back.

"Motherfucker." Devries groaned.

"Where is he being held?" I repeated.

"Nowhere," the vampry roared, spitting blood and saliva.

Fury erupted. Moving toward him, I raised my leg, but Kieran grabbed my arm, stopping me before I brought my boot down on the vampry's head.

"You level?" Kieran asked.

Inhaling deeply, I stepped back and nodded. I didn't even know what level meant at the moment. "Okay. Moving on, Devries. I want you to tell me about the Maiden."

The Lord moaned, rolling onto his side.

"Why is she important to the Blood Crown?"

"She's Chosen," the vampry groaned. "By the Queen. By the gods."

Kieran looked over at me.

"You forget who you're speaking to," I advised. "We know the gods have Chosen no one, least of all a mortal girl."

"She *is* Chosen, you fool. The bringer of a new era," he gasped, pale features contorting in pain. "And you are a fool."

"I think he wants to die," Kieran remarked, his brow raised.

One black eye opened and fixed on me. "I...I remember when you wanted to die. When...when you begged for it."

My chest lurched.

Kieran's head whipped back to the vampry. "What did you say?"

"He doesn't recognize me. Do you? Of course, not." Lord Devries' laugh was bloody and wet. "You were out of it, screaming and biting at the air one second..."

I stiffened.

What the Lord spoke of hit Kieran in an instant. "Shut up."

"Then pleading for death the next," the Lord said, laughing as he eased onto his back. "I was there in the capital when they had you."

I'd frozen, but my chest moved with each rapid breath.

"Shut the fuck up," Kieran growled.

"I remember where they kept you underground and in that cage." His arms flopped uselessly at his sides as images of those damp bars flashed in my mind. Glimpses of bloodless skin. Dark eyes. Sharp nails. "How you writhed in pain and then ecstasy—"

Lord Devries' words ended in a gurgle, startling me. I blinked, my surroundings coming back into view. The hung meat. The thick blocks of ice. Blood and clumps of matter strewn across the stone. Lord Devries' body twitched as Kieran moved back, his steps smearing gore.

"Cas?"

When I didn't answer, Kieran clasped my shoulder. "You okay?"

I closed my eyes and nodded, but I wasn't. Kieran knew that. No matter how many times I said I was, I wasn't.

I never would be.

PRESENT IV

"I'd forgotten all about that," I said, eyeing the elegant curves of her jaw and then the brave lines cut through her cheek and brow. "Lord Devries. What he said about you." I dragged in a ragged breath. "What he said to me."

It was late, sometime in the middle of the night. Kieran had left to check on things. I lay beside her now, my body cradling hers. There wasn't even an inch of space between us. I found her hands in the candlelit chamber without taking my eyes off her face. They rested on her stomach, just below her chest. I ran my fingers over hers. They were incredibly still between mine, smooth. The bones beneath felt so damn fragile.

Her skin was still icy.

"He was right, you know? About you being Chosen. Neither Kieran nor I got it then." I threaded my fingers through hers. Seconds ticked by, turning into minutes. "I think we both blocked that whole thing out. I…I did because it was something I didn't want to remember. Kieran would've done the same because he knew it caused me pain."

I wanted to close my eyes. It was hard thinking about my time in captivity, let alone speaking about it. It was that lingering shame. Still as difficult to talk about as it was to admit I'd hurt myself.

"I didn't recognize him, Poppy, and I thought I wouldn't forget a single face of those who had taken part. But I did, and it…it fucked with my head. Made me wonder how many I'd blocked out. I don't even know why it mattered. I don't think it does now." My gaze flickered over her profile. "But it gets to me, you know? That I can't remember what this Lord bore witness to. Did he see me used? Was he there when I hurt others—when I fed from them until there was nothing left? Was he there with Malik in the beginning?"

I dragged my thumb over the top of her hand. "He was also right about Malik." A low, rough laugh left me. "He said, 'There is no kept Prince,' and he'd spoken the truth."

In the silence, I had to ask if that really was the truth.

Malik may not have been kept in a cage and chained the entire time he was with the Blood Queen, but he had been *kept*.

"His chains were invisible," I said aloud, glancing toward the closed chamber door. "And those chains had a name."

Millicent.

His heartmate.

I looked at Poppy and didn't even want to imagine our roles reversed. Poppy in place of Millie. Me instead of Malik. But I knew one thing. "I'd *gladly* serve any monstrous being if it meant you were safe. I can't fault him for that. I really can't. But…" My gaze returned to her cheek. To those scars. I leaned over, kissing the one on her temple. "I don't know how I can forgive him for what he planned to do to you. He may not have harmed you with his own hands, but his actions left their marks on you."

Marks that were both physical and emotional. Ones she still carried and likely always would.

"You probably want me to forgive him. I want to, but…" But I needed time. I needed to talk to him. I needed to understand, and none of that would happen right now. Still, I wanted to.

Because I'd seen Malik die in the Bone Temple. Struck down. And, fuck. That had taken a part of me out there. He was my brother, fucked-up choices and all.

Pushing the mess with Malik aside, a faint smile returned as I thought of my first day guarding Poppy. "Do you remember when you finally spoke to me? It was after you were in the atrium."

My smile quickly faded when I thought of what came next.

The Duke.

And her nightmares.

THE MAIDEN
SPEAKS

The following afternoon, the Maiden was quiet as we stood outside one of the halls that led to the kitchens, waiting for Tawny to return.

She stood as quiet as ever, her chin dipped, and her hands clasped loosely at her waist. "Is there anything you need while we wait?"

She shook her head.

"Did you rest well last night?"

She nodded.

I bit the inside of my cheek. That was how she responded to any question I asked. A nod or a shake of the head. She hadn't spoken to me. Nor had she talked in front of me.

Thinking about what I'd overheard her and Tawny discussing, I fought a grin. She would have to speak in my presence at some point. She had to know that.

Tawny returned before I could pester her with any more inane questions, the edges of her skirt snapping at her heels. She lifted a plate of sliced sandwiches. "Look what I got!" she exclaimed. "Your favorite."

The Maiden smiled. Kind of. The corners of her lips at least curved upward.

"What's your favorite?" I asked, my hand resting on the hilt of my sword.

The Maiden quickly turned her head away.

"Cucumber," Tawny answered, several tight, caramel-hued curls slipping free of their twist to fall over her shoulder as she shot a not-so-covert, narrowed-eye look at the Maiden as she started walking down yet another hall. "What's your favorite, Hawke?"

"My favorite sandwich?" I pondered, noticing how the Maiden tilted her head slightly to listen. "I'm not sure I have one."

"Everyone has a favorite sandwich," Tawny insisted. "Mine is salmon-cucumber, which Poppy thinks is disgusting."

Poppy. That nickname was…cute. Fitting in an odd way since the Maiden wasn't exactly someone I'd think of as being *cute*. Although her refusing to speak in front of me was…decidedly adorable. "I have to agree with her."

Tawny scoffed, her lips pursing. "Have you tried it?"

I shook my head. "And I don't plan to."

The Maiden's lips twitched, but there was no smile.

"Then what is your favorite?" Tawny asked after giving a rather dramatic sigh that even Emil would've found impressive.

"I suppose anything with meat," I decided, shrugging the weight of what I liked to refer to as my how-to-get-yourself-killed-quickly-in-battle mantle over my shoulder. If I were fighting someone wearing one, it would be the first thing I grabbed.

"Well, that is the most typical guy thing I've ever heard," Tawny retorted.

Chuckling, I trailed after them, and like the day before, any servant or member of the household staff we passed stopped in their tracks and stared. Tawny and the Maiden proceeded as if unaware, but there was no way they didn't notice. Unless they had grown accustomed to it.

Entering a hall with shimmering white and gold tapestries, we ended up in the bright, airy atrium Wardwell had said the Maiden preferred. I chose a position where I had a view of the entire space and the section of the garden it overlooked. Tawny did most of—if not all—the talking while they picked at the sandwiches. She spoke about the upcoming Rite and then relatively harmless gossip about which Lords and Ladies were suspected of sneaking off together. All the while, I kept my focus on the Maiden. She was meticulous while eating, each small movement seeming thought out beforehand, even if it were to sip from her tea or handle the linen napkins.

Footsteps and the sound of giggles drew my attention to the entryway. Two young Ladies in Wait appeared, one dark-haired and carrying a pouch, and the other blond. I'd seen them on the castle grounds a few times, watching the guards training. What were their names? Loren and Dafina? I thought so, but which was which was beyond me. And, honestly, it didn't matter as my attention shifted to the Maiden.

I closely watched as the two Ladies in Wait took the chairs near the

Maiden, wariness creeping its way through me. From what Wardwell had explained, the Maiden wasn't to interact with others except for Tawny, but neither attempted to leave.

I had a choice. I could either behave as her guard and escort her back to her chambers, where she would likely stay for who knew how long, or I could follow her lead on this. And since I thought the rules were a load of crap, I went with the latter.

A part of me regretted it within the first few minutes after the two Ladies in Wait arrived.

They quickly became quite the...handful, prattling excitedly and loudly about everything. Yet I somehow had no idea what it was they spoke about. The thread of their conversation was hard to follow.

But what I did take note of was the subtle change that came over the Maiden. I couldn't say she had appeared all that relaxed when it was just her and Tawny, but she had at least been...comfortable, I supposed. Her posture not nearly as rigid as it was now. I couldn't even fathom how someone sat that straight and still. Was she forced to wear one of those bone corsets I knew many of the wealthy favored beneath the gown? The dress she wore today was different than the one the day before. More elaborate. Her sleeves were long and flowing, leaving me to wonder how she managed not to drag them across the sandwiches each time she stretched for her tea. The gown's neckline damn near reached her neck, causing my throat to itch. My gaze dropped to her shoulders and the beaded bodice. The material appeared thin, so I doubted a corset was beneath it. The posture was all her. I eyed her lower half. Her hands were folded in her lap.

Was she carrying that dagger?

I shifted my stance, then noticed that her white-slippered feet had disappeared beneath the hem of her gown. The way she sat made it appear as if she had no hands or feet.

The blonde snapped her fan, reflexively catching my attention. That was likely one of the reasons I found it hard to decipher what they spoke about. She peered at me from behind the laced edges of her fan, her large blue eyes filled with more than just a welcome. It was a promise.

Ladies in Wait weren't required to be all that strict with whom they spent their time or how they chose to do so, but I was already very well aware of that.

The dark-haired one could not stay seated, leaving the mask she had been sewing tiny jewels onto on the table as she peered out into the garden, watching some bird outside. She was likely only at the windows for a few moments before a soft thump and the subsequent tinkle of crystals could be heard. I looked to see jewels of all colors under the sun spill out from the pouch the dark-haired one had been carrying for some reason.

"Oh, no!" she gasped, staring at the mess in such a desperate, helpless manner one would've thought she'd dropped a babe. "My crystals!"

"That was entirely clumsy of you, Loren," Tawny drawled from where she sat watching her.

"I know!" Loren knelt in a dramatic flourish of silk and lace and began picking up each crystal, one by one.

"Allow me to be of aid." I strode forward.

"Oh, that is so kind of you," Loren beamed, straightening. "You're so incredibly gallant."

"I try," I murmured, scooping up the crystals and dumping them into the pouch. Rising, I offered it back to her.

"Thank you." Loren took the bag, her hand gliding over mine in the process. "Thank you so very much."

Fighting a grin, I nodded and gave her a curt bow before returning to my corner. I wasn't there long before the blonde halted midway to the table with refreshments.

"Oh, my." Dafina lifted a limp hand to her forehead. "I feel so dizzy." She began to sway.

Good gods…

I went to her side before she ended up in a pile of blue silk, like the crystals scattered upon the floor. "Here." I took hold of her elbow, and she all but fell into my side. "You should sit," I advised, leading her back to the chaise near the Maiden. "Would you like me to retrieve a drink for you?"

"If you'd be so kind." Dafina batted her thickly lashed eyes. "Mint water, if you could." She looked at the others, waving her fan. "It is so terribly warm in here, is it not?"

"Not really." Tawny looked on, unimpressed.

I had no idea what the Maiden thought as I poured a glass of the mint water.

"It must be the warmth that has made me so clumsy," Loren chimed in as I handed the water to the other Lady in Wait, once more having my hand touched in a way that felt more like fondling. Loren had now sprawled herself across the chaise, curving her body so one would have to be utterly unobservant *not* to notice how low-cut her gown had become. How suddenly low-cut *both* of their gowns had become. "I do say, it has given me such a frightening headache."

Tawny sighed, rolling her eyes.

Beside her, the Maiden dipped her chin.

Unperturbed, Loren pressed two delicate fingers to her temple, and I suspected she was on the verge of slipping from the chaise.

"Then I suggest you make sure you stay seated," I said, thinking to nip any attempts of her rising in the bud. I gave her a smile that had opened many closed doors to me in the past, flashing a dimple. "All right?"

Loren stared at my mouth as she dropped her hand from her temple to the lace of her bodice, her boldness amusing. She nodded.

Giving them all one more smile, I returned to my station. When both Ladies turned their attention to Tawny, I breathed a small sigh of relief.

"You know what I heard?" Dafina asked, snapping her fan as she glanced in my direction. She lowered her voice, but I easily heard everything she said. "Someone has been a rather frequent visitor of one of those…one of those dens in the city."

"Dens?" Tawny asked, and I realized this was the first time she'd interacted with them outside of commenting on their clumsiness and apparent weak constitution.

Dafina tipped her upper body forward. "You know the kind, where men and women often go to play cards and *other* games."

Tawny lifted her brows. "You're talking about the Red Pearl?"

The Maiden sat as still as the limestone statues I could see in the garden.

"I was trying to be discreet." Dafina sighed, looking at the Maiden. "But, yes."

I bit the inside of my mouth as I briefly shifted my attention to the glass panels above us.

"And what have you heard he does at such a place?" Tawny asked, the skirt of her gown moving and the toe of her slipper appearing—

The Maiden jerked slightly.

Did Tawny just *kick* the Maiden under the table?

"I imagine he's there to play cards, right? Or do you…?" Tawny pressed a hand to her chest, leaning back in her chair. "Or do you think he engages in other more illicit…games?"

"I'm sure playing cards is all he does." Loren raised an eyebrow as she pressed her fan against her chest. "If that is all he does, then that would be a…disappointment."

I didn't think she'd be disappointed.

Mostly.

I hadn't returned to the Red Pearl since the night the Maiden was there, and I had been there nearly every night before that.

"I imagine he does what everyone does when they go there," Tawny said. "Finds someone to spend…quality time with." She tilted her head slightly to the Maiden.

I had to bite harder on the inside of my lip.

"You shouldn't suggest such things in current company," Dafina admonished.

Tawny choked on her tea while I almost choked on my breath.

"I imagine if Miss Willa were alive today, she would've snared him in her web," Loren said. "And then wrote about him in her diary."

Who was this Miss Willa?

"I heard that she only wrote about her most skilled…*partners*," Dafina added, laughing softly. "So, if he made it onto those pages, you know what that means."

I was flattered they'd already decided I would be skilled enough to make it into this diary.

Unfortunately, their conversation moved on from my perceived *skills* to the Rite, though I still occupied their thoughts based on how Loren and Dafina continued stealing glances in my direction.

But they weren't the only ones.

The Maiden looked, too.

I couldn't see her eyes, but there was a slight tilt of her head in my direction. What really let me know was the odd prickle at the nape of my neck that I would not ask Kieran about because, knowing him, he'd probably say it was my conscience.

"I do hope you-know-who isn't in the city like some are saying," Dafina said. "If so, they may cancel the Rite."

"They won't cancel the Rite," Loren assured. "And I don't think it's an if." She glanced at the Maiden, then sent her friend a meaningful look. "You know that it has to mean that he's near." Her chin lifted. "Prince Casteel."

Damn.

Did she just say my actual name? Usually, I was only referred to as the Dark One.

Dafina frowned. "Because of the…" She glanced not-so-coyly at the Maiden. "Because of the attack?"

"Besides that." Loren's attention returned to the mask she was currently sewing a red crystal to. The corners of my lips turned down. How many damn colors were on that thing? "I overheard Britta saying so this morning."

"The maid?" Dafina scoffed.

"Yes, the maid." Loren lifted her chin even higher. "They know everything."

That was true.

Mostly.

Dafina laughed. "Everything?"

She nodded. "People speak about *anything* in front of them. No matter how intimate or private. It's almost like they are ghosts in a room. There is nothing they don't overhear."

"What did Britta say?" Tawny placed her cup down.

"She said that Prince Casteel had been spotted in Three Rivers," Loren said. "That it was he who started the fire that took Duke Everton's life."

I did start the fire.

But Duke Everton was already dead by then.

"How could anyone claim that?" Tawny demanded. "No one who has ever seen the Dark One will speak of what he looks like or has lived long enough to give any description of him."

"I don't know about that," Dafina countered. "I heard from Ramsey that he is bald and has pointy ears, and is pale, just like...you know what."

Well, that was...offensive. I did not look like a Craven, which was what they insinuated.

"Ramsey? One of His Grace's stewards?" Tawny challenged. "I should've stated, how could anyone *credible* claim that?"

"Britta claims that the few who've seen Prince Casteel say he's actually quite handsome," Loren tacked on.

"Oh, really?" Dafina murmured.

Loren nodded. "She said that was how he gained access to Goldcrest Manor. That Duchess Everton developed a relationship of a physical nature with him without realizing who he was, and that was how he was able to move freely through the manor."

Part of that was true. My appearance had gotten me easy access to the manor. That was about it, though.

"Nearly all of what she says turns out to be true." Loren shrugged, picking up a green jewel, an emerald one that reminded me of the

Maiden's eyes. "So, she could be right about Prince Casteel."

"You should really stop saying that name." Tawny smiled thinly as the two focused on her. "If someone overhears you, you'll be sent to the Temples faster than you can say 'I knew better.'"

Loren laughed. "I'm not worried. I'm not foolish enough to say such things where I can be overheard, and I doubt anyone present will say anything."

"What…what if he was actually here?" Loren shuddered. "In the city now? What if that was how he gained access to Castle Teerman?" Something akin to excitement filled her tone. "Befriended someone here or perhaps even poor Malessa."

"You don't sound all that concerned by the prospect," Tawny pointed out, picking up her cup. "To be blunt, you sound excited."

"Excited? No. Intrigued? Possibly." She lowered the mask to her lap, sighing. My brows rose. "Some days are just so dreadfully dull."

"So, a good old rebellion may liven things up for you? Dead men and women and children are a source of entertainment?"

The looks of surprise on Loren's and Dafina's faces surely mirrored mine as shock rolled through me. I slowly turned my head to the Maiden. That had been her. She had spoken. *Finally.*

Loren recovered first. "I suppose I…I might've misspoken, Maiden. I apologize."

"Please ignore Loren," begged Dafina. "Sometimes, she speaks without any thought and means nothing by it."

Loren nodded emphatically.

The Maiden said nothing as her head remained turned in their direction. However, there was no doubt in my mind they felt that hidden stare because they quickly departed after that.

"I think you scared them," Tawny remarked.

The Maiden took a drink, and my eyes narrowed at how her hand trembled slightly. I stiffened, glancing at the door.

"Poppy." Tawny touched her arm. "Are you okay?"

She nodded, placing the cup on the table. "Yes, I'm just…" She seemed unsure what to say in those moments.

I imagined that Dafina's and Loren's careless words had made her think of Keal. My jaw flexed.

"I'm okay," the Maiden continued, her voice low. "I just can't believe what Loren said."

"Neither can I," Tawny agreed. "But she's always been…amused by the most morbid things. Like Dafina said, she means nothing by it."

She nodded.

Tawny leaned toward her. "What are you going to do?" Tawny whispered.

"About the Dark One possibly being in the city?" The Maiden sounded confused.

"What? No." Tawny squeezed her arm. "About him."

"Him?"

Me?

The Maiden's head tilted in my direction.

"Yes. Him." Tawny let go of her arm. "Unless there's another guy you've made out with while your identity was concealed."

Okay, this was a far better conversation.

"Yes. There are many. They have an actual club," the Maiden replied with the dryness I'd heard in her voice at the Red Pearl. "There's nothing for me to do."

"Have you even spoken to him?" Tawny asked.

"No."

"You do realize you will have to actually speak in front of him at some point," Tawny informed her, and yet again, she proved she was my favorite person in the kingdom.

"I'm speaking right now," the Maiden argued, and I swallowed a laugh. She was speaking so low I knew she believed I couldn't hear her.

Tawny called her out on that in the next heartbeat. "You're whispering, Poppy. *I* can barely hear you."

"You can hear me just fine."

Tawny shook her head. "I have no idea how you haven't confronted him yet. I understand the risks involved, but I would have to know if he recognized me. And if he did, why hasn't he said anything?"

"It's not like I don't want to know, but there's..." She trailed off, her veiled face turning to mine.

Again, I felt that stare, and the odd prickle at the nape of my neck worked its way down my spine. And as crazy as it all sounded, I didn't see that damn veil. I saw *her*: face bare, stubborn and proud, with her chin lifted.

Left uneasy by the intensity of that vision and irritated with myself for standing there thinking idiotic things, I looked at the entry when I heard someone approaching. One of the Duke's Royal Guards appeared. He gave a curt lift of his chin. Glancing over at the two women, I quickly made my way to the doors.

"His Grace has summoned the Maiden to his offices on the fourth floor."

"Understood." I turned from the Royal Guard, wondering what the Duke could want.

"He's just doing his job," the Maiden was saying. "And I...I just lost track of what I was saying."

"Is that so?" Tawny replied, tone as dry as the Wastelands of the east.

"Of course." She smoothed her hands over the lap of her gown.

"So, he was just making sure you're still alive and—"

"Breathing?" I suggested, coming to stand by their table. Both jumped slightly. "Since I am responsible for keeping her alive, making sure she's breathing would be a priority."

The Maiden stiffened.

Tawny lifted a napkin to her mouth, appearing as if she were attempting to smother herself. "I'm relieved to hear that," she managed.

I grinned at her. "If not, I'd be remiss in my duty, would I not?"

"Ah, yes, your duty." Tawny removed her napkin. "Between protecting Poppy with your life and limb and gathering spilled crystals, you're very busy."

"Don't forget assisting weak Ladies in Wait to the nearest chair before they faint," I added, glancing at the Maiden and in no hurry to answer the Duke's summons. "I am a man of many talents."

"I'm sure you are." Tawny returned my grin.

"Your faith in my skills warms my heart." I looked at the Maiden. "Poppy?"

Her mouth clamped shut so quickly, I wondered if she cracked a molar.

"It's her nickname," Tawny explained. "Only her friends call her that. And her brother."

"Ah, the one who lives in the capital?" I asked of her—the Maiden.

The tension in her jaw eased a bit, and then she nodded.

"Poppy," I repeated. "I like it."

The corners of her lips turned up. It wasn't much of a smile, but it was something.

"Is there a threat of stray crystals we need to be aware of, or is there something you need, Hawke?" Tawny asked.

"There are many things I'm in need of," I said, giving the Maiden a grin. I was immediately rewarded with a faint flush spreading across her jaw. "But we'll need to discuss that later. You've been summoned by the Duke, Penellaphe. I'm to escort you to him at once."

I hadn't been around the two that long, but I noticed their moods change immediately. Tawny's teasing vanished, as did her grin. The Maiden had stilled again for a few heartbeats, and then a smile appeared as she rose. A tight, *practiced* smile.

"I'll await you in your chambers," Tawny told her.

Their reactions had alarm bells ringing as the Maiden eased past me. I followed behind and walked slightly at her side as we entered the foyer. Her hands were twisting once more, but no servants moved about as we neared the staircase. The alarms continued going off.

"Are you all right?" I asked.

She nodded.

I didn't believe that for one second. "Both you and your maid seemed disturbed by the summons."

"Tawny is not a maid," she responded and immediately sucked in a sharp breath.

She hadn't meant to respond to me.

I hadn't expected her to be so defensive regarding her companion. Her *friend*. I thought of how the Duke had claimed the Maiden had a habit of not setting boundaries. I was really glad to hear that was apparently the truth. It made things easier for me. But why in the whole wide realm of fucks did it matter if the Maiden had a friend?

Either way, I wanted to shout in triumph that I'd gotten her to speak to me and now knew how to get her to respond.

Irritate her, and that tongue of hers would move.

I kept my expression blank as I asked, "Is she not? She may be a Lady in Wait, but I was advised that she was duty-bound to be your lady's maid." I had been told no such thing, and I also knew the difference between a maid and a lady's maid. The latter held rank. The other didn't. "Your companion."

"She is, but she's not. She's..." She turned her head in my direction as the staircase curved. "It doesn't matter. Nothing is wrong."

I looked down at her, a brow raising.

"What—?" Her foot snagged on the gown, causing her to misstep. I caught her by the elbow, steadying her. "Thank you," she muttered.

There was that...spunky attitude—the fire I'd seen in her. "No insincere thanks are required or needed. It is my duty to keep you safe. Even from treacherous staircases."

She drew in a deep, audible breath. "My gratitude was not insincere."

Noting the irritation in her tone, I grinned. "My apologies, then."

We reached the third-floor landing, taking the left that led to the castle's newer wing. She was quiet once more, as usual, and I used the time to plot what to say to her next. She was clearly worried I'd recognized her and would report it, which was just silly. But did she really believe I didn't recognize her voice? Or hadn't seen enough of her features that night at the Red Pearl to know it was her when she was unveiled? She didn't strike me as being that foolish. Perhaps she *wanted* to believe I hadn't recognized her, despite what she had said to Tawny.

Reaching the wide, wooden doors at the end of the hall, I purposely made sure my arm brushed hers as I opened one side. Her lips parted slightly in response. I held the door for her, waiting for her to enter.

"Watch your step," I said, even though the spiral staircase was well-lit from the numerous oval-shaped windows along the wall. I didn't think she'd trip again, but I was confident I'd get another response out of her. "You trip and fall here, you're likely to take me out on your way down."

She huffed. "I won't trip."

"But you just did."

"That was a rarity."

"Well, then, I feel honored that I bore witness to it." I eased past her, fighting a laugh. "I've seen you before, you know."

Her breath hitched.

"I've seen you on the lower balconies." I held open the door to the fourth floor. "Watching me train."

"I wasn't watching you. I was—"

"Taking in the fresh air? Waiting for your lady's maid, who is not a maid?" I caught her elbow once more, stopping her. I lowered my head until I was a few inches from her veil-covered ear. "Perhaps I was mistaken," I spoke, my voice low. "And it wasn't you."

There it was again, the catch in her breath. Those tiny reactions were a good sign. "You are mistaken," she said, her voice softer but not in that submissive way.

One side of my lips tipped up as I let go of her arm. That veiled head tilted toward mine, a ghost of a smile on her lips. One not as tight. Nor as practiced. I stepped into the hall, spotting two Royal Guards stationed outside the quarters where I'd first spoken to the Duke. I waited for her, but she had gone still again. I looked down, finding that she wasn't looking at me but at the two Royal Guards down the hall.

"Penellaphe?" I questioned.

She jerked slightly and then took another deep breath. She clasped her hands together and moved forward. The two Royal Guards stared ahead, not looking at her as she stopped before them. One started to open the door, but she turned her head back to me.

Something about that made me wish I could see all of her face. Those warning bells renewed as my gaze flicked to the doors of the Duke's office.

"I'll wait for you here," I assured her.

There was a moment of hesitation, and then she nodded, turning away. The Royal Guard opened the door wide enough for her to enter, just enough for the Ascended's faint, stale-sweet scent to waft out. As she left my line of sight, the urge to follow hit hard and unexpectedly. More of those warning bells I'd been experiencing. They were even louder now.

I strained to hear anything beyond the doors, but there was nothing. The walls in the newer parts of the castle were thicker.

My hand tightened on the hilt of the sword as I eyed the two Royal Guards. I didn't recognize either of them. "Is this common?" I asked, nodding at the door.

The darker-skinned one answered after a moment. "Not too common."

That wasn't much of an answer. "How long do these…meetings take?"

Again, the one who spoke hesitated. "Depends."

I glanced at the other guard. He stared straight ahead as if he heard nothing of the conversation. I looked between the two, sure they had witnessed some horrific shit.

Atrocities they had decided they could live with knowing.

I could force them to tell me what they'd seen—the things involving her—but using compulsion was too great a risk. Some mortals were resistant, remembering everything they were compelled to do.

Instead, I sent a steward to get Vikter. Maybe he could tell me what was going on.

A muscle ticked in my jaw, as did the time while I committed both guards' faces to memory. About ten minutes passed before the doors at the end of the hall swung open, and Wardwell entered, his white mantle streaming behind him. He motioned me forward as he stopped several feet away.

I didn't move. Not for several seconds. It was like my damn feet were rooted to the floor. Glancing at the doors to the Duke's office, I forced myself to move and join Wardwell.

"How long has she been in there?" he asked, dragging a hand over the sandy strands of his hair.

"A little over ten minutes," I answered, noting how the creases at the corners of his eyes had deepened. "What does the Duke want with her?"

"He likely wanted to discuss her upcoming Ascension," he answered, attention focused on the doors behind me. "I will take over from here and continue for the rest of the day."

Everything in me went on alert. "My shift doesn't end for several hours."

"I know." His gaze shifted to mine. "But I'm here now. You got a problem with that, take it up with the Duke."

Irritation flared deep, and energy ramped up in my core. I felt the compulsion to make him tell me what was going on building in me as I snagged Wardwell's gaze. I had to fight it back. Knowing my luck, this fucker would be one who remembered everything they did while under compulsion.

Taking a deep breath, I pushed the urge down. I looked over my shoulder at those closed doors. "She…"

"She what?" he pushed when I didn't finish.

She'd looked at me as if she needed assurance that I'd be out here, waiting for her.

And that should've pleased me. It meant that she was already starting to trust me, despite my short time as her guard. I figured the Red Pearl had a lot to do with that, but either way, I needed it from her. Trust. However, nothing about this sat right with me.

"Hawke," Wardwell snapped.

"Nothing," I said, tearing my gaze from the doors. I smiled at the older Royal Guard. "Good day."

Then I walked away.

I left the fourth floor.

I left the Maiden.

A TWISTED IRONY
OF SORTS

The reason for the meeting between the Duke and the Maiden remained a mystery, much to my ever-growing displeasure.

Especially when Vikter changed up the schedule, moving me to guard over her the following night when I was supposed to be watching over her that day. He'd done the same today, and when I demanded to know why, he'd pulled rank while calling me a *boy*. I wasn't sure which of those two things irritated me the most as I stood outside the Maiden's chambers, the dark hall lit by a few scattered wall sconces.

I hadn't seen the Maiden since I'd left her in the Duke's office, and as far as I knew, she hadn't left her chambers. Tawny had been with her, though, late into the night both yesterday and today.

"She's feeling under the weather," Tawny had claimed when I asked how the Maiden was. Then, she'd hastily entered her adjoining chambers, not lingering long enough for me to ask anything else.

I fisted and flexed my hand as I told myself my irritation had everything to do with yet another delay in my plans. The Rite would be here sooner rather than later, and I needed the Maiden's irrevocable trust by then—for her to be at a point where she didn't question orders or suspect anything. We weren't there. We weren't anywhere near there. And I wouldn't delay what was to come.

Malik didn't have the time.

That was the source of my frustration. It had nothing to do with how she had turned to look at me outside the Duke's offices or the feeling that she sought reassurance.

Cursing under my breath, I peered at the small window at the end of the hall. The faint, acrid scent of smoke reached me. There had been fires earlier in the day. One of the homes in Radiant Row had burned to the foundation, thanks to a group of Descenters. A smile tugged at my mouth. They had gotten a few of the Ascended, not that the Teermans would fess up to the loss.

Fools.

They could've used those losses as a way to fuel hatred and fear. Instead, they didn't want their weaknesses known. They wanted to be seen as godlike. Immortal.

The Descenters had acted on their own, propelled by what had occurred at the last City Council. The Tulises' plight not only had those who'd been against the Ascended seeking revenge, but it had also changed a few minds. More and more no longer shuddered in fear upon hearing about the Dark One. Instead, resolve had replaced the fear, as did hope for a different, better future. I wanted it to continue beyond freeing my brother.

I wanted the people of Solis to fight back.

They just needed to know the Ascended were not who they claimed. The gods hadn't Blessed them, and the entire kingdom was built on a foundation of lies. Freeing Malik would be the first crack. Without him, there would be no more Ascensions, and because of what they'd led their people to believe, it would look like the gods had turned on the Ascended. After all, the Blood Crown couldn't admit that they used the blood of those they had made villains for their Ascensions. Their lies would be their downfall.

But that didn't fix everything.

Not in my father's or Alastir's eyes.

There were the Ascended who still ruled—Queen Ileana and King Jalara, and all their Dukes, Duchesses, Lords, and Ladies that would need to be dealt with. There was still the fact that Atlantia was running out of land and on the brink of being overfarmed and overpopulated. We had time, but not a lot. Not a—

A sudden, abrupt scream jerked my head to the Maiden's door. Bad dreams. Vikter had warned me, but I wasn't willing to risk that.

Withdrawing the dagger strapped to my hip, I opened the door to the Maiden's dark chambers. It was a cloudy night, leaving no moonlight to find its way in through the windows, but I immediately found her in the darkness.

She was in her bed, lying on her side, asleep and alone. Clearly, she wasn't being attacked.

At least not by anything I could see.

Her hands opened and closed where they lay a few inches from her parted lips. Only a cheek was visible, the left one. The one I thought was just as beautiful as the other. It was damp, glistening. Tears. She moaned, shifting onto her back. Her gasp shattered the silence.

It was the only warning.

Fuck.

I moved lightning-fast, pressing myself against the wall where the shadows of the night were the deepest and clung the heaviest.

Thick hair fell forward as she jerked back onto her side, rising on one elbow. Her breaths were ragged. I held myself completely still as she lifted a trembling hand and shoved the hair back from her face.

My heart lurched.

She was staring right in my direction, but I knew she couldn't see me.

But I saw her—and the horror in her eyes. Pure terror.

"Just a dream," she whispered, settling onto her side again. Her body curled inward, arms and legs tucked close. Her eyes remained open as she lay there, gently rocking herself back and forth. Each time her eyes closed, it took longer for them to reopen.

I knew what she was doing—fighting falling back to sleep. Gods, I'd done that more times than I could count. Several minutes passed before she finally lost the battle, slipping back to sleep. I didn't move, though. I just...watched her. Like a creep. A slight laugh shook me. I was actually doing the least creepy thing I'd done in a long time; however, I had no good reason to watch her now. The Maiden was fine.

The Maiden.

She has a name, an unwanted voice in the back of my head reminded me. Penellaphe. The Duke and Duchess called her that, but according to Tawny, her friends called her Poppy. But she was just the Maiden to me.

She won't scream if she's under duress.

Still having no clue what Vikter had meant by that, I approached her bed. The blanket had gathered at her waist, exposing the long-sleeved robe she must have fallen asleep in or normally wore to bed. I wouldn't be surprised. I glanced around the bedchamber—the *sparse*, chilly bedchamber. There was hardly anything in here. A table. A chest. A wardrobe. I frowned. No personal items to speak of. I'd seen the poorest of the kingdom have more things in their homes.

Was that another prohibited thing? Personal items? My attention shifted back to her. She was breathing deeply, if a bit unevenly, as if she were wary of those unpleasant dreams returning, even in sleep. Did she

184/Jennifer L. Armentrout

remember them when she woke? I didn't always. Sometimes, there was just a general sense of apprehension upon waking, a feeling of dread that lingered all day.

I bent, catching the scent of pine and sage, reminding me of arnica—a plant used to treat all manner of things. I carefully lifted the blanket, placing it over her shoulders. I glanced at her face. Those eyes were closed, lips relaxed. I saw the scars and thought of the source of her nightmares.

Backing away, I left the bedchamber, finding a twisted sense of irony in the fact that the same people were responsible for what found us both in the darkest hours of the night.

PRESENT V

"I don't think I've ever told you about that. It wasn't that I was hiding it from you. I just didn't want you to feel embarrassed," I told Poppy as she slept, curling my arm around her waist. "I also figured you'd probably stab me if you ever learned I had been in your bedchamber while you slept." I paused. "More than once."

My laugh stirred the wisps of hair at her temple, but my amusement faded. "I didn't know about the Duke. I just knew something was up. The way you and Tawny responded. How Vikter was when he showed up. Now, I know why he dismissed me. He knew you wouldn't have wanted me—or anyone really—to see you after you finished with your *lesson*. He was protecting you the best he could."

His best wasn't good enough in my opinion. He'd known what was being done to her, yet he stood by. But I kept that opinion to myself. She didn't need to hear it.

I stared at her. Dawn quickly approached. I should try to sleep while Delano was here, resting at the foot of the bed in his wolven form. I could try to find her in our dreams. But my mind wasn't shutting down, and maybe I was too afraid that we *wouldn't* find each other. Neither of us knew how to walk in each other's dreams—if it was something that happened naturally when we both slept or if one of us initiated it. But this wasn't normal sleep. She was in stasis.

Still, resting would be wise either way. I needed it. Except there was no way I could until she opened those beautiful eyes of hers and knew me. Knew herself.

And she would.

I believed that.

Because she was strong and stubborn as hell. She was brave.

I hadn't always known just how strong she was.

A smile tugged at my lips as I thought of the first time I'd truly grasped how brave and skilled she was. "When we were at the Red Pearl, and I found that dagger? You said you knew how to use it. I wasn't sure I believed you. Why would I? You were the Maiden, but then you cut Jericho, and I should've realized then that you were nothing like I expected. Nothing at all."

I dipped my head, kissing the bare skin of her shoulder beside the thin strap of the gown Vonetta had found for her. "But the night on the Rise, when the Craven attacked, I realized then that Kieran and I really *had* underestimated you." In my mind, I could see her now, her cloak billowing around her in the wind right before she threw a dagger at me. "That was when it began to change—how I thought of you. Saw you. You were no longer the Maiden. You were becoming... You were becoming Poppy."

THE MONSTER
IN ME

The atmosphere shifted.

I felt it in the air as I walked the Rise after Vikter relieved me. I was already on edge, brimming with unspent energy. Part of it was due to the frustration of it going on the second day of the Maiden being an absolute no-show. Whatever that shit was with the Duke. Her nightmares. Mine. That fucking dead Lord Devries.

But what caused the small hairs all over my body to rise was something else entirely.

The silence on the Rise was unsettling as I stalked toward the front, the cold breeze catching the godsdamn mantle. Up ahead, I saw a whole damn line of guards staring out over the barren lands. Spotting Pence's fair head, I went up to where he stood at an archer's nest, bow in hand. "What's going...?" I trailed off as my gaze left his pale face and focused beyond the Rise and the steel row of lit torches.

Then, I didn't need an answer.

I saw it.

The mist.

It was so thick that it nearly obscured the Blood Forest, and it moved under the moonlight, churning and slipping across the ground in a way that was not at all typical.

"Fuck," I muttered.

"Yeah," Pence rasped. "The mist was normal, you know? Just a foot or so above the ground, but then it started thickening and moving. It's already tripled in size in the last three minutes."

That was undoubtedly not a good sign.

Everyone on the Rise knew that—knew what was in that mist.

The Craven.

I hadn't seen it get like this here, but it reminded me of the Primal mist that blanketed the Skotos Mountains in the east—the magic of the gods that shielded the Kingdom of Atlantia. And it was all kinds of fucked-up how that magic had somehow become so distorted here. How it protected the monsters the Ascended created.

No one could really answer why the mist behaved this way in Solis. Not even the Elders in Atlantia. But the reason wasn't the most pressing issue at the moment. The mist had already spread out on both sides as far as the eye could see, and while the distance between the Rise and the mist was about the width and length of the Lower Ward, it was not far enough as I watched tendrils seep out, stretching yards ahead. It was like a collective breath was held on the Rise as the mist reached the standing torches.

The breeze stilled.

But the flames began to flicker and then dance wildly, the fire casting frenzied shadows across the ground. What I wouldn't give for one of our Atlantian crossbows. They were far superior and did a hell of a lot more damage than the recurve bows. I reached for the hilt of my broadsword.

The middle torch was the first to go out. The rest followed rapidly, plunging the land outside the Rise into utter darkness.

"Light it up!" Lieutenant Smyth's command cracked the silence.

All down the Rise, guards hurried forward with arrow tips wrapped in tight cloth containing a gunpowder mixture behind the arrowheads. One after another, fire sparked. Then they were released, slicing through the night sky and sharply veering down, slamming into a tinder-filled trench. Flames erupted from the furrow, casting a wide, orangey-red glow across the land and the mist.

Silence fell once more along the Rise as the mist rushed forward. The closer it got, the more solid it became. I squinted as it seeped into the trench and beneath the tinder, crawling above it, smothering the flames within moments of them being lit.

Dark, silvery-moonlit shapes could be seen in the mist. Twisted bodies. The entirety of the mist was filled with them.

"Sound the alarms," someone shouted from the ground below. "Sound the alarms."

Horns went off at the four corners of the Rise, signaling the impending attack on the city. More like a siege as I turned and headed for the nearby stairs. Within moments, lights were extinguished all throughout Masadonia as homes and still-open businesses went dark—all except for the Temples—the air going quiet with fear.

Because Craven hordes had breached the cities before, and even if none made it past the Rise, many families would lose loved ones tonight.

As archers were ordered to fire, I heard a distant rumble, the grinding of iron against stone. I cast a glance at the castle. Thick and heavy iron doors were already beginning their descent at every entry point to the stronghold. Everyone inside would be safe—most importantly, the Maiden. She would be behind feet of stone and iron in a few minutes, and Vikter was with her.

"Where are you going?" Pence called as he grabbed a quiver of arrows.

"To fight."

Knowing what that meant, Pence's mouth dropped open. "You don't have to. You're a Royal Guard. You're the Maiden's—"

I cut him off. "I know." As I reached the stairs, I added, "Stay alive."

Pence stood dumbfounded as I went down the narrow steps. I couldn't blame him. No one in their right mind would want to go beyond the Rise on a good day, let alone now, but while the Ascended cowered in their fancy homes, I didn't fear a Craven's bite. No Atlantian did. It had no effect on us.

But I was also not of the right mind on most days, because a Craven could still fuck an Atlantian up. They could even kill one if they gained the upper hand.

I didn't plan on that happening.

Instead, I intended to work out some pent-up aggression, and it looked like I would be able to do just that based on the size of the horde. There was no way the archers would be able to take them all out.

Once on solid ground, I kept to the shadows of the Rise as I unclasped the mantle. Nearing the gatehouse, I tossed it onto one of the benches and quickly joined the group of about a hundred guards who waited at the Rise gates.

I didn't look at any of them as arrows whizzed through the air. I had no need to see the faces of those who wouldn't return. Many black flags would be raised tomorrow.

Seconds ticked into minutes as the anxiety of those waiting around me ramped up. I reached down at my sides and unhooked the short swords, their slightly curved blades glistening like blood in the moonlight. Beside me, a guard trembled as he murmured a prayer under his breath.

"We are the only ones standing between the failure of the Rise," Commander Jansen yelled from above, "and the beasts in the mist who wish to feast upon your flesh and blood. They take us, they take the Rise. And then the city. Will we gladly meet the god Rhain tonight?"

Denial thundered all around me as hilts of swords thumped off shields and chests.

"Then we will defend the Rise and the lives beyond it with our shields, arrows, and swords." Jansen thrust his blade into the sky. "Go forth and do unto them as they would do unto you and yours, for the gods Theon and Lailah ride at your sides. Split their rotten flesh and soak the ground with their blood."

In any other situation, I would've laughed at Jansen talking of the gods like that, but not now. Not as bloodthirsty roars echoed along the wall.

"Open the gates," Lieutenant Smyth ordered from down the Rise. "Open!"

Iron creaked and groaned, unlatching. None of the waiting guards spoke as the gap between the gates grew wider. Foot by foot, the land beyond was revealed, and there was nothing but thick, rapidly approaching mist and the bodies within it.

"May the gods be with you!" shouted the Commander. "And may the gods welcome those who come into their embraces as heroes!"

Not a single guard hesitated. No matter how pale their faces were or how badly they'd shaken seconds ago. They ran forward, swords drawn and battle cries splitting the air, headed out into the land just beyond the Rise. As the gates slammed shut behind us, and arrows continued raining down ahead, striking the monsters in the mist, several lines of guards formed. They braced themselves, many who I knew had never seen battle before. Who were likely facing their first Craven.

I waited, eyes trained on the mist—on the forms inside it.

I didn't have to wait long.

A sound came next. The low, keening wail of the Craven rising in a crescendo that even sent a chill down *my* spine as the archers released another volley of lit arrows, reigniting the trench.

I slowly stretched my neck from left to right, firming my grip on the swords.

Then they came, pouring out of the mist, their bodies in various states of decomposition. Some were fresh, still mostly dressed in the clothing they wore when they turned, their faces pale. Others had been Craven for a while, their clothing hanging in rags from milky-white bodies, arms and legs as thin as the bones beneath, faces even more sunken and skeletal.

All of their eyes burned crimson.

They flooded the ground and swamped us within *seconds*, clawing with elongated fingers and nails as sharp as the two sets of jagged fangs. Claws that had left their mark behind on the Maiden. Claws that had dug into my skin.

The horde swallowed the first line of guards, the men driven to the ground in screams and sprays of blood. The second line engaged, and then there was no more waiting. The Craven were everywhere.

It was time to let my monster out.

I shot forward, launching over a fallen guard as I swiped out with the short sword, cleaving the head from the shoulders of a nearby Craven.

Spinning, I brought the other sword up, catching another at the groin and splitting it straight up the middle. Rotten insides spilled, splattering off the ground. The stench of decay and that stale sweetness increased as I jerked back. Another Craven had taken the spot of the one before me, its clawed hand scraping off the armor of my chest.

Bastard.

Kicking the Craven in the sternum, I knocked it back. Another came at me from the side. I swung the sword across its neck as I twisted, bringing my other blade around as other guards fought, holding their ground. Some fell, and not even I, as fast as I was, could reach them before the Craven smothered them. There were no more wild volleys of arrows, but skilled, purposeful shots. Sharpened arrowheads that flew between guards, striking the Craven.

But for those of us out beyond the Rise, there was no skill in this kind of battle. No art. There was no thinking, and in a way, it was kind of a release. It was all about moving. Staying on your feet. Keeping out of reach. It was hacking and cleaving my way through what seemed like an endless wave of dry, gray flesh. I chopped off limbs. Tore skin open. Dark, oily ichor flowed, joining the brighter, redder blood spilling across the packed ground. There was no way to tell how many I took down. A dozen. Two? Three? Still, it got my heart and blood pumping.

It silenced my mind.

I spun, slamming my elbow into a Craven's face, feeling the bones cave in as I snapped forward, kicking another off a fallen guard. A mortal brought his broadsword down on the Craven, a flash of white snagging my attention. My head jerked up just as an arrow whizzed past me, slamming into the skull of a Craven sneaking up on a guard.

A *Royal Guard*.

Vikter.

He stood several feet away, his cheeks splattered in blood as he turned to the Rise. There was this moment—a brief one—where I knew I could strike now and take him out, wound him enough that a Craven would quickly finish him off. It was necessary because then he wouldn't be around when it came time for me to take the Maiden out of the city. This was my chance. A perfect one. My fingers twitched around the hilt of a sword. No one would know. No one would suspect a thing.

But I didn't.

I didn't even know why.

Vikter turned back around and spotted me almost instantly. Our gazes locked for a heartbeat, and it was as if we both realized the same thing in that instant.

If he was out here, and so was I, that meant...

Motherfucker, Vikter mouthed.

"Shit." I spun, sheathing one sword.

I bolted over the slippery, body-clogged crowd. The Maiden was safely tucked away in the castle, where no Craven could reach her, but that didn't mean she was safe.

Especially since she was locked away with the Ascended, and even though she was important to them, I didn't trust a single one.

Grabbing the half-torn tunic of a Craven, I tossed it to the ground and brought the bloodstone sword down, straight through its chest. Cursing, I withdrew the blade and pressed on. I didn't like leaving the fight, not when a decent number of the horde was still standing, but the Maiden was unguarded, and knowing my luck...

Near the foot of the Rise, a guard drew his blade free of a Craven's chest. The man stumbled back, lifting his sword arm. The skin of his hand was a mangled mess.

He'd been bitten.

The guard turned, and in the chaos of the battle, his wide gaze collided with mine. I didn't recognize him. Had no idea who he was, but I knew he understood what was coming for him now. One bite. It was all it took. His jaw set in determination.

The man dropped his sword and withdrew the dagger attached to his hip. I knew immediately what he was about to do. He didn't hesitate. Not for a damn second, and he couldn't if he hoped to *finish* this. The bite would make it impossible in minutes.

The mortal guard showed more honor in that moment than most were capable of—more than the Ascended ever deserved.

He cut his own throat.

Fuck.

I looked away. The quickness it required to be successful? The bravery to do that for what was basically the greater good?

Fuck.

At the gates, I looked up. "Commander!" I shouted, catching a Craven with an uppercut of my sword, splitting the bastard in two.

Jansen whipped around, looking down. The way his jaw hardened, I knew he wasn't pleased to see me—the only free Prince of his kingdom—outside the Rise, but he would have to suck it up.

"Open the gate!" he yelled.

Stepping over the fallen Craven, I hurried forward and squeezed through the minuscule opening. I didn't waste time with being checked out, I just ran to the nearest steps and climbed the Rise. It was the quickest way to get back to the castle. Jansen shot me a look as I reached the top. Hiding a smile, I took off down the wall, passing an empty battlement and then another, nearing the portion of the Rise that hadn't been manned earlier. There simply weren't enough skilled archers to fill each—

Something caught my attention. I slid to a quiet stop and turned. My eyes narrowed. One of the nests was no longer empty, but that wasn't what had stopped me. Frowning, I crept back and peered inside. At first, I wasn't sure what I was looking at.

Someone knelt in the archer's nest, hidden behind the stone ledge. Someone who was cloaked as they pulled the bowstring back, releasing an arrow, firing at a Craven approaching the top of the Rise.

I dragged in a deep breath, scenting the air. I smelled the decay of blood and Craven on me, but there was also a distinctively fresh, sweet scent that belonged to only—

The godsdamn *Maiden.*

YOU'RE AN ABSOLUTELY STUNNING, MURDEROUS LITTLE CREATURE

"You must be the goddess Bele or Lailah given mortal form," I murmured, thinking I had to be wrong.

There was no way it was her.

The figure spun on one knee, the cloak and *gown* flowing out around them as they aimed an arrow right at my head.

Holy shit.

I couldn't see her features beneath the hood, but I knew it was her. It was the Maiden, out here on the Rise—not in her quarters where she should be—with a godsdamn arrow aimed at my head.

I didn't know if I should laugh.

Or shout.

Her inhale was audible, but she said nothing as she remained kneeling, and fuck, those fingers holding the arrow didn't tremble.

"You are…" I sheathed my sword and found myself somewhat speechless, but not for long. "You're absolutely magnificent. Beautiful."

I saw a slight reaction from her. Her hooded head turned a fraction of an inch, but that was all.

My mind raced as I eyed her. Clearly, she recognized me, but she likely believed her identity remained unknown, and that was understandable. She had no idea that I could pick out her scent.

My heart was still pumping from adrenaline, but that wasn't all that had my blood pulsing. I briefly glanced down the Rise. No one was near us, nor would anyone pay attention. Not with the barely controlled chaos on the ground.

I made a quick decision then, deciding to humor her. To see how far she would take this. How far *I* would take this.

And I already knew I often took things way too far.

"The last thing I expected was to find a hooded lady with a talent for archery manning one of the battlements," I said, a grin tugging at my lips as she remained silent. I extended my hand. "May I be of assistance?"

She didn't take my hand. Of course, not. But she lowered the bow, switching it to one hand. She said nothing as she motioned for me to back up.

My gods, she really wasn't going to speak.

I raised a brow as I folded the hand I offered over my chest and moved back. Then, fighting a laugh, I bowed.

She made a soft sound I couldn't quite decipher as she placed the bow on the ledge below her. I felt her stare as she made her way to the ladder and climbed down.

She hadn't taken her eyes off me.

And she'd picked up that bow again.

Smart girl.

"You're a..." I fell silent once more. My eyes narrowed as she slipped the bow *beneath* her cloak, hooking it to her back.

It was her bow?

What the fuck did she have a bow for?

To kill Craven with, obviously, but that led to my next query. How the fuck did she know how to use a bow to kill a Craven?

Oh, I had so many questions.

The Maiden stepped to the right, making a move to exit the battlement.

I blocked it. "What are you doing up here?"

There was no answer.

Instead, she strode past me with all the haughtiness of a...of a *Princess.* My lips curled. I'd forgotten I'd called her that at the Red Pearl.

I spun, catching her arm. "I think—"

The Maiden whirled, twisting under my arm. My mouth dropped open. Shock froze me. I didn't even move as she dipped low behind me and kicked out, sweeping my legs out from under me.

She'd swept *my* legs out from under *me.*

"Fuck," I gasped, catching myself on the wall to stop my fall. Shock kept rolling through me. I couldn't believe it.

The Maiden had almost taken my ass down.

The Maiden, who was currently running away from me.

Oh, hell no.

Pushing off the wall, I reached down, unhooking the dagger at my hip. I threw it with precision, catching the back of her cloak. It spun her around and jerked her against the wall. Her hooded head dipped.

I smirked as I prowled toward her. "That wasn't very nice."

She gripped the handle of my blade, wrenching it free. To my utter disbelief...and rapidly growing *interest*, she flipped the godsdamn dagger like a pro, catching it by the blade.

I halted. "Don't."

She threw it right at my face, but I moved fast, catching it by the handle. Half-irritated and half, well, enthralled by her utter audacity, I started walking toward her as I tsked beneath my breath.

She took off once more, running down the narrow, dangerously high Rise while wearing...slippers. She was *mad*.

Swallowing a laugh, I launched myself onto the ledge, picking up speed. I was nothing more than a shadow as I passed her from above. I jumped off the ledge, landing in a crouch before her.

She jerked, her feet sliding out from under her. She went down on her hip, and I almost felt bad.

Except she'd thrown a dagger at my *face*.

"Now that really wasn't nice at all." I rose as her head jerked to the ledge. "I'm aware that my hair is in need of a trim, but your aim is off. You should really work on that since I'm quite partial to my face."

I walked up to her and saw she'd gone completely still, and I should've known better. I really should have. But a part of my mind hadn't caught up to what I was seeing yet. What I was learning. And the other half was still enthralled by her actions—by the fire in her.

She kicked out, hitting my lower leg. I grunted at the dull flare of pain as she jumped to her feet, whirling to her right. I went to block her, but the damn vixen darted to the left, playing me like a novice.

And I felt like one just then.

I cut off that path, too.

She wasn't happy about it. Clearly. Because she spun, kicking out from the folds of her cloak—

Catching her ankle, I held on as the sides of the cloak parted, revealing her bare leg from the knee down. I raised a brow at her. "Scandalous."

She growled.

The Maiden actually *growled* at me.

A laugh burst free—one I couldn't even hope to stop. "And such dainty little slippers. Satin and silk?" I said. "They're as finely tailored as your leg. The kind of slipper no guard of the Rise would wear."

She pulled at my hold.

"Unless they are being outfitted differently than I am." I dropped her ankle, but I was a quick learner. I caught her arm, yanking her against my chest, leaving no room for her to kick. That was my plan.

Except her scent, all that sweetness, surrounded me, and I felt her body against every part of mine that wasn't covered by leather and iron. There wasn't an inch separating us, and the last time I had been this close to such a soft body was...

Damn, it was when I was with her.

A pulse of arousal throbbed through me as I stared at her hooded face, so sudden and intense that I dragged in a breath—

Her scent thickened around me, turning even sweeter, which was really, *really* intriguing.

My head dipped as I lifted my other arm. "You know what I think—?" The warm press of a blade against my throat stopped me.

The Maiden had a knife at my throat.

That damn wolven-bone dagger.

I'd forgotten she had that.

Anger sparked because this was taking things a bit too far, in my honest opinion. It was all fun and games until a blade was at—

A prick of pain stunned me. Not so much because it hurt. It barely did. And not because it silenced my mind. The pain did nothing this time. It was the shock.

She'd drawn blood.

My blood.

Anger faded with the shock as I stared, amusement rising in their places, along with something else. Something far stronger. Lust. Pure, hard, and hot lust. And good gods, I knew that said some fucked-up shit about me. But it wasn't the pain that got me rock-hard in an instant. Pain never did that for me.

It was her boldness.

Her bravery.

Her skill.

Her utter recklessness and the fire that burned so bright in her.

And I never wanted someone more than I wanted her. Right here.

Dear gods, if she were anyone else, I would act on the arousal I'd picked up from her. I'd have her against the wall and my cock in her so fast, so hard, both our heads would spin. But she wasn't anyone else.

"Correction," I said, another laugh leaving me as the blood trickled down my neck. "You're an absolutely stunning murderous little creature." I glanced down at the dagger, no longer humoring her by allowing her to think I didn't recognize her. "Nice weapon. Bloodstone and wolven bone. Very interesting…" I paused. "*Princess.*"

Shock went through her like a wave. She jerked the blade back.

I caught her wrist. "You and I have so much to talk about."

"We have nothing to talk about," she snapped.

A surge of savage satisfaction went through me. "She speaks! I thought you liked to talk, Princess. Or is that only when you're at the Red Pearl?"

She went quiet once more.

"You're not going to pretend that you have no idea what I'm talking about, are you? That you're not her?"

She pulled at my arm. "Let me go."

"Oh, I don't think so." I turned sharply, pinning her against the wall before she decided to use her free arm against me. I leaned in, all up in her space. "After all we shared? You throw a dagger at my face?"

"All we shared? It was a handful of minutes and a few kisses," she said, jerking slightly.

"It was more than a few kisses," I reminded her, glancing at where her breasts rose and fell with her deep breaths. "If you've forgotten, I'm more than willing to remind you," I offered.

The scent of her arousal increased, and my dick answered with an almost painful throb.

Her head lifted. "There was nothing worth remembering."

Such a little liar. "Now you insult me after throwing a dagger at my face? You've wounded my tender feelings."

"Tender feelings?" She snorted. "Don't be overdramatic."

"Hard not to be when you threw a dagger at my *head* and then cut my neck," I shot back.

"I knew you'd move out of the way."

"Did you? Is that why you tried to slice open my throat?"

"I *nicked* your skin," she countered. "Because you had a hold of me and wouldn't let go. Obviously, you haven't learned anything from it."

"I've actually learned a lot, Princess. That's why your hands and your dagger aren't getting anywhere near my neck." I slid my thumb across the inside of her wrist. "But if you let go of the dagger, there's a whole lot of me I'll let your hands get close to."

And I would, too.

In that moment, I'd let her do just about anything.

Except go silent on me.

"How generous of you," she retorted.

Liquid heat hit my blood, and fuck, there was nothing teasing about how that felt. "Once you get to know me, you'll find that I can be *quite* benevolent."

Her breath caught. "I have no intention of getting to know you."

"So, you just make a habit of sneaking into the rooms of young men and seducing them before running off?"

"What?" she gasped. "Seducing men?"

"Isn't that what you did to me, Princess?" I moved my thumb back and forth over her wrist.

"You're ridiculous."

"What I am is *intrigued.*" And I truly was.

She groaned, pulling at my hold. "Why do you insist on holding me like this?"

"Well, besides what we went over already, which is the whole being partial to my face *and* my neck thing, you're also somewhere you're not supposed to be. I'm doing my job by detaining and questioning you."

"Do you typically question those on the Rise who you don't recognize like this?" she asked. "What an odd method of interrogation."

"Only pretty ladies with shapely, bare legs." I leaned into her, amused that she thought I didn't connect her and the Red Pearl with her being the Maiden. "What are you doing up here during a Craven attack?"

"Enjoying a relaxing evening stroll."

I grinned. "What were you doing up here, Princess?"

"What did it look like I was doing?"

"It looked like you were being incredibly foolish and reckless," I said.

"Excuse me?" Disbelief filled her voice. "How reckless was I being when I killed Craven and—"

"Am I unaware of a new recruitment policy where half-dressed ladies in cloaks are now needed on the Rise?" I asked. "Are we that desperately in need of protection?"

"Desperate?" The disbelief was gone in that one word. Now, there was anger. "Why would my presence on the Rise signal desperation when, as you've seen, I know how to use a bow? Oh, wait. Is it because I happen to have breasts?"

My brows shot up. "I've known women with far less beautiful breasts that could cut a man down without so much as blinking an eye, but none of those women are here in Masadonia. And you are incredibly skilled. Not just with an arrow. Who taught you how to fight and use a dagger?"

Silence.

"I'm willing to bet it was the same person who gave you that blade," I wagered. "Too bad whoever they are didn't teach you how to evade capture. Well, too bad for *you*, that is."

That got a reaction from her.

She brought up her knee, aiming for a rather cherished part of my body.

I blocked the blow before she had me talking several octaves higher. "You're so incredibly violent." I paused. "I think I like it."

"Let me go!" she demanded.

"And be kicked or stabbed?" Sensing she was about to do the former again, I thrust my leg between hers, preventing just that. "We've already covered that, Princess. More than once."

She lifted her hips off the wall, and I thought she was attempting to throw me back. No, I *knew* what she was trying to do. It was a smart move, actually.

But that wasn't what she got.

She ended up basically *riding* my thigh, and I wasn't complaining. Not at all. Except the arousal thundering through me left me a little off-kilter. It was too damn intense. Too quick. Like if she kept it up, I may do something I hadn't done since I was a young man and find release in my pants without even being touched.

And, damn, that was...

I didn't know what that was.

It made the floor of the Rise feel like it was shifting as I lowered my cheek to her hooded head. Rattled by my response and her—everything, I said, "I came back for you that night. Just like I told you I would. I came back for you, and you weren't there. You promised me, Princess."

Her inhale was soft. A faint tremor went through her. "I...I couldn't."

"Couldn't?" I let my eyes close for a moment, and that was foolish. She'd likely headbutt me, but I liked that soft breath and those quiet words. "I have a feeling that if there's something you want badly enough, nothing will stop you."

She laughed, and it was cold and hard. My eyes opened. "You know nothing," she said.

I thought she was right about that.

"Maybe." I let go, but before she moved, I slipped my hand inside her hood and cupped her right cheek. She gasped as I let myself soak in the feel of her warm skin against mine, just for a moment. "Maybe I know more than you realize."

She was still.

She didn't pull away.

That pleased me. Immensely. Except she likely didn't realize that I knew the two versions of her. The curious, responsive young woman with a surprising knack for fighting, and the quiet, submissive Maiden in white. Or she was going to pretend that I didn't know she was one and the same.

I wouldn't allow that.

I pressed my cheek to the left side of her hood. "Do you really think I have no idea who you are?"

She tensed against me.

Yep. I was right.

I smiled. "You have nothing to say to that?" I dropped my voice to a whisper. "*Penellaphe?*"

She exhaled loudly. A moment passed, one she used to sharpen that tongue of hers. "Are you just now figuring that out? If so, I'm concerned about you being one of my personal guards."

I chuckled. "I knew the moment you removed the veil." I'd known before then, but she couldn't know that.

"Why…why didn't you say something then?"

"To you?" I asked. "Or to the Duke?"

"Either," she whispered.

"I wanted to see if you'd bring it up. Apparently, you were just going to pretend that you're not the same girl who frequents the Red Pearl."

"I don't frequent the Red Pearl," she said. "But I hear you do."

"Have you been asking about me? I'm flattered."

"I haven't."

"I'm not sure if I can believe you. You tell a lot of lies, Princess."

"Don't call me that," she snapped.

"I like it better than what I'm supposed to call you. *Maiden.*" Fuck if that wasn't the truth. "You have a name. It's not that."

"I didn't ask for what you liked," she told me.

"But you did ask why I didn't tell the Duke about your little explorations," I countered. "Why would I do that? I'm your guard. If I were to betray you, then you wouldn't trust me, and that would definitely make my job of keeping you safe much harder."

Her head tilted slightly. A few more moments passed. "As you can see, I can keep myself safe."

"I see that." I drew back, brows furrowed, and then I remembered what Vikter had said.

"Hawke!" Pence called, causing me to stiffen. "Everything okay up there?"

My gaze flicked down, making sure the hood was still in place before I yelled back, "Everything is fine."

"You need to let me go," she whispered. "Someone is bound to come up here—"

"And catch you? Force you to reveal your identity?" I said. "Maybe that would be a good thing."

She sucked in a sharp breath. "You said you wouldn't betray me—"

"I said I *didn't* betray you, but that was before I knew you would do something like this. My job would be so much easier if I didn't have to worry about you sneaking out to fight the Craven...or meet random men in places like the Red Pearl," I reasoned, mostly to myself. "And who knows what else you do when all believe you're safely ensconced in your chambers."

"I—"

"I imagine that once I brought it to the Duke's and Duchess's attention, your penchant for arming yourself with a bow and climbing to the Rise would be one less thing I had to worry about."

"You have no idea what he'd do if you went to him. He'd—" She went silent.

I locked up. "He'd what?"

She lifted her chin. "It doesn't matter. Do what you feel you need to do."

I had no intention of telling the Duke anything. I'd only been messing with her. Mostly. "You better hurry back to your chambers, Princess." I stepped back. I had more questions, but they'd have to wait. "We'll have to finish this conversation later."

THAT DRESS WILL BE THE DEATH OF ME

I wasted no time, stopping only long enough to wash the blood from my face and ditch the heavy broadsword. I had no idea when Vikter would return to his post, and I had questions for the...

I couldn't think of her as the Maiden anymore. Truth be told, I'd had a hard time since the Red Pearl thinking of her as that.

Now, she was...Penellaphe.

My hands spasmed at my sides. Before, I could force myself to think of her as just the Maiden. Not anymore. The change was like a switch being thrown. Though when, I wasn't exactly sure. It could've been the moment I realized that was her on the Rise. Or when she nearly took my legs out from under me.

Or when she threw that dagger at my face.

A wry grin tugged at my lips as I climbed the steps. The *when* didn't matter. The why did, even though it shouldn't, but I couldn't ignore what had happened out on the Rise. Or what hadn't.

I hadn't thought of why I was there. My past. The future. My brother. I hadn't thought about any of my plans. I'd just been...*living* in the moment. Not existing. Not plotting. Not thriving on the idea of vengeance. Surviving on the knowledge that I was doing all of this for Malik.

I hadn't been myself.

Or maybe I *had* been, if only for those minutes.

And that was unsettling as fuck.

However, that ultimately changed nothing.

Blowing out a ragged breath, I went down the empty hall and

stopped outside Penellaphe's chambers. I could hear Tawny speaking.

"There'll be a lot of black flags raised tomorrow," she said.

Yes, unfortunately, there would be.

I knocked on the door.

"I'll get it," Tawny announced, and quick, light footsteps followed. The door swung open, and an array of emotions flickered across the Lady's pretty face before a smile appeared. "The Maiden is sleeping—"

"Doubtful." I walked right on in, having no patience for politeness or etiquette. My gaze swept the quarters, finding her—

I stopped just inside the door as she…as *Penellaphe* rose from the bed and spun, her fingers tangled in the braid she was unraveling.

She was unveiled.

And I was frozen for a few heartbeats as I took in her features. The proud brow. The stubborn curve of her jaw. Her open mouth, lips parted in surprise. She was—

Snapping out of it, I kicked the door shut behind me. Irritation with myself built. "It's time for that talk, Princess." I glanced over to where Tawny stood. "Your services are no longer needed this evening."

Tawny's mouth dropped open.

Penellaphe's hands slipped from her hair. "You don't have the authority to dismiss her!"

"I don't?" I arched a brow. "As your personal Royal Guard, I have the authority to remove any threats."

"Threats?" Tawny's brows snapped together. "I'm not a threat."

"You pose the threat of making up excuses or lying on behalf of Penellaphe. Just like you said she was asleep when I know for a fact that she was on the Rise," I pointed out.

Tawny closed her mouth, then turned to Penellaphe. "I have a feeling I'm missing an important piece of information."

"I didn't get a chance to tell you," Penellaphe began. "And it wasn't that important."

I snorted. "I'm sure it was one of the most important things to have happened to you in a long time."

Penellaphe's eyes narrowed. "You have an overinflated sense of involvement in my life if you really think that."

"I think I have a good grasp on just how much of a role I play in your life."

"Doubtful," she shot back.

My lips twitched as I met her glare. "I do wonder if you actually believe half the lies you tell."

"I am not lying," she said as Tawny's attention jerked back and forth between us. "Thank you very much."

I lost the fight then and smiled. "Whatever you need to tell yourself, Princess."

"Don't call me that!" She stomped her foot.

My brow rose. That was…adorable. Her foot stomping. Especially because I suspected she'd prefer my face under that foot. "Did that make you feel good?"

"Yes!" she exclaimed. "Because the only other option is to kick you."

I'd been right. I chuckled, thoroughly enjoying this side of her. "So violent."

Her hands fisted. "You shouldn't be in here."

"I'm your personal guard," I replied. "I can be wherever I feel I am needed to keep you safe."

"And what do you think you need to protect me from in here?" She made a show of looking around. "An unruly bedpost I might stub my toe on? Oh, wait, are you worried I might faint? I know how good you are at handling such emergencies."

"You do look a little pale," I said. "My ability to catch frail, delicate females may come in handy."

Penellaphe sucked in a sharp breath.

"But as far as I can determine, other than a random abduction attempt, you, Princess, are the greatest threat to yourself."

"Well…" Tawny drew out the word. "He kind of has a point there."

"You're absolutely no help," she snapped.

"Penellaphe and I do need to speak," I said. "I can assure you that she is safe with me, and I'm sure that whatever I'm about to discuss with her, she'll tell you all about it later."

Tawny crossed her arms. "Yes, she will, but that's not nearly as entertaining as witnessing it."

Penellaphe sighed. "It's okay, Tawny. I'll see you in the morning."

"Seriously?" Tawny cried.

"Seriously," she confirmed. "I have a feeling that if you don't leave, he's just going to stand there and drain precious air from my room—"

"While looking exceptionally handsome," I added, just to get a rise out of her. It worked. Her brows slammed down. "You forgot to add that."

Tawny giggled.

"And I would like to get some rest before the sun rises," Penellaphe said.

Tawny exhaled loudly. "Fine." She glanced at me. "*Princess.*"

"Oh, my gods," Penellaphe muttered.

I watched Tawny leave. "I like her."

"Good to know," she said. "What is it you wish to talk about that couldn't wait until the morning?"

Turning back to her, I allowed myself to look at her—to really see her. The remaining braid had unraveled. She had...a lot of hair. I hadn't really noticed that at the Red Pearl, and any other time I'd seen her, it had been bound. "You have beautiful hair."

She blinked, seeming caught off guard. Fuck, I caught *myself* off guard. She recovered quickly, though. "Is that what you wanted to talk about?"

"Not exactly." I lowered my gaze then, my attention not straying very far from her face until then.

I shouldn't have allowed myself to do so because courtesy of the flickering light from the fireplace and the lamps, I saw *a lot.*

She wore a thin, white sleeping gown that left only the most hidden parts of her to my imagination. And the gods knew I had a vast imagination. But what I saw...

Was perfection.

From the slope of her shoulders to the very tips of her toes curled against stone was utter perfection, especially everything in between. The gown was loose, but the ample curves of her body were visible beneath it. The swells of her full breasts. The slight inward curve of her waist, the flare of her hips, and those lush thighs.

Godsdamn.

I dragged my gaze back to hers. A pretty flush had appeared on her cheeks as she started for the robe lying at the foot of the bed.

One side of my lips curved up.

She stopped, lifting her gaze to mine. That chin rose a notch as I waited for her to cover herself, half of me hoping she would.

The other half silently begging her not to.

She didn't. She held herself still in an odd, intriguing mix of shyness and boldness that was...just devastating. I needed to leave this chamber and clear my head. Center myself.

I didn't.

"Was that all you were wearing under the cloak?" I asked.

"That's none of your concern," she responded.

She *had* been. For fuck's sake, she'd been fighting me practically nude beneath the cloak. That realization got my blood pumping even hotter, which was the last thing I needed. "Feels like it should be," I said.

Her chest rose sharply. "That sounds like your problem, not mine."

A laugh crawled up my throat as I stared at her, completely bemused. And aroused. Wholly intrigued. And, gods, I couldn't remember the last thing that truly intrigued me. Honestly, I shouldn't enjoy this side of her. A submissive, frightened Maiden would be easier to deal with.

Nothing about her would be easy.

"You're…you're nothing like I expected."

She stared at me for a long moment. "Was it my skill with an arrow or the blade? Or was it the fact that I took you to the ground?"

"*Barely* took me to the ground," I corrected. "All of those things. But you forgot to add in the Red Pearl. I never expected to find the Maiden there."

She snorted. "I imagine not." Holding my stare for a moment more, she turned. The way she walked was completely different than I had seen from her before. Her steps were graceful and measured as the bare length of her leg peeked through the slit in her gown. Was it because she wasn't weighed down, literally or figuratively, by the chains of her veil?

"That was the first time I was in the Red Pearl." She sat, hands falling to her lap. I'd seen her sit like that as the Maiden, but it was different now. "And the reason I was on the second floor was because Vikter came in." Her nose wrinkled. "He would've recognized me, mask or not. I went upstairs because a woman told me the room was empty. I'm not telling you this because I feel like I need to explain myself, I'm just…telling the truth. I didn't know you were in the room."

"But you knew who I was," I said.

"Of course." Her attention turned to the fire. Flames rippled over the thick log. "Your arrival had already stirred up quite a bit of…talk."

"Flattered," I murmured.

Her lips curved up slightly. "Why I decided to stay in the room isn't up for discussion."

Discussion of that wasn't exactly necessary. "I know why you stayed in the room."

"You do?"

"It makes sense now." And it had made sense then. She was there because she wanted to live.

"What are you going to do about me being on the Rise?" she asked, her fingers twisting in her lap.

Did she think I would tell on her? I went over to where she sat and gestured at the empty seat. "May I?"

She nodded.

I sat across from her, elbows resting on my knees as I watched the shadows from the fire dance over her features. "It was Vikter who trained you, wasn't it?"

There was no answer, but her pulse jumped.

"It had to be him," I surmised. "You two are close, and he's been with you since you arrived in Masadonia."

"You've been asking questions."

"I'd be stupid not to learn everything I could about the person I'm duty-bound to die to protect." Or steal away.

"I'm not going to answer your question."

"Because you're afraid I'll go to the Duke, even though I didn't before?" I figured.

"You said out on the Rise that you should," she reminded me. "That it would make your job easier. I'm not going to bring anyone else down with me."

I tilted my head. "I said I *should*, not that I *would*."

"There's a difference?"

"You should know there is." My gaze flickered over the elegant slopes of her cheekbones. The scars did nothing to detract from her appearance. Was her beauty why they kept her veiled? It made keeping her...*virtue* safe easier. I shoved those thoughts aside. "What would His Grace do if I had gone to him?"

Her fingers curled inward. "It doesn't matter."

Bullshit. "Then why did you say I had no idea what he'd do? You sounded as if you were going to say more but stopped yourself."

Inhaling deeply, she looked at the fire. "I wasn't going to say anything."

I didn't believe that for a second. I thought back to when she had gone to see the Duke. Her absence. "Both you and Tawny reacted strangely to his summons."

"We weren't expecting to hear from him," she explained.

"Why were you in your room for almost two days after being summoned by him?" I watched her closely, not missing how her fingers pressed hard into her palms, and thought of the nightmare she'd had last night. What I'd smelled on her. Pine and sage. Arnica. The plant was used for many things, including healing wounds and bruises.

Sitting back, I folded my hands around the arms of the chair as an icy anger built inside me. "What did he do to you?"

"Why do you even care?"

"Why wouldn't I?" I asked. She knew nothing of my plans, and they didn't include her being harmed—well, harmed more than she had been already.

Slowly, she tilted her face back to me. "You don't know me—"

"I bet I know you better than most."

Her cheeks were pink again. "That doesn't mean you know me, Hawke. Not enough to care."

"I know you're not like the other members of the Court," I reasoned.

"I'm not a member of the Court," she stated.

My brows flew up. "You're the Maiden. You're viewed as a child of the gods by the commoners. They see you as higher than an Ascended, but I know you're compassionate. That night at the Red Pearl, when we talked about death, you genuinely felt sympathy for any losses I'd experienced. It wasn't a forced nicety."

"How do you know?"

"I'm a good judge of people's words," I said. "You wouldn't speak out of fear of being discovered until I referred to Tawny as your maid. You defended her at the risk of exposing yourself." I paused, thinking of what I'd seen during the City Council. "And I saw you."

"Saw what?"

I tipped forward again, lowering my voice. "I saw you during the City Council. You didn't agree with the Duke and Duchess. I couldn't see your face, but I could tell you were uncomfortable. You felt bad for that family."

She'd gone still. "So did Tawny."

I almost laughed. "No offense to your friend, but she looked half-asleep throughout most of that. I doubt she even knew what was going on."

Her fingers stilled a bit in her lap.

"And you know how to fight—and fight well," I continued. "Not only that, you're obviously brave. There are many men—*trained* men—who wouldn't go out on the Rise during a Craven attack if they didn't have to." I watched her closely as I said, "The Ascended could've gone out there, and they'd have a higher chance of surviving, yet they didn't. You did."

She shook her head. "Those things are just traits. They don't mean you know me well enough to care about what does and doesn't happen to me."

It didn't pass me by that she had no response to what I said about the Ascended, which was intriguing. "Would you care what happens to me?"

"Well, yes." Her brows knitted in a frown. "I would—"

"But you don't know me."

Her lips pursed.

I sat back, exhaling heavily. Respect for her took root. "You're a decent person, Princess. That's why you care."

"And you're not a decent person?"

I huffed. "I'm many things. Decent is rarely one of them."

Her nose scrunched as she appeared to mull that over.

It was time for me to get back to what she wouldn't speak of. "You're not going to tell me what the Duke did, are you?" I stretched a bit. "You know, I'll find out one way or another."

A faint smile appeared. "If you think so."

"I know so," I said, and that prickle at the nape of my neck came again. My grip on the chair relaxed as we sat in silence for a few seconds. The strangest, most inexplicable feeling came over me. "It's weird, isn't it?"

"What is?"

Our gazes locked, and I felt it again. That prickle at my neck. A hitch in my chest. The sensation that I… "How it feels like I've known you longer. You feel that, too." The moment the words left my mouth, I thought I should perhaps punch myself in the dick. They sounded foolish. They *were* foolish. Didn't change what I felt, though.

Her lips parted, and I thought she might respond. Or, at the very least, laugh at me. She did neither, apparently having more sense than I did and keeping her innermost thoughts quiet. She looked away, her gaze dropping to her hands.

I decided to change the subject. "Why were you on the Rise?"

"Wasn't it obvious?"

"Your motivation wasn't. At least tell me that," I persisted. "Tell me what drove you to go up there to fight them."

She was quiet as she relaxed her fingers, sliding two of them under her right sleeve. "The scar on my face. Do you know how I got it?"

"Your family was attacked by some Craven when you were a child," I said. "Vikter..."

"He filled you in?" A tired smile appeared as her hand slid out from under the sleeve. "It's not the only scar. When I was six, my parents decided to leave the capital for Niel Valley. They wanted a much quieter life, or so I'm told. I don't remember much from the trip other than my mother and father being incredibly tense throughout the whole thing. Ian and I were young and didn't know a lot about the Craven, so we weren't afraid of being out there or stopping at one of the smaller villages—a place I was told later hadn't seen a Craven attack in decades."

I stayed quiet as she spoke, my focus solely on her. I didn't even blink.

"There was just a short wall, like most of the smaller towns, and we were staying at the inn only for one night. The place smelled like cinnamon and cloves. I remember that." Her eyes closed. "They came at night, in the mist. There was no time once they appeared. My father...he went out onto the street to try and fend them off while my mother hid us, but they came through the door and the windows before she could even step outside."

My grip on the arms of the chair tightened as she swallowed. Good gods, she must have been so terrified.

"A woman—someone who was staying at the inn—was able to grab Ian and pull him into this hidden room, but I hadn't wanted to leave my mom and it just..." Her brows knitted together as her face paled. "I woke up days later, back in the capital. Queen Ileana was by my side. She told me what had happened. That our parents were gone."

"I'm sorry," I said, and I meant it. "I truly am. It's a miracle you survived."

"The gods protected me. That's what the Queen told me," she said. "That I was Chosen. I came to learn later that it was one of the reasons the Queen had begged my mother and father not to leave the safety of the capital. That...that if the Dark One became aware of the Maiden being unprotected, he'd send the Craven after me."

My jaw ached from how tightly I clenched it. I had absolutely nothing to do with what had happened to her family. I hadn't even known about her at that point.

"He wanted me dead then, but apparently, he wants me alive now." She laughed, and it sounded pained as she looked at me.

I forced my tone level. "What happened to your family is not your fault, and there could be any number of reasons for why they attacked that village." I lifted a hand from the chair, dragging it through my hair. "What else do you remember?"

"No one...no one in that inn knew how to fight. Not my parents, none of the women, or even the men. They all relied on the handful of guards." She rubbed her hands together. "If my parents knew how to defend themselves, they could've survived. It might've been just a small chance, but one nonetheless."

Then I got it. Right then. Why she'd learned how to fight. "And you want that chance."

She nodded. "I won't...I refuse to be helpless."

I knew that promise all too well. "No one should be."

A soft breath left her as her fingers stilled. "You saw what happened tonight. They reached the top of the Rise. If one makes it over, more will follow. No Rise is impenetrable, and even if it were, mortals come back from outside the Rise cursed. It happens more than people realize. At any moment, that curse could spread in this city. If I'm going down—"

"You'll go down fighting."

She nodded again.

I was quiet for a moment, processing all of that. "Like I said, you're very brave."

"I don't think it's bravery." Her gaze returned to her hands. "I think it's...fear."

"Fear and bravery are often one and the same." I told her what my father had once told Malik and me, when we were first learning how to wield a sword. "It either makes you a warrior or a coward. The only difference is the person it resides inside."

Her gaze lifted to mine. "You sound so many years older than what you appear."

"Only half of the time," I replied with a small grin. "You saved lives tonight, Princess."

"But many died."

"Too many," I agreed. "The Craven are a never-ending plague."

Her head fell back against the chair as she wiggled her tiny toes at the fire. "As long as an Atlantian lives, there will be Craven."

"That is what they say." I turned to the dying fire, reminding myself she didn't know any better. Most mortals didn't. They... Something else occurred to me. Things began to click into place. The admiration people held for her went beyond being told she was Chosen by the gods. What Jole Crain had said. Those white handkerchiefs and the people who helped bring peace to those afflicted. "You said that more come back from outside the Rise cursed than people realize. How do you know that?"

Silence

"I've heard rumors," I lied. My gaze slid to her. "It's not spoken about a lot, and when it is, it's only whispered."

"You're going to need to be more detailed."

"I've heard that the child of the gods has helped those who are cursed," I told her, thinking of Jole. "That she has aided them, given them death with dignity."

She wet her lips. "Who has said such things?" she asked.

"A few of the guards," I said, which wasn't true. One guard had said it—one dying guard. "I didn't believe them at first, to be honest."

"Well, you should've stuck with your initial reaction," she said. "They're mistaken if they think I would commit outright treason against the Crown."

I knew she wasn't been truthful. "Didn't I just tell you that I was a good judge of character?"

"So?"

"So, I know you're lying and I understand why you would. Those men speak of you with such awe that before I even met you, I half-expected you to be a child of the gods," I told her. "They would never report you."

"That may be the case, but you heard them talking about it. Others could hear them, as well."

"Perhaps I should be clearer in what I said about hearing rumors. They were actually speaking to me," I clarified. "Since I, too, have helped those who are cursed die with dignity. I did so in the capital and do so here, as well." Which was true. Jole wasn't the first, nor would he be the last.

Her lips parted as she stared at me. Clearly, she hadn't expected me to say that.

"Those who come back cursed have already given all for the kingdom," I told her. "Being treated as anything other than the heroes they are, and being dragged in front of the public to be murdered is the last thing they or their families should have to go through."

She continued staring, but a faint sheen appeared in those jewel-green eyes. A moment passed. Then another as we stared at each other. I didn't know what she was thinking. Damn, I didn't know what *I* was thinking. She'd shocked the fuck out of me tonight. Multiple times. It was a lot to process. And I was sure she didn't know what to think of me, either. It was clear that she didn't entirely trust me, not with her secrets, at least, and I needed her trust.

I *wanted* it.

But I wouldn't get that tonight.

I leaned forward in the chair. "I've kept you up long enough."

She raised an eyebrow. "That is all you have to say about me being on the Rise?"

"I ask only one thing of you." I rose. "The next time you go out, wear better shoes and thicker clothing. Those slippers are likely to be the death of you." I glanced at the too-thin gown and almost groaned. "And that dress...the death of me."

GOOD GRACES

"Why are you keeping your silence?"

Frowning, I turned to Vikter. We'd been standing in the quiet while Tawny helped Penellaphe ready herself for the summons. The Teermans had to address the people of the city following the Craven attack. Too many had died for them to write it off as a small incident. "What am I keeping my silence on?"

Alert and always-wary blue eyes met mine. "That she was on the Rise."

I spared a glance at the door, images of her aiming an arrow at me alternating with the vision of her standing in her bedchamber, unveiled with her hair a wild tumble over her shoulders. "Why didn't you ask this of me when I came to you last night?" I'd gone to him as soon as I left her chambers, partly out of irritation and strategy. I wanted to know why the fuck he'd been out beyond the Rise when he was supposed to be guarding her. I also figured that if she told him before I did, he would think I was keeping something from him. That could lead to him being more wary than he already was, which would further lead to him poking around until he began discovering all the other, more important things I was keeping from him.

"I had a chance to sleep on it," Vikter retorted. "So, I'm asking you now."

"Am I not supposed to keep what I saw a secret?" I asked. "Should I have reported her to His Grace?"

I took a deep breath as he turned to face me. "I asked you a serious question, Hawke."

"As did I of you," I countered.

His patience was about as thin as his mouth was becoming. So was mine. We had that in common at the moment. "You know damn well she's not supposed to be outside the castle without a guard, let alone on the Rise."

"Technically, I did report her. To you—the one who was supposed to be watching her last night," I pointed out, and he snapped his jaw shut so hard I swore I heard his bones creak. "Perhaps she wouldn't have been out on the Rise if you had remained at your station." I let that sink in. "At least now I know *why* you would leave the Maiden unguarded during a Craven attack."

Vikter said nothing to that.

"However, I have a feeling that she would've found her way out there even if you had remained at her door," I continued, returning my attention to the closed door, thinking of her reasons for being on the Rise. "She told me why she needed to be out there."

·"And?" Vikter pressed.

Eyeing the grain of the wood, I wondered exactly what she had shared with the Royal Guard to prompt this round of questions. "And I respect that—needing to do something other than relying on others to protect oneself."

"Because of what she's been through?"

Yes.

And no.

My respect for that—for *her*—was a complicated mess. "Even if she hadn't experienced what she did with the Craven, I can still understand why someone would want to be more active in their protection and defense of those they care about."

"Most would not, especially given who she is."

Frustration flared. "I'm not most people." I looked at him. "And neither are you."

His eyes narrowed. "What's that supposed to mean?"

"Come on now, Vikter." I chuckled, shaking my head. "You think I don't know who trained her to fight and use a bow? You did one hell of a job. She almost knocked me on my ass."

"Obviously, not a good enough job," he muttered. "If so, you would've been on your ass."

I smiled at that. He had no idea how truly impressive that *almost* was. "Like I told her, I'm not going to report her to the Teermans or anyone else."

Vikter was quiet for only a few moments. "Doesn't make sense."

I sighed.

"You could earn the Teermans' favor by keeping them informed," Vikter reasoned. "Get in even better with them."

Reminding myself that punching Vikter wouldn't earn me any of those so-called favors, I said, "I have no desire to be in their good graces."

He stood so close now that I'd feel his chest move against my arm if he breathed. "Then is it your desire to get into *her* good graces?"

Irritation sparked as I slowly turned to him. "Now it is I who is asking what that's supposed to mean."

His gaze locked with mine for several tense moments. "She is the Maiden. It's best you not forget that."

I knew what he was getting at, and he had every reason to remind me of that. More than he realized because I didn't think of her as the Maiden any longer. For the last dozen or so hours, when I did think of her, I saw her as I had last night, not on the Rise but in her bedchamber, in that barely there nightgown. I saw no problem with the latter. The former, though? Not thinking of her as the Maiden? That could be problematic.

Because just like with the respect, it was a complicated mess.

"I spent the better part of the day thinking about why you would keep her secret. What you'd gain from doing so," Vikter went on. "You know what I came up with?"

"I'm sure you'll tell me," I muttered.

"You're trying to gain her trust."

Vikter was right. I needed her trust. I wanted it, and there was a whole realm of difference between wanting and needing. And that was the third complicated mess I found myself in.

"Of course, I want her trust," I said. "I won't be able to do my duty if she doesn't trust me."

"That's true." Vikter faced the door. "And that'd better be the only reason you seek her trust."

"Correct me if I'm wrong," I said, "though I'm pretty sure I'm not. However, I do believe you said that you didn't need to know what I was thinking for either of us to carry out our duties."

I watched the muscle throbbing in his jaw. Smiling, I returned to staring at the door.

"You weren't wrong," Vikter admitted after a moment.

"I know. I rarely am." I heard footsteps nearing from the other side, thank the gods.

"Hawke?"

"Yeah?"

"You can be right." He moved in front of me as the door finally opened. "And still be wrong."

FROM BLOOD AND ASH

"Because of the gods' Blessing, the Rise did not fall last night." Duke Teerman shouted his lie for everyone in Masadonia and then some to hear.

I could barely stop myself from laughing my ass right off the balcony as I stood behind Penellaphe and Tawny. The Rise had held because of those who defended it, many who died doing so. *Too many*, I thought as I eyed the crowd below. The air was still heavy with the smoke of the funeral pyres and incense. I couldn't even count how many wore the white of mourning or who had hung black flags from their homes.

"They reached the top!" a man yelled from below, where the throng of people stood in the light of the oil lamps and torches. "They almost made it over the Rise. Are we safe?"

"When it happens again?" Duchess Teerman replied. "Because it will happen again."

"That will surely ease fears," I murmured.

"The truth is not designed to ease fears," Vikter responded just as quietly.

I smirked. "Is that why we tell lies, then?"

"And what lie has been spoken?" he countered.

As if there was only one. "That the gods were responsible for the Rise not falling. Those who defended it are."

"Those two things aren't mutually exclusive," he replied.

For a moment, I entertained the idea of picking Vikter up by the throat and tossing him off the balcony. However, I supposed that wouldn't help me gain Penellaphe's trust.

"The gods didn't fail you," Duchess Teerman said as she walked forward, placing her hands on the waist-high railing. "We didn't fail you. But the gods *are* unhappy. That is why the Craven reached the top of the Rise."

A wave of fear swept through those below like a flood.

"We have spoken to them," the Duchess continued with what had to be the least reassuring speech I'd ever heard in my life. Those in the crowd were growing paler by the second. "They are not pleased with recent events, here and in nearby cities. They fear that the good people of Solis have begun to lose faith in their decisions and are turning to those who wish to see the future of this great kingdom compromised."

What a load of bullshit.

Effective bullshit, though. The crowd shouted their protests, much like the guards had last night, when Jansen had asked if they would let the Rise fail. The horses' nervous prancing drew my attention as I scanned the crowd, spotting Kieran on horseback.

"What did you all think would happen when those who support the Dark One and plot with him are standing among you right now?" the Duke demanded. "As I speak, at this very moment, Descenters stare back at me, thrilled that the Craven took so many lives last night."

Kieran inclined his head, and I knew he was likely struggling as much as I was, doing nothing as the Ascended spewed their ridiculous lies.

"In this very crowd, there are Descenters who pray for the day the Dark One comes," the Duke said. And that was true. "Those who celebrated the massacre of Three Rivers and the fall of Goldcrest Manor. Look to your left and to your right, and you may see someone who helped conspire to abduct the Maiden."

My eyes narrowed as Penellaphe shifted from one foot to the other.

"The gods hear and know all. Even what's not spoken but resides in the heart," the Duke said from where he stood beside his wife. "What can any of us expect? When those the gods have done all to protect, come before us, questioning the Rite?"

What in the fuck?

Penellaphe went still as my narrowed-eye gaze swung back to the Duke. What happened last night had nothing to do with the gods, let alone the Tulises, who he was clearly speaking of.

"What can anyone expect when there are those who wish to see us dead?" the Duke asked, lifting his hands. "When we are the gods given form and the only thing that stands between you and the Dark One and the curse his people have cast upon this land."

It took everything in me not to laugh. The Ascended wouldn't stand between the people and a mouse.

The Duke continued jabbering on with his nonsense, riling up the crowd and filling them with anxiety and anger just like a damn Soul Eater would. This was how you controlled the masses. Give them something to fear, to blame for all your losses, and to hate. It never ceased to amaze me how effective it was, and yet—

Kieran caught my attention, jerking his chin toward the front of the crowd. Checking out the faces below, I stopped on a familiar blond-haired and broad-shouldered male making his way forward.

Lev Barron.

Shit.

What was he up to? For the last half an hour or so, he'd been steadily creeping closer to the front of the mass of people. He wasn't the only one. Three more flanked him, those I didn't recognize. Contrary to what the Duke would say, I didn't know every single Descenter.

Penellaphe suddenly stepped back.

Vikter caught her by the shoulder. "Are you all right?"

I focused on her. She was still, but she was trembling. I didn't think anyone else noticed. Who could blame her given what the Duke was shouting at the top of his godsdamn lungs?

"But if we continue as we have, the gods may not bless us again. The Craven will breach the Rise and then there will be nothing but sorrow," Duke Teerman said. "And, if you're lucky, they'll go for your throat, and it will be a quick death. Most of you will not be so fortunate. They'll tear into your flesh and tissue, feasting on your blood while you scream for the gods you've lost faith in."

Good fucking gods… "This is perhaps the least calming speech ever given after an attack," I muttered.

Penellaphe jerked slightly, but the trembling appeared to have ceased a few moments later. Tension brewed in my gut as I stared at the straight line of her back. Based on what I had seen last night and what I knew before then, she wasn't someone who scared easily.

But she knew exactly what it felt like to have what the Duke spoke of done to her. That was pain and fear she knew firsthand.

Yet she still went out and helped those infected, knowing they could turn at any second.

My reluctant respect for her grew.

Penellaphe tipped her head to Vikter. "Do you see him?" she

whispered. "The blond male near the guards. He's large-shouldered. Tall. Wearing a brown cloak. Clearly angry."

Surprise swept through me as she described Lev. How in the whole wide realm had she caught sight of him?

"Yes." Vikter inched closer to her.

"There are others like him," she said.

"I see them," Vikter confirmed. "Be alert, Hawke. There—"

"May be trouble?" I interrupted, finding Lev once more in the crowd. Yes, he was clearly angry. It was written all over the hard set of his features, and others appeared just like him. Silent. Fury etched on their faces. "I've been tracking the blond for twenty minutes. He's slowly working his way to the front. Three more have also inched closer."

"Are we safe?" Tawny asked quietly.

"Always," I murmured. They were. Lev? I had a feeling he wouldn't be.

Penellaphe nodded when Tawny looked at her, her hand lowering to the right side of her gown. The corners of my lips kicked up. She had that dagger on her, didn't she?

Cheers rang out suddenly, and I guessed the Teermans had finally said something inspiring.

"And we will honor their faith in the people of Solis by not shielding those you suspect of supporting the Dark One, who seek nothing but destruction and death," the Duchess said. "You will be rewarded greatly in this life and in the one beyond. That, we can promise you."

The crowd was joyous in their response, even shouting how they would honor the gods during the Rite.

If the gods were actually awake, they'd probably strike the Duchess down right where she stood.

The Duchess pushed back from the ledge, standing by the Duke's side. "What better way to show the gods our gratitude than to celebrate the Rite?"

"Lies!" Lev shouted from the crowd. "*Liars.*"

Dammit, what was he thinking?

"You do nothing to protect us while you hide in your castles, behind your guards! You do nothing but steal children in the name of false gods!" Lev yelled. "Where are the third and fourth sons and daughters? Where are they really?"

A murmur of shock swept through the crowd and from Penellaphe.

Lev reached inside his cloak, and damn, he was fast. He cocked back his arm—

"Seize him!" shouted Jansen.

Vikter shouldered Penellaphe back a second before I folded an arm around her waist, drawing her against me as an object flew past us, smacking into the wall and falling to the balcony floor.

Lev had thrown a hand—a Craven hand.

Vikter bent, picking it up. "What in the name of the gods?"

Holding onto Penellaphe, I found Lev on his knees, arms twisted back, and blood smeared across his mouth. My arm tightened around Penellaphe's waist as I fought the instinct to intervene. I couldn't. There was nothing anyone could do for Lev now. He knew that, yet he still glared up at the balcony with defiance—he stared at Penellaphe.

At *me* as he yelled, "From blood and ash—" A guard gripped the back of his head. "We will rise! From blood and ash, we will rise!"

We would.

For him.

For all those who stayed silent, who couldn't speak.

We would rise.

THERE IS A
CHOICE

"Where in the world did that man get a Craven's hand?" Tawny asked as we crossed under the banners, moving past the Great Hall while Vikter remained behind to speak to the Commander.

"He could've been outside the Rise and cut it off one of those who was killed last night," I figured, walking beside Penellaphe but staying a step back, my thoughts on Lev and his inevitable fate. I didn't know the man all that well, but I hated not knowing a damn thing about what would happen to him.

He should've stayed quiet, but he'd hit a breaking point, and I was sure the babe that had turned Craven had a hell of a lot to do with it. It was understandable. There would be more like him. That should thrill me. It didn't because they would meet the same fate as Lev.

"That's…" Tawny swallowed as she pressed her hand to her chest. "I really have no words for that."

"I can't believe he said what he did about the children—the third and fourth sons and daughters," Penellaphe said.

"Neither can I," Tawny agreed.

What he asked was a damn good question. Those children were not serving the gods. They were nothing more than cattle.

"I wouldn't be surprised if more people thought along those same lines," I said, raising my brows as they looked at me in shock. Well, I could only assume that was how Penellaphe looked at me. She was wearing the damn veil. "None of those children have been seen."

"They've been seen by the Priests and Priestesses and the Ascended," Tawny said.

"But not by family." I scanned the atrium, seeing nothing but statues. "Perhaps if people could see their children every so often, beliefs like that could easily be dismissed. Fears allayed."

"No one should make claims like that without any evidence," Penellaphe argued. "All it does is cause unnecessary worry and panic— panic that the Descenters have created and then will exploit."

"Agreed," I murmured, glancing down as we reached the staircase. "Watch your step. Wouldn't want you to continue with your new habit, Princess."

"Tripping once isn't a habit," she stated. "And if you agree, then why would you say you wouldn't be surprised if more felt the same way?"

Because I didn't agree. However, I couldn't say that. "Because agreeing doesn't mean I don't understand why some would think that. If the Ascended are truly concerned about those claims being believed, all they need to do is allow the children to be seen. I can't imagine that would interfere too badly with their servitude to the gods."

Penellaphe glanced at her friend. "What do you think?"

"I think you are both saying the same thing," she said.

One side of my lips curled as we climbed the steps in silence and entered the floor for their chambers. Upon reaching Tawny's room, I stopped. "If you don't mind, I need to speak to Penellaphe in private for a moment."

Tawny looked at Penellaphe as if she were on the brink of either shouting or laughing.

"It's fine," Penellaphe assured her.

Tawny nodded, opening her door. "If you need me, knock." She gave a dramatic pause. "*Princess.*"

Penellaphe groaned as the door shut.

I laughed. "I really do like her."

"I'm sure she'd love to hear that."

"Would you love to hear that I really like you?" I teased, facing her.

"Would you be sad if I said no?"

"I'd be devastated."

Penellaphe snorted. "I'm sure."

I grinned. Her snarkiness… I liked it.

She went to open her door. "What did you need to talk about?"

I stepped in front of her. "I should enter first, Princess."

"Why? Do you think someone could be waiting for me?"

"If the Dark One came for you once, he'll come for you again," I said with an impressively straight face as I walked into her quarters.

Two oil lamps were on by the bed and the door. Wood burned in the fireplace. Yet the chamber felt cold and devoid of life.

I took note of another door, one closer to the windows. I hadn't noticed it the other night—I'd been too busy looking at her—but I thought I'd discovered how she left her chambers unnoticed. I had a feeling that door led to one of the many unused servants' staircases in the old wing. I smiled.

"Is it okay for me to enter?" she asked from behind me. "Or should I wait out here while you inspect under the bed for stray dust bunnies?"

I looked over my shoulder. "It's not dust bunnies I'm worried about. Steps, on the other hand? Yes."

"Oh, my gods—"

"And the Dark One will keep coming until he has what he wants," I said, looking away. "Your room should always be checked before you enter it." Facing her, I thought of how shaken she'd been earlier. "Are you all right?"

"Yes. Why do you ask?"

"Something appeared to happen to you as the Duke addressed the people."

"I was…" One shoulder lifted. "I got a little dizzy. I guess I haven't eaten enough today."

Unable to see anything above her mouth, I couldn't tell if she spoke the truth. "I hate this."

Her head tilted. "Hate what?"

"I hate talking to the veil."

"Oh." She reached up, touching the chains. "I imagine most people don't enjoy it."

"I can't imagine *you* do."

"I don't," she admitted, and a surge of…something went through me. Satisfaction upon hearing she didn't like wearing the veil? I didn't think that was it. "I mean, I'd prefer if people were able to see me."

I preferred that. "What does it feel like?"

Her lips parted, but she was quiet, unbearably so, as she walked to one of the chairs and sat. I didn't think she would answer.

Then she did. "It feels suffocating."

My chest clenched as I watched her. I almost wished she hadn't answered. Or I hadn't asked the question. "Then why do you wear it?"

"I didn't realize I had a choice."

"You have a choice now." I knelt in front of her. "It's just you and me, walls, and a pathetically inadequate supply of furniture."

Those lips twitched.

"Do you wear your veil when you're with Tawny?" I asked.

She shook her head.

"Then why are you wearing it now?"

"Because...I'm allowed to be without my veil with her."

"I was told that you were supposed to be veiled at all times, even with those approved to see you," I said.

She had no response to that.

So, I waited.

She sighed. "I don't wear my veil when I'm in my room, and I don't expect anyone to come in other than Tawny. And I don't wear it then because I feel...more in control. I can make—"

"The choice not to wear it?" I guessed.

Penellaphe nodded slowly.

"You have a choice now," I told her.

"I do," she whispered.

I searched the veil, unable to see anything but shadows beneath it. But her hands...they were twitching in her lap again, revealing what I couldn't see in her features. I rose. "I'll be outside if you need anything."

Penellaphe was silent as I left her quarters. I took up my position outside her door, my heart pounding too fast for not having done anything. I stared at the wall across from me. Why had I spoken of choice? I wasn't sure, except that I felt it was important she understood it existed. That she knew it was okay to go unveiled around me. And that had nothing to do with me needing her trust.

It had nothing to do with my plans at all.

A TOUCH OF PEACE

"Skotos," Priestess Analia interrupted Penellaphe. "It's pronounced like Sko*tis*."

My eyes narrowed on the Priestess's back. That was *not* how Skotos was pronounced.

"You know how it's pronounced, Maiden," the Priestess continued in that sharp tone that had been grating on my nerves since we'd entered the chamber. Every word the woman spoke was delivered with a hornet's sting. "Do so correctly."

Penellaphe took a breath and began again, reading from a tome that was far too large to be filled with only lies.

And, apparently, mispronunciations.

Then again, who really knew what was in the book or what the purpose of reading from it was when the Priestess continually interrupted Penellaphe every five fucking seconds? I wanted to snatch the book from her hands and whack the woman upside the head with it. Better yet, I would pay good coin to see Penellaphe pick up the hard stool she sat upon and throw it at the Priestess. I smirked. That may be extreme, but damn if I wouldn't find satisfaction in watching it go down.

I would also find satisfaction in tossing the Priestess's ass out the window.

Needless to say, I was in a bad mood.

And there was a whole slew of reasons for that, namely lack of sleep. Which hadn't been any easier to come by in my quarters than in the dorm. Part of it was due to what was surely happening to Lev, and the baseless accusations the Teermans' least motivational speech of the decade had already inspired, at least according to Jansen. Five people, none who had a damn thing to do with the Descenters, had been reported to the Commander. Then, when I'd managed to find sleep, nightmares found me, but instead of ones where I was caged, they were about my brother.

"*Which sat at the foot of the Skotis Mountains—*'"

"It's actually pronounced Skotos," I interrupted, unwilling to let this go.

Her veiled head shot toward me as the red-dressed Priestess stiffened where she sat across from Penellaphe. She turned to give me a once-over. Her brown hair was pulled back so sharply from her hawkish features it was a wonder the strands of hair hadn't snapped.

Priestess Analia's dark brown stare turned dismissive. "And how would you know?"

"My family originates from the farmlands not too far from Pompay, before the area was destroyed and became the Wastelands we know today," I said, which technically wasn't a lie. My family originated from that general vicinity. "My family and others from that area have always pronounced the mountain range as the Maiden first said. The language and accent of those from the Far East can be difficult…for some to master. The Maiden, however, appears to not fall into that group."

Penellaphe sucked her lower lip between her teeth and dipped her chin as if she sought to hide a smile.

The Priestess did not have a similar reaction. Her bony shoulders beneath the crimson gown went stiff. "I did not realize I asked for your thoughts."

"My apologies." I bowed my head. *Just a few more days*, I reminded myself. That's all.

Priestess Analia nodded. "Apology—"

"I just didn't want the Maiden to sound uneducated," I continued, enjoying the flush of anger creeping into the Priestess's cheeks, "if any discussion were to arise about the Skotos Mountains, but I will remain quiet from here on out." I looked at Penellaphe. Her mouth formed a perfect oval now. "Please, continue, Maiden. You have such a lovely reading voice that even I find myself enthralled with the history of Solis."

Her grip slowly loosened around the tome. "'*Which sat at the foot of the Skotos Mountains, the gods had finally chosen a side.*'"

That was bullshit.

"'*Nyktos, the King of the gods, and his son Theon, the God of War, appeared before Jalara and his army*,'" Penellaphe continued with yet another lie. Theon was not Nyktos's son. "'*Having grown distrustful of the Atlantian people*

230/Jennifer L. Armentrout

and their unnatural thirst for blood and power, they sought to aid in ending the cruelty and oppression that had reaped these lands under the rule of Atlantia. Jalara Solis and his army were brave, but Nyktos, in his wisdom, saw that they could not defeat the Atlantians, who had risen to godlike strength through the bloodletting of innocents—"'

"They killed hundreds of thousands over the time of their reign," the Priestess elaborated yet again, this time sounding damn near orgasmic. "Bloodletting is a gentle description of what they actually did. They *bit* people."

I would like to bite her right about now.

"Drank their blood and became drunk with power—with strength and near immortality," she continued. "And those they didn't kill became the pestilence we now know as the Craven. That is who our beloved King and Queen bravely took a stance against and were prepared to die to overthrow."

Penellaphe nodded.

"Continue," the Priestess ordered.

"'*Unwilling to see the failure of Jalara of the Vodina Isles, Nyktos gave the gods' first Blessing, sharing with Jalara and his army the blood of the gods,*'" Penellaphe read, giving a faint shudder. "'*Emboldened with the strength and power, Jalara of the Vodina Isles and his army were able to defeat the Atlantians during the Battle of Broken Bones, therefore ending the reign of the corrupt and wretched kingdom.*'"

Was this really what they were teaching people in Solis? My gods, it was all a load of crap. There was no Blessing given by the gods. They were already asleep. Nor did the counterfeit King defeat the Atlantian armies. Atlantia had retreated for the sake of the people—to end the war destroying the lives and futures of Atlantians and mortals alike.

Penellaphe started to turn a page, and, man, I couldn't wait to hear what was next.

"Why?" Priestess Analia demanded.

She looked over at her. "Why, what?"

"Why did you just shudder when you read the part about the Blessing?"

"I..." She trailed off, her fingers tightening around the edges of the book once more.

"You seemed disturbed," the Priestess said. "What is it about the Blessing that would affect you so?"

"I'm not disturbed. The Blessing is an honor—"

"But you shuddered," the Priestess pressed. "Unless you find the act of the Blessing pleasurable, am I not to assume that it disturbs you?"

What in the fuck kind of question was that? I didn't like the Priestess's tone nor the way she pitched forward toward Penellaphe.

The lower half of Penellaphe's face turned red. "It's just that…the Blessing seems to be similar to how the Atlantians became so powerful. They drank the blood of the innocent, and the Ascended drink the blood of the gods—"

"How dare you compare the Ascension to what the Atlantians have done?" Priestess Analia grasped Penellaphe's chin. My hand slid off the hilt of my sword. "It is not the same thing. Perhaps you've grown fond of the cane, and you purposely strive to disappoint not only me but also the Duke."

The cane?

"I didn't say that it was," Penellaphe said as I stepped forward. She didn't appear to be in pain, but this woman should not be touching her. "Just that it reminded me of—"

"The fact that you think of those two things in the same thought greatly concerns me, Maiden. The Atlantians took what was not given. During the Ascension, the blood is offered freely by the gods." The Priestess lashed out, delivering another verbal sting. "That is not something that I should have to explain to the future of the kingdom, to the legacy of the Ascended."

"The future of the entire kingdom rests on me being given to the gods upon my nineteenth birthday?" Penellaphe asked. "What would happen if I didn't Ascend?" she demanded, and I halted, needing to hear the answer to this. "How would that stop the others from Ascending? Would the gods refuse to give their blood so freely—"

Priestess Analia swung her free hand back. I shot forward, grasping the Priestess's wrist. I was done with this. "Remove your fingers from the Maiden's chin. Now."

The Priestess's wide eyes met mine. "How dare you touch me?"

Hell. I wanted to do more. Crack those bones beneath my fingers for even having the gall to touch Penellaphe. "How dare you lay a single finger on the Maiden? Perhaps I was not clear enough for you. Remove your hand from the Maiden, or I will act upon your attempt to harm her," I warned, and a huge part of me hoped she lacked common sense. "And I can assure you, me touching you will be the least of your concerns."

A moment passed.

Then another. And, gods, I hoped she didn't. I really did.

I started to smile.

Unfortunately, the Priestess had a smidgen of common sense. She removed her hand from Penellaphe's chin. I had to force myself to let go of her wrist. I didn't want to. I wanted to make sure she couldn't use those hands to harm Penellaphe or anyone ever again.

The Priestess's rage was evident as she turned back to Penellaphe. I stayed close, right behind her. I didn't trust the woman at all. She'd raised a hand to Penellaphe far too casually, too easily for it to have been the first time. It was also clear to me that no one—no guard, and not even Penellaphe—had stopped her in the past.

I couldn't fathom how Penellaphe, who could wipe the floor with this woman's face, sat and took it. My anger built as I stared at the top of the Priestess's head.

"The mere fact that you would even speak such a thing shows that you have no respect for the honor bestowed upon you," Priestess Analia said to Penellaphe. "But when you go to the gods, you'll be treated with as much respect as you have shown today."

"What does that mean?" Penellaphe asked.

"This session is over." The Priestess rose. "I have too much to do with the Rite only two days away. I have no time to spend with someone as unworthy as you."

My eyes narrowed as my nostrils flared. This woman wouldn't know worthiness if it fell into her lap.

"I'm ready to return to my chambers," Penellaphe announced before I could tell the Priestess what I thought of her idea of worthiness. She nodded at the woman. "Good day."

Forcing myself to follow Penellaphe from the chamber, I added the woman to my list of those who may find themselves answering for their lies sooner rather than later.

Penellaphe didn't speak until we were halfway across the banquet hall. "You shouldn't have done that."

Disbelief thundered through me. "I should've allowed her to hit you? In what world would that have been acceptable?"

"In a world where you end up punished for something that wouldn't even have hurt."

I couldn't believe what I was hearing. "I don't care if she hits like a baby mouse, this world is fucked-up if anyone finds that acceptable."

Penellaphe halted and looked up at me through that damn veil. "Is it worth losing your position over and being ostracized for?"

She was worried about my position? Disbelief crashed into the simmering anger. "If you even have to ask that question, then you don't know me at all."

"I hardly know you at all," she whispered.

Dammit, she was right. She didn't know me. Fuck. I didn't even know myself half the time, but I did know this. "Well, now you know that I will never stand by and watch someone hit you or any person for no reason other than they feel they can."

Penellaphe appeared as if she were about to say something but changed her mind. She turned and began walking. I joined her, trying to cool my rage.

"It's not like I'm okay with how she treats me," she said quietly after several moments. "It took everything in me not to throw the book at her."

Admittedly, I was relieved to hear that. The idea of her just sitting there and taking it... "I wish you had."

"If I had, she would've reported me. She'll probably report you."

"To the Duke? Let her." I shrugged. "I can't imagine that he's okay with her striking the Maiden."

She snorted. "You don't know the Duke."

The way she said that... "What do you mean?"

"He would probably applaud her," Penellaphe remarked. "They share a lack of control when it comes to their tempers."

It came together then, though part of me had already figured it out. I just didn't want to consider it. "He's hit you," I bit out, aware of the servants' nervous glances in our direction as they passed. "Is that what she meant when she said that you'd grown fond of the cane?" I grasped her arm, my mind flashing to those canes in his private office and how she'd been absent for days after meeting with him. And the smell of arnica...? Fucking gods, I was going to kill the bastard. "Has he used a cane on you?"

She jerked a bit and then pulled her arm free. "I didn't say that."

"What were you saying?"

"J-just that the Duke is more likely to punish you than he is the Priestess. I have no idea what she meant by the cane," she quickly added. "She sometimes says things that make no sense."

She wasn't speaking the truth right now, but I knew. Fuck, *I knew*. The Priestess had hit her before. The Duke had caned her. She was accustomed to these punishments—punishments she didn't want me to know about.

I went cold inside.

Not hollow or empty.

Icy rage filled me, and only by sheer effort did I stop myself from finding the Duke right then and ending his miserable, pathetic existence. I briefly closed my eyes. "I must've misread what you said then."

"Yes," she confirmed. "I just don't want you to get into trouble."

She was worried about me? Again? "And what about you?"

"I'll be fine." Penellaphe began walking again. "The Duke will just...give me a lecture, make it a lesson, but you would face—"

"I'll face nothing," I promised. And neither would she. I forced the tension out of my neck. "Is she always like that?"

Penellaphe sighed. "Yes."

"The Priestess seems like a..." I couldn't think of anything appropriate to say. "A bitch. I don't say that often, but I say it now. Proudly."

A half-smothered laugh came from her. "She...she is something, and she's always disappointed in my...commitment to being the Maiden."

"Exactly how are you supposed to prove you are?" I asked, genuinely curious. "Better yet, what are you supposed to be committed to?"

Her veiled head turned to me sharply, and then she nodded. "I'm not quite sure. It's not like I'm trying to run away or escape my Ascension."

I glanced over at her as we entered a short, narrow hall full of windows. What an odd thing for her to say. "Would you?"

"Funny question," she murmured.

"It was a serious one."

Penellaphe didn't answer, and my heart started thumping a bit erratically. Had she considered doing that? Running away from her Ascension? If so...

I watched her go to a window overlooking the courtyard. She was so quiet and still, appearing as if she were a spirit garbed in the white of the Maiden. Then she looked up at me.

"I can't believe you'd ask that," she finally said.

I moved so I stood behind her, keeping my voice low. "Why?"

"Because I couldn't do that," she admitted, but there was no passion in her voice. Only hollowness. "I wouldn't."

My heart was still pounding. "It seems to me that this *honor* that has been bestowed upon you comes with very few benefits. You're not allowed to show your face or travel anywhere outside the castle grounds.

You didn't even seem all that surprised when the Priestess moved to strike you. That leads me to believe it's something fairly common. You are not allowed to speak to most, and you are not to be spoken to. You're caged in your room most of the day, your freedom restricted. All the rights others have, are privileges for you, rewards that seem impossible for you to earn."

She opened her mouth but only looked away. I couldn't blame her for that.

"So, I wouldn't be surprised if you did try to escape this *honor*," I told her.

"Would you stop me if I did?" she asked.

Hell, no. I'd hold the door for her. I stiffened. What was I thinking? My heart raced now. "Would Vikter?"

"I know Vikter cares about me. He's like…he's like I imagine my father would have been if he were still alive," she said. "And I'm like Vikter's daughter, who never got to take a breath. But he would stop me."

He would.

And so should I if she were to do that in the next two days. I needed her—

"So, would you?" she asked again.

I didn't know how to answer that, so I went with the truth. "I think I would be too curious to find out exactly how you planned to escape to stop you."

She laughed faintly. "You know, I actually believe that."

Shoving the conversation aside, I focused on what was important in this moment as I stared at the vibrant colors of the garden. "Will she report you to the Duke?"

"Why would you ask?"

"Will she?" I insisted.

"Probably not," she answered. I didn't believe her. "She's too busy with the Rite. Everyone is." She exhaled long and slow. "I've never been to a Rite."

"And you've never snuck into one?"

She lowered her chin. "I'm offended that you'd even suggest such a thing."

I chuckled, the noise sounding strange to my ears. "How bizarre that I could think that you, who has a history of misbehaving, would do such a thing."

She gave me a small grin.

Not a smile.

I didn't think she really smiled.

"You haven't missed much, to be honest. There's a lot of talking, a bunch of tears, and too much drinking," I told her, thinking of the Rites I'd seen in my time in Solis. "It's after the Rite where things can get...interesting. You know how it is."

"I don't know," she said.

One side of my lips kicked up. I had a feeling she knew exactly what happened after the Rite. "But you know how easy it is to be yourself when you wear a mask," I reminded her. "How anything you want becomes achievable when you can pretend that no one knows who you are."

"You shouldn't bring that up." Her voice was breathy.

I cocked my head. "No one is close enough to overhear."

"That doesn't matter. You...we shouldn't talk about that."

"Ever?"

I waited for her to say yes, but she didn't as she turned her attention back to the courtyard.

I knew Penellaphe had no issue speaking her mind to me. If she never wanted me to bring it up, she would've made that clear. The thing was...that wasn't what she wanted.

I didn't think she wanted a lot of what occurred around her—what happened to her.

My heart was doing that pounding thing again, and that prickle at the nape of my neck decided to join in. "Would you like to go back to your room?"

She shook her head, causing the golden chains to chime softly. "Not particularly."

"Would you like to go out there instead?" I pointed outside.

"You think it would be safe?"

"Between you and me, I would think so."

A faint grin appeared again. "I used to love the courtyard. It was the one place where, I don't know, my mind was quiet, and I could just be. I didn't think or worry...about anything. I found it so very peaceful."

"But not anymore?"

"No," she whispered. "Not anymore."

A kernel of something akin to guilt seeded itself in my gut. I was the cause of her loss of peace. Something I was only just beginning to realize she had very little of. And that didn't sit well with me.

It never would have.

"It's strange how no one speaks of Rylan or Malessa," she continued. "It's almost as if they never existed."

"Sometimes remembering those who died means facing your own mortality."

"Do you think the Ascended are uncomfortable with the idea of death?"

"Even them," I told her. "They may be godlike, but they can be killed. They can die."

Penellaphe fell quiet as a handful of Ladies in Wait appeared in the otherwise vacant hall. They looked out at the gardens while speaking about the Rite. I kept glancing at her, wishing she would ask to go out into the courtyard.

"Are you excited about attending the Rite?" I asked when she didn't say anything.

"I am curious," she shared. The Rite was only two days away.

Two days. Instead of thinking of what that really meant, I found myself thinking about *her*. All wore red to the Rites, and I imagined it would be the same for the Maiden. "I'm curious to see you. You'll be unveiled," I assumed since all wore masks to the Rite.

"Yes," she confirmed. "But I will be masked."

"I prefer that version of you."

"The masked version of me?"

"Honest?" I leaned my head down, keeping my voice low. "I prefer the version of you that wears no mask or veil."

A faint tremor coursed through her as her lips parted on a soft exhale—lips I clearly recalled were incredibly soft. Heat pumped through my veins. I inched back before I caved to the urge and did something that would be entirely unwise.

She cleared her throat, but when she spoke, there was still a tantalizing breathiness to her words. "I remember you said your father was a farmer. Do you have any siblings? Any Lords in Wait in the family? A sister? Or...?" She took a shallow breath. "There's only Ian for me—I mean, I only have one brother. I'm excited to see him again. I miss him."

Ian.

The brother who'd Ascended.

The one who was in the capital, where mine was being held.

I cooled. "I had a brother."

I looked away. Sometimes, it felt like that. Had. In the past tense. Other times, it felt like I would be too late. That he would be lost to me before I could free him, and his death and all his pain...

238/Jennifer L. Armentrout

It was my fault.

Anguish built in my chest, and no matter how many breaths I took, the pain settled there with the weight of a hundred boulders. Malik should never have—

The feeling of her hand settling over mine shocked me. I started to look at her, but she squeezed my fingers, and…gods, that simple gesture of comfort meant a lot. The pressure in my chest eased, the anguish retreating.

"I'm sorry," she said.

I took a breath to speak, but it was looser and deeper than any I had taken in weeks—maybe months or even years. I blinked, barely aware of the fact that she was no longer touching me.

"Are you okay?" she asked.

My brows knitted as I pressed my hand to my chest. Was I? I felt okay. Good, even. Lighter.

Like I had tasted peace.

WHO I WAS BECOMING

Something beckoned me, slowly coaxing me from the calm chasm of sleep into consciousness.

I'd gone to bed early, at least for me. I hadn't cracked open the old book I'd picked up from the chamber Penellaphe took her lessons in. Pure curiosity had led me to grab the book, a much thinner version of Solis's history than what she was forced to read, but no less insane. I hadn't found myself staring at the thin cracks in the ceiling of my quarters that were even sparser than Penellaphe's. Memories of the past weren't dredged up in the long, dark hours of the night. Instead, I felt...I wasn't sure. Lighter? Unencumbered? Eased?

At peace?

Either way, the moment my head hit the pillow, I fell asleep and *stayed* that way, and that hadn't happened in *decades*. I had no idea why, but I knew better than to look a gift horse in the mouth.

That *thing* came again. A soft touch on my hand, then my arm. A graze of fingers against my skin. Then the craziest thing happened. I thought of *her*. Penellaphe. The tentative way she had touched me at the Red Pearl. The way her body had eagerly responded and the brief feel of her hand wrapped around mine. Half-asleep, my mind conjured images of her fingers curling around a far more interesting part of me. My dick reacted to the heated thoughts, hardening as pulses of lust throbbed through me. I groaned.

Gods, I wanted—

"Hawke."

The voice. That touch. It didn't come from my dreams, and it wasn't *hers*.

Inhaling deeply, I caught the scent of tart lemon as I pried my eyes open. Dust danced in the slice of sunlight cutting between the gap in the drapes over the single window. The brightness told me it was well past the time I usually woke as I turned my head to the right.

Britta sat perched on the edge of my bed, her tight, blond curls bare. My gaze shifted to my arm, where her hand rested.

"What are you doing in here?" I asked, voice rough with sleep.

The centers of her cheeks pinkened. "I'm here to clean your chambers. Normally, you're gone by now," she explained. And I *would* be training at this hour most days.

"I knocked like I usually do, but…" She trailed off, her blue gaze leaving mine, lowering to my bare chest and past it where the sheet tangled at my waist, where I knew damn well my arousal was evident against the thin cover. "But there was no answer."

Her voice had thickened, as did an earthy scent that beat back the lemony smell. "I tried waking you upon entering. I called your name several times. You sleep deeper than I imagined."

I normally didn't.

"But I suppose it's my lucky day," she added, her breath quickening as she continued staring at the thick ridge beneath the sheet. "You're quite the fetching surprise to find in the morning." Her fingertips trailed over my arm. "A very nice, unexpected one."

I said nothing as I watched her draw her lip between her teeth. She leaned in, skating her hand off my arm to my stomach. The pads of her fingers were a little rough from cleaning as they traced the dips and swells of my lower abdomen. She was saying something about my sleep or my body, but I wasn't listening as I stared at her hand and racked my memories for any detail regarding my previous time spent with her. There had been a lot of whiskey. I had the distinct impression that the fucking had been fast and hard, something we'd both enjoyed. She'd come. Loudly. So had I. Quietly. That was about it.

"We won't be interrupted," she said as her fingers trailed over my navel.

My body reacted, muscles tensing as I watched her hand through half-open eyes. Based on how much sunlight was coming through the gap in the drapes, I knew I had time before I was due to guard Penellaphe. She was likely still engaged with her prayers and breakfast, though I wasn't quite sure that was what she did in the mornings. But that was neither here nor there because Britta *was* here, and I hadn't found release outside my own hand in…shit, it had been a while.

My cock throbbed with need, something I was sure Britta was well aware of, because she hadn't taken her gaze off the outline of my dick since she first looked. The almost painful hardness had nothing to do with her presence, though. Most mornings, I woke up with a godsdamn hard-on, but this morning? Today, there had been a reason. I lifted my gaze to the blond curls. The cause of my current arousal had hair the color of rich red wine.

Fuck.

But that was no reason to stop this. Britta was fun. I remembered that. And she liked to have fun with many. I knew that, too. There were no attachments here. No complications. We could fuck, find pleasure, and be on our merry ways.

There was absolutely nothing wrong with that.

Britta's hand slipped under the sheet, her fingers mere inches—if that—from my cock—

I reached down, grasping her slim wrist.

Britta's wide eyes flew to mine.

"Sorry," I said, gently but firmly pulling her hand out from under the sheet.

"Oh," she whispered, blinking. "I thought—"

"It's okay. Just not the right time," I cut her off as my dick demanded to know exactly when the right time would be. Fuck if I knew.

She dropped her hand to her lap, where her white cap lay as her gaze flicked down and then returned to mine. "You sure about that?"

"Positive." Tossing the sheet aside, I swung my legs off the other side of the bed and rose. "I need to get ready for the day."

Britta stood, her gaze tracking my steps as I crossed the chamber. "Would you like me to come back later?" A pause. "To clean your chambers?"

As I opened the door to my bathing chamber, I had a feeling that cleaning my chambers was code for riding my dick. I stopped, looking over my shoulder at her. She wasn't looking at my face. Her stare was glued to my cock. "That will not be necessary."

Not waiting for a response, I closed the door and turned on the oil lamp. Clasping the edges of the vanity, I stared at my reflection in the oval mirror, somewhat shocked with myself—stunned that I had walked away from easy, uncomplicated pleasure.

"What the fuck?" I muttered.

There was no answer as golden eyes stared back at me. I recognized my features, but I had no idea who I was…who I was becoming.

PRESENT VI

"I really hope you don't remember much of that last part when you wake," I said, tracing the tendons of her hand.

"Out of everything you've told her, Britta in your bedchamber will be the one thing she'll definitely remember," Kieran said with a laugh. "She'll probably want to do some damage to that cock you keep speaking of."

Chuckling, I looked over to where Kieran sat on Poppy's other side. "Nah, I think she's far too interested in having my cock pierced for that."

Kieran arched a brow. "I would pay an insurmountable amount of coin to witness you allowing someone to pierce your dick."

"It has to be fucking painful." I grinned. "But worth it."

"Don't know about that last part, and I feel like I need to spend some time talking you out of this."

Another laugh left me as I dipped my head, kissing Poppy's shoulder. "I only thought of the bit with Britta because it really threw me that I wasn't down for it."

"You were down for it," Kieran remarked. "Just not with her."

"Yeah." I shifted, rising slightly on my elbow. The thick fringe of Poppy's lashes didn't flutter as I scanned her features. "Do you think the shadows under her eyes have lessened?"

"A little." He leaned over and brushed a stray wave off her cheek. "I really think so."

"That's good." I swallowed.

"It's mind-blowing what she did for you that night. What she was capable of before all of this," Kieran said, his brows furrowing. "She gave you real peace with just a touch of her hand without even knowing what plagued you."

"I know." My damn chest ached with the intensity of emotion swelling there. "She did it out of kindness—something she didn't have to show me, especially when I was striving to be an utter irritation to her."

"Yeah, but I think she liked that kind of irritation even then."

A smile surfaced as I nodded. "She couldn't resist my charm."

Kieran snorted.

Exhaling heavily, I looked over at him. He was watching Poppy, his features soft in a way I hadn't seen in a long time.

"Have any updates for me?" I asked. He'd returned in the middle of my storytelling and hadn't interrupted.

"Things are calm in the city for now. Several Descenters have come out and helped with that." He scratched a hand over the shadowy growth on his jaw. "Dozens of Ascended have been located—maybe even hundreds. I don't have the exact number. Still waiting on that."

"And?"

"And they are all basically under house arrest, as was ordered."

"How did that go?"

"From what I understand, many did as requested." His stare was grim. "Some did not, and they met an unfortunate end."

That wasn't something I would stress over. "We are giving them a chance. That's more than many of them would have given us."

Kieran nodded. "A Descenter, I think her name is Helenea? Not sure. But anyway, she went to Emil and warned him about the tunnels and how the Ascended use them to travel during the day," he told me. We expected that, but it was still good to know that we had supporters here in the city willing to help. "Hisa is leading a group into them now."

I felt myself nodding as my hand clenched at my side.

"I know it's hard," Kieran said. "Not being out there while our people are taking risks. It's hard for me, but you need to be here."

"We need to be here." I forced my hand to relax. "Any news on Malik?"

"Not yet."

Gods, where the fuck was he? Wherever Millicent was, which was anyone's guess. I didn't doubt that Naill would eventually track his ass down, but I hoped it was sooner rather than later. That would be one less thing to worry about. At least for now.

"Your father and the others were likely delayed at Padonia, but they will be here," Kieran said. "You should rest, Cas."

"Have you rested?"

"We're not talking about me."

I smirked. "I did rest. While you were gone." I picked up Poppy's hand. Her skin was still cold. "I fell asleep for an hour or so. I didn't walk in her dreams."

"That's not why I'm saying you should sleep."

"I know." I brought her hand up and pressed a kiss to her palm. "I'm fine." I found his gaze. "You?"

He nodded. The thing was, though, if either of us managed to sleep more than an hour or two, it wouldn't be restful. Not until Poppy woke up. Not until we knew.

"When was the Rite?" Kieran asked. "From that point in your story?"

"Hell. About…two days, I think." I tipped my head back, delving into my memories of that time. "Miss Willa."

Kieran's brows rose.

I looked down at Poppy. "Her diary." My lips split into a smile. "But there was also the meeting with you." I briefly glanced at Kieran. "And the night before that."

HOT, HEAVY
WANTING

I strode forward, entering Penellaphe's chambers before her after her evening stroll. The space was empty and chilled despite the crackling flames in the fireplace.

"Will you also be checking beneath the bed?" Penellaphe asked as I crossed the chamber. "Or in the bathing chamber?"

Grinning, I nudged open the door to that exact room. "I'm very thorough when it comes to my duty, Princess."

"Uh-huh." She clasped her hands loosely in front of her. "There's no one here but us."

One quick glance at the darkened bathing chamber confirmed as much. Not that I expected anyone to be in here. It was just the perfect excuse to ask her a few questions in private and spend some time with her.

I faced her, noting that she'd partially closed the chamber door, leaving it open a scant few inches. Which meant no one would be able to see inside the chamber unless they put some effort into it. The door was supposed to be left open, and each time it had been closed, I did it. This was progress.

"Your chambers are always so cold." I went to the fireplace and picked up the poker.

"I never noticed that," she replied dryly.

"I imagine it's those windows." I nodded in their direction as I knelt by the hearth. "The stone around them is degrading."

"I suppose that is one of the many causes. There are many drafty sections along the outer wall." Her veiled head tipped back as she looked. "The high ceilings also don't help, but I like them—the height. It makes the chamber seem more...spacious."

I was sure she did when she spent most of her time in here. I moved the logs around, creating air pockets. "There must be more spacious chambers in the newer wings of the castle."

"There are."

I looked over my shoulder at her. She'd inched closer. "Is there a reason they would place you, the Chosen child of the gods, in the most decrepit part of the castle?"

Penellaphe's lips twisted in a wry grin. "They didn't." She moved a few more inches toward me. "I did."

That hadn't been the answer I'd expected. "And why would you choose that?"

One white-draped shoulder rose. "I just prefer the older wing."

I stoked the flames, taking stock of the chamber once more. The narrow door by the windows, the one I was sure led to the old servants' staircase. The corners of my lips tipped up. "That seems like an odd preference."

"Perhaps." She was quiet for a moment. "Your chambers? They are in this wing also?"

"Do you ask because you'd like to visit?" I placed the poker aside.

The lower half of her cheeks pinked. "That was not why I was asking."

"You sure?" I teased, damn well knowing it wasn't the reason, but I enjoyed the flush creeping along the lower half of her face. "It's okay if it was."

Her chin rose. "It wasn't."

"I wouldn't mind at all." Waking to her would be an unexpected delight, unlike what had occurred with Britta.

"Forget I even asked," she muttered.

I chuckled, also enjoying her quick-to-surface ire. "Yes, my chambers are a floor below." Brushing my hands on my pants, I rose. "Though the ceiling is not as high as your chambers, nor is it as cold."

"I'm glad to hear that. I mean that your chambers are comfortable." Her clasped fingers relaxed, even as the skin beneath her veil continued to deepen in color. "Do you still have your quarters at the dorm?"

I nodded.

"Do you stay at them?" The hem of her white robes glided silently over the stone as she came forward. "I don't think Vikter stays at his often."

"I haven't since I became your servant."

"You're not my servant," she quickly corrected.

"But I am here to serve you." I tilted my head, watching the lower half of her face closely. The skin there. Her mouth. "In whatever way necessary."

Penellaphe huffed out a noise that almost sounded like a laugh. "You are my guard, not my servant. You serve as my protection and…"

"And?"

"And you serve as a source of irritation."

I laughed deeply. "You wound me yet again, Princess."

"Doubtful." There was a twitch to her lips as if she were fighting a smile. "And don't call me that."

I grinned at her. "I was disappointed this evening, by the way."

"By what?" She'd stopped coming closer. The gold chains of her veil twinkled in the lamplight.

"I hoped you would ask to take a walk in the garden."

"Oh." She drew her plump lower lip between her teeth as she looked at the windows. "I…I thought about it." A forlorn sigh left her, tugging at my chest. "I do miss those walks."

An emotion I didn't want to recognize festered. Guilt. My gaze followed hers to the blue-black sky beyond. Just for a moment, I allowed myself to wish I had chosen a different location in which to move my plan forward—somewhere she hadn't found peace. Then I wouldn't have stolen that from her.

"Maybe another night this week, after the Rite," she said.

I turned to her, finding that she had been watching me. "Of course," I lied. Clearing my mind of what I'd already cost her wasn't easy, but I thought of my brother. The peace that had been stolen from him. That did the job. "As I said, I live to serve you."

Her sigh was impressive. "Then you must live a rather boring life."

"I did." I dipped my chin as I slowly made my way to where she stood, just beyond the little sitting areas she had created by the fire. "Until I became your…" I swore I felt her eyes narrowing. "Protector."

"Guard," she clarified.

"Now, *I'm* a bit confused." I crossed the distance, stopping when there was only about half a foot between us. I watched her closely, trying to gauge her reaction to my proximity. Her pulse kicked up, but she didn't back away. "Aren't guard and protector the same thing?"

"I don't believe so. One is simply guarding, the other is protecting."

My brows knitted as I looked over at her. "Again, are they not the same?"

"No."

"Explain." I saw that two of the chains on the top of the veil were twisted together.

"Guarding...is more passive. Protecting is proactive," she said, a small grin appearing, one I could only describe as her being pleased with herself.

"Both require passiveness and preparedness," I countered.

One shoulder lifted again. "Well, it's just my opinion."

"Clearly," I murmured.

Penellaphe's head tilted to the side. "I don't believe your services are needed any longer this evening."

"So, I am at your service?"

"Apparently not, if you're still standing here," she quipped.

Another laugh left me, tugging at the corners of my mouth. "I will be out of your...veil soon enough."

"Out of my veil?" she repeated. "Shouldn't that be out of my hair?"

"Yes, but since I can't see your hair, I thought veil made more sense."

"You are..."

"What?"

Silence.

"Don't be shy."

The chest of her lacy robes lifted with a deep breath. "You are strange."

"Well, I for sure thought you would say something far more insulting than that, but speaking of your veil," I said, lifting a hand. She stiffened as I reached for her. Her pulse skittered now. "Your chains are tangled."

"Oh," Penellaphe whispered, clearing her throat. She lifted her hand.

"I got it." My hand brushed hers as I slid my fingers under the chains. Her soft inhale and the sudden thickness of fresh, sweet scent brought a tight smile to my lips as I leaned in. "I did wonder something."

"And what would that be?"

The breathiness of her words touched my throat and heated my blood. "I was thinking about when the Teermans addressed the people." I gently began untangling the chains, discovering that they were as heavy as I had imagined. "Many in the crowd weren't happy, and not just because of the attack."

She said nothing as I worked the length of chain, but her hands had unclasped and fallen to her sides.

"How did you know some in the crowd may grow violent?" I asked, though I wouldn't call Lev's actions all that violent.

"I...I didn't know for sure," she answered. Her fingers twitched. "I just saw the way they were moving closer and their expressions."

"You have very good eyesight, then." I continued tugging the chains apart, even though a small child could've completed the task by now, but I was taking my time.

"I suppose."

"I was surprised." I kept an eye on her as I slowly worked the chains free, catching every tiny reaction. Her breathing had picked up, along with her pulse. Her fingers had stilled. "You caught sight of what many of the guards didn't."

"But you noticed."

"It is my job to notice, Princess."

"And because I am the Chosen, I suppose it is not my duty to take note of such things?"

"That's not what I'm saying."

"Then what are you—?" Her breath snagged as I reached the end of the chains, and the backs of my fingers brushed her shoulder. "What are you saying?"

My attention shot back to her face. Those lips parted as I turned a single chain so it faced up. I could feel that the material of her gown was thinner than expected. Her reaction surprised me, yet didn't. I hadn't forgotten how incredibly responsive she was to touch, but the graze of my hand wasn't much of a caress. Then again, other than Tawny and perhaps Vikter, who touched her? With kindness? Any contact would likely feel extreme to her, sensual or not. She would be easy to seduce and coax into all manner of things forbidden to her.

"I was saying that your observational skills were a surprise," I answered her question. "And that has nothing to do with who you are. There were a lot of people out there. A lot of faces, and a lot of bodies moving."

"I know." Her right hand lifted a few inches, then she jerked it back to her side. "I just happened to look at them at the right moment."

Had she been about to touch me? I thought so. Instead of feeling a surge of satisfaction, all I felt was want. Hot, heavy *want*.

"What do you think will happen to that man?" she asked.

Drawing my hand from the chains before I tore the damn veil from her head and did something reckless but also very pleasurable, I looked down at Penellaphe. Her head was tipped back, and she had—

Shock rolled through me.

Penellaphe had moved closer. Maybe an inch or so separated us, but that wasn't what surprised me. It was the fact that I hadn't been aware of it.

A huge part of me wished I hadn't noticed it now, either. With as close as we stood, it would be all too easy to lower my mouth to hers. I wanted to know how she would react. Would she protest? Or relent?

But it was too risky for various reasons. One of them even more so than the knowledge that anyone could walk by the chamber and peer inside, or that I may even frighten and overwhelm her. I wanted to know what her lips tasted like without whiskey on mine too badly.

"Hawke?"

I blinked. "I'm sorry. What did you ask?"

"I asked what you thought would happen to that man."

That question should've cooled my blood. "He'll probably be questioned and then sentenced." I stepped back, my shoulders tensing at the thought of Lev. Word from Jansen was that the Descenter still lived. I wasn't sure if that was a good thing or not. "There will be no trial, but I imagine you already know that."

"Yes." Her fingers went to a row of small beads down the center of her bodice. "But sometimes they…"

I waited for her to continue, but she didn't. "Sometimes they what?"

Penellaphe shook her head. "Do we even know if he truly is a Descenter?"

The question intrigued me. "Does it matter?"

Her head cut away. "Likely not."

"He recited the words the Descenters often use," I said. "I imagine that is what he is."

She nodded, and I watched her as silence fell between us. I always watched her, but it felt different at the moment. Like I was searching for something. What, I wasn't sure. I couldn't even figure it out after I bid her goodnight and returned to the hall before Vikter arrived for his shift. But I had the distinct feeling—one that was so strong, even though I had no idea what it was I looked for—that it would be better if I didn't find whatever it was.

PLANS HAVE NOT CHANGED

I moved through the hall of one of the upstairs floors of the Red Pearl, a bottle of whiskey I'd helped myself to in one hand and a canvas sack in the other. The floor wasn't quiet. Moans and grunts came from each side of the hall, so many of them it was hard to tell exactly which chambers were in use and which weren't.

Taking a swig of the whiskey as I reached the room designated for meetings, I didn't bother knocking. I pushed open the door.

The smell of sex was the first thing to reach me.

Then the soft, breathy gasp of pleasure turning to surprise.

Lowering the bottle as I kicked the door closed behind me, my gaze swung to the bed—the very same bed I'd laid Penellaphe on.

It was definitely not her on that bed.

The woman on her knees was all lush curves, but her hair was a color somewhere between black and brown. Her eyes, a deep shade of brown, were wide and fixed on me as the hands on her hips tightened, pressing into the flesh. I squinted, thinking I recognized the woman.

"I would ask if you'd considered knocking," Kieran remarked, the muscles in his hips and ass flexing as he slowed behind the woman. "But obviously that didn't cross your mind."

I raised a brow as he lifted the woman's ample ass that shook with his thrust. "I didn't realize you'd have company."

"I assume not." His skin glistened with a faint sheen of sweat. "You're earlier than I expected."

"Clearly," I drawled.

"Well, since you're here…" Kieran drew one hand from the woman's hip, dragging it up the soft skin of her belly and then between her swaying breasts. "Care to join in?"

The woman moaned, rocking forward on the length of his glistening cock.

Kieran chuckled as his fingers curled around the base of her neck and he pulled her back, bringing her flush with his chest. "I don't think Circe would mind."

"Not at all," Circe panted, extending a hand. "Join us."

It struck me then, as Kieran's other hand left her hip and delved between her thighs. I knew why I thought she looked familiar. She was a Descenter.

One I was pretty sure I'd fucked.

Kieran's grin kicked up a notch as he locked eyes with me. Dipping his head, he nipped at her throat, wringing a startled cry of pleasure from her. My gaze went back to his large hand between her thighs, both promising a welcome and pleasant diversion. And considering my cock had just been about as hard as Kieran's while in Penellaphe's chambers, I should dive headfirst into what they offered.

But like the morning with Britta, the desire wasn't there.

"Thanks," I said. "But I'm good.

"You sure?" Kieran gave her clit a playful smack.

"Positive." I turned, making my way to the settee. There was something fucking wrong with me. I sat, whiskey bottle in hand as I placed the canvas sack on the floor. "But please, pretend I'm not even here," I said, knowing damn well neither of them would do that, but both would thoroughly do what I said next. "And enjoy yourselves."

Kieran made a sound that was a cross between a laugh and a groan. I smirked. Taking another drink of whiskey, I propped my feet on the low table.

Circe must've whispered something that earned a warning from Kieran to leave me be. My smirk grew, and I could practically feel his heated glare.

I'd be lying if I said the sounds of their bodies coming together or how Kieran fucked, the tight control of his thrusts, and how he ground on her ass had no effect, but as my gaze flickered over the jut of Circe's rose-tipped breasts, it wasn't her body I saw in my mind.

It was *hers*.

Penellaphe's.

My fantasies decided to put her on that bed between Kieran and me, and man, just imagining that packed a sensual punch.

Gods, I shouldn't be thinking of her like that for a multitude of reasons, the least of which was that while Penellaphe was curious about sensuality, this would likely scandalize her into an early death.

It didn't take long for Circe to find her release, thank the gods. Kieran took her to her stomach, driving into her, and I knew how hard he could fuck—something Circe very noisily approved of. By the time he found his release, I had a feeling she would find herself comparing every future lover to him.

My eyes drifted shut as they disentangled themselves and rose from the bed. Kieran whispered something that made her giggle. The soft click of the door closing announced her departure.

"Did you enjoy yourself?" I asked.

"What do you think?"

I grinned, opening my eyes. "Actually, I'm glad you had company tonight. You could use the practice."

Kieran snorted as he dipped a cloth into a basin of water. "You feeling okay?"

"Of course." I took a drink of the whiskey. "Why do you ask?"

"You're sitting over there with a hard dick," he pointed out, drawing the wet cloth over his. "By choice."

"Yeah," I said. "Not like I haven't chosen more disconcerting things in the past."

"True." He tossed the cloth aside. "Got an update for me?"

"I do," I said, filling him in on what had occurred, which wasn't of much interest to him until I got to the part about what I planned to do to the Duke.

"You cannot kill the Duke," Kieran said, dressing as he joined me.

"Oh, I'm going to kill him." I straightened my leg. "There's no way around that." And if I had the time and opportunity, Lord Mazeen was another dead motherfucker.

So was that damn Priestess.

And I couldn't forget Lieutenant Smyth.

There would be a bloodbath.

"When the Craven attacked the Rise, she was out there," I told him, and he did a double-take. "She kept her identity hidden, but she saved guards that night. She's damn good with a bow and arrow and likely just as skilled with a dagger. She's a fighter, Kieran. You know what that means for her to have taken what the Duke has been doing to her? To not be able to stop him?"

"Hawke—"

"He has been *caning* her, Kieran," I cut him off, anger pulsing through me, chasing away the last of the strange feelings of peace. "And only the gods know what else. He must die. Maiden or not, what is being done to her is inexcusable."

His jaw tightened. "I'm not down with anyone being abused, but what you're talking about is revenge."

"And?"

Kieran's stare met mine. "That's not the same as stopping an abuser."

"Seems like the exact same thing to me."

"One is an act to protect another," he countered. "The other makes it about you."

"And those two things cannot be true at the same time?" I asked, letting out a harsh laugh. "Because they are."

"I didn't say they couldn't be."

"Then what are you saying?"

For several moments, there were only the muted cries of passion from an adjoining chamber, and then Kieran said, "You care about her."

"What?" My booted foot slipped from the low table and landed near the canvas sack I'd filled with clothing for Poppy that I was about ninety percent confident would fit. Pants. Sweater. A cloak. Kieran would take it with him when he left, as it would be less suspicious than me running around with it the night of the Rite. "You need to say that again because, surely, I didn't hear you right."

"You heard me right." Kieran crossed his arms.

For a moment, all I could do was stare at him, wondering if he had suffered some sort of ailment of the mind. "Then that is a ridiculous question."

"It wasn't a question," he said. "It was a statement. You must care about someone to want revenge for the harm done to them."

Was that true? I didn't think so. Not in every case. Not in this case.

"And honestly, I'm not all that surprised. You're forced to spend a lot of time with her. To protect her," he continued. "I suppose it's only natural that you would develop some sort of feelings for her."

"The Duke's soon-to-be death has very little to do with her or any perceived feelings and everything to do with him. Because if he's doing this to her? He's doing it to others. I'm not going to leave here and allow that, and I know damn well you wouldn't want him able to continue harming others, either." I searched his gaze. "The plans haven't changed, Kieran. The Rite will happen. The Descenters will make their move, and I will take her. None of that has changed."

Kieran stared, inhaling roughly through his nose. "Glad to hear it."

My brow pinched. "Did you think it had?"

"I don't know." His stare fixed on the unlit fireplace. A couple of moments passed. "Have I told you what a bad idea this whole plan of yours is?"

A grin tugged at my lips. "You have. Many times."

"Have I told you that I think it's a colossal mistake, then?" he asked.

"You've said it's an enormous mistake. I also believe you've called it gargantuan in the past. Mammoth another time," I reminded him. The expression etched into his face was something I'd seen a million times. It was the one that warned he was on the verge of a lecture that would make his father proud. "At this point, you've got to be running out of adjectives."

"I have a whole list stored up, starting with humongous."

I laughed. "You're starting to remind me of Emil, you know."

Kieran snorted. "Unlikely." His pale blue gaze turned serious. "You're not going to be swayed about this whole Duke thing, are you?"

"No." I figured it was best to keep the others I wanted dead to myself. "I believe he will be an unfortunate victim of the attack the night of the Rite."

He squinted. "The Descenters won't be laying siege to the castle."

"No, but I will make it look like at least one managed to infiltrate," I said. "Either way, we will be gone, so it matters little."

The pinch of his brow said that it still mattered. "How the fuck did the Maiden learn how to use a bow?"

"That's not all she can do. She can also fight hand-to-hand. She almost took my ass down."

"Well, I want to know more about that."

A dry laugh left me. "It's not as interesting as you think."

"Disagree," he murmured.

"I think it was her other guard. Vikter," I answered his question. "He must have trained her."

"That is unexpected, and a potential problem down the road."

I sighed, looking at my empty hand. "Don't I know it?"

A heartbeat passed. "Caning her?"

Anger simmered in my gut as I nodded.

"Fucking gods." His eyes, a brighter shade of blue now, met mine. "Make it hurt."

"I plan to."

"Good." He scratched his jaw. "I cannot wait to be free of this cesspool."

"You and me both," I said, and we would be. Soon. *Our* plan would work.

But things would get messy and bloodier than they already were, and I didn't want Kieran anywhere near any of it. I hadn't wanted him here at all.

He knew that, and still insisted on joining me. But that didn't mean I couldn't try to talk some sense into him.

I rose, and Kieran's eyes immediately narrowed. "You know I'd prefer if you—"

"Don't start," he interrupted, his voice dropping low, even though not a soul could hear us. "I know exactly what you're going to say, Cas."

"I didn't want you here in the first place," I told him. "If I had my way, you would be back in Atlantia, or at the very least, in Spessa's End, annoying the hell out of your sister."

"Didn't I just ask you not to start with this shit?"

"You didn't ask. You demanded that I not, and I'm ignoring that." I clasped his shoulder. "Besides the risks—"

"What you mean to say is besides the fact that my father would have your ass if something happened to me."

"That, too." I cracked a grin despite the truth of what Kieran said. His father would have my ass if something happened to his son. Who I was wouldn't stop him. "I know being here, having to stay in this form, hasn't been easy."

"I make do. I'll keep making do, so don't worry about me."

Of course, he'd say that. But no wolven enjoyed being confined to their mortal forms, even if it was by choice. "You can ride ahead to New Haven."

"I'm with you," Kieran said, folding his hand around my outstretched forearm. "Always. Even if I think what you're doing is idiotic."

Just like he'd known there would be no changing my mind about the Duke, I knew there was no chance I'd change his regarding this. I had to try, though. I squeezed his shoulder, then dropped my hand. "I've done far more idiotic things."

"Name one."

I knocked back a strand of dark hair. "I could name a hundred, but then we'd be here until the Rite."

"We would be." The humor dissipated as he bent, picking up the sack. "If all goes well, the next time we see each other…"

I took a deep breath. "Will be when we're leaving Masadonia."

MISS WILLA COLYNS

I didn't know if I should laugh or shout.

The very ill-behaved Maiden had snuck out again, and I only knew because I had entered her chambers when there'd been no answer to my knock. I'd been bored. Vikter was nowhere near, and it was the perfect opportunity to get closer to her. But her quarters were empty.

My suspicions concerning that door by the windows had been spot-on. It led to a dusty-ass, cobweb-filled stairwell that appeared as if it were mere minutes from crumbling.

I'd figured she would use the broken section of the inner wall to leave the castle grounds and then take Wisher's Grove to wherever she planned to go. I'd been right, catching up to her just as she left the woods.

I didn't stop her, which inarguably made me a bad guard *and* question my sanity because, yet again, another prime opportunity to make a run for it with her had presented itself, and I didn't take it.

But I would have to get in touch with Kieran, which wasn't exactly quick, and we'd still have to make it past the fully staffed Rise.

Besides, I was curious as to what she was up to. Was she going to the Red Pearl? Meeting with someone? I didn't think that was the case.

I lost her for a bit once she entered the packed streets, and it took an ungodly amount of time to pick up her scent again near the Atheneum.

She was sneaking off to the city library, which was disgustingly cute…until I thought about the fact that she had to actually *sneak out* to go to a place as harmless as the Atheneum. This was her life. I felt bad for her.

Until I looked up and spotted her standing on a godsdamn window ledge that faced the Grove, too far from the very hard ground. I couldn't even allow myself to fathom what in the hell she was doing as I entered the Atheneum. There'd been many scents, halls, and staircases to get to the floor I believed her to be on. And I'd finally tracked what I was sure was a lovely ass down to a private and quite chilly chamber despite the warmth of the other spaces. I zeroed in on the open window.

And that was approximately when my humor faded.

Making sure the door to the private chamber was locked, I stalked toward the godsdamn *window*.

"You still out there, Princess?" I called out. "Or have you fallen to your death? I really hope that's not the case since I'm pretty positive that would reflect poorly on me since I assumed you were in your room." I placed my hands on the windowsill. "*Behaving.* And not on a ledge, several dozen feet in the air, for reasons I can't even begin to fathom but am dying to learn."

"Dammit," she whispered.

I fought back a grin, reminding myself I was angry with her. Rightfully so. She was endangering her life—and my plans. I leaned out the window and looked to my right. There she was, plastered against the stone wall, a book clutched to her chest. I raised an eyebrow.

"Hi?" she squeaked.

That was all she had to say? "Get inside."

She didn't move.

Sighing, I extended a hand. I swore to the gods, if I had to climb out there… "Now."

"You could say *please*."

My eyes narrowed. "There are a whole lot of things I could say to you that you should be grateful I'm keeping to myself."

"Whatever," she muttered. "Move back."

I waited, wanting to take her hand just so I was confident she wouldn't slip and fall to her death, but when she made no move to take it, I swallowed a carriage full of curses and stepped back. "If you fall, you're going to be in so much trouble."

"If I fall, I'll be dead," she quipped. "So, I'm not quite sure how I'd also be in trouble."

"Poppy," I snapped.

A second later, the lower half of her cloaked body appeared in the window. She gripped the upper windowsill, then dipped. She started to let go—

I snapped forward, wrapping an arm around her waist. Her sweet, fresh scent curled around me as I hauled her inside. The front of her body was pressed to mine as I lowered her feet to the floor. Keeping my arm around her, I reached for the back of her hood. If I were going to yell at her, I would do so while looking upon her and not at a shadowy space.

"Don't—"

I yanked her hood down. Her features were still only partially exposed to me. Disappointment surged, but this was better than a veil. "A mask." I eyed the silky strands of hair that had escaped her braid and fell against her cheek. "This brings back old memories."

Her cheeks warmed as she tugged at my hold, getting nowhere. "I understand you're probably upset—"

"Probably?" I laughed.

"All right. You're definitely upset," she corrected. "But I can explain."

"I sure hope so, because I have so many questions, starting with, how did you get out of your room?" I said, even though I knew exactly how. I just wanted her to admit it. "And ending with why in the gods were you on the ledge?"

That stubborn chin lifted. "You can let me go."

"I can, but I don't know if I should. You might do something even more reckless than climbing out onto a ledge that can't be more than a foot wide."

Behind the white mask, her eyes narrowed. "I didn't fall."

"As if that somehow makes this whole situation better?"

"I didn't say that. I'm just pointing out that I had the situation completely under control."

She considered that being under control? She really did. I blinked, my amusement returning as I laughed. "You had the situation under control? I'd hate to see what happens when you don't."

Actually, I'd probably enjoy seeing it when she didn't.

A shiver swept through her. I almost didn't catch it, but the cloak had parted, and whatever she wore underneath wasn't that thick. Gods, I hoped it wasn't a damn nightgown again. Or maybe I did.

She wiggled, trying to slip free. It didn't work. What it did do was bring our lower bodies even closer together. I bit back a curse when her soft belly brushed my pelvis, sending a sharp, pulsing bolt of arousal through me.

Poppy stilled, her breathing picking up. I didn't dare move as we stood there, our bodies pressed together. Then, slowly, she tipped her head back, and those green eyes locked with mine. I inhaled deeply, catching the thickness in her scent. Fuck, my damn heart kicked heavily in my chest in response.

A hundred different things went through my mind as I stared down at her, waiting for her to try to pull away again. But she didn't. Her attraction to me had control of her, and I knew that was good. I could use that to further gain her trust. The Rite was tonight, and things— things would be happening fast after that. Seduction was a need.

And it was also a *want*.

I lifted a hand, placing my fingers just below the curved edges of the mask. My jaw loosened at the feel of her soft skin beneath mine. I didn't move my hand, and I should've because I knew she enjoyed being touched. Seducing her wouldn't be hard, but I waited to see what she would do. That was important to me.

Poppy didn't move away.

It wasn't satisfaction that surged through me but pure, raw lust. I drew my fingers just below the bottom of the mask and then down over the corner of her parted lips. Gods, they were soft and pillowy.

I dipped my head, liking how her breath caught—how her sweetness increased. My lips followed the path of my fingers before I even realized they had touched her skin. Her desire thickened in the air as I tilted her head back. Our mouths were now mere centimeters apart. I could kiss her. I could likely do a hell of a lot more, but my chest was too tight.

So, I didn't.

I couldn't even say why. Because I needed to. I wanted to. I just couldn't.

You care about her.

Cursing myself and Kieran for even putting that thought out there, I tilted my head, bringing my mouth to her ear. "Poppy?" My voice sounded thick to my ears.

"Yes?" she breathed.

I slid my fingers down the elegant line of her throat. "How did you get out of the room without me seeing you?"

She gave a little jerk. "What?"

I'd surprised her with that question. Disappointed her even, because she wanted my mouth doing something more than questioning her. I smiled at that. "How did you leave your chambers?"

"Dammit," she muttered, tugging at my hold once more.

I let go this time, my body immediately missing the heat of hers and regretting the decision.

Her face flushed as she retreated and lowered the book she held, but her chin lifted. "Maybe I walked right past you."

"No, you didn't. And I know you didn't climb out of a window. That would've been impossible. So, how did you do it?"

Poppy turned from me, raising her face to the cool air coming in through the window. "There's an old servants' access to my chambers."

I smiled widely, enough that if she'd faced me, she would've seen all my lies.

"From there, I can reach the main floor without being seen."

"Interesting." I kept my voice level. "Where does it empty out on the main floor?"

She faced me. "If you want to know that, you have to find out for yourself."

"All right." I let that go since I already knew the answer. "That's how you got onto the Rise without being seen."

Poppy shrugged.

"I'm assuming Vikter knows all about this. Did Rylan?"

"Does it matter?"

Yes, it did. "How many people know about this entrance?"

"Why do you ask?" she shot back.

"Because it's a safety concern, Princess." And it truly was. "In case you've forgotten, the Dark One wants you. A woman has already been killed, and there has already been one abduction attempt that we know of." I took a step toward her. "Being able to move unseen through the castle, directly to your chambers, is the kind of knowledge he'd find valuable," I told her, even though it wasn't valuable in the way I implied. I was more worried about the Ascended making use of the access.

She swallowed. "Some of the servants who've been at Castle Teerman for a long time know about it, but most don't. It's not a concern. The door locks from the inside. Someone would have to break down the door, and I'd be ready if that happened."

"I'm sure you would be," I murmured.

"And I haven't forgotten what happened to Malessa or that someone tried to abduct me."

"You haven't? Then I guess you just didn't take any of that into consideration when you decided to go gallivanting through the city to the *library*."

"I didn't go *gallivanting* through anything. I went through Wisher's Grove and was on the street for less than a minute," she argued. "I also had my cloak up and this mask on. No one could even see a single inch of my face. I wasn't worried about being snatched, but I also came prepared, just in case."

"With your trusty little dagger?" I grinned.

"Yes, with my trusty little dagger," she retorted. "It hasn't failed me before."

"And that was how you escaped abduction the night Rylan was killed?" I asked another thing I knew, but we hadn't spoken of. "The man wasn't scared off by approaching guards?"

She exhaled loudly and a bit dramatically. "Yes. I cut him. More than once. He was wounded when he was called off. I hope he died."

"You are so violent."

"You keep saying that," she snapped. "But I'm really not."

I laughed again, enjoying how quickly her ire rose. "You really aren't all that self-aware."

"Whatever," she muttered. "How did you even realize I was gone?"

"I checked on you," I lied, dragging my hand over the back of the settee. "I thought you might want company, and it seemed stupid for me to stand out in the hall bored out of my mind with you inside your room, most likely bored out of yours. Which, obviously, you were since you left."

"Did you really?" She took a deep breath. "I mean, did you really check on me to ask if I…I wanted company?"

I nodded. "Why would I lie about that?"

"I…" She looked away, her lips pursed. "It doesn't matter."

But I thought it might've.

I leaned against the settee. "How did you end up on the ledge?"

"Well, that's kind of a funny story…"

"I imagine it is. So, please, spare no details." I crossed my arms.

She sighed. "I came to find something to read, and I stopped inside this room. I…I didn't want to go back to mine yet, and I didn't realize that anything about this room was special."

I followed her gaze to the liquor cabinet. That hadn't given away that this was a private chamber?

"I was in here, and I heard the Duke outside in the hall. So, hiding on a ledge was a far better option than having him catch me here."

"And what would've happened if he had?"

She shrugged again. "He didn't, and that's all that matters. He had a meeting here with a guard from the prison. At least, I think that's who it was. They were talking about the Descenter who threw the Craven hand. The guard got the man to talk. He said that the Descenter didn't believe that the Dark One was in the city."

"That's good news," I forced out.

She glanced over at me. "You don't believe him?"

"I don't think the Dark One has survived as long as he has by letting his whereabouts be widely known, even by his most fervent supporters," I replied.

"I think…" Her grip on the book she held tightened. "I think the Duke is going to kill the Descenter himself."

I remembered what she had asked me. "Does that bother you?"

"I don't know."

I tilted my head. "I think you do, and you just don't want to say it."

Her lips pursed. "I just don't like the idea of someone dying in a dungeon."

"Dying by public execution is better?"

She stared at me. "Not exactly, but at least then it's being done in a way that feels…"

My heart was kicking faster now. "Feels like what?"

Poppy gave a shake of her head. "At least then it doesn't feel like it's…" She glanced at me.

I was holding my fucking breath for her answer.

"Something being hidden," she said.

I stared at her. She didn't like how the Ascended handled things. I'd already suspected as much, but to see how uncomfortable she truly was with it was something…

Important.

And I would have to think about that later when it was quiet, and I could figure out what it really meant.

"Interesting," I said.

"What is?"

"You." I eyed the book she held.

"Me?"

Nodding, I then struck, grabbing the book.

"Don't!" she gasped.

Too late.

I freed the tome from her grasp and stepped back, glancing down at it. "The Diary of Miss Willa Colyns?" My brows furrowed as I turned it over. "Why does that name sound familiar?"

"Give it back." She reached for it, but I moved away. "Give it back to me now!"

"I will if you read it for me. I'm sure this has to be more interesting than the history of the kingdom." Smiling, I opened the book, quickly scanning the page. One sentence stood out boldly.

He took me from behind, pounding the iron steel of his manhood into me.

My mouth parted as I blinked. I flipped a few more pages, my brows rising as I caught sight of words like *nipples* and *salty come*.

What in the world was she reading? Better yet, why was she reading it?

"What interesting reading material," I remarked, glancing over at her.

Poppy looked like she wished to throw a blunt or sharp object at my face.

My grin returned. "*Penellaphe*." I feigned shock. "This is…just scandalous reading material for the Maiden."

"Shut up." She crossed her arms.

"Very naughty," I teased.

That chin went up as if on cue. "There's nothing wrong with me reading about love."

"I didn't say there was." I glanced down at a page that included the oh-so-romantic verse—*Gods, I'm soaking wet just sitting here penning this.* I looked at her. "But I don't think what she is writing about has anything to do with love."

"Oh, so you're an expert on this now?"

"More so than you, I imagine."

She pressed her mouth shut. Only a second passed. "That's right. Your visits to the Red Pearl have been the talk of many servants and Ladies in Wait, so I suppose you do have a ton of experience."

"Someone sounds jealous."

"Jealous?" She laughed, rolling her eyes. "As I said before, you have an overinflated sense of importance in my life."

I snorted, returning to skimming the book. Damn, this Miss Willa was a very…descriptive writer.

"Just because you have more experience with…what goes on at the Red Pearl," she said, "doesn't mean I don't know what love is."

"Have you ever been in love?" I asked half-jokingly, but as soon as the question left my tongue, it no longer felt much like a joke. My eyes narrowed. "Has one of the Duke's stewards caught your eye? One of the Lords? Or perhaps a brave guard?"

Poppy shook her head as she stared at the liquor cabinet. "I haven't been in love."

"Then how would you know?"

"I know my parents loved one another deeply." She toyed with the jeweled top of a decanter. "What about you? Have you been in love, Hawke?"

"Yes," I answered honestly, my chest twisting. I then stared at the book, seeing none of the words as I thought about Shea.

Poppy looked over her shoulder at me. She dragged her teeth across her lower lip. "Someone from your home?"

"She was," I said. "It was a long time ago, though."

"A long time ago? When you were what? A child?" she asked.

I chuckled at the confusion in her tone, welcoming how her question made it easier than normal to tuck away everything related to Shea. I refocused on the page, giving a paragraph a quick read. "How much of this have you read?"

"That's none of your business."

"Probably not, but I need to know if you got to this part." I cleared my throat.

"I only read the first chapter," she added quickly. "And you look like you're in the middle of the book, so—"

"Good. Then this will be fresh and new to you. Let me see, where was I?" I ran a finger over the page, stopping at the halfway mark. "Oh, yes. Here. *'Fulton had promised that when he was done with me that I wouldn't be able to walk straight for a day, and he was right.'* Huh. Impressive." I paused, sneaking a glance at her.

Her eyes were wide behind the mask, but perhaps I'd been wrong in thinking what Kieran had offered the night before would scandalize her.

"*'The things the man did with his tongue and his fingers had only been surpassed by his shockingly large, decadently pulsing, and wickedly throbbing—'*" I chuckled. "This woman has a knack for adverbs, doesn't she?"

"You can stop now."

"*'Manhood.'*"

"What?" Poppy gasped.

"That's the end of that sentence," I told her, glancing up. I beat back my smile. "Oh, you may not know what she means by manhood. I do believe she's talking about his cock. Prick. Dick. His—"

"Oh, my gods," she whispered.

I kept going. "His—apparently—extremely large, throbbing and pulsing—"

"I get it!" she yelled, unfolding her arms. "I completely understand."

"Just wanted to make sure." It took everything in me not to laugh as she inhaled deeply, holding her breath. "Wouldn't want you to be too embarrassed to ask and think she was referencing his love for her or something."

The air punched from her lungs. "I hate you."

"No, you don't."

"And I'm about to stab you," she tacked on. "In a very violent manner."

Since her hand was near her thigh, that was a real concern. "Now that, I believe."

"Give me back the journal."

"But of course." I handed it over, grinning as she held it against her chest like a precious jewel. "All you had to do was ask."

"What?" Her mouth dropped open. "I have been asking."

"Sorry. I have selective hearing."

"You are…" Her eyes narrowed. "You are the worst."

"You got your words wrong." Pushing away from the settee, I strode past her, patting her head. She swung at me—and fast, too—almost catching me in my back. "You meant, I'm the best."

"I got my words right."

Smiling too widely again, I went to the door. "Come. I need to get you back before something other than your own foolishness puts you at risk." I stopped, waiting for her. "And don't forget your book. I expect a summary of each chapter tomorrow."

Poppy huffed but came forward, and not quietly. She stomped. "How did you know where I was?"

I looked over my shoulder at her, my smile fainter now. "I have incredible tracking skills, Princess."

JUST A NAME

"You don't have to follow me," Poppy said as she walked ahead, her dark cloak blending into the darkness of Wisher's Grove. "I know my way back to the castle."

"I know." I kept pace, a step behind her. "But what kind of guard would I be if I let you walk through the woods all alone and at night?"

"A less annoying one?"

The retort brought a genuine laugh.

"I'm glad you find that amusing." Her hooded head turned slightly. "Because I don't."

I was glad she was speaking again. She'd been quiet as we left the Atheneum, which had allowed my mind to wander to unsettling places, like how the earlier need and then want to seduce her hadn't felt mutually exclusive.

You care about her.

Fucking Kieran.

"You know what I find amusing?" I asked.

"I cannot wait to hear."

A grin played on my lips as I kept scanning the shadows for any stray Ascended. "How you manage to dull your tongue with everyone else."

"That amuses you?" She skirted an outcropping of boulders.

"Only because I imagine that whatever you're thinking during those moments would burn the ears of sailors."

She snorted. "Sometimes." The hem of her cloak snagged on a bush. Being the helpful albeit annoying guard I was, I untangled it for her. "Thank you," she murmured, clutching the diary to her chest.

"You sound a bit more genuine than the last time you thanked me," I pointed out.

"I was genuine then, too."

"Uh-huh."

Her heavy sigh made me smile. She walked ahead, avoiding the jagged rocks and uneven terrain one would only know if they often traveled this section of Wisher's Grove. "It's not easy," she said after a couple of moments.

"What's not?"

Poppy didn't answer right away. "Staying quiet," she said. "Dulling my tongue."

I almost asked why she did it, but I already knew the answer. It was the same reason she allowed the Priestess to mistreat her. She had no choice.

"Anyway," she continued, clearing her throat, "did you know these woods are rumored to be haunted? At least that is what Tawny believes."

I let the change of subject go. "I have a friend who thinks the same."

"You have friends?"

I laughed. "Yes, I know. Shocking, isn't it?"

A soft sound came from the depths of her hood, one that could've been a laugh. Did she ever laugh—one that was loud and uncontrolled? I didn't know, but I...I hadn't laughed or even smiled as easily as I did around her in a very long time.

I didn't know why *that* was, either.

Rubbing at my chest, I stepped over a few fallen branches and pushed those thoughts aside. "So, you like to read?"

"I...I do."

"What do you like to read? Other than extremely detailed tellings of thick, throbbing—"

"I'll read anything," she cut in quickly. "It doesn't always have to be something like...like that, and I've read mostly everything that I'm allowed to read."

"Allowed?" I questioned.

"Priestess Analia believes that I should only spend time reading appropriate things, like the histories or prayers."

"Priestess Analia can go fuck herself."

Poppy laughed then—it was short and full of surprise but loud and real. And I was glad she had, but there was nothing humorous about that Priestess.

"You shouldn't say that," she said, her voice lighter.

"Yeah, I know."

"But you don't care?"

"Exactly."

"It must be an amazing feeling not to."

The wistfulness in her voice drew my gaze and caused pressure in my chest to build. "I wish you knew the feeling."

Her hooded head cut toward me and then faced forward again. Silence fell between us, and it wasn't good because I was thinking of how Poppy was only *allowed* to read certain things, as if she were a child or not trusted to choose for herself. There truly was nothing the Ascended didn't control when it came to her.

Well, that wasn't exactly true. The fact that we were strolling through the Grove after she'd snuck out was proof, as was the time she'd stolen for herself at the Red Pearl. But those were just minutes here and there over the years.

It wasn't right.

But it would change when—

I stopped myself, the back of my neck prickling. What would change for her once I got what I wanted? She would end up back with those monsters, the false Queen and King. Her life would return to this or possibly become even stricter while the Blood Crown searched for more Atlantian blood to complete their Ascensions. At least until they were stopped. The only thing that would change would be where her gilded cage was located, and she would no longer be subjected to the Duke. However, there were far worse Ascended in the capital. That, I knew for sure.

I stared at her hooded figure, my heart thumping. How would she react once she learned the truth of the Ascended—of her precious Queen Ileana? She would eventually discover the truth, sooner rather than later. Based on what I already knew, I didn't think she would continue going along with the charade the Ascended had fostered for her. But so what?

I could give her a choice once I had Malik, could I not? Allow her to remain with us. Doing so would be tricky, presenting a whole slew of risks that my people nor I needed. They'd signed up to free Malik. Not free him and the Maiden. And would my people accept her? Likely not. Atlantians could hold a grudge with the best of them.

Fuck. Now wasn't the time to think about any of that shit.

"There's something I've been wondering." Spying several low-hanging branches, I moved so I walked to her left. "What is it that you do every morning?"

"My daily prayers." Her hooded head tilted toward mine. "And breakfast."

I reached out, holding one of the branches up so she could pass underneath. "Would you be angry if I said I didn't believe you?"

Poppy huffed. "I've given you no reason not to believe what I say."

"Really?" I drawled, lifting another branch. "I think I know."

"Do you?"

"I just need to ask one question to be sure," I said as we crossed under thinner branches. Streaks of moonlight pierced the darkness all around us. "Does Vikter happen to be with you during your...prayers?"

Poppy said absolutely nothing.

I smiled, getting my answer without her confirming it. She was likely training how to use that dagger and to fight when she was with him.

"I was wondering something myself," she said, both arms folded over the book now as if she worried I'd snatch it from her once more. "About you."

"Yes. I find women who can wield a dagger and nearly knock me on my ass to be extremely alluring," I answered, glancing in her direction. "And arousing."

Her soft inhale turned into a gasp as she tripped over something in the foliage. I caught her upper arm, steadying her.

"I was not going to ask that." She quickly recovered, clearing her throat.

"It's true, though."

"That, I couldn't care less about."

Little liar. My hand slipped away from her cloak. "What were you wondering?"

She was quiet again for a few moments. "You...you called me Poppy back there, in the Atheneum."

I had?

"You'd been calling me Penellaphe," she continued. "Why?"

"Does it bother you?" I asked.

"No." She peeked at me from under the hood. "You didn't answer the question."

I couldn't answer the question. Hell, I hadn't even realized that I *had* called her Poppy. Or that I now thought of her as such. I frowned. It didn't matter. A name was just a name. "I'm not sure why." I remembered what Tawny had said. "I suppose that means we're friends."

There was another soft inhale, betraying her sharp words. "I wouldn't go that far."

I chuckled. "I would."

Poppy sighed.

Another laugh left me. "We are most definitely friends."

PRESENT VII

"How badly did you want to stab me when I took that diary from you?" I laughed, the sound echoing in the quiet chamber. "I imagine it was a lot. Would've been worth it, though."

Dipping my chin, I pressed a kiss to the top of Poppy's head. She was tucked against me, her head resting on my chest and my legs bracing hers. Delano was still at the foot of the bed in his wolven form, a big mound of white fur. Still, I knew he was awake and alert. He hadn't strayed far from Poppy's side.

It was near evening, and Kieran was currently making use of the adjoining bathing chamber. Poppy remained as she was, but I didn't think her skin was as cold as it had been before, and the shadows under her eyes had faded even more. A nearly untouched plate of sliced meat and fruits sat on a nearby table. I managed to eat a few bites and hadn't fallen back to sleep, but oddly, I wasn't tired. Neither was Kieran, who hadn't slept or eaten much more than I had. Sure, there was weariness, but it stemmed from concern. Otherwise, I felt fine, and there was only one thing I could think of to explain that. The bond between the three of us. Poppy's life force—all that eather in her that Nektas had spoken of— fueled us, keeping us strong. I didn't think either Kieran or I felt particularly worthy of that strength.

"But when I saw you standing on that ledge? I was furious. I couldn't even fathom what the hell you were thinking," I continued. "I couldn't stay mad long, though. Not after realizing what you had to do just to be able to read a book of your choosing."

Old anger that was never quite far away rose, and it was hard to push back down. This wasn't the time or place for that kind of emotion. "I'm glad you took the diary. You know how much I fucking love that book."

The thing I loved more about Miss Willa's journal was how pretty Poppy flushed whenever I or anyone else brought it up. Well, that and the throaty sexiness of her voice when she read from it—and how wet she became doing so.

Fuck.

My dick swelled against the curve of her ass. Now *really* wasn't the time for that.

I tipped my head back. "I suppose we have Miss Willa to thank for many things," I murmured, thinking of how the Atheneum was the first time I'd called her Poppy. And how that was who she'd become to me after that night. "I should've known then, and maybe I did on some subconscious level because that's when I started rethinking my plans, wondering how I could give you choice and freedom. I think I knew even then, before we spent time under the willow and left Masadonia, that I couldn't just send you back to the Ascended. But I didn't know how to acknowledge it. I don't think I was capable of doing so then, to be honest."

You care about her.

"But Kieran knew, or at least he started to suspect as much because of what I wanted to do to the Duke," I said, and Delano's ears perked. "Killing him wasn't in the initial plans. If he had been somewhat decent, he could've lived, or at the very least, his death would've been quick." My lips thinned. "It wasn't."

I ran my fingers through her hair, brushing the silky strands back from her cheek as I thought back to that day in the Duke's quarters. "I didn't even know the full extent of what he had put you through—what he'd allowed—until much later. And, gods, I've lost count of how many times I wished I could go back and make it even worse for him."

A warm breeze flowed through the chamber. "But I made it hurt, just as I told Kieran I would." A cold, brutal smile spread across my mouth. "I've taken lives I've regretted. But the Duke's? That is one death I will *never* regret."

THE DUKE

The day of the Rite, I sat in Duke Teerman's study, at *his* desk, in *his* chair, and waited impatiently.

Patience wasn't typically a skill of mine, nor did I see it as a virtue in general.

However, for this, I'd deal with it.

I looked down at the back of the Royal Guard my boots rested upon. With compulsion, I'd gotten what I needed to know from the fair-haired man before I snapped his neck. Killing him wasn't necessary. I didn't plan to be here when the compulsion wore off, but the thing was, he'd known what was going on in here during the Duke's *lessons*. I was sure the other Royal Guard who often watched the door also knew, but this one had gotten hard as he recounted how the Duke made her undress from the waist up and then bent her over the very desk I sat at. Then he took a cane to her skin. Sometimes, Lord Mazeen *watched*. More than once, she'd left this room barely conscious. There was no telling what they'd done to her.

"Fucking bastard." I kicked the dead guard in the side, sending him skidding across the floor.

My stare fixed on the long, slender cane propped against the corner of the mahogany desk. Was it this one he'd used to punish Poppy? Or one of the others by the credenza? Anger simmered in my gut, hard to keep in check.

I'd done a lot of terrible things. Horrific shit. I'd killed in cold blood. I'd killed in anger. Blood that I'd never be able to wash away stained my hands. I was a monster capable of monstrous acts, but what Duke Teerman had done to Poppy? What he'd likely been doing to her for years? That was below even me.

You care about her.

My fingers curled around the arm of the chair. I truly didn't believe a person needed to care about someone to be infuriated and disgusted by how others treated them, but I'd lied to Kieran.

This wasn't about revenge.

It was about her.

I turned my head from side to side, easing the building tension as I stared at the cane. All I saw was the blood draining from the lower half of Poppy's face when she realized what she'd said the day we left her lessons with Priestess Analia. I could hear that slight tremor in her voice even now. I knew what it was.

Fear.

Actual fear, from the girl who snuck out and roamed the city at night. Who went up onto the Rise during a Craven attack. I felt my anger rising. And it was more than that. It was the role these bastards had played in everything forbidden to Poppy—what they'd taken from her. Friendship. Physical contact. The freedom to explore. To experience. She couldn't even choose what she read. And because of the lengths she'd had to go to, the risks *she'd* had to take to have just a taste of those things. But worse yet, it was the shame I heard in her denials.

All of that factored into why I was willing to take these risks.

It didn't matter what came next. That I'd inevitably become the cause of the fear filling her voice. That she was another monstrous act I was in the process of committing. I hadn't thought of that as we walked back to the castle the night before when I was thinking of choices. She would not choose to stay with us once she knew our truth.

But I would not cause her to feel *shame.*

If I did?

Then that would become yet another act I would never be able to cleanse from my soul.

The sound of footsteps reached me. My grip on the chair arm relaxed.

Duke Teerman opened the door to his study, letting it swing shut behind him. I caught the faint scent of iron. Blood. He'd taken about three steps before the bastard realized the chamber wasn't empty.

"What in…?" Teerman halted. One side of my lips curled up as I slowly turned the chair to face him. Those dark, soulless eyes went wide. They widened even more when he noticed the dead guard. "The *fuck?*"

"Good afternoon." I leaned back, propping my booted feet on the smooth, shiny surface of his desk. I made a grand show of crossing my ankles. He hadn't yet dressed for the Rite—too busy getting a snack in. "*Your Grace.*"

The pale-haired fucker recovered quickly. I had to give him that. He straightened and dropped his cloak on the settee. Anger tightened the skin around his mouth. "I must admit, the utter disrespect of your actions has me at a loss for words, but I assume you must be here to turn in your resignation."

I tilted my head. "And why would you think that?"

His nostrils flared. "Because you'd have to be a fool to believe you'd keep your role as a guard when you leave this office."

"Well, for starters, I'm not going anywhere." My smile spread as the Duke went rigid. "And secondly, I cannot behave disrespectfully toward someone I never respected in the first place."

His too-red lips parted. My gaze dropped to the crisp collar of his white shirt. There was a small red drop there. Messy eater.

"You're out of your mind."

"I'm out of many things." Reaching over, I picked up the cane. His gaze shot to it. He took a step forward, his large hands curling into fists at his sides. "Patience is one of them. I've been waiting for you to return for some time." I paused. "Dorian."

He halted once more, his back going straight as he stared at me. Understanding dawned in his features. He'd finally figured it out. Who I was. What he'd gladly welcomed into his guard and allowed to sleep beneath his roof. Why I was here. His eyes shot to the door.

"*Run,*" I urged. "I dare you."

Duke Teerman locked up.

"Ah, there it is." Running my fingers up the length of the cane, I leaned forward. "A flicker of intelligence *is* to be found."

"You," he snarled.

I folded my hand around the end of the cane. "Me?"

Teerman's lip peeled back. His chin dropped as a low growl rumbled from him. "The Dark One."

"So they say." I gave him a tight-lipped smile. "But I'd prefer if you addressed me properly. It's *Prince* Casteel Da'Neer."

"And here I thought it would be traitorous bastard."

I laughed softly. "That works, too, but you forgot a part of that title. It's traitorous, *murderous* bastard."

His throat worked on a swallow. "Is that so?"

I nodded.

"Do you plan to commit an act of murder?"

"Always," I murmured.

A muscle throbbed at his temple as a long moment passed. "I know what you're planning. You won't get away with it. You have to know that."

"I do?"

"You're in my home, in my city—both of which are full of my guards." He tipped up his chin. "All I have to do is yell, and you'll be surrounded. There's no way you'll escape."

"Then what?" I asked.

He smiled. "Then I'll send your head back to the Queen."

I snorted. "That sounded entirely dramatic and grossly incorrect."

"And what exactly was incorrect?" He inched back a step, clearly thinking I hadn't noticed.

"Your city is not full of guards loyal to you. It hasn't been for a while," I told him. Somehow, the Ascended grew even paler. "And you have no idea what I plan."

Teerman laughed then. "You think I don't know?"

"Well, you had no idea we've been in your city and home for quite some time," I remarked. "You see, I wouldn't want to give you too much credit."

He laughed, low and hard. "You know, the Queen said you had a smart mouth."

"Did she?" I asked. "I'm not surprised to hear she's still obsessed with my mouth after all this time."

"That's not the only thing she said."

"I'm sure it wasn't." There would be no repeat of Lord Devries. There wasn't much time. I had a Rite to ready myself for. "But I didn't come here to talk about that bitch."

"Then why are you here?" He glanced at the cane. "Your brother?"

I shook my head.

His cheeks hollowed. "The Maiden."

I smiled.

"You will not get your hands on her," he swore, his dark eyes glinting. "I promise that. You won't—"

"You know what I find fascinating about the trees that grow in the Blood Forest?" I interrupted, drawing my palm down the smooth side of the reddish-brown cane, enjoying the rumble of his anger. "Besides the fact that you clearly treat these canes as if they are an extension of your withered cock?"

Air hissed between his clenched teeth.

I chuckled. "While bloodstone leaves nothing left of an Ascended, the wood of a Blood Forest tree simply kills a vampry. Slowly. Painfully." One side of my lips curved up as I met his stare. "Leaving the remains to rot and decay, just like any other body."

Teerman swallowed. "And what does it do to an Atlantian?"

"Not much." I smirked. "I bet that gets to you. The Ascended want so badly to pretend they're Blessed by the gods. You and I both know that is a load of shit. You're nothing special. You never have been. None of you are. You're just a poor imitation of us, desperately clinging to the last vestiges of your waning power and privilege."

"And do you think you're any better than us?" he retorted.

"Most of us are. Me? No. I'm not that much better. Hell, perhaps I'm even worse than some of the Ascended. But you?" I pointed the cane at him. "You're not even horse shit compared to me."

"You insolent—"

"Traitorous, murderous bastard. I know." I sighed. "Anyway, back to these canes." I watched him through half-open eyes. "I know what you do with them."

Teerman went silent.

"I know you've used them against her."

His shoulders straightened. "And did she tell you that?"

"Poppy hasn't said a word."

Teerman's brows shot up. "Poppy?" he repeated, and I knew I'd made a mistake there. I'd *slipped*. The Duke stared, a slow smile creeping across his cheeks. "You've got to be fucking kidding me."

Now, it was I who fell silent.

He tipped his head back and laughed. "Anyone else taking an interest in her wouldn't have surprised me all that much. She has a…certain way about her. A fire." He laughed again, and I went cold. "Her last guard had a soft spot for her. But you? The Dark One? Didn't see that coming." One side of his lips curled up. "Then again, *Poppy* is beautiful. Well, at least half of her i—"

I moved then, leaving the cane on the desk as I vaulted over it. In a heartbeat, I had the Duke by his shirt collar and his back against the spot my boots had just dirtied. I clamped one hand around his throat, just below his chin, pressing my fingers into his cold skin until the fragile bones there started to crack. I didn't break them, though. I wanted the fucker to still breathe but not scream.

"You will not say her name again," I said as a thin rush of air wheezed from his gaping mouth. "Not Penellaphe. Especially not Poppy."

Teerman grabbed for the cane.

I caught his arm, snapping it at the elbow. The crack of bone made me smile as a low moan rattled out of him. He swung his other arm. I broke that one at his shoulder.

"Make one more move, and your legs will be next," I warned as his skin dampened along his brow. "Do you understand? Blink once for yes."

Teerman blinked.

"Perfect." I patted his chest. "There is something I want you to understand. You were already dead before you ever laid eyes on me. You were already running out of time. But your death, why it's coming now, it has absolutely nothing to do with the Blood Queen or the throne and lands you've taken part in stealing. It has nothing to do with my brother. You were right when you said it was because of her. You're dying right now, right here, because of her."

A tremor went through Duke Teerman as he struggled to breathe. He went as still as a fucking statue, though, when I picked up the cane.

"You're dying because of *this*." I watched him track the cane as I moved it above his face. "The last time you used it on her, how many times did you bring it against her skin?"

He moaned, flopping unsteadily on the desk.

I leaned in until our faces were inches apart. "Use your eyes. Blink," I instructed. "Blink once for each lash you delivered."

Teerman's eyes remained wide for several moments, then he blinked. Once. Twice. When he got to five, a rage that tasted of blood unfurled in my chest. When he finally stopped blinking, I shook.

I fucking *shook*.

It was part horror for what he'd subjected Poppy to, and part awe that she had withstood it. And a couple of days later was out on that Rise. Godsdamn.

"Did you break her skin?" I demanded. "Once for yes. Twice for no."

He blinked two times rapidly.

"Have you drawn blood before?"

Duke Teerman blinked once as his lips thinned and pulled back over his teeth.

I inhaled deeply as I pushed up. Of course, he had.

Gripping him by his ruined shoulder, I roughly flopped him onto his stomach. His muffled groan of pain was just a precursor. I tore open the back of his shirt, exposing the pale line of his spine as I leaned over him and whispered into his ear the number of times he'd blinked.

Then I brought the cane down on his back that many times, each lash whistling through the air, sending his body into spasms, each blow opening thin slits in the skin.

I delivered an extra one just because I fucking felt like it.

When I finished and flipped him onto his back once more, he was a quivering mess, and the scent of piss was strong in the air. I shook my head in disgust.

His lips moved as he tried to speak around the cracked larynx, finally pushing the words out in a broken wheeze only Atlantian or wolven ears could've picked up. "Once...she...finds out who...you are, she...will...*hate you.*"

"I know." I gripped the cane. "And just so you know, every part of Poppy is beautiful."

"She...is." Something flashed in his eyes. A flicker of dying sunlight amidst the darkness. "And...she will...always be...mine."

"You sick bastard," I snarled. "She has never been yours."

Then I drove the cane through his chest.

Duke Teerman's body reared, arms flopping as I let go of the cane. It remained in his chest as I stepped back. This time, I had all the patience in the realm to wait. His death wasn't quick. I'd purposely nicked his heart, so it took several minutes for the blood tree to do its thing.

The Duke of Masadonia went out without even a whimper, body broken and urine staining his pants. The surge of savage satisfaction from watching the life go out of his eyes was short-lived, though. He wouldn't lay a hand on Poppy again—or anyone for that matter—but it wouldn't erase the pain and humiliation he'd inflicted upon her. Wouldn't undo any of that.

I wished I could kill the sick bastard all over again.

Turning from the Duke, I stopped. I thought of what was to come tonight and the opportunity for a bit of dramatic flair I was now presented with.

"Well, Your Grace,"—facing him, my smile returned—"I do believe you will make a fine centerpiece for the Rite."

I LOST MY BREATH

I was running late.

My visit with the Duke and subsequent arrangement took longer than expected.

Freshly bathed, I was finally dressed for the Rite in crimson, my mask in place as I strode through the packed foyer. The plan was to find Poppy, separate her from Vikter and Tawny, then get her into the garden, where Kieran would eventually be. My steps slowed, though. The place was a fucking madhouse.

Commoners moved among the Ascended and Lords and Ladies in Wait like waves of red. I spotted a handful of guards only because of the weapons they wore. There were so many people, and the scent of roses was heavy in the air, nearly choking me as I neared the Great Hall.

I'd cleaned the Duke's blood from my hands, but nothing had washed away my smirk. It was firmly plastered across my face and would likely remain there for the foreseeable future.

Especially when I thought of his prized Blood Forest cane.

I saw hundreds milling about through the open doors, filling the floor and alcoves. The gold and white banners had been stripped, replaced by the red of the Rite, reminding me of the ones that hung in Wayfair. My upper lip curled. There were vases of roses in every shade placed every couple of feet, and the sight of them reminded me of when I'd overheard Tawny complaining about them. A wry grin tugged at my lips as I stopped at the pillars, scanning the scene before me. Everyone looked the same to me, dressed and masked in the color of fresh blood. My gaze skipped over an alcove and then shot back to one of the columns—

Good gods.

I saw Poppy standing there with Vikter and Tawny, and that odd damn prickling sensation hit the nape of my neck again as I lost my breath.

Staring at Poppy from the pillars, still several yards from her, the air just went right out of my lungs as if I'd forgotten how to fucking breathe. And how idiotic did that sound? One didn't simply forget how to breathe, but never in my life had I felt that...that *whoosh* in my chest. Never. I didn't know if it was because she wasn't veiled, or because she wasn't in white.

Or perhaps because she was simply the most beautiful creature I'd ever seen.

Her hair was swept back from her face and fell in loose waves down her back, the color reminding me of raspberries in the light of the Great Hall. The red domino mask was leagues above the veil, and even from where I stood, I thought her lips appeared darker, lusher. And that gown...

The sleeves were a gossamer crimson, as was much of the rest. Only the fabric from the bodice to the thighs was opaque. The remainder was translucent, and all of it hugged the tempting curves of her body.

Poppy turned, angling away from where I stood. Her hair ended just above the sweet, lush swell of her ass.

That gown.

It was the likely source of my lost breath because it was obscenely decadent and made for sin.

And my imagination ran wild, filling my mind with all the fun and various ways one could sin as I started toward her. The nape of my neck tingled as I wove in and out of the crowd, my heart thumping.

The slope of Poppy's shoulders tensed, and then she turned. Her rosy-hued lips parted, and fuck...so much want seized me. Too much. The breeches and tunic were far too thin for what I currently felt.

"Hi," Poppy said and then clamped her mouth shut.

I grinned as her cheeks pinked. "You look..." There really wasn't a single word that would do her justice, so I settled for the best I could think of in the moment. "Lovely." I turned to Tawny, and honest to gods, she could've been nude or wearing a sack for all I knew. "As do you."

"Thank you," Tawny replied.

I glanced at Vikter. "You, as well."

He snorted, and Tawny laughed, but I felt rewarded when I saw Poppy's smile.

She turned to Vikter. "You do look exceptionally handsome tonight."

The older man flushed as he gave a faint shake of his head.

I moved to stand behind Poppy, as close as I could. "Sorry for the delay."

"Is everything okay?" she asked, sounding nervous.

"Of course," I assured her. "I was pulled to assist with security sweeps." Which wasn't entirely untrue. I did speak with Jansen to discuss the fires the Descenters planned to set. No one would be harmed tonight—well, no mortals, anyway—but many of the Ascended would find it difficult to return to their homes. "I didn't think it would take as long as it did."

Poppy appeared as if she wished to say something more but only nodded as she turned her attention to the dais. Music began playing as servants entered from the many side doors, carrying trays of fragile glasses and delicate foods.

"I need to speak to the Commander," Vikter said, looking at me.

"I have her," I told him.

Instead of reminding me exactly how important she was like he normally did, he only nodded before curtly pivoting. Relief swept through me. I wouldn't have to work around Vikter and what that would inevitably lead to.

I moved to take Vikter's place, standing at Poppy's right. "Have I missed anything?"

"You haven't," Tawny answered. "Unless you were looking forward to a bunch of prayers and teary-eyed goodbyes."

"Not particularly," I commented dryly.

Poppy looked at Tawny. "Did they call out the Tulis family?"

Her brow creased. "You know, I don't think they did."

I bit back a smile. If they had, the Tulises would not have been able to answer. They were well on their way to New Haven.

Movement caught my attention. The Duchess made her way toward us, followed by several Royal Guards.

"Penellaphe," the Duchess said, smiling.

"Your Grace," Poppy replied so politely it was almost hard to believe I'd ever heard her curse.

The Duchess nodded at Tawny and me, her gaze sweeping over

my form in the exact way I'd looked at Poppy. Would she miss her husband? I didn't think so.

I smiled.

"Are you enjoying the Rite?" she asked Poppy. Apparently, it didn't matter if Tawny or I were having a good time.

Poppy nodded. "Is His Grace not attending?"

My smile kicked up a notch.

"I believe he is running late." The corners of the Duchess's mouth tensed, giving away her worry.

She shouldn't be.

The Duke was already here.

She moved in closer to Poppy, her voice low, but I heard her clearly. "Remember who you are, Penellaphe."

My smile slipped from my face.

"You are not to mingle or socialize," the Duchess continued.

"I know," Poppy assured her as my hand tightened into a fist at my side.

I watched the Duchess move into the crowd of adoring Ascended and Lords and Ladies in Wait, that muscle ticking in my jaw again. "I have a question."

Poppy tilted her head. "Yes?"

"If you're not supposed to mingle or socialize, which are the same thing, by the way," I said, feeling my anger fading a bit with the slight curve of her lips, "what is the point of you being allowed to attend?"

That small grin disappeared.

"That is actually a good question," Tawny stated.

Poppy's lips pursed. "I'm not sure what the point is, to be honest."

Neither was I.

I looked out over the crowd, but after a few moments, my gaze was drawn back to Poppy—to her loose hair and that damn gown. Gods, why did she have to be so beautiful? So *fierce*?

Her hands were twisting together, and I looked at her face. She watched Tawny. A moment passed, and then she called her friend's name.

Tawny twisted toward her. "Yes?"

"You don't have to stand here beside me," she said. "You can go and have fun."

"What?" Tawny's nose wrinkled. "I'm having fun. Aren't you?"

"Of course," Poppy said, but I doubted that. "But you don't have to be right beside me. You should be out there." She gestured at those on the main floor. "It's okay."

Tawny protested, but Poppy wouldn't allow it, eventually convincing her that it was all right for her to leave. To socialize. Then Poppy smiled. Not a huge one, but I caught just a glimpse of white teeth. Her friend having fun made her happy—made her smile.

Fuck me.

I wanted her to have fun.

To be happy.

I wanted that smile.

And in a little bit, it would be a long time before she smiled again. Poppy was alone with no effort on my part. The relief I should feel was nowhere to be found.

I stepped in closer to her. "That was kind of you."

"Not particularly. Why should she stand here and do nothing just because that's all I can do?"

"Is that really all you can do?"

"You were standing right here when Her Grace reminded me that I am not to mingle or—"

"Or fraternize."

"She said socialize," Poppy said.

"But you don't have to stay here."

"I don't." She turned back to the floor. "I would like to go back to my room."

I clenched my teeth. "You sure?"

"Of course."

I stepped aside. "After you, Princess."

Her eyes narrowed. "You need to stop calling me that."

"But I like it."

She brushed past me and lifted the hem of her skirt. "But I don't."

"That's a lie."

Her lips twitched as she shook her head. I followed her through the throng of masked attendees, none seeming aware of who walked among them. The air was cooler outside the Great Hall. Poppy glanced at one of the open doors that led to the garden.

"Where are you going?" I asked as she continued, hastily looking away from the garden.

Poppy faced me, her nose scrunched against the mask in confusion. "Back to my rooms, as I..."

I started to speak, but my gaze snagged on the fall of her hair and then on the delicate lace of her bodice. "I was wrong earlier when I said you looked lovely."

"What?" she whispered.

"You look absolutely exquisite, Poppy. Beautiful." And she really did. "I just…I needed to tell you that."

Her eyes widened behind the mask as she stared at me—at my face, luckily. If she looked lower, I feared she would see just how true the words were. My gaze returned to the lace of her bodice.

I really needed to get better control of myself.

And I needed to get on with this.

I hadn't expected to get her alone this quickly or easily. I had some time before Kieran arrived. I could take her to her chambers and coax her back out later, but…

The garden was her place, and I wanted her to see it one last time. I wanted that smile from her.

And if I were being honest with myself, getting her out in the garden now wasn't just about my plans. It also had to do with the fact that something happened when I spent time with her. Something damn near magical.

I was…I was just me.

Cas.

And fuck if that didn't feel dangerous. Maybe even idiotic. Because I was self-aware enough to recognize that in my short time of knowing her, a connection had formed between us—a bond that wasn't at all one-sided. If I had any common sense or were more like I had been before the Blood Crown held me captive, I would nip this shit in the bud. But I wasn't him anymore. Hadn't been in decades. I was now far more impulsive and reckless. Selfish. When I wanted, I *wanted*.

And it wasn't like there would be many more opportunities for this after tonight.

"I have an idea," I said, forcing my gaze to hers.

"You do?"

I nodded. "It doesn't involve returning to your room."

She drew her lip between her teeth. "I'm confident that unless I remain at the Rite, I would be expected to return to my room."

"You're masked, as am I. You're not dressed like the Maiden," I pointed out. "To use your own ideology from last night, no one will know who either of us is."

"Yes, but…"

"Unless you wish to go back to the room." I started to grin. "Maybe you're so engrossed in that book—"

Her cheeks turned pink. "I am not engrossed in that book."

I found that somewhat disappointing. "I know you don't want to be cooped up in your chambers. There's no reason to lie to me."

"I…" Her gaze darted around us. "And where do you suggest that I go?"

"Where *we* go?" I tilted my chin toward the garden entrance.

Her chest rose with a deep breath. "I don't know. It…"

"It used to be a place of refuge. Now, it's become a place of nightmares," I said, stomach churning with the knowledge I was the reason she no longer had that. "But it can only stay that way if you let it."

"If I let it? How do I change the fact that Rylan died out there?"

"You don't."

The corners of her mouth tensed. "I'm not following where you're going with this."

I moved in closer to her, meeting her stare. "You can't change what happened in there. Just like you can't change the fact that the courtyard used to give you peace. You just replace your last memory—a bad one—with a new one—a good one," I told her, having learned that myself. "And you keep doing that until the initial one no longer outweighs the replacement."

Poppy's lips parted as her attention shifted to the garden door. "You make it sound so easy."

"It's not. It's hard and uncomfortable, but it works." I offered her my hand. "And you won't be alone. I'll be there with you, and not just watching over you."

Her gaze flew to mine. She seemed to lock up as if my words startled her. At first, I wasn't sure what I'd said to cause such a reaction, but then I thought about what I knew of her. Other than perhaps Tawny, those who spent time with her did so because it was their duty. Even Vikter, to some extent. Even me.

Fuck. That sat like a boulder on my chest.

Poppy brought her hand to mine but then stopped short. "If someone saw me," she said. "Saw you—"

"Saw us? Holding hands? Dear gods, the scandal." I grinned, looking around. "No one is here. Unless you see people I can't."

"Yes, I see the spirits of those who've made bad life choices," she replied dryly.

I laughed. "I doubt anyone will recognize us in the courtyard. Not with both of us masked, and just the moonlight and a few lamps to light the way." I wiggled my fingers. "Besides, I have a feeling anyone out there will be too busy to care."

Poppy placed her hand in mine. "You're such a bad influence."

She had no idea.

I folded my hand around hers. The back of my neck tightened. "Only the bad can be influenced, Princess."

THE WILLOW

"That sounds like faulty logic to me," Poppy commented.

I laughed, leading her toward the cooler air of the outdoors. "My logic is never faulty."

That got me a slight smile. "I feel like that's not something one would be aware of if it was."

But in the lantern light, the small grin faded too quickly as she glanced around the garden and the breeze rattled the bushes crowding the walkway. Her steps slowed. Even without my senses, I knew she practically hummed with anxiety.

Seeking to distract her, I spoke the first thing that came to mind. "One of the last places I saw my brother was a favorite place of mine."

Her attention darted from the darkened pathways that neither the lanterns nor the moonlight penetrated. Wide eyes met mine.

I tightened my hand around hers, but her fingers remained straight. I held her hand. She wasn't holding mine. "Back home, there are hidden caverns that very few people know about. You have to walk pretty far in this one particular tunnel. It's tight and dark. Not a lot of people are willing to follow it to find what awaits at the end."

"But you and your brother did?" she asked.

"My brother, a friend of ours, and I did when we were young and had more bravery than common sense." My brows knitted. "But I'm glad we did because at the end of the tunnels, was this huge cavern filled with the bluest, bubbling, warm water I'd ever seen."

She glanced to our left, where the low murmur of conversation seeped out from the darkness. "Like a hot spring?"

"Yes, and no. The water back home... There's really no

comparison."

"Where are—?" Her head swiveled to the right at the sound of a soft moan. I grinned as she swallowed. "Where...where are you from?"

"A little village I'm sure you've never heard of," I said, squeezing her hand. Her fingers remained straight. "We'd sneak off to the cavern every chance we got. The three of us. It was like our own little world." A wistfulness I hadn't felt in a long time filled me as I spotted the marble and limestone fountain sculpted in the likeness of the veiled Maiden. Water tumbled from the pitcher she held, spilling into the basin at her feet. "And at the time, there were a lot of things happening—things that were too adult and grown-up for us to understand then. We needed that escape, where we could go and not worry about what could be stressing our parents, and fretting over all the whispered conversations we didn't quite understand. We knew enough to know they were a harbinger of something bad. It was our haven."

I stopped at the fountain and faced her. "Much like this garden was yours. I lost both of them. My brother when we were younger, and then my best friend a few years after that," I told her, which was only partially true. I lost both of them at once. One because of my foolishness. One at my hands. "The place that was once filled with happiness and adventure had turned into a graveyard of memories. I couldn't even think about going back there without them." A slight tremor went through my arm as the knot of sorrow and bitterness loosened. "It was like the place became haunted."

"I understand," she said, looking up at me with clear eyes. "I keep looking around, thinking that the garden should look different. Assuming there'd be a visible change to represent how it now feels to me."

I cleared my throat. "But it is the same, isn't it?"

Poppy nodded.

"It took me a very long time to work up the nerve to go back to the cavern. I felt that way, too." I hadn't gone back alone. Kieran was there. I didn't think I would've been able to go myself. "Like the water surely must've turned muddy in my absence, dirty and cold. But it wasn't. It was still as calm, blue, and warm as it always was."

"Did you replace the sad memories with happy ones?" Poppy asked.

I shook my head. "Haven't gotten a chance, but I plan to." I told her yet another lie. I doubted that was something I would achieve. And honest to gods, I didn't think I deserved to.

"I hope you do." She said it so earnestly. And, gods, that was a punch to the gut as I watched the breeze play with the strands of her hair, tossing them across her shoulder and chest. "I'm sorry about your brother and friend."

Yeah, I really didn't deserve that.

"Thank you." I looked up at the star-riddled night sky. I knew I was a monster. But I also knew I wasn't the only monster here. "I know it's not like what happened here, to Rylan, but I do understand how it feels."

"Sometimes, I think...I think it's a blessing that I was young when Ian and I lost our parents," she said after a moment. "My memories of them are faint, and because of that, there's this...I don't know, level of detachment? As wrong as this will sound, I'm lucky in a way. It makes dealing with the loss easier because it's almost as if they're not real. It's not like that for Ian. He has a lot more memories than I do."

"It's not wrong, Princess. I think it's just the way the mind and heart work," I said. "You haven't seen your brother at all since he left for the capital?"

Poppy shook her head as she stared at my hand holding hers. "He writes as often as he can. Usually, once a month, but I haven't seen him since the morning he left." Slowly, she curled her fingers around mine, and fuck, that surge of triumph came again. I wasn't only holding her hand any longer. "I miss him." She lifted her chin, her gaze finding mine. "I'm sure you miss your brother, and I hope...I hope you see him again."

Fuck.

That was said as earnestly as her earlier words. I started to tell her that I would, but damn, it felt all kinds of wrong to tell *her* that.

The breeze caught another strand of her hair. I snagged the curl, the backs of my knuckles grazing the bare skin just below her throat. A tremor went through the hand I held. Her scent thickened, her body eagerly responding to that barely there touch.

Poppy dropped my hand and stepped back, turning away. "I..." She cleared her throat, and a smile started to tug at my lips. "My favorite place in the garden is the night-blooming roses. There's a bench there. I used to come out almost every night to see them open. They were my favorite flower, but now I have a hard time even looking at the ones cut and placed in bouquets."

"Do you want to go there now?" I asked.

"I...I don't think so."

"Would you like to see my favorite place?" I offered.

Poppy glanced over my shoulder. "You have a favorite place?"

"Yes." I extended my hand once more. "Want to see?"

She hesitated for only a heartbeat, then returned her hand to mine.

My heart thumped as I led her away from the Maiden fountain and down another pathway toward the southern side of the garden. Her sweet, fresh scent invaded all my senses, even crowding out the lavender blooms we neared, leaving me thinking she was anxious because of that. Her desire concerned her.

"You're a fan of the weeping willow?" she inquired.

The old and large willow she spoke of appeared in the lantern light, its branches nearly reaching the ground.

I nodded. "Never saw one until I got here."

"Ian and I used to play inside. No one could see us."

"Play? Or do you mean hide?" I asked. "Because that's what I would've done."

She gave me a tiny grin. "Well, yes. I would hide, and Ian would tag along like any good big brother." Her head tilted back. "Have you gone under it? There're benches, but you can't see them now. Actually, anyone could be under there right now, and we wouldn't know."

I gave the willow a quick glance, able to see through the darkness of the canopy of branches. "No one is under there."

"How can you be sure?"

"I just am. Come on." I tugged her forward. "Watch your step."

Poppy was quiet as I took her around the low stone wall. I parted the branches with one hand, letting her enter, and kept my other hand firmly around hers as I joined her beneath the willow, knowing she wouldn't be able to see a damn thing.

"Gods," she murmured. "I forgot how dark it is in here at night."

"It feels like you're in a different world under here," I said. "As if we've stepped through a veil and into an enchanted world."

"You should see it when it's warmer. The leaves bloom—oh!" Excitement filled her voice, bringing a grin to my lips. "Or when it snows, and at dusk. The flakes dust the leaves and the ground, but not a lot makes it inside here. Then it really is like a different world."

"Maybe we'll see it."

"You think so?"

"Why not?" I said, knowing we wouldn't. I turned to her in the darkness. We stood close, our bodies inches apart. "It will snow, will it not?" I asked, letting myself...well, pretend. "We'll sneak off just before dusk and come out here."

"But will we be here?" she asked, sending a bolt of surprise through me. "The Queen could summon me to the capital before then."

"Possibly." I forced my tone to remain light. "If so, then I guess we'll have to find different adventures, won't we? Or should I call them *mis*adventures?"

Poppy laughed quietly, and the soft sound did two things simultaneously: It warmed my chest and my blood. The chest part confused me. The blood side of it did not. "I think it will be hard to sneak off anywhere in the capital," she said. "Not with me...not with me being so close to the Ascension."

"You need to have more faith in me if you think I can't manage to find a way for us to sneak off," I told her instead of saying that wouldn't happen. "I can assure you that whatever I get us involved in won't end with you on a ledge." I brushed a wisp of hair back from her cheek. "We're out here on the night of the Rite, hidden inside a weeping willow."

"It didn't seem all that difficult."

"That's only because I was leading the way," I teased.

That brought another soft laugh from her. "Sure."

"Your doubt wounds me." I turned from her. "You said there were benches in here? Wait. I see them."

"How in the world do you see those benches?"

"You can't?"

"Uh, no."

I grinned at the darkness. "Then I must have better eyesight than you."

"I think you're just saying you can see them, and we're probably a second away from tripping—"

"Here they are." I stopped by one, taking a seat.

Poppy gaped at me.

"Would you like to sit?" I asked.

"I would, but unlike you, I can't see in the dark—" She gasped as I tugged her down so she was perched on my thigh.

I was glad she couldn't see, because my smile was so wide, there was no doubt my fangs were visible. "Comfortable?"

There was no answer from Poppy, but her scent was rich and lovely, ever increasing.

"You can't be comfortable," I told her, sliding an arm around her and drawing her closer so her entire side was pressed firmly to my chest, and the top of her head was just below my chin. "There. That has to be much better."

Her breath came out in short, shallow breaths.

"I don't want you getting too cold," I tacked on, grinning. "I feel like that's an important part of my duty as your personal Royal Guard."

"Is that what you're doing right now?" Her voice was thicker, smoother. Did she notice? Because I sure as hell did. "Protecting me from the cold by pulling me into your lap?"

I carefully and lightly placed my palm against her waist, thinking of what little experience she had. While I might have been bold with her seating arrangement, I knew this was also a first for her. "Exactly."

Her breath tickled my throat. "This is incredibly inappropriate."

"More inappropriate than you reading a dirty journal?"

"*Yes*," she insisted.

"No." I laughed. "I can't even lie. This *is* inappropriate."

"Then why?"

"Why?" That was a good question. My chin grazed the top of her head as I looked at the branches concealing us. There were many reasons, and all of them came before killing time. Her need of me. My want of her.

My gaze tracked over her bow-shaped lips, the proud tip of her nose. "Because I wanted to," I said, giving her another bit of honesty.

"And what if I didn't want to?"

I chuckled. "Princess, I'm confident that if you didn't want me to do something, I'd be lying flat on my back with a dagger at my throat before I even took my next breath. Even if you can't see an inch in front of you."

She didn't deny that.

I glanced down at the curve of her leg. "You have your dagger on you, don't you?"

She sighed. "I do."

"Knew it." Desire surged through me as I let go of her hand. It wasn't so much the dagger that turned me on. It was what the blade symbolized. Her resilience. Her capability. Her strength. The proof that she had taken the nightmares and the fear and turned them into power. *That* was what turned me on. "No one can see us. No one is even aware that we're here. As far as anyone knows, you are in your room."

"This is still reckless for a multitude of reasons," she countered. "If someone comes in here—"

"I'd hear them before they did," I told her. I had my reasons for being under here. Many reasons. One of them was that I wanted her to have at least a handful of minutes where she was just Poppy. Not the Maiden. Minutes where she didn't have to worry about being caught. I wanted her to be as she was at the Red Pearl, free to experience. To live.

"And if someone did, they'd have no idea who we are."

Poppy leaned back, trying to see my face in the shadows. "Is this why you led me out here to this place?"

"What is *this*, Princess?"

"To be…inappropriate."

It hadn't been at first. Now? Most definitely. I touched her arm. "And why would I do that?"

"Why? I think it's pretty obvious, *Hawke*," she said. "I'm sitting in your lap. I doubt that's how you normally hold innocent conversations with people."

"Very rarely is anything I do innocent, Princess."

"Shocker," she muttered.

"So, you're suggesting I led you out here, instead of toward a private room with a *bed*." Knowing how touch was so forbidden to her, I exploited that, skimming my fingertips down her right arm. "To engage in a particular type of inappropriate behavior?"

"That's exactly what I'm saying, though my room would've been a better option."

"What if I said that isn't true?"

"I…" Her exhale teased my jaw as I moved my hand to her hip. "I wouldn't believe you."

"Then what if I said it didn't start off that way?" I moved just my thumb along the soft, rounded flesh there. I spoke the truth. I hadn't planned on this. Especially not right before I betrayed her. That would make me the kind of bastard that I…well, that I was. "But then there was the moonlight and you, with your hair down, in this dress, and *then* the idea occurred to me that this would be the perfect location for some wildly inappropriate behavior."

"Then I…I would say that's more likely."

I glided my hand down. "So, there you have it."

"At least, you're honest." She bit her lip as her eyes drifted halfway closed.

"Tell you what," I said, watching her closely. "I'll make you a deal."

"A deal?"

"If I do anything you don't like…" I drew my hand down her upper thigh, stopping when I felt the dagger beneath the thin panels. Closing my hand over it, I smiled. "I give you permission to stab me."

"That would be excessive," she stated.

"I was hoping you'd give me just a measly flesh wound," I said. "But it'd be worth finding out."

Her lips curved into a grin. "You are such a bad influence."

"I think we've already established that only the bad can be influenced."

Poppy's eyes closed as my fingers slipped off the hilt of her dagger and trailed over the blade. "And I think I already told you that your logic is faulty."

My heightened senses picked up on how her breath and pulse quickened. I could feel the heated restlessness building inside her.

It was building in me.

"I'm the Maiden, Hawke," she said, sounding more like she was reminding herself of that fact.

"And I don't care."

Her eyes snapped open. "I can't believe you just said that."

"I did." And I fucking meant it, because even with all the lies I'd told, this was the truth. Right now, under this willow, the only thing that mattered was *who* she was. "And I'll say it again. I don't care what you are." I moved my hand from her back and cupped her cheek. "I care about who you are," I said, and...fuck, godsdamn Kieran was right. I did care about her.

Her lower lip trembled as the muscle in my jaw flexed. "Why?" she whispered. "Why would you say that?"

I blinked, her question catching me off guard. "Are you seriously asking me that?"

"Yes, I am. It doesn't make sense."

"You don't make sense," I said.

She punched me in the shoulder, and not that lightly either.

I grunted. "Ouch."

"You're fine."

"I'm bruised," I teased.

"You're ridiculous," she retorted. "And it's you who makes no sense."

"I'm the one sitting here being honest." Which was entirely fucked-up if I thought too long about it. I didn't plan on doing that because I was sure to pay for it later. "You're the one hitting me. How do I not make sense?"

"Because this whole thing makes no sense. You could be spending time with anyone, Hawke—any number of people you wouldn't have to hide in a willow tree to be with."

That was true. "And yet, I'm here with you. And before you even begin to think it's because of my duty to you, it's not. I could've just walked you back to your room and stayed out in the hall."

"That's my point. It makes no sense. You can have a slew of willing participants in…whatever this is. It would be easy," she argued. "You can't have me. I'm…I'm un-have-able."

I frowned. *Unhaveable?* "I'm confident that's not even a word."

"That's not the point. I'm not allowed to do this. Any of this. I shouldn't have done what I did at the Red Pearl," she went on. "It doesn't matter if I want—"

"And you *do* want," I said, my voice low because it felt like I would send her fleeing if I said it too loudly. "What you want is me."

"That doesn't matter," she said.

That was bullshit. "What you want should always matter."

A brutal laugh left her. "It doesn't, and that's another thing that isn't the point. You could—"

"I heard you the first time, Princess. You're right. I could find someone who would be easier." I traced the edge of her mask, over her cheek. "Ladies or Lords in Wait, who aren't burdened by rules or limitations, who aren't Maidens I'm sworn to protect. There are a lot of ways I could occupy my time that don't include explaining in great detail why I'm choosing to be *where* I am, with *whom* I choose."

Poppy's nose scrunched.

"The thing is," I continued, "none of them intrigue me. You do."

"It's really that simple for you?" she asked.

No.

Not at all.

Not even here under the willow.

"Nothing is ever simple." I pressed my forehead to hers. "And when it is, it's rarely ever worth it."

"Then why?" she whispered.

My lips quirked. "I'm beginning to believe that's your favorite question."

"Maybe. It's just that…gods, there are a lot of reasons why I don't understand how you can be this intrigued. You've seen me," she said. I couldn't have heard her right. "You've seen what I look like—"

"I have," I cut her off, because holy fuck, I *had* heard her right, and that shouldn't have even crossed her mind. But because of bastards like the Duke, it did. Gods, I wanted to murder the fucker all over again. "And I think you already know what I think. I said it in front of you, in front of the Duke, and I told you outside the Great Hall—"

"I know what you said, and I'm not bringing up what I look like for you to shower me with compliments. It's just…" She shook her head. "Never mind. Forget I said that."

"I can't. I won't."

"Great."

"You're just used to assholes like the Duke." I snarled his title. "He may be an Ascended, but he's worthless."

She stiffened. "You shouldn't say things like that, Hawke. You—"

"I'm not afraid to speak the truth. He may be powerful, but he's just a weak man." And a dead one. "Who proves his strength by attempting to humiliate those more powerful than he is. Someone like you, with your strength? It makes him feel incompetent—which he is. And your scars? They are a testament to your fortitude. They are proof of what you survived. They are evidence of why you are here when so many twice your age wouldn't be. They're not ugly. Far from it. They're beautiful, Poppy."

The tension eased from her as she whispered, "That's the third time you've called me that."

"Fourth," I corrected. "We're friends, aren't we? Only your friends and your brother call you that, and you may be the Maiden, and I'm a Royal Guard, but all things considered, I would hope that you and I are friends."

"We are."

I should feel like shit for that—for becoming what I needed to be. Her friend. Gaining her trust. That festering guilt spread. My gaze flicked to the willow's swaying limbs. I didn't need to take it this far. I knew that. Fuck, I knew that in the Atheneum when I didn't kiss her. I had what I needed. The rest would be history.

I sighed, palming her cheek. "And I'm not…I'm not being a good friend or guard right now. I'm not…" I moved my hand beneath the heavy fall of her hair and curled my fingers there, holding her close to me. Just for a few more moments because I liked the way she felt in my arms, and I figured that after tonight, the only time I'd be holding her this close would be to stop her from punching me. "I really should get you back to your room. It's getting late."

Her exhale was ragged. "It is."

Fighting the desire to do the exact opposite, I started to lift her from my lap—

"Hawke?" she whispered. "Kiss me. Please."

Shock held me still, but my damn heart punched at my ribs as I stared at her. I knew what I should do. There was a past. There was a future outside this willow. I needed to do what I had done last night. There was no need for this.

Except she'd asked me to kiss her.

And I *wanted* this.

Fuck good intentions and the sliver of me that was a decent man.

"Gods," I rasped, sliding my hand back to her cheek. I would surely pay for this later, but right now, no price seemed too steep. "You don't have to ask me twice, Princess, and you never have to beg."

Closing the distance between us, I brushed my lips over hers. It wasn't a kiss. Not at all. But she gasped against my mouth so damn sweetly that I smiled. And I slowed without much conscious thought. Not because I thought she couldn't handle it. I knew she could. Whether I could handle it was debatable at the moment, but I also wanted her to enjoy this. I wanted her to feel as much as she could.

I wanted her to have more experiences.

She *could* have that, no matter how this all turned out. She *would*.

I moved my mouth over hers as I shifted my hand so my thumb reached the pulse at her throat. It beat a wild tempo. So did mine as she fisted the front of my tunic. She tugged on the fabric. I wasn't sure she was even aware of the demand, but I was.

She wanted more.

I could give her more.

Tilting my head, I deepened the kiss, drawing her plump lips into mine, and she liked that, pressing into me more. When the kiss ended, I drew back just enough to see her swollen, glistening lips. I really liked how that looked on her. A lot.

Poppy moved toward me a second before I could reclaim her lips— and fuck, I liked that even more. Her eagerness set fire to my blood. As I drew my hands down her shoulders, I had to be careful that she didn't feel my sharp canines, but there was no teasing now. She shuddered, returning the kiss with an inexperienced passion that surpassed any kisses that'd come before. A growl of approval rumbled up from my chest and danced against her lips. I nipped at her lower one, grinning at the way her breath caught. Her fingers dug into the tunic, her hold almost desperate as she squirmed in my embrace, and I knew what that meant, too.

She wanted more.

And I was more than willing to give it to her.

Gripping her by the waist, I lifted her and brought her down so her legs opened and slid to my hips. I tugged her against me, her softness against my hardness. And I knew she could feel me. The scent of her arousal spilled into the air around us. Her hips jerked, causing the sweetness between her thighs to drag along the ridge of my cock. I moaned at the friction.

And Poppy…

She showed me just how much she liked the feeling of me against her. She gripped my hair as her mouth moved against mine. My arms tightened around her as I sipped from her lips. The fingers in my hair clenched, and fuck, her hips moved. She rolled them out of pure, raw instinct, pressing her softness against my cock. I caught her lower lip again. She gave a breathy little whimper as her movements rewarded her with pleasure. Gods, she was *hungry*.

And I was willing to let her devour me.

Moving my arms, I grabbed her skirts, lifting just enough to get my hands under them. My palms hit her bare calves, and she trembled.

"Remember," I reminded her as I slid my grip up the sides of her legs. "Anything you don't like, say the word, and I'll stop."

Poppy nodded, finding my mouth in the darkness. My hands skimmed up as we kissed. She shifted closer, pressing down on me. Needing more. Wanting more. She was greedy.

Good thing I was, too.

A bolt of pure desire pounded through me as she arched into me. My fingers pressed into the flesh of her thighs as I rocked my hips up. She shook, grinding down on me, and fuck, it was the most exquisite torture there was. I gripped her legs, dragging her just a bit to the right, where she was fully pressed against my hard length.

"Hawke," she moaned against my mouth, squirming against me and then moving back and forth. And, gods, I helped her find that pace.

Poppy rode me through my breeches and whatever flimsy undergarment she wore, the heat I felt between her thighs as addictive as her kisses. Her knees clenched my hips, and fuck, I wanted to take her to the ground and lose myself in her. Lose everything in what I knew was her slick heat. My arms trembled. I shuddered with want. The image of her beneath me, her bodice tugged down, baring those dark nipples I'd seen through her nightgown, and the skirt bunched to her hips was so real that I started to draw my hands there. To lift her once more, to do just what I imagined because that sliver of decent man was even thinner now—

Poppy's tongue slipped between my lips, flicking against my teeth.

Fuck.

I jerked away before she could accidentally come across something she didn't expect. Something that would terrify her.

"Poppy." Panting, I squeezed my eyes shut as I let my forehead drop to hers. My entire body was primed with want. My dick throbbed.

Her hands spasmed around the strands of my hair. "Yes?"

Struggling to rein in my desire, I said, "That was the fifth time I've said your name, in case you're still keeping track."

"I am."

"Good." I forced my hands out from under her gown before I gave in to the temptation and slipped up. I didn't want to, but I'd just come way too damn close to taking from her what I did not deserve. I swallowed, unsettled by how quickly I'd gotten swept up in her.

Letting out a ragged breath, I palmed her cheek, the tip of my finger finding her mask. I traced it. "I don't think I was being honest a few moments ago."

"About what?" Poppy lowered her hands to my shoulders.

"About stopping," I admitted. "I would stop, but I don't think you would stop me."

"I'm not exactly understanding what you're saying."

I opened my eyes. "Do you want me to be blunt?"

"I always want you to be honest."

Guilt festered like an old, nasty wound, but I could be honest with her in this as I kissed her temple. "I was seconds from taking you to the ground and becoming a very, very bad guard."

Her chest rose sharply against mine, and her scent flooded me. "Really?"

"Really," I told her.

"I don't think I would've stopped you," she whispered.

I moaned. "You're not helping."

"I'm a bad Maiden."

"No." I kissed the other temple. "You're a perfectly normal girl. What is expected of you is what's bad." I thought that over. "And, yes, you're also a very bad Maiden."

Poppy then did what I'd wanted from her at the start of this misadventure.

She laughed.

And it was a real, deep one. Her head tipped back, and she laughed loudly, the sound traveling through me.

Good gods.

My arms folded around her as I brought her back to my chest. I closed my eyes again, guiding her cheek to my shoulder as I fought the renewed desire to do what we both wanted: Take her to the ground. Fuck her until neither of us knew who we were. And she'd been telling the truth. Poppy wouldn't stop me. She would've welcomed me into her. And I knew she wouldn't have regretted it.

Until later.

Later, she would regret every moment spent with me.

Kissing the top of her head, I pressed my cheek to the soft strands of her hair. I needed to get her back, safely tucked away in her chamber. Things would be happening soon, or perhaps they'd already started, which meant Kieran had to be close.

"I need to get you back, Princess."

Poppy's grip tightened on me. "I know."

I chuckled. "You have to let me go, though."

"I know." She sighed, remaining where she was. "I don't want to."

I held her to me, likely a little too tight. A bit too long. But I was reluctant to let go of her warmth and weight because the feel of her in my arms like this, relaxed and trusting, elicited an array of emotions that came at me fast and hard. I couldn't describe most of them.

Except for one.

A feeling of rightness.

As if pieces fell where they were supposed to be and clicked together. I knew it sounded fantastical and made little sense, but it left me unsettled.

"Neither do I," I admitted, then I shut it all down. I was good at doing that. Just like I did when the memories became too harsh and dark. It was like separating myself into two people. There was Cas. Then there was this, the one that had control.

I stood, gently lifting Poppy to her feet, but we were still holding on to each other, our bodies pressed tightly together. Maybe I wasn't all that in control.

Poppy was the one to step back. Chest oddly hollow, I grabbed her hand. My hold on her was gentle as was my tone when I spoke, but inside? Man, anger and frustration built. "Ready?" I asked.

"Yes," she whispered.

I led her out from under the willow in silence, taking us back to the lamplit walkway. The garden was quiet but for the wind rattling the stems and branches. We neared the fountain when a familiar scent reached me—

Vikter.

Fuck.

That was all I could think.

Fuck.

Kieran was ready. He was here. I needed to take her, but I'd stayed too long beneath the willow and now...now Vikter was an obstacle I'd have to go through, and I was about to erase the good memory of the garden I'd just given Poppy, replacing it with one even more horrifying than what had happened with Keal.

Every part of my being rebelled. I couldn't do it even though I'd snapped one Royal Guard's neck tonight. I'd done much worse to the Duke, but I couldn't take out Vikter in front of her.

Fuck.

My thoughts quickly raced. This wasn't a big deal. Just a slight change in plans. I would have to take her later tonight—make use of that servants' door.

We rounded another corner, and Poppy jerked back a step as we came upon a maskless Vikter. My grip on her hand tightened as I turned to catch her, but she'd regained her footing.

"Oh, my gods," she whispered. "You about gave me a heart attack."

Vikter's hard gaze flicked from her to me. His nostrils flared as he looked down to where I still held Poppy's hand.

I probably should've let go, but I didn't. Couldn't fucking explain why as Vikter lifted his glare to my face.

Poppy tugged on my grip, and not breaking eye contact with the man, I held on for a moment more before letting go.

"It's time to go back to your room, *Maiden*," Vikter growled, facing Poppy.

She winced.

Fuck. I didn't like that. "I was in the process of escorting *Penellaphe* back to her room."

Vikter's head whipped in my direction. "I know exactly what you were in the process of doing."

"Doubtful," I murmured, purposefully stoking Vikter's ire.

"You think I don't know?" Vikter came level with me. "It only takes one look at both of you to know."

He was probably right. "Nothing happened, Vikter."

"Nothing?" Vikter snarled. "Boy, I may have been born at night, but I wasn't born last night."

"Thanks for pointing out the obvious, but you're stepping way over the line."

"*I* am?" Vikter choked out a laugh. "Do you understand what she is?

Do you even understand what you could've caused if anyone other than I had come upon you two?"

Poppy moved toward him. "Vikter—"

"I know exactly who she is," I cut in. "Not what she is. Maybe you've forgotten that she's not just a godsdamn inanimate object whose only purpose is to serve a kingdom, but I haven't."

"Hawke." She spun.

"Oh, yeah, that's rich, coming from you. How do you see her, Hawke?" Vikter was so godsdamn close, only a gnat could get between us. "Another notch in your bedpost?"

Poppy gasped, whirling back around. "*Vikter.*"

"Is it because she's the ultimate challenge?" he continued.

"I get that you're protective of her." My chin dipped as my voice dropped. "I understand that. But I'll tell you just one more time, you're way out of line."

"And I'll promise you this…it will be over my dead body before you spend another moment alone with her."

I smiled then, my anger calming, but that wasn't good news for Vikter. I tended to do the worst things when I was calm, and I could make his promise come true. Right here. Right now. End him and take Poppy. That's what I should be doing.

But I didn't want to do that in front of Poppy. "She thinks of you as a father," I said softly. "It would hurt her greatly if something unfortunate were to happen to you."

"Is that a threat?" Vikter demanded.

"I'm just letting you know that is the only reason I'm not making your promise come true this very second," I said. "But you need to step back. If you don't, someone is going to get hurt, and that someone won't be me. Then Poppy will get upset." I turned to her. She stared with wide eyes. "And that's the sixth time I've said it," I told her, and she blinked. I faced Vikter once more. "I don't want to see her upset, so step. The fuck. Back."

Vikter looked like he was going to do the exact opposite.

My grin kicked up a notch.

"Both of you need to stop." Poppy grabbed Vikter's arm. "Seriously. This is escalating over nothing. Please."

I held Vikter's stare even as another scent reached me. I looked straight into Vikter's eyes and let a little bit of what I was come to the surface. Just enough that he recognized who we really were to each other at the end of the day.

Predator.

And the prey.

Then, Vikter stepped back. The man had balls. I had to give him that.

"I'll be guarding her for the rest of the evening," Vikter told me. "You're dismissed."

I smirked, my eyes dropping to where Vikter took hold of Poppy's arm and turned away from me. The grip was gentle. That was the only reason he still had an arm.

Stepping back, I gave Poppy one last glance, taking in the fall of now-tangled hair and the lush curves I'd had my hands on. Then I moved into the shadows of an unlit pathway. The wind picked up, tossing several strands of hair across my forehead as I walked under the jacaranda trees. I caught a faint acrid smell as I spotted Kieran leaning against one of the older, moss-adorned statues, dressed in the black of the City Guard. No one, not even Nyktos himself, would've gotten him to wear the red of the Rite.

"Are you forgetting something?" he asked.

"No." Reaching up, I tore the domino mask off and tossed it aside. "Her other guard showed up."

"So?" He pushed off the statue, frowning. "You could've taken him out—ripped the heart from his chest if you wanted to."

"I would never do such a thing."

He snorted, giving me a knowing look. "What the fuck?"

"It's not a big deal. Just a slight delay," I told him. "I'll get her in a bit, and we'll meet in the Grove instead."

Kieran made a low sound in his throat. "I don't like this, man…"

"I know." Frustration with myself, with Vikter, and this whole godsdamn thing rose. "Look, if I took him out, she'd be fighting us even more than she already will be. We don't need that headache."

"I think I already have a headache," he shot back. "Anyway, the Descenters have set things in motion, so you'd better get her to the Grove."

PRESENT VIII

"That strange feeling I'd felt when we were beneath the willow?" I said to Poppy, brushing my lips over the crown of her head, just like I had then. "The sensation of rightness? It was a part of my soul recognizing yours. Heartmate. That's what I felt falling into place. I had no idea that was what I was feeling then."

"And you didn't want to believe it," Kieran remarked. He sat cross-legged between Poppy and Delano, rooting through a small bowl of almonds. "When I told you she was your heartmate."

"Who would believe it?" I countered.

He pinned me with a dry look. "Anyone who saw you two together."

I huffed out a laugh, shaking my head. "It was just hard to believe. Heartmates are rare."

Kieran's gaze shifted to Poppy. "Yeah, but she's rare."

I glanced down at her. "Understatement of a lifetime." I brushed aside the strand of hair that kept finding its way onto her face. "What she allowed herself under the willow? It was brave. I know it wouldn't seem that way to us, but it was."

"No. I get it." Kieran popped an almond into his mouth, chewing softly for several moments. "I didn't really know her then, but I knew enough about the society the Ascended had created and what was expected of her—what she was forbidden."

I nodded slowly.

"By the way, I had my suspicions even then." He threw an almond, and I caught it. "I knew something was up."

"Because of the Duke?" I tossed the nut into my mouth.

Kieran chuckled, shaking his head as he offered Delano a handful of almonds. "Before that."

I arched a brow as Delano took the nuts, somehow managing not to bite Kieran's hand off in the process.

"After the Red Pearl, when you didn't want to talk about her. I knew then." Kieran leaned down, placing the bowl on the floor. "You were already protective of her."

I had been, and it seemed a little ridiculous even now, but that was the thing about heartmates. It didn't mean that any other love was less than. Fuck, I knew others who loved each other just as strongly as Poppy and I loved one another. Heartmates were just a whole other breed. An emotion that was stronger and more secure, creating an undeniable pull. It hadn't mattered that I didn't know Poppy then. We were two pieces that fit together, and our souls had recognized that, even if neither of us had.

And it made me think of my brother. What he claimed. What I knew had to be true for him to stay in Carsodonia and not attempt to escape any number of times. But Millicent? I exhaled a long breath. Could she even *have* a heartmate? I supposed it wasn't impossible, but... "What the fuck *is* Millicent?"

Kieran's brow rose. "That was random."

It was. But it was a legitimate question. "I mean, she's not exactly a Revenant, right? She's still Ires's daughter. That would make her a god."

"But not," Kieran said, his dark brows furrowing. "Because she didn't Ascend. Your blood wasn't..." He frowned. "Good enough."

"Thanks."

A brief smile appeared as he straightened the hem of Poppy's nightgown. "We still don't for sure know how Revenants are even made. Or how the hell that Callum fuck has managed to stay alive so long." He leaned back, patting Delano as the wolven gave a low growl. "But I bet Millicent knows."

"Yeah." Head tipped back, I stared at the ceiling as I ran my thumb in slow circles across Poppy's shoulder. "The night of the Rite..."

"Things got out of hand," Kieran finished.

Out of hand? It was both a success and a disaster.

"What happened that night wasn't what you planned," Kieran stated. "You didn't order the Descenters to attack the Rite—to attack mortals. They were just supposed to set a few dozen or so fires and take out some

Ascended and their enablers. That was all."

"I know." My jaw worked. "But I'm still responsible. They found their own power and strength to fight back. That's what I wanted, and they did it in my name. I have to own that. We all do."

Kieran went silent, but I knew he understood.

I drew my teeth over my lower lip. "I had to kill some of them. Men who risked everything for me—for Atlantia and freedom. It made me sick."

"It made us all sick," Kieran said quietly. He, too, had to end some Descenters' lives.

"But it had to be done." The circles I drew on Poppy's skin calmed me. "My father would say that just because one starts out on the right side of history doesn't mean they remain there," I said, knowing the same could be said about me at any point. But what happened that night had been different. I thought of the two Ladies in Wait who had fluttered about the atrium like hummingbirds. Dafina and Loren. They hadn't deserved to die. Many of the Lords and Ladies in Wait had no idea what the Ascended truly were, but the beaten-down, broken people of Masadonia couldn't tell the difference between those who didn't know better and those who enabled their oppressors.

"My father would also say that the deaths of innocents are an unfortunate consequence of the fight against tyranny," I said. "And he would be genuine. Not dismissive or dispassionate like someone who's never lifted a sword in battle. He knows the cost of each life lost. It was why he pulled the Atlantian forces back at the end of the last war." I squinted. "But what I know? What I've learned? The line between right and wrong is a thin one that is often crossed without intention or knowledge. Most of us live with one foot planted on each side.

"That night?" My thumb stilled as I took in how Poppy's lips were parted and the still lashes fanning her cheeks. "Few found themselves on the right side." I pressed a kiss to her brow. "Gods know, I didn't."

NOT WHAT I PLANNED

"From blood and ash!" The muffled shout came from behind the silver mask carved to resemble a wolven. The man charged, his thin steel blade raised high. "We will—"

Cursing, I shoved the sword deep into the man's chest, ending his life before he hit the floor. I tore my sword free and spun, scanning the horror the Great Hall had become.

Bodies lay scattered about, a sea of crimson fabric and bright, fresh red among the crushed roses and fallen wolven masks. Limbs had been hacked off. Skulls crushed. Chests impaled with arrows. Faces disfigured. People whimpered. Cried out. The Great Hall looked like a battlefield. I turned, spotting a blonde on the floor. Glass jutted from her eye. I knew her. Dafina.

This wasn't supposed to happen.

I looked at the dais, to where I'd left the Duke. Nothing but ash and a black smear against stone remained of him now.

I had to find Poppy.

She wasn't in here, nor were Tawny or Vikter, but I knew she wouldn't be safe even if she had made it to her chambers. The moment this shit started, she would've been in the thick of things. The only benefit was that no one would know who she was, which was good. Because if the Descenters got their hands on her?

Her blood would be spilled.

Spinning around, I left the Hall. Heart pounding, I dragged the back of my hand over my cheek, wiping away the blood splatter.

Fury built with each step, every mortal I passed that lay dead or dying, some attendees and others Descenters. It was never supposed to get this far. None of this should have happened.

I entered the foyer. There were bodies there, too. Someone whimpered. My head cut to the side. A Descenter was crouched in the corner, holding a small blade too large for his hand. A kid. He was just a fucking *kid*. I didn't recruit children.

Seething, I turned at the sound of rapidly approaching footsteps.

Lieutenant Smyth strode into the circular chamber, his sword out and dripping blood. Of course, that motherfucker was still alive.

"Do you know where the Maiden is?" I demanded.

He sent me a look as he headed straight for the kid. "She's secure with the Duchess. No thanks to you, it seems." He sneered, turning his attention to the boy. I started to leave. "Get up."

The kid didn't move.

"Get up and face the sword, you little shit." Spittle flew from Smyth's mouth.

A whimper came from behind the mask. He dropped the knife. I glanced at the main hall, my grip tightening on my sword. I didn't have time for this shit. I needed to get to Poppy.

"Too late for that." Smyth bent, grabbing a bony arm. He hauled the kid to his feet and shoved him against the wall.

Fuck.

"Rhain awaits." Smyth drew back his sword. "You piece of—"

Snapping forward, I thrust my sword into Smyth's back.

Smyth jerked free, stumbling to the side, his sword slipping from his hand as he looked down at the jagged tear in the chest of his tunic. Blood seeped from the corner of his mouth as he lifted his head.

"Fuck, that felt good," I said.

"Bastard," Smyth rasped, falling back against the wall.

"Yeah, well, you're fucking annoying." I watched him slide to the floor, the light going out of his eyes. "And now you're dead. Whatever."

The kid stood frozen.

"You need to get the hell out of here." I approached him, grabbing the side of the mask. I broke the strap, baring his face. A jolt of surprise went through me. It wasn't a boy. It was a *girl*. The one I'd seen outside the meatpacking warehouse the day Kieran had made a new friend out of Lord Devries. Fucking gods. I leaned down, catching her wide and terrified eyes. I tossed the mask aside. It landed at the base of the statue of Penellaphe and shattered. The child flinched. "Go *now*."

The little thing stared at me for a moment longer and then spun, taking off as fast as her twig-thin legs and bare feet could carry her.

"Gods," I spat. I would need to have a really long chat with Mac.

I left the foyer, picking up speed as I hit the hall. Every few feet or so, there were fallen guards and Descenters. I neared the end of the corridor, the sound of a sword clanging off another echoing. Silence followed.

Then I heard Poppy scream. "No!"

The hairs rose all over my body as I took off, moving faster than a mortal eye could track. I saw that one door of a greeting room was open. A wounded Descenter stood at the threshold. Beyond him, I saw Vikter's familiar weathered face, but it wasn't right. I could tell that even as I raced forward, vaulting over a settee. The sun-warmed skin was leached of all color.

Several other guards flooded in, but I crossed the space as the bloodied Descenter jerked a sword back, tearing it free of—

This wasn't supposed to happen.

Slowing, I arced the sword high, cleaving the Descenter's head from his body. I couldn't even say who else was in the chamber.

I only saw what I'd brought upon Poppy, not by my hand but by my actions.

She was on her knees beside Vikter, her hands pressed against his chest. Blood pumped between her fingers as Vikter's chest rose too fast, his breaths too shallow. That wound. All that blood. My lips parted as I lowered my sword. This was not what I'd planned.

"No," Poppy said, and the horror in that one word. The sorrow...

My eyes closed as pressure clamped down on my chest. I didn't want this.

"No. No. No," Poppy repeated, and I opened my eyes. "No. Gods, no. Please. You're okay. Please—"

"I'm sorry," Vikter rasped, lifting a trembling hand and folding it over hers.

"What?" she cried. "You can't be sorry. You're going to be okay. Hawke." Her wide gaze swung to mine. "You have to help him."

I knelt at Vikter's side, placing a hand just below his shoulder. I felt what I already knew. The crackling and bubbling in his chest. I said her name quietly.

"Help him," she demanded. "Please! Go get someone. Do something!"

Gods, there was nothing I could do. If I could, I would have. Just to stop the panic and remove the horror from her voice. It didn't matter that I'd basically threatened his life earlier. Or that this was—fuck, this was inevitable. None of that mattered.

Because Poppy...

She was breaking.

"No. No." She closed her eyes, shaking her head in denial.

"Poppy," Vikter wheezed. Blood leaked from the corner of his mouth. "Look at me."

She shuddered, lips pressed together, but she was, damn, she was strong. Her eyes opened.

"I'm sorry," he said. "For...not...protecting you."

She tipped toward him. "You have protected me. You still will."

"I...didn't." He blinked rapidly, lifting his gaze.

I followed it to where Lord Mazeen stood. The dark-haired Ascended looked *amused* and like he hadn't lifted a hand to defend a single person tonight. And he could have. Any of the vampry could have. My nostrils flared as I made a mental note to deal with that fucker later tonight.

"I...failed you...as a man," Vikter told her. "Forgive me."

"There's nothing to forgive you for," she swore. "You've done nothing wrong."

"Please," Vikter rasped.

"I forgive you." Poppy pressed her forehead to his, and fuck, I wanted to stop this. "I forgive you. I do. I forgive you."

Beneath my hand, Vikter shuddered.

"Please don't," Poppy said. "Please don't leave me. Please. I can't...I can't do this without you. Please."

Gods.

Poppy's gaze frantically swept over Vikter's face, searching for signs of a miracle, but she would find none. He was gone.

"Vikter?" She pressed down on his chest as I became aware of Tawny. She stood nearby, weeping. "Vikter?"

"*Poppy.*" I folded my hand over hers, stopping her from looking for a heart that would not beat.

She looked up at me. "No."

"I'm sorry." And I was. I lifted her hand. "I'm so sorry."

"No," she repeated, her breath coming in short, rapid pants. "*No.*"

Lord Mazeen spoke. "I do believe our Maiden has also crossed a certain line with her Royal Guards. I don't think her lessons were at all effective."

Slowly, I looked to where the Lord stood. That was about when I realized the Duchess was here. I couldn't give a fuck about her as I warned, "Speak one more word to her and you will not have a tongue."

Lord Mazeen raised a brow. "I'm sorry?" he said, lip curling as he eyed me. I felt Poppy's hand ease out from under mine. "Are you speaking to me?"

I was going to do a lot more than speak to him.

The soft scrape of metal over stone drew my attention to a fallen sword. To Poppy's bloody fingers wrapping around the hilt.

I watched her rise, her hands and arms covered in blood and the knees of her gown soaked with it. She turned to him.

Lord Mazeen smirked.

I rose.

"I won't be forgetting *that* anytime soon." Lord Mazeen tilted his chin at Vikter, his smirk growing.

I could've stopped Poppy. Could have taken the sword from her. Gotten her away from this chamber and dealt with the fucker myself. Easily.

But I *knew*.

Crazy as it sounded, I knew on an instinctual level that nothing in this godsdamn realm or beyond would've made me stop her.

Poppy's scream was one of such pain and anger that I flinched. It was a sound I'd heard before. I'd made it myself when I realized what Shea had done.

And maybe that was why I didn't stop Poppy. At least one of the reasons, anyway. Because I knew what she was about to do.

I'd done it myself.

Poppy was quick, swinging the sword. The vampry lifted a hand, to do what was anyone's guess. Whatever it was, it went horribly wrong for him. The blade sliced right through muscle and bone, taking that fucking smirk right along with his arm.

My brows shot up. That was so incredibly...violent of her.

Someone screamed as the Lord gasped. The Duchess? Tawny shouted at Poppy.

I smiled as blood gushed from the stump where the Lord's arm should be. He stumbled back, staring down at his severed arm like the dumb fuck he was.

She brought that sword down again, chopping off the Lord's left hand. The screaming. It was *hers*. My smile faded.

And Poppy...she spun, and she was *glorious*, arcing that sword high. She caught him at the throat. The Lord's head went in one direction and his body in the other.

Then she struck him across the chest, the stomach, and she *screamed*, her rage and grief taking her, breaking her even further.

This, I couldn't allow.

I snapped forward, folding an arm around her waist. I hauled her back against me as I clamped down on the hilt of the sword—shit, it was Vikter's. I wrenched it free from her grip, but she fought to get back to the Lord, slamming her foot into my leg, twisting and beating on my arm.

"Stop." I spun her away from what was left of Mazeen. I dipped my head, pressing my cheek to hers. "Gods, stop. Stop."

Her foot snapped back, catching me in the shin and then the thigh. Hard. I grunted as she reared, causing me to stumble.

Gods.

I clamped both arms around her, dragging her toward the door, past the body of the Descenter. Guards backed away, giving us a wide berth as she screamed, her nails digging into my skin, scratching until there was a fiery sting.

Forcing her onto her knees, I held her there so she couldn't rise. "Stop. Please. Poppy—"

Her head kicked back against my chest. The skin of her jaw and throat was flushed a bright red. Her breathing was erratic, and her screams...

My chest cracked in a way I hadn't thought possible. I leaned over her, caging her with my body. And still, she screamed. I didn't know how long she could keep it up before she hurt herself. And she would. Those screams... They sounded as if they were killing her.

I turned my head, pressing my mouth to her too-hot temple. "I'm sorry," I whispered. She couldn't hear me over the pained shrieks.

Knowing I wouldn't be able to reach her with compulsion in this state, even if we had the privacy to do so, I did the next best thing. I eased an arm from her and reached around, pressing my fingers into points at her throat, the pulse there. I pushed. Her screaming cut off abruptly. A staggered heartbeat later, her body went limp in my arms, her head falling back.

"Poppy," Tawny whispered behind me. "Poppy?"

I rose with her in my arms and began walking. The Duchess spoke, but all I heard were Poppy's screams.

HER PAIN

"She'll be okay," Tawny said, placing Poppy's limp hand on the bed. "She just needs time."

"How much more time?" I demanded from where I stood by the windows.

Tawny glanced over as she tucked the blanket around Poppy. "She's been through a lot, Hawke, and Vikter…" Pressing her lips together, she took a moment. "Vikter was important to her."

"I know." The question had come out harsher than intended. My gaze shifted to Poppy, and then I looked away, running a hand through my hair. "She's slept for so long. That can't be healthy. Has she even eaten?"

"She woke a few times." Tawny's brows pinched as she stood. "And I've managed to get her to drink water and take some soup." A faint, tired smile crossed her features as she came around the foot of the bed, smoothing her hands over her pale mint-green gown. "But you already know that. You've asked that every time we've spoken."

I had, but I had only seen Poppy awake once, which hadn't counted because she hadn't been able to use her voice at all. The screaming had damaged her throat. The Duchess had arrived with the Healer, and then Tawny had helped her bathe the blood from her skin. But after that? All I'd seen was grief that she couldn't even escape in sleep. Sleep that seemed too deep. And sips of water and soup weren't enough for anyone.

Turning my stare back to the window, I looked at the cold stone of the Rise looming against the gray sky of dusk. It was fucked-up. A lot of things were. One of them was that I actually missed that prickly bastard. I couldn't say I liked Vikter. The gods knew he wasn't fond of me, despite Poppy thinking he had been warming up to me. But I respected him. For his loyalty to Poppy—not to what she was. No other guard would've taught her what he had—taken those risks. Poppy lived because of him.

Vikter's death hadn't been inevitable. If I'd just done what I'd planned. I would've gotten her to Kieran before Vikter even found us, using compulsion if necessary. He would still be alive, and Poppy would never have seen what I'd sought to prevent. To witness that. To live it.

She didn't need those memories.

But that wasn't the only fucked-up thing. Obviously, I hadn't met Kieran in the Grove. Jansen had gotten word to him, and I knew he was probably going stir-crazy, but I couldn't do that to Poppy right now. I just fucking couldn't.

The delay didn't matter anyway.

I felt Tawny watching me. She'd been doing a lot of that these past days as we shared the same space, waiting for Poppy to return to us. What she hadn't done at any point was ask why I was always inside Poppy's chambers. Not that Tawny struck me as a rule follower, but she had to be curious, considering what she knew when it came to Poppy and me.

But she wasn't the only one who hadn't said anything about where I guarded Poppy. There was no doubt in my mind that the Duchess was well aware that I kept a very close and personal vigil.

Tawny cleared her throat. "You…" She trailed off.

"What?" I faced her.

She gave a small shake of her head, sending tight curls tumbling against the sides of her cheeks. She turned back to the bed. "You care about her."

I stiffened, hearing Kieran saying the same damn thing. I didn't need to hear any of their voices when I had mine annoying the ever-loving fuck out of me.

Because my inner voice answered her question without hesitation. Yes, I did care about Poppy. And it didn't stop there. Oh, no, it had been doing a whole lot of chattering, reminding me that I shouldn't care any more than I would for anyone who'd suffered a loss. That I shouldn't care deeply because of who she was.

Who I was.

And what I would do to her.

"It's okay," Tawny said quietly. "I won't tell anyone."

My head whipped toward her.

"I have lessons to attend. You'd think they'd be suspended, but of course not." Tawny bowed her head. "I will see you later."

I watched Tawny leave the chamber, quietly closing the door behind her. "Fuck," I muttered, pushing away from the windows.

Unsheathing the short swords, I placed them on the chest beside the broadsword. The chamber was too quiet as I walked to Poppy's side, but it was always this way, wasn't it? Likely long before I arrived in Masadonia.

I sat beside Poppy as I'd done well over a dozen times now. Her hair was splashed across the pillow like spilled red wine, lips parted, and breaths steady and even. The skin around her eyes was red and puffy, evidence that the peaceful sleep of the moment was rare.

Nightmares had plagued her. If they were from years ago or from the night of the Rite, I didn't know, but she'd cried in her sleep. I'd never seen anything like it. Tears fell faster than I could wipe them away, but she would calm as I spoke to her. Telling her that it was okay. And it would be.

And...it wouldn't.

I looked down at my arms, the sleeves of my tunic rolled up to my elbows. I stared at where Poppy had dug into my flesh with her nails in her panic and desperation—her fury and agony. The scratches she'd left on my forearms had faded, but I swore I could still see them.

Exhaling roughly, I dropped my head into my hands, pressing the tips of my fingers to my forehead and temples. Guilt churned as I sat there. What had gone down during the Rite hadn't been what I'd planned—what I wanted. But I was still responsible. Hundreds had died, and the overwhelming majority of them were mortal. Some had been enablers, but too many had been innocent. There had been so many funerals that multiple ones had been held at once. Their blood was on my hands.

And as fucked-up as it sounded, I could live with that. I had to. But what was hard to swallow? That I'd caused her pain. A rough laugh left me as I smoothed my palms down my face. It wasn't like I hadn't known the kind of hell I would unleash when I set out to take the Maiden and use her to free my brother. I knew I would stir the Descenters, likely inciting them to a violent insurrection. I knew I would cause innocent people to lose their lives. And I'd known that I would come into the Maiden's life like a storm, destroying everything she knew in the process—perhaps even her.

I'd accepted that.

It was a price I'd been willing to pay, and the cost I would force others to endure because I knew that no matter how many died at my hands or because of my actions, it would pale in comparison to the lives lost if my father rode our armies into Solis. Millions would die. This was the whole greater-good shit...

With a dose of retribution.

But what I hadn't expected was her. Poppy. Any preconceived notions I'd had about her had been wrong. Poppy wasn't quiet and submissive, nor was she a willing participant. She was like so many others who either didn't know better or, out of self-preservation, didn't want to look too closely at all the things that didn't add up around them. I hadn't wanted her to be kind, but I could've dealt with that. What I couldn't deal with was how brave she was. How much of a fighter she was.

I hadn't expected to *like* the Maiden, not enough that I would strive to make her happy, smile, and laugh.

I hadn't expected to care for the Maiden, not enough that I would sit and think of another way for this to work. For me to get what I needed *and* for her to have what she wanted: a life. Freedom.

I hadn't expected to desire the Maiden, not enough that even now, my blood quickened at the memory of the taste of her lips and the feel of her bare flesh beneath my hands.

And I sure as hell hadn't expected how I changed around her, enough that I quickly found myself not thinking about the past or the future and forgetting why I was here. Feeling calm. At peace.

Simply, I hadn't expected to want. Because I hadn't. Not in the years and decades since I'd been free. I hadn't truly wanted a damn thing.

But I wanted those things for Poppy, and I wanted *her*.

So, now what?

I dropped my hands to the space between my knees and lifted my gaze. The wind lashed at the windows, chilling the chamber. I'd been summoned to the Duchess the day before. Jansen had been there. It had been a quick meeting. No coy smiles. She'd told me the Crown had grown concerned about the Maiden's safety due to that last abduction attempt, just as the Duke had said during our initial meeting, and since word had already been sent to the capital notifying them of what had occurred at the Rite, she was confident the Crown's response would be a summons. So much so, she had ordered the Commander to put together a group that would travel with the Maiden to Carsodonia.

I was getting what I came for. What I needed. I would be escorting her out of Masadonia with the Crown's permission.

But it wasn't what I wanted.

Scenario after scenario played out as I sat there, trying to figure out how I could at least give Poppy freedom when this was over. Different options. Choices. But they were all half-baked impossibilities.

A soft whimper drew me from my thoughts. I twisted at the waist as Poppy shuddered, her hands clenching at the blanket Tawny had so carefully tucked around her.

Her cheeks were damp.

Pressure settled in my chest as I smoothed the tears from her face. "It's okay," I told her. "You're not alone. I'm here. It's okay."

I chased away the dampness, the tips of my fingers grazing the rougher skin of the scar on her left cheek. "I'm sorry," I said to her, like I'd said it damn near a hundred times now. "I'm sorry for everything—for Vikter. Despite our last conversation, he didn't deserve that. He was…he was a good man, and I'm sorry this happened."

I'd said that to her before, too. I kept whispering to her, and the grip on the blanket eased after a few moments. Her breathing steadied, and some of the pressure in my chest lifted.

Minutes ticked by. Gods only knew how many before I realized I'd kept touching her, lightly tracing the curve of her jaw. I hadn't even been aware I was doing it. Just like I hadn't the last two nights when I'd fallen asleep comforting her.

And woke up still lying beside her.

I didn't think she'd appreciate any of this. Not so much my actions but that I was here and witnessed what she was going through. I drew my thumb over her chin.

"Now what?" I whispered to her, my stomach clenching.

There was no answer, but I caught sight of something red jutting out from the pillow next to the one she slept on. Reaching over her, I lifted it. A faint grin tugged at my lips when I recognized the red, leather-bound journal. Miss Willa's diary. Letting the pillow go, I glanced back at Poppy. Was she reading it at night?

I cut those thoughts off before I could wonder about how she felt reading those pages and if she acted upon any of it. Now wasn't the time to think about that.

Once night had fallen, I heard the sound of approaching footsteps. Knowing there was more than one, I rose from the bed and grabbed the short swords, sheathing them as I took my spot at the window.

The door opened without a knock, revealing the Duchess dressed in white. The color of mourning. Her flawless skin bore no signs of grief, but I'd also never seen an Ascended cry. It may not be possible. Her dark eyes immediately fixed on where I stood.

I gave her a curt bow.

The Duchess entered the chamber, but her two guards remained at the door. "I was coming to check on Penellaphe. Has there been any change?"

"No, Your Grace. She continues to sleep."

"I imagine very deeply." She stopped at the foot of the bed, her hands clasped loosely together. "But it will do her some good, I suppose, making use of the sleeping draft."

"Sleeping draft?" I repeated.

The Duchess nodded. "The Healer brought some with him when he examined her to make sure she hadn't been injured," she explained.

The Healer's visit must've happened when Tawny was with her when she first woke, and I was in my quarters to bathe.

That explained how she could sleep this long and not be disturbed by anything happening around her.

"It is a shame, is it not?" the Duchess started. "For one person to suffer such loss."

It was.

She turned to me, and I waited for her to say something about my presence. It wouldn't change where I was.

"Where is your mantle?" she asked.

"Forgot it."

"Hmm. Understandable. I'm sure your mind is...occupied with guarding her," she said.

What the fuck? That was all she had to question?

"Your loyalty to her is admirable." She glanced back at Poppy. "Would you like anything sent here? Dinner, perhaps?"

"I'm good," I said. Tawny had been bringing food.

"Then I will leave you to your duty." The Duchess made her way to the door, then stopped. She smiled then, and a chill hit my spine. "The Queen will be most pleased with your devotion, Hawke. I'm sure she'll reward you greatly for your service to the Crown."

HER VENGEANCE

I'd found the sleeping draft shortly after the Duchess left. The vial was in the drawer of her nightstand. I removed it from the chambers. Poppy could get as angry as she wanted with me. I didn't care. She needed to be eating and drinking, not drugging herself into oblivion.

The good news was that Poppy was no longer sleeping.

The bad news was me.

I was the bad news for her as I stalked through Wisher's Grove, spotting Poppy's cloaked figure ahead of me in the moonlight. I would've left her ass drugged if I'd known she would sneak out of her quarters the first chance she got. And while I was all about letting her explore to her heart's content and more than curious to know exactly what she was up to, now wasn't the time for that.

Not when the Ascended were finding their vengeance at night for what had gone down at the Rite. Even now, the wind carried the scent of fresh blood. Come morning, bodies would be found in their homes and the streets, cold and waxen. And since many had no idea what Poppy looked like, her status would not protect her.

I reached down and unsheathed the dagger at my hip as Poppy's steps slowed, and she made her way through a tangle of exposed roots. Flipping the dagger so I held the blade between my fingers, I narrowed my eyes. Wind gusted through the pines, sending needles to the ground as her cloak billowed around her.

Smiling, I threw the dagger.

Poppy yelped as the blade snagged her cloak, wrenching her backward. Catching herself, she reached for the dagger, tearing it free from where it had embedded in the roots.

"Don't," I warned as she started to turn to me, her arm already cocking back, "even think about it."

She spun around. "You could've killed me!"

"Exactly," I snarled, crossing the distance between us. "You wouldn't have even seen it coming."

Her gloved hand tightened around the dagger's hilt. I couldn't see her face within the shadows of her hood, but I sensed she was about to do something foolish with that blade.

I caught her wrist before she could. "I'll take that back." I pulled it free of her grasp as I glared down at her, but I kept an eye on her, knowing she'd likely brought a weapon with her, even though she wasn't in possession of the wolven dagger. I was. "I see I will have to bar that door in your chamber."

She let out a growl of frustration.

"That was adorable." I sheathed the dagger. "It reminded me of a small, angry creature. A fluffy one."

Poppy pulled on my hold.

"Not going to let you go. I prefer not to be kicked in the shin, Princess." Another shower of needles rained down on us. "Where were you going?"

Nothing but silence came from her.

I wasn't surprised to get that response. She hadn't said much since she woke, but neither had I. Because I'd found myself in this weird predicament of not knowing what to say, and I also had something to say.

This was different.

She was.

I was.

This whole fucking *thing* felt different.

"Fine," I snapped. "Don't tell me. I don't need to know what reckless thing you plotted to do. But what you need to know is that you're not going to do something like this again. Things are far too unstable right now, and you are—"

"What? I'm too important to die? While no one else is?" she seethed, the sound of her voice like a punch to the chest. It was still raspy from the damage done by the screaming. From her pain. "Because I'm the Maiden—"

I hauled her against my chest, her words ending in a gasp. Anger pumped through me. I wasn't sure if I was pissed at her or myself at the moment. "Like I said before, I don't give a fuck that you're the Maiden. I would think you would've realized that by now."

She had no response for that either, which was great. Just dandy. I led her out of the jumble of roots, the sound of her voice still getting to me, and my chest still feeling like a three-hundred-pound wolven was sitting on it. This was why I hadn't spoken much to her since she awakened. It was because of the role I'd played in her pain. The big role. The fucking only role. I would have to get over that.

We'd only taken a handful of steps when she spoke. "She knew," she rasped.

A muscle ticked at my jaw. "Who?"

"Agnes."

I frowned.

"She was at the Rite and warned—" Poppy drew in a shaky breath. "She warned us that the Dark One was planning something. Agnes knew more than she told us, and she could've warned us earlier."

"Then what?" I questioned, keeping an eye on the darkness ahead as I heard a distant scream, one Poppy couldn't hear.

"She could've prevented what happened," she argued.

I shook my head. "One person couldn't have prevented what occurred."

"It would've helped," she insisted, her voice giving out halfway.

It really wouldn't have, but I knew there was no convincing her. "So, what were you planning to do? Find this Agnes and tell her this?"

"I didn't plan to talk to her."

"You planned to take your anger out on her?" I thought of that chest of weapons in her bedchamber. I'd likely have to remove that. "The one who attempted to warn you."

"It wasn't enough," she hissed.

I could respect her desire for revenge and that damn fire in her. In any other situation, I might not have stopped her. But this? "It's a good thing I'm here," I said and almost laughed at my words as I slid my grip from her wrist to her hand.

"Really?" she said, no derision in her voice.

Now, it felt like two wolven were on my chest. "If you accomplished what you set out to do, you would've regretted it. Maybe not right now, but later, you would have."

Poppy was quiet for several moments. "You really think that?"

I glanced down at her as her fingers curled around mine, but I

324/Jennifer L. Armentrout

couldn't see her face.

"You'd be wrong," she said.

"I'm never wrong."

"This time, you would've been."

Lifting my gaze to the crowded pines ahead, I squeezed her hand as I felt a reluctant smile hit my mouth. Somehow, that was more frustrating and infuriating than her midnight escapades.

More worrying.

SO I LIED

"I was beginning to think something had happened to you." Kieran looked up from where he sat as I entered the private chamber at the Red Pearl. "I expected to hear from you sooner than this."

"Yeah." Closing the door, I crossed the room and sat on the chair across from him. "This was the first I could get away."

Kieran arched a brow.

Well, it had been the first time I felt comfortable leaving the castle—leaving Poppy. She was with Tawny, and with the old servants' door barred, and her stash of weapons removed—which had been shockingly diverse—I felt confident she'd stay put. For a little while. But I hadn't left her unguarded. Jansen watched over her from the hall. Not that I currently worried about any threats to her. With the Duke and Mazeen both out of the picture, I was her greatest danger.

I was more concerned about her going on a rampage.

"I heard the other guard will no longer be an issue," Kieran stated.

I took a shallow breath. "No, he won't be."

"You don't sound that happy about it."

Feeling his stare on me, I forced a smile. "Should I be?"

"Not overly so, but you sound..." Picking up the decanter of whiskey, he poured me a drink. "Regretful."

I sighed, taking it. And then leaned back, holding the glass on the arm of the chair. "You sure you don't have a Seer in your bloodline?"

Kieran laughed. "Doesn't take one to notice the conflict in your voice." His head tilted. "Or the beard you're growing."

Snorting, I ran my hand over my jaw, realizing I hadn't shaved. I squinted, dropping my hand back to the other arm of the chair. "The

Duchess expects word from the capital either today or tomorrow."

"I heard." Kieran propped a booted foot on the low table between us. "Jansen told me. I've also been promoted." He gave a broad, mocking smile. "To Huntsmen."

"I don't think that's considered a promotion."

He laughed. "Neither do I, but I've been cleared to escort the Maiden to the capital once the time comes."

The *Maiden*.

I took a drink of whiskey. The shit scorched my throat as I glanced at the bed. I didn't see Kieran and Circe there. I saw Poppy and me. Gods, this fucking chamber.

"You know, we could already be gone." Kieran scratched at his chest. "We should be."

"I know, but…things got rough." I wasn't sure how much Jansen had shared with Kieran, but he didn't speak up. "Her other guard? Vikter? He was like a father to her and died in front of her." The second drink of whiskey was easier to swallow. "She sort of lost it after that. Killed an Ascended."

"That, I hadn't been told." His brows rose. "Why did she do that?"

"The bastard laughed at Vikter's death. She hacked him to pieces." A brief smile tugged at my lips. "And I fucking mean pieces."

"Shit," he murmured.

"Yeah."

Kieran was quiet as he eyed me. Didn't last. "And you couldn't get her to the Grove in the days before you learned that the Crown would likely summon her back?"

"Could I?" I laughed dryly, downing the rest of the liquor. "She was self-medicating, and before you think that would've made it easier, she wasn't eating or drinking. Having her weak for the kind of journey we have to take her on wouldn't be good."

I set the glass aside. "But here we are now, given a boon, have we not?"

"I suppose that's one way of looking at it, but yes. Now, we have permission. That means we can get a hell of a lot farther before we raise any suspicion," he said, fingers tapping his bent knee. "But that also means we'll have others to deal with."

"It does, but we can probably make it to New Haven before she ever finds out the truth," I countered. "Before, we'd have been fighting to keep her under control from here to there—and trust me, we want to delay that, she can kick some ass."

"I imagine she can if she hacked an Ascended to pieces." Kieran was still eyeing me in that fucking annoyingly astute way of his. The tapping of his fingers halted, and I tensed. "You're acting weird, just so you know."

I started to deny it, but what was the point? My head was a fucking mess. I flicked my gaze to the rafters in the ceiling. "She's survived some horrible shit and has the scars and strength to prove it. She's brave, Kieran. Passionate. Hungry for life and experience." My jaw worked. "She's fierce, even a little vicious when provoked." I paused. "Or a lot vicious. You were right when you said we'd underestimated her. She's nothing like we expected."

"Sounds like I'll like her."

"You will." I smiled at that. "She doesn't know the truth about the Ascended, but I know she doesn't agree with a lot of the practices, especially regarding the Rites, and even her position among them. She doesn't understand why she's Chosen, and I know…" I worked my neck from side to side. "I know that if she had a choice, she wouldn't have picked the life of the Maiden."

"You sure about that?"

"Positive." I exhaled roughly. "And even though we still don't know why she's Chosen or what role she plays in the whole Ascension, it's safe to assume it's going to be some fucked-up shit."

"No doubt." He reached for the decanter and poured himself a drink. "What are you thinking?"

"I'm thinking she…she doesn't deserve whatever the fuck they have planned for her. She deserves a chance to have a life," I said.

"Well, if the plans haven't changed, Cas," he said, and my gaze shot to his. "Then what does all of that mean?"

"Nothing." I laughed, but the sound was without humor. "It means nothing at the end of the day."

Kieran shook his head. "You sure about that?"

Absolutely not. It meant that Poppy deserved a future, one that allowed her to live, but that wasn't something I would involve Kieran in.

So, I lied. "Yes."

THIS IS PROGRESS

I waited until the Duchess's guard left the hall outside Poppy's room before I approached her door.

Reaching for the handle, I stopped. I doubted I was interrupting anything. Poppy was likely sitting by the window. That was all she'd been doing since she left her chambers in the middle of the night to seek revenge.

Poppy had grown even quieter than usual, more withdrawn. The jut of her chin more stubborn. Not once since I'd seen her awake had she cried or had her eyes even looked glassy. At first, I thought that was good.

But now?

I didn't think so.

The gods knew I was no expert when it came to dealing with one's emotions—obviously—but she'd lost someone important to her. That pain didn't go away simply upon waking.

Knocking on the door, I gave it a moment and then entered. Poppy was by the window as I expected, but as I stood there, taking in her tired eyes and paler-than-normal skin tone, something occurred to me.

She hadn't donned that damn veil in the days since she woke.

Poppy's eyes narrowed. "What?"

I crossed my arms. "Nothing."

"Then why are you here?"

Her churlishness threatened to bring a smile to my face. One that would likely irritate her further. "Do I need a reason?"

"Yes."

"I don't." I had a reason to be in her chambers this time; however, she was actually speaking instead of staring at me silently.

"Are you just checking to make sure I haven't figured a way out of the room?"

"I know you can't get out of this room, Princess."

"Don't call me that," she snapped.

I fought a grin but welcomed the anger over the silence. "I'm going to take a second to remind myself that this is progress."

Poppy frowned. "Progress with what?"

"With you," I told her. "You're not being very nice, but at least you're talking. That's progress."

"I'm not being mean," she shot back. "I just don't like to be called that."

"Uh-huh."

"Whatever." Poppy looked away, squirming a little on the stone ledge.

I watched her as she stared down at her hands, the tension seeping from her rigid shoulders. I quietly moved closer. She looked...I wasn't sure. A little lost? Or maybe stuck between anger and grief. I knew that feeling.

"I get it," I told her.

"You do?" Her brows rose. "You understand?"

"I'm sorry."

"For what?" The coldness had faded from her voice.

"I said this to you before, shortly after everything, but I don't think you heard me," I said. "I should've said it again sooner. I'm sorry for everything that has happened. Vikter was a good man. Despite the last words we exchanged, I respected him." I meant every word. "And I'm sorry that I couldn't do anything."

She stiffened. "Hawke—"

"I don't know if me being there—like I should've been—would've changed the outcome," I continued, "but I'm sorry that I wasn't. That there was nothing I could do by the time I *did* get there. I'm sorry—"

"You have nothing to apologize for." She rose, her hands falling to the skirt of her gown. "I don't blame you for what happened. I'm not mad at you."

"I know." Part of me wished she was. I looked away from her, finding the Rise in the distance. "But that doesn't change that I wish I would've done something that could've prevented this."

"There are a lot of things I wish I would've done differently," she shared. "If I'd gone to my room—"

"If you'd gone to your room, this still would've happened. Don't put this on yourself." I turned to her. She was staring at her hands. I placed my fingers beneath her chin, gently lifting her stare to mine. "You're not to blame for this, Poppy. Not at all. If anything, I—" My heart lurched, and my throat dried. What had I been about to say? I drew in a shallow breath. "Don't take on the blame that belongs to others. You understand?"

Her weary eyes searched mine. "Ten."

"What?"

"Ten times, you've called me Poppy."

I grinned, relaxing a little bit. "I like calling you that, but I like calling you *Princess* more."

"Shocker," she replied.

My gaze tracked over the lines of her brows, the delicate arch of them, and the proud scar cutting through the left one. I thought about how I'd felt after Malik had been taken—after Shea's death. There had been moments when I'd felt too much, and others when I felt nothing at all. And the latter? There had been shame in that. I imagined she was going through something similar. Grief, then nothing, and perhaps even normalcy, then guilt for feeling somewhat okay.

Holding her gaze, I lowered my chin. "It's okay, you know?"

"What is?"

"Everything that you're feeling and everything that you're not."

Her chest rose with a sharp inhale, then she moved fast, wrapping her arms around me. A jolt of surprise ran through me, but before I knew it, my arms were around her. I embraced her as tightly as she held me, folding my hand around the back of her head as she pressed her cheek to my chest. She needed this.

Maybe I did, too.

We held each other for a while, and I thought that maybe in a different life, I would've been built just for this.

But this wasn't my life.

And it wouldn't be hers.

Leaning back, I caught sight of the wisps of hair that always seemed to escape her braid. I smoothed them back. "I did come here with a purpose. The Duchess needs to speak with you."

Poppy briefly closed her eyes. "And you're just telling me now?"

"Figured what we had to say to each other was far more important."

"I don't think the Duchess would agree," she said. "It's time for me to find out how I'll be punished for what I...for what I did to the Lord, isn't it?"

I frowned. "If I thought I was delivering you for punishment, I wouldn't be taking you there."

Her eyes widened. "Where would you take me?"

"Somewhere far from here," I said, a little stunned by the truth of my words. It caused a lurching sensation in my chest again. "You're being summoned because word has come from the capital."

PRESENT IX

I fell silent as I lay at Poppy's side, thinking about the days after the night of the Rite. I could still hear Poppy's screams so clearly that thinking of them even now caused me to flinch.

I knew learning what Vikter really was hadn't lessened the blow of his loss.

"Those days when you slept and I watched over you?" I said, "It makes me think about what Kieran must have gone through when I first returned home. The situations were different, and I stayed much longer in that grief and anger, even long past awakening."

I curled my arm around her waist. "And everything with the Duke? Knowing what you had to deal with—how it made you feel? How I know it still gets to you sometimes?"

And I knew it did.

Sometimes, it was when she slept, her memories taking her back to the Duke's study. It was how she'd go unnaturally still on the rare instance someone mentioned Duke Teerman.

We didn't go through the same shit, but trauma was trauma. It affected everyone differently, but it always affected.

I cleared my throat. "I used to tell myself that what was done to me didn't matter because I'd processed it. Dealt with that shit. But telling myself that proved I hadn't really dealt with it. Because what I experienced will always matter in some way—sometimes, insignificantly and barely noticeable, and other times, it can ruin your entire fucking day. But that's okay. And I mean that. Because saying someone *chooses* to live in the past, rehashing bad shit done to them, is bullshit. You can't choose that. Things inside you? Parts of your mind and body that you don't control decide that. And it took a hell of a long time for me to learn that what I *can* control is how I act in response to those memories—to those emotional wounds. How I treat myself. How I treat others because of it. It's not as simple as saying that. I know. Nothing is simple."

I inhaled deeply. "Even though my idiotic actions led to my capture, I know what was done to me wasn't my fault. Took a long time for me to understand that, but I do. How I respond to it? Figuring out a good way to deal with it was my responsibility." I smiled at her. "But I think you already know that. Because you deal with all you've gone through. I just wanted you to know that when you feel like you're not dealing?" I leaned over, kissing her cheek. "It's okay."

Pressing another kiss to the bridge of her nose, I settled back beside her. "I should've known something was up with the Duchess when she had no problem with me being in your chambers, but things always seem different in hindsight, don't they? I couldn't even consider then that they knew who I was and not only allowed me to take you but practically helped facilitate it."

My gaze shifted to the ceiling. It still amazed me how much Isbeth had manipulated or controlled, but in the end, even with all her plotting and planning, she failed when it came to Poppy.

I turned my head to her. For Isbeth to bring Kolis back to full power, she had chosen to sacrifice someone she loved and decided to let her heartmate go over her daughter—her *daughters*. Fuck. I couldn't wrap my head around that slice of decency in Isbeth.

It was just a tiny sliver, but it had been there. And if I didn't know what to think about that, how could Poppy?

And I couldn't say for sure I wouldn't do the same.

Then again, I didn't have a child. I had no idea what that kind of love felt like. What type of bond it forged—one that could lead to choices you'd never believed yourself capable of.

But I'd seen it in action.

Look at what it had done to Isbeth. The loss of her son had tipped her over the edge. My parents? They'd lied for centuries, believing they were protecting Malik and me. They'd killed. And that bond was not one forged in blood. Coralena and Leopold were examples of that. They'd not only risked their lives but lost them, attempting to protect their son and Poppy, who they'd raised as their daughter.

That love made one capable of the greatest acts of selflessness, but it could also cause one to spiral into the depths of evil. And Isbeth, as depraved as she was, she still loved her daughters in her twisted, sick way.

"It's hard not to wonder what would have become of Isbeth if Malec had made different choices. Hell. If my mother hadn't gone after him, entombing him," I said. "Would she and Malec have simply gone off and lived their lives? Would the Ascended never have taken root as strongly as they did with her and her knowledge guiding them?"

I didn't think so.

In all reality, the realm would be a different place. A better one. Kolis wouldn't be a threat. So many lives would've been saved. But it also meant I wouldn't be here right now.

Poppy wouldn't be alive.

I shook my head. There was really no point in dwelling on what'd never happened or could've happened.

Blowing out a long breath, I thought back to our last day in Masadonia. "Do you remember," I asked softly, "standing by the Rise with your eyes closed and your face turned to the sun? I do."

A SIGNIFICANT
MOMENT

"I know you're anxious to get out of here," I murmured to Setti, my gaze not on the steed but her. "But it won't be too much longer."

Poppy stood at the Rise, a cool morning breeze toying with the wisps of hair at her temples.

She was unveiled.

And she clearly reveled in the sensation of the sun and wind against her skin. Her head was tipped back, her eyes closed, and a soft smile appeared on her mouth. It made me wonder when the sun had last kissed the skin of her cheeks or brow. Likely years. This was a significant moment for her.

I didn't want to rush her, but the others would be joining us soon. So, I got my ass moving, leading Setti to her side. "You look like you're enjoying yourself."

Poppy's eyes opened as she angled her body toward mine. I didn't know if she was still angry with me over my refusal to allow Tawny to accompany her. If she was, I didn't hold it against her. Tawny was her friend, and she needed her, but I was doing them both a huge favor by ensuring that Tawny did not accompany her.

But the longer Poppy stared at me, I didn't think she was holding it against me. The tips of her cheeks pinkened as her gaze moved over me, her focus seeming to get a little hung up on the stretch of the tunic across my chest, and the brown breeches I wore.

I raised a brow, waiting for her to finish checking me out. Not that I was complaining. I liked that she did.

Her gaze lifted to mine. "It feels nice."

"For the air to touch your face?"

Poppy nodded.

"I can only imagine that it does," I said. "I much prefer this version."

She bit her lip as her attention shifted to the black steed. She rubbed the side of Setti's nose. "He's beautiful. Does he have a name?"

"Been told it's Setti," I said, unable to tell her that I'd chosen the name and raised him from a colt.

"Named after Theon's warhorse?" Her lips curved up as Setti nudged her hand, always looking for attention. "He has big hooves to fill."

"That he does," I replied. "I'm assuming you can't ride a horse."

She shook her head. "I haven't been on one since..." Her smile grew. "Gods, it was three years ago. Tawny and I snuck out to the stables and managed to climb on one before Vikter arrived." The smile vanished as she dropped her hand and moved back. "So, no, I can't ride."

"This will be intriguing," I said, seeking to distract her from the pain associated with Vikter's name. "And torturous since you'll be riding with me."

Poppy tipped her head to mine. "And why is that intriguing? And torturous?"

I grinned. "Besides the fact that it will allow me to keep a very close eye on you? Use your imagination, Princess."

Her brow knitted and then smoothed. "That's inappropriate," she muttered, proving she had a damn fine imagination.

"Is it?" I dipped my chin. "You're not the Maiden out here," I told her. "You're Poppy, unveiled and unburdened."

Those stunning green eyes lifted to mine once more. "And what of when I arrive at the capital? I will become the Maiden once more."

"But that's neither today nor tomorrow." I turned back to one of the saddlebags. "I brought something for you."

She waited a bit impatiently, trying to peer around me as I pushed aside extra clothing. Finding what I was searching for, I worked it free and quickly unraveled the cloth I'd wrapped it in.

"My dagger," she gasped. "I thought...I thought it was lost."

"I found it later that night," I shared. "I didn't want to give it to you when I had to worry about you running off and using it, but you'll need it for this trip."

"I don't know what to say." She cleared her throat, drawing my gaze to hers as I handed the dagger and sheath over. Her eyes were damp, and her fingers trembled slightly as she grasped the hilt. "Vikter gave me this on my sixteenth birthday. It's been my favorite."

I wasn't surprised to hear that it had been a gift from Vikter. "It's a beautiful weapon."

She nodded, turning slightly as she parted the folds of her cloak, giving me a brief glimpse of the breeches she wore as she secured the dagger to her right thigh.

Breeches.

She was wearing nice tight breeches. My gut clenched. It wasn't that I was surprised. There was no way she could wear a gown out on the roads we'd be traveling, but I hadn't thought about how she would be wearing something that would reveal every lush curve of her body.

This would be a very intriguing trip.

"Thank you," she whispered.

I nodded, turning at the sound of the others. "The party has arrived."

Poppy followed my gaze, stepping closer to me in a way I wasn't sure she was aware of as I introduced her to them. None met her stare as they greeted her, but as soon as I moved onto another, their gazes lifted, and every single one of their features immediately filled with either awe or surprise. None of them had seen the Maiden unveiled before, and they now saw what had always been beneath that veil.

A beautiful young lady.

My eyes narrowed on brown-haired Airrick, the youngest of the guards tasked with escorting her. He stared in open-mouthed wonderment, like a godsdamn fish out of water.

Jaw ticking, I turned to the final member of the group. "This is Kieran," I announced. The wolven slid me a quick sideways look. "He came from the capital with me and is familiar with the road we must travel."

"A pleasure to meet you," Kieran said as he mounted his horse.

"Same." Poppy's head tilted slightly as she looked up at him.

Kieran's attention lingered on her for a moment, his expression appearing blank to anyone who didn't know him. But I did. I caught the slight widening of his eyes and the faint upcurve of one side of his lips. He, too, was now finally seeing her.

"We need to be on our way," he said. "If we have any hope of crossing the plains by nightfall."

"Ready?" I asked Poppy.

She glanced past us toward the center of Masadonia and the castle she'd called home for the last several years. Where her friend Tawny and all her most recent memories—the good and the bad—remained. And I was struck again by how enormous this moment was for her. She truly was leaving the city not as the Maiden but as Penellaphe Balfour.

As Poppy.

ENCHANTED

Never in my life did I think I would be so thrilled by another's inability to ride a horse on their own.

But with Poppy seated in front of me and little, if any, space between our lower bodies, I thought perhaps I needed to give a prayer of thanks.

I swallowed a groan as Poppy moved in front of me. With the saddle flat and having no seat, the curve of her ass was pressed fully between my thighs, and when she squirmed, which was a lot, that lovely ass of hers brushed my cock.

Which made what would normally be a boring ride through the empty lands quite intriguing and a bit challenging for my self-control.

And this was only day one.

We hadn't headed straight into the Blood Forest. It would've been the quickest route, but it would've also meant traveling through the thickest section. No one, not even Kieran and I, wanted that. So, we were skirting that, riding more toward Pensdurth, where the Blood Forest thinned out. We would enter there.

Watching where Kieran rode ahead with Phillips, one of the more seasoned guards, Poppy wiggled again.

I shifted, sliding my arm through the opening of her cloak and clasping her hip.

She stilled.

I tipped forward, lowering my head to hers. "You doing okay?"

"I can't really feel my legs."

I laughed. "You'll get used to it in a couple of days."

Her sudden inhale as I moved my thumb across her hip brought a grin to my face. "Great."

"You sure you ate enough?" I asked. She'd only had a little of the cheese and nuts earlier, and I knew she wasn't accustomed to eating and riding at the same time.

She nodded. "Are we stopping?"

"No."

"Then why are we slowing?"

"It's the path—" Airrick cut himself off as he caught my glare.

For once, he managed to stop himself from calling her the Maiden. My promise to knock his ass off his horse likely helped with that. I saw Poppy grin at the young guard.

Airrick just may end up being knocked off his horse either way.

"The path gets uneven here," Airrick continued. "And there's a stream, but it's hard to see through the growth."

"That's not all," I said, moving my thumb in a circle on Poppy's hip.

"It's not?" she asked.

"You see Luddie?" I said, referencing the quiet Huntsman who rode beside us. "He's keeping an eye out for barrats."

Her lip curled. "I thought they were all gone."

"They're the only thing the Craven won't eat."

Poppy shuddered. "How many do you think are out here?"

Likely thousands, but I didn't think she needed to know that. "I don't know."

She looked at Airrick.

The young guard quickly averted his gaze. Smart man.

Poppy was, as always, undaunted. "Do you know how many, Airrick?"

"Eh, well, I know there used to be more," he said, his gaze flicking toward me. I raised my brows. "They didn't used to be a problem, you know? Or at least that was what my grandfather told me when I was a boy. He lived out here. One of the last ones."

"Really?" Interest filled Poppy's voice.

Airrick nodded. "He grew corn and tomatoes, beans and potatoes." A small smile formed. "He would tell me that the barrats used to be nothing more than a nuisance."

"I can't imagine rats weighing nearly two hundred pounds being only a nuisance," Poppy stated.

"Well, they were just scavengers and more scared of people than we were afraid of them," Airrick explained. "But with everyone moving out, they lost their…"

"Food source?" she surmised.

Airrick nodded, scanning the horizon. "Now, anything they come across is food."

"Including us," she murmured, glancing at Luddie.

I nudged Setti forward, putting some distance between us and the others. "You're intriguing."

"Intriguing is your favorite word," she replied.

"It is when I'm around you."

Poppy grinned. "Why am I intriguing now?"

"When are you *not* intriguing?" I replied. "You aren't afraid of Descenters or Craven, but you're shuddering like a wet kitten at the mere mention of a barrat."

She huffed. "Craven and Descenters don't scurry about on all fours, and they don't have fur."

"Well, barrats don't scurry," I told her. "They run, about as fast as a hunting dog locked onto prey."

She shuddered once more. "That is not helping."

I laughed. "You know what I would love right about now?"

"For there to be no talk of giant, people-eating rats?" she suggested.

I gave her a quick squeeze. "Besides that."

Poppy snorted, and I liked when she did that. It was a cute little sound.

I frowned at myself. "Do me a favor and reach into the bag by your left leg. Be careful, though. Hold onto the pommel."

"I'm not going to fall off."

"Uh-huh."

She listened, though. Holding on, she reached the bag and lifted the flap.

I eyed her closely as she rooted around. I knew the exact moment she found it. She frowned and pulled out the red leather-bound journal.

Poppy gasped. "Oh, my gods." She shoved it back into the bag.

Her reaction undid me. A laugh burst out of me, loud enough that Kieran and Phillips both looked over their shoulders.

"I can't believe you." She twisted in the saddle. Some of the heat faded from her tone. "How did you even find that book?"

"How did I find that naughty diary of Lady Willa Colyns?" I grinned. "I have my ways."

"How?" she demanded.

"I'll never tell."

Poppy smacked my arm.

My grin went up a notch. "So violent."

She rolled her eyes.

"You're not going to read to me?"

"No. Absolutely not."

I dipped my head closer to hers, unable to stop myself from teasing her. "Maybe I'll read to you later."

Her chin lifted. "That's not necessary."

"You sure?"

"Positive," she muttered.

I laughed, enjoying the warmth that invaded her cheeks. "How far did you get, Princess?"

She stubbornly mashed her lips together. I waited for an answer. It came with a sigh. "I almost finished it."

Surprise flickered through me, along with something hot and smoky. That was much, much further than I thought she would have read. "You'll have to tell me all about it."

Her nose scrunched. The corners of her lips twitched, and then it happened.

Poppy smiled, and it was wide, crinkling the skin at her eyes. It was beautiful.

Then she laughed, and it was no quiet chuckle, but a deep, throaty one.

And I...I lost my breath for the second time in my life. The nape of my neck tingled. I'd never seen her smile like that. I'd never heard her laugh like that. And there was another clenching sensation in my gut. I was...enchanted.

It took me a few moments to realize that Poppy had relaxed into me. She had been sitting straight, keeping her back rigid, but not anymore. She leaned into me, her head resting against my chest and fitting rather perfectly against my body. Again, I couldn't help but think like I had before I took her to the Duchess. That in a different life, I would've been built for this. My arm tightened around her.

The ease in which she sat—how she allowed me to hold her—didn't last. Not with the sun setting. Not with what I could now see in the distance.

A horizon of red.

Our pace picked up, and it wasn't long before Poppy saw it. She tensed, then sat straight as each step carried us forward, until all any of us could see was the gray, twisted bark and leaves the color of dried blood.

We were on the outskirts of the Blood Forest now. There was no teasing. Hands were at the ready, including Poppy's. Hers had fallen to the hilt of her dagger. All of us were on alert. The only sound was the horses' hooves passing over rock, and then the crunching of something much more fragile.

Poppy started to look.

"Don't," I warned her. "Don't look down."

But, of course, she did.

I glanced at her, seeing her face pale as she stared at the dull, scattered bones along the path.

Gasping, she jerked and face forward. "The bones..." She swallowed. "They're not all animal bones, are they?"

"No."

Her left hand went to my arm. "Are they the bones of Craven who died?"

"Some of them," I said, knowing I shouldn't coddle her. This was far more dangerous than barrats. I felt her tremble, and I cursed beneath my breath. "I told you not to look."

"I know," she whispered.

I kept scanning the spaces between the trees, but mostly the ground. We were good. So far. There was no mist.

The ground became a tangle of exposed roots and larger boulders, forcing us to slow and ride in a tight line. Airrick's mount reared, catching the scent of something it didn't like. Kieran had caught it, too. His head turned to the north, his jaw tight. As we traveled farther, and the temperature dropped, I picked up on what they had already scented. The faint stench of decay.

"No leaves," Poppy whispered.

I saw that she was staring at the forest floor. She then looked up at the thick canopy of red leaves above us. They had glistened in the fading sun. Not anymore. Now, they were dark as puddles of blood against the rapidly approaching night.

"What?" I leaned into her, speaking low.

"There are no leaves on the ground," she said. "It's just grass. How is that possible?"

"This place is not natural," Phillips answered from ahead of us.

"That would be an understatement." Airrick wrinkled his nose.

That, I could agree with. I leaned back. "We will need to stop soon.

The horses need rest."

Poppy's hold on my arm tightened. I could feel the press of her fingers through the sweater I wore beneath my cloak. She didn't protest or complain nor lose her nerve. No one would've blamed her if she did. The rest of us had been in the Blood Forest before. She hadn't. And with her experience as a child?

Poppy had to be afraid, but she wasn't terrified. I knew that by her easy breathing, the calm way she kept an eye on our surroundings, and that right hand steady on her dagger.

I smiled.

HER PLEASURE

After checking on Setti to make sure he had enough hay to nibble on, I crossed the campsite, my attention not straying far from where Poppy lay, having wrapped herself in a blanket. I moved quietly, not wanting to wake the four guards currently sleeping as I joined Kieran—they would be up soon enough to relieve the rest.

"What're you looking at?" I asked, noting that he was staring ahead.

"The stream," he answered, voice low. "The water is red."

I squinted, catching sight of what he spoke of several yards out in the moonlight. "When Airrick said this place isn't natural, he wasn't wrong."

"No shit," Kieran remarked as he folded his arms.

I scanned the shadows, my gaze settling on Poppy. She was awake, her eyes popping open every time a twig snapped, or the wind shook a branch. Even from where I was, I saw that she shivered. It was damn near frigid. But when she did fall asleep, would it be peaceful? Or would nightmares find her? Seemed likely in a place like this.

I looked at Kieran again. "The Craven you picked up on earlier today? How far do you think they were?"

"Far enough." He paused. "For now."

I knew what he was saying. We wouldn't be able to rest here for too long. Sooner rather than later, the Craven would realize that fresh blood and flesh were moving about their domain.

"Been talking with Phillips a bit," he said.

"I've noticed."

"He asks a lot of questions and is observant as fuck. He's suspicious."

"Of us?" I found Phillips in the distance, guarding the western side of our camp.

"So far, just in general," Kieran answered.

"*So far* is a common theme, I see." I checked Poppy. Her eyes were closed. She was still shivering.

"You surprised me earlier," Kieran remarked.

"Yeah?" I turned my attention back to him.

Kieran was looking in Poppy's direction now. "You laughed." He squinted. "You laughed in a way I haven't heard you do in years."

I didn't know what to say to that, and we stood there in silence for several moments.

"She's cold," I finally stated.

"She appears to be a moment away from shaking herself across the forest floor," he observed dryly.

"She's not used to this." My eyes narrowed on Poppy. "And she's not us."

"I was just pointing out that she's cold." Amusement filled his tone. "No need to get defensive."

"I wasn't—" I cut myself off. I *was* being defensive. Of her. My shoulders tightened.

"You should see if you can warm her up," he said, and I arched a brow. "Before any of the others get the idea to do so."

My spine stiffened. "That will not happen."

"I wouldn't count on it."

I ignored that as I watched her. "She has bad dreams sometimes," I said, lowering my voice even more as I faced Kieran. "Night terrors."

Kieran, who'd witnessed mine hit more than either of us cared to admit, glanced back at her. "The scars?"

I nodded.

"Well, now you have even more reason to join her."

"Shut up." I turned back to Poppy. Her eyes were open again, and she was shivering even harder now.

I left Kieran's side, his quiet laugh following me across the small clearing. Stopping, I knelt in front of Poppy, who now had her eyes closed, but I knew she was awake. I looked at her, grinning at how she'd wrapped herself in some sort of cocoon, leaving only her head visible.

"You're cold."

"I'm fine," she muttered, teeth chattering. The tip of her nose was red, but her cheeks were pale.

My smile faded as I tugged off a glove, shoving it into the pocket of my cloak. I touched her cheek, drawing open her eyes. Shit. "Correction. You're freezing."

"I'll warm up. Eventually."

I appreciated the front she was putting on and her unwillingness to complain, but this could turn dangerous. "You're not used to this kind of cold, Poppy."

Her red-tipped nose scrunched. "And you are?"

"You have no idea what I'm used to." I'd been in far colder and more...unpleasant situations than this, but I wasn't mortal.

Poppy was.

I rose, going to where my bag sat a few feet from her head. I unhooked what I needed. Stepping over Poppy, I laid it out behind her. She watched me as I spread out the bedroll, then lowered myself next to the heavy fur blanket.

"What are you doing?" she asked.

"Making sure you don't freeze to death." I draped the pelt over my legs. I wasn't that cold moving around, but lying still like this on the ground? My body would cool off. "If you did, that would make me a very bad guard."

"I'm not going to freeze to death."

"What you're going to do is lure every Craven within a five-mile radius with your shuddering." I stretched out next to her, briefly reminded of those few hours I'd fallen asleep beside her after the night of the Rite. She'd basically been unconscious then, and I hadn't noticed how the entire length of my body so easily curved around hers.

"You can't sleep beside me," she stated.

"I'm not." I rolled onto my side. Facing her, I took my blanket and draped it and my arm over her, but kept my hand hanging in the air.

Poppy blinked. "What do you call this, then?"

"I'm sleeping *with* you."

Her eyes, only a few inches from mine, went wide. "How is that any different?"

"There's a huge difference."

She turned her head to the branches above us. "You can't sleep with me, Hawke."

"And I can't have you freezing or getting sick. It's too dangerous to light a fire, and unless you'd rather I get someone else to sleep with you," I said, and other than Kieran, that was so not going to fucking happen, "there really aren't many other options."

"I don't want anyone else to sleep with me," she argued.

"I already knew that," I teased.

"I don't want *anyone* to sleep with me," she corrected, head whipping toward mine again.

I met her gaze and held it. "I know you have nightmares, Poppy, and I know they can be intense. Vikter warned me about them."

"He did?" Her voice was thick, hoarse.

"He did."

Her eyes closed, and damn, I wished I could ease the pain I saw skittering across her pale, tight features.

But I knew I couldn't.

"I want to be close enough to intervene in case you have a nightmare," I continued, which was true. So was the fact that I was worried it may be too cold for her. "If you scream..."

Poppy exhaled slowly.

"So, please, relax and try to rest. We have a hard day ahead of us tomorrow if we have any hope of not being forced to spend two nights in the Blood Forest."

She was quiet as she eyed me. So, I stayed that way, too. She didn't know I'd fallen asleep beside her before. Having someone of the opposite sex sleeping beside her wasn't something she'd experienced.

But she kept staring at me.

My lips twitched. "Go to sleep, Poppy."

The exhale she let out was impressive, as was how she dropped her cheek back to the sack she used as a pillow. I sort of wondered if she'd hurt herself.

Silence fell between us, but I knew she didn't sleep. Her shivering and the constant little movements gave her away. It was like being with her on Setti once more.

"This is wildly inappropriate," she muttered.

I chuckled, always amused by what she found inappropriate compared to what she willingly engaged in. "More inappropriate than you masquerading as a wholly different kind of maid at the Red Pearl?"

She went silent.

"Or more inappropriate than the night of the Rite, when you let me—"

"Shut up," she hissed.

"I'm not done yet." I inched closer to her. "What about sneaking off to fight the Craven on the Rise? Or that diary—?"

"I get your point, Hawke. Can you stop talking now?"

I grinned at the back of her head. "You're the one who started this."

"Actually, no, I did not."

"What?" I laughed. "You said, and I quote, 'This is wildly, grossly, irrefutably...'"

"Did you just learn what an adverb is today?" she asked. "Because that is not what I said."

"Sorry." I wasn't sorry. "I didn't realize we were back to pretending we hadn't done all those other inappropriate things. Not that I'm surprised. After all, you're a pure, untainted, and untouched Maiden. The Chosen. Who's saving herself for a Royal husband," I went on. "Who, by the way, will *not* be pure, untainted, or untouched—"

Poppy attempted to hit me but only managed to uncover half of herself.

I laughed.

"I hate you." She tugged the blanket back to her chin.

"See, that's the problem. You don't hate me."

Poppy couldn't deny that.

"You know what I think?" I said.

"No. And I don't want to know."

Of course, that was a lie. "You like me."

Again, Poppy couldn't deny that.

"Enough to be *wildly inappropriate* with me," I pointed out. "On multiple occasions."

"Good gods, I'd rather freeze to death at this point."

I grinned at her snippiness. "Oh, right. We're pretending none of that happened. I keep forgetting."

"Just because I don't bring it up every five minutes doesn't mean I'm pretending it didn't happen."

"But bringing it up every five minutes is so much fun."

Poppy jerked up the edge of her blanket, but I caught the small grin before her mouth disappeared beneath it.

"I'm not pretending none of that stuff happened," she said after a few moments. "It's just that..."

"That it shouldn't have happened?" I asked, no longer teasing. What did she think about what had happened under the willow? I didn't need to know, but I *wanted* to know.

"It's just that I'm not supposed to...do any of that," she said finally. "You know that. I am the Maiden."

But that wasn't *who* she was. "And how do you really feel about that, Poppy?"

She was quiet for so long, I didn't think she'd answer. "I don't want it. I don't want to be given to the gods." The moment she spoke, the rest came out in a rush that sounded almost painful. "And then, after that, if there is an after part, I don't want to be married off to someone I've never met, who will probably…"

"Probably what?" I asked softly.

"Who will probably be…" Poppy sighed. "You know how Royals are. Beauty is in the eye of the beholder, and flaws, well, they are unacceptable. If I end up as an Ascended, I'm sure whoever the Queen pairs me with will be the same."

I had to take a deep breath because I feared I may start cursing. Loudly. I hated the Ascended for a lot of reasons, but this? How they'd made Poppy feel as if she were flawed? Someone to be ashamed of? This had moved to the top of the reasons to hate them.

"Duke Teerman was a cunt," I bit out. "And I'm glad he's dead."

Her laugh was forceful but quick. "Oh, gods, that was loud."

I smiled, uncaring if her laugh drew a horde of Craven. "It's okay."

"He was definitely that, but it's…even if I didn't have these scars, I wouldn't be excited. I don't understand how Ian did it. He barely even knew his wife, and I…I don't think he's happy," she said, and it was clear that bothered her. "He never speaks about her, and that's sad, because our parents loved each other. He should have that."

And why shouldn't she have that? "I heard that your mother refused to Ascend."

"It's true. My father was a firstborn son. He was wealthy, but he wasn't Chosen," she told me. "Mom was a Lady in Wait when they met. It was accidental. His father—my grandfather—was close to King Jalara. My father went to the castle with him once, and that's when he saw my mother. Supposedly, it was love at first sight." She wiggled a little inside her cocoon. "I know that sounds silly, but I believe it. It happens—at least for some."

"It's not silly. It does exist." I lifted my gaze to the branches and the dark leaves, chest hollowing. What would happen to her once she was returned to the Blood Queen? Would they give her my brother's blood and turn her into a cold, soulless monster? Would they marry her off to some bastard like the Duke? My chest tightened. I couldn't—

I couldn't what? Let that happen? I almost laughed. Once the deal was made, Poppy would become the Maiden once more. She would become that again long before that moment.

I shook my head. "Is that why you were at the Red Pearl? Looking for love?"

"I don't think someone goes looking for love there," she said dryly.

"You never know what you'll find there." I sure as hell hadn't. "What did you find, Poppy?"

"Life."

"Life?"

Her head nodded. "I just want to experience things before my Ascension. There's so much I haven't experienced. You know that. I didn't go there looking for anything in particular. I just wanted to experience—"

"Life," I finished. "I get it."

"Do you? Really?"

There was so much hope in her words that I knew I'd been right to talk with Kieran about an exit strategy for her. "I do. Everyone around you can do basically whatever they want, but you're shackled by archaic rules."

"Are you saying that the word of the gods is archaic?"

"You said it, not me."

"I've never understood why it is the way it is," she admitted, so quietly it was barely above a whisper. "All because of the way I was born."

"The gods chose you before you were even born." My chest brushed her back. "All because you were *'born in the shroud of the gods, protected even inside the womb, veiled from birth.'*"

"Yes. Sometimes, I wish…I wish I was…"

"What?" I waited.

And waited.

"Never mind," she said eventually. "And I don't sleep well. That's another reason why I was at the Pearl."

"Nightmares?"

"Sometimes. Other times, my head doesn't…go quiet. It replays things over and over."

I knew that all too well. "What is your mind so loud about?"

There was another wiggle from inside her cocoon. "Lately, it's been the Ascension."

"I imagine you're excited to meet the gods." I rolled my eyes.

She let out that cute little snort. "Far from it. It actually terrifies—" She stopped herself with a sudden inhale.

"It's okay," I told her, relieved that she felt that way. "I don't know much about the Ascension and the gods, but I'd be terrified to meet them."

"You?" Disbelief flooded her voice. "Terrified?"

"Believe it or not, some things do scare me. The secrecy around the actual ritual of the Ascension is one of them." And that was true because I knew exactly how they *Ascended* others. What they were doing to my brother to make it happen. "You were right that day when you were with the Priestess," I continued, choosing my words carefully. "It is so similar to what the Craven do, but what is done to stop aging—stop sickness for what has to be an eternity in the eyes of a mortal?"

"It's the gods—their Blessing. They make themselves seen during the Ascension. To even look upon them changes you," she shared, but her words were odd, hollow.

"They must be a sight to behold," I replied dryly. "I'm surprised."

"About?"

"You. You're just not what I expected."

She surprised me each time we talked. Either it was curiosity and her questions, her thirst for knowledge and understanding. Or simply what she thought. Believed. Her hopes. Fears. All of it. But what really surprised me was that curiosity. How did she never see more than what the Ascended presented themselves as? How had she not recognized the inconsistencies? Seen through the lies?

But that wasn't fair.

Recognizing and seeing those things would've collapsed her entire world. And it took more than bravery and strength to do that.

It took having nothing to lose.

Not even yourself.

"I should be asleep," she said, drawing me from my thoughts. "So should you."

"The sun will be up sooner than we realize, but you're not going to sleep anytime soon. You're as tense as a bowstring."

"Well, sleeping on the hard, cold ground of the Blood Forest, waiting for a Craven to attempt to rip my throat out, or a barrat to eat my face isn't exactly soothing."

I bit back a laugh. "A Craven will not get to you. Neither will a barrat."

"I know. I have my dagger under my bag."

"Of course, you do." I smiled. She was genuinely afraid of the barrats, but if they came, I had a feeling she'd be the first to kill one.

In the moments of quiet that followed, what she had shared with me cycled over and over. And as I lay there, I thought about why she had gone to the Red Pearl. To live. To experience.

To experience something other than the feelings of suffocation and pain. She had gone to find pleasure.

A truly inappropriate idea came to me as I drew my teeth over my bottom lip, and that impulsive, wholly indecent side of me that reared its head when around Poppy seized control. I could give her what she'd sought that night at the Red Pearl and help her sleep.

Which she still wasn't doing, based on the wiggling.

I grinned. "I bet I can get you relaxed enough that you sleep like you're on a cloud, basking in the sun."

She gave me another little snort.

"You doubt me?"

"There is nothing anyone or anything in this world could do that would make that happen."

"There is so much you don't know," I said to her.

"That may be true, but that is one thing I do know."

"You're wrong. And I can prove it."

"Whatever." She sighed.

"I can, and when I'm done, right before you drift off to sleep with a smile on your face, you're going to tell me I'm right."

"Doubtful."

I pressed my hand flat to her stomach.

Her head jerked around. "What are you doing?"

"Relaxing you." I lowered my head close to hers.

"How is this relaxing me?"

"Wait," I told her. "And I'll show you."

Poppy's questions ceased as I worked my hand through what seemed like insurmountable layers of material bundled around her, finally finding the thin undershirt beneath her sweater. Listening to her breathing, I went slow, trailing my fingers in small circles while I glided my thumb back and forth, brushing against the sweet swells of the undersides of her breasts until I felt some of the stiffness leave her body, even though she was still looking at me—or at least trying to. Then I moved my fingers in larger circles, sweeping them just below her navel.

Her breathing quickened. "I don't think this is making me relaxed."

"It would if you'd stop trying to strain your neck." I dipped, letting my lips brush her cheek as I said, "Lay back down, Poppy."

She did as I requested. I was shocked.

"When you listen to me, I think the stars will fall," I admitted quietly. "I wish I could capture this moment somehow."

"Well, now I want to lift my head again."

My lips curved up. "Why am I not surprised?" I inched my fingers lower, below her navel. "But if you did, then you wouldn't find out what I have planned. And if I know anything about you, it's that you're curious."

She shivered against me, and it was nothing like she had done before from the cold. "I...I don't think this should happen."

"What is *this*?" The tips of my fingers coasted over the band of her breeches. "I have a better question for you. Why did you go to the Red Pearl, Poppy? Why did you let me kiss you under the willow?" My lips brushed against her cheek once more. "You were there to live. Isn't that what you said? You let me pull you into that empty chamber to experience life. You let me kiss you under the willow because you wanted to feel. There's nothing wrong with that. Nothing at all. Why can't tonight be that?"

Poppy was silent.

My heart started thumping. She was only quiet when she wanted something. "Let me show you just a little of what you missed by not coming back to the Red Pearl."

"The guards," she whispered.

It didn't pass me by that her concern had nothing to do with the rules imposed on her and the consequences she had been forced to believe in.

That brought a smile to my face as I shifted slightly behind her, sliding my hand between her thighs. "No one can see what I'm doing."

Poppy gasped as I cupped her through her breeches, growing hard at that soft, breathy sound.

"But we know they're there. They have no idea what's going on. No clue that my hand is between the thighs of the Maiden." I tugged her back so my hips cradled her ass. I groaned at the feel of her, reminding myself this wasn't about me. This was about her. Her pleasure. A faint tremor ran through me. "They have no idea that I'm touching you."

I could only see her profile. Her eyes were open as I touched her through the pants, stroking two fingers along the seam of the crotch. Her sweet scent rose all around me. I imagined I could taste her on my lips as I followed that perfectly placed stitching, featherlight at first and then a little harder with each pass. Her breath snagged as I pressed down. Her hips twitched, and I briefly closed my eyes at the rush of hot, hard desire.

But my eyes snapped open a heartbeat later, not wanting to miss a second of this as I drew my hand up, causing her undershirt to bunch above my wrist. Her bare skin was warm against my arm.

Finding that spot that had made her hips move, my jaw clenched as I teased her clit through the pants. "I bet you're soft and wet and ready," I whispered into her ear. "Should I find out?"

Poppy shuddered, and fuck, I wanted nothing more than to get my hand beneath her pants. Feel her hot, warm flesh against my skin, and discover the damp heat I knew I would find.

"Would you like that?" I asked.

Poppy answered with a roll of her hips, pressing herself into my hand as she had a white-knuckled grip on the blanket.

A low sound of approval rumbled from me before I could stop it. My gaze lifted to where Kieran stood guard. There was a very good chance he'd heard that. And could sense what I was doing. What *we* were doing. If I had an ounce of decency in me, I would stop. Hell, I wouldn't have even started this to begin with. Surely, there were other ways to help her sleep.

But I wasn't decent.

"I would do more than this," I promised, my head filling with all sorts of things I wanted to do, starting with discovering just how sweet she tasted.

Her lips had parted, and her eyes closed halfway as she continued responding to how my fingers stroked. The movements of her hips were these little subconscious jerks, each one ratcheting up the pleasure until the roll of her hips was purposeful.

And, good gods, the way she rocked against my hand turned my blood to liquid fire. "You feel what I'm doing, Poppy?"

She nodded.

"Imagine what my fingers would feel like with nothing between them and your skin." I shuddered. Or she did. Perhaps we both did at the same time. "I would do this." I pressed harder, and her legs curled. "I would get inside of you, Poppy. I would taste you." My mouth watered with want of doing so. "I bet you're as sweet as honeydew."

She bit down on her lip as she let go of the blanket. I about held my fucking breath as her hand moved beneath the blanket, and I felt her fingers on my forearm. I waited to see if she would pull my hand away or not.

Poppy's fingers pressed into the upper part of my hand as she lifted her hips.

That's my girl, I thought as I returned to stroking her. "You would like that, wouldn't you?"

"Yes," she whispered.

Fuck.

Sharp lust pounded through me. I almost lost it right there. "I would work in another finger. You'd be tight, but you're also ready for more."

Her breathing was a series of quick pants as she held my hand down, feeling what I was doing with my fingers. Her hips followed my lead.

"I would thrust my fingers in and out," I said against the curve of her ear. "You'd ride them just like you're riding my hand right now."

Poppy shuddered, clutching my arm as she did just that: rode my hand.

"But we won't do that tonight. We can't," I reminded myself more than her. "Because if I get *any* part of me in you, *every* part of me would be in you, and I want to hear every sound you make when that happens."

I rolled my thumb over her clit. A moan escaped her, and that sound…good gods, I could live on it, drink and feed on that moan. But when her thighs clamped down on my hand? *Fuck.*

Working my other arm under her, I folded it over her upper chest, holding her tightly to me as her hips began moving against my hand in a frenetic way. I knew she was close. Her entire body trembled. Her breaths were shallow and quick. The grip on my arm increased. Those low moans danced in the dark air, driving me to near insanity. I could feel her release roaring up on her as I pressed my mouth to the space behind her ear. My lips peeled back from the brutal need pounding through me. I kissed her there. Licked her skin. My jaw throbbed. My head tilted. I felt my fangs graze her flesh. Poppy's body went taut. So did mine.

I closed my hand over her mouth, smothering her cries as she came. It took sheer effort to rein in my body. I tried focusing on my fucking breathing as I clamped my jaw shut while she trembled and writhed against me.

Kissing her throat, I shuddered as I fought back my need. As I tried to understand the warmth in my chest. The sudden feeling of being *full.* Of being complete without reaching completion.

Poppy's shaking eased, and her grip on my hand did also. I drew it from between her thighs and brought it to her stomach. I held her, my heart pounding damn near as fast as hers. And I kept holding her, even as her body went limp against mine, sated and relaxed while I remained rock-fucking-hard. I held her in the silence as the night continued around us.

Drawing in a deep breath, I lifted my head just enough to see Poppy's face. Her eyes were closed, the lashes forming little crescent moons against her cheeks, and I thought that was the silliest fucking thing I could've thought, but godsdamn, she was absolutely breathtaking in the afterglow of pleasure.

"I know you're not going to admit it," I said, my voice thick with unspent desire. "But you and I will both always know that I was right."

A tired smile appeared on Poppy's lips, and mine responded in kind as I settled behind her, keeping my arms wrapped around her. My cock fucking ached, and it would be sometime before that eased up, but damn, that minor discomfort was more than worth it.

Because my release would never compare to the knowledge that I had been the first person she'd ever experienced pleasure with. A primitive sort of satisfaction seized me. One I should be damn ashamed of but wasn't. I couldn't be. Not when I'd helped her find pleasure.

Experience it.

Live it.

HOW COULD I?

I'd been reluctant to leave Poppy as the gray skies of the approaching morning dawned, but I'd been awake for a while, just watching her and thinking.

Thinking about what we'd talked about last night. What she'd experienced. How it'd felt like an honor to bear witness to her *living*. What was to come.

And all the while, Poppy looked so damn peaceful, as if she were where monsters could never find her.

But they already had.

I was one of them, no better than the Ascended.

Because once I got what I wanted, I would be sending her right back to the beasts capable of unthinkable atrocities. I had to because she was the only thing the Blood Crown would negotiate for. She was the only way I could free my brother and prevent a war.

But how did I do that?

After last night? After how brave she'd been to seek something for herself—to vocalize that this was not the life she would've chosen, confirming what I already suspected? After how she'd clung to me before I took her to the Duchess? After I'd seen all her pain the night of the Rite and what we did beneath the willow? After I found her in the Atheneum, reading such a dirty little journal? After she'd admitted she didn't agree with the Rite? After the Duke had brutalized her, yet she worried about me getting in trouble for stopping the Priestess? After finding her on the Rise, discovering her at the Red Pearl, and all those seconds, minutes, and hours in between, when she showed me again and again that she was not what I expected? How, when I was around her, I didn't think of the past or the future? I simply lived.

But how could I not?

She was important to the Blood Crown. She, and she alone, was the thing they were willing to do anything for. And even if that weren't the case, I was already in this too deep. Too many bodies lay between the moment I'd started this and now—too many lives were already on borrowed time to back out.

Fuck, this wasn't even the first time I'd thought this.

From the moment I'd realized it was her at the Red Pearl, doubt had steadily crept in and grew. I'd done my damnedest to ignore it, to erase the doubt and guilt, telling myself that my reasons were just. That everything I did was for my brother and the greater good.

Pressure clamped down on my chest as I carefully brushed a wisp of hair from her cheek. She wiggled, snuggling against me in sleep.

I closed my eyes as a yawning hollowness opened in my chest. Fuck, I didn't want this for her.

So why did it have to be this way?

A muscle ticked at my temple as I opened my eyes, finding Kieran moving about, checking on the horses. There had to be another way. My thoughts raced as fast as my heartbeat. In the eerie silence of the Blood Forest, scenario after scenario played out like they had before. Unless I could somehow get the Blood Crown to release Malik before handing over Poppy, there were no feasible options. And that wasn't even a choice. The Blood Crown was a lot of things, but they weren't fucking idiots.

There had to be something.

I just needed time to think of a solution that wasn't a half-baked impossibility.

A stray breeze caught a strand of hair. I pinched it, tucking it back. I didn't have a lot of time, though. My gut clenched. Sooner rather than later, Poppy would learn the truth. She would know that I'd been lying to her, using her.

That I was no better than the Ascended.

I needed to come up with an exit plan for her before then, because once she learned that? Poppy wouldn't trust anything I told her. She'd actively work against me.

She would hate me.

Hate herself.

I didn't want to—

Cursing under my breath, I cut off that thought. I needed time. Not this. I eased my arm from around her, halting when she squirmed. The back of my neck prickled as I stared down at her, her left cheek exposed to me. The scarred one. What she'd said last night about how a potential Ascended would see her repeated itself in my mind.

If anyone didn't see her for the beauty she was, then they were irrelevant.

Then again, most Ascended were fucking irrelevant.

Lifting the fur, I draped it over Poppy. I began to rise but stopped again. I fixed the blanket, pressing into the bedroll. Bending, I kissed the top of her head. Then I made myself get the hell up. Rising, I caught sight of Kieran. He stood near the cluster of blood trees, watching. Probably wondering what the fuck I'd been doing this whole time.

Turning, I grabbed the sack and pulled out my brush and paste. I quickly cleaned my teeth, having to make do with only a sip of water to wash out the grit. Then I traveled a bit deeper into the trees to relieve myself. When I returned, Kieran was still waiting, and Poppy still slept.

I joined him. "Sleep well?"

He arched a brow. "Not as good as you."

I narrowed my eyes and shot him a look as I picked up his bedroll, folding it.

"And how often do you sleep that well?" Kieran asked.

I knew what he was getting at. "That was a first." I hooked his bedroll to his pack. "A first in a very long time."

Kieran was quiet as I stood. "She likes you."

I frowned. "And what makes you think that?"

"Besides the fact that she let you do whatever it was you were doing under that blanket?"

I ignored that, carrying his sack to his horse.

"I noticed it before then." Kieran followed as I dipped under a low-hanging branch. "Saw it as soon as you two were together."

"You didn't say shit about it last night."

"No, I didn't say it last night. Didn't feel the need to say it."

"And you feel the need now?"

"I do." His jaw was hard.

Strapping the pack to the saddle, everything I was just thinking about came to the surface, which made what I had to say come out harshly. "Her liking me means I've gained her trust," I bit out, wanting to fucking peel off my godsdamn skin. "That is part of the plan."

"Last night was a part of the plan?" His eyes turned to chips of ice. "Just so you know, I really want to punch you. She's a—"

"I know what she is, Kieran."

"But do you know who you are?" His hand fisted.

I stiffened, taking a deep breath. "I do."

He eyed me long and hard before exhaling.

"We need to be leaving soon."

Nodding, I faced him. Time. I was running out of time. Squinting into the gloom, I tried to think of where I could possibly pick up a day or two before we reached New Haven. Obviously, the Blood Forest wasn't ideal. That left only Three Rivers, but that was a potshot.

"We made it farther than I thought we would," I stated, crossing my arms. "We should reach Three Rivers before nightfall."

"We can't stay there," Kieran said, almost as if he somehow knew I was seeking to delay the inevitable. "You know that."

"I know," I repeated, frustrated. Lingering there would draw too much attention from the others who rode with us, requiring us to deal with them sooner rather than later. "If we break halfway to Three Rivers, we can ride through the night and make it to New Haven by morning."

"You ready for that?" Kieran asked.

I met his stare. "Why wouldn't I be?"

"You think I haven't noticed what's been going on?" His voice dropped to just above a whisper. "Really? That I've forgotten what we just spoke about? Her having feelings for you isn't the only thing I'm worried about, *Hawke.*"

Irritation flared.

Sensing it, Kieran gave me a tight smile. "Remember what your task is."

We'd wanted to knock each other on our asses many times in our lives, but I'd never wanted it more than I did right now.

"Remember your task," he repeated.

"I haven't forgotten for one second." My tone hardened. "Not one."

Kieran lifted his chin. "Good to know."

The way he looked at me as I stepped around him told me he didn't quite believe what I was saying. I'd have to key him in on the shit in my head, but now wasn't the time for that, either.

I crossed the distance, kneeling in front of Poppy. I still didn't want to wake her, but time...yeah, we were running out of it.

I touched her cheek, and her lashes lifted. Green eyes met mine, and how easy it was for me to let go of that frustration and irritation was sort of miraculous.

Sliding my thumb along the line of her cheek and then across her lower lip, I smiled. That was easy, too. "Good morning, Princess."

"Morning,"

"You slept well."

"I did."

"Told you," I teased.

Poppy grinned as she blushed. "You were right."

"I'm always right."

She rolled her eyes. "Doubtful."

"Do I have to prove it to you again?"

Poppy's scent thickened, a lovely and welcome reprieve to the staleness of the Blood Forest. "I don't think that will be necessary."

"Shame," I murmured. "We have to get moving."

"Okay." She sat, wincing. "I just need a couple of minutes."

I took her hand after she'd unraveled herself from the blankets, helping her stand. Because I'd rather be in a helpful mood than a pissy one, I straightened her sweater, tugging it down her hips.

Poppy's gaze lifted to mine, and the conversation with Kieran felt like it had happened a dozen years ago. There was uncertainty in her gaze and the set of her mouth, and it took only a heartbeat to remember that what she'd experienced the night before had been a first for her. Only the gods knew what was going on in her head. It was likely as messy as mine, even though the reasons were different.

I lowered my voice. "Thank you for last night."

Her lips parted. "I feel like I should be thanking you."

"While it pleases my ego to know you feel that way,"—and it really did—"you don't need to do that." I threaded my fingers through hers. "You trusted me last night, but more importantly, I know that what we shared is a risk."

In so many ways.

I stepped closer to her and spoke a truth that was as sad as it was beautiful. Something that cut so deep it left me reeling. "And it is an honor that you'd take that risk with me, Poppy. So, thank you."

BLOOD IN THE FOREST

Snow began falling as we traveled deeper into the Blood Forest. The blood trees were less dense here, allowing us to spread out a bit more, but we couldn't pick up much speed unless we wanted to risk injuring one of our horses. The forest floor was a gnarled tangle of thick roots and rock.

I glanced down at Poppy. She was staring at the ground, likely searching for barrats. A wry grin came to my lips. She had been gazing at the trees. They were a lot stranger in this part of the Blood Forest, their limbs and boughs twisted and tangled, the bark glistening in a way that wasn't at all natural—as Airrick would say.

Poppy had been quiet for most of the trip. All of us had been this far into the Blood Forest, but she'd immediately relaxed against me the moment I mounted Setti behind her. There was still that little breathy inhale that I so enjoyed hearing when I put my arm around her and folded my hand over her hip. I'd contented myself with drawing circles with my thumb and lines with my forefinger, but my hand had stilled.

My senses tingled as I scanned the unforgiving shadows between the tangled trees. My jaw locked. Icy wind whirled through the branches, carrying the smell of rot and decay.

Kieran's horse suddenly reared up ahead. My grip tightened on Setti's reins as Kieran calmed his steed, rubbing the horse's neck. I eased my arm from around Poppy's waist.

"What is it?" a Huntsman named Noah said from in front of us as I signaled those behind me to stop.

Near Kieran, Phillips lifted a finger to his lips. My eyes narrowed on the trees. Poppy tensed as Setti's muscles twitched, and he began backing up, whinnying nervously. I moved to calm him, but Poppy beat me to it. She stretched forward, rubbing his mane. The horses all around us started fidgeting.

Something was coming.

Something that scurried on four legs and would likely give Poppy a heart attack.

I tapped Poppy's sheathed dagger. She needed no other instruction. She nodded, reaching inside her cloak.

Kieran's head jerked to our left at the same time I caught sight of the reddish-black fur. Neither of us said a damn thing because, well, one less guard was one less to deal with.

The barrat came out of nowhere. A burst of black and red about the size of a boar leapt into the air, slamming into the side of Noah's horse as Poppy jerked back against me. Startled, the steed reared, throwing the mortal. The barrat, ever the opportunist, was instantly on the man, snapping at his face as the Huntsman struggled to hold on to its oily fur.

Phillips turned in his saddle, bow in hand. He released the nocked arrow, striking the bastard in the neck.

The barrat shrieked as Noah threw him off. The mortal didn't waste time. He pulled his short sword free, the blade a gleaming crimson as he brought it down, ending the rodent's suffering. Or ours. I turned my attention back to where it had come from. That wasn't the only one.

"Gods," Noah grunted. "Thanks, man."

"Don't mention it," Phillips said, another arrow at the ready.

"If there's one, there's a horde," I said. "We need to get—"

Barrats were suddenly everywhere, racing out of the foliage, surprising even me with how close they'd been. Poppy pressed back against me.

"Shit," Noah cursed, jumping to a low-hanging branch. He hauled his legs up as a sea of reddish-black fur flooded us.

The chattering and yelping barrats flew past us, rushing between the nervous horses. They disappeared into the thick foliage on our other side.

That wasn't good at all.

Neither were the tendrils of mist gathering along the exposed roots. The scent of rot increased, and the mist rose and thickened to our left.

"We need to get out of here," Kieran stated. "Now."

Finally deciding to stop hanging from a tree, Noah dropped to the ground. The mist was already deep enough that his legs disappeared in it. Withdrawing his sword, he hurried to his horse and grabbed the reins as Setti tensed—

A Craven ran out of the mist faster than the damn barrats, its shredded clothing hanging from its body in tatters. Noah, the poor bastard, didn't have a chance. Not even with the warning. It was suddenly on him, tearing into the man's chest with its sharpened nails and his throat with its jagged fangs. I cursed as Noah fell back, dropping his sword as his horse took off.

Then the howls came, the low moan of unending hunger.

"Shit," I snarled as Luddie spun his horse around, catching the Craven who'd taken out Noah with a bloodstone spear.

"We won't make it if we run." Luddie flipped his weapon upward. "Not in these roots."

He was right.

The mist was already at our waists. It would be over our heads if we tried to make a run for it.

I looked down at Poppy and didn't hesitate to say, "You know what to do. Do it."

Poppy nodded.

Swinging off Setti, I landed on one of the thicker roots. Poppy was right behind me, one leg off Setti, dropping to land on the roots. Out of the corner of my eye, I saw Airrick raise his brows as he got an eyeful of her dagger.

"I know how to use it," she said.

The curve of Airrick's lips was goofy as hell. "For some reason, I'm not surprised."

My eyes narrowed on the young man.

"They're here," Kieran announced, lifting his sword.

And they were.

Unsheathing the short sword, I braced myself as they raced toward us, a horde of pale gray skin, tattered clothing, and bones. I stepped forward, driving my sword through a Craven's chest.

Spinning, I drew the blade across another's neck as I caught sight of Poppy. She slammed a hand into a Craven's shoulder, holding it back as she plunged her dagger into its heart. She turned as I did, grabbing the Craven making a run for Setti without a second's hesitation. Damn, the way she moved... How sure she was of her movements. Strands of hair fell across her cheek as she twisted at the waist, her features set in determination and utter fearlessness as she left a wake of blackish-red blood through the mist. There was simply nothing...sexier than that. I caught a Craven in the back, piercing its heart. Poppy looked up, her gaze finding mine.

"Never thought I'd find anything having to do with the Craven sexy." I took the head off the closest Craven. "But watching you fight them is incredibly arousing."

"So inappropriate," she muttered, shoving aside a limp Craven.

Laughing under my breath, I danced along a root, cleaving a Craven in half as Kieran swung both of his short swords, lip curled in disgust as rotten blood spewed into the air. Shrieks rose all around us as I swung my sword through a Craven's neck. I grabbed the torn cloth of one heading toward the group and kept an eye on Poppy. It wasn't that I didn't trust her ability. She slammed her dagger into the chest of another. She was fucking *magnificent*, but her weapon required her to get close to the Craven. I caught sight of Luddie jabbing with his spear as the mist reached our knees. A Craven grabbed for me, his bloodstained teeth snapping at the air. I kicked the fucker back. Kieran turned, bringing his sword down on it as an arrow zinged between us, slamming into the back of another fresher Craven's head—one recently turned.

I jumped off the root, landing on the ground. Mist scattered. A Craven turned, stringy hair falling from the patchy scalp flapping against the side of her head. She opened her mouth. Gods. I drove the sword into her chest, ending the piercing wail. She fell back, on top of Noah. Spotting his fallen sword, I picked it up. My head snapped toward Poppy.

She tugged her dagger free of a sunken chest and staggered back.

"Princess," I called out, rising. "Got a better weapon for you." I tossed her the sword.

Poppy caught it, quickly sheathing her dagger. "Thanks." She spun, cutting down a Craven.

Godsdamn, she was…

A Craven shrieked, racing toward me. Another was right behind that one. Neither resembling anything living any longer. Both were more bone and thin tissue than anything else. Annoyed that I couldn't watch Poppy be, well, a total badass, I sliced the head from one and then the other. Mist whirled along the ground as a smaller Craven charged forward. I stiffened, drawing back a step as the small, pale face of…of a *child* came into view.

"Godsdamn," I muttered, taken aback.

There was always pity for the Craven, even the ones who'd torn into my flesh with insatiable hunger while the Blood Crown held me captive. I used to wonder who they'd been before that. Farmers? Huntsmen? Villagers? Innocent mortals who had lives, families, and futures of wants and needs stolen from them? I'd long since stopped asking those questions. It was easier to see them as they were now: creatures that had died a long time ago.

But this? A child? And one that couldn't have been older than the two I'd seen outside the meatpacking warehouse. Perhaps even the age of the little girl who had somehow ended up in the castle wearing a Descenter's mask and frightened out of her mind. This could very well be her fate unless the Ascended were stopped.

Focusing on the brutal task at hand, I stepped forward and caught the child with my hand under its chin. It snapped and hissed like a feral animal. This would be hard to unsee. To forget. I thrust my sword through its chest. *"Godsdamn."*

"The mist is letting up." Kieran kicked a Craven back, looking past me. "Shit."

I spun just as Poppy tumbled backward. I started forward as Airrick reached Poppy, shoving her aside. Claws snagged my damn cloak, jerking me back. Cursing, I turned, cleaving off the Craven's head. Whirling around, my heart lurched. I didn't see Poppy. Panic took root. If something had happened to her—

She rose from where the mist was the thickest along the ground. With a shout, she thrust her sword through the chest of a hairless, emaciated Craven.

Relief nearly took the air out of my lungs. She was good. More than good as she pulled the sword free and prowled forward, the edges of her cloak billowing around her, scattering more of the thinning mist. She brought her foot down on a wounded Craven's back, driving it to the ground. With a quick jab, she ended its shrieking with a savage smile.

"Gods," I muttered, my blood heating despite the death and decay all around us. "Did you see that?"

"I did." Kieran dragged the back of his sleeve across his cheek, wiping away spots of blood.

One side of my lips kicked up. "It was hot."

Kieran smirked. "It was."

Laughing under my breath, I turned and scanned the trees. The mist was almost all but faded now, revealing the ashy-hued bark of the blood trees and their glistening crimson leaves. Luddie speared a Craven with an arrow protruding from its gut. I spotted another struggling in the roots, hissing and growling as snarled, reddish-brown-colored hair hung in clumps. Bony, bloodstained hands clawed at the air as I hopped over a fallen Craven. A slice of sunlight cut through the trees, glancing off the thin, waxen flesh of its cheek and the soulless, crimson eyes. It swiped out at me in mindless hunger. I thrust my sword through its chest.

Withdrawing my blade, I started to survey the damage. We'd taken some losses. Only four guards remained standing. Kieran and Luddie were looking down at a Huntsman whose chest and stomach had been torn open. Looking up, I found Poppy kneeling beside Phillips. The older man had his hands pressed to Airrick's shredded, bloody chest.

Cleaning my blade on a Craven's tattered clothing, I sheathed my sword and trained my eyes on Poppy. Her brows were pinched with sorrow as she dropped to her knees beside the brown-haired Airrick, placing the sword beside her. I stepped over a fallen Huntsman's legs, slowly walking toward them. Poppy's face had paled. I was used to this kind of death, but...

But she was, too, wasn't she?

"You saved me," Poppy said softly.

Airrick's laugh was weak. Blood trickled from his mouth. "I don't...think you...needed saving."

"I did," she told him, glancing at his stomach. I followed her gaze and immediately wished she hadn't looked. The Craven had done a number on the young man. There was so much damn blood and gore. "And you were there for me. You did save me, Airrick."

I knelt on Phillips' other side as Airrick writhed in pain. Poppy looked up at me with desperate hope as the poor bastard's chest rose and fell rapidly. I shook my head, telling her what she surely already knew. The only thing we could do now was end his pain with an act of mercy. There was no coming back from this kind of wound.

Poppy briefly closed her eyes, and then she picked up Airrick's pale hand. Her brow furrowed even more as she pressed the young guard's trembling hand between hers. She seemed solely focused on the young man, the skin at the corners of her mouth taut—

Something happened.

Airrick stopped trembling. The pain eased from his features. At first, I thought he'd passed, but the man still lived. And he was looking at Poppy again with those wide, awed-filled eyes.

"I don't...hurt anymore," he whispered.

"You don't?" She smiled at him, her hands still wrapped around his.

"No." Airrick's head relaxed against the cold ground. "I know I'm not, but I feel...I feel good."

"I'm relieved to hear that," Poppy said as a look of peace settled into Airrick's face.

I started to frown. What in the hell was going on here? I glanced at

Airrick's nasty wound. The man's guts were half-strewn across his legs. This wasn't a peaceful death.

"I know you," Airrick spoke, his breaths slowing, his words no longer thick and garbled with pain. "Didn't think...I should say anything, but we've met." More blood leaked out of his mouth. "We played cards."

Her smile spread. "Yes, we did."

They'd played cards? Had it been when she snuck into the Red Pearl? Or another time when she was somewhere she shouldn't be? Not that any of that mattered. What was going on with Airrick right now did.

The man clearly felt no pain. Not only that, he looked relaxed and at *peace.*

"It's...your eyes," Airrick said. "You were losing."

My heart started to pound. A lock of hair had fallen forward, brushing the tip of her nose. What in the fuck was going on here?

"I was." Poppy leaned over him. "Normally, I'm better at cards. My brother taught me, but I kept being dealt bad hands."

Airrick laughed—the man whose insides were exposed, *laughed.* "Yeah...they were bad hands. Thank..." His gaze shifted beyond Poppy, his bloodied lips spreading in a trembling smile. "Momma?"

Airrick took a breath. A moment passed. Another. I stared at Poppy as she lowered his hand to his chest, unable to believe what I had just seen.

She was born in a shroud.

My heart was still pounding as Poppy looked up. "You did something to him."

"It's true," Phillips rasped, the seasoned guard clearly shaken. "The rumors. I heard it, but I didn't believe it. Gods. You have the touch."

THREE RIVERS

You have the touch.

Phillips' words kept cycling over and over as I stalked past Noah's horse. We'd found the steed a few hours after leaving the Blood Forest, grazing in a meadow without a care in the realm. We'd ridden hard, reaching the outskirts of Three Rivers at dusk with plans to take a few hours to rest and then ride the remainder of the way to New Haven.

Nearing the cluster of trees, I looked back to where Poppy sat near a fire, eating a supper of cured meat and cheese—mostly cheese, from what I'd noticed. We were on high ground with only a few scattered pines and a clear view in every direction. A small fire to beat back the chill was safe, but I didn't wander far. Phillips was beside her, and although he hadn't mentioned what we'd witnessed with Airrick, he kept looking at her in wonder.

And why wouldn't he?

Phillips had witnessed Poppy—the godsdamn Chosen—ease a dying man's grave and painful wounds with her *touch.*

Fuck, *I* was filled with awe and a little disbelief.

She's Chosen, born in a shroud.

Gods.

I looked for Kieran. We hadn't had a chance to talk until now. Luckily, he hadn't gone far.

He appeared in the trees, the collar of his tunic damp from the stream he must've used to wash the blood away.

"Did you see what happened back in the Blood Forest?" I didn't waste time.

"I heard Phillips saying some weird stuff about a touch." He stopped in front of me. "But I didn't see what was going on."

"Remember what you said about the shroud?" I kept my eyes on Poppy as my thoughts ran a hundred miles a minute. They'd been like that for the last couple of hours. "That it wasn't impossible for a mortal to be born in one? Well, I think that part about Poppy is true."

"Poppy?" Kieran repeated.

"That's what she—it doesn't matter. It's just a nickname," I said. "Have you actually heard of a mortal being born in one?"

"Not that I can recall at the moment," he answered, eyeing me closely. "Doesn't mean one hasn't been at some point." His head tilted. "What happened back there?"

Brows raised, I shook my head. "She eased his pain with her touch—and I'm one hundred percent sure that's what happened."

"That's not—"

"Possible," I cut in. "I know. She's mortal." My heart fucking skipped as I looked at him. "Unless she's not."

"Half-Atlantian? I'm not even sure that would explain these abilities—this kind of gift," Kieran argued. "The bloodline of Atlantians capable of such died out ages ago. And, yeah, sometimes certain abilities skip a generation or two, but that is a hell of a lot to skip."

"Her brother is a vampry, and unless that's not her full-blooded brother, her being part Atlantian doesn't make sense."

"And nothing has ever indicated that her parents aren't who she believes they are?" He scratched his jaw when I shook my head. "Are you sure that's what you saw? The mortal body goes through some weird shit at the end."

"It's what I saw. Her touch took his pain. Gave him...gave him peace." Exhaling slowly, I watched Poppy as Phillips offered her one of the canteens. "I don't think that was the first time she's done it. Phillips said it's true—the rumors." I thought about Jole Crain. "One of the guards spoke of the child of the gods—her. Saying she would've eased his suffering and given him dignity." I dragged a hand over my head. "He was infected, so I dismissed it." I turned to him. "But that's what she did with Airrick."

Kieran stared at me, his mouth opening and then closing. "How is that even possible, though?"

"No fucking clue."

A bird hopped from one branch to another, peering down at us. "Well, this could be why she's so important to the Blood Crown—at least part of the reason." He, too, was staring at Poppy, his brows raised.

"Definitely." But while the ability to ease another's anguish was remarkable and astonishing, why would that be of value to the Ascended? They sought power and endless life. They didn't seek to give others peace. Poppy handed the canteen back to Phillips as she looked over her shoulder, searching out where Kieran and I stood in the shadows of the pines. "I'm guessing you've also never heard of a mortal with those kinds of abilities?"

Kieran's laugh was gruff. "You've been around them more than I have. If you haven't, I sure as hell haven't. My father? Different story. He may have, but…" He cursed. "What if she is Chosen?"

I met Kieran's gaze. "The gods are asleep."

"Do we know if that means they can't do whatever it is they do to choose someone?" he challenged. "We don't know. What we *do* know is that life and death and everything in between carries on while they sleep."

"True," I murmured. The last of the sunlight pulled back from the western valley below. "We need to figure out what her gifts are and how the Ascended likely plan to use them before we make this trade. This has to be tied to why she is so important to them."

A keenness entered his eyes. "I agree that we need to know more about what she can do, but is that the only thing *I* need to know before we make this trade?"

"Yes." But it wasn't the only thing. I needed to know exactly where Poppy stood when it came to the Ascended. Sure, she didn't want to be the Maiden. She questioned everything about that and didn't support the Rite, but she hadn't outright voiced any real dissent against the Ascended, and especially not her beloved Queen Ileana. I would have to know her stance before the exchange.

But then what? What if she wised up to the Ascended? Her brother was one of them. Could I make the exchange, free my brother, and then recapture Poppy once more? I'd gotten into the capital before without being caught. I could do it again. That was an option.

A risky fucking option.

Going into Carsodonia was like falling face-first into a viper's nest. My gaze flicked to where Poppy was redoing the braid in her hair.

Poppy…she was worth the risk. To give her a chance to actually live.

But I wouldn't ask any of my people to help me with it. Not even Kieran. I'd have to do it alone.

"What's going on in your head?" Kieran asked, drawing my attention back to him. "I can practically see the wheels of something really bad turning."

I let out a dry laugh. "Just thinking about everything." I sighed. "I'll talk with her once we get to New Haven and see what I can find out. Right now, we need to get some rest."

Kieran nodded. "Yeah, but you and I need to talk about her real quick."

The muscles along my spine tensed. "What about her?"

"I thought her name was Penellaphe."

I frowned. "It is."

"But you called her Poppy."

What the fuck was he getting at? "Out of everything that just went down, you want to talk to me about a nickname?"

He raised a brow. "Just wanted to say that it seems like a...cute nickname."

"So?"

"Also sounds like a nickname someone close to her would use."

"Let me repeat myself—so fucking what?"

Kieran stepped in close, keeping his voice low, even though the other guards weren't within earshot. "Okay, I'll be more blunt. She *is* still a maiden, yes?"

Everything went quiet in me as I locked eyes with Kieran.

"I know you said you were willing to do anything to gain her trust," Kieran went on. "Clearly, you've gotten it."

I gritted my teeth as I looked away. This was not the conversation I wanted to have with him. Not now. Not when I even thought about the trust I'd gained but didn't deserve.

Kieran saw it and kept going. "So, there is no reason for you to do *anything*—to do *that* to her. Especially if what you've told me about her is true. She doesn't deserve how that will fuck with her."

My head whipped in his direction. "You think I don't know that?" I seethed. "You think I haven't thought about that?"

Kieran's jaw locked down, his nostrils flaring. "I don't know what you're thinking half the time anymore."

I inhaled sharply, feeling those words like a punch in the chest. I started to tell him that wasn't true. That out of everyone in this fucking realm, he knew me—my thoughts and all, but *fuck*. He really had no idea what I was thinking when it came to Poppy. Did *I* even know? I dragged my fingers through my hair as my attention shifted past Kieran, landing on Poppy.

"She will leave me as she came to me," I said, meeting his stare. "I'm not that much of a piece of shit."

The skin at Kieran's mouth grew taut. "I didn't say you were."

I huffed out a low laugh.

"Seriously." He clasped my shoulder. "The whole point of this awkward-as-fuck conversation is so you aren't feeling that way about yourself when this ends."

When this ends…

With me just handing Poppy over to the Ascended.

"I know." I cleared my throat, knowing that Kieran was also looking out for Poppy—a girl he didn't know but didn't want to see hurt. It was one of the reasons I loved him. He cared when he didn't need to. "Get some rest," I told him, clasping the back of his neck and squeezing. "We're going to need it."

"Yeah," Kieran murmured.

We started back to the fire, parting ways, but I knew Kieran worried. He had good reason to. I went to Setti and grabbed the bedrolls and a blanket. Phillips took note of my approach and rose. Nodding at me, he strode off.

The breeze stirred the flames, sending sparks into the air. Poppy's features were softened in the firelight, giving her an almost ethereal appearance.

What if she was Chosen?

I shook the bedrolls out, placing hers on the side that would be the warmest. "We should get some rest."

"Okay." Poppy rose, dusting off her hands. She looked up at me with such brilliant green eyes.

She moved to where I placed the bedrolls and sat as the stars appeared. Unstrapping the swords, I put them within arm's reach, then draped the blanket over her legs.

"You don't need this?" she asked, smothering a yawn.

"I'll be fine." It wasn't too cold for me here. "Got you to keep me warm."

That got a pretty flush out of her as she hastily looked around the campsite. No one was close enough to hear us.

I dropped onto the bedroll beside her. "We only have a few hours to rest, then we'll ride through the night."

"Okay," she repeated, nibbling on her lower lip. She peeked at me. "What you saw back there? With Airrick?"

I shook my head. "We'll talk about that later."

"But—"

"Later." I caught her hand, tugging her down. I didn't want anyone to potentially overhear us when we talked about this. "We need to rest. The ride will be hard from here on out."

The breath Poppy let out could've blown out the fire if she faced it. My lips twitched as I watched her close her eyes. They didn't stay closed.

"Hawke—"

"Sleep."

Those eyes narrowed. "I'm not tired."

"You just yawned as loud as a tree bear."

"I did not—" A yawn interrupted her words.

I laughed.

A second passed. Maybe two. Her head turned toward mine.

"Do you need help relaxing again?" I offered. "I'm more than happy to help you fall asleep."

"Not necessary," she snapped, all but throwing herself onto her side, turned away from me. The sudden, heady increase of her scent completely ruined her denial.

And the fact that she peeked at me from over her shoulder.

I smiled, but it didn't last. What if Poppy was Chosen by the gods? If the impossible were somehow possible?

That had to be the reason she was so important to the Blood Crown.

What did it mean for them? How could they use that, other than they did now? I suspected it was somehow tied to the planned Ascensions, but how? I didn't know, but I was sure it was terrible.

ON THE ROAD

"Here." Kieran reached inside his saddlebag as we rode through the northern valley, pulling out a chunk of cheese wrapped in wax paper.

Poppy eyed his offering. "You sure?"

Kieran nodded.

She hesitated. "But won't you be hungry later?"

"We'll be arriving in New Haven in a few hours," he said. "I'll eat then."

"I can eat then, too."

Staring at Phillips' and Bryant's backs, I grinned.

"But you ate all your cheese," Kieran replied.

"And mine," I added.

Her head whipped to the side. "You said you didn't want it."

"I didn't." I glanced down at her. "You know you want his cheese."

Poppy's chin rose stubbornly. "I'm not going to eat his food."

"If he was planning on eating it, he wouldn't have offered it."

"He speaks the truth," Kieran said, arm still extended, cheese lifted between his steed and Setti.

"Take it, Princess," I said. "If not, you'll hurt his feelings."

Kieran sent me a droll look.

I ignored it. "He's very sensitive, you see. He will take it personally."

"I will not take it personally."

Dipping my head, I whispered, "He most definitely will."

"Fine," Poppy relented, the corners of her mouth curling upward. She took the cheese. "Thank you."

"More like thank the gods," Kieran muttered.

Poppy eyed him as she popped a tiny piece of the cheese into her mouth. "So, will you be staying in the capital, Kieran?"

My grin went up a notch as I raised my brows at him. When Kieran first started riding beside us, Poppy had stayed quiet as she stole glances at him. She was nervous at first, seemingly unsure what to think of him, and then she'd started peppering him with questions, much to his rising discomfort. Where was he from? How long had he been a guard? Had he lived in Masadonia long? Did his horse have a name? That was my favorite question, because it was the first time Kieran had looked genuinely amused by the litany of questions Poppy came up with.

"Name's Pulus," he'd answered, which was amusing to me for two reasons.

That wasn't the horse's name. I wasn't even sure Kieran knew what the steed was called.

And Pulus was also the name of a lesser god, one who had served under the goddess Penellaphe and was known in our histories for asking a lot of questions.

"I have no plans to stay in Carsodonia," Kieran answered, scanning the hills to our right.

"Oh." Poppy nibbled on the cheese. A few moments passed. "Then will you travel back to Masadonia?"

"I will be traveling again," he said.

She looked up as a thick cloud passed overhead, letting a bit of the fading sunlight reach us. It was later in the day than I'd hoped. "It must be tiresome making such long trips and then having to turn around and do it again."

"I don't mind it." Kieran shifted on his saddle. "I prefer being out in the open."

Her brows rose. "You prefer being outside the Rise?"

Kieran nodded.

"But it's so dangerous." She lowered the cheese. "You saw what happens to those who live outside the Rise, or even those who live in cities that have walls like Masadonia or the capital. They end up becoming what we faced in the Blood Forest."

"What's inside those walls can be just as dangerous as what's outside them," he told her.

Poppy's head tilted. She started to speak, but then took another bite of the cheese as I drew my thumb over her hip. "I suppose you are correct."

She was likely thinking about the Descenters and the night of the Rite. The so-called Dark One and the Atlantians the Ascended swore lived hidden among them.

"I have a question for you," Kieran said as a cool breeze caught in the nearby trees, rattling the limbs. The scent of snow was in the air. "If you had a choice, what would you be doing right now?"

"Instead of annoying you with questions?" she responded.

"Yes," Kieran stated dryly. "Instead of that."

"You're not annoying him," I said, cutting Kieran a dark look as I gave her hip a light pat. "He enjoys being asked questions because it means someone is paying attention to him. He likes attention."

Kieran huffed.

"He doesn't seem like someone who likes attention," she noted, looking at him. "But to answer your question—what would I choose to do? I think...I think I would choose this."

"You would choose traveling to the capital?" he asked as my stomach clenched.

"No. I'm not saying that." Poppy fiddled with what was left of the cheese in the wax paper while a somewhat unsettling wave of relief went through me. "I mean, I would choose to be out here." She looked up at the graying sky. "Just out here."

Kieran looked over at her, the skin furrowing between his brows.

"I know that doesn't make much sense." Poppy laughed self-consciously. "It's just that I've never been here before. I've never been anywhere, really. That I can remember much of, that is. And I don't know what..." She trailed off, squirming a little. "Anyway, I would choose this, but with more cheese."

I had a feeling I knew what she had been about to say. That she didn't know what was out there to even choose something different than this. And, fuck, that was...it was tragic.

I could tell Kieran had sensed what she was trying to say, too. I saw it in the tension of his shoulders.

"You're making sense," I told her, well aware of Kieran's attention shifting to me. My arm tightened around Poppy, drawing her back against my chest. "I would choose the same."

PRESENT X

"Neither Kieran nor I could figure out how you had these gifts. It just didn't make sense to us. Nothing I'd found on Ian or what was said about who you believed your parents to be indicated anything like that," I said as I sat beside her, keeping my voice low.

Kieran slept beside her in his wolven form, as did Delano, who was at the foot of the bed. I didn't want to wake either of them.

"I hadn't fully figured out yet that you'd used your abilities on me. I had an inkling then, but not until we spoke about it." I leaned over, fixing the strap on her slip. "And when I did? It blew me away that you'd do that for me."

I swallowed thickly. It still blew me away that she'd taken that risk, and it had been just as risky as what she'd done for Airrick in the Blood Forest.

"I don't know if you picked up on what I was feeling during that time. I was a..." A low, rough laugh left me. "I was a fucking mess of guilt and worry, and this desperation I didn't fully understand then. I just knew I couldn't allow you to remain under the Blood Crown's control. That you deserved a shot at a real life."

Pressing a kiss to her temple, I stayed there for several long moments, the bridge of my nose pressed against her cheek, until I heard footsteps approaching from the hall outside.

"What are you doing here?" Emil's voice demanded from beyond the chamber.

Kieran stirred at once, lifting his head as I frowned, straightening.

At the foot of the bed, Delano's ears flattened. He jumped down, his claws rapping softly off the floor. A low growl started to rumble from his chest. I rose, grabbing the dagger from the nightstand.

A grunt came, followed by the sound of someone hitting a wall. Kieran moved, planting two massive paws on the other side of Poppy's legs so he stood over her as I stepped forward, flipping the dagger. Holding the blade between my fingers, I cocked my arm back as the door swung open, revealing a glimpse of a pale-haired figure in black—

Millicent walked in, the hem of her tightly fitting tunic snapping at the knees of her black tights. She drew up short, pale blue eyes narrowing. "Please don't," she said. "I would really appreciate not having to do the whole dying and coming back to life thing at the moment." Her attention shifted to the growling wolven before her and then the one on the bed. "Or having to regrow limbs. That shit sucks. Growing skin and bone isn't fun. It's painful, in case anyone is wondering."

"I'm not wondering." I didn't lower the blade as my gaze shifted to the hall. I could only see half of Emil. A golden-brown-haired fucker had him pinned to the wall. My brother. "But I'm guessing Naill located you two."

"Actually," came Naill's disembodied voice from the hall, "I did, and then I didn't. Found one but not the other—"

"You know," my brother drawled, "none of that is important right now." Letting go of Emil, Malik turned and faced the chamber.

I tensed. Malik didn't look well-rested. His golden-brown hair was swept back into a knot at the nape of his neck. His eyes were just as shadowed as Poppy's, and he had a fading bruise on his jaw. He, too, wore black, but his linen shirt was wrinkled and torn across the chest. I was confident the breeches were the ones he'd worn the last time I'd seen him.

"Heard you were looking for me," Malik said, crossing his arms as Emil flipped him off over his shoulder. "And yet, when I came here, I was told that I could not see you—by Naill, Emil, Hisa, and some other random-ass female wolven—"

"And yet, you are here," I cut in. "Both of you."

"Yeah, we are." Malik's golden gaze flicked to the dagger I held. "Is that necessary?"

"What do you think?" I answered as Kieran growled low in his throat. I lowered the dagger, but I sure as fuck wasn't putting it down.

Malik started forward. "You have got to be fucking kidding—"

"What is wrong with her?" Millicent demanded, bending sideways to see around Kieran.

Every muscle in my body locked up. "Nothing is wrong with her."

"Liar, liar," she sang, slowly straightening. "No one sleeps through a five-hundred-pound wolven standing over them and growling."

Kieran's ears flattened.

"What's wrong with her?" Millicent repeated. "Is she...okay?"

"None of that is any of your business," I said.

Her head whipped toward me. "None of my business? That's my *sister.*"

"You share her blood, but you're a stranger to her—one who thought it would be better if she was dead," I reminded her.

"I never said that."

"You said you failed at killing her." I bit out the words. "That gives the impression you wanted her dead."

"I needed her dead, we all needed that, and you know why. But that's neither here nor there now, is it?" Her fingers twitched at her sides. "But I never *wanted* her dead."

Her choice of words caused me to stiffen. "Is there a difference?"

"Cas," Malik snarled. "She is not going to hurt—"

"No one is talking to you," I snapped. "So, how about you shut the fuck up?"

Malik's eyes narrowed, but there was no mistaking how his pupils constricted, or the look he gave me. I'd seen that a thousand times when we were boys and I annoyed him.

"Besides the fact that I can't do shit to a Primal," Millicent began, "I have no desire to harm her."

"She killed your mother."

"Mother?" Millicent laughed, the sound high-pitched and maybe a little crazed, causing Delano to tense. "Yeah." Her laughter faded as she clasped her hands together. "That was our mother, but if you think I'm going to seek revenge, you must think I'm an idiot."

"Well..." I drew out the word, smirking as Malik growled. "I wouldn't say an idiot, but a little off balance? Yes."

"I would be offended if that wasn't true," she remarked, her fingers beginning to twist together. She shook her head, looking at the ceiling. "I'm not a stranger to her. I spent time with her when she was a child." Her gaze went back to where Kieran stood, no longer growling. "She probably doesn't remember that. Probably blocked it out. Either way, she didn't know, but I...I watched over her. She was always in the underground chambers…" She trailed off, the knuckles of her fingers turning white.

"Your father has been freed," I said after a moment.

Millicent's eyes closed, the skin tightening around them. Behind her, Malik had gone silent, his focus fully on her. "Good."

A heartbeat passed. "He asked about you."

Her eyes flew open as her chest rose but did not fall.

"We told him you were okay," I said.

The breath she released was a ragged one. I looked at Millicent then—really looked at her. There was no dark color in her hair. It was a blond so pale it was nearly white and hung in curls to the middle of her back. There was no black or red mask painted on her face, nor was there anything painted on her arms. Freckles dotted her upturned nose and covered the high cheekbones of her oval face. She was leaner, but her mouth, strong brow, and stubborn chin? A jolt of shock hit me, just as it had when I'd first seen her free of the ink and paint. She looked so damn much like Poppy.

Millicent had asked me if Poppy rambled liked her. That and their appearance weren't the only things they shared. I looked at her hands, how she twisted her fingers just like Poppy did whenever she was anxious or uncomfortable.

I glanced at Kieran, then refocused on Millicent. I was torn. Technically, Poppy hadn't completed her Ascension, and I bet that made her somewhat vulnerable. I didn't want to take any risks, especially with Poppy, but I thought about what I'd said to her while she slept. And about all the shit Millicent had likely gone through being raised by that bitch of a mother. I saw Malik, still watching her. I knew firsthand what he'd gone through before he started to play Isbeth's game, and I knew he only did that because of her.

Millicent.

Poppy's sister.

And Poppy had lost so much. Vikter. Her brother. The two people who were her parents. Time spent with her biological father. Time with Tawny. I didn't know what kind of relationship Poppy would want with Millicent. There'd been no time to really discuss it, but I couldn't stand in the way. Even if it disturbed me to know my blood had been used to attempt to Ascend Millicent into her godhood.

"Why did you run?" I asked. "Why did you flee the Temple?"

"Maybe that's none of your business," Malik shot back.

Since it was something I'd say if our roles were reversed, I ignored him.

"I thought..." Millicent blinked rapidly. "When I saw the silver light, the realms split open, and...and that draken come through, I thought it was her at first." Her lashes lowered. "The Primal of Life. And even when I realized it wasn't her, I knew...I know she awakened."

I frowned. "Why would you run because of that? She's your grandmother," I said, and yeah, that still sounded weird.

Millicent's eyes flicked to me. "No one hates Revenants more than the Primal of Life, and it's not because we're abominations—"

"You're not an abomination," Malik interjected.

She smiled, but there was nothing to it. No emotion. "Yes, we are. But with the Primal of Life, it's personal, and I...I ran because I thought..." A heavy exhale left her as she focused on what she could see of Poppy. "I thought she would take me out." One shoulder lifted. "I was afraid."

"Poppy wouldn't do that," I said.

"How was she supposed to know that?" Malik countered from the doorway.

I started to respond, but there was no way for Millicent to have known that. However... "You're not someone who strikes me as being afraid of death."

Millicent's gaze flicked back to me. She said nothing, and I was right. Millicent wasn't afraid to die, be it final or not. It wasn't her death she'd been afraid of.

I looked at my brother and cursed under my breath. "She sleeps— in stasis until she fully completes her Culling," I said quietly, and that was all I said. Neither she nor Malik needed to know there was a chance—a small one—that Poppy could wake with no knowledge of herself.

Millicent jerked. "Is that common?"

"You don't know?"

She shook her head. "I know what stasis is, how they can go to ground. How long will it last?"

"Not much longer." I hoped.

Kieran slowly backed off, sinking onto his belly beside Poppy. Delano did the same, returning to the foot of the bed but remaining on the floor.

And Millicent...she stared at the bed. "She looks the same," she said after a few moments. "I mean, she's paler than normal."

I didn't tell her it had been much worse before. I noticed she was twisting her fingers again. I glanced at Malik. There were things I needed to ask—about how the fuck Revenants were made, and everything with Callum, but now wasn't the time.

"Do you want to visit with her?"

Millicent's head jerked toward me. She said nothing, but she nodded. I looked once more at Malik. He'd quietly stepped back into the hall. I needed to talk with him, but...

Kieran rose from the bed and quickly shifted. His eyes locked with mine. "I'll stay with them."

"Are you going to put some clothing on?" Millicent asked.

"Do I need to?"

"I mean, it's your dick hanging out, not mine." Millicent shrugged and then came forward, eyeing Delano but not Kieran as she sat on the very, very edge of the bed.

I caught Kieran's eye, and he nodded. I tossed him the dagger. He smiled at Millicent. "Are you afraid of wolven?"

"That's like asking if you're not afraid of draken," she retorted, glancing at Delano. I'd swear the fucking wolven smiled. "Everyone should be afraid of anything with claws and sharp teeth."

I walked out then, pulling the door after me but leaving it cracked open. Malik didn't protest. He knew Kieran wouldn't do anything unless given reason to, and I supposed that also said he knew Millicent wouldn't give cause.

I glanced to where Emil stood with Naill. "Can you give us a moment?"

Naill nodded, but Emil said, "I kind of want to witness this awkward meet and greet—"

"Emil," muttered Naill, catching the back of his tunic. "I swear to the gods."

Malik watched Naill drag the other Atlantian down the hall. "I see Emil really hasn't changed."

"What the hell happened to you?" I asked.

He faced me. "I'm not sure what you're referencing, exactly."

"Your face." I crossed my arms. "Looks like you've been in a fight."

"I was. We were, actually."

"With?"

"Other Revs." He leaned against the wall. "Those loyal to Isbeth."

Surprise flickered through me. "And how did that go?"

"Bloody. There are still a few out there, running about, but we took out most of those who would be a problem."

"And by *took out*, you mean killed? 'Cause that's interesting." I eyed him. "I was under the impression that draken fire was the only thing that could kill them."

One side of his lips twisted up. "There are things that can kill a Rev."

"Really?" I wasn't sure if I believed him. This wasn't what we'd been told.

"The Primal of Death can, and I assume that means *both* of them," he said, referencing Nyktos and Kolis. "Since Kolis created them—and before you ask, I don't know how he did it. And she can. The Primal of Life."

"And Poppy."

Malik's jaw tightened.

"But neither of you is either of those two things, so how the hell did you kill some of those troublesome Revs?"

A muscle ticked in his temple.

"I get it," I said when he didn't answer. "You don't want me to possess the knowledge of how to kill one, which is idiotic, considering my wife is one of those ways, but mainly because if I wanted knowledge on how to kill Millicent, I wouldn't have left her in the chamber with Poppy."

"You didn't leave her alone with Millie," he countered. "Not really."

I stepped closer to him. "Would you have if the roles were reversed?"

"No." Malik's laugh was dry. "Draken fire and draken blood can kill them," he shared. "Lucky for us, Millie knew where Isbeth kept vials of it. You either make them ingest it or dip a blade or arrow in it. As long as it gets into their heart or head, they're done. I got the impression that Reaver was unaware of that—where is he?"

"He took Malec back to Iliseeum."

"Shit," he said, brows raised. "He was still alive?"

"Barely, from what I gathered." I glanced down the hall. "Are there more of those vials?"

His stare sharpened. "There are."

"And do either you or Millie know if the draken Isbeth got that blood from is being held?" I asked, even though we knew. "That's Nektas's daughter—you know, that big-ass draken."

"I was kind of temporarily dead when he came through," he said, and my stomach twisted sharply. Malik had died. I'd seen that, too. "So, I didn't see him in that form, but to answer your question, I don't. Millie? Possibly. There were many things she wasn't supposed to know that she found out, but I seriously doubt that draken will be in a good way. So, when you go for her, make sure another draken is with you. They can fuck up a Primal really bad."

"Noted," I murmured.

"I'm surprised our father hasn't arrived yet," Malik stated.

"We delayed him a bit."

"Because of Poppy?" When I said nothing, he laughed. "You don't trust him, either."

"There's only one person I irrevocably trust. Not taking chances with anyone else."

Malik eyed me. "You're a little overprotective of a being who is literally immortal."

Just because Poppy was a Primal didn't mean she was indestructible. I didn't know a lot about Primals. None of us did. But there were *always* checks and balances. Besides, I didn't fear my father attempting to harm Poppy.

It was that slim chance that Poppy didn't remember who she was when she woke.

"Why do I have a feeling there's something you're not telling me?" he asked.

I said nothing to that.

"All right." Malik smiled, but it didn't reach his eyes. I realized none of his smiles had since we'd been reunited. "So, what is your game plan here, Cas? You took down the Blood Crown, but there's been no public address. Only Descenters on the streets, acting as Priests and Priestesses, preaching the goodness of Atlantia and their new King and Queen."

"Poppy and I are not their King and Queen."

His brows shot up. "I'm sorry, you two rule Atlantia, correct? You just seized the capital and destroyed the reigning monarch. Does that not make you their sovereign rulers?"

I got what he was saying, but this was another thing that Poppy and I hadn't had a lot of time to really hash out. "No decisions on that will be made until she's awake."

"Okay, then, but they think you two are their new rulers—an Atlantian and a god, by the way. They have no idea she's a Primal—"

"I know." I rubbed my temple. "Those are bridges we'll cross when we get there."

Malik stared and then laughed. This time, it reminded me of one of his old laughs, and that hit me in the chest.

Hard.

I cleared my throat. "What?"

"It's just…" Trailing off, he shook his head. "When we were kids, you were always at your lessons on time. I had to be tracked down. You learned what it took to handle land disputes and which crops grew best where, and I forgot everything the moment our tutors were gone. You always would've made a better King than me." His gaze flicked back to mine. "And yet, I get the impression you don't want to be King."

"Being King meant accepting that you were dead," I said, and his mouth tensed. "Or, at the very least, incapable of ruling. So, maybe when I was younger and jealous of what you had, I wanted that, but I don't now."

"But you did it anyway," he said quietly.

"Poppy took the throne," I reminded him. "She superseded all of us. She is the Queen. I am the King because of her. If she had chosen differently? Our mother and father would still sit on that throne. It would still be yours." Anger festered. "Hell, it could've been yours years before Poppy arrived in Atlantia if you had come home."

"I couldn't." Malik pushed off the wall, anger flaring in his eyes. "I wouldn't leave Millie alone, and it's not like you wouldn't have done the same thing. You just admitted that you'd abdicate the throne for her. And I'm sure you've done a whole lot of other shit for her that goes against what is right or wrong. So how about you knock off this self-righteousness a bit, okay? You're no better than me—"

"I never said I was," I seethed, stepping toward him. "I spent the last fucking century torn up, thinking about what was being done to you, exactly the kind of horrors they were putting you through. All the while knowing that I…it was my actions that put you there."

Malik went rigid. "Cas—"

"If I hadn't been so foolishly obsessed with proving myself, I wouldn't have gotten captured. You never would've had to come for me. That is an inarguable fact. It wasn't Shea who put you there. It was me, so I drowned in that guilt until I learned to exist with it." My nostrils flared as my lips flattened against my teeth. "And look, I don't blame you for doing what you needed to do to survive, playing whatever fucked-up game you had to. I don't blame you for staying because of Millicent. And the shit with Poppy when she was a child? I'm not going to even think about that because it makes me want to fucking choke you. But you know what I can't understand? Your silence. You could've sent word to me. You could've let me know you were surviving."

Malik held my stare, his jaw working.

"You had to know what I was doing these last several years to free you," I told him, hands clenching. "All the people I've killed? Those I've harmed? Those who died to free you? But no. You just let me exist all these fucking years fearing, believing I would be too late. That you would be dead or beyond help, consumed by the guilt—" I cut myself off, taking a step back, and it took me a moment before I could trust myself to speak again. "Why didn't you send word?"

"It's not..." Malik swallowed, head still shaking. "I thought about it, Cas. A hundred times. A thousand."

"Then why?" I asked, voice hoarse. "You could've told me that you'd joined them. You could've said *anything*."

"That's not true, and you know it."

"Bullshit." I started to turn before I did something I'd thoroughly enjoy at the moment but might regret later.

Malik moved fast, blocking the door. "You want to have this conversation now? Then we're going to have it. If I sent word and told you that I'd joined the Blood Crown, would you have believed me? Or would you have thought it was some sort of farce?"

My head snapped back to him.

"Would it have stopped anything you did?" he demanded, the centers of his cheeks flushing with anger. "And if I told you about her? Would you have even believed I'd found my heartmate? Back then? Because I know you wouldn't have. You didn't really believe in it. Neither did I. So, you would've still done what you've been doing."

"Maybe you're right," I spat, and fuck, maybe he was. "But there had to be other options, Malik. You could've said anything, starting with the truth—"

"I didn't want you coming after me!" Malik shouted, shoving me. "I didn't want you anywhere near the capital—"

"But I already was!" I yelled, pushing him right back. "Not saying anything sure as fuck didn't prevent it."

"I know that. Gods, do I fucking know. But I was fucked, Cas. Damned if I did, damned if I didn't," he said, chest rising and falling. "Because I knew if I told you the truth about what Isbeth was trying, you would've dropped your plans to free me. You wouldn't have gone for her. Instead, you would've come straight to the capital." He jabbed his finger at the doors. "And if I told you that I'd joined the Blood Crown, you still would've come straight to the capital under the pretense of doing the same thing. And if you had? What do you think Isbeth would've done?"

"You knew her better than me," I snapped. "You tell me."

Malik's smile was a cruel twist. "You'd be dead."

I barked out a harsh, short laugh. "Doubtful."

"Oh, you really think that?" His laugh mirrored mine. "I think you're forgetting the original plan, the one where Isbeth had no need of you. It was supposed to be me who Ascended Poppy when the time was right."

My head cranked to the side, lips peeling back as I grabbed Malik by the collar of his shirt and slammed him into the wall.

"Growl at me all you want, Cas, but the truth is, Isbeth had no need of you before you went off and decided to take the Maiden. She hadn't planned on that. She'd just adapted her plans, but if you had come for me before that? She would've made me kill you." Malik swept his arms up, knocking mine aside. Then he was right in my face. "Isbeth knew about Millie—what she is for me. And trust me when I say she took every opportunity to use that as leverage. She would've made me choose, Cas. Millie or you."

I stiffened.

"And I wouldn't have relied on whatever motherly bond she might have had." His stare held mine. "Because they can dish out worse things than death, as you are well aware. So I think you know what I would've chosen."

I did.

I turned from him, shoving a hand through my hair. Because I knew exactly what I would've done if the situation were reversed. *Fuck.*

"I hated it," Malik added quietly. "Knowing you were out there, risking your life to free me. I wanted nothing more than for you to return home and forget about me—"

"I never would've been able to do that." I faced him.

"I know, but I wanted it." His shoulders tensed. "I wanted you to go home and *live* without guilt, because you wouldn't have needed to feel as if you had to prove yourself if I'd been a better brother—a better heir."

"Malik," I started.

"Come on, the only reason you paid attention in our lessons was the same reason you felt you needed to take care of the Blood Crown. Because you knew that once I took the throne, I would've started a war and gotten myself killed."

"No, you wouldn't have," I denied. "You didn't want war."

"I didn't want it, but I could've been talked into it. You know Alastir would've gotten to me," he said when I shook my head. "He wanted that long before shit went bad with us and Shea. And I would've listened. Fuck, I would've let him run the damn kingdom as long as I could do what I wanted, which was whatever required the least amount of effort."

"You don't give yourself enough credit," I muttered. "You never did."

"That's something else we'll have to disagree on." A few short moments of silence fell as we locked eyes. He exhaled slowly. "I'm sorry, Cas."

"Don't."

"I am. I'm sorry for what you had to believe. I'm sorry for all you had to do. For the pain. For all the death." His voice dropped. "For Shea."

I closed my eyes.

"I wish the past was different for us," he said. "But it's not, and I don't think either of us would change very much, would we?"

Not if it jeopardized where we were today, as fucked-up as that was. Rubbing the heel of my palm over my chest, I looked at my brother and thought about how I knew I wouldn't have done a damn thing differently if I were in Malik's place.

I dropped my hand, sighing. Knowing that and this conversation didn't erase all the messy-ass feelings we both had surrounding everything. Our lies. Our guilt. Our fuckups. The blood on our hands.

But we were brothers, and I loved the fucker.

I exhaled long and slow, gaze moving to the door. When I spoke, I kept my voice low. "I'm guessing Millicent still has no idea you're heartmates?"

Malik's attention shifted to where mine had. He shook his head.

"You going to tell her?"

"I haven't really even acted upon it," he murmured.

My brows flew up. I could only assume he meant getting physical and not the kind that left him bloody. "So, I'm guessing that's a no?"

Malik nodded.

"Why?" I asked.

A wry smile appeared. "Because she hates me."

"I don't think that's true," I said, crossing my arms. "When you got hurt out there, she—"

"It's true," he cut me off. "She hates me and has every damn reason to."

I didn't know what to say to that at first. I had no knowledge of her reasons or what he believed them to be. "Poppy hated me at one point."

"Yeah, but you haven't done the things I have," he said, clearing his throat. "Anyway, there is something you should know. It's about the Revenants and Kolis."

His change of subject didn't pass me by, but I let it slide. "What?"

"Callum made sure all of them knew who their creator was, so those who were loyal to Isbeth? That only went surface-deep. They were loyal to Kolis. And the ones we couldn't find?" Malik's eyes met mine. "They're going to be a problem. They're going to try everything to bring him to full power and stop anyone who attempts to thwart that."

Millicent didn't stay when I re-entered the chamber. Without saying a word, she rose and left. According to Kieran, she'd said nothing while she sat beside Poppy.

She'd only held her hand.

"Everything cool with you?" Kieran asked, picking up a pair of clean breeches. The fact that he'd remained nude by Poppy's side, not leaving Millie alone, brought forth a smile that was part amused and part, well, proud.

"You heard Malik and me?" I returned to my place beside Poppy.

"Everyone on this floor likely heard you two," he stated dryly. "At least parts of the conversation."

I snorted, taking the cup from the nightstand. "Everything is...as good as it can be."

Kieran pulled up his breeches, fastening the flap. "You think they'll get better?"

"Possibly." I took a drink of water, then offered the glass to Delano. He shook his head. "Did you hear what he said about the Revs?" I asked, returning the cup to the nightstand.

"Parts of it." Bootless, he returned to the bed and sat on Poppy's other side.

I filled him in, and none of what I'd shared was particularly good news.

But as I'd once told Poppy, I wouldn't borrow from tomorrow's problems.

Picking up the hand that Millicent had held, I brought it to my lips. I tabled the shit with Kolis and my brother as I searched for where I'd stopped in my story. We'd been on the road.

To New Haven.

Where everything truly changed.

NEW HAVEN

We arrived in New Haven at dusk, and I knew Poppy had to be tired. We'd been riding for almost twenty-four hours, taking minimal breaks, and there was definitely no more cheese to be found. But as soon as we entered the city, Poppy sat straight and looked around, taking in everything with an expression damn close to wonderment. She probably hadn't expected much from the small trading town, especially since the mortal elite didn't flock to the distant city. That benefited us. The Ascended had no reason to check on Lord Halverston, who had once overseen the city, so New Haven was run entirely by Descenters and mortal descendants of Atlantia—unbeknownst to the Blood Crown. That was why the Rise was in good condition, and the rows of homes we rode past were well-kept and far more spacious than what one saw near the Rise in Masadonia.

Since we'd arrived at suppertime, I'd hoped to make it to the keep unnoticed.

We didn't.

Doors and windows opened, and there were smiles and waves. A small horde of children followed our progress, smiling up at us. Poppy gave a short, jerky wave, bringing a grin to my face.

She leaned back into me and whispered, "This is a little odd."

"I don't think they get a lot of visitors," I said, squeezing her waist.

"This is an exciting day for them," Kieran commented drolly, knowing damn well they recognized us. Me.

"Is it?" I eyed Kieran.

"They behave as if royalty is among them," Poppy murmured.

"Then they truly must not get many visitors," I replied.

Kieran gave me a long, sideways glance.

"Have you been here before?" Poppy asked.

"Only briefly," I told her, smiling at the young girl with dark braids and deep brown skin waving from one of the second-floor windows of a golden-doored home.

Poppy turned to Kieran. "You?"

"I've passed through a time or two."

More like a time or two dozen, but luckily the greenish-gray stone of the two-story Haven Keep appeared ahead, framed by the heavy woods that separated the town from Whitebridge. The structure was old, built before the War of Two Kings, and it looked it.

Snow began falling as we crossed into the keep's yard, and I spotted several guards in black. To Poppy, they likely looked like normal Rise Guards. They weren't.

I relaxed a little at seeing a few familiar faces as I led Setti toward the stables. Once inside the lamplit barn, I swung down, giving the horse a quick pat before lifting my arms to help Poppy.

She looked at my hands, arched a brow, and then slid off the other side of the saddle.

I sighed, and Poppy grinned as she rubbed Setti's neck, who was busy sniffing the straw.

Grabbing the saddlebag, I draped it over my shoulder and went to where she stood. "Stay close to me."

"Of course."

My eyes narrowed on her. That was a far-too-quick agreement. She clasped her hands together, fixing what she likely thought was an innocent look on her face, but it only made her appear impish.

Kieran and the others joined us as we left Setti's stall, where he'd found fresh hay in the racks. Outside the stables, the snow was coming down harder. We'd made it just in time. Poppy tugged her cloak around her as we crossed the yard. Catching the eyes of several of my men, I nodded. Their expressions were a mixture of relief and anticipation.

I felt the same.

But didn't.

The doors of the keep opened, and godsdamn, it was good to see the tall, blond wolven in the entryway. It had been far too long since I'd last seen Delano Amicu.

"It's good to see you." Delano clasped Kieran's hand as he glanced at me, then at Poppy. His gaze lingered a second or so on her and then returned to Kieran. "It's good to see all of you."

"Same, Delano," Kieran answered as I placed my hand on Poppy's lower back. "It's been too long."

"Not long enough."

I cracked a grin at the deep voice booming from inside the keep. A second later, the massive, bearded, dark-haired Elijah Payne strode out, hand resting on the short sword strapped to his side. Not that the mountain of a man needed it. I'd seen the half-Atlantian pick up a Craven and *throw* it like it was nothing more than a sack of potatoes.

Kieran smiled, and I saw Poppy do a double-take. "Elijah," he drawled. "You missed me more than anyone else."

Elijah proved just how strong the fucker was, capturing Kieran in a hug. He lifted the heavy-ass wolven off his feet as his golden-brown gaze landed on Poppy and me.

A half grin appeared on Elijah's face as he dropped Kieran. He strode forward, giving Kieran only a heartbeat to move out of the way. "What do we have here?" Elijah asked.

"We're in need of shelter for the night," I said.

Elijah threw back his head, laughing. I stifled a sigh as he said, "We have plenty of shelter."

"Good to hear." I sent Elijah a look of warning as I guided Poppy into the keep's foyer.

The space was packed. I kept my hand on Poppy's back, knowing the looks of distrust coming from some of them were simply because they didn't recognize Poppy or the guards who traveled with us, but it made me tense. I needed to make sure none of them would be a problem, especially if any happened to figure out who Poppy was. She kept looking around, and I bet she searched for the Lord or Lady in charge of the city.

She would not find either.

"We do have a lot of…catching up to do." Elijah clapped Kieran on the shoulder, causing him to stumble again. Elijah's grin spread. The fucker loved to mess with the wolven like a child who kept poking a sleeping bear.

A flash of forest green tunic and a cream shawl caught my attention. I turned to see the true lady of the keep striding forward, her raven-hued hair swept back from her face, and her knee-length tunic and breeches seeming to snag Poppy's attention. That wasn't what held mine. It was the growing belly of Elijah's niece.

Little Magda was pregnant? Again?

Well, she wasn't exactly little anymore, but it was hard not to think of her as the long-limbed, pigtailed girl who could throw punches just as well as her uncle.

Who currently eyed Poppy, looking like he was seconds away from saying something that didn't need to be said.

"I must speak with a few people, but Magda will show you to your room." I glanced at Magda, who I trusted to be far more circumspect than her uncle. "Make sure she has a room to bathe in, and she's sent hot food."

"Yes—" Magda started to dip into a curtsy but stopped herself. Her cheeks turned pink as she sent me an apologetic glance before turning to Poppy. "Sorry. I'm a little off balance some days." She patted her stomach. "I blame baby number two."

"Congratulations," Poppy said, her cheeks flushed. She turned to me. "Hawke—"

"Later," I said, hating to cut her off like that, especially surrounded by strangers and with how out of her element she was. But I had to because Phillips was now inside the keep, and things...some things would begin to happen quickly.

Resolved, I joined Elijah. "Where are the others?"

"Making sure the outside is secure," Phillips answered, his attention trained on Magda and Poppy.

Elijah chuckled. "The outside can't be any more secure."

Phillips turned dark eyes on the man, giving him the once-over. "We'll see that for ourselves, sir."

The smile on Elijah's face grew as I briefly met Kieran's gaze. "Whatever makes you happy."

Kieran stepped forward, clasping Phillips' shoulders. "Let's see what we can get from the kitchens while we get a better idea of the layout here."

Phillips hesitated, still watching the side door that Poppy had disappeared through. "Should she be alone with that woman?"

"That woman?" The smile faded from Elijah's face.

I moved between the two. "I've been told these are good and trustworthy people. Let's not offend them," I suggested, more than aware of Elijah glowering behind me. "Plus, Poppy is not helpless."

"Yes, but—"

"She is fine," I cut in. "Go with Kieran so I can make sure everything we need here will be provided."

His lips pressed into a thin line, but he went with Kieran this time.

"Are we going to kill him?" Elijah asked. "I hope the fuck so."

I sighed, facing him. "We need to talk."

"That we do." Elijah looked over at the crowd of people. "Y'all get going. You got stuff to do. Do it." He held up a hand. "And do it *quietly*. We have guests." He paused. "Special guests."

Delano briefly closed his eyes, shaking his head as there were a few grumbles. A giggle or two. Still, the crowd dispersed, most disappearing into the numerous rooms or heading for the dining hall. All except for one. A tall, rich-brown-skinned Atlantian.

"Naill," I said, meeting him halfway. I clasped his arm. "Been a while, hasn't it?"

"Too long." His grip was as tight as mine as he smiled, the skin crinkling at the corners of his golden eyes. "Glad you made it here."

"Same," I said.

"I'm kind of sad I didn't get the same welcome," quipped Delano.

Laughing under my breath, I turned to the pale-haired wolven. "Might be a wee bit suspicious if I know every single one of you."

"I know." Delano came forward. "I just wanted to complain."

I took hold of his arm. "It is good to see you."

Wintry blue eyes met mine. "I was worried we wouldn't…" He forced a smile. "You good?"

Yanking the younger wolven in for a hug, I cupped the back of his head. "I'm good."

"Oh, fuck," Elijah muttered. "You're going to make him an even bigger marshmallow."

"Marshmallow?" I repeated, pulling back.

Delano rolled his eyes. "Yeah, he says I'm like a marshmallow, all gooey and soft on the inside."

"Am I wrong?" Elijah threw up his hands.

"You're going to realize just how not soft I am when I knock your ass through that stone wall," Delano warned, pointing at said wall.

"You wouldn't dare." Elijah chuckled, motioning us to follow him to one of the closed wooden doors. "Wanna know why? You'd be all kinds of sad afterward for hurting me."

"I'm not so sure about that," Delano muttered, but he did so as he grinned.

Smiling, I shook my head as I followed them into a study. I'd missed them—fucking missed them all. It had been a year since I'd seen some of them. Years for others. It was so damn good to hear them rib one another. All we were missing was my brother. My chest tightened, and I forced myself to inhale and hold the breath until I felt the knot loosening. Only then did I exhale. Malik would be with us soon.

Holding that close to my heart, I looked around as Naill closed the door behind us. Gas sconces cast a faint yellow glow throughout the study. An ancient-looking oak desk sat in the corner. The walls were bare except for a credenza stocked with liquor, and a faded painting of Haven Keep above the fireplace. Several chairs were situated near the lit hearth.

"Want anything to drink?" Elijah walked behind the desk, taking a seat there as Delano went to the credenza. "Got some whiskey and, well, more whiskey."

"I'm good." Unhooking my cloak, I dropped it over the back of a chair. "But help yourself."

Naill shook his head when Delano glanced at him, and then Elijah asked, "So, that's her? The Maiden?"

"It is." I adjusted my baldric strap as Delano poured a glass for himself and Elijah. "I want to thank you again, Elijah, for taking the risk to house us."

"I would do anything for you and our Prince," he said, tone serious. "Anything to stop those bastard Ascended. There is no risk too great." He took the glass from Delano, giving him a nod of thanks. "And there's not anyone here, in this keep or this town, who isn't willing to take the risk."

"I know, but being willing to take the risks isn't the same as living them," I told him. "The Blood Crown will likely send a division of their armies. Their Royal Knights."

"And we'll be ready for them if they do." Elijah leaned forward. "We all know what is ultimately at risk here. Not just what we've carved out in New Haven, but our lives. Our futures. Our children's futures. And if we've got to bleed for that, we will. Look, we all know that everything we built here can come crashing down on us at any moment," he said, speaking the truth. "And if freeing your brother and preventing this whole damn land from breaking out into war is what does it? Fucking hell of a way to go, if you ask me."

My respect for the man—for all of those here—knew no limits.

"All of this has been such a long time coming." Disbelief colored his tone. "Almost can't believe we're here. That you have her and Malik's freedom within our grasp."

I had a hard time believing it myself, and there was all this anticipation and determination to see it through, but also an undercurrent of unease. Guilt. And a rising sense of loss I couldn't shake.

"I'm not asking to be an ass," Delano said, drawing me from my thoughts, "but what happened to her?"

One thing I could count on was Delano never being an ass. "She was attacked by Craven as a child."

"Holy shit," Elijah breathed. "She survived a Craven attack as a child? Damn me." He chuckled, taking a drink. "Maybe she is Chosen."

I thought of what she'd done for Airrick.

"Gods," Delano murmured, leaning against the desk. "She's lucky."

"Or unlucky," Naill commented, sitting near the fire. "All things considered." He looked over at me. "You run into any problems on the way here?"

I filled them in on the Blood Forest, leaving out the part about Poppy. "Other than that, it's been pretty smooth."

Elijah eyed me over the rim of his glass. Most of his whiskey was already gone. The man could drink any of us under the table. "So, you're down a few guards already. What about the rest?"

"I will handle them," I told him.

Delano lowered his glass. "None of them can be swayed to join our side?"

I smiled faintly at his optimism. "I don't believe so."

"See? Marshmallow." Elijah leaned back, kicking his feet up onto the desk. "First thing he asks? How did the Maiden get scarred? The second thing?" He finished off his whiskey as Naill hid his smile behind his hand. "Can any of the guards be saved? Soon, he's gonna ask—" He cursed as Delano turned, knocking his legs off the desk with a swipe of his arm, nearly toppling Elijah out of his chair. He righted himself with one hand. "My apologies."

"Uh-huh." Delano turned. "Want a refill?"

"Does today end in a Y?" Elijah countered, chuckling as Delano took his glass. "I'm guessing we gotta handle the others with quickness."

"The sooner, the better," I told him.

"I know you said you'd take care of them yourself, but we got it." Naill tipped his head back to look at me. "Even the resident marshmallow."

Delano sighed, handing the glass to Elijah.

"I don't want that blood on your hands," I said. I'd brought the guards here. They were my responsibility.

"You shouldn't be the only one getting your hands dirty," Delano argued. "We got this, and we're not going to take no for an answer." He paused, a sheepish grin appearing. "My Prince."

I snorted.

"Seriously. We have this." Naill's eyes met mine. "We will take care of it."

My jaw worked as I took in their resolute faces—well, Delano's and Naill's, anyway. Elijah just looked eager, which made me want to laugh.

"They're not your responsibility," Naill said, knowing where my mind was with this. Not surprising. Besides Kieran and his family, Naill had known me the longest. "You've done enough."

But I hadn't even begun. Still, I nodded. I didn't thank them. This wasn't something you expressed gratitude for.

"Speaking of bloodied hands," Elijah began, his feet back on the desk, "I see Jericho is missing one."

My gaze flicked to the half-Atlantian. "He earned that."

"No one in this room is surprised to hear that," Delano remarked.

"He hasn't said what made you take it. Neither has Ivan or Rolf," Elijah said, referencing the two who had been with Jericho in Masadonia. "You going to key us in on what caused that? Dying to know."

"He was told not to harm the Maiden. He did. So, I took his hand," I explained. "And the same goes for all of you and all who reside at New Haven. No one is to harm her."

"Understood," Delano said when my stare met his. Naill nodded.

"Your wish is my command, as always," Elijah said with a cheeky grin. "But I got questions."

"I'm sure you do."

He lifted one large shoulder in a shrug. "I'm nosy, what can I say? I'm assuming the Maiden is unaware of who you are—who we are."

The knot returned to my chest. I nodded. "At this time, yes."

Elijah's bushy brows lifted. "At this time?"

"She expects that we will only be here for the night," I explained. "When we don't leave in the morning, she'll start asking questions."

"And?" Delano asked.

"I will tell her what I can of the truth. Who I am. Who the Ascended really are," I said, knowing that conversation was coming, likely by the time the sun set tomorrow.

Elijah met my stare. "I'm also assuming she isn't going to handle it well."

No, she likely wouldn't.

"Then what?" Naill asked.

"I will handle her," I told them, chest icing over. "No one else will."

UNWORTHY AND UNDESERVING

Magda had proven once more how she always thought ahead, giving Poppy a chamber on the second floor of the keep, accessible only by the covered outdoor hall. Escape options were limited in these chambers, with only one door and a small window.

I had a feeling I'd be thanking Magda for that later because I didn't believe Poppy would take the truth well. I wouldn't expect her to.

Before I checked on her, I used a room near hers to grab a quick bite to eat, bathe, and change into fresh clothing. When I stepped back out into the outdoor hall, more snow had fallen, and it was still coming down, blanketing the courtyard and the nearby pines in about an inch or so. I went to Poppy's door and stopped.

The meeting with the others had taken longer than expected, and considering how hard we'd been traveling, Poppy was likely asleep. She could use the rest, but I also needed to talk to her. I had to find out what I could about her abilities before I told her everything else. I doubted she would be exactly forthcoming with information from that point forward. Or maybe she would once she learned the truth. Poppy was smart and kind. Forgiving—I stopped those thoughts. None of that mattered. Poppy could be understanding or not. She could take my offer of eventual freedom or not. Either way, she would not forgive me. I didn't deserve it. That much I knew.

Dragging my hand through my damp hair, I knocked on the door before opening it.

Poppy wasn't sleeping.

In fact, she was standing by the bed with her dagger in hand.

"Hawke," she breathed.

My brows rose. "I thought you'd be asleep."

She lowered the dagger. "Is that why you barged in?"

"Since I knocked, I don't consider that barging in." Shutting the door, I took a closer look at her. She wore a velvet robe of some dark color somewhere between green and blue. All that damp hair was down and curling at her throat and flushed cheeks. She looked beautiful, even more so with the dagger in her hand. "But I'm glad to see that you were prepared just in case it wasn't someone you wanted to see."

"What if you're someone I don't want to see?" she asked.

"You and I both know that's not the case. At all," I said, speaking the truth for the time being. Later? I had a feeling I would have to take that dagger and all sharp, heavy, and blunt objects from her.

She placed the weapon on the nightstand and then sat on the edge of the bed. "Your ego never fails to amaze me."

"I never fail to amaze you," I corrected her.

Poppy smiled, and it was a rare one—big and bright. "Thank you for proving what I just said."

I chuckled. "Did you eat?"

She nodded. "You?"

"While I bathed."

"Multi-tasking at its finest."

"I am skilled." I came closer, stopping a few feet from her. "Why aren't you asleep? You have to be exhausted."

"I know the morning will come sooner rather than later, and we'll be back out there," she said, and it took effort for me not to react to that. "But I can't sleep. Not yet. I was waiting for you." She toyed with the sash. "This place is…different, isn't it?"

"I imagine if one was used to only the capital and Masadonia, it would be," I said. "Things are far simpler here, no pomp and circumstance."

"I noticed that. I haven't seen a single Royal Crest."

I tilted my head. "Did you wait up for me to talk about Royal banners?"

"No." Poppy dropped the sash. "I waited up to talk to you about what I did to Airrick."

I watched her brush her hand through the sides of her hair, tucking the length back on her left side. Something struck me then. When speaking with Kieran or the others, she always turned her head so her right side faced them. She didn't do that with me.

"Is this later enough for you?" she said. "A good time?"

I grinned. "This is a good time, Princess. It's private enough, which is what I figured we would need."

Poppy appeared as if she might speak but seemed to change her mind. A look of chagrin settled in her features.

"Are you going to explain why neither you nor Vikter ever mentioned that you had this...touch?" I asked.

"I don't call it that," she said after a moment. "Only a few who have heard...the rumors about it do. It's why some think I'm the child of a god." The delicate brows, a shade or so darker than her hair, knitted. "You, who seems to hear and know everything, haven't heard that rumor?"

"I do know a lot, but no, I have never heard that," I admitted. "And I've never seen anyone do whatever it was that you did."

She was quiet for a moment. "It's a gift from the gods. It's why I'm Chosen." Her brow creased once more, then smoothed out. "I have been instructed by the Queen herself to never speak of it or to use it. Not until I am deemed worthy. For the most part, I have obeyed that."

I felt like Elijah in that moment because I had a lot of questions. "For the most part?"

"Yes, for the most part. Vikter knew about it, but Tawny doesn't. Neither did Rylan or Hannes. The Duchess knows, and the Duke knew, but that was all." She paused. "And I don't use it often...*ish*."

Often-ish? "What is this gift?"

Her lips pursed with a long exhale. "I can...sense other people's pain, both physical and mental. Well, it started off that way. It appears that the closer I get to my Ascension, the more it evolves. I guess I should say I can sense people's emotions now," she explained, nervously plucking at the blanket she sat on. "I don't need to touch them. I can just look at them, and it's like...like I open myself up to them. I can usually control it and keep my senses to myself, but sometimes, it's difficult."

Immediately, I thought about when the Teermans had addressed the city after the attack. "Like in crowds?"

Poppy nodded. "Yes. Or when someone projects their pain without realizing it. Those times are rare. I don't see anything more than you or anyone else would see, but I feel what they do."

What she was telling me was...it sounded impossible for a mortal. "You...just feel what they feel?" Wait. My eyes widened. "So, you felt the pain that Airrick, who had received a very painful injury, felt?"

Poppy's gaze lifted to mine, and she nodded once more.

Fucking gods. I briefly closed my eyes. "That had to be..."

"Agony?" she said. "It was, but it's not the worst I've felt. Physical pain is always warm, and it's acute, but the mental, emotional pain is like...like bathing in ice on the coldest day. That kind of pain is far worse."

My mind was racing again, pulling out the times I'd seen her uncomfortable—her hands twisting nonstop. "And you can feel other emotions? Like happiness or hatred? Relief...or guilt?"

"I can, but it's new. And I'm not often sure what I'm feeling. I have to rely on what I know, and well..." She shrugged. "But to answer your question, yes."

I had no fucking clue what to say because even though I'd seen her do it, my brain rebelled against the news.

"That's not all I can do," she added.

"Obviously," I said dryly.

"I can also ease other people's pain by touch. Usually, it's not something the person notices, not unless they're experiencing a great deal of obvious pain."

Something tugged at the recesses of my memories. "How?"

"I think of...happy moments and feed that through the bond my gift establishes through the connection," she shared.

"You think happy thoughts and that's it?"

Her nose scrunched. "Well, I wouldn't say it like that. But, yes."

Hold on... My gaze shot to hers. "Have you sensed my emotions before?"

Her throat worked on a swallow. "I have."

I sat back. Holy fuck, only the gods knew what she'd picked up from me.

"I didn't do it on purpose at first—well, okay, I did, but only because you always looked like... I don't know," she said, and I looked at her again. "A caged animal whenever I saw you around the castle, and I was curious to find out why. I realize I shouldn't have. I didn't do it...a lot. I made myself stop. Sort of," she added as my brows rose. "For the most part. Sometimes, I just can't help it. It's like I'm denying nature to not..."

My stomach clenched. "What did you feel from me?"

Poppy gave me a small shake of her head as she faced me. "Sadness."

I stiffened.

"Deep grief and sorrow." Her stare fastened on my chest. "It's always there, even when you're teasing or smiling. I don't know how you deal with it. I figure a lot of it has to do with your brother and friend."

My lips parted. The niggling in the back of my mind? I suddenly thought of what had happened after we'd left her studies. The inexplicable *peace* I'd felt.

"I'm sorry," she said. "I shouldn't have used my gift on you, and I probably should've just lied—"

"Have you eased my pain before?" I asked.

She pressed her hands into her thighs. "I have."

"Twice. Right? After you were with the Priestess, and the night of the Rite." When we'd been in the garden, and I'd been speaking about the caves. There had also been a strange easing of sorrow and bitterness then, I now realized. It hadn't been as strong, nor had it lasted as long, but those heavy emotions *had* eased.

Poppy nodded.

"Well, now I understand why I felt…lighter. The first time it lasted—damn, it lasted for a while. Got the best sleep in years." I coughed out a short laugh, a little stunned. Okay, a lot stunned.

"Too bad that can't be bottled and sold."

"Why?" The demand burst from me. "Why did you take my pain? Yes, I do…feel sadness. I miss my brother with every breath I take. His absence haunts me, but it's manageable." Now. *Now* it was manageable.

"I know," she said quietly. "You don't let it interfere with your life, but I…I didn't like knowing that you were hurting, and I could help, at least temporarily. I just wanted—"

"What?" I asked.

"I wanted to help. I wanted to use my gift to help people."

I drew back, exhaling roughly. "And you have? More than just me and Airrick?"

"I have. Those who are cursed? I often ease their pain. And Vikter would get terrible headaches. I would sometimes help him with those. And Tawny, but she never knew."

"That's how the rumors got started." Godsdamn. "You're doing it to help the cursed."

"And their families sometimes," she told me in a voice that was too small, too quiet for someone so fucking caring. "They often feel such sorrow that I have to."

"But you're not allowed."

"No, and it seems so stupid that I can't." Poppy threw up her hands. "That I'm not supposed to. The reason doesn't even make sense. Wouldn't the gods have already found me worthy to have given me this gift?"

"One would think so." And it was a damn good question. "Can your brother do this? Anyone else in your family?"

"No. It's only me, and the last Maiden. We were both born in a shroud," she said. "And my mother realized what I could do around the age of three or four."

I frowned. The last Maiden? There was no other Maiden that I knew of.

"What?" She peeked at me.

I shook my head, then my gaze cut to hers. "Are you reading me now?"

"No," she insisted, lowering her gaze to her hands. "I seriously try not to, even when I really want to. Doing so feels like cheating when it's someone I..."

Poppy stiffened. She went so damn still, then her wide eyes swung back to mine. Her lips parted as she stared at me. Kept staring at me as pink crept into her cheeks.

"Now, I wish I had your gift," I said. "Because I would love to know what you're feeling at this moment."

"I feel nothing from the Ascended," Poppy blurted out, and I blinked. "Absolutely nothing, even though I know they feel physical pain."

"That's..."

"Weird, right?" she said.

"I was going to say disturbing, but sure, it's weird."

"You know?" She leaned in, lowering her voice as if someone was hidden in her bathing chamber. "It always bothered me that I couldn't feel anything. It should be a relief, but it never was. It just made me feel...cold."

I wanted to tell her there was a reason for that. It was because they had no souls, but that would basically be shouting in her face that her brother didn't have one.

"I can see that." I mimicked her movements, inching closer. "I should thank you."

"For what?"

"For easing my pain."

"You don't have to," she whispered.

"I know, but I want to," I said, still sort of blown away by the fact that she would do that for me. For anyone. Especially knowing how the Duke treated her. "Thank you."

"It's nothing." That thick fringe of lashes swept down, shielding her eyes from me.

"I was right."

"About what?"

"About you being brave and strong," I told her. "You risk a lot when you use your gift."

"I don't think I've risked enough," she said, her fingers tangling. "I couldn't help Vikter. I was too...overwhelmed. Maybe if I wasn't fighting it so much, I would've at least taken his pain."

"But you took Airrick's," I reminded her. "You helped him." And countless others. I brought my brow to hers. "You are utterly nothing like I expected."

"You keep saying that," she said. "What did you expect?"

"I honestly don't know anymore," I admitted, only knowing that I never expected her. Ever.

Gods.

She was...

Fuck, I was simply blown away by *her*. Who wouldn't be? Those who'd stared at her with distrust earlier would be on their knees before her if they knew her kindness and strength. Hell, I was half-tempted to get on mine.

"Poppy?"

Her soft breath danced across my lips. "Yes?"

I brought my fingers to her cheek. "I hope you realize that no matter what anyone has ever told you, you are more worthy than anyone I've ever met."

"You haven't met enough people, then," she said.

"I have met too many." Closing my eyes, I kissed her forehead. I had to force myself to lean back instead of tilting her head and bringing my lips to hers. I wasn't worthy of kissing her. My thumb slid along her jaw. Or even touching her. "You deserve so much more than what awaits you."

My gods, that was the truest thing I'd ever spoken. Even if I was able to give her freedom, she didn't deserve the position I was putting her in. She didn't deserve what the Ascended had already stolen from her. And she wouldn't deserve the sense of security I would take from her.

Poppy shuddered, her eyes opening. The green was so bright, so clear.

Jaw clenching, I drew back, really hoping I wasn't—what did she call it? Projecting. I really hoped I wasn't projecting what I was feeling. "Thank you for trusting me with this."

She didn't answer as she looked at me, her lips parted as if she were mid-breath. And she wasn't just looking at me. Those bright green eyes were slowly tracking over my face, then down my shoulders to the hand that rested between us. Her gaze slowly made its way back up to mine, and the breath she let out caused mine to snag for the third damn time.

"You shouldn't look at me like that," I warned her.

"Like what?" Poppy's voice had taken on a breathy quality that stroked every part of me.

"You know exactly how you're looking at me." I closed my eyes. "Actually, you might not, and that's why I should leave."

Because I *knew* the look in those beautiful eyes, even if I didn't catch the scent of her rising desire. She looked at me like she wanted to be kissed.

Stared at me like she needed more than that. Wanted more.

And fuck, I was a little shocked that she would come to that choice because of what it meant for her—for the role she had been placed in. That was huge. My body, however, was not shocked, and was immediately on board—blood heating and cock hardening. I started to lean toward her, answering the need and want I saw in her stare. Every fiber of my being demanded it. Wanted it.

But she was real. The entirety of her.

And I wasn't. Everything about me was a lie.

"How am I looking at you, Hawke?"

I stiffened, eyes opening. "Like I don't deserve to be looked at. Not by you."

"Not true," she swore.

My chest clenched. "I wish that was the case. Gods, I do. I need to leave." I stood quickly, backing up.

I needed to get out of this chamber before the fragile hold I had on my self-control snapped. And it was already nearly nonexistent. Because what I'd said to Kieran before? That I wasn't that much of a piece of shit? It was a lie. I was. Because with Poppy, it was too easy to forget who I really was. It was too easy to lose myself in her, let go of all the nasty shit that had brought me to her. It was too damn easy to...to live right alongside Poppy.

And, gods, I wanted that. Badly. But I couldn't even fool myself into believing that I could stay and show her pleasure. I was not altruistic. This wasn't the Blood Forest. There were no barriers here.

I had to leave.

"Goodnight, Poppy." I did one of the hardest damn things I'd ever done and turned for the door. I made it halfway.

"Hawke?"

I stopped, even though I knew I shouldn't. It was like her voice was a compulsion.

"Will you...?" Her voice strengthened. "Will you stay with me tonight?"

I shuddered to my bones. "I want nothing more than that, but I don't think you realize what will happen if I stay."

"What would happen?"

I turned then, and I could see her pulse thrumming in her throat from where I stood. "There is no way I could be in that bed with you and not be all over you in ten seconds flat. We wouldn't even make it to the bed before that happened. I know my limitations."

The chest of her robe rose with a sweet, sharp breath.

"I know that I'm not a good enough man to remember my duty and yours or that I'm so incredibly unworthy of you it should be a sin," I told her. "Even knowing that, there is no way I wouldn't strip that robe from you and do exactly what I told you I'd do when we were in the forest."

And that was the godsdamn truth. Despite what I knew. Despite my lies. Despite how she deserved so much fucking better than me. I would take her.

Poppy's stare met mine. "I know."

I sucked in a breath. "Do you?"

She nodded.

"I'm not just going to hold you. I won't stop at kissing you. My fingers won't be the only thing inside you," I promised, blood thickening. "My need for you is far too great, Poppy. If I stay, you will not walk out this door the Maiden."

Poppy shivered. "I know."

I'd moved without realizing it, taking too many steps away from the door—away from what was right—and toward her—toward what was so damn wrong. "Do you truly, Poppy?"

She didn't speak as she held my heated stare. Instead, steady hands lifted to the sash at her waist, and everything in me stopped and then sped up as she undid it. The robe parted, revealing a sliver of the inner swells of her breasts, a glimpse of her stomach, and the shadowy paradise between her thighs.

Then Poppy let the robe slip from her shoulders and fall to the floor.

I wanted to be a good man who would walk away from what he knew he wasn't worthy or deserving of. The kind Kieran believed I was. The type I had been raised to be. But I wasn't a good man.

I was just hers.

THIS IS REAL

Poppy hid nothing as she bared herself to me, even though she trembled. Even though no one had seen her like this. She was that brave, that bold, and I was rooted where I stood, my heart thundering in my chest as my gaze left hers, following the sweet flush down her throat.

I'd seen a lot of bodies. Women. Men. Slim ones. Round ones. Those in between. Bodies that were smooth and absent of perceived flaws. Others whose flesh reflected a life lived. I'd seen bodies I'd completely forgotten, but I knew I'd never seen anyone like her.

Poppy had to be a goddess.

Because, my gods, she was absolutely *breathtaking*—every bit of the unending, lush softness of her curves. The fullness of her breasts and their deep rosy tips. The slight indentation of her waist and the way her hips flared, the lushness of her thighs and the hidden valley between them. I saw the scars she'd told me about before—the marks Craven claws had left behind on her strong forearm, the softness of her belly, and the ones on her inner thighs, and they too were beautiful—a testament to her strength and resilience.

"You're so damn beautiful and so damn unexpected." I rasped as I lifted my gaze to hers, more eloquent words failing me because looking upon her felt like both a sin and a blessing. A reward I had not earned.

But one I would take.

I moved faster than I probably should've, but I wasn't thinking. I'd stopped the moment she undid that sash on her robe. I wrapped her in my arms, and then I took her mouth. There was nothing gentle in the way I kissed her. All my hunger and want came through.

And then I lost myself in her.

Poppy reached for my tunic at the same time I did. It hit the floor as I kicked off my boots. My breeches went next, and then there was nothing between us.

I stood where I was, letting Poppy look her fill, and she did. Her gaze traveled slowly over my chest and stomach, then lower.

"The scar on your thigh," she said, staring at the faded brand. "When did you get it?"

"Many years ago, when I was dumb enough to get caught," I said, brushing several strands of her hair back. Normally, I hated when someone mentioned the brand or looked at it, but with Poppy? I didn't care.

I didn't care about *anything* but her, nothing but right now.

Poppy's gaze inched away, and I knew the moment she saw exactly how much I wanted her. She drew her lower lip between her teeth as she stared. My cock throbbed.

"You keep looking at me like that," I told her, "and this will be over before it starts."

Her cheeks flushed an even deeper pink. "I...you're perfect."

My chest seized because, fuck, I wished I were. If I were, I wouldn't be here. "No, I'm not. You deserve someone who is, but I'm too much of a bastard to allow that."

The skin between her brows creased as she stared up at me. "I disagree with everything you just said."

"Shocker," I murmured, curling an arm around her waist.

The way she inhaled at the contact of our bodies was fucking addictive. I lifted her, taking her to the bed. I carefully laid her down and then came down over her.

I held myself back, giving her time, even though every part of my being strained to feel the length of her body against mine, to discover what it felt like to be deep inside her. But this...this was a first for her. A lot of firsts. And I'd never been anyone's *first*. I wasn't perfect, but I wanted this to be that for her.

I slowly let some of my weight settle against her. I shuddered at the feel of her legs against mine.

Poppy swallowed. "Are you—?"

"Protected? I take the monthly aid," I assured her, speaking of the herb that ensured unions weren't of the fruitful variety. "I assume you're not."

She gave me that cute little snort.

"Wouldn't that be a scandal?" I teased, skimming my hand over her right arm. The scars there were deep. How she hadn't lost the arm or her life was beyond me.

"It would, but this…"

My gaze lifted to hers, and it felt like the entire keep shifted beneath and all around us. There was a skipping motion in my chest. The nape of my neck tingled as we looked at each other. My heart sped up. This moment…it felt like it had always been coming. As if every choice I'd made—that we'd made—had led to this. It was a crazy feeling, completely senseless, and yet… "This changes everything."

I brought my mouth to hers, and this time I held myself in check. I mapped the line of her mouth with mine. I kissed her slowly, drawing her lip into my mouth and then parting her lips. I wanted to kiss her harder, deeper, but I couldn't. I couldn't let her feel the evidence of who I was like this, but I kissed her until she trembled beneath me, until I knew she wanted more.

Then I let myself explore.

I trailed my fingers down her throat and over the slope of her shoulders to the sweet swell of one breast. I flicked my tongue against hers as I felt her hardened nipple beneath the pad of my thumb. Her back arched, and her breaths against my lips turned quick and shallow. I drew my fingertips down her stomach, skating over the thin, jagged scars there and then lower, slipping my fingers between her thighs, through the soft dusting of curls.

Poppy cried out at the featherlight touch. I grinned, obsessed with how responsive she was. It would be a dream to tease and taunt her, to be cruel in the most decadent way and drive her to the brink of insanity with need. But there was no time for that.

There likely never would be.

Pain sliced through me, and for a moment, I thought she had drawn that dagger and put it to my chest. I stilled, my fingers moving gently over the softest part of her as my gut twisted—

She lifted her head, artlessly pressing her mouth to mine, jarring me from my thoughts. Her inexperienced kiss was…it was truly fucking magical, more seductive than any I'd experienced before.

I shuddered as I lifted my mouth from hers and then followed the path of my fingers. I kissed the side of her throat, a little startled by the urge to linger at her pulse. As I kept going, my jaw throbbed almost as intensely as my cock. I drew my lips over the delicate line of her collarbone and then tasted the skin of her chest. I slowed, my gaze flicking up. Her eyes were half-open as I pressed my lips to her nipple. She gasped, fingers clenching the sheet beneath us. Watching her, I drew the turgid flesh into my mouth.

Poppy's moan brought an answering groan from me as she moved restlessly, guided by instinct. I grinned and then went lower, drawing my tongue over her stomach. She tensed as I neared her scars, and even as brave as she was, I knew having me so close to them worried her.

I would show her she had no reason to worry.

Drawing my mouth over the healed wounds, I pressed a kiss to them, paying them the respect they were due. Her breath caught, and I went even lower, below her navel. I hooked a hand around her thigh, spreading her to fit the width of my shoulders. My mouth inches from the damp curls, I looked up at her.

"Hawke," she whispered.

I grinned. "Remember that first page of Miss Willa's diary?"

"Yes."

Holding her gaze, I kissed between her thighs. Poppy's back bowed. I didn't look away. Neither did she, but my heart pounded as I drew my tongue over her, sampling her, and gods, she tasted so damn good. So fucking sweet. I dipped my tongue into her heat, muscles throughout my body clenching with want. I shifted my head, flicking my mouth over the taut bundle of nerves.

Poppy's hips rose, drawing a rumble of approval from me. I watched as I drew her clit into my mouth. Her head fell back as she writhed.

Fucking gods, I could come just from the taste of her, the sight of her breasts rising and falling rapidly, the jut of that stubborn chin, and the way she so sweetly gave herself over to the wildness building in her.

And I could feel it, the tremor in her legs, the quiver in her breath. I *feasted* on her, licking and sucking until I was drowning in her scent. Until I knew I could survive on her taste.

"Oh, gods," she gasped, fingers digging into the sheet. Her legs straightened. "Oh, gods, Hawke—" She cried out, her body jerking and trembling as she came. Her spine flattened against the mattress as her unfocused gaze met mine.

I took one last taste of her, then lifted my head. As she watched, I drew my tongue over my lower lip.

"Honeydew," I groaned. "Just like I said."

Poppy shook, and I smiled.

The ache in my cock and jaw intensified as I prowled up the length of her body, clasping the nape of her neck. She watched me with those hooded emerald eyes and shivered as my thighs brushed hers. My godsdamn arms trembled when I positioned myself above her once more. Her eyes closed.

"Poppy," I whispered, the desire for her becoming primal. I kissed her, letting her taste herself on my lips as my cock pressed against the hot dampness. My heart raced as I stared down at her. "Open your eyes."

She did as I asked. "What?"

"I want your eyes open," I said.

"Why?"

I laughed. "Always so many questions."

She let out a soft little gasp. "I think you would be disappointed if I didn't have any."

"True." I slid my hand from her neck to her breast.

"So, why?" she asked.

"Because I want you to touch me," I said. "I want you to see what you do to me when you touch me."

She shivered. "How…how do you want me to touch you?"

The way she asked that… It fucking killed me. "Any way you want, Princess. You can't do it wrong."

Slowly, she let go of the sheet. I watched her as she brought her hand to my cheek. Her touch was so gentle. She trailed her fingertips along my jaw, then my lips, and I felt that caress in every part of my body.

Then she explored as I had, gliding her hand down my chest, drawing a quick, deep breath from me. She continued between us, tracing the muscles of my lower stomach. When she reached the line of coarse hair below my navel, I might've stopped breathing. I sure as fuck didn't move, other than to make lazy little circles around her nipple with my thumb. Not until the tips of her fingers brushed my cock.

My entire body jerked. "Please. Don't stop," I begged when she halted. "Dear gods, do not stop."

Poppy did as I pleaded, her gaze locked onto me as she drew her fingers along the base of my cock. My lips parted as she followed the vein, stopping midway to curl her fingers around me. My head kicked back. I trembled as exquisite pleasure rippled through me. Her grip loosened, and my breathing picked up as she slid her hand to the tip. My entire body shuddered as her hold tightened once more.

"Gods," I growled.

"Is this okay?"

"Anything you do is more than okay." I groaned as she dragged her palm against my cock. "But especially that. Totally that."

Poppy laughed and then did it again. My hips followed her movement, need rumbling from my chest.

"You see what your touch does to me?" I asked, pumping against her palm.

"Yes," she whispered.

"It kills me." I lowered my head, soaking in how she looked up at me. I'd never felt such anticipation, such pleasure. "It kills me in a way I don't think you'll ever understand."

Her gaze searched mine. "In a...in a good way?"

Gods, it undid me. I lifted my hand, cupping her cheek. "In a way I've never felt before."

"Oh," she said softly.

Lowering my head, I kissed her as I eased onto my left arm. I slid my hand from her cheek down the length of her as I reached between us. My hand replaced hers. "Are you ready?"

Her chest rose against mine as she nodded.

"I want to hear you say it."

The corners of her lips tugged up. "Yes."

Thank fuck. "Good, because I might have actually died if you weren't."

Poppy giggled, causing the skin at her eyes to crease.

"You think I'm kidding. Little do you know." I kissed her as I guided the head of my cock to her entrance. I pushed in, just a little, before stopping. I groaned at the feel of her heat and dampness. "Oh, yeah, you're so ready." I lifted my gaze to hers once more, seeing the flush had heightened. I grinned. "You amaze me."

"How?" She sounded so confused.

"You stand before Craven with no fear." I dragged my lips over hers. "But you blush and shiver when I speak of how slick and wonderful you feel against me."

"You're so inappropriate," she muttered.

"I'm about to get really inappropriate," I warned her. "But first, it may hurt."

Her chest rose again with another deep breath. "I know."

"Reading dirty books again?"

She bit her lip. "Possibly."

I laughed, and fuck, that was stupid. It brought me deeper. Taking a deep breath, I pressed in slowly. She was slick with arousal, but she was tight. I didn't want to hurt her. I'd rather tear out my fucking heart than do that, and maybe that should've concerned me, but I was too lost in the feel of her body accepting mine, her taking me, to dwell on that. Poppy's hands went to my shoulders. I liked the feel of them there. A lot. Shaking, I clenched my jaw as I pushed in to the hilt. Gasping, her eyes closed, and she went rigid beneath me. Breathing heavily, I forced myself to remain still, even as I twitched all over.

"I'm sorry." I kissed the tip of her nose, then each of her closed eyes, and both cheeks. "I'm sorry."

"It's okay," she said.

I kissed her lips, then dropped my forehead to hers. I still didn't move. Her body needed time. She needed it, not because of the pain she felt, but because pain, no matter how brief, tended to make everything real. She could change her mind now, and I would leave her, but it wouldn't undo the choices we'd made to this point. It wouldn't change that she'd crossed that line with me. That I'd crossed it with her.

Poppy's chest rose against mine, and then her hips lifted—

Fucking gods, my beautiful, brave Poppy. I squeezed my eyes shut against the sensation of her moving along my length. I shuddered as she did it again, holding myself still until her grip on my shoulders loosened. I opened my eyes.

Then I moved slowly, watching her closely for any signs of discomfort. If I saw it, this would stop. I pulled back until only an inch or so remained inside her and then slowly eased back in.

Poppy's arms slid around my neck, and another shudder took me. Her hips lifted, following my lead once more. Then we were moving together, her rising as I pushed down. A rhythm of give and take took hold. I still moved slowly, keeping myself in check. This was enough— the friction of her heat and my hardness, her soft moans, the feeling of her so damn tight around me. This was her first time. She didn't need to be fucked. She needed gentleness.

But then Poppy...my beautiful, brave, and *wicked* Poppy, curled her legs around my hips, and my restraint snapped.

I shoved an arm under her head, clasping her shoulder as firmly as I held her hip. My mouth closed over hers. I thrust harder, faster, as I held her beneath me. Her mouth moved with mine as she moaned.

Tension built, and I knew I wouldn't last long. Not after tasting her. Not after feeling her come against my mouth. Not when she was taking every plunge of my hips. I let go of her hip, moving my hand between us, finding her clit as I ground against her, my release building. It felt like descending into madness as I tore my mouth from hers, my gaze fixed on her features.

Poppy cried out, her legs tightening around my hips, and her body clamping down on my cock. She came, and that was it. Her spasms took me to the edge of that madness. My jaw throbbed. My lips parted as she unashamedly found her pleasure. I slipped my hand from between us and planted it on the bed beside her head, my fingers pressing into the mattress. My want for her was spiraling, tightening, and another kind of need took shape, a darker one. My gaze tracked over her swollen lips, her throat. Her pulse. My fangs pressed against my lips. Every part of my body tensed. My head started to lower, lips parting.

Poppy's eyes fluttered open, locking with mine. She placed a hand against my cheek. "Hawke," she whispered.

The sound of her voice caught me. I ground my molars as dual needs roared through me. My hand pressed into the space beside her head more, and I fought back the desire to sink my fangs into her as deeply as my cock and give in to my other desire.

My arm around her shoulders tightened, and then I fucked her. I took her hard—harder than I probably should've—driving our bodies across the bed. She felt too damn good, too damn perfect, and I'd wanted her from the first moment my lips touched hers. The tension spiraled. Release powered down my spine. I thrust into her once, sealing our bodies together as I came in waves of pleasure. I got a little lost in them, and the instinct I'd been fighting took over. I bowed my head, pressing in beneath her chin, forcing hers back. I found her pulse with my mouth as my hips churned against hers. My lips peeled back. My fangs grazed her skin. Poppy shivered, and a smile tugged at the corners of my mouth. I was poised, ready to strike—

Fuck.

I clamped my mouth shut, swallowing a groan as I pressed my chest against hers. My heart thundered as I fought back the hunger. It had been weeks since I'd fed, but I didn't need to. I could go much longer. The desire for her blood had nothing to do with that. It had everything to do with *her*, and never in my life had I experienced that kind of need with a mortal.

I had no idea how long it took for that to happen, for me to trust myself with her. I slowly became aware of her fingers sifting through my hair, but I remained as I was, still joined with her. I didn't think I had a choice. The nearly all-consuming need to take her blood rattled me, not to mention the feeling of completion without even feeding from her. I'd never felt this before. Never. I didn't know what it meant. Or maybe I did because I knew this was real. What was between us. What she felt for me. What I felt for her. This. It was real.

A rough breath left me, and I shifted my weight to my elbows. I turned my head, finding her mouth. I kissed her. "Don't forget this."

She splayed her fingers across my jaw. "I don't think I ever could."

"Promise me." I lifted my head, catching her stare. "Promise me you won't forget this, Poppy. That no matter what happens tomorrow, the next day, next week, you won't forget this—forget that this was real."

"I promise," she swore with hesitation. "I won't forget."

HIGHLY INAPPROPRIATE

I came back to the bed, a glass of mulled wine in one hand and a damp cloth in the other. Poppy hadn't moved since I left her, actually listening to me. She lay on her side, her arms crossed over her chest, knees slightly bent, and gloriously nude. My gaze traced the decadent curves of her body. I could stand here all night and look at her, but that, admittedly, would be weird.

"Princess."

Poppy opened her eyes as I planted a knee on the bed. "Don't call me that."

"But it's so fitting," I murmured, grinning where her brows snapped together. "I brought you something to drink."

"Thank you." Poppy sat, her chin dipped as she unfolded her arms and took the glass.

Sensing her shyness, I made myself act like a gentleman. For once. I waited until she was finished before I took a sip and then placed it on the nightstand beside her dagger. My grin spread. "Lie down."

Arms pressed tightly to her sides and her hair tumbling in a wild mess over her shoulders and breasts, she stared up at me. She didn't move.

"You look thoroughly debauched," I said. Her cheeks turned pink. "I like it."

"It's inappropriate for you to point that out," she said.

"More inappropriate than me licking between your thighs?"

Poppy's lips parted.

"Did Miss Willa ever write what that was called in that diary of hers?" I asked, leaning over her. I pressed my fingers under her chin, tipping her head back so her gaze met mine. I kissed her. "There are many names for it. I could list them for you—"

"That won't be necessary."

"You sure?" I kissed the corner of her mouth as I eased her down onto her side and then onto her back.

"I'm sure." Her hand went to my arm, loosely holding on as I sat beside her.

I chuckled. "Whatever you say, Princess." I lowered the cloth I held, tearing my gaze from the tips of her breasts that peeked through the strands of her hair. "Can you do me a favor?"

"What?"

"Open your legs for me."

Poppy blinked. "What…what for?"

I bent my head, kissing her cheek. "I would like to clean you," I explained. Her inhale was sharp, the hold on my arm tightening. "I'm afraid I may have left an…inappropriate show of my affections behind."

"Oh," she whispered.

A heartbeat passed, and Poppy did as I requested. I spared a glance at the slickness along her upper thighs. I didn't look long because I didn't want to embarrass her, but I saw the evidence of my *inappropriate affections* and faint traces of a darker color I'd also seen on myself when I made use of the bathing chamber. Blood. I'd scented it the moment my body left hers. It wasn't much, but I wanted to…I wasn't sure…wipe away the remnants of the brief pain I'd caused her.

Which was fucking ridiculous, considering I was going to cause her—

I silenced those thoughts, not ready to face them. I'd have to do it soon enough.

Gently but quickly, I took care of her. We were both quiet through the intimate moments. When I was done, I bent and pressed my lips to where the cloth had just been, eliciting a soft gasp from Poppy, and a slight, needy jerk of her hips. Smiling at the response I doubted she was even aware of, I went to the fire and tossed the cloth into it. Flames crackled, spitting sparks. When I turned around, I found she had returned to her side and was watching me.

I could practically feel her stare as I walked back to her. "You know," I drawled, picking up the fur blanket from the foot of the bed. "Some would say the way you're staring at me and my unmentionables is inappropriate, but you know what I think?"

Her eyes narrowed. "I'm half-afraid to ask."

Stretching out beside her, I drew the blanket up to our hips. "I rather enjoy you staring at my unmentionables as if they were good enough to eat."

"I am not staring at them in that manner."

"Oh, but you were." I shoved her pillow back, working my arm under her head. "It's okay." I brought my mouth to hers. "Anytime you want to taste me, just let me know."

"Oh, my gods." She laughed.

I caught that laugh with my lips. "And the same goes for whenever you would like me to...*eat you.*"

Her hands went to my chest. "Why do I have a feeling that last part is highly inappropriate?"

"Because it most definitely is."

"You are so—"

"Wonderfully wicked and devastatingly charming?"

Poppy laughed again, and damn, she truly didn't do that enough. "Incorrigible."

"I would've suggested incomparable," I said, leaning back as her fingers danced over my skin, letting her touch me as much as she wanted. I watched her as she trailed two fingers down my sternum. "How are you feeling?"

Her eyes lifted to mine. "Okay. More than okay—"

"Are you in any pain?" I cut in softly.

"No. Not at all."

I raised a brow.

Poppy's fingers halted as one shoulder lifted. "I'm just a little sore, but nothing major. I swear."

"Good."

She smiled at me, a soft and sweet one that made me think anything was possible. Her fingers halted just below a pec. "How...how did you get this scar?"

I had to think about it. "Fighting, I believe. I was likely being overconfident and nearly took a blade to the heart."

She winced, trailing her fingers to another shallow nick in my skin. "And this?"

"The same." I plucked up a strand of her hair, grinning when the back of my hand brushed her breast, and she inhaled sharply. "A Craven caused the one beside it. The same on the right side of my navel."

"You...you have a lot of them." She peeked up at me through her lashes. "Scars."

"I do." I twirled her hair around my finger. It took a lot for an Atlantian of the elemental bloodline's skin to scar. The same for a wolven. It usually only happened when one was weakened, or something was done to prevent the skin from healing as quickly as it normally would. "Most of them were from when I was a much younger, reckless sort."

"And when was that?" She yawned, her fingers skating over my stomach. "A handful of years ago?"

I smiled faintly. "Yeah, something like that."

"How did you get them when you were a younger, reckless sort?"

"Training. Picking fights on the training yard with those bigger and faster than me, trying to prove myself," I said. Some of that was true. The Commanders who trained the Atlantian armies were notorious for knocking the ego right out of your ass, but the other scars, the Craven marks? The brand? They had come while I'd been held captive. "The father of a good friend helped train me—and my brother. We both learned fairly quickly that we were not as skilled as we thought we were."

She grinned. "The ego of boys…"

"Was your brother flawed in such a manner?"

"No." Poppy laughed as I tugged gently on her hair. "Ian's never had any interest in learning how to wield a sword. He's far more interested in making up stories."

"Smart man, then," I murmured.

She nodded. "Ian abhors violence of any kind, even in self-defense. He believes that any conflict can be resolved with conversation—the more entertaining, the better. He…" She peeked at me again. "He didn't like that I trained to fight—well, he didn't like the idea of the violence, but he knew it was necessary for me."

"He sounds like he was a good brother."

"He is."

Is.

As in present tense.

But he likely wasn't anymore. Whatever ideas of anti-violence Ian held had long since left him—the moment he Ascended.

That weighed heavily on my mind as I told her how I earned the scar on my waist, an inch-long slash courtesy of the tusks of a wild boar that my brother had dared me to attempt to capture.

Poppy struggled to stay awake through the conversation, and the way she kept blinking her eyes was…it was fucking adorable. Finally, sleep took her, but it evaded me as I lay there, my finger still wrapped around the strand of hair.

When she woke, I would have to tell her the truth and what was to come. I would need to convince her that the Ascended were the monsters. That way, I could prepare her for what she'd find in the capital when I exchanged her for Malik. She was a fighter. She would survive until I got to her again.

I can't do this.

Fuck. The idea of handing her over to the Blood Crown sickened me. Anything could happen to her. Anything. They needed her for something. There was no reason for them to position her as a Chosen and convince an entire kingdom of that fact, unless it benefited them somehow. But even if they truly only planned to Ascend her? My chest lurched. I couldn't let that happen—let her be turned into a cold, soulless creature who no longer sought to take away the suffering of others but thrived on causing agony.

But I had to free my brother, and the only way to do that was through Poppy.

The reality of the situation sat like a fucking boulder on my chest. There were so many what-ifs—what if I couldn't return to her in time? What if she didn't believe me? What if she chose to stay with the Ascended? And why wouldn't she? Her beloved brother was one of them. The Queen she knew was like a mother to her. Sure, she understood that some of them were capable of evil, but she would also know that I'd been lying to her.

I would be telling her that the Ascended were using her to back their claims of being Blessed by the gods and could hurt her, but I had also used her. Was still using her.

And I *would* hurt her with the truth.

I watched Poppy sleep, fucking knowing that the moment she learned the truth there would be no more of *this*. No more just...just *living*. No more peace. I would become the one she'd been taught to fear as a child. She would hate me. And I deserved that, but she had to remember that what we'd shared was real. It wasn't a lie. She had to.

No matter what, I needed to find a way out of this for Poppy.

Godsdamn it, there had to be another way. One that worked to free my brother, would prevent a coming war, and also ensure her safety even if she never stopped believing in the Ascended. Because it wasn't like I could let her roam free, even here, not with those who believed she willingly symbolized the Crown that had taken so much from them. There were people I'd trust with her in Spessa's End, which sat at the cusp of the Skotos. She could live a full, happy life there. But I couldn't endanger all we'd worked for if she betrayed us in the end, running back to the Ascended the moment she had a chance.

I laid the strands of hair on her arm, my mind doing what it always did in the dead of night, but it wasn't rehashing old memories. It was racing to find a solution.

But I already knew the answer, didn't I?

Closing my eyes, I cursed under my breath. That was the only option…unless we reneged on the deal immediately after I made the exchange, not allowing the Crown to make it far with her. And it was *we* reneging on the deal. Not just me. I was honest enough with myself to acknowledge that it would take not only those who could fight here but also more.

And I was smart enough to realize that act alone might very well ignite the war I sought to prevent.

IT WAS OVER

Sometime later, I woke to find myself entangled with Poppy. She was still using my arm as a pillow but had turned herself while asleep, so her back was against my chest. My other arm was already at her waist, and one of my legs was nestled between hers.

I lay there in the quiet of the chamber, still lit by the gas lamp. The fire had died down a bit, but the space was warm. I couldn't have been asleep that long, and I had no idea what had woken me. I'd never slept this close to anyone before. I usually wanted my space. But this was comfortable. More than that. More than pleasant. I could sleep like this, with her body pressed to mine, for an eternity.

A quiet knock came. Frowning, I lifted my head. It had to be the middle of the night, so I doubted whoever was at the door brought good news. Could I just pretend I didn't hear it?

No. I couldn't.

Biting back a curse, I glanced down at Poppy. Reluctant to leave her but not wanting continuous knocking to wake her, I slipped my leg out from between hers as I skimmed my hand down her arm and across the soft skin of her waist. Grabbing hold of the blanket, I drew it up to her shoulders. I eased my arm out from beneath her and placed her head on the pillow as I rose. Thrusting a hand through my hair, I scanned the floor, spotting my breeches. I tugged them on and went to the door before the knocking started up again.

Magda stood there. "Three things. Two of the guests have been dealt with."

She was speaking about the guards. "The others?"

"Working on it," she answered, keeping her voice low. "The second thing is that Elijah needs to see you." She lifted the bundle she held, expression bland. "And thirdly, I have the *Maiden's* clothing."

I took Poppy's clothes. "Elijah can't wait?"

"No." Magda tilted her head to the side, trying to see around me. I shifted, blocking her. "There's been word from home."

I stiffened. "I'll be right out."

Magda nodded, still trying to see around me, a look of concern on her face.

Closing the door, I sat the bundle of laundered clothing on the chair. Word from home. That likely didn't bode well. I turned.

Poppy was awake.

Silent, I went to her side and reached down, catching that same piece of hair that always made its way onto her face. I tucked it back.

Hi," Poppy whispered, eyes closing as she pressed her cheek against my palm. "Is it time to get up?"

"No."

"Is everything okay?"

"Everything is fine. I just need to go handle something," I told her, dragging my thumb across her cheek, just under the scar. "You don't need to get up yet."

"Are you sure?"

I grinned at her sleepy yawn. "I am, Princess. Sleep." I tugged the blanket back up. "I'll be back as soon as I can."

Poppy had fallen back to sleep before I'd even finished pulling on my sweater and boots. I went to the door once more and then stopped, wanting to look back at her, to make sure she was comfortable, but I stopped myself. If I did, I'd likely say *fuck it all* and climb back into bed with her.

I quietly left the chamber, not liking the idea of leaving her alone, even though Kieran was only two doors away and would hear anything of concern.

Not bothering with the steps, I placed a hand on the railing and leapt over it. Cold, night air and flurries reached up, swallowing me. Landing in a crouch, I rose. My boots swept through the snow as I crossed under the roof of the second-floor hall and entered through a side door. The keep was quiet as I made my way back to the study.

Elijah was there, once more behind the desk. Delano was with him. There was a good chance neither of them had left, but another had joined them. A fair-haired man who worked alongside Alastir. Irritation pricked at my skin as he turned to me, issuing a stiff bow. Delano raised his brows at me as he took a drink from the same glass of whiskey he'd likely been nursing for hours.

"Orion," I greeted the Atlantian with a handshake. "Haven't seen you in a while."

"No, you haven't." Orion smiled tightly. "It's been quite some time since you were at the capital."

"It has." I crossed my arms. "Didn't expect to see you in this neck of the woods."

"I'd rather carve out my heart than be here, but I've been sent to deliver a letter of the utmost importance." Orion reached inside his cloak and pulled out a folded piece of parchment.

I took it, turning it over as Elijah asked Orion about his travels. The golden seal bearing the Atlantian crest—the sun with a sword and arrow—had me feeling some kind of something. Nostalgia for home? Maybe. But the faint line cutting through the center of the seal told me it had been broken and the wax remelted.

Smiling tightly, I glanced up at Orion as I broke the seal. He returned my smile as he answered Elijah's question. Not a single part of me was surprised he'd read it. He was, after all, loyal to the Crown and Alastir, and he would want to know what Emil had to say to the Prince of Atlantia.

Unfolding the letter, the muscle in my jaw started ticking the moment I read the first line. I gave the rest a quick scan. The letter was written in a way that most wouldn't understand. Clever Emil had encoded it, but it was clear to me. He had done his best to run interference with Alastir, but somehow word of my whereabouts and plans had still managed to make it back to the Advisor's ears.

Which meant my father, the King, was also aware of what I was doing. That I sought to capture the Maiden.

I couldn't be shocked that word had finally made it back to Alastir. However, I didn't expect to read the last part.

My father, the King, was en route to New Haven.

Fucking gods.

"Glad to hear you made it here before the storm," Delano said. "But I'm confused."

I glanced up, gaze flicking from Delano to Orion.

Orion raised a brow. "What are you confused about?"

"Well, maybe *confused* isn't the right word," Delano mused, setting his glass on the table. "I suppose awed is a better choice. I'm awed that you would show up with a missive for the Prince the same day he arrived in New Haven."

I slowly folded the letter.

"Now that leaves me in awe," Elijah added, his booted feet on the desk and a big-ass smile on his bearded face. "Perfect timing."

"It truly was," Orion stated blandly. Nothing about his tone hinted at deceit, but the corner of his right eye twitched. "I suppose I'm lucky."

"I suppose you are." Delano smiled, and his blue eyes brightened. "Oh, wait. There is something both Elijah and I are confused about. You arrived shortly after the Prince did."

"And yet you waited until now to summon me?" I asked.

"I rode long and hard to get here, Your Highness." Orion lifted his chin. "I was hungry and needed a moment to collect myself."

"Well, we all need moments to collect ourselves." I smiled. "When did my father leave for New Haven?"

Elijah's gaze shot to me, the smile slipping from his face.

"I'm sorry?" Orion frowned.

"Let's not pretend you didn't read this missive and then attempt to conceal that fact." I tossed the letter onto the desk.

Orion's shoulders stiffened. A moment passed. "It is my duty to keep Alastir informed, therefore the King and Queen informed—"

"Yes. Yes. I know. You were just doing your duty. Now, do it again," I said. "When did my father leave?"

"I imagine shortly after Alastir sent me. He will likely arrive within a day or so, depending on the track of this storm," Orion told us. "I'm to rejoin him at Berkton."

I hid my shock. Berkton was about half a day's ride from here if one pushed it—a village on the cusp of the Dead Bones Clan's woods and long since forgotten. No Rise existed there any longer. The homes had all turned to rubble, but the manor still stood and was often used as a hideout. One unfit for a King and the Crown's Advisor, because if my father came, so would Alastir.

Fucking gods, this was a highly problematic development. One I would have to deal with shortly.

I eyed Orion. I didn't know the man well, but I did know Alastir. He was like a second father to me. The only reason he'd let Orion deliver a missive from Emil was because it fed him additional information. Alastir always liked to know more than what he was told. He'd sent Orion to snoop, which was why he would be rejoining them at Berkton instead of waiting for them to arrive here, where much nicer accommodations awaited.

"Oh, no," Delano murmured. "He's got that look."

Orion frowned as he glanced at the blond-haired wolven.

"Yep." Elijah nodded. "He does."

Delano leaned forward. "Do you know what that look means?" He gestured with his chin in my direction.

My tight smile remained.

The Atlantian shook his head as he looked me over. "No, I don't."

"I've seen it, well, a time or a hundred," Delano went on. "That smile you see? It's always a warning."

Orion's inhale was swift as his gaze darted between us.

"It usually comes right before a lot of blood is spilled," Delano said.

"A lot," Elijah added.

"They speak the truth." My smile grew, baring a hint of fang. "I'm going to make something very clear to you, Orion. I know you're serving Alastir, therefore the Crown, and you must be a terribly loyal man to travel alone into vampry-infested lands."

"I am very loyal." His chin lifted a notch.

"Here's the thing, though. I don't care about your loyalty to Alastir or my father. Here?" I spread my arms wide. "I am not my father's son. I'm not your Prince. I'm just a man not to be fucked with, so I will only ask you this once. What do you plan to tell the King when you return to them?"

Orion's lips thinned as he locked his amber eyes on me. "I will tell them that the rumors are true. That you have captured the Maiden, and she is here with you."

"I imagine that should make my father very happy," I murmured. "I assume he already has plans for her."

Orion relaxed. "He does."

My head cocked. "And what are the plans?"

"I'm unaware of the details," he said.

"But I'm sure Alastir is aware of them," I countered. "Which means you are. What are his plans?" I paused. "That, I *am* asking as your Prince."

Orion's laugh was as thin as ice. "It's interesting how you use your title only when it suits you."

I smirked. "Isn't it?"

"You should be at home, Casteel." Orion took a step toward me. Over his shoulder, I saw Elijah's lips purse. "Your father and your mother need you there. Alastir needs you. The kingdom needs you."

"What do you think I'm doing here, Orion?" I said.

"I know what you think you're doing. So do your parents and Alastir, but if you want to save your people? You should do so at home, where you belong," he implored, shaking his head. "The crown should've been passed onto you years ago—"

"The crown belongs to my brother," I cut him off. "Prince Malik is the heir."

"Prince Malik is—"

"I wouldn't finish that sentence," Delano warned.

Orion clamped his mouth shut.

I forced the building fury down. "You still haven't answered my question."

Orion shoved his cloak aside, placing a hand on his waist. "He plans to send a message to the Blood Crown."

Everything in me slowed, but the rage... I could taste its hot bitterness. "And the message is?"

"The Maiden," he answered. "He will return her to them. Her head, that is. Then, our armies—"

I struck, punching my hand into Orion's chest. Bone and cartilage cracked and gave way.

"Welp," Delano murmured.

Hot blood spurted as Orion's eyes went wide. His mouth dropped open as my fist snapped his ribs. He spasmed as my fingers dug into his heart.

Smiling, I jerked my hand back. "Perhaps I will send this back to my father in place of you."

Slowly, Orion's chin lowered as he looked down at the gaping wound in his chest.

A bloody, wordless breath escaped him as he dropped to his knees and then fell forward.

"But I won't do that." I turned, tossing the Atlantian's heart into the fire. Flames crackled and whirled, spitting embers. "I have more class than that."

Delano's lip curled as he stared at the fireplace. "That's kind of disgusting."

"Well," Elijah drawled, picking up his glass of whiskey and finishing it off. "Was not expecting to learn that our King would arrive." He then leaned over, swiping a meaty hand across the desk. Taking Delano's drink, he downed what was left in the glass. "Also didn't expect to see a man's heart tonight."

"But here we are." I knelt, using Orion's cloak to wipe the blood and gore from my hand. Didn't do much good. I rose. "Unfortunately, our loyal courier will have met an untimely demise on his return to Berkton."

"Understood," Elijah replied as Delano snorted. The wolven rose, going to the credenza. The chair behind the desk creaked when the half-Atlantian leaned back once more. "The King is really in Solis?"

"Sounds like it." The flames calmed.

"And you think that's what your father really plans?" Elijah asked. "I mean, that's brutal. Even more so than that." He nodded at Orion's prone body as Delano picked up a pitcher of water. "He was a smug bastard—like far too many of you elementals. No offense."

I snorted. "None taken."

"But taking the Maiden's head?" He blew out a low whistle. "She's just a girl."

Just a girl.

Poppy wasn't *just* anything. "My father isn't a cruel man," I said as Delano came to me, a wet towel extended. "Thank you," I murmured, taking it to clean my hand. The irony of me having done a similar thing earlier tonight was...well, it was something. "Years ago? Before everything? He wouldn't have considered that." Especially if he had spent any time with Poppy and saw that she hadn't chosen this life. "But after what was done to me? To Malik? And all those who have been taken by the Blood Crown?" I rubbed at the blood on my hand. "He is capable of anything."

Delano took his seat. "And what are you going to do with her, Cas?"

Tossing yet another stained towel into the fire, I laughed, and it sounded just like the spitting, hissing flames. "I don't plan to do that."

"No shit." Elijah snorted. "I figured keeping her head on her shoulders fell under the whole no-one-touches-or-harms-her warning from earlier." He smirked at Orion's body. "But I suppose he was too busy collecting his thoughts to have heard that."

"You knew he was here?" I stepped over Orion's legs as I went to the credenza, feeling a sudden dull twinge of discomfort in the side of my stomach. It came and went fast.

"I knew he was here, but I didn't know *who* he was. Only that he was Atlantian," Elijah said. "You going to Berkton?"

Pulling the cork from the whiskey, I took a swig. The liquor was smooth. "I have to." I took another drink and waited for that fleeting sensation to return. It didn't. "What is the condition of the Berkton manor?"

"We keep it together and stocked with supplies," Elijah said.

"Good." They would have to make use of those supplies because I could not allow my father to come here. Not yet. "I'll leave in the morning. Make it there by the afternoon and then come back."

"You'll have to ride fast to beat this storm. It looks like nothing right now, and there will be weaker bands, but once it gets going, it'll be a big one," Delano said, resting his elbows on his knees.

"Fucking wolven," Elijah laughed, shaking the table. "They're like your own little forecasters."

Delano ignored that. "It's blowing in from the east, so if you spend just an hour too long in Berkton, you'll get stuck there or in between."

"I won't."

"I'll go with you," Delano said.

"No. I want you here." I put the cork back on the whiskey. "To guard her."

"The message has been sent and received by those in Haven Keep," Elijah assured, staring pointedly at the floor. "No one here would be foolish enough to cross you."

"I'd rather not risk that." I scratched my fingers through my hair. "By the way, her name is Penellaphe. It would be better to call her that instead of the Maiden."

"Yeah." Elijah nodded, chuckling softly. "It would be." He pulled his boots off the table. "Magda said she was nice if a bit nervous."

"She is—" I turned at the sound of pounding footsteps. "What the hell now?"

The door swung open, and Naill burst in. "We have a problem."

I raised a brow at the crossbow he held. "What kind of problem?"

"The remaining guards are attempting to run off with your Maiden," Naill answered, frowning at the body on the floor.

"What the fuck?" I spat, snapping into action. I stalked forward. "Where are they?"

"In the stables," Naill answered, and Delano and Elijah rose, their long-legged gait keeping pace with mine as I entered the hall. "Cas, we have a bigger issue than just the guards trying to run off with her," Naill added. "They saw Kieran." Bright golden eyes met mine. "In his wolven form."

"Fuck," Delano rasped.

Ice drenched my veins. "How? How did that happen?"

"From what I could quickly gather from what I saw, Phillips tried to take her. She put up a fight, and Kieran intervened. He was wounded—

he's okay," Naill quickly added.

That odd sensation earlier—

"But he shifted," Naill continued. "He's at the stables. They barred the door from the inside."

They.

Poppy.

For a moment, I was frozen where I stood in the hall of the keep. I couldn't move. Something akin to *terror* exploded in my gut. I could've told her. I should have told her. It would've prevented her from finding out this way, but it was too late. It was over. Everything with Poppy. The closeness. Her warmth. The ability to be in the now and not the past, not the future. The peace I'd found with her. I knew it immediately. *It was over.* I moved then, staggering back under the weight of the pain. It felt like a hand had gone through my chest and ripped my heart out. I looked down just as Orion had, but there was no gaping wound. Still, I felt pure agony.

"Kieran couldn't control it if he was wounded," Delano said, and I looked at him somewhat dumbly. He was eyeing my fists. Worry filled his tone. "It kicks in our instinct."

I knew that.

"You didn't tell her anything, did you?" Elijah asked.

Finally, I found my fucking voice. "No. I didn't get…I didn't get the chance."

"Okay, then what's the game plan?" Elijah's eyes were narrowed, alert—watchful and *knowing.* "Do we let them make a run for it? Get them out there? We can have Kieran lay low for a while, play it off as if we had no idea what he was. That would give you time to deal with your—"

"No." There was no point in doing that. It was over. "They will not take the Maiden. She stays here."

I shut it down like I had under the willow—all of it. The pain. The guilt. The terror that she would forget that what we shared wasn't a lie. That it was real. I had to pull it together. There would barely be time for any explanations, let alone a convoluted lie to temporarily soothe Poppy. I put all those emotions behind a wall so thick that I couldn't even feel them. Ice filled my chest and gut, and I felt nothing when I took the crossbow from Naill's hands. That wouldn't last, but right now…

I was nothing.

"Delano, circle around the back of the stables." I glanced at Naill. "Go with him."

Both nodded.

"They won't be able to get the horses through the back doors," Elijah told me. "If they plan to make a run for it, they'll need to be on horseback."

"If any of them have truly discovered who we are, they'll go on foot," I said, then turned to Naill and Delano. "Take out the guards, but do not touch her."

"Understood," Delano answered.

Pivoting, I prowled out of the keep and onto the frozen ground. The snow had stopped. The night was quiet, except for the sound of wood cracking coming from the stables. My jaw locked.

"Hold on," Elijah said.

I kept walking. The stables came into view, the windows glowing with the yellow light of lanterns. A large fawn-colored wolven was at the entry, clawing and digging at the door.

"Dammit." Elijah grabbed my arm. "Give me a sec."

I stopped, looking down at where his hand was around my arm. Slowly, I lifted my gaze to his.

"Yeah, I know. I just saw you tear a man's heart out. I probably shouldn't be grabbing you, but you need to listen to me," Elijah said. "I don't know what the hell is going on between you and that girl, but it ain't nothing. Don't even bother telling me it is. I know better."

My jaw locked.

"And I don't care about that right now. What I do care about is you—what you've been working toward for years. Not just your brother. What you have going on here and at Spessa's End. It's been working because these men and women are loyal to you. They believe in you," he said, his face inches from mine. "And right or wrong, they will only see the Maiden for what they know her as: a symbol of what has taken so much from them."

His stare held mine. "And while they will follow your orders, more than a few brows were raised when they heard about what you did to Jericho. And more than a few tongues were wagging after you all arrived, with how you were acting with her. This keep is big but not so big they don't know where you spent several hours tonight."

Fucking gods.

"And I'm betting that was also what Orion was being fed before he decided to bring his ass to my study," he said, the wind catching the snow on the ground and whipping it into a frenzy. "You go in there, treating her like anything other than what she is supposed to be? With your father making his way here? Wanting her head?" Over his voice, Kieran rammed the wood. "The people here will even stand against their King for you, but if they think you've gotten yourself wrapped around the godsdamn Maiden, you run the risk of losing their support. You don't want that."

Elijah was absolutely correct. My father was coming. He wanted her head, and he was the King. His command superseded mine, except for here. In Solis, they were loyal to me. It was the only reason I was even standing where I was. But if I lost their support?

Poppy lost her life.

That panic and pain threatened to return, but I didn't allow it. I would do anything to make sure that didn't happen. Anything. Even if it meant becoming what she loathed the most.

The Dark One.

"I know," I told him.

Elijah nodded and dropped my arm. I turned and rounded the corner of the keep.

Kieran backed off from the barn doors, his head whipping toward me. His growl was low and furious.

"It's okay." I ran my left hand over his back as I passed him. Fury at the scent of blood and the sight of it matting the fur on his leg and waist broke through the ice encasing my insides.

I let that anger in as I went up to the barn doors. I wasn't keeping my strength in check as I leaned back, kicking the center of the door. Wood splintered and gave way. The doors swung open, and all I allowed myself to feel was the anger as I quickly took in what was playing out in front of me.

I saw the guards. The rearing horses. Fucking Jericho. And Poppy. I saw her, brave and bold as ever, the bloodstone dagger in her grasp.

"Hawke!" Poppy cried out, relief evident in her voice, and I didn't let myself feel a damn thing. She started for me. "Thank the gods you're okay."

Phillips lurched forward, grabbing her arm. "Stay back from him."

My gaze swiveled toward him—toward his grip on her arm. Poppy tugged herself free.

She turned to Jericho. "Kill him!" she shouted, "He was the one—" Her eyes went wide, having caught sight of Kieran coming up behind me. "Hawke, behind you!"

Phillips grabbed her again, this time around the waist.

"It's okay," I told her, lifting the crossbow and pulling the trigger.

The bolt slammed into my target, knocking Phillips back from Poppy with such force that the guard was impaled on the pole behind them as Poppy toppled forward onto her knees.

I lowered the crossbow as she looked to where Jericho stood, the shaggy-haired bastard smiling. Then she saw Phillips' fallen sword lying among the straw. I knew the exact moment she saw the blood dripping onto it—saw Phillips. She jerked.

Luddie, the other guard, shouted, lifting his sword as he charged forward. "With my sword and my—"

Delano fired a bolt as he stepped out of the shadows of the stalls, catching Luddie from behind and taking him to the straw-strewn ground.

The last guard made a run for it. I couldn't remember his name.

Kieran was faster, leaping into the air. He landed on the mortal, his claws digging into his back as he clamped his powerful jaws around the Huntsman's neck, snapping it.

There was silence.

That didn't last either.

Jericho strode forward, smirking as he looked down at Poppy. "I'm so glad I'm here to witness this moment."

"Shut up, Jericho," I bit out, the wind whipping at my back.

Poppy lifted her head, her eyes locking with mine. Her braid had fallen over her shoulder, and that one strand of hair was in her face, as always. I realized she wasn't wearing her cloak. Had Phillips planned to take her out unprotected in the weather? She would've frozen or become ill. I didn't feel a smidgen of guilt for killing the imbecile.

"Hawke?" she whispered, her empty hand grasping at the damp straw.

I felt nothing.

Poppy recoiled, her chest rising rapidly.

I was nothing.

"Please tell me I can kill her," Jericho said. "I know exactly what pieces I want to cut up and send back."

"Touch her, and you'll lose more than a hand this time," I warned him, my gaze never leaving hers. "We need her alive."

A BROKEN BREATH

"You're no fun," Jericho muttered as Poppy stared up at me. "Have I told you that before?"

"A time or a dozen," I said.

Poppy flinched.

She'd *flinched* because of me. I couldn't let myself process that. Nor could I allow myself to see what I did in her eyes. I already knew what was there. Disbelief. Dawning understanding. Horror. Pain. Betrayal—

I looked away, my gaze skipping over the bloodied straw and bodies. "This mess needs to be cleaned up."

Kieran shook his head, then rose. The sound of his bones shortening and cracking back into place only lasted seconds. Once more, he stood beside me in his mortal form. I looked for signs of his injury, seeing only a faint mark on his side. I raised a brow at the torn breeches. Usually, he made no attempt to make sure his clothing survived the transition. I imagined he'd done it for her. My jaw locked once more.

"This isn't the only mess that needs to be cleaned up," Kieran said, stretching his neck muscles.

I knew he wasn't talking about her. He was talking about me. This mess I'd created—one gaining an audience. People were filling the shadows of the barn and behind me, drawn by the commotion.

I looked at Poppy. She'd sat back, her chest still rising too fast, too shallowly. "You and I need to talk."

"Talk?" Poppy laughed, but it reminded me of crackling flames.

"I'm sure you have a lot of questions," I said, softening my voice as I saw her grip on the dagger tighten.

She flinched again.

I inhaled sharply through my nose.

"Where…?" Poppy tried again. "Where are the other two guards?"

"Dead," I admitted, watching her closely. "It was an unfortunate necessity."

Poppy went silent. I kept an eye on that dagger. Needing to get her out of here before she did something that provoked the others to react, I took a step toward her.

"No." Poppy launched to her feet. "Tell me what's going on here."

I stopped, forcing my voice even lower. "You know what's going on here."

Poppy opened her mouth. Her gaze darted to where Elijah stood beside Magda behind me. Soft footsteps sounded, and I knew at least Magda had left. She had a good heart and soul. She didn't want to see this.

"Phillips was right," Poppy said, her voice trembling.

"He was?" I handed the crossbow to Naill as he came up behind me.

"I do believe Phillips had begun to figure things out," Kieran answered. "They were coming out of the room when I went up to check on her. She didn't seem to believe whatever it was he'd told her, though."

I saw it again in Poppy's face—another moment of realization. The way her face paled, causing the scars to stand out more. How her chest rose sharply. The tremor that went through her.

I pressed my lips together as I felt that wall I'd fortified, that mess inside me, begin to crack. *Elijah was right*, I reminded myself. No one here could see any of that, not even Poppy.

"Well, he's not going to be figuring anything out again," Jericho drawled, gripping the bolt that held Phillips. He tore it free, letting the mortal fall. He nudged the man. "That's for sure."

One of these days, I was going to kill that fucker.

"You're a Descenter," Poppy rasped.

"A Descenter?" Elijah laughed. Because, of course, he would find that funny.

Jericho frowned at Poppy. "And here I said you were smart."

Poppy ignored him. "You're working against the Ascended."

I nodded.

The breath she took sounded broken. "You…you know this…this thing that killed Rylan?"

"Thing?" Jericho drew back. "I'm insulted."

"That sounds like your problem, not mine," Poppy snapped, and I had to fight back a grin. That wouldn't help anything. She faced me. "I thought the wolven were extinct."

"There are many things that you thought to be true that are not," I said. "However, while the wolven aren't extinct, there aren't many left."

Poppy's nostrils flared. "Did you know he killed Rylan?"

"I thought I could speed this up and grab you, but we know how that turned out," Jericho chimed in.

Her attention shot to him. "Yes, I clearly remember how that turned out for you."

Jericho's snarl came from deep within him.

I stepped closer. "I knew he was going to create an opening."

"For you...to become my personal Royal Guard?"

"I needed to get close to you."

Poppy shuddered. "Well, you succeeded at that, didn't you?"

That wall inside me shook. "What you're thinking...?" I knew she was thinking about earlier tonight. Us. "You could not be further from the truth."

"You have no idea what I'm thinking." Poppy's grip on the dagger was a white-knuckled one. "And all of this was...what? A trick? You were sent here to get close to me?"

Kieran's brows lifted. "Sent—"

I shut Kieran up with a look.

"You were sent by the Dark One," Poppy stated.

She didn't... Fuck. She had yet to realize that I was the so-called Dark One—or was, at the very least, refusing to acknowledge what was clearly in front of her. I couldn't blame her for that, but I would do what I did best. I would exploit it. There was a good chance I could talk to her...sensibly if she didn't let herself believe that the Dark One and I were one and the same.

"I came to Masadonia with one goal in mind," I said. "And that was you."

"How?" Poppy lifted her chin, swallowing. "Why?"

"You'd be surprised how many of those close to you support Atlantia, who want to see the kingdom restored," I told her. "Many who paved the way for me."

"Commander Jansen?" Poppy guessed.

"She is smart," I said, smiling just a little because, godsdamn, she was fucking amazing. Even right now, faced with my betrayal. She held on to calm. She was figuring shit out. I was in awe of her. "Like I told you all."

Poppy blinked rapidly. "Did you even work in the capital?" Her gaze flipped to Kieran. "The night at the..." She couldn't finish, but I knew she was thinking about the Red Pearl. "You knew who I was from the beginning."

"I was watching you as long as you were watching me," I said quietly. "Even longer."

A tremor, stronger than the ones before, ran through her. "You...you were planning this for a while."

"For a *very* long time," I confirmed.

"Hannes." Her voice was thick, hoarse. "He didn't die of a heart ailment, did he?"

"I do believe his heart did give out on him," I said. "The poison he drank in his ale that night at the Red Pearl surely had something to do with it."

"Did a certain woman there help him with his drink?" she demanded. "The same one that sent me upstairs?"

What woman was she speaking of? The one at the Red Pearl that she thought was a Seer?

"I feel like I'm missing vital pieces here," Delano murmured under his breath.

"I'll fill you in later," Kieran commented.

Poppy's trembling increased as she whispered, "Vikter?"

I shook my head. I was responsible, but I hadn't ordered his death.

"Don't lie to me!" Poppy screamed. "Did you know there'd be an attack on the Rite? Is that why you disappeared? Why you weren't there when Vikter was killed?"

I could see the calm beginning to thin. I needed to get her out of here before it disappeared because if I knew anything about Poppy, she was like me when cornered. Dangerous. And too many were getting too close to her. Idiot Jericho. Rolf, who usually knew better. A half-Atlantian with a sword drawn. Delano.

"What I know is that you're upset. I don't blame you, but I've also seen what happens when you get really angry." I lifted my hands, keeping them where she could see them. "There is a lot I need to tell—"

I saw it coming a second before she moved.

Poppy did what I feared. Cornered, she lashed out, and with that damn dagger, too. Her arm cocked back, and she hurled the blade right at my damn *chest*.

"Fuck," I spat, spinning to the side as I reached out, catching the dagger before it found a new victim.

Naill whistled softly.

I spun back to her. Godsdamn, she was vicious.

And she was also clever.

Poppy had to know I would catch it, which meant…

Godsdamn it.

She dipped, snatching up Phillips' fallen sword. I halted for half a second. That was all she needed. She twisted, swinging out with the sword. Not at me. At Jericho.

The wolven jumped back, but it caught him off guard, still obviously underestimating her. She sliced him right across the stomach.

I *almost* laughed, except she'd spilled blood, and shit was about to get out of hand.

"Bitch," Jericho snarled, smacking his remaining hand on his wound.

Poppy turned as several charged her. I shot forward, catching one of the half-Atlantians in the chest, shoving him back as Kieran snapped forward. A sword sliced through the air as Kieran caught Poppy around the waist, pulling her away from Rolf and another. I caught the wolven by the hem of his shirt, hauling him back.

"No," I growled, thrusting him into the half-Atlantian. I turned only to see Kieran go down on his back.

Poppy kicked her head back into his face, causing him to yelp. His hold on her loosened.

Poppy tore free, scrambling for the sword. She got there before Delano. He wisely backed off as she rose. I saw her spin, her wild eyes connecting with mine.

She locked up.

I seized the moment. "That was very naughty." I grabbed the sword, wrenching it from her grip. I needed to keep her attention—her anger—focused on me. If she went after another of them, I would have to kill every fucker in this barn. "You are so incredibly violent." I dipped my chin and whispered what I knew would ensure she paid no mind to anyone else. "It still turns me on."

She screamed, jabbing her elbow right into my chin.

"Dammit," I said, laughing as pain—which I deserved—went down my spine. "Doesn't change what I just said."

Poppy whirled to the door.

Elijah blocked the entrance, tsking under his breath as he shook his head.

Stepping back, she turned to her left, where Kieran stood. He blinked slowly. She twisted and took off.

I caught her before she made it two steps, spinning her around. Her legs tangled with mine, tripping us. We went down, her first. I twisted with a second to spare, hitting the floor hard on my back.

"You're welcome," I grunted.

Shrieking like a cave cat, she brought the heel of her foot down on my shin. Pain radiated up my leg, forcing the air out of my lungs as she twisted, straining against my arms until I was afraid she would hurt herself. I let go just enough. She turned in my hold, straddling me—

I grinned at her. "I'm liking where this is headed."

Poppy punched me in the cheek fucking *hard*, knocking my head back against the straw. She cocked that arm back again.

I caught her wrist, yanking her down so she couldn't get the leverage needed for that other hand. "You hit like you're angry with me."

She shifted, thrusting her knee between my legs, and while I'd let her get a couple of good hits in, that was a hell no.

I blocked her with my thigh. "That would've done some damage."

"Good," she spat, her braid hanging over her shoulder and that strand of hair in her face. I'd move it out of the way for her, but she'd likely take that moment to claw my eyes out, or worse, go after someone else.

"Now, now." I kept my voice low, knowing that only Kieran was possibly close enough to hear. "You'd be disappointed later if I couldn't use it."

Her lips parted as she stared down at me, disbelief filling her eyes. "I would rather cut it from your body."

I lifted my head from the straw and whispered, "Liar."

Perhaps I'd gone too far in my attempt to keep her focused on me because the rage that poured from her reminded me of the sound she'd made when she turned on Mazeen.

Fuck.

That kind of anger gave a person unbelievable strength. She reared back, breaking my hold. Then, jumping to her feet above me, she lifted her foot. I caught it before she could stomp on my throat, pulling her leg down so she didn't run. If she did, she would likely engage another.

Poppy hit the floor beside me, and not even one breath later, I felt her fist hitting my side with enough force to crack my ribs.

"Damn," Kieran drawled.

"Should we intervene?" Delano asked as she moved to punch me again. I blocked her with my arm.

"No." Elijah laughed. The fucker. "This is the best thing I've seen in a while. Who would've thought the Maiden could throw down?"

"This is why you don't mix business with pleasure," Kieran commented.

"Is that the case?" Elijah whistled. I knew damn well he already suspected that, but he was a bastard. "My money is on her then."

"Traitors," I gasped as I knocked Poppy's hands aside as she started grabbing for my head, likely trying to snap my neck. Honestly, I would've let her just to see if she could do it, but this had to end before she hurt herself.

Or me.

I moved faster than she could stop, coming over her and forcing her onto her back. She went for my face this time. I caught her wrists. "Stop it."

Poppy was not ready to stop.

She lifted her hips, trying to throw me. She then pushed with her upper body, but I kept her pinned and scanned the front of her shirt. The material was dark, but it looked darker at the waist.

"Get off me!" she screamed.

"Stop it," I said. "Poppy. Stop—"

"I hate you!" She tore one hand free, shocking me with her strength. She was strong—stronger than even I realized. Then she—

Her fist snapped my head back *again*. Stinging pain erupted across my mouth.

"I hate you!" she shouted as I caught her hand once more.

I pressed it back to the ground, lips peeling back as blood trickled from my mouth. "Stop it!"

Poppy stopped.

Finally.

Only her chest rose as she stared up at me.

"That's why you never really smiled," she whispered.

At first, I didn't realize what she meant, and then I knew she'd seen what I'd barely managed to hide from her this entire time. My fangs.

Poppy shuddered beneath me, her arms going limp. "You're a monster."

I stilled above her, the pain of her words, the truth of them, stabbing deep, but I shut it off. I felt nothing. I *was* nothing as I said, "You finally see me for what I am."

Poppy's lips trembled, her eyes glistening. She pressed her mouth shut, holding back tears. The desire to comfort her, the want to see how she was injured, threatened to shatter the hold I had on myself. The fight was out of her. I needed that.

But it wasn't what I wanted.

Still, it was what I deserved.

NOT EVERYTHING
WAS A LIE

"When I told Delano to put her somewhere safe…" I told Kieran, who was waiting for me in the now-empty stables as I washed the blood from my face with a clean bucket of water.

He'd waited after I handed Poppy off to Delano and warned the others not to touch her as I went out into the cold woods.

I had to cool off. Physically. Mentally. Everything. Because I was on the brink of losing control, likely to do something I'd regret.

Like tearing out the hearts of those who'd demanded Poppy's death.

If I did that, shit would go south. Poppy's life was on the line. So was Malik's. The entire fucking kingdom was at risk. I needed that calm. I found it.

I dragged the towel over my face. "I didn't mean the dungeons."

"Yeah, well, it's likely the only place she won't be able to escape and slaughter everyone," he replied dryly.

"True. Do you know how Phillips figured shit out?"

"Not sure, but like I said before, he'd been asking questions since the moment we left Masadonia."

I supposed it didn't matter now, but if he'd only kept his suspicions to himself—fuck, it wasn't the man's fault. He'd only been doing his duty.

"Word arrived from home." Shoving open the barn door, I started across the packed snow. "Alastir finally learned of my plans."

Kieran cursed. "We knew this would happen no matter what Emil managed."

"Yeah, except that's not all." Yanking open the side door to the keep, I held it for Kieran. "My father is en route."

He stopped, his brows lifting. "What the fuck?"

"That was my reaction." I quickly told him about Berkton and my plan to hold them off there. "I'll have to convince him that keeping her alive is the best course of action."

"And if not?"

"Then war between Solis and Atlantia will be the least of our people's concerns." I passed the closed doors to the Great Hall. "I will not allow my father to harm her." Stopping, I faced Kieran. "And I don't expect you to stand with me on that."

He stiffened.

"You stand with me against my father, it's treason," I reminded him. "I will not have you ousted from the kingdom—from your family."

"The bond—"

"That's an order," I said, knowing it gave Kieran an out.

Kieran's eyes turned a vivid, luminous blue. "That's fucking bullshit, Cas."

"More like it's me doing the right thing for once."

"No, it's more like you being a stubborn asshole, per usual," he shot back. "What do you think Delano will do if it comes down to you and your father? Naill? Elijah? My sister? Emil? I can keep listing all those who will back you."

"They will be given the same order."

"Do you think that will matter? Fucking gods, Cas. You know better than that." Kieran shook his head. "They aren't just loyal to you because you're the Prince. They're loyal to you because they care about you."

"I know," I shot back. "And that's why I don't want them getting messed up in this."

"I have a spoiler alert for you—all of us are already messed up in this."

"No, not this." I shook my head, looking down the hall. "Everyone agreed to support me in freeing my brother. No one agreed to this."

"And what is *this*?"

I wasn't sure I could even answer that question. All I knew was that I wouldn't allow anyone to take Poppy's life from her.

"It is what it is," I answered, walking once more. "I want Jericho out of here. Send him to Spessa's End or back to Atlantia, but he needs to be gone."

"Wise idea. He's a problem." Kieran paused. "So is this."

A dry laugh left me as I reached for the exit. "Don't I fucking know it?"

"We need to talk." Kieran planted his hand on the door, stopping me from opening it. "You were with her tonight."

"Of course, I was."

His frosted blue eyes met mine. "I'm not talking about that, and you know it."

I did.

"I thought you said she would leave you as she came to you," Kieran said, voice quiet. "Clearly, that isn't the case. What the fuck, Cas?"

I ran a hand through my hair. "Turns out I'm that kind of a piece of shit. Okay?" I reached for the door again.

Kieran's palm flattened against it. "No, it's not okay."

My hand fisted as I stared at his, anger sparking. "We really don't have time for this conversation, Kieran."

"We're going to make time because what I saw back there in the stables? You let her get the upper hand on you. Multiple times."

I huffed out a laugh. "You know she can fight."

"No shit, but you're a fucking elemental Atlantian. She is still just a mortal, gifted or not. You could've easily gotten her under control. You didn't. Anyone else, no matter if they were of the fairer sex or not, you would've handled that—" Kieran jabbed a finger toward the stables "—in seconds. You didn't with her. Why?"

Running my tongue over my upper teeth, I shook my head.

"What is going on with you? With her? And don't give me a bullshit answer, not when you're ready to go against your father over her." Anger tightened Kieran's features. "You don't keep shit from me, Cas. We've been through too much for you to start doing that again, so let's not have a repeat. What is it?"

What is it?

"I don't have time to get into this. We don't have the time. We'll talk," I told him, pushing down the irritation. He had every right to question things. "I promise."

Kieran held my stare for a moment. The line of his jaw was tight as he lifted his hand. He said no more, letting me pass. I was being a shit for keeping things from him, but this…whatever this was with Poppy, was different.

I entered the narrow staircase, already fucking troubled. The underground level of Haven Keep was damp and dank. Foreboding. Comfort hadn't been in the minds of those who'd built the keep. Fear had.

Poppy didn't belong down here.

She belonged in the sun.

Steeling myself, I dipped under a low doorframe and entered a dimly lit hall. The dull gleam of the old gods' twisted bones that adorned the ceiling haunted my steps as I went to where Delano waited.

"Leave," I told him. The wolven hesitated, glancing back to the cell, but he left.

I stepped forward, my gaze drifting over her. She sat on a thin, dirty mattress, her back pressed against the wall. Her face was pale, but her stare was as defiant as ever. Brave. Bold.

"Poppy." I sighed, hating that she was here. Loathing that she was here because of me, but knowing the moment I let her out, things would be worse. "What am I to do with you?"

"Don't call me that." She shoved to her feet. Chains rattled, drawing my attention.

My jaw clenched. Delano wouldn't have put her in chains unless he had a reason, meaning she'd likely attacked him.

I lifted my stare to her. "But I thought you liked it when I did."

"You were mistaken," she shot back. "What do you want?"

The hardness in her voice? The coldness? It was brutal, but it was all blade-thin. Fragile. "More than you could ever guess," I said.

"Are you here to kill me?"

Her question surprised me. "Now why would I do that?"

Poppy raised her arms and rattled the restraints. "You have me chained."

Actually, I didn't, but there was no reason for her ire to turn on Delano more than it likely already was. "I do."

Her nostrils flared. "Everyone outside wants me dead."

"That is true."

"And you're an Atlantian," she said, with as much disgust as she had when she'd spoken about the barrats. "That's what you do. You kill. You destroy. You curse."

I huffed out a short laugh. "Ironic coming from someone who has been surrounded by the Ascended her whole life."

"They don't murder innocents, and they don't turn people into monsters—"

"No," I stopped her. "They just force young women who make

them feel inferior to bare their skin to a cane and do the gods only know what else to them," I reminded her. "Yes, Princess, they are truly upstanding examples of everything that is good and right in this world."

Her chest rose sharply as her lips parted.

"Did you think I wouldn't find out what the Duke's *lessons* were?" I asked of her. "I told you I would."

She staggered back, the skin of her throat and cheeks flushing.

"He used a cane cut from a tree in the Blood Forest and he made you partially undress." I reached up, grasping the bars as fury resurfaced. "And he told you that you deserved it. That it was for your own good. But, in reality, all it did was fulfill his sick need to inflict pain."

"How?" she whispered.

"I can be *very* compelling."

Poppy turned her cheek, squeezing her eyes shut. A tremor ran through her, then her gaze snapped back to mine. "You killed him."

Recalling the way the Duke had died, I smiled. "I did, and I've never enjoyed watching the life seep out of someone's eyes more than I did while watching the Duke die. He had it coming." I held her stare. "And trust me when I say his very slow and very painful death had nothing to do with him being an Ascended. I would've gotten to the Lord eventually, but you took care of that sick bastard yourself."

Poppy stared at me for several moments, then shook her head, sending that piece of hair across her face. "Just because the Duke and the Lord were horrible and evil, that doesn't make you any better. That doesn't make all Ascended guilty."

"You know absolutely nothing, Poppy." Moving to the side, I unlocked the cell door. I wasn't going to talk to her through bars.

Keeping my eyes on her, I entered, but did so cautiously. Knowing her, she'd use those chains to choke my ass. I closed the cell door behind me. "You and I need to talk."

Her chin lifted. "No, we don't."

"Well, you really don't have a choice, do you?" I glanced at the cuffs on her wrists as I took a step forward. I stopped, inhaling deeply. Her scent reached me, but so did the smell of blood. Her blood. And I knew it was hers and not anyone's who'd died in the stables. It was too sweet, too fresh. Concern took root. "You're injured."

Poppy stepped back. "I'm fine."

"No, you aren't." I scanned her, my stare stopping on the damp spot on her shirt. "You're bleeding."

"Barely."

No longer giving a shit about her strangling me with the chains, I crossed the distance between us. It startled her. She gasped, stumbling back into the wall. I took advantage of that, reaching for the hem of the coarse linen shirt.

"Don't touch me!" She jerked to the side, wincing.

Everything in me stilled as I looked down at her. The panic I heard in her voice. The *pain*.

"Don't," she repeated.

Putting everything behind that wall inside me was harder than ever. "You had no problem with me touching you last night."

Her lips pulled back in a snarl. "That was a mistake."

"Was it?"

"Yes," she hissed. "I wish it never happened."

No doubt that was the truth. A bitter one I already knew. Still, it fucking hit deep to hear her say it. Those walls weren't as fortified as I thought.

"Be that as it may," I said, "you are still wounded, Princess, and you will allow me to look at it."

That chin of hers went right back up. "And if I don't?"

I laughed, genuinely amused with her resistance—impressed by it. But I would not fight her again. "As if you could stop me. You can either allow me to help you or..."

"Or you will force me?"

I didn't want to, but I would. She was hurt. Fucking gods, I almost prayed that she submitted.

Poppy stared at me for so long I started telling myself that compulsion may be necessary. I didn't know how badly she was injured, but even small wounds could turn bad for a mortal.

She looked away. "Why do you even care if I bleed to death?"

"Why do you think I would want you dead?" I countered. "If I did, why wouldn't I have agreed to what was demanded outside? You are no good to me dead."

"So, I'm your hostage until the Dark One gets here? You all plan to use me against the King and Queen."

"Clever girl," I murmured, relieved that she still hadn't acknowledged the truth. "You are the Queen's favorite Maiden." I tried again. "Will you let me check you now?"

Poppy said nothing, which I knew meant she was relenting. I reached for the shirt, this time slower. She tensed but didn't pull away. I lifted the hem as I looked down. The smell of her blood increased, even before I reached the seeping wound just below her breast. The gash was thin. I clenched my teeth together, my mind flicking through those who had been close enough to cause such a wound—a cut that could've taken her life if it had been an inch deeper. She would've bled out on that fucking stable floor.

"Gods," I said, lifting my gaze to hers. "You could've been disemboweled."

"You've always been so observant," she snapped.

And I was also glad to see her temper hadn't been wounded. "Why didn't you say anything? This could become infected."

"Well, there really wasn't a lot of time," she said, standing there with her arms at her sides. "Considering you were busy betraying me."

"That's no excuse."

She let out a cutting laugh. "Of course, not. Silly me for not realizing that the person who had a hand in murdering the people I care about, who betrayed me and made plans with the one who helped to slaughter my family to use me for some nefarious means, would care that I was wounded."

She was right.

She was completely right to think that.

And also utterly fearless.

"Always so brave," I murmured, dropping her shirt. I turned. "Delano," I called out, knowing he wouldn't have gone too far. The wolven appeared in a heartbeat. I quickly told him what I needed, then I waited. I knew Poppy had returned to leaning against the wall and could come at me at any moment.

But I didn't think she would. That wound was causing her pain.

Delano returned, handing the items to me in a basket. I could tell he wanted to ask about her before he left.

I faced her. "Why don't you lie—?" I looked around, shoulders tensing once more upon seeing the mattress. "Why don't you lie down?"

"I'm fine standing, thanks."

Impatience grew as I moved toward her. There was no way I could do this with her standing. "Would you rather I get on my knees?"

Poppy held my stare as her lips started to curve up—

"I don't mind." I drew my lower lip between my teeth. "Doing so would put me at the perfect height for something I know you'd enjoy. After all, I'm always craving honeydew."

Her eyes went wide as anger heightened the color in her cheeks. It wasn't the only thing, though. For a moment there, a different kind of heat hit her blood.

Poppy pushed off the wall and stomped her way to the mattress. She sat. "You're repulsive."

I laughed as I walked over to her and knelt, having gotten what I needed from her. For her to sit. And I also discovered that she was still attracted to me despite everything. "If you say so."

"I know so."

I grinned, placing the basket on the floor. She checked it out, probably looking for something that could be turned into a weapon. She would be disappointed there. I motioned for her to lie back.

"Bastard," she muttered but did as I requested.

"Language." I reached for her shirt again, but she grabbed it herself. That reminded me of something very important. Control. She needed control because she never had any. "Thank you."

Her lips thinned.

I smiled slightly, pulling a bottle from the basket. A bitter, sharp scent crowded the cell the moment I unscrewed the lid.

"I want to tell you a story," I said, eyeing the wound.

"I am not in the mood for story time—" Poppy gasped and grabbed my wrist with both hands as I took hold of the clothing. "What are you doing?"

"The blade damn near ripped out your rib cage." Anger sparked. "It extends up the side of your ribs." I waited for her to deny that. She didn't. "I'm guessing this happened when the sword was wrestled from you?"

Poppy stayed silent, but her grip remained on my wrist. Did she think…?

I sighed. "Believe it or not, I'm not trying to undress you so I can take advantage of you. I'm not here to seduce you, Princess."

Her lips parted as she stared up at me. Her shoulders lifted from the mattress, and her fingers were too damn cold against the skin of my wrist. A tremor ran through her once more, and I had no idea what was going through her head at the moment. It could be anything, but the longer she stared at me, the more I knew it wasn't good. Her thoughts were painful. I saw that in how her eyes started to glisten.

And I heard it in the hoarseness of her voice when she asked, "Was any of it true?"

Was any of it…?

I knew then what I should've made myself see while we were in the stables. That she had forgotten that our time together earlier was real.

Poppy let go of my wrist, closing her eyes. Mine followed. Anger rose. She'd forgotten. The anger I felt was wrong. I knew that, but I was also furious with myself for expecting her to remember. There was no point in telling her otherwise. She wouldn't believe me.

Opening my eyes, I got to work. Lifting her shirt again, I looked closer at the wound's jagged edges. I needed to close the gash, and there was a much easier, quicker alternative to what was to come. I could give her my blood, but I would have to force her to take it. This would hurt her, but completely stripping her of control? I had a feeling that would do lasting damage.

"This may burn," I warned as I leaned over her, tipping the bottle. The astringent hit the wound, causing her to jerk. The liquid immediately bubbled in the cut as I gritted my teeth. I knew it had to sting, but Poppy didn't make a sound.

"Sorry about that." I set the bottle aside. "It will need to sit for a bit to burn out any infection that may have already been making its way in there."

She said nothing, just let her head fall back against the mattress. The hair that was always in her face slipped down her cheek.

I stopped myself from moving it out of the way and instead focused on what I had to tell her. "The Craven were our fault," I said. "Their creation, that is. All of this. The monsters in the mist. The war. What has become of this land. You. Us. It all started with an incredibly desperate, foolish act of love, many, many centuries before the War of Two Kings."

"I know." Poppy cleared her throat. "I know the history."

"But do you know the true history?"

"I know the only history." Her eyes opened, fixing on the bones above her.

"You know only what the Ascended have led everyone to believe, and it is not the truth." I picked up the chain that lay across her lower stomach, moving it off her. "My people lived alongside mortals in harmony for thousands of years, but then King Malec O'Meer—"

"Created the Craven," she interrupted. "Like I said—"

"You're wrong." I sat, drawing a leg up to rest my arm on. There wasn't a lot of time to tell her this, but I had to if I had any hope of her understanding. "King Malec fell hopelessly in love with a mortal woman. Her name was Isbeth. Some say it was Queen Eloana who poisoned her. Others claim it was a jilted lover of the King's who stabbed her because he apparently had quite the history of being unfaithful," I told her, imagining my mother conspiring to poison someone. It wasn't exactly that hard to imagine. "But either way, she was mortally wounded. As I said, Malec was desperate to save her. He committed the forbidden act of Ascending her—what you know as the Ascension."

Poppy's gaze shot to mine.

"Yes," I confirmed what I knew she was putting together. "Isbeth was the first to Ascend. Not your false King and Queen. She became the first vampry. Malec drank from her, only stopping once he felt her heart begin to fail, and then he shared his blood with her." I stretched my neck. "Perhaps if your act of Ascension wasn't so well-guarded, the finer details would not come as a surprise to you."

Poppy started to rise but stopped. "Ascension is a Blessing from the gods."

I smirked. "It is far from that. More like an act that can either create near immortality or make nightmares come true. We Atlantians are born nearly mortal. And remain so until the Culling."

"The Culling?" she repeated.

"It's when we change." I curled my upper lip, showing the tip of a fang. "The fangs appear, lengthening only when we feed, and we change in...other ways."

"How?" Curiosity filled her.

"That's not important." I reached for a cloth. There wasn't enough time to explain all of that. "We may be harder to kill than the Ascended, but we *can* be killed. We age slower than mortals, and if we take care, we can live for thousands of years."

Poppy stared at me. She didn't counter that, so I figured I'd made progress. Or it was just her curiosity. Probably the latter.

"How...how old are you?" she asked.

"Older than I look."

"Hundreds of years older?" she whispered.

"I was born after the war," I told her. "I've seen two centuries come and go."

She gaped at me, and I figured it was best I continue.

"King Malec created the first vampry. They are...a part of all of us, but they are not like us. Daylight does not affect us. Not like it does the vamprys," I said. "Tell me, which of the Ascended have you ever seen in the daylight?"

"They do not walk in the sun because the gods do not," she answered. "That is how they honor them."

I snickered. "How convenient for them, then. Vamprys may be blessed with the closest possible thing to immortality, like us, but they cannot walk in daylight without their skin starting to decay. You want to kill an Ascended without getting your hands dirty? Lock them outside with no possible shelter. They'll be dead before noon. They also need to feed, and by *feed*, I am talking about blood. They need to do so frequently to live, to prevent whatever mortal wounds or illnesses they suffered before they Ascended from returning." I glanced at her wound. The fizzing had eased. "They cannot procreate, not after the Ascension, and many experience bloodlust when they feed, often killing mortals in the process."

I gently dabbed the cloth on the wound, soaking up the astringent. "Atlantians do not feed on mortals—"

"Whatever," she cut in. "You expect me to truly believe that?"

I met her glare. "Mortal blood offers us nothing of any real value because we were never mortal, Princess. Wolven don't need to feed, but we do. We feed when we need to, on other Atlantians."

Poppy sucked in a soft breath, shaking her head.

"We can use our blood to heal a mortal without turning them, something a vampry cannot do, but the most important difference is the creation of the Craven. An Atlantian has never created one. The vamprys have." I lifted the cloth. "And in case you haven't been following along, the vamprys are what you know as the Ascended."

"That's a lie." Her hands fisted at her sides.

"It is the truth." I frowned, looking at the wound. The astringent that remained no longer bubbled. That was good. "A vampry cannot make another vampry. They cannot complete the Ascension. When they drain a mortal, they create a Craven."

"What you're saying makes no sense," she argued.

"How does it not?"

"Because if any part of what you're saying is true, then the Ascended are vamprys, and they cannot do the Ascension." Her voice hardened. "If that's true, then how have they made other Ascended? Like my brother."

"Because it is not the Ascended who are giving the gift of life," I bit out. "They are using an Atlantian to do so."

Her laugh was scathing. "The Ascended would never work with an Atlantian."

"Did I misspeak?" I challenged. "I don't believe I did. I said they are *using* an Atlantian. Not working with one." I picked up the smaller jar, unscrewing the lid. "When King Malec's peers discovered what he'd done, he lifted the laws that forbade the act of Ascending. As more vamprys were created, many were unable to control their bloodlust." I dipped my fingers into the thick, milky-white substance. "They drained many of their victims, creating the pestilence known as the Craven, who swept across the kingdom like a plague. The Queen of Atlantia, Queen Eloana, tried to stop it. She made the act of Ascension forbidden once more and ordered all vamprys destroyed in an act to protect mankind."

Her gaze dipped to the jar. "Yarrow?"

I nodded. "Among other things that will help speed up your healing."

"I can—" Poppy jerked as I touched the skin below the angry red flesh. I spread the ointment.

"The vamprys revolted," I continued as I scooped out more of the balm, somehow finding the willpower to ignore the warmth building in her. "That is what triggered the War of Two Kings. It was not mortals fighting back against cruel, inhuman Atlantians, but vamprys fighting back. The death toll from the war was not exaggerated. In fact, many people believe the numbers were far higher."

I glanced up to see her watching me. "We weren't defeated, Princess. King Malec was overthrown, divorced, and exiled. Queen Eloana remarried, and the new King, Da'Neer, pulled their forces back, called their people home, and ended a war that was destroying this world."

"And what happened to Malec and Isbeth?" Poppy asked.

"Your records say that Malec was defeated in battle, but the truth is, no one knows. He and his mistress simply disappeared." I returned the lid to the jar and picked up a clean bandage. "The vamprys gained control of the remaining lands, anointing their own King and Queen, Jalara and Ileana, and renamed it the Kingdom of Solis." I took a breath to calm the fury. "They called themselves the Ascended, used *our* gods, who'd long since gone to sleep, as a reason for why they became the way they did. In the hundreds of years that have passed since, they've managed to scrub the truth from history, that the vast majority of mortals actually fought alongside the Atlantians against the common threat of vamprys."

"None of that sounds believable," Poppy said after a moment.

"I imagine it is hard to believe that you belong to a society of murderous monsters, who take the third daughters and sons during the Rite to feed upon. And if they don't drain them dry, they become—"

"What?" she gasped. "You have spent this entire time telling me nothing but falsehoods, but now you've gone too far."

Shaking my head, I placed the bandage over her wound, pressing down on the edges so it stayed in place. "I've told you nothing but the truth." I leaned back. "As did the man who threw the Craven hand."

She sat up, lowering her shirt. "Are you claiming that those given in service to the gods are now Craven?"

"Why do you think the Temples are off-limits to anyone but the Ascended and those they control, like the Priests and Priestesses?"

"Because they're sacred places that even most Ascended don't breach."

"Have you seen one child that has been given over? Just one, Princess?" I pressed her. "Do you know anyone other than a Priest or Priestess or an Ascended who has claimed to have seen one? You're smart. You know no one has. That's because most are dead before they even learn to speak."

She started to deny it.

"The vamprys need a food source, Princess, one that would not rouse suspicion. What better way than to convince an entire kingdom to hand over their children under the pretense of honoring the gods? They've created a religion around it, such that brothers will turn on brothers if any of them refuse to give away their child," I told her. "They have fooled an entire kingdom, used the fear of what they have created against the people. And that's not all. You ever think it's strange how many young children die overnight from a mysterious blood disease? Like the Tulis family, who lost their first and second children to it? Not every Ascended can stick to a strict diet. Bloodlust for a vampry is a very real, common problem. They're thieves in the night, stealing children, wives, and husbands."

"Do you really think I believe any of this?" Poppy demanded. "That the Atlantians are innocent, and everything I've been taught is a lie?"

"Not particularly, but it was worth a shot," I said, also knowing it wasn't something she'd believe immediately. She had to sit with it. I just hoped we had enough time. "We are not innocent of all crimes—"

"Like murder and kidnapping?" Poppy tossed out.

"That among other things," I admitted. "You don't want to believe what I'm saying. Not because it sounds too foolish to believe, but because there are things you're now questioning. Because it means your precious brother is feeding on innocents—"

"No," she cut in.

"And turning them into Craven."

"Shut up," she growled, launching to her feet.

I followed her, coming to stand before her. "You don't want to accept what I'm saying, even as logical as it sounds because it means your brother is one of them, and the Queen who cared for you has slaughtered thousands—"

Poppy swung at me, dragging the chain across the floor.

I caught her hand an inch from my jaw. I twisted her, forcing her to turn away from me. Hauling her back against my chest, I trapped one arm with mine and caught her other hand. A sound of pure frustration tore from her as she lifted a leg.

"Don't," I warned, my mouth against her ear.

Poppy, of course, did not listen.

I grunted as her foot connected with my shin, likely bruising it as she had Kieran's. A huge part of me was more than impressed by her tenacity. Hell, it *was* a turn-on—her willingness to fight her way out. Her strength. But we didn't have all day for this.

Moving too fast for her to react to, I spun her and took several steps. Trapping her between the wall and me, I was...somewhat confident she couldn't kick me.

"I said, don't," I repeated, my mouth now against her temple. "I mean it, Princess. I don't want to hurt you."

"You don't? You already hur—" Poppy cut herself off.

"What?" I lifted her arm away from her stomach and the wound I'd just covered, placing her palm against the wall. She didn't answer me, and I knew she was thinking of ways to take me out. Again, that was admirable and arousing, but also pointless.

I shifted my head, resting my cheek against hers. "You know you can't seriously hurt me," I said.

Every muscle of her body tensed. "Then why am I chained?"

"Because getting kicked, punched, or clawed still doesn't feel good," I drawled. "And while the others have been ordered to not touch you, it doesn't mean they'll be as tolerant as I am."

"Tolerant?" She tried to push away from the wall—*tried* being the keyword there. "You call this tolerant?"

"Considering that I just spent time cleaning out and covering your wound, I would say so." I paused. "And a thank you would be nice."

"I didn't ask you to help me," she snapped.

"No. Because you're either too proud or too foolish to do so. You would've allowed yourself to rot instead of asking for help," I said. "So, I'm not going to get a thank you, am I?"

Her head thrust back, but I saw it coming. I pushed against her until there was no space between her and the wall, which she didn't like. She started to squirm, pressing back—wiggling soft, shapely parts of her, and my body reacted immediately.

Fucking gods.

"You are exceptionally skilled at being disobedient," I growled. "Only second to your talent of driving me crazy."

"You forgot one last skill."

"I did?" I frowned.

"Yes," she hissed. "I'm skilled at killing Craven. I imagine killing Atlantians is no different."

I laughed, enjoying her threats. "We're not consumed by hunger, so we're not as easily distracted as a Craven."

"You can still be killed."

"Is that a threat?" I asked, grinning.

"You take it however you want."

It likely was a threat. My smile faded. "I know you've been through a lot. I know that what I've told you is a lot, but it is all the truth. Every part, Poppy."

"Stop calling me that!" She wiggled, shifting slightly. Her ass rubbed against my cock.

"And you should stop doing that," I bit out, unsure if I really wanted her to stop. "Then again. Please continue. It's the perfect kind of torture."

Poppy inhaled sharply as a tight, sweet shiver hit her. "You're sick."

"And twisted. Perverse, and dark." I drew my chin across her cheek, smiling as her back arched in response. Her body knew what it wanted. Against the wall, I spread my fingers over hers. "I'm a lot of things—"

"Murderer?" she whispered. "You killed Vikter. You killed all the others."

The breath I took was a heavy one. "I've killed. So have Delano and Kieran. I and the one you call the Dark One had a hand in Hannes' and Rylan's deaths, but not that poor girl," I said, speaking of Malessa Axton. "It was one of the Ascended, most likely caught in bloodlust.

And I am willing to bet it was either the Duke or the Lord."

Poppy seemed to exhale the same heavy breath.

"And none of us had anything to do with the attack on the Rite," I told her, which was true. They were never supposed to be near the Rite. "And what happened to Vikter."

I could feel each breath she took as she asked, "Then who did?"

"It was those you call Descenters. Our supporters," I told her. "There was no order given to attack the Rite, however."

"You really expect me to believe the *thing* the Descenters follow didn't order them to attack the Rite?"

"Just because they follow the Dark One, doesn't mean they are led by him. Many of the Descenters act on their own. They know the truth. They no longer want to live in fear of their children being made into monsters or stolen to feed another. I had nothing to do with Vikter's death," I said, even though I felt responsible because I *was* responsible.

Poppy shivered. "But the others you claim. You killed them. Owning it doesn't change it."

"It had to happen." I moved my chin without thought, much like a cat seeking touch. "Just like you need to understand that there is no way out of this. You belong to me."

You belong to me.

My eyes opened, fixing on our joined hands against the cold stone wall. The back of my neck prickled.

"Don't you mean I belong to the Dark One?" she countered.

I swallowed. "I meant what I said, Princess."

"I don't belong to anyone."

"If you believe that, then you *are* a fool." I moved my head, preventing her from retaliating. "Or you're lying to yourself. You belonged to the Ascended. You know that. It's one of the things you hated. They kept you in a cage."

"At least that cage was more comfortable than this one."

"True," I admitted, and fuck if that wasn't a kick in the nuts. "But you've never been free."

"True or not, that doesn't mean I'll stop fighting you," she warned. "I won't submit."

"I know." Admiration for her rose once more, but so did concern. I didn't need her to submit. I needed her to see the truth, and there was so much I hadn't told her. There wasn't time. I needed to get to Berkton.

Poppy stiffened against me. "And you're still a monster."

Another truth. "I am, but I wasn't born that way. I was *made* this way. You asked about the scar on my thigh. Did you look at it closely, or were you too busy staring at my co—"

"Shut up!"

"You should've noticed that it was the Royal Crest branded on my skin." I wasn't going to shut up. "Do you want to know how I have such intimate knowledge of what happens during your fucking Ascension, Poppy? How I know what you don't? Because I was held in one of those Temples for five decades," I hissed. "And I was sliced and cut and fed upon. My blood was poured into golden chalices that the second sons and daughters drank after being drained by the Queen or the King or another Ascended. I was the godsdamn cattle."

My lips peeled back over my teeth. "And I wasn't just used for food. I provided all sorts of entertainment. I know exactly what it's like to not have a choice." I went there because she had to know. "It was your Queen who branded me, and if it hadn't been for the foolish bravery of another, I would still be there. That is how I got that scar."

I let go of her then, burning with anger and grief, shame and desperation. The walls were down. Backing away, I saw that she trembled. I knew that what I'd shared shook her. Good. It was terrible. Horrific. It was the truth of those she wanted so badly to believe were the heroes.

The thing was, there were no heroes here. Not really. But my people weren't monsters.

I left the cell before she turned around, crossing her arms over her waist.

I gripped the bars as she stared at me. "Neither the Prince nor I want to see you harmed," I said, speaking of my brother. "As I've said, we need you alive."

"Why?" she whispered. "Why am I so important?"

"Because they have the true heir to the kingdom. They captured him when he freed me."

Her brows knitted. "The Dark One has a brother?"

"You are the Queen's favorite. You're important to her and to the kingdom. I don't know why. Maybe it has something to do with your gift. Perhaps it doesn't." I forced myself to say what I needed to, because now wasn't the time to tell her I had no plans of letting her go back to or stay with them. That conversation would have to come once she accepted the truth. "But we will release you back to them if they release Prince Malik."

"You plan to use me as ransom."

"That's better than sending you back in pieces, isn't it?" I countered, grip tightening on the bars.

Disbelief filled her expression. "You just spent all this time telling me that the Queen, the Ascended, and my brother, are all evil vamprys who feed on mortals, and you're just going to send me back to them once you free the Dark One's brother?"

There was nothing I could say that she'd be willing to listen to.

A harsh, *hurt* laugh left her, and the bars dented under my hands as she lifted hers to her chest.

"A more comfortable sleeping arrangement will be made." I pushed back from the bars. "You can choose not to believe anything I've said, but you should so that what I'm about to say doesn't come as such a shock to you. I will be leaving shortly to meet up with King Da'Neer of Atlantia to tell him that I have you."

Her head jerked upright.

"Yes. The King lives. So does Queen Eloana. The parents of the one you call the Dark One and Prince Malik." I turned from her, stopping. My hands fisted at my sides. "Not everything was a lie, Poppy. Not everything."

PRESENT XI

"I never wanted you to find out the way you did," I told Poppy. "And I know that's no excuse—I knew that then. It doesn't matter that I planned to tell you the truth. I should've told you everything before we spent that night together, and I know I should've also forced you to confront what you already had to know." I took a shallow breath. "That I was who you believed to be the Dark One. That would've been the right thing to do. I knew that then, too, but I was selfish. I wanted you, and I didn't have the decency to do the right thing."

I lay beside Poppy, running my fingers over her arm. Her skin had warmed in the last few hours.

Hope was such a fragile creature, so I held it in check. "The thing is, Poppy? If I had to do it all over again, the first thing I would change is leaving you in that room. And I know that sounds fucked-up—that there is a whole slew of other things I should've done differently. But knowing what I should've done and what I would've done are two entirely different things. I was greedy then with you, even before I realized it, but that night…"

I traced the elegant lines of the bones and tendons in her hand. "I'd already fallen for you, despite what I said to Kieran. I didn't know it wasn't only lust and obsession. That I was already deeply and madly in love with you—your stubbornness and bravery, your kindness, and that delightful vicious streak that runs deep in you." I grinned. "I just didn't know that was what I was feeling because love…it wasn't something I thought I deserved. Not after all my mistakes, the lives I'd taken, and the pain I'd caused others—the pain I caused you. The agony my actions were still going to bring you. It wasn't even that I thought you'd never forgive me. It was that I couldn't be forgiven and…" I trailed off, thinking about my brother and what he'd said about not telling Millicent they were heartmates.

My chest constricted. That was likely what drove Malik's choice. He believed she couldn't understand or forgive the things he'd done. That he wasn't worthy of her love—of anyone's, really. And despite our issues, that made me hurt for him.

I blew out a breath, forcing the tightness in my chest to loosen. "I hated seeing you in that cell, and I loathed leaving you there. Delano and Naill were to move you as soon as they could. They had to wait till they believed Jericho had left." My lips thinned. "And for others in the keep to be occupied. They didn't want to run the risk of being seen while moving you because New Haven had become a powder keg—more so than we even realized."

A warm breeze rolled in through the window, playing with the strands of her hair. "I rode to Berkton as fast as I could, pushing Setti to his limits in that weather. The snow had eased off, but I knew I didn't have long before it picked up again. When I arrived at the old manor, I…"

I really had no idea what I would have done if it *had* been my father there.

"Alastir was there, not the King. He'd convinced my father to remain in Atlantia because it was too much of a risk for him to be that deep in Solis. You already know that, but the relief I felt? I could've fallen to my knees. Alastir…he was a traitorous bastard at the end, and fuck him, but to this day, I'm glad he came." I lifted her hand and pressed a kiss to the top.

"I was able to convince him that I had things handled and that the roads were too bad for his group to travel." I glanced at the closed doors. "Emil helped there, being his ridiculous self. And Alastir? He didn't push me. Wouldn't. Honestly? I think the delay was a relief to him. You see, he didn't know who you really were then. All he knew was that he was about to go and do something I'm not sure he wanted to do—something he'd assured my father he would do."

I mulled that over, reconciling the Alastir I had grown up with, with the one who had killed. Who had ultimately betrayed us. "I used to think it was because he was a good—sometimes irritating—man. Now, I realize he just didn't want more innocent blood on his hands. But that was before he saw who you were."

My smile faded. "If my father had been there? He would've ridden to New Haven anyway, and I don't know if I would've been able to change his mind," I admitted in the quiet. "But I do know I would not have allowed him to hurt you."

Turning her hand, I kissed the golden imprint. "I would've gotten people banished. Others killed. I would've split the kingdom." The truth tasted like ash on my tongue. "I would've killed him," I whispered. "Honest to gods, even then, before I could really understand what I felt for you—that you were my soul—I would've killed him."

I lowered her hand. "But that didn't happen. I got lucky there, but the luck didn't last." I soaked in the sight of the pink slowly returning to her cheeks, even as the image of her bloodless body being handed to me filled my mind, a memory I wouldn't forget.

The breath I took burned a little. "The fear I felt when word of your attack reached me on the way back to the keep? I should've known then. Kieran did." I threaded my fingers through hers. "More so than before. He saw my panic, what I was willing to do to save you. Anyone else? Kieran would've destroyed them for stabbing me. But you? Don't get me wrong. There was a moment when instinct took over. You hurt me. That initial response is beyond his control. But me stopping him wasn't the reason he didn't give in to it. He *knew*. That was why he let you live." I squeezed her hand. "He already knew that I was in love with you."

THE DARK ONE

The *howling*.

About an hour into our return trip to Haven Keep, the wolven's sharp, high-pitched yips and keening, powerful howls whipped the woods between Berkton Manor and New Haven into a frenzy. Perched high above us in the pines, birds took flight, scattering into the air. Small creatures scurried under bushes and boulders. From the deeper, darker parts of the forest, the Craven answered with wails.

I'd heard the wolven's alarm call a hundred times in my life, but this raised every hair on my body and caused the nape of my neck to prickle.

Because I *knew*.

I didn't know how. It made no sense for me to know, but every fiber of my being knew that something had happened to Poppy.

My head snapped to Kieran. "*Go*."

He didn't hesitate. He slowed his horse and jumped off, shifting into his wolven form mid-run. He was nothing more than a fawn-hued blur as I caught the reins of his horse. Pitching forward on Setti, I rode hard through the maze of pines as the flurries picked up, coming down faster and harder.

Wind stung my cheeks as we leapt over boulders and fallen trees, my heart pumping. I didn't feel the icy dampness or the jarring landings as Setti's hooves kicked up snow and soil. The horses' panting breaths joined mine. The relief that it had been Alastir who'd come instead of my father was long gone as I pushed Setti and the other steed hard. Now, I felt only mounting dread.

Something had happened to Poppy.

The inexplicable knowing only increased with each passing minute and hour. Had she escaped? Had she fallen ill despite me cleaning her wound? Had someone harmed her?

If anyone had touched an inch of her skin, they would die. No matter who they were. Their life was already over.

When the pines began to thin, I knew I was close. Slowing Setti and the other horse, I leapt from the saddle and hit the ground running. I darted through the trees, flying over rocks and thick branches littering the slick, snow-covered ground. My boots slipped several times, but I didn't slow. Some sort of primal instinct warned me there was no time to waste.

The faded gray stone of Haven Keep appeared through the pines, and I dug in, pulling on every bit of elemental strength I had in me. I burst from the tree line, racing across the courtyard—past the anxious, pacing wolven, past blurred faces. I only slowed when I spotted Naill running out of the keep's doors.

"Where is she?" I demanded.

His eyes were wide—wider than I'd ever seen them, the whites stark against his skin. "Kieran took her upstairs, to your chambers."

I spun, heading for the entrance to the stairs. "How bad?"

Naill was just a step behind me. "It's…it's bad."

My chest hollowed as I wrenched open the door, and the scent of her blood hit me. "Those responsible?"

"The ones that still live are in the cells," Naill answered as I rushed the steps. "We tried to stop them, but we were fucking outnumbered. She fought back, and she…fuck, she saved Delano's life down there. I swear to the gods she did. And I don't even know why."

Neither did I. I shoved open the door and hit the outdoor hall of the second floor. The scent of her blood was even stronger. "I want them kept alive. They are mine to deal with."

"Understood."

"I left Setti and Kieran's horse in the woods," I told him. "There are Craven—"

"I'll get them." Naill turned, grasping the railing as he leapt onto it. He crouched. "Cas, I'm…I'm sorry. We failed you."

"No, you didn't," I growled as the chamber door swung open, and Elijah appeared. "It was I who failed."

Hands clenching, I stalked past the noticeably subdued Elijah and came to a complete stop.

Kieran was by the crackling fire, cradling Poppy in his lap. He had a hand pressed against her stomach. Red seeped through his fingers and splattered the floor. And Poppy…her eyes were closed, her skin far too pale. For a moment, I thought she—oh, fuck, I thought she was already gone. But then I saw the dagger clenched in her hand.

Kieran's head lifted, his features somber. "Cas…"

I knew that look.

I heard the finality in his voice.

I refused to acknowledge either as I strode forward, unclasping my cloak and letting it fall to the floor. Aware of Elijah closing the door, I tugged off my gloves, tossing them aside. I reached for her as Kieran rose and took her in my arms.

She made no sound. Did nothing as I turned, my heart thundering. I could feel how chilled her skin had grown beneath her clothing. I inhaled sharply at the fresh, jagged tears across her arm and beneath her shoulder. A wolven had clawed her.

Sickened, I brought her to the floor beside the fire, shifting her so she rested on her side. Kieran followed silently, once more placing his hand on the wound—one far too close to her heart.

"Open your eyes, Poppy. Come on." I pried the dagger loose from her grip, letting it fall to the floor. The fact that she clung to it like that fucking cut me up. My hand shook as I took hold of her chin. "I need you to open your eyes."

I dragged in a ragged breath as her blood continued pumping between Kieran's fingers. It was bad. The wound was deep, and no one here could fix it with some balm and a bandage. She was… Fucking gods, she was going to—no, I would not allow it.

"*Please*," I demanded—begged, really.

The skin around her eyes pinched. Those thick lashes fluttered, then lifted.

"There you are." I forced a smile because I didn't want her to be scared. I didn't want her to see what I knew. I didn't want her to have this memory to add to her other terrible ones because she *would* survive this. I knew that the moment I heard the wolven howling.

"It hurts," she rasped.

"I know." Shuddering, I held her gaze. "I'm going to fix it. I'll make the pain go away. I'll make it all go away. You won't carry one more scar."

Her chest moved with a shallow breath. "I'm… I'm dying."

"No, you're not," I snarled, terror crashing into fear. "You cannot die. I will not allow it."

There was no hesitation. No second thoughts as I lifted my wrist to my mouth and bit down deep. Poppy cried out, and Kieran jerked his hand away from her wound, stumbling back a step as my blood touched my tongue. I tore my flesh open.

I saw a brief look of concern flash across her face.

"I'm going to die an imbecile," Poppy whispered.

Lifting my wrist, I frowned. "You're not going to die, and I'm fine. I just need you to drink."

Kieran had gone rigid. "Casteel, do you—?"

"I know exactly what I'm doing, and I don't want your opinion or your advice." Blood trailed down my arm. "And I don't require either."

He got the message and stayed silent.

Poppy did not, however. She tried to pull away. "No," she rasped. "No."

I held her against me. "You have to. You'll die if you don't."

"I'd rather...die than turn into a monster," she swore.

"A monster?" I laughed at the absurdity. "Poppy, I already told you the truth about the Craven. This will only make you better."

She turned her head from me.

The hollowness in my chest spread. "You will do this. You will drink. You will live. Make that choice, Princess." My voice thickened. "Do not force me to make it for you."

She shook her head weakly, still struggling to free herself.

Fuck, there was no time to argue with her, to try to convince her of what she didn't believe. I'd given her a choice. She'd given me none.

"Penellaphe." I spoke her name as I summoned the eather from deep within. It flowed through my veins and filled my voice with the power of the gods. "Look at me."

Slowly, her gaze met mine. Her lips parted.

"Drink," I commanded, pushing hard with the compulsion as I brought my wrist to her mouth. "Drink from me."

A drop of blood fell from my arm to her lips. It slipped between them, and she jerked slightly. I pressed my wrist to her mouth. My blood seeped in, coating her tongue, coursing down her throat, but I held my breath and waited.

Poppy *swallowed*.

"That's it," I rasped. "Drink."

Those green eyes locked onto mine as she drank, drawing my blood into her. She didn't look away as she swallowed again and again, even after I eased up on the compulsion, letting her go. She drank from me on her own, the repulsion of doing so passing the moment she tasted my blood. It wouldn't be like she expected.

Poppy's eyes drifted shut as her fingers pressed into my forearm, but I didn't close mine. I watched her intently, vaguely aware of Kieran quietly leaving the chamber. It was just us as she fed. I focused on her breathing, her pulse. Both strengthened and steadied, her overtaxed heart becoming stronger as I cleared my mind of the fury and terror. I didn't want her to pick up on any of that. I wanted her to feel safe.

Her steady pulls against my wrist became almost languid, and still she took from me, hungrily, greedily. I let my head rest against the wall. For some reason, I thought of the Stroud Sea, how it had looked to me when I climbed my way out of the tunnels. The sun had hurt my eyes after being held underground for so long, but even with them stinging and watering, I hadn't been able to look away from the sparkling blue waters. Pence had been right. The Stroud Sea was beautiful.

The image of the water scattered as Poppy squirmed a little against me. From the depths of my memories, another image took shape. Smooth rock. Clearer water drenched in shadows that smelled of lilacs. The *cavern.*

I swore I felt Poppy's presence as my last memory of there started to piece itself together. As if she were inside my mind. My breath snagged.

I opened my eyes, heart racing as I looked down at Poppy. "Enough," I rasped. The color had returned to her flesh. "That's enough."

Poppy...gods, as gloriously stubborn as ever, was latched on to my wrist. Clearly, she didn't believe she'd had enough. She pulled on the punctures I'd created, and those greedy drags hit every sensory point in my body.

"Poppy," I groaned, pulling my wrist from her.

She started to follow but then relaxed against me, her eyes closing again. The way she looked reminded me of when she'd fallen asleep as I told her about my scars. Sated. Peaceful. *Happy.*

I tucked that rebellious strand of hair back, my fingers sifting through the silken tangles as I let my head rest against the wall once more. Admittedly, I got a little lost in just holding her in the quiet. I wasn't even sure how much time had passed, but I wouldn't forget the calm moments even if the world outside demanded I do so.

"Poppy," I called out to her. "How are you feeling?"

"I'm not cold," she answered after a moment. "My chest...it's not cold."

"It shouldn't be."

"I feel...different," she added.

A small smile tugged at my lips. "Good."

"I feel like my body...isn't attached."

"That will go away after a few minutes," I told her. Feeding caused a high. It wasn't the only thing it did, but as long as she remained as she was, the effects would pass. "Just relax and enjoy it."

"I don't hurt anymore." Poppy was quiet for a few moments. "I don't understand."

"It's my blood." That strand had already made its way to her cheek. I really liked that piece of hair. I brushed it back. Poppy shivered, and a scent other than her blood reached me. I ignored it. "The blood of an Atlantian has healing properties. I told you that."

"That...that is unbelievable," Poppy murmured.

"Is it?" I reached over her, picking up her arm. "Were you not wounded here?"

She looked, but nothing but dried blood and dirt marred her flesh.

"And here?" I moved my hand so my thumb swirled around her upper arm, right below the shoulder. "Were you not clawed here?"

Once more, her gaze followed where I directed. Wonder filled her. "There's...there are no new scars."

"There will be no new scars. That is what I promised," I reminded her.

"Your blood..." She swallowed. "It's amazing."

I was glad she thought that now. Later? Likely a different story.

Poppy's gaze snapped back to mine. "You made me drink your blood."

"I did."

Her nose scrunched. "How?"

"It's one of those things that occur during maturity," I explained. "Not all of us can...compel others."

"Have you done it before?" she asked. "On me?"

"You probably wish you could blame your prior actions on that," I stated dryly. "But I haven't, Poppy. I never needed nor wanted to."

Confusion settled, causing her to purse her lips. "But you did it now."

"I did."

Her eyes narrowed. "You don't even sound remotely ashamed."

"I'm not," I admitted, fighting a grin. "I told you that I would not allow you to die, and you would've died, Princess. You were dying." A cold, harsh slice of pain cut through my stomach. "I saved your life.

Some would suggest a thank you as the appropriate response."

"I didn't ask you to do it," she said, and I'd never been more grateful to see that stubborn chin of hers lift.

"But you're grateful, aren't you?" I teased.

Poppy pressed her lips together.

Amusement rose. "Only you would argue with me about this."

"I won't turn—"

"No." I sighed, lowering her arm to her stomach. "I told you the truth, Poppy. The Atlantians did not make the Craven. The Ascended did."

Poppy stared at me, her chest rising sharply, and I thought I saw it then. A smidgen of acceptance before she looked at the exposed wooden beams of the ceiling. "We're in a bedchamber."

"We needed privacy."

Her brow pinched. "Kieran didn't want you to save me."

"Because it's forbidden."

"Will I turn into a vampry?"

I laughed. I couldn't help it because she *was* beginning to accept the truth.

"What about that is funny?"

"Nothing." I grinned. "I know you still don't want to believe the truth, but deep down, you do. That's why you asked that question." I glanced at the door as I heard footsteps approach, then retreat. "To turn, you would require far more blood than that. It would also require me to be more of an active participant."

The breath she took was soft. "How...how would you be more of an active participant?"

My smile spread. "Would you rather I show you instead of telling you?"

"No," she said, even as her desire increased.

I closed my eyes. "Liar."

Poppy fell quiet again, and I knew I should get her cleaned up and then into bed so she could rest. *Alone.* There were things I needed to take care of. People I wanted to kill. Slowly. Painfully.

But she was warm and alive, safe in my arms, and I wasn't ready to leave.

I would pay for that, sooner rather than later because Poppy's breathing had changed. Her pulse had quickened. The other effects of my blood that I'd foolishly hoped would pass her by were now hitting her.

"Are…Naill and Delano okay?" she asked, her voice thicker, lusher.

"They will be fine," I told her. "And I'm sure they'll be happy to know you asked about them."

Poppy didn't respond to that. Perhaps she had, and I just didn't hear her over my pounding pulse. I inhaled deeply and swallowed a groan. Her scent surrounded me, and I felt her heated stare on me. I could fucking feel exactly where her mind was going.

"Poppy," I warned.

"What?" she whispered.

I gritted my teeth. "Stop thinking what you're thinking."

"How do you know what I'm thinking?"

Opening my eyes, I lowered my chin. "I know."

Poppy stared back at me, her skin flushed as she shivered. Her hips wiggled, and I about cursed as my arm tightened around her. Wasn't sure how that helped. It didn't. Not when her ass was snug against my cock.

"You don't know," she denied, watching me through half-hooded eyes. She bit down on her lip and moaned. "Hawke."

Fucking gods.

Poppy took that exact moment to stretch like a feline. Her back bowed, pressing her breasts against the shirt. "Hawke."

"Don't," I bit out, stiffening. "Don't call me that."

"Why not?"

"Just don't." Not after this. Not after…*oh, fuck.*

Poppy's hand was on the move, sliding up the length of her torn shirt. My mouth dried as I watched her fingers curl around her breast and press into the plump flesh.

"Poppy," I forced out. "What are you doing?"

"I don't know."

That was an utter, complete lie.

Her eyes were closed as her back arched. She drew her thumb over the tip of her breast. "I'm on fire."

"It's just the blood," I said, hearing how thick my voice was as I watched her. "It'll pass, but you should…you need to stop doing that."

To the surprise of no one, least of all me, Poppy didn't listen.

She drew her thumb over the hardened nipple I could see clearly through the coarse, thin shirt. And she liked how it made her feel. Her breath was sharp.

Desire rippled through me as she shifted, pressing her thighs together—thighs I could clearly recall pressing against my shoulders as I tasted her.

"Hawke?"

A taut bolt of pleasure cut through me. "Poppy, for the love of the gods."

Her eyes opened as her hand left her breast. There was a moment of reprieve, but then her fingers were on the move again, sliding down her stomach, and any relief vanished.

"Kiss me?" Her sultry whisper taunted me.

Every muscle in my body tensed. "You don't want that."

"I do." The tips of her fingers reached the loose band of her breeches. "I need it."

"You only think that right now." What I would've given to hear her say that any other time. "It's the blood."

"I don't care." Her hand slipped lower. "Touch me? Please?"

Need shredded me as I groaned. "You think you hate me now? If I do what you're asking, you'll want to murder me." My lips tipped up. On second thought... "Well, you'll want to murder me more than you already do. You don't have control of yourself right now."

The skin of her brow creased. "No."

"No?" I repeated, watching her hand inch its way down.

"I don't hate you."

A low rumble came from me. It wasn't just need that seized me. So much desire did that I'd grabbed her wrist before I even realized what I was doing. I wanted to replace her hand with mine—my fingers, my lips, my tongue. My cock thickened.

"Hawke?" she whimpered.

I stretched my neck. "I plotted to take you from everything you knew, and I did, but that is nowhere near the worst of my crimes," I bit out. "I've killed people, Poppy. There is so much blood on my hands that they will never be clean. I will overthrow the Queen who cared for you, and many more will die in the process. I am not a good man, but I am trying to be right now."

"I don't want you to be good." She gripped my tunic. "I want you."

I shook my head. I wouldn't do this. Poppy tugged on the hand I held. Drawing in a shallow breath, I leaned over her. "In a few minutes, when this storm passes, you'll return to loathing my very existence, and for good reason," I told her, our mouths inches apart. "You're going to hate that you begged me to kiss you, to do more. But even without my blood in you, I know you've never stopped wanting me." The words came out of me in a heated rush. "But when I'm deep inside you again, and I will be, you won't be able to blame the influence of blood or anything else."

Poppy stared as I pulled her hand from between those lovely thighs and lifted her palm to my mouth. I kissed the center, eliciting a gasp from her.

A heartbeat passed.

Maybe two.

Then, the blood-fueled lust began to clear, just as I said it would.

I let go of her hand when she pulled at my hold. Seconds ticked by. Minutes.

"I never should've left," I said, now that I was sure she had a somewhat clear mind. "I should've known something like this could happen, but I underestimated their desire for vengeance."

"They...they wanted me dead," she said.

"They will pay for what they did," I promised.

She moved a little, but nothing like before. "What will you do? Kill them?"

"I will, and I will kill anyone who thinks to follow their path."

Poppy swallowed. "And me...what are you going to do with me?"

I looked away from her, so fucking tired. "I already told you. I will use you to barter with the Queen to free Prince Malik. I swear, no more harm will come to you."

Poppy started to speak, but her entire body seemed to jerk. "Casteel?"

I froze.

"Kieran...Kieran said the name Casteel."

Had he?

I hadn't noticed. I'd been too preoccupied with saving her. I sensed her pulse picking up, and instead of anger or panic, there was actual relief as one last lie came crumbling down. She was finally accepting what she already had to know.

"Oh, my gods." Her hand folded over her mouth. "You're him." Her hand slipped to curl around the collar of her torn shirt. "That's what happened to your brother. Why you feel such sadness about him. He's the Prince you hope to use me to get back. Your name isn't Hawke Flynn. You're him! You're the Dark One."

Only past pain stopped me from reacting to being called the Dark One. "I prefer the name Casteel or Cas," I stated. "If you don't want to call me that, you can call me Prince Casteel Da'Neer, the second son of King Valyn Da'Neer, brother of Prince Malik Da'Neer, but do *not* call me the Dark One. That is *not* my name."

Poppy was still for a second, and then her anger and sorrow boiled over. I let it. And took it. The punch to my chest. The stinging slap across my cheek. She pushed at my shoulders as she screamed. I let her until I saw the dampness gathering in her eyes. I couldn't sit by and do nothing about that.

"Stop it." I grasped her upper arms, pulling her to my chest. "Stop it, Poppy."

"Let me go," she demanded, trembling so bad I feared she would break if I let her go.

That she would shatter this time, and there would be no one to blame but me. So, I held her tightly to me. I pressed my head to hers. "I'm fucking sorry," I whispered. "I'm sorry."

Not a single tear escaped Poppy, but she shook, beyond hearing me. I started to pull back, easing my hold. Her heart was racing. "Poppy?"

She twisted again, rolling onto her side as she gulped air. "Let me go."

"Poppy," I repeated, pressing my fingers to her pulse. I swore. "Your heart is racing too fast."

"Let me go!" she shouted so loud and fiercely it carried weight, had its own power.

I dropped an arm but didn't let go completely. No mortal's heart could beat like that continuously. She had to calm, but she was beyond that. Fuck. She planted her hands on the floor, her body still shaking. This was too much for her—too much for anyone. I knew what I would have to do. It would be yet another reason for her to hate me, but I'd rather her curse my very existence than be dead. I started to pull her back to me as she suddenly whipped my way. "*Poppy.*"

She pushed against my chest—

The breath I took was stolen.

She…she hadn't *pushed* against my chest. That wouldn't have caused the sudden, stunning, red-hot agony there. Pain that took my breath.

Poppy's wild, wide eyes locked with mine. Slowly, I looked down.

A dagger jutted from my chest.

Disbelief thundered through me. Poppy had stabbed me. Just as I'd told her to do under the willow if I did something she didn't like.

She jerked her hand off the hilt of the dagger and scuttled back. "I'm sorry," she whispered.

Dragging my stare from the dagger, I saw the tears she'd been fighting spill over. I'd only seen her cry for Vikter. For someone she cared about. "You're crying," I rasped, tasting blood. My blood.

Pure, unadulterated horror filled her beautiful eyes. She shot to her feet, backing away. Her entire body shook. "I'm sorry," she repeated.

I choked on a laugh as I pitched forward, slamming my hand against the floor. That laughter cost me, causing my chest to burn. "No," I gasped. "No, you're not."

Poppy shook her head. A sound came from her as she turned, ripping open the door. And then she did something I didn't think she'd ever really done before.

She *ran*.

IN THE SNOW

"Fucking gods," I grunted, stunned by the myriad of emotions. I was shocked that she'd actually done it, furious because she'd meant it, and also *amused*. I gripped the dagger's hilt.

Kieran suddenly appeared in the open door. "Good gods." He staggered forward a step, his breathing ragged. "She stabbed you."

"Just a little." I jerked the dagger free. Pain exploded as I thrust the blade into the floor. "*Fuck*."

"A little?" Kieran snarled. "Did she get your heart?"

"Almost." Or maybe just a little. Perhaps a nick. "And with bloodstone. A half an inch to the left?" Another wet, bloody laugh left me as anger seeped through my veins like a fire. "That would've…really hurt."

A low rumble of fury radiated from Kieran. My head jerked up as the predator in me woke. His skin had thinned, jaw elongating. The blue of his eyes was as brilliant as stars. His head swung toward the door as his chest expanded, stretching the seams of his tunic. It was more than just the bond kicking in, demanding he go after the one who'd harmed me. If he did, he would capture Poppy…

"No." I shoved to my feet, ignoring a burst of fresh agony. "Do not go after her. I will get her." I took a breath. It stung, but the blade was out. The wound would heal quickly. The pain would stop. "I will handle her."

Tendons stood out in his neck as his head whipped back to me. He vibrated with rage. "I'm going to—"

"*No*," I roared, lunging. I edged Kieran back from the door, fangs bared. "She is mine."

Kieran locked up, then took an unsteady step back, his mouth going slack. "Cas…"

There was nothing else for me to say. I turned from him, taking off. *She is mine* repeated itself as I leapt over the second-floor banister. I hit the ground hard, sending another wave of pain through me. Rising among the falling snow, I scanned the covered courtyard, dragging a hand over my chest. The wound was already closing.

"The woods." Elijah stood at the keep's entrance. "She ran into the woods."

Where did she think she was going, unprotected from the elements and without a weapon? My chin dipped, lips curving into a snarl. Whatever humor I'd found in the situation vanished. Stabbing me was one thing. Risking her life like this was something entirely different.

Poppy was bound and determined to get herself killed.

And perhaps I was, too.

The pain and blood loss sharpened my senses, leaving little room for anything beyond anger. That was dangerous for anyone, but especially an elemental Atlantian.

Crossing the courtyard in the blowing snow, I hit the woods and picked up speed. The snow-dusted branches were a blur as I caught her scent. Veering to the left, I rushed beneath a half-fallen pine.

I noticed a flash of dark red among the world of white and green, and a savage smile split my lips. There she was.

Warning bells rang in a distant part of my head. I'd felt this kind of madness before. I'd lived it. Regretted it. Accepted it. Only once. Decades ago, when I locked eyes with Shea and realized that she'd betrayed my brother. That madness was like standing on the precipice of a cliff, staring down at the fall.

And here I was, on that edge once more.

Like a predator, I made no sound. I gave no warning as I hunted Poppy and caught her with an arm around her waist.

She shrieked as her feet left the ground. I hauled her back against my chest, and the anguish I felt had nothing to do with the pain of the still-healing wound. It was for her. Me. This situation. Us. And the madness I was teetering on the verge of—the kind that erased all that mattered and left no winners. I gripped her chin, forcing her head back with the very hand that had killed so many. Those who had it coming. Those who didn't. My fingers pressed into Poppy's jaw just as they had *hers*.

"An Atlantian, unlike a wolven or an Ascended, can't be killed by a stab to the heart," I snarled into her ear. My anger at her reckless flight faded. The disbelief that she'd actually stabbed me vanished. All that was an agony that ran deeper than the physical. "If you wanted to kill me, you should've aimed for the head, Princess." My jaw throbbed. "But worse yet, you *forgot*."

"Forgot what?" she gasped.

"That it was *real*," I growled.

I began to fall into that madness.

I struck, sinking my fangs into the side of her throat. I felt her entire body jerk against mine as my arm clamped down on her. Hot blood hit my tongue. I didn't even taste it. I was falling, my mouth sealed to her throat, my fangs still buried deep in her flesh. I knew exactly what it felt like when the fangs remained in. The bite would feel like being burned alive, creating a firestorm of pain. Fragile skin would eventually tear. Her neck wouldn't be broken by my hands, but Poppy would—

No.

This wasn't Shea.

This was the Maiden.

The Chosen.

Penellaphe Balfour.

Poppy.

Mine.

Heart thundering, I withdrew as her warm blood splashed over my tongue, coating the inside of my mouth. I started to let her go, but then...

The taste of her hit me in a stunning, unexpected burst of sensation. Sweet. Fresh. *Power*. My mouth was still fused to her throat, and her blood flowed freely. The pain I'd caused had retreated the moment my fangs left her flesh. Now, my bite would create a wholly different kind of storm within her. In me.

Her taste was lush and rich, utter decadence. Her rapidly building arousal was pure sin. The heat of mine burned as I drank greedily. I groaned, lost in it all as I held her to me, but the taste of her...

Her *blood*, it was an awakening. There was something about it. Something *in* it. The inside of my mouth tingled. My skin hummed. There was something in her blood that shouldn't be there. That couldn't be. It was a charge of energy. Power. The pain of the wound was nowhere near as fierce.

Good gods.

That could only mean one thing.

She was—

Shock ripped through me. I tore myself away from her in disbelief.

Poppy stumbled, catching herself. She turned to me. I stood there, trembling as I watched blood seeping from my bite.

My chest rose and fell rapidly as she lifted a hand to her throat. She took a step back, and the shock of what I'd discovered faded.

Poppy was mortal, but her blood was also of my people. Atlantian.

"I can't believe it." I ran my tongue across my bottom lip, tasting her. Tasting the truth. My eyes closed as a groan of pleasure rumbled from my chest. She was half-Atlantian—and that part of her was fucking strong.

In an instant, so much made sense. My eyes opened. "But I should've known."

I did now.

Once more, *everything* changed. I was on her before I could take another breath. I took her mouth with mine as I fisted her hair. Relief crashed into *joy*—brilliant and airy. There was a way out of this for her, one that would truly ensure her safety.

But right now, relief and elation weren't the only things pumping through me—through *her*. Need and want came together. I kissed her as I wanted to from the first. No hiding my fangs, concealing who I was. And Poppy kissed me back just as fiercely, as desperately. She clung to me as I took her to the snow-covered ground, my mouth never leaving hers. Part of that was my bite. Once the pain left, pleasure came, but that only *partly* fueled her hungry little kisses as I rolled my hips against hers. I nipped at her lip, drunk on her breathy moan, on how she moved beneath me, rocking her hips, straining for more, wanting more.

From me.

Poppy wanted me.

That hadn't stopped when she learned of my betrayal. Our attraction couldn't be denied, but I needed to hear her say it.

Ending the kiss, I lifted my head to see her. "Tell me you want this." I rocked against her. "Tell me you need more."

"More," she whispered.

"Thank fuck," I growled, reaching between us, too needy and too fucking eager to be inside her. Because she *knew*. She knew the truth of me. There were no lies between us. I had to be inside her. Now. I grabbed the front of her breeches and yanked. Buttons sprang free.

"Goodness," she gasped.

I laughed, shoving her pants down. I bared one lovely leg. That was enough. I lifted my gaze to hers. "You know this shirt was beyond repair, right?"

Her brows pinched. "Wha—?"

Curling my hand in the front of the bloodstained shirt, I ripped it open, baring her breasts to me. Fuck. I tore open my breeches as my gaze hungrily traveled across her creamy skin, dampened by the falling snow that found its way through the trees. Her plump nipples, a darker pink, were hard and puckered. I saw the dried streaks of blood leftover from when she was attacked. I froze. I'd come so close to losing her…

"I will kill them," I swore. "I will fucking kill them all."

Poppy shuddered as I claimed her mouth, settled myself between her thighs, and sank into her slick, tight heat. Her kisses muffled my shout. I went at her, fast and hard, and it was fucking mind-blowing. The way she met each thrust. How she clutched at me, my shoulders, my hair, and any part of me she could get her hands on. The snow fell harder, heavier, as if it were answering our fierceness with its own.

But I wanted this to last.

I drew her tongue into my mouth, obsessed with her taste, then left her lips. Kissing my way down her throat, I came to my bite. A growl of raw satisfaction escaped from me as I licked the tiny punctures, grinning as she gasped and strained against me. Her grip on my shoulders tightened as I swirled my tongue over the bite.

But I couldn't stay there.

If I did, I'd reopen the wounds and drink more of her. I couldn't do that. She had my blood in her, but I'd been greedy earlier, and she had been so gravely wounded before.

Kissing her throat, I lifted my head. Our gazes locked. Her eyes were wide and a stunning shade of green as the snow dotted the loose strands of her crimson hair.

Gods, she was…she was so godsdamn unexpected in every way. So beautiful. So brave. So vicious.

Trailing my hand down her chest, I cupped her breast as I moved in and out of her, each thrust nearly undoing me and unraveling her. She felt too hot, too wet, and too damn good. My mouth returned to hers. She was just as hungry, as greedy. She lifted her hips, urging me deeper, harder, faster. I held back, a laugh giving way to a groan as she cried out in frustration.

I lifted my head. "I know what you want, but…"

She pressed her hips fully against mine, and I shook. "But what?"

My jaw hardened as I locked eyes with her. "I want you to say my name."

"What?"

I moved against her in slow circles. "I want you to say my real name."

Her lips parted on a sharp inhale.

I stilled inside her, heart pounding. "That's all I ask." My voice dropped as I toyed with her nipple. "It's acknowledgment. It's you admitting you are fully aware of who is inside you, who you want so badly, even though you know you shouldn't. Even though you want nothing more than to *not* feel what you do. I want to hear you say my real name."

"You're a bastard," she whispered, rolling her hips against mine.

I grinned. "Some call me that, yes, but that's not the name I'm waiting to hear, Princess."

Her lips pressed into a firm, tight line.

"How bad do you want it, *Poppy*?" I asked.

She gripped my hair, yanking my head down hard enough that my eyes widened. "Bad," she seethed. "Your *Highness*."

That was not—

Poppy lifted her legs, folding them around my waist. Before I could even fathom what she was up to, she rolled me onto my back. She planted her hands on my chest and rocked back as if to rise, taking me so deeply inside her that I forgot my fucking name.

"Oh." Poppy gasped, breaths ragged.

I stared at her through half-open eyes. "You know what?"

"What?" she whispered, her body twitching all around me.

"I don't need you to say my name," I told her. "I just need you to do that again, but if you don't start moving, you might actually kill me."

A sudden laugh left her. "I…I don't know what to do."

That soft chuckle. Those even softer words. My chest felt too fucking full as I grasped her bare hips. "Just move," I told her, showing her what I meant. I lifted her up the length of my rigid cock and then brought her back down. "Like that." I groaned at the heated friction of our bodies. "You can't do anything wrong. How have you not learned that yet?"

Poppy followed my instructions, tentatively moving up and down as the snow continued to fall. Her breath caught. She moved her palm up my shirt as she pitched forward. Her moan was the best kind of agony. "Like that?" I breathed.

I gripped her hips tighter. "Just like that."

Drawing her lip between her teeth, she rocked her hips, and with each torturous rise and fall, her movements grew more confident, and I became more enthralled.

I couldn't take my eyes off her as she rode me. The pleasure on her face, in her parted lips and glazed-over eyes. The sway of her heavy breasts, the tips of them disappearing behind the shredded shirt, only to reappear as she found an angle that caused her to gasp. My gaze dropped to where our bodies were joined as she began moving faster, grinding down on me until she came. Watching her take control like this, finding her pleasure, was the hottest fucking thing I'd ever seen.

And it undid me.

I moved, rolling her beneath me again. Closing my mouth over hers, I thrust into her heat as she held on, her nails digging into my skin. Release barreled down my spine as I took her, slamming my hips into her as pleasure erupted. I stayed seated deep inside her, the intensity of the pleasure shocking.

Fucking gods, the release lasted a small eternity. I was still twitching deep inside her when I pressed my forehead to hers. We remained like that for some time, our bodies joined, my hand at her waist, my thumb moving idly as our hearts and breathing slowed. We stayed in the falling snow longer than we probably should have, but I was reluctant to leave her because she was...gods, she was *mine*.

The possessiveness was a little shocking. I'd never felt that way for anyone. My brow furrowed.

"I don't...I don't understand," Poppy whispered.

"Don't understand what?" I shifted slightly above her, lifting my head.

"Any of this. Like how did this even happen?"

I started to pull out, but I caught the sudden tightening of her features. I halted. "Are you okay?"

"Yeah. Yes."

Poppy's eyes were closed. I wasn't sure I believed her. Worry grew. Had this been too rough? Had I been too rough?

"Are you sure?" I asked, rising onto an elbow.

She nodded.

"Look at me and tell me you're not hurt."

Thick lashes swept up. "I'm fine."

"You winced. I saw you."

Poppy slowly shook her head. "That's what I don't understand. Unless I completely imagined the last couple of days."

"No, you didn't imagine anything." I scanned her face as she blinked the snow from her lashes. "Do you wish that this, right here, hadn't happened?"

Her gaze darted away and then returned to mine. "No," she whispered. "Do…do you?"

"No, Poppy. I hate that you even have to ask that." I turned my head to the side, unsure what to say. To put to words anything I felt. "When we first met, it was like…I don't know. I was drawn to you. I could've taken you then, Poppy…"

The truth of that was something I hadn't allowed myself to see until that moment. I could've taken her the night at the Red Pearl. When she left there. Or when she snuck off to the library. I had so many chances. I would've found a way out of the city. She would've fought me, but she wouldn't have been able to stop me.

I shuddered. "I could've prevented a lot of what has happened, but I…I lost sight of a lot of things. Each time I was near you, I couldn't help but feel as if I knew you." I thought of what I'd tasted in her blood. A part of me had recognized what was in her. "I think I know why it's been like that."

At least, I thought that explained the strange sensations I felt when around her. We didn't always recognize half-Atlantians in such a manner, but there'd been stories of such—of the eather in our blood recognizing the eather in others.

I felt Poppy shiver, and it suddenly occurred to me that we were half-naked in the snow.

"You're cold." I rose above her, tugging my breeches up as I ignored the sharp pain when the tender skin on my chest pulled. I fastened what buttons remained, then extended a hand to her. "We need to get out of this weather."

Poppy had sat up, holding the torn sides of her shirt. She hesitated and then placed her hand in mine. "I tried to kill you."

She said it as if I'd forgotten, and I had to fight a grin as I pulled her up. "I know. I can't really blame you."

Her mouth dropped open as I knelt, grasping her pants and lifting them to her hips. "You don't?" she asked.

"No," I said. I had blamed her, but then again, I'd been angrier with her for running out here. "I lied to you. I betrayed you and played a role in the deaths of people you love. I'm surprised that was the first time you tried."

Poppy stared in silence.

"And I doubt it will be the last time you try." I lost the fight, and one side of my lips curled up as I tried to fasten her pants. Unfortunately, there were no buttons left. "Dammit." I then tried to, well, do something with the shirt. That wasn't working either. I cursed again. Reaching up, I pulled off my tunic. "Here."

Poppy was still standing there, looking at me as if I were the most confounding individual she'd ever met.

I probably was.

"You're...not mad?" she asked.

Our eyes locked. "Are you not still mad at me?"

"Yes," she answered without hesitation. "I'm still angry."

"And I'm still angry that you stabbed me in the chest." And then ran from me, but whatever. "Lift your arms."

Poppy did as I said.

"You didn't miss my heart, by the way. You got it pretty good," I admitted. It had definitely been more than a *nick*. I pulled my shirt down her arms. "That's why it took a minute to catch up to you."

"It took more than a minute." Her voice was muffled for a moment, and then her cute, irritated expression appeared.

She didn't need to know exactly what had delayed me. It hadn't been the stab wound. It had been Kieran. "It took a *couple* of minutes," I said, tugging down the sleeves.

Poppy looked down at the shirt she now wore and then at my chest. The wound was bright pink, the flesh a little jagged. "Will it heal?"

"It will be fine in a few hours. Probably sooner."

"Atlantian blood," she rasped.

"My body will immediately start to repair itself from any non-fatal wounds," I explained. "And I fed. That helped."

Her hand went to her throat before she quickly jerked it away. I raised a brow. "Will anything happen to me from...from you feeding?"

"No, Poppy. I didn't take enough, and you didn't take enough of mine earlier," I assured her. "You'll probably be a little tired later, but that's all."

Poppy was once more fixated on my chest. "Does it hurt?"

"Barely," I told her.

She lifted a hand, placing it flat against my chest. I stilled. She wasn't going to—

Warmth splashed my chest, rippling through my body in soft waves. It washed over me, taking with it the pain of the wound and the anguish that lived deeper.

A tremor rocked me as my jaw loosened. She'd taken the pain away.

I couldn't believe her generosity.

Hand trembling, I placed it over hers. "I should've known then," I said, voice thick as I lifted her hand to my mouth. It was stained with both of our blood. I kissed her knuckles.

"Known what?" she asked.

"Known why they wanted you so badly that they made you the Maiden."

The skin at the corners of her mouth pinched.

"Come." I held on to her hand as I started walking.

"Where are we going?"

"Now? We're going back inside so we can get cleaned up and…" I saw she had to hold up her pants. I sighed. I really should've taken my time with those buttons. Turning, I dipped, threading an arm behind her knees. I lifted her to my chest. "And, apparently, to find you some new pants."

Poppy blinked rapidly. "These were my only pair."

"I'll get you new ones." I strode forward. "I'm sure there is some small child around here who would be willing to part with their breeches for a few coins."

I grinned as her brows snapped together.

"And after that?" Poppy insisted as I stepped over a thick branch.

"I'm taking you home."

"Home?" Her breath snagged. "Back to Masadonia? Or to Carsodonia?"

"Neither." I looked down, my smile spreading wide. It was the kind of smile that hid nothing. "I'm taking you to Atlantia."

I WAS RIGHT

Our return to Haven Keep didn't go unnoticed. Everyone simply made themselves scarce as I crossed the courtyard in the falling snow with Poppy cradled to my chest.

Except for Kieran.

He stood at the second-floor railing, his arms folded across his chest. Our eyes locked. He raised a brow at the sight of me, shirtless— at the sight of us.

"You can put me down," Poppy muttered. "I can walk."

That was not the first time she'd said that. It was more like…the twentieth. I'd ignored the nineteen variations that came before. "If I do that, your pants will fall right off you." I kicked open the door to the stairwell. "And then you would expose your thighs—your very lovely thighs."

The flush in her face was visible, even in the darkened stairwell. "Only because you destroyed my clothing."

"Be that as it may, I doubt you want to flash anyone." I paused mid-step, glancing down at her. "Or is that what you'd prefer?"

Poppy blew out an exasperated breath. "No. That is not what I prefer."

I grinned as I started back up the steps. "I didn't think so."

She was quiet as we rounded the landing and I climbed the remaining steps. I imagined she was reliving the moment she'd plunged the dagger into my chest. Truth be told, her pants weren't the reason I'd insisted on carrying her. After all, I wouldn't complain if she flashed me. Her thighs were so very lush. But the snow was coming down in sheets, soaking the rest of her clothing. She was cold. Hell, I was even getting cold. But keeping her close also kept her as warm as possible. Plus, I was faster.

Entering the second-floor hall, her hands curled tighter in the shirt she now wore, and her face burned brighter. I shifted her higher, allowing her cheek to reach my shoulder. She turned her head, pressing her forehead against me.

It wasn't necessary for her to hide her face, though. Kieran's attention remained fixed on the heavy snowfall and the forest beyond.

Wanting her in my chamber since it was bigger and a bit nicer, I passed the room she'd been kept in and took her to mine. A faint smile tugged at my lips. Kieran had cleaned up the blood.

And removed the dagger I'd plunged into the floor. Smart move there.

I carried Poppy to the much larger bed and set her down, grateful that the flames in the fireplace were still strong. As I straightened, her mouth opened. "I know you have questions," I cut in. "I will answer them, but there are a few things I need to take care of."

Poppy's lips pinched but she didn't argue for once. Turning from her, I stopped with my hand on the door, once more reluctant to leave her. I looked back at her. She was still where I'd put her, hands now resting on the bed.

"I'll be back," I promised, then stepped out into the hall. Forced myself.

Dragging a hand through my damp hair, I turned to Kieran.

"Do I even want to know why she is wearing your shirt and you are without one?" Kieran asked.

"Probably not." Lowering my hand, I joined him at the railing. "Thank you for cleaning up the room."

Kieran nodded. "No one needs to smell your blood."

A wry smile tugged at my lips as I rested my hands on the railing. "I need you to watch over her for a little bit."

"You trust me with that?" was all he asked. He likely already knew what I intended to do. "After I wanted to go after her?"

"But you didn't," I reminded him. "And you won't."

"Because she's..." Kieran looked at me then. "How did you say it? 'She is mine?'"

"That's not exactly why." I rolled my neck. "She's half-Atlantian."

Kieran pushed back from the railing. "You are certain?"

"I tasted her blood. I'm sure."

His forehead creased as his brows lifted. "Well, I have a lot of questions about that."

"I bet you do." The snow was already well on its way to covering the tracks I'd left. "But what's important right now is that she's one of us—and, Kieran, the part of her that's Atlantian? It's *strong*. Look at my chest," I said, and he did just that. "The wound is far more healed than it normally would be."

Kieran stared, then his gaze cut to the door I'd exited from. "Damn." He ran his hand over his hair, clasping the back of his neck. "It explains so much. Her abilities. Why the Ascended want her."

"It does." I looked down at my hands. They were still stained with blood. Fresh streaks would join them soon. "And it doesn't."

It took a moment for Kieran to understand. "Her parents? Her brother…"

I nodded slowly. There was no way they were her parents—at least one of them couldn't have been. But Ian? He could still be a half brother. Regardless, all of this would still come as a blow.

Kieran squinted. "They planned to use her to Ascend the Lords and Ladies in Wait? But why? They have Malik. They…"

I tensed all over. I knew what he was thinking. That they needed Poppy because Malik was… "He's still alive."

"I didn't say he wasn't."

My heart thumped heavily. "He's probably weakened, and using him to Ascend all those in Wait would likely kill him. That's why they need Poppy. It's the only thing that makes sense, especially if her blood is strong."

"And for them to know that, they must have…"

Drank from her at some point, likely without her knowledge. My hands tightened on the cold railing until I heard the wood groan. I pushed away. "This won't take too long."

"You're wrong, by the way," Kieran stated when I was halfway down the hall.

I stopped, looking back at him.

"The reason I won't hurt her has nothing to do with her being half-Atlantian or because she's one of us." Kieran faced me. "It has everything to do with the fact that I was right."

I lifted my brows. "About what?"

"You. Her." His head tilted to the side, and when he spoke again, his voice was low. "She's yours, and you care about her. That's why. And don't even try to deny it. Not after the lengths you've gone to in order to keep her safe." He took a step forward. "The lengths you are about to go to, to ensure that what happened in that cell doesn't happen again."

A faint tickle of sensation hit the nape of my neck. There was no point in denying it. "I do. I care about her."

Kieran smiled like a kid who'd just run off with a handful of sweets.

"That wasn't the reaction I expected," I stated, tone dry.

"Honestly?" He lifted his hands. "I'm relieved."

My brows inched up. "Really?"

"Yeah. It proves you aren't the piece of shit I knew you weren't."

"How in the fuck does it prove that?"

"Because being with her wasn't about getting off. It's because you care about her. That changes things."

Everything *had* changed.

Kieran shook his head. "In any other situation, it would be funny for you to fall for her—"

"Fall for her?" My stomach dipped as if I were standing on the edge of the cliffs in the Skotos. "I said I care about her, Kieran. I didn't say I'd fallen in love with her. Lust? Yes. Respect and admiration for her? Fuck yes."

Kieran's brows creased further as he looked at me like I was missing half a brain. "What do you think lust, respect, admiration, and caring for someone adds up to?"

"Not what you think it does. Maybe for some people, but not me. I don't—" I stopped myself, but what I didn't say hung in the air between us.

I didn't deserve to be in love—to experience that. Not after my actions had led to Malik's capture. Not after Shea. Not with all the blood on my hands. Not after what I'd done to Poppy.

And Kieran knew that. He just didn't want to say it. However, this otherwise pointless conversation about love and shit sparked an idea. A fucking insane one, but one that would not only give me what I needed and Poppy what she deserved, but so much more.

"Cas," Kieran started.

I held up my hand, stopping him. My mind raced, filling in the blanks. This would give Poppy all the protection she'd ever need and then some while ensuring the Blood Crown did anything they could to prevent the knowledge of what she was. No one would dare touch her—not Atlantian or Descenter. Not even my father. My lips curved up.

"Why are you smiling like that?" Kieran asked.

"Look, I do care about her, but that's not the point here. She is one of us, and there's no way they didn't know that." I crossed the space, stopping in front of him. "Think about what that means."

"For once, I'm not sure I follow."

"The Blood Crown rules through lies, Kieran. Everything about them and everything they tell their people is a lie. And Poppy?" I jerked my chin at the chamber door. "She is the foundation of those lies."

Kieran's eyes widened as it began to click. "They've told the people she's Chosen by the gods and, fuck, maybe she is, but we know she's half-Atlantian."

"And based on the lies they've told? Wouldn't that make her half-monster?" I said, smirking. "And wouldn't they do anything to prevent that knowledge from getting out?"

Kieran nodded as a slow smile began tipping up his lips. "Fuck yeah, they would, because if it's revealed that she's part Atlantian?" He huffed out a laugh. "It would begin their end, collapsing all their other lies." His smile faded. "But how are you going to prove that? Better yet, how are we going to keep her alive? Alastir will still come, and half-Atlantian or not, your father could still make demands."

"My father can." I started backing up, my smile spreading. "But he won't."

Kieran stiffened. "Cas."

"Don't worry," I told him. "I have a plan."

"But that *does* worry me."

I laughed, the sound traveling down the hall. "Keep watch over her."

Leaving Kieran to do just that, I made my way to the main floor of the keep. I found Magda and Elijah in his study.

The bearded Descenter looked up from the ledgers piled on his desk. "Not sure if you realize this or not, but you're half-undressed."

"And it appears as if you've been stabbed." Magda's hand fluttered to her belly. "In the chest."

"I'm fine, but speaking of clothing, is it possible for you to find something that would fit Penellaphe?"

Magda frowned as she rose from her chair. "Is the clothing I brought before unable to be laundered?"

My lips pursed. "That would be a no."

"Okay." She drew out the word. "Do you need clothing?"

"Likely, but that can wait. First, can you have hot water sent to my chambers? Kieran is there with her, and she will remain there."

"Oh, man," Elijah murmured while Magda nodded.

"And bloodstone." I looked at Elijah. "I'm going to need bloodstone. Lots of it."

"You're going down to the cells?" Elijah asked.

"No," I said. "I want them brought to the Great Hall."

He stood, rubbing his chin through his beard. "Oh, man, oh, man."

I smiled.

It didn't take long to wrangle a couple dozen bloodstone stakes. They'd been placed in a canvas bag and dropped in the center of the Great Hall, the space all had to pass through to enter the dining hall. It was empty now except for Delano, the doors closed on either end.

"You feeling up to this?" I asked him as I waited.

Delano nodded, the set of his jaw hard. There was nothing boyish about his features. "I'm more than feeling up to this."

"Good." I glanced at him. "I'm glad you're okay."

"So am I." A quick grin appeared. "I wouldn't be if it weren't for her. She saved my life, Cas, and she didn't have to," he said, and I had a feeling that was why he was so willing to carry this out. "I owe her. You know what that means."

I did know what it meant when a wolven made that pledge. It was damn near an unbreakable oath. He would guard her with his life. Even against me, if it came to it.

I glanced at the door, hearing footsteps. I bent, reaching into the canvas. My fingers curled around a smooth bloodstone spike. "You never have to worry about me harming her, Delano."

"I know," he said, stretching his neck from side to side. "That I know."

The door opened, and a trembling mortal was escorted inside.

One who had been given a second chance to live out his life with his wife and child.

He'd thrown that away.

Naill and Elijah let go of Mr. Tulis. The man staggered forward, his hands not bound but clasped. His wide, frightened eyes were unfocused. "I'm sorry—"

"You're not here to apologize. We are past that." I went to where he stood, each step slow and measured. "She had nothing to do with what happened to your other children, nor did she have anything to do with the Rite."

"She is the Maiden—"

I caught him by the throat, silencing him. "Her name is Penellaphe Balfour. You should know the name of the person who felt sorrow for you and your family. You should know the name of the one you plotted to kill." I lifted him to the tips of his toes. "And you should know the name of the one I told you not to harm."

His eyes bulged. "I-I'm—"

"No." I tightened my grip. "You threw away your life, not that of your wife or son. Let that be your last thought as you leave this realm."

With the spike in my other hand, I drove it through his chest, the bloodstone slicing through mortal tissue and bone like warm butter. His death wasn't instantaneous—I left the spike in, after all—but it was quicker than he deserved. He was dead before I impaled him to the wall.

They brought the next one in. Ivan. He already knew what was coming. Didn't say a word. He didn't beg or fight, and he, too, ended up on the wall. The rest were brought in, one after another. Wolven. Atlantian. Mortal. Some fought, swinging fists, baring fangs, and shifting into their wolven forms. Some pleaded, dropping to their knees. Some were already dead, having been dealt with during the attack. They all ended up the same. A spike to the chest or head and hanging on the wall.

I showed them more kindness than they'd shown Poppy. Those alive all died either immediately or within minutes, and I didn't feel a fucking ounce of remorse. None of *them* did. All they felt was regret for the life they'd forfeited: theirs.

Blood splattered both Delano's and my chest when Elijah and Naill dragged in the last one.

Jericho.

They shoved him forward. The wolven caught himself before toppling over. His pale blue eyes widened as he saw the wall of the Great Hall. "Cas," he said, lifting both arms. "We can—"

"We can do what, Jericho?" I flipped a spike in my hand. "Talk this out?" I laughed. "We are beyond that, my friend. You were warned, and you were given grace." I pointed at his stump. "And yet you betrayed me. Not once, but twice."

"Betrayed you?" Jericho stiffened, his skin thinning. Beside me, Delano sighed. He was going to shift. "I have stood beside you for *years*. I've done all you've asked and more."

"And yet you *continuously* did the thing I asked you not to do. I know I sound repetitive, but you were warned multiple times not to touch her." I flipped the spike again. "You only lived the first time because Kieran managed to talk me out of killing you. He didn't even try this time."

"Of course, he didn't," Jericho snarled, voice guttural. "If you're getting your dick wet in the Maiden, then so is he—" He yelped, falling backward under the force of the spike I threw. He hit the floor hard. "Fuck."

I prowled toward him. "You know what the funny thing is, Jericho?" As he reached for the spike, I stomped my foot down on his right arm, breaking the bones. "I always knew I would kill you one day."

"You...you missed my heart," he grunted. "You prick. I...I never thought you'd kill me...over the fucking Maiden," he rasped, blood trickling from his mouth.

"No." I pushed down harder with my foot. Another bone crunched. Jericho screamed. "I wasn't aiming for your heart, you fucking cunt."

Understanding dawned, and then, *then* I saw fear. I gave his ruined arm one more punishing grind of my boot before stepping back. Delano was there, grasping Jericho by the arm.

"You will live," I told him. "Until I'm ready for you to die."

"How can you...do this?" Jericho growled, snapping at Delano as Elijah took hold of his other arm. They lifted him as I went to the canvas bag and pulled out two more spikes. "You're making a mistake—"

"You never learn, do you?" Delano snarled. "Can you at least shut the fuck up?"

"How about you suck my—?" Jericho yelped as Delano drove his knee into said cock.

Elijah laughed. "Damn, my little marshmallow's getting kinda crispy."

With Naill's help, they got him to the wall, holding his arms outstretched. Jericho, of course, did not shut the fuck up. "You've all...betrayed your kin and...kingdom. And for what? She's...basically the Ascended."

"She is not," I said, thrusting a spike through his forearm. He shouted.

His lips peeled back over bloodstained teeth. "You...you think you can just will people...into forgetting what she is?"

I sighed.

"She'll never be...safe here!" he shouted, spitting blood as it coursed down his chest.

"Oh, yes, she will be." I drove the final spike through his remaining hand as the others backed off.

"You're out...of your mind," he swore, breathing labored. "If you...really think that."

"I know it." I caught his jaw, forcing his head back against the wall as I leaned in close and whispered the truth about Poppy and what I'd planned.

And Jericho?

That motherfucker finally shut his mouth.

PLANS HAVE CHANGED

I made use of the chamber Poppy had originally been placed in to bathe and change into fresh clothing. The water was fucking freezing, but I didn't want to return to her covered in blood and smelling like death. Hair damp, I stepped back into the hall. Kieran was waiting outside.

He hadn't been earlier. "She's likely asleep again."

"Again?"

"She fell asleep while bathing," he answered.

"You woke her from a *bath*?" My eyes narrowed.

"She was in there for quite some time. I called out to her more than once," he explained. "When she didn't answer, I figured I should check on her."

"How did she handle your intrusion?"

A small smile appeared. "She said that among her people, it was impolite to stare."

I faced him. "And were you staring?"

His smile kicked up a notch. That was...interesting. "A little." His eyes met mine. "I saw her scars. Some of them."

I tensed, though not because he'd obviously been staring more than just a little. Anyone else? They'd already be dead. But I knew she was self-conscious of those scars.

"I told her that among my people, scars are never hidden," Kieran continued. "That they are always honored."

I relaxed. Poppy...she needed to hear that. Know that. "You're lucky she had no weapon on her."

Kieran snorted. "Before her nap, she asked some questions about Atlantia."

"I imagine she did." I glanced at the closed door. "I told her I was taking her home. To Atlantia."

One eyebrow rose. "Is that a part of the plan I'm not supposed to worry about? Because I am."

I went to stand beside him. "I plan to marry her."

Kieran slowly turned his head to me. A moment passed, his expression remaining unreadable. "Is that so?"

I nodded. "What happened to her in that cell won't happen again if she is my wife. It offers her protection."

The other eyebrow rose.

"And with her as my wife, the threat of us tearing down all their lies becomes more real. After all, if the gods have forsaken the Atlantians as the Ascended claim, then surely the Chosen—the child of the gods—would not be able to marry one. It's more likely the Blood Crown will release my brother."

Another moment passed. "And?"

"And once Malik is free, Poppy will be free of me." I lifted my chin. "I told you that I care about her, so I have no intention of forcing her to remain married to someone she hates."

"Someone she hates?" Kieran repeated, one side of his lips curling up. "When you went to bring her back to the keep, you were with her. I know you were. I smelled you on her."

"Just because she's attracted to me doesn't mean she would want to remain married to the man who kidnapped her."

"Or set her free," he said, to which I frowned. "That's a different way to look at what you've done, isn't it? Set her free."

Watching the snow fall, I supposed that was a lovely revisionist version of how we'd gotten to this point. "I killed those she's cared about, both directly and indirectly. I don't expect nor seek her forgiveness, Kieran. We will not remain husband and wife."

"If you say so."

"I know so." The back of my neck prickled again, stronger than before.

Kieran watched me, head tilted. "You've been doing that a lot of late."

"Doing what?"

"Rubbing the back of your neck."

I was? My hand was on the nape of my neck, so yeah, I'd been doing that. "Think I pulled a muscle."

Kieran snorted.

"What? Like that's not possible?"

"Yeah." He looked away. "You really think Alastir won't see through this ploy? Your father?"

"Well, for starters, I plan to be gone before he gets here. If the snow ends. We'll leave in the morning if possible. Either way, they won't see through this—if I'm convincing enough," I told him. "Which I plan to be."

Kieran's eyes narrowed on me. "Please tell me you're going to tell her about these plans. That you're not—"

"I will announce to those here that we are to marry. That is only to ensure her safety while we're here."

"That's smart."

"But she is no longer a pawn, Kieran. She will be fully aware of this ploy," I swore.

"And if she doesn't agree to it?"

I exhaled heavily. "If she doesn't, then I...I won't force her. And I know what that means, what I will be choosing," I said before Kieran could. "But I will just have to convince Poppy to go along with this."

Kieran choked on a laugh, and I couldn't help but smile. "By the way," he said, "your plan is...insane."

"I know." I followed his gaze to the snow. "But not only will it work, it's the least I can do for her."

Kieran was silent for several heartbeats. "But will it be enough?"

I knew what he meant. It was something I hadn't allowed myself to dwell on. Freeing Malik took priority, but bringing him home wouldn't fix everything in Atlantia, not with us running out of land. Our people had strengthened in the years since the war, replacing the numbers we'd lost and then some. That was good, except it wasn't. We were running out of territory, and in the not-too-distant future, resources would become limited. If we didn't expand beyond Spessa's End, the future of Atlantia would be a troubled one. And besides that, would Malik be ready to take the crown? My chest hollowed as my throat dried. He'd be fine. Eventually. I would be there to help him. Our parents. Kieran and everyone else. He'd just need time.

"None of Atlantia's struggles are Poppy's," I said. "She is not to be burdened with them."

"A Princess who is to remain unburdened by the plight of her kingdom?" Kieran murmured.

"A Princess in name only," I reminded him.

He turned, angling his body toward mine. "If she goes along with this, that means a part of her accepts the truth about the Ascended, and I don't know her all that well, but you do. Do you think she will be satisfied with just freedom? While the Ascended continue on?" he asked. "Will she be able to remain unburdened?"

That was a damn good question. One I didn't have an answer to.

I stepped back. "It's almost time for supper. I'm sure she's hungry."

Kieran nodded, his lips curving into a faint smile as he looked away. "I'll be waiting."

Turning, I crossed the hall and entered my chamber, closing the door behind me.

I didn't make it far at first. I saw her curled on her side, the dark crimson strands of her hair spread across the pillow. The sight of her seemed to rob me of the ability to move.

Sounded fucking silly as hell, but I had to will myself to take a step. I went to her side and sat on the edge of the bed. The movement didn't wake her. I hadn't taken that much blood from her, but she'd been through a lot. She was exhausted, but she needed to eat.

And if I told her about my plans before then? She likely wouldn't consume a single bite. She would be mad at me by the end of supper, but I preferred her anger over her being harmed. Besides, I always found myself somewhat bemused by her ire.

There was likely something wrong with me.

I reached over, brushing her hair back from her neck. The two puncture wounds caused a visceral reaction. The sudden, sharp pulse of lust was damn strong. I couldn't remember ever reacting that way to the sight of my bite before.

My fingers drifted from her cheek to the skin just above the bite. Poppy...things were just different with her.

Always.

Her eyes fluttered open, locking with mine. She didn't speak. Neither did I while I waited for her to demand that I not touch her. She didn't, but I withdrew my hand anyway, knowing better than to push my luck. "How are you feeling?"

Poppy's nose scrunched, and then she laughed.

Completely caught off guard by the reaction, I felt myself grin. "What?"

"I can't believe you're asking me if I'm okay when I stabbed you in the heart."

"Do you think you should be asking me that question?" I countered. When she didn't answer, my smile spread. "I'm relieved to hear that you care. I'm perfectly fine."

"I don't care," she muttered, sitting up.

"Lies," I murmured. The thing was, I knew she did. She wouldn't have taken my pain away earlier if she didn't, but she didn't *want* to care. My chest tightened. I couldn't blame her for that. "You didn't answer my question."

"I'm fine." She stared at the dull yellow of the quilt draped over her.

"Kieran said you dozed off in the bath."

"Did he tell you he came into the bathing chamber?" she asked.

"Yes."

Her gaze shot to mine.

"I trust Kieran," I said. "You've been asleep for several hours."

"Is that not normal?"

"It's not abnormal. I guess I'm…" I frowned. "I guess I'm feeling guilty for biting you."

"You guess?" she stammered.

I wasn't sure. If I hadn't bitten her, I never would've discovered that she was half-Atlantian. Then again, there was a lot with Poppy that I felt guilt for but didn't regret. "I believe so."

"You should feel guilt!" she exclaimed.

I raised a brow. "Even though you stabbed me and left me to die?"

Her mouth clamped shut. "You didn't die. Obviously."

"Obviously. I was barely winded."

"Congratulations." Poppy rolled her eyes.

Amused, I chuckled.

Poppy, however, was not amused. Shoving the quilt aside, she scooted to the other side of the bed. "Why are you here? To take me back to the cell?"

"I should. If anyone other than Kieran knew you had stabbed me, I would be expected to."

Poppy stood. "Then why don't you?"

"I don't want to."

Her hands opened and closed as she stared. "So, what now? How is this going to work, Your *Highness*?"

My jaw clenched.

"You'll keep me locked up in a room until you're ready for us to leave?" she asked.

"Do you not like this room?"

"It's far better than a dirty cell, but it's still a prison," she said. "A cage, no matter how nice the accommodations are."

She was right. "You would know, wouldn't you? After all, you've been imprisoned since you were a child. Caged and veiled."

Surprisingly, she didn't deny that as she turned to the small window, her arms folded over her chest.

My gaze dropped. The breeches she wore fit her like a second skin. I liked it. A lot. "I came here to escort you to dinner."

"Escort me to dinner?" Her eyes widened.

"I feel like there's an echo in this room, but yes, I imagine you're hungry," I said. "And we'll discuss what will happen next when we have some food in our stomachs."

"No."

"No?" I repeated. When there was no further explanation, I stretched out on my side, plopping my cheek on my fist. "You have to be hungry."

Poppy shook her head, but the act didn't match her words. "I am hungry."

I sighed. "Then what's the problem, Princess?"

"I don't want to eat with you. That's the problem."

I fought a grin. "Well, it's a problem you're going to have to get over because it's your only option."

"See, that's where you're wrong. I have options." She turned from me.

Big mistake.

I rose silently.

"I'd rather starve than eat with you, *Your Highness*—" Poppy squeaked as I stepped in front of her. "Gods," she gasped, pressing her hand to her chest.

"That's where you're wrong, Princess." I met her stare. "You don't have options when it comes to your own well-being and your own foolish stubbornness."

Her brows shot up. "Excuse me?"

"I won't let you weaken or starve yourself because you're mad. And I do get it. I get why you're upset. Why you want to fight me on everything, every step of the way." I took a step toward her. She didn't back down. Her chin lifted, and I knew she was digging in for a fight, but little did she know, it wouldn't get the desired effect. "I want you to, Princess. I enjoy it."

Poppy blinked. "You're twisted."

"Never said I wasn't. So, fight me. Argue with me. See if you can actually injure me next time." I paused. "I dare you."

Her arms unfolded. "You're...there's something wrong with you."

"That may be true, but what is also true, is the fact that I will not let you put yourself in unnecessary danger."

"Maybe you've forgotten, but I can handle myself," she retorted.

"I haven't forgotten. I won't ever prevent you from lifting a sword to protect your life or those you care about," I told her. "But I won't let you shove that sword through your own heart to prove a point."

She was quiet as she appeared to process what I shared, and then she let out a shriek of frustration. "Of course, you won't! What good am I to you dead? I imagine you still plan to use me to free your brother."

"You are nothing to me if you're dead," I snapped, my irritation flaring to life. That wasn't at all what I'd been getting at.

Poppy's sharp inhale stung like a lash against my skin.

This was not a good start.

"Come. The food will grow cold." I took her hand, but she didn't budge. "Don't fight me on this, Poppy. You need to eat, and my people need to see that you have my protection if you have any hope of not finding yourself spending your days locked in a room."

Poppy clearly wanted to fight, but in this, she relented.

For now.

MY PRINCESS

Glasses and plates clinked, and laughter and conversation hummed while Poppy stared at the dining hall's closed doors.

She was not pleased.

It could've been the argument before we left for supper, or Kieran's knowing chuckle when she all but stomped out of the chamber. But what really bothered her was what she'd seen in the hall outside.

What everyone in the dining hall had seen.

My message.

My warning to others that I'd left hanging on the wall.

Poppy had been horrified and disturbed, especially when she realized Jericho still breathed, though what disturbed her wasn't the fact that he lived. It was that he suffered.

The fucker had tried to murder her. Yet she felt bad for him. That was a level of basic decency many didn't have when it came to someone who sought to harm them. I sure as fuck didn't.

And I sure as fuck didn't like that it made me wish I was that decent.

The things done to me had nearly killed that within me. What had been required of me and still was finished it off.

I shifted in my seat, sipping wine as others at the table talked. My gaze flicked to her plate. Kieran had offered her some of his beef. She'd accepted, but the meat remained untouched. He'd also placed a piece of roasted duck on her plate. I'd added some potato and broke off a hunk of cheese, her favorite. It all remained.

"Poppy," I said softly.

She looked up at me as if coming out of a daze.

"Eat," I said, voice low.

She speared a piece of meat, then moved on to the potatoes. I could tell she was forcing herself.

My grip on the glass tightened. I'd clearly shocked her. Maybe even made her afraid of me, so much so that it had dampened the fire inside her. An ache settled in the back of my throat. "You don't agree with what I did to them?"

Poppy looked at me wordlessly.

I sat back, glass still in hand. "Or are you so shocked, you're actually speechless?"

She swallowed, placing her fork down. "I wasn't expecting that."

"Can't imagine you were." I lifted the glass.

"How…?" Poppy cleared her throat. "How long will you leave them there?"

"Until I feel like it."

"And Jericho?"

"Until I know for sure no one will dare to lift a hand against you again," I answered, smirking as those seated at the table listened in.

"I don't know your people very well," Poppy said quietly. "But I would think that they have learned a lesson."

Right now, I didn't give a fuck what they thought. I took a drink. "What I did disturbs you."

Poppy's stare shifted from me to her plate. The non-answer was answer enough.

"Eat," I insisted, lowering the wine. "I know you need to eat more than that."

Her eyes narrowed, and I could practically see her tongue sharpening, but she didn't unleash the swift verbal cut I knew she was capable of. Instead, I got an answer. One that surprised me.

"When I saw them, it horrified me. That was shocking, especially Mr. Tulis. What you did was surprising, but what disturbs me the most is that I—" Poppy drew in a deep breath. "I don't feel all that bad. Those people laughed when Jericho talked about cutting my hand off. Cheered when I bled and screamed and offered other options for pieces for Jericho to carve and keep," she continued in the silence as those around us listened. "I'd never even met most of them before, and they were happy to see me ripped apart. So, I don't feel sympathy."

"They don't deserve it," I assured her.

"Agreed," Kieran murmured.

Poppy's chin lifted. "But they're still mortal—or Atlantian. They still deserve dignity in death."

I eyed her. "They didn't believe you deserved any dignity."

"They were wrong, but that doesn't make this right," she countered.

I searched the beautiful lines of her face. Poppy was vicious, but she was still decent. "Eat."

"You're obsessed with ensuring that I eat," she snapped.

There was that fire. I grinned. "Eat, and I'll tell you our plans."

That got her eating.

I took a drink to hide my smile. I waited until she'd made some progress before sharing, "We're leaving in the morning."

"Tomorrow?" Poppy's voice pitched.

I nodded. "As I said, we'll be going home."

She took a long drink. "But Atlantia is not my home."

"But it is," I reminded her. "At least, partly."

"What does that mean?" Delano asked from where he sat across from her.

"It means it's something I should've figured out sooner. So many things now make sense when they didn't before. Why they made you the Maiden, how you survived a Craven attack. Your gifts," I said, lowering my voice so only those immediately around could hear. "You're not mortal, Poppy. At least, not completely."

Delano's blue eyes sharpened. "Are you suggesting that she's...?"

"Part Atlantian?" I finished for him, eyes on Poppy. Her hand trembled slightly as she took another drink. "Yes."

"That's impossible," she whispered.

"Are you sure?" Delano asked, but then his attention cut to Poppy—to what she thought she hid behind her hair. He jerked back in his seat.

"One hundred percent," I said.

"How?" Poppy demanded.

I grinned, looking at the same spot on her Delano had been. I raised my brows.

Her gaze swung to Delano and then moved to Kieran.

"It's rare, but it happens," Kieran stated, running his thumb over the rim of his chalice. "A mortal crosses paths with an Atlantian. Nature takes its course, and nine months later, a mortal child is born. But every so often, a child of both kingdoms is born. Mortal and Atlantian."

"No. You have to be mistaken." Poppy twisted toward me. "My mother and father were mortal—"

"How can you be sure?" I asked. "You thought I was mortal."

"But my brother," she said. "He's an Ascended now."

"That's a good question," Delano remarked.

And it was, which meant I had to point out something I honestly, truly, did not want to, but there was no way around it. "Only if we're working off the assumption that he is your full, blooded brother."

"Or that he even has Ascended," Naill murmured as Poppy drew back, face paling. I knew her mind went to the worst-case scenario there. The glass she held started to slip.

I reached out, catching it. I placed it down and then folded my hand over hers, drawing it to the table. "Your brother is alive."

"How can you be sure?" she whispered.

"I've had eyes on him for months, Poppy," I told her. "He hasn't been seen during the day, and I can only imagine that means he is an Ascended."

Elijah cursed. Another spat on the floor. Poppy's eyes closed, but only briefly. This was a lot to take in, but she was strong. Likely more so than many of us in the hall.

"Why would they keep me alive if they knew?" she asked.

My lips thinned. "Why do they keep my brother?"

She jolted. "I can't do that. Right? I mean, I don't have...the, uh, parts for it."

"Parts?" Kieran coughed. "What have you been filling her head with?"

I shot him a bland look. "Teeth. I do believe she means these." Curling my upper lip, I ran my tongue over one fang. "They don't need that. They just need your blood for them to complete the Ascension."

Poppy shuddered as she slowly shook her head.

"I'm curious, Cas. Why must we go home?" Kieran asked, even though he already knew the answer. "When we will be going farther away from where your brother is held." He raised his voice on purpose.

"It is the only place we can go," I replied, eyes fixed on Poppy. "Did you know that an Atlantian can only marry if both halves are standing in the soil of their land? It's the only way for them to become whole."

The entire hall went as quiet as a tomb as those bright, beautiful green eyes fastened on mine. I could see it dawning on her. Poppy's lips parted.

And I knew that what I was about to do would stoke the fire in her to a violent inferno. My lips started to curve up in anticipation, and yes, there was definitely something very wrong with me.

I lifted our joined hands and spoke loud enough for the entire dining hall to hear. "We go home to marry, my *Princess*."

PRESENT XII

"I really thought you were going to stab me again after I announced my plans to marry you," I said, grinning as I lay beside Poppy.

The lamplit chamber was quiet as I talked, the surprisingly cool breeze stirring the curtains of the open windows. Word had arrived that my father was a few hours out from Carsodonia, and Kieran had left to ensure that his arrival didn't ignite any unrest in the still-calm capital. I'd sent Delano with him, knowing that Perry would want to see him. It had taken some urging, but Delano finally relented.

I was actually…relaxed. The shadows beneath Poppy's eyes were gone. Her skin *almost* felt normal. That fragile hope had grown, but it wasn't the only reason I felt at ease.

Poppy would wake soon.

I couldn't answer how I was certain of that, other than the knowledge, the sense, coming to me through the bond. Soon, those beautiful eyes would open, and she would know herself. I wouldn't allow myself to believe anything else.

"So, I wasn't at all surprised that you made a run for it. Picking a lock? Did I tell you how impressed I was? Not just with that but your utter fearlessness. Don't get me wrong. I was also furious you'd make a run for it in the cold and with just—what was it? A supper knife?"

I could vividly recall how fiercely she'd fought me—and her desire that night and the days and weeks that followed. She hadn't been the only one, though. I'd been in a state of denial.

I smothered a yawn as I tightened my arm around her waist. I searched my memories, looking for the moment I'd stopped pretending.

Had it been in the pantry when I stole a few kisses? Or before that, when Lord Chaney took her? I'd descended into a black rage when I saw her with those bite marks. But I hadn't stopped pretending. Not even after that morning when I woke in bloodlust and feasted between her thighs instead of on her blood. Had it occurred when we arrived in Spessa's End, and I saw her wonderment upon seeing the Atlantian outpost? Or had it been when I took her to the cavern?

"It wasn't any of those moments," I whispered. "I never pretended when it came to my want of you. From the first time in the Red Pearl to this moment, what I felt was real. It was always real because I…I'd fallen in love with you long before I realized it. I was on the edge before we even left Masadonia, and I began falling when we arrived in New Haven. By the time we made it to Spessa's End, I knew I was in love with you."

I swallowed, letting my eyes drift shut. In truth, the process of falling in love with Poppy had started in Masadonia. It had just taken me that time to realize I could be worthy of such an emotion after betraying her—after all I'd done. That I could allow myself to love and be loved without hesitation or conditions.

I turned my cheek, pressing a kiss to her temple, then told her about our time in Spessa's End and how I'd felt when we talked—when we were finally honest with each other. I shared with her how it'd felt when we exchanged vows and struggled to put those emotions to words because none known did them any justice. And then I told her how stunned I'd been when we fought the Ascended in Spessa's End and what she'd been willing to do to ensure my safety.

"There are similarities between your actions when we were surrounded and what…what Shea did. She, too, had been willing to do anything. But…" I cleared my throat. "I'll tell you about that when you wake. What really happened."

Kieran was right.

Poppy would understand.

It was just something I still had to come to terms with.

Kissing the spot beside her ear once more, I began telling her more. Those moments in the carriage after the battle in Spessa's End, and then the trip to the Skotos. My eyes stayed closed through it all, and the pauses between what I said grew longer and longer until I drifted off to sleep.

I wasn't sure how long I'd slept, but what felt like icy fingertips against the nape of my neck stirred me—a primordial warning that went deeper than the elemental instinct. It woke me at once.

There was a stale, sweet scent, and then a brief glimpse of a figure in black. Then a flash of something milky white, like polished bone, arced down.

I threw up my arm, blocking the swing before what turned out to be a really fucking sharp edge plummeted into my chest. My forearm connected with another as I jackknifed up, thrusting the assailant back.

Swinging my legs off the bed, I got a good look at the dark-haired fucker as I shot to my bare feet. I immediately knew at once what he was.

A Revenant.

And since they'd been all over the castle before thanks to the Blood Queen, they obviously didn't need to be invited in.

The mask obscuring half his face gave what he was away. It was shaped like wings that reached to the shaggy hairline and swept down to his jaw on either side—deep gold, not red or black.

The pale-as-fuck, silver-blue eyes were a clue, too.

This had to be one of the ones Malik had said were still out there and would be a problem.

"You picked the wrong fucking chamber," I warned, baring fangs.

"But I didn't." The Rev smirked. "You should've closed those windows."

"Is that so?" I watched as the Rev edged to the side.

He nodded. "And perhaps been a little less arrogant in your belief that you were safe. That you won a war that hasn't—"

"Even begun yet. I know." Muscles coiled as my chin dipped, sending locks of hair across my forehead. "Can we skip this cliché-as-hell conversation and just get to the point where I make you wish you could die?"

The Rev's laugh was low and as dry as bones. "How about we skip the conversation and get to the point where *you* die?"

I smiled. "And how are you going to do that? By talking me to death? Or with your little white knife?"

"White knife?" Another sandpaper laugh grated my skin. "This is a bone of the Ancients, you fucking idiot false Primal."

The Rev came at me before I could even question why the fuck he'd called me that. I braced myself, my smile growing. "I always wanted to know how a Rev regrew a head. Guess I'm going to find out because I'm going to rip yours fucking off."

He darted to the side about a foot from me. Anticipating the move, I laughed under my breath and spun, kicking out. I caught the Rev in the stomach. He skidded back onto one knee. Our eyes locked as I straightened.

Another glimpse of white appeared—a second dagger in his other hand. One side of the Rev's lips curled up.

The cold press of unease hit my chest as the prickle at the nape of my neck gave off a warning. I heard Vikter's voice as if he were standing right beside me, speaking the same words he had that morning in the training yard.

All it takes is a second for your enemy to gain the upper hand.

The Rev was shockingly fast, letting one of the daggers fly.

He didn't throw it at me.

He'd gone for Poppy.

Nothing more than the length of a heartbeat given to either arrogance or vengeance to then lose all which truly matters.

It had been an omen then. A lesson Vikter had promised me I'd learn. One I still hadn't.

Cursing, I jumped to the side faster than I ever had, tapping in to every bit of agility and speed I had in me. My fingers curled around the blade as I snagged it from the air—

I hissed in pain, my fingers spasming open reflexively. The dagger hit the floor as I landed in a crouch. Only a thin cut crossed my palm, but it wasn't that which caused the stingy burn. It was the blade itself. It was scalding to the touch—hot enough that the skin around the cut on my palm *smoked.*

"What the fuck?" I rose, twisting at the waist.

Swinging out, I grabbed the Rev's arm, but he twisted both of us with a burst of unnatural-as-fuck strength. He thrust his right arm out, hitting me in the chest—

Red-hot agony exploded as I careened backward, short-circuiting all my senses. My back hit the wall, and then I was on my ass, staring down at the iron hilt of a dagger embedded in my chest—in the same damn spot Poppy had gotten me in New Haven. Which had been a bit more than a nick of the heart.

Blood flowed from the wound, drenching my bare stomach, but my skin—fuck, I could feel it burning, peeling back from where the blade had penetrated. That pain. Fuck. I'd never felt anything like it before. My teeth gritted as it rippled through me.

The Rev spoke quietly as he bent, picking up the fallen dagger. "Bones of the Ancients. Sharper than bloodstone. Harder than shadowstone." One golden wing lifted with his half smile. "And deadlier than both, able to kill a god with just a prick and incapacitate a Primal."

The fucking Rev winked and rose. "Should have closed those windows, Your Highness." He flipped the milky-white dagger.

My gaze shot to the bed.

Poppy.

Terror was an icy shock to the system, momentarily freezing the fire in my chest. I pushed to my feet—or thought I had. My brain sent the message, but my legs didn't move. I remained slumped against the wall as the Rev chuckled, turning to the bed. I couldn't get enough air into my lungs—any air. I couldn't breathe.

Get up, I ordered. *Get the fuck up.*

Muscles twitched but didn't respond as the Rev approached the bed. Panic crashed into terror as my mouth opened, my throat issuing no sound.

I was frozen. Couldn't move. Voiceless. Couldn't yell for help. I didn't know who was in the hall—either Emil or Naill, but the walls were thick. If they stood down a ways, they wouldn't hear shit—

Good gods, this couldn't be happening.

Not now.

Not when we didn't know what it felt like to have each other when the realm was at peace. Not when we hadn't gotten the chance to know what our love was capable of—what we could create together.

Not ever.

"What a pretty little flower," the Rev *sang* softly.

For a second, the scorching pain faded, replaced by the raw horror of his words as I stared at the Rev's back. That godsdamn rhyme—Poppy had heard it for years, actual *years.*

"What a powerful poppy," he said, grabbing the thin blanket.

It started low, coming from outside of me, a low hum—no, it came from within me.

"Pick it," he continued to sing, yanking the blanket back. "And watch it bleed."

Get up.

Nothing moved. Not a godsdamn thing as Poppy remained asleep, her features relaxed and peaceful.

"Not so powerful any longer." The Rev reached for Poppy, grabbing a fistful of her hair—

He touched her.

He was fucking *touching* her, and she was completely vulnerable. My heart shattered—it had to be shattering. She was *vulnerable,* and she'd promised herself she would never be that again. I'd sworn I would never allow it.

I couldn't.

I *wouldn't.*

The Rev jerked her head back, exposing the back of her skull. "He's been waiting so, so, so long for what is his."

Like a chasm splitting open, pure, unfettered rage exploded from deep within me, but there was…there was more. Not knowledge. I was fucking beyond that. It was instinct—ancient, powerful instinct. *Primal.* The hum in my ears intensified and then hit my blood. My skin buzzed as I latched on to the fury. My muscles quivered as I took all that feral rage and let it pour into me, flooding every vein and filling every cell in my body until the violence tasted like ash in my mouth and became ice in my veins.

Blood full of ash and ice…

A streak of lightning tore through the sky outside, turning night to day as my arm lifted.

The Rev's head jerked to the window as another bolt lit up the realm, and for a moment, I swore I saw silvery cords draping the chamber—flowing from Poppy and rippling across the floor, covering my legs. My body. The Rev's head tilted.

A rumble started in my chest as I willed my fingers around the red-hot hilt. My arm moved, jerking the dagger free. Air poured into my lungs as I shifted sideways. The dagger fell and clattered—

Power, ancient and unyielding, flooded my senses as my hand slammed into the floor. And then it seized control of my body.

Tiny specks of silver appeared along my flesh, filling every pore. My lips peeled back as my jaw popped out of its socket. Canines jutted out. My palms roughened as my fingers spread out, fingernails growing and thickening, sharpening, digging into the stone floor. The linen pants split at the thighs as bones throughout my body shifted, breaking at joints and then rapidly fusing back together, lengthening and hardening. The cloth fell away as my back bowed. I could feel my skin thinning, *moving.* From the silvery-lit pores, fur sprouted—glossy, onyx-and-gold-hued fur. I pushed back onto my knees, then rose to my hands and feet—no, my paws. It had only taken seconds. A stuttered handful of heartbeats. And I was still me, but not.

I was something else.

I rose onto all fours, shaking myself as the sound of the Rev's fast breaths echoed in my head. His stale-sweet scent reached me, tinged in…fear. I *smelled* his fear. Something in my peripheral vision snagged my attention—a reflection in a standing mirror propped against the wall. A large black and gold feline with a shoulder height of over five feet and nearly double the length—and eyes a luminous silver.

That rumble came again from my chest as I turned my head to the Rev.

Pale blue eyes were wide behind the golden mask. "Impossible."

There was no thought, no need to figure out how to get these much larger limbs and body to move. It was more than just an instinct that took over. It was a long-buried knowledge that had been waiting for decades, maybe centuries, to be awakened and tapped into.

I leapt, clearing the distance between us as the Rev jabbed out with the dagger. My reflexes, already fast, were now sharper. I caught his arm, clamping down with my jaws. Skin gave way like fragile silk. Hot, strange-tasting blood poured into my mouth. Bones cracked as if they were nothing more than twigs.

The man howled as I twisted my head, tearing through tissue. I yanked him away from the bed, the dagger falling from his grasp. He fell back, away from me. I spat the lower half of his arm onto the floor.

"Fuck," he rasped, lurching for a fallen dagger.

Powerful, sleek muscles coiled and stretched as he darted to my side, attempting to go around me. I swiped out with a clawed paw, slicing through his leg. His shout of pain turned into a grunt as I latched onto his calf with my canines, dragging him across the floor. With my hold on his muscle, I lifted him and flung him aside. Blood spurted as his leg came off from the knee down.

He skidded across the floor, slamming into the wall. His head jerked up as he rolled onto one knee. I stalked him, a low hiss coming from the back of my throat as he half-crawled, half-slid.

I let him get close enough that his fingers brushed what he sought, then I pounced. Driving him onto his back, I dug my claws into his chest, his thighs, shredding skin and muscle.

I was brutal, clawing through his chest until the cavity gave way beneath me. Savage satisfaction filled me. Then I moved onto his shoulders, ripping apart the tendons, removing what was left of his arms and legs as his screams turned to pitiful whimpers.

Lifting my blood-soaked head, I prowled up his writhing form as I brought my face to his. His mouth opened, revealing blood-streaked teeth—

I snapped down on his throat, twisting my head back and forth sharply, snapping the neck and then severing it.

Spitting the bad-tasting blood from my mouth, I brought one paw down on the Rev's skull, crushing it as I stepped over the remains, scanning the chamber.

Every part of my being focused on the female asleep on the bed, one arm at her side, the other lying across her stomach. Her head was turned toward me, leaving a waterfall of crimson hair to trail over the side of the bed.

She was...important.

My claws rapped off the floor as I prowled toward her, stretching forward. Her scent. My muzzle drew close to her still arm. Whiskers twitched. Fresh. Sweet. *Mine.* I turned my head, nudging her hand. She was *mine.* My Princess...

My heartmate.

My Queen.

Mine.

And I was *hers.*

My head swung toward the chamber doors. Footsteps pounded. A raspy, guttural snarl reverberated from me as I lowered my head, tensing.

The doors flew open, and a panting, brown-skinned male entered—one who smelled of rich, dark soil and us. Of her. His ultra-bright-blue gaze found Poppy first and then me.

"Holy fuck," he whispered, taking a step forward.

I leapt onto the bed, crouching over her. I gave a warning growl.

The male went completely still, then threw up a hand—

Another skidded to a stop behind him, sword in hand and auburn hair windblown. "Is that...is that a fucking cave cat? A really large, strangely colored one?"

"That's Cas," the male said—the one who smelled of the woods and her. He smelled of us. *Mine.*

My eyes narrowed on the newcomer as my lips peeled back. He didn't smell of us.

"What the fuck?" that one gasped, making another choking sound as he saw the blood and pieces scattered across the floor. "I mean, what in the actual fuck?"

I eased down to the foot of the bed, my claws scratching the polished wood. He was not us. He was a risk.

"No, he's not," the male said. "Emil is annoying as fuck."

The one called Emil frowned.

"But he is not a risk," the male continued. "He is one of us."

He was not one of us. He was not *mine*. He was nothing but meat and blood. A meal.

"Meat and blood—oh, fuck," the male said. "Emil's more than that. He is yours, too." He paused while this other thing's entire face creased. "Just not in the same way."

"Okay," the soon-to-be dead one drawled. "I'm going to say it one more time. What in the actual fuckity fuck?"

I came down onto the stone floor, my tail swishing as I eyed the pile of talking meat.

"Fuck." The blue-eyed male twisted at the waist, pushing the meat aside. "Keep his father and the others away," he ordered.

Father?

Something stirred in the back of my thoughts.

"Tie them up. Knock them out," the male demanded. "I don't care what you have to do but keep them the fuck away from here."

The meat sack didn't get a chance to respond. The door was closed in his face and locked. The first male faced me.

"Cas?" he said, voice soft.

My head tilted. The name stirred something inside me. *Cas.*

"The name is familiar because it's yours." He slowly lowered himself and knelt before me. "Your name is Casteel Hawkethrone Da'Neer, and I'm Kieran Contou."

Wisps of memories drifted from the recesses of my mind. Flashes of him much younger—of us as boys and then men.

Kieran glanced to where she slept. "And that is—"

Mine.

One side of Kieran's lips tipped up. "Yeah, she's yours, but depending on her mood, she may not be all that thrilled to hear you continuously snarling that."

My eyes narrowed as I backed up so my head was level with her arm.

He took a deep breath. "I'm guessing by the state of the chamber, someone attempted to attack her, and it didn't end well for them." His blue eyes drifted over me. "And it changed you." A bit of awe crept into his voice. "Holy fuck, you *shifted*."

I… I had. Because this wasn't my normal…existence. I didn't see the spotted gold and black fur but a male with golden-bronze skin and dark hair.

"Cas?"

My attention swung back to him. He'd inched closer, on one knee now.

"Do you remember when we were boys, and I first shifted after being in my mortal form for a while? I had trouble separating myself from the wolf, but you were there. You helped remind me who I was," he said, voice low and soothing as more disjointed images flashed and collided, building atop one another. "I know it can be difficult to pull yourself out of this, but you're still in there, and I'm going to need you to come back to me as Cas." His gaze held mine. "*She* needs you to come back as Cas."

Kieran.

She.

Penellaphe.

Poppy.

My Queen.

She *needed* me.

At once, my sense of self came roaring back, clicking into place beside this new part of me, fusing. I took a step forward, then stopped as I shook my fur out.

"You just will it," Kieran explained. "Like you would a compulsion. You will your body back into its mortal form. That's how it works."

I widened my stance. Like a compulsion? I tapped into the eather like I would for a compulsion, doing as Kieran instructed. I willed myself into mortal form, but the rush of power came at me faster and harder than ever before. Silvery specks of light appeared, seeping out of my pores and washing over me. The shift happened much more fluidly. Bones in my arms and chest shrank, muscles and tendons loosening to allow room for them to snap back into place. Canines retreated as my jaw reformed. I rocked back on instinct, my paws changing into feet. I rose, a little unsteady, as flesh replaced fur. I straightened, cracking my back as my ribs settled.

"Gods," I bit out, throat scratchy as I watched my nails retract and my hands return to normal. "I thought you said shifting doesn't hurt."

A shaky laugh of relief left Kieran as he rose. "The very first time can be a bitch, but it gets easier—more comfortable each time." He blinked several times. "Then it doesn't hurt."

"Good to know." There was still a...a distinctive purr to the tenor of my voice as I looked down at my chest. I was fucking drenched in blood, but most of it was the Rev's. The wound in my chest had closed, leaving behind a puckered line of almost charred skin.

I looked up at Kieran. "I think I was about to eat Emil."

The skin crinkled at the corners of his eyes as he laughed again.

"Yeah, you were definitely thinking that."

Fucking Emil.

"What in the hell happened in here?" Kieran asked, moving to stand in front of me. He touched the skin under the wound. "What is this?"

"A Rev came in through the window while I was sleeping. I woke just as he was about to—" My hand fisted as I confirmed that Poppy was okay. She was alive, and she wasn't *vulnerable*. "He got me in the chest with this dagger."

I bent, picking up the one nearest me. "Get the other."

Kieran went to where the other one had fallen near a few scattered Rev pieces. "What kind of blade is this?" he asked, eyeing the milky-white stone. "It looks like the same kind that fucker Callum used to curse me."

"It does." I frowned. "This Rev said it was made of the bones of the Ancients and that it could incapacitate a Primal."

Kieran's stare shot to Poppy. "Ancients? Like the Primals?"

"I don't know, but it did fuck me up. I couldn't move. It was like the blade severed all control of my body the moment it penetrated my skin," I said. "I couldn't move until this...this power filled me. I've never felt anything like it. It tasted like ash and felt like ice in my veins." I swallowed, wiping the blood from my chin with my other hand. "Then I was able to move. I pulled the dagger out, and I don't even know how, but I...I shifted."

Kieran came forward, his gaze searching mine. "When you shifted back to your normal self, it looked just like her father when he shifted." He looked down at Poppy, and when he spoke again, he sounded awed. "It has to be the bond forged during the Joining. It connected the three of us, somehow giving you the ability to shift like me." His brows knitted. "But then wouldn't you have shifted into a wolven?"

"No." I started to reach down and touch Poppy but stopped when I saw the blood and gore smearing my hand. "Her father shifts into a cave cat. My ability to shift might've come through the connection with you, but it was her eather. That's what I felt. Primal eather," I said, but it had felt like more. Like it had been something inside me, always there. Waiting. But that made no sense. "I bet that was what Nektas was referencing."

"Makes sense," Kieran murmured. He was quiet for a moment, and then his gaze shot to mine. "Then wouldn't that mean Poppy can shift...?"

A slow grin spread across my lips. "She's going to be so excited when she realizes that."

Kieran laughed. "Yeah, she will." Another laugh left him. "Gods, you two are going to be obnoxious with your abilities to shift."

"You can count on it." Something occurred to me as Kieran disappeared into the bathing chamber and returned with a towel. I took it, quickly wiping away as much blood as possible. I turned, picking up a pair of breeches from a nearby chest. There wasn't time to clean up. "You heard my thoughts, didn't you?"

Kieran nodded as I pulled the pants up. "You heard mine, too. After Emil left, I wasn't speaking out loud."

Surprise rippled through me. I wanted to see if that was something we could do in this form or if it was like what Poppy could do with the wolven. I wanted to know if this bond had changed Kieran somehow. There were a whole lot of things I wanted to know—that I wanted to sit down and dwell on for a bit. Because I'd just shifted into a godsdamn spotted cave cat, but there were more important things that needed to be handled.

Starting with the current mess that was the chamber.

I didn't want Poppy to wake up to whatever horror show a Revenant regenerating themselves from pieces would end up being.

"I don't know how the fucker is going to come back from this," I said. "And it might be a good idea to see if we can find Millicent to ask about that, but I'm guessing we should gather up the pieces and put them in one of the cells below."

Kieran's lip curled. "How about we just toss them into the sea? Or burn them?"

"I would love to, but I need him alive."

"Is that up for discussion?"

"He was saying the messed-up rhyme—fucking singing it. And the Rev said he had been waiting a long time for what was his. I know he was speaking of Kolis and…" Anger tightened my gut. "And Poppy."

Tension poured into Kieran's jaw. "Absolutely fucking—"

A rumble came from below, rattling the floors and walls. Something toppled over in the bathing chamber as Kieran's gaze flew to mine. "That can't be another god waking up."

I didn't think it was.

The back of my neck prickled as a sudden charge of power hit the air, raising the hairs all over my arms. Kieran's. too.

The sound of stone cracking came from the floor. A thin fracture appeared on Kieran's other side, rapidly spreading in a circle around us—

around the bed. Another fissure appeared on the floor at the foot of the bed, at the head, and along both sides.

Kieran stepped back as another shallow rift cut through the floor beneath the bed. "What the—?"

Silvery light sparked, racing across the ruptures in the stone. Moonlight pulsed and held, revealing the shape of a circle with an overlapping, pointed cross in the center. A symbol in old Atlantian—no, it was two symbols. The circle and the line through the center were life. The one from the top represented death.

Life and Death.

Blood and Bone.

The intense bright light faded, and the rumbling stopped. We both turned to Poppy.

A glow appeared beneath her flesh, lighting up the delicate network of veins throughout her entire body with…with eather.

"My gods," Kieran whispered.

I swayed, hope and fear I'd kept in check since she went into stasis crashing together.

Poppy would know herself.

She would recognize us.

I said that over and over like a prayer to the gods I knew no longer slept. "*Please*," I whispered, voice cracking.

The light in her veins faded. A streak of silver appeared, and then shadows gathered like pulsing storm clouds beneath her flesh. They slid together down her chest, over her arms and legs, a kaleidoscope of light and darkness—the power of life and death reaching her fingertips.

Poppy's fingers twitched.

I dropped to my fucking knees beside the bed, went right down on them as Kieran lurched forward, planting his palms on the bed. Time seemed to slow to an infinite crawl, every second passing too quickly yet not fast enough as the powers whirled together beneath her skin.

Her arm spasmed. A knee bent slightly. Her toes wiggled, then stretched.

I picked up her hand and shuddered like a godsdamn leaf. "Her skin is warm. See?"

Kieran folded his hand over ours. "It is," he exhaled roughly.

I felt fucking weak with giddy relief as her left arm jerked. Then her chest rose with a deep breath, and I swore to the gods ours did the exact same thing. Her brows tensed. Eyelids twitched. Lush, rosy lips parted, and then the eather slowed under her flesh, slowly disappearing. She inhaled deeply, and it was the most beautiful sound.

"Poppy," I whispered, pitching forward. Her hand squeezed mine, and Kieran squeezed both of ours. I felt dampness gathering in my eyes. She was going to open those lids and know herself. She would recognize—

Thick lashes fluttered, lifting to reveal eyes that held no trace of dewy green. Eyes that weren't even those of a god. They were the pure molten silver of churning eather as they locked with mine. They were the eyes of not just a Primal.

But the Primal of Life and Death.

Of Blood and Bone.

DISCOVER MORE FROM JENNIFER L. ARMENTROUT

A Shadow in the Ember
Flesh and Fire Series
Book One

Available in hardcover, e-book, and trade paperback.

#1 New York Times bestselling author Jennifer L. Armentrout returns with book one of the all-new, compelling Flesh and Fire series—set in the beloved Blood and Ash world.

Born shrouded in the veil of the Primals, a Maiden as the Fates promised, Seraphena Mierel's future has never been hers. *Chosen* before birth to uphold the desperate deal her ancestor struck to save his people, Sera must leave behind her life and offer herself to the Primal of Death as his Consort.

However, Sera's real destiny is the most closely guarded secret in all of Lasania—she's not the well protected Maiden but an assassin with one mission—one target. Make the Primal of Death fall in love, become his weakness, and then…end him. If she fails, she dooms her kingdom to a slow demise at the hands of the Rot.

Sera has always known what she is. Chosen. Consort. Assassin. Weapon. A specter never fully formed yet drenched in blood. A *monster*. Until *him*. Until the Primal of Death's unexpected words and deeds chase away the darkness gathering inside her. And his seductive touch ignites a passion she's never allowed herself to feel and cannot feel for him. But Sera has never had a choice. Either way, her life is forfeit—it always has been, as she has been forever touched by Life and Death.

A Light in the Flame
Flesh and Fire Series
Book Two

Available in hardcover, e-book, and trade paperback.

The only one who can save Sera now is the one she spent her life planning to kill.

The truth about Sera's plan is out, shattering the fragile trust forged between her and Nyktos. Surrounded by those distrustful of her, all Sera has is her duty. She will do anything to end Kolis, the false King of Gods, and his tyrannical rule of Iliseeum, thus stopping the threat he poses to the mortal realm.

Nyktos has a plan, though, and as they work together, the last thing they need is the undeniable, scorching passion that continues to ignite between them. Sera cannot afford to fall for the tortured Primal, not when a life no longer bound to a destiny she never wanted is more attainable than ever. But memories of their shared pleasure and unrivaled desire are a siren's call impossible to resist.

And as Sera begins to realize that she wants to be more than a Consort in name only, the danger surrounding them intensifies. The attacks on the Shadowlands are increasing, and when Kolis summons them to Court, a whole new risk becomes apparent. The Primal power of Life is growing inside her, pushing her closer to the end of her Culling. And without Nyktos's love—an emotion he's incapable of feeling—she won't survive her Ascension. That is if she even *makes* it to her Ascension and Kolis doesn't get to her first. Because time is running out. For both her and the realms.

From Blood and Ash
Blood and Ash Series
Book One

Available in hardcover, e-book, and trade paperback.

Captivating and action-packed, From Blood and Ash is a sexy, addictive, and unexpected fantasy perfect for fans of Sarah J. Maas and Laura Thalassa.

A Maiden...

Chosen from birth to usher in a new era, Poppy's life has never been her own. The life of the Maiden is solitary. Never to be touched. Never to be looked upon. Never to be spoken to. Never to experience pleasure. Waiting for the day of her Ascension, she would rather be with the guards, fighting back the evil that took her family, than preparing to be found worthy by the gods. But the choice has never been hers.

A Duty...

The entire kingdom's future rests on Poppy's shoulders, something she's not even quite sure she wants for herself. Because a Maiden has a heart. And a soul. And longing. And when Hawke, a golden-eyed guard honor bound to ensure her Ascension, enters her life, destiny and duty become tangled with desire and need. He incites her anger, makes her question everything she believes in, and tempts her with the forbidden.

A Kingdom...

Forsaken by the gods and feared by mortals, a fallen kingdom is rising once more, determined to take back what they believe is theirs through violence and vengeance. And as the shadow of those cursed draws closer, the line between what is forbidden and what is right becomes blurred. Poppy is not only on the verge of losing her heart and being found unworthy by the gods, but also her life when every blood-soaked thread that holds her world together begins to unravel.

A Kingdom of Flesh and Fire
Blood and Ash Series
Book Two

Available in hardcover, e-book, and trade paperback.

Is Love Stronger Than Vengeance?

A Betrayal...

Everything Poppy has ever believed in is a lie, including the man she was falling in love with. Thrust among those who see her as a symbol of a monstrous kingdom, she barely knows who she is without the veil of the Maiden. But what she *does* know is that nothing is as dangerous to her as *him*. The Dark One. The Prince of Atlantia. He wants her to fight him, and that's one order she's more than happy to obey. *He may have taken her, but he will never have her.*

A Choice...

Casteel Da'Neer is known by many names and many faces. His lies are as seductive as his touch. His truths as sensual as his bite. Poppy knows better than to trust him. He needs her alive, healthy, and whole to achieve his goals. But he's the only way for her to get what she wants—to find her brother Ian and see for herself if he has become a soulless Ascended. Working with Casteel instead of against him presents its own risks. He still tempts her with every breath, offering up all she's ever wanted. Casteel has plans for her. Ones that could expose her to unimaginable pleasure and unfathomable pain. Plans that will force her to look beyond everything she thought she knew about herself—about him. Plans that could bind their lives together in unexpected ways that neither kingdom is prepared for. And she's far too reckless, too hungry, to resist the temptation.

A Secret...

But unrest has grown in Atlantia as they await the return of their Prince. Whispers of war have become stronger, and Poppy is at the very heart of it all. The King wants to use her to send a message. The Descenters want her dead. The wolven are growing more unpredictable. And as her abilities to feel pain and emotion begin to grow and strengthen, the Atlantians start to fear her. Dark secrets are at play, ones steeped in the blood-drenched sins of two kingdoms that would do anything to keep the truth hidden. But when the earth begins to shake, and the skies start to bleed, it may already be too late.

The Crown of Gilded Bones
Blood and Ash Series
Book Three

Available in hardcover, e-book, and trade paperback.

Bow Before Your Queen Or Bleed Before Her...

She's been the victim and the survivor...

Poppy never dreamed she would find the love she's found with Prince Casteel. She wants to revel in her happiness but first they must free his brother and find hers. It's a dangerous mission and one with far-reaching consequences neither dreamed of. Because Poppy is the Chosen, the Blessed. The true ruler of Atlantia. She carries the blood of the King of Gods within her. By right the crown and the kingdom are hers.

The enemy and the warrior...

Poppy has only ever wanted to control her own life, not the lives of others, but now she must choose to either forsake her birthright or seize the gilded crown and become the Queen of Flesh and Fire. But as the kingdoms' dark sins and blood-drenched secrets finally unravel, a long-forgotten power rises to pose a genuine threat. And they will stop at nothing to ensure that the crown never sits upon Poppy's head.

A lover and heartmate...

But the greatest threat to them and to Atlantia is what awaits in the far west, where the Queen of Blood and Ash has her own plans, ones she has waited hundreds of years to carry out. Poppy and Casteel must consider the impossible—travel to the Lands of the Gods and wake the King himself. And as shocking secrets and the harshest betrayals come to light, and enemies emerge to threaten everything Poppy and Casteel have fought for, they will discover just how far they are willing to go for their people—and each other.

And now she will become Queen...

The War of Two Queens
Blood and Ash Series
Book Four
Available in hardcover, e-book, and trade paperback.

War is only the beginning...

From the desperation of golden crowns...

Casteel Da'Neer knows all too well that very few are as cunning or vicious as the Blood Queen, but no one, not even him, could've prepared for the staggering revelations. The magnitude of what the Blood Queen has done is almost unthinkable.

And born of mortal flesh...

Nothing will stop Poppy from freeing her King and destroying everything the Blood Crown stands for. With the strength of the Primal of Life's guards behind her, and the support of the wolven, Poppy must convince the Atlantian generals to make war her way—because there can be no retreat this time. Not if she has any hope of building a future where both kingdoms can reside in peace.

A great primal power rises...

Together, Poppy and Casteel must embrace traditions old and new to safeguard those they hold dear—to protect those who cannot defend themselves. But war is only the beginning. Ancient primal powers have already stirred, revealing the horror of what began eons ago. To end what the Blood Queen has begun, Poppy might have to become what she has been prophesied to be—what she fears the most.

As the Harbinger of Death and Destruction.

ON BEHALF OF BLUE BOX PRESS,

Liz Berry, M.J. Rose, and Jillian Stein would like to thank ~

Steve Berry
Doug Scofield
Benjamin Stein
Kim Guidroz
Chelle Olson
Hang Le
Chris Graham
Tanaka Kangara
Jessica Saunders
Malissa Coy
Jen Fisher
Stacey Tardif
Laura Helseth
Jessica Mobbs
Erika Hayden
Dylan Stockton
Kate Boggs
Richard Blake
and Simon Lipskar